Praise for
Santa Steps Out

"The only two rules in *Santa Steps Out* are that everything is sacred and nothing is sacred. I wish I could hope to ever attain one-thousandth the perversity of Robert Devereaux's least toenail clipping. I also wish—despite its enticing/cautionary subtitle—that this Santa story might be read to children everywhere on Christmas Eve."
  —Poppy Z. Brite

"There are scenes from this book that will haunt me forever. I know I'll never innocently or absent-mindedly suck on a candy cane again. Reading this book made me want to bitch-slap Robert Devereaux. So icky, yet so magnificently rendered."
  —Elizabeth Engstrom

"The kind of fairy tale that could make Walt Disney burst from his cryogenic ice cube and go on a mad killing spree."
  —Ray Garton

"A delirious slice of Nabokovian porno whimsy. Wholesome, savory, weird and blasphemous, all at the same time—just like the best sex. I believe in Robert Devereaux."
  —Tim Lucas

"In its violation of our sensibilities and our cherished childhood icons, in its topping of its over-the-top scenarios, Santa Steps Out manages to be at once fascinating, funny, and enlightening. Devereaux's most outrageous achievement is that as he destroys our childhood myths, he rebuilds them in a twisted yet equally magical and compelling way."
  —Jeanne Cavelos

"Exactly the kind of dangerous book that a small press should publish: the kind that makes mainstream publishers sweat."
  —Hank Wagner

"Robert Devereaux is a master of vivid scene-setting, especially gory scenes and sex scenes. There is a lot of sex in this book—mostly happy, lubricious sex that is sometimes downright amazing. Prepare for a strange and stimulating ride when you hop in the sleigh with Santa and witness all his adventures."
—Fiona Webster

"Never until now have so many sacred childhood deities been subjected to such vile reinvention, in what has to be one of the most perversely hilarious books ever written."
—Brian Hodge

"Santa Steps Out is breathtaking. It's almost life changing. A novel so refreshing and inspiring to read that it breaks down the walls of genres and sits comfortably outside of everything."
—Andy Fairclough

"A perfectly sincere, seriocomic exploration of myth and taboo, sexuality and relationships, and the evolution of the godhead. Yes, Virginia, there really is a Robert Devereaux."
—Edward Bryant

"By the time Mrs. Claus is exacting her revenge with the help of Santa's elves, and the Tooth Fairy and Easter Bunny are tearing each other apart in an act of sexual congress, any comfort we may find in these figures is way out the window."
—Thomas Deja

"Devereaux breaks every mold imaginable, and he does it with élan, and with an unabashed glee."
—Monica J. O'Rourke

So, grab a cup of hot cocoa, snuggle up in your warmest blankie, and settle back for a reading experience the likes of which you've never had. One warning should accompany this book, however: KEEP THIS and all other dangerous objects OUT OF THE REACH OF CHILDREN!"
—P. D. Cacek

deadite
press

DEADITE PRESS
205 NE BRYANT
PORTLAND, OR 97211
www.DEADITEPRESS.com

AN ERASERHEAD PRESS COMPANY
www.ERASERHEADPRESS.com

ISBN: 978-1-62105-013-1

Printed in the USA.

SANTA STEPS OUT

ROBERT DEVEREAUX

deadite
press

OTHER DEADITE PRESS BOOKS
BY ROBERT DEVEREAUX

Slaughterhouse High
Baby's First Book of Seriously Fucked-Up Shit
Walking Wounded
Santa Steps Out
Santa Claus Conquers the Homophobes

For Caitlin and Lianna
beloved lovebunnies
whose childhood
(as if their dad could possibly know)
must surely have been
perfectly normal

Robert Devereaux Boldly Goes:
Santa Steps Out

---

by David G. Hartwell

Robert Devereaux is a pleasant man, a passionate reader of contemporary fiction, involved in a decades-long affair with what we used to call "the legitimate theater," and a writer of extraordinary originality and technical accomplishment. He's also a practical man, with a job in the computer industry. What we normally like to think of as a real adult.

You might imagine then how surprised I was to find him in his late thirties a student at the infamous Clarion West writing workshop in Seattle in the summer of 1990 expressing the desire to become a Splatterpunk.

I believe I tried to discourage him, but it didn't work. He had an answer that I know would have confounded most of the members of the Splat pack at the time—he'd always really liked Jacobean drama. It stopped me cold. I have always liked Jacobean drama, which is more violent, bloody, sexy, and disturbing than 90% of splatterpunk fiction, but also I think of incomparably higher merit. I'd match *The Duchess of Malfi* against any work of horror of the eighties or nineties. And I'd bet Devereaux is the only writer among the genre contemporaries who knows the play.

The other thing that sets Devereaux apart is his sheer outrageousness. The image of "over the top" is outworn and useless when applied to his work. His ability is more turbulent and oceanic—the outrageousness comes in like huge Pacific rollers, wave after wave, inundating you. This is, after all, an introduction to the single most outrageous novel I have ever read: *Santa Steps Out*.

This novel reminds me of nothing so much as the centerfold Wallace Wood, the great comic artist, did for Paul Krassner's magazine, *The Realist*, in the mid-60s: "The Loss of Innocence in Disneyland." In one panoramic landscape, Wood showed every famous Disney cartoon character involved in sex acts with another or others, as Dumbo flew over and shit on them. It was the single dirtiest thing I had seen in my life to that time and a powerful work of cultural deconstruction. This novel is like that. It is so dirty it overwhelms you.

What Devereaux does in *Santa Steps Out* that is so powerful is to set up a mythic frame and an internal logic and then plug in figures of childhood sentiment and make them fuck each other and real people too. I cannot offhand think of any sexual taboo still extant in American society that this book does not violate. It wishes to offend, and thereby destroy certain normal defenses against deep involvement in art by shock and surprise. Each individual incident is raised to a fantastic and hyperbolic pitch, it assaults our sensibilities, it violates our sentimental attachments, page after page, chapter after chapter.

Of what use, or to what artistic purpose, is this done? Well, it seems to me that carrying the sentimentalities of childhood into grown-up life leads one to behave as if those around you were cartoons, not real people with problems and passions, and especially powerful sexual desires. Especially yourself. Our children's myths are emasculated, and Devereaux is giving them, and us, back our sexuality, and with it our adulthood. It's not very comfortable, nor comforting. But it is better than a pet-like existence of extended pre-adolescence. It's a very post-modern project, at least in principle.

Much of this is in my opinion absurd and very funny. Like horror, humor doesn't work consistently, is indeed very subjective. But this book is supposed to be funny. I am sorry for any reader who does not in the least see the humor in this novel. Perhaps it might help you to think of this as a film like *Who Framed Roger Rabbit?*, except that it is about sex, not murder. I do think that some readers will be overwhelmed before they reach the end, but I don't think the effect will be lessened, except that there is a plot and one might like to know how it all turns out.

You hold in your hands one of the most interesting and unusual literary artifacts of the late 20th century in America.

—David G. Hartwell, Pleasantville, NY

INTRODUCTION

by Patrick LoBrutto

You hold a dangerous book in your hands.

Looks normal and innocent, don't it? It's not. *Santa Steps Out* by Robert Devereaux is a dangerous book. A NASTY book. Publishers and editors refuse to look this book in the eye; marketing managers cringe; sales executives make elaborate signs to ward off evil. And—just you wait—reviewers will rage and sputter, citizens will protest and object. A lot of people are going to be offended . . . deeply. Some will have even read the book.

So what's the big deal? There's an awful lot of fucking and sucking in this book—get out the pencil, for there's a lot to underline; lubricious twats and engorged pricks and stiff nipples and blow jobs and . . . well, you get the idea. Okay, so that's not so new—whatinhell IS the big freakin' deal? Like books and movies and TV and the Internet and *toothpaste ads* aren't filled with jiggling boobs and sexstuff fercryinoutloud. That's bad enough, but *Santa Steps Out* has *Santa and the Tooth Fairy* screwing and licking like crazy, and something to say about myths and human behavior and gods and . . . now, now, that would be telling, wouldn't it?

Anyway, that's all offensive, see? I mean, there are just some things that are sacred; like Mom and Apple Pie and the Flag and God . . . and good ol' Saint Nick (no relation to Old Nick . . . I think). There are just some things that shouldn't be written about, should never be questioned, can never be lampooned. There are some screens we should never look behind. There are some things that just shouldn't be fucked with! Right? EVERYbody says so. And they are right. People shouldn't have to think about this stuff. The Public shouldn't be subjected to this kind of filth.

Something should be done.

Now, you just go ahead and read this book. Then you'll see what I mean.

Dangerous book, *Santa Steps Out*. Filthy pervert, that Robert Devereaux.

Bless him and keep him, oh gods; may his light shine on and on; long may his pecker wave.

Let's wave back! Thank you, Robert! Thank you for disturbing our peace and upsetting the applecart and making us think the unthinkable and smile and wonder. Thank you for writing a dangerous book for us.

PROLOGUE
CUPIDITAS RESURGENS

Love is not the dying moan of a distant violin—it is the triumphant twang of a bedspring.
   —S. J. Perelman

I wonder why men can get serious at all. They have this delicate long thing hanging outside their bodies which goes up and down by its own will. . . . If I were a man, I would always be laughing at myself.
   —Yoko Ono

Human life is mainly a process of filling in time until the arrival of death or Santa Claus.
   —Eric Berne

In the beginning, the Father heard rumblings from Above and cut His vacation short.

Regained His throne.

Surveyed the scene.

Flew into a towering rage.

The archangel Michael had gone berserk, his thick white wings now twitching. As he staggered before the throne, the glowering God-mask angled upon his face. Shards of Hermes jagged out of his body. The six other archangels looked on, wringing their hands. Raphael's eyes were moist with tears.

"How long has he been like this?" God asked them. Gesturing toward Michael, He expunged all evidence of the trickster-god, putting him under as He had done during the great transformation.

"Two decades and more, Father," said Gabriel, he who had been Apollo in the old times. "We couldn't stop him. As Your surrogate, he had absolute power. He wouldn't listen to reason."

The Father lifted the God-mask from Michael's face. The penitent looked pale as moonlight.

"Dear Lord, forgive me," he begged. "One of the cherubim—that one up there—whispered a suggestion in my ear. It sounded so splendid and proper at the time. But now I see it wasn't, not in the least."

God glanced upward.

As He suspected.

He flared a finger at the impish grin and plunged Eros deep inside the plump winged babe; its face became smooth and innocent once more.

"And what was the cherub's suggestion?"

Michael told Him.

God erupted. "*Omanko!*" He swore. "*Hijo de puta! Scheissdreck! Jaevla dritsekk! Oh, c'est vraiment con! Gott verdammi hure seich! Madonna damigiana con tutti i santi dentro e Dio per tappo!*"

Now the Son, once Dionysus, spoke. "Michael," He said,

"you know that Santa Claus and the Tooth Fairy are never to cross paths. It's one of our Father's most solemn injunctions."

Michael hung his head. "It only happened once, for a moment, in Idaho, Christmas of 1969. They had the barest glimpse, then she vanished and it was over. Except that they began . . . doing things on their own."

"Christ!" God peered down in disbelief at the earth below. His all-seeing eye traced the effect of the lapsed cherub's suggestion, short range and long, watching it ramify over three-and-twenty years. "Oh Jesus, will you look at 1991, it's all *three* of them. They're going haywire down there!"

"Easy, Father. No need for apoplexy. I'm sure it's fixable."

And it was.

At a cost.

The twenty-fourth of December, 1970.

The Tooth Fairy, wearing nothing but a necklace of huge blood-flecked teeth, squatted on the eastern shore of her island and looked out to sea. A storm was kicking up out there, a real corker.

Good, she thought, chewing over the remains of an eagle she had dropped from the heavens with a high-flung silver dollar. Whatever resentments she harbored against the being who these days called himself God, she liked the way he made his creatures: with the tastiest part, the skeleton, on the inside.

Staring seaward, she mapped out the evening's itinerary. As always, instinct told her which dwellings to visit, which bedrooms to enter, which brats to loom over, longing to rip the teeth clean out of their skulls like moist sweet kernels of corn, but confined, alas, to the meager leavings beneath their pillows.

But this night, this Christmas Eve, the Tooth Fairy had a second agenda. Centuries of God-imposed isolation had created an itch inside as deep and omnipresent as a toothache. She sorely missed the old frolics through glen and dale, the thud of randy hoofs at her heels, the goat-breath blasting hot against her shoulderblades.

She needed a lover. Someone all-giving, warm, and cheery, whose stamina went beyond that of mere mortals.

She needed Santa Claus.

In the days before God had laid a veil of forgetting over his mind, she had enjoyed him often. A thing of danger and abandon he had been then, beautiful to behold and incredible to couple with.

She pictured him as she had seen him in Boise the year before, kneeling by the tree in the Sloane residence off Cloverdale Drive, his distressingly cherubic face radiant with philanthropy. The memory made her quim throb. Before this night was out, she vowed, she would enjoy him once more.

Until then, the ocean harbored a treasure of its own, something that would do as a stopgap.

Digestion's clink and jingle sped the masticated eagle through her system. Inside her rectum, thin disks of metallic waste stacked up neat and heavy as rolled coins. There in the sand, as the wind skimmed along the shore and blasted her full in the face, she relaxed her sphincter and shat a quick clatter of quarters.

Relieved, she rose to outface the wind.

Into the restless surf she strode. The undertow ate at the seabed on which she stood. Her palms lowered to the churning surface, straightened toward the horizon, then swept about until her thumbtips touched her navel. Again and again, as sheets of rain whipped at her cheeks, she repeated the movement, chanting words of summoning.

In an instant, the waves vanished, the wind dropped, the rain relented. It fell about her in a gentle mist, pelting the calm sea with the muted sound of hundreds of herons taking flight. Long before her drowned sailor surfaced, she saw him rise from the ship, blink his lidless eyes, look down in wonder at the tattered remnants of his body. The force of her lust had drawn his manflesh up into the crude semblance of an erection. That same lust now made what was left of his limbs thrust and kick stiffly through the sea in a mockery of swimming.

Thigh-deep in water, holding sea and sky at bay, the Tooth Fairy watched his approach, skin and bones breaking the surface not fifty yards away.

Closer, he rose to a lurch. Two things about him drew her attention. The first was the ragged column of flesh at his groin, nibbled here and there by small sharp teeth but serviceable enough, she judged, for one last tumble in surf and sand.

The second was the seductive gleam of bone. The nearer he came, the more aroused she grew at hints of the stuff peeking out coquettishly from behind curtains of flesh: a succulent patch of skull, a long curve of rib, the lower half of one femur begging for the viselock of her jaws.

Above all, the teeth.

They grinned across his skull, a full set of them, molars, bicuspids, canines, incisors, laid out in logical array like a mapped sampler of chocolates. All hers from crown to root, from enamel to pulp.

When he was six feet away, she released storm and ocean, letting them fury about her once more. Then she grabbed him, dragged him to the beach, and straddled him, filling her hungry channel with raw dead flesh. As she rode him, she prised apart his jaws and sucked seawater from his incisors.

By the time orgasm seized her, her mouth was stuffed full of dead man's teeth. Yet even in the high delirium of gustatory and clitoral ecstasy, part of her mind leaped into the night ahead and fixed on the jolly old elf in his bright red suit, remembering the generous gifts that hung beneath that shiny black belt of his, behind the large red buttons of his fly.

She knew what she wanted for Christmas.

PART I
BETRAYAL

Give me chastity and continence—but not yet.
        —Saint Augustine

The advantage of the emotions is that they lead us astray.
        —Oscar Wilde

A lie is an abomination unto the Lord and a very present help in trouble.
        —Adlai Stevenson

1.

SEDUCTION IN THREE ACTS

With Anya's kiss tingling warm upon his cheek and her grandmotherly smile of devotion dancing in his eyes, Santa Claus bounded through cheering throngs of elves and lifted the worn leather reins of his sleigh. He loved their heft, how they took to his hands like tendons stretched from his snorting stamping team straight up through the brawn of his arms to his shoulders.

As far off as his eyes could see, elfin hands lifted lanterns high and elfin voices—strong, high-pitched, and spirited—beat back the silence of the night. "Farewell, Santa!" they shouted. "God speed! God bless! *Auf Wiedersehen!*"

"Merry Christmas to you all!" boomed Santa, to which his elves cheered and sent their caps jingling skyward. The whip cracked smartly over his reindeer, whose powerful bodies responded as if to ravenous hunger. "Into the sky with you, my four-footed wonders!" came Santa's command. "Let's not keep our beloved little boys and girls waiting a moment longer!"

Random snorts and stamps assumed order and purpose. Nine antlered heads drew a bead on the stark silhouette of treetops pasted against the sky above the skating pond. Nine harnessed bodies, taut with sinew and muscle, surged forward. Like a blare of sirens, the fiery effulgence of Lucifer's antlers split the dusk in twain. Eighteen pairs of hoofs beat soundless against the night breeze, tossing up divots of wind.

They were away.

Shifting the reins, Santa raised his right hand for a final wave to his friends and loved ones. His wife beamed up at him from the porch. In her eye, a tear. In her hand, a handkerchief edged with bobbin lace. For an instant, he saw only her, felt only the love that bound them in wedded bliss.

Santa knew their holiday separation took its toll on Anya, she delighted so in his company. He missed her too, working Christmas Eve with no one but the likes of Comet and Cupid to talk to. But he loved the world's wee ones with all his heart, and he knew that Anya loved them too. For the sake of the children, then, a loss of consortium, bitter though it was for them both, had to be endured.

Behind him, his wife and fellow workers grew tinier. The stable, the workshop, the cottage itself became as miniatures folded into the night. Santa leaned forward into the jingle of bells and the busy haunches of his team, feeling the sleigh's dip and rise in his testicles.

"That's the way, pretty ones! Straight on into the night!"

A wrist-snap. The impulse traveled the length of his whip, stinging the air over a forest of antlers. Lucifer, his lead reindeer, scattered a guiding white light in all directions, and the delicious aroma of vanilla dipped and rolled along the backs of the remaining eight. Overhead, stars huddled into the depths of night like millions of impulses eager to be acted upon.

As always, and thank God for that, the winter world which opened before him kissed the hem of perfection and the children were his to bless on this most wondrous night of the year.

The first time Santa encountered the Tooth Fairy was barely six million residences into his rounds, in a modest ranch house on Elm Street in North Merrick, New York. He had just finished setting out gifts for the Draper children—Bobby, ten; Davey, eight; Anne Marie, five—and had his face pressed against their Douglas fir, hung with lights and ornaments. Santa loved the hint of forest in his nostrils.

When he rose, she was standing there where the living

room spilled into a long dark hallway, wearing nothing but a pair of yellow panties, her necklace of outsized teeth, and a beguiling smile.

He drank her in, all of her carnality at once, glory enfleshed. Her necklace spoke boldly, its wide arc of glistening white teeth sweeping from shoulder to shoulder, large and canine every one. Like rough surf, they slapped cruelly at her breasts, which thrust out full and defiant. Her nipples seemed forever aroused, pointed and prominent as constellated stars, with fire to match.

Her eyes flared seduction.

Santa gave a sharp cry as a shockwave of sensuality engulfed him. He had known of course that the Tooth Fairy existed, had even on occasion cast a kind thought her way. But her sudden appearance in the flesh set off ancient echoes in his mind, brought forgotten aromas to the fore, thrilled him in shameful ways.

"Santa Claus," she whispered. Her splayed fingers framed the bright stretch of fabric that hugged her sex. More discovering than covering was that splash of yellow, so guileful the gold silk, so tight its stretch from pubis to perineum. Santa, his mouth dry as gauze, watched her arousal darken the cloth from canary to maize to mustard.

He ached to look elsewhere, anywhere but there. But something told him he was staring at the true core of his life, long forgotten, and he couldn't tear his eyes away. He felt the Clausean kindness drain from him, turning him light in the head and pendulous at the groin. *Anya is not going to like this; nosirree, not one bit.*

"What—?" His voice was thick as rope. "What are you doing here?" He sounded lost already and that stirred anger in him.

"Look at me," she commanded him.

"No. I mustn't," said Santa, but he couldn't look anywhere else. She hovered there over the carpet, beauty and terror wrapped up in one tantalizing package.

Santa's sack, which enroute from house to house grew heavy with gifts behind him in the sleigh, now hung slack and exhausted from his hand. In spite of himself, beneath the vast bulge of his belly, his manhood grew tightfisted as a skinflint.

She dipped a hand beneath the silk. Her body flexed. "Oooh, Santa, I wish this hand were yours." Her urgency gripped him like a fist of fragrance.

He shuddered. "You'd better stop that right now."

But she kept at it, burning the dark lasers of her eyes into him as her left hand joined her right, writhing this way and that with her passion.

An agonized inner voice warned him to shun the Tooth Fairy, to turn instead to the task at hand. But Santa chose not to hear it—or hearing, not to heed—fixing his ears on the immensity of her moans and gasps. Even the impatient jingle of sleighbells out on the lawn scarcely registered.

His lips moved. *Shame on you*, he thought he said, but the blood was pounding too loud in his ears to know whether he spoke at all.

Then she peaked. Above the exudacious swell of her breasts, her mouth elongated into a stretched oval and she unleashed the hell-hounds of passion from the depths of her throat. "Oh Jesus God," she gasped. They issued from her, invisible guttural mongrels nipping like flames of frost at Santa's ears. She clawed at the yellow silk, rending it, ripping it away. Her hipbones writhed into view, then the taut skin below her navel and a few stray hints of curls. The shredded cloth lemoned away like a streak of sunlight and flew across the room into Santa's face.

All sights vanished then, and all scents but one: the aroma of her arousal, fecund and fleshy, soaked into the weave of her undergarments. Santa snatched them from his face, greedy for the sight of her. But only a visual echo, fleeting as a phantom, hung in the hallway.

He starved for the sight of her, he wanted her in the woods, any woods, a copse of trees, hell a manicured backyard by moonlight would do, *Good God, what's come over me?*, he wanted her up against a tree, his hands locked around her shoulders, bark biting into his arms, his bloodpulse thrust up into her, *No I'm Santa Claus*, his muscular backlegs tense and tight as his hoofs struck sparks from exposed roots, channeling into her, feeling her thighs grip his flanks, feeling the rich spring air wash in and out of his lungs.

"No!" he screamed, more astonished than angered.

He pressed the torn cloth to his face and filled his lungs. It was a pure whiff of peace and joy, the lushness of forest and tidepool. It called out for procreation, for the rough and tumble of rutting lust, the insistent commingling of generous fluids.

Sobbing, Santa fumbled at the big red buttons of his fly. Out sprang his sex, its tip moist with pre-ejaculate. Silk tatters he fisted about it, rubbing as the bony hand of a science teacher vigorously strokes a glass rod to demonstrate the wonders of static electricity. Into the wet folds of silk the jolly old elf shot his spunk, voluminously, with great pitch and moment.

But even as orgasm overtook him, Clausean goodness came rushing back into him. His fingers twitched against the soaked and clotted panties, which bloomed into a large package wrapped in soft paper the color of lemon chiffon, topped with a large bow of a deeper yellow. Feeling low and mean, he set it down beneath the tree and fled to his sleigh, fumbling his buttons up as he went.

Outside, Lucifer's soulful eyes glinted with incriminating sparks; but Santa tossed the spent sack behind him, threw himself into the driver's seat, and with nary a word of explanation whipped the team skyward.

"Off with you!" he shouted in a voice thick with self-loathing.

On Christmas morning, John and Mary Draper awoke, to their delight, in the midst of a lovemaking most amazing. When at last they lazed down from the dizzying heights of orgasm, uncoupled, and donned robes and slippers, they found their home infused with the most delicious aroma imaginable.

The kids noticed it too. They bubbled with life, more than could be accounted for by the excitement of Christmas Day alone. Even Bobby, usually the soul of fifth-grade cynicism, raced to and fro before the tree, heady with childish greed.

Little Anne Marie sniffed out its source: the pale yellow package sitting apart from the piled gifts. Its curiously quaint card read: "For John and Mary, to be opened in the privacy of your bedroom. May the coming year be new and happy in a multitude of ways. Much love, Santa." Despite the pleas of the children, Mary refused to open it but set it upon the cedar chest at the foot of her bed.

Her hands tingled as she touched it.

All through the exchange of gifts, the visits from friends and family, and the endless holiday feasting, she and John exchanged looks of suppressed excitement.

And after a day of revelry, with the kids tucked safely away for the night, they tore into the yellow enigma and brought forth sex toys galore. A profusion of them splashed across their comforter: dildos and cock-rings and ben-wa balls; frilly fuckwear for her, leather briefs with strategic zippers for him; flavored creams and gels of every variety; and condoms without number—ribbed and stippled, latex and lambskin, clear and opaque and every color of the rainbow.

Each denied the giving but delighted in the gift, as much for the sheer naughtiness these playthings suggested as for anything inherently exciting in them.

And their sex life, hitherto a dim porchlight over the dark doorway of their marriage, became thereafter a blazing hearth-fire, lending abundant light and heat to all of life's endeavors.

The second time Santa saw the Tooth Fairy, he had nearly succeeded in putting her out of his mind. For a time, he dreaded seeing her again. He couldn't shake her image, her aroma, nor his overwhelming sense of guilt. If Saint Anthony had resisted temptation of all sorts, he agonized, then why couldn't jolly old Saint Nick?

Good God in Heaven, Claus, another part of him shot back. Anthony was an ascetic, an oddball, a loner, thin as a rail and half as exciting. You're as corpulent as they come, a lover of food and drink, fond of realizing spiritual good in material form. When you saved that Lycian merchant's three daughters from whoredom by tossing a bag of gold in at each of their windows, please recall how you yielded at once to the youngest's gratitude: you followed your money through her casement, taking joy in the sweet paroxysm of her loins.

Dear Jesus, I'd forgotten that. Yes, but that was before I met and married my beloved Anya, before I vowed to cleave to her alone. If she knew about tonight, it would hurt her heart. It would wither her soul.

So keep it from her. Heavens, man, you didn't even *touch* the temptress. So unfret that brow, put your worries behind you, let's see some *jolly* light those eyes. If she presses you again, you'll be ready to resist, to play at Saint Anthony, or even Jesus in the Wilderness, if you wish.

So it went, the turmoil in Santa's mind.

But by the time he reached the Midwest, all was once more bright and calm, nothing in his mind but sleighbells and candycanes.

Humming with joy and contentment, Santa reached into his burgeoning sack and pulled forth gift after gift for the Gilberts, long-time Iowa City residents in the blue and white Victorian at 925 North Dubuque Street: Sandra, a full professor in the School of Dentistry; Paul, head dispatcher for the Coralville transit system; and their daughters—Karen, Julie, and Jane—arrayed in age from nine to five. Theirs was a lovely tree, dusted white and decorated in motifs of gold and silver. Much love filled their house. True, Paul was boffing one of his bus drivers, an earthy young woman named Debbie Travers. But his heart, Santa knew, belonged to Sandra and the girls.

This time his nose found her first.

One moment he was on his knees adjusting the ribbon

around the neck of a rocking horse and breathing in the apple-cider and cinnamon-stick air of the ticking house. The next, his nostrils were ravished by the sharp thrust of the Tooth Fairy's woman-scent, alluring and arousing and monstrous all in one.

He tossed his head back in panic. There she stood at the sliding doors to the front parlor. A luminous trail of fairy dust sparkled down the dark stairway. Apparently she had already paid her visit to Julie's room upstairs, taken up her tiny tooth, and left a cache of coins behind. Now she hovered, one hand on the dark wood of the sliding door, and spoke his name.

"Santa," she said, "you know why I'm here."

Fright seized the unwary elf. He stood up in a rush, upsetting the rocking horse. A string of silver bells on the tree *ting-ting*'d in protest. "All right," he said, his voice trembling. "This has gone far enough."

"Has it?" Her body choked his eyes. Silken panties as orange as hissing bonfires hugged her hips. She cupped and caressed her dark-tipped breasts.

He faltered. "Look, I'm trying to do my job here. You're distracting me. You're spoiling the mood, the purity of the . . . of the holiday spirit. Now be a good little fairy and . . ."

Santa's mouth moved but suddenly nothing would come out. He wanted to be firm with her, abrupt as a dictator, but it refused to happen.

The Tooth Fairy tilted her head just so and hung a smile upon her lips.

Santa staggered. *Oh Jesus, I'm going to fall.* The Persian carpet's elaborate weave funneled him toward the delectable devourer.

"For the sake of the children," he moaned, "please go away. You're so beautiful—good God the word doesn't do you justice—but I can't give you what you want." Had he called her beautiful? Yes, he thought. As beautiful as an earthquake swallowing whole cities.

In a blink she wafted over to him and pressed her body against his, her breasts pushing the sharp necklace of teeth into his red-suited chest, her pantied pelvis molding and encouraging his arousal.

"You can," she insisted, "and you will."

"I have a wife," Santa protested weakly. He was losing himself in the wilds of her scent.

"Forget her," she rasped. She swirled her tonguetip inside the dips and folds of his left ear. Santa's knees buckled, taking his last vestige of resolve with them. The steady voice of conscience, the troth he had plighted long ago, proved no match for this insistent female, whose moist lips now played upon his mouth. Her tongue licked greedily at Santa's teeth and gums, deftly probing his oral cavity.

It suddenly occurred to him that he was Santa Claus, God damn it, that three innocent children slept overhead, and that what he was now engaged in was an unforgivable violation of the sanctity of the Gilbert household. Santa seized upon the Tooth Fairy's shoulders and rudely thrust her away.

Drunken rage flared in her eyes, but she masked it and glided back against him. "So, we're playing hard to get, are we? Or maybe we're just getting hard. Is that what this is about?"

"No more, please."

"Shall we see just how hard we're getting?"

"Don't, please don't." But in the physical struggle she had begun, her playful combativeness made her body shift and arch in alluring ways and Santa felt the demon again, the not-Santa in him, surge up, robbing him of all resistance.

Now her fingers snaked down his paunch, past the shiny black belt to the bright red bulge in his trousers. His buttons must have undone themselves, for in no time, the ineffable thrill a man feels when a woman grips his loveshaft surged through him.

"No," he gasped.

Santa's hands felt numb and alien. His left splayed across her shoulderblade like a starfish on a beach. *This is not happening.* His right sculpted her neck, her hard-tipped breasts, her belly, then plunged beneath the orange silk and found the swell of her desire. *Please God, let this not be happening.*

Thus they led one another, by hand and lip—though Santa kicked and screamed inside like a caged saint—to the brink of orgasm.

With a shudder, she gripped his inserted middle finger and bellowed out a world-splitting groan. That sound was enough to tilt the balance for him as well. Santa's low taut baritone came up under her full-throated gasps, and his seed arced out of him and spattered the topmost branches of the tree, dripping downward in dribs and drabs.

Oh Lord, I'm damned indeed, he thought, but it didn't stop him from wanting suddenly to embrace the Tooth Fairy in all her monstrosity. His massive red arms encircled her to hold her tight. And closed on nothing. His sex hung suddenly free and unstroked and spurting, and his mouth, still a-tingle, gaped empty and unkissed.

Fighting back tears of humiliation, Santa gestured toward the tree and watched his semen turn to gleaming white candycanes on the branches it had befouled.

He fell to his knees. "Heavenly Father," he prayed, "give me strength. Help me withstand the temptress. Be with me in my hour of need. This I pray by all the saints in heaven and on earth. Amen." Then he gathered his things together, dematerialized through the front door, and dove into his sleigh.

Lucifer took one look at him and rolled his eyes at Prancer. But Santa's whipsmack split the air above his antlers, distressed shouts of "Up and away, damn you!" filled his ears, and before he knew it, his hoofs had left the snowy lawn and the sleigh was airborne.

The Gilberts' Christmas that year was the best any of them could recall. It wasn't so much the presents, nor the food, nor the folks who dropped by, though all of that was tinged as usual with the special clarity and goodness of Christmas Day. It seemed rather that the house itself, from attic to basement, from front porch to back, was infused with the deepest comfort and warmth.

But the girls' favorite moment was Karen's discovery of the off-white candycanes on the tree. They went wild over them, the young ones especially, licking the stiff glistening columns of white like Ponce de Leon indulging himself at the Fountain of Youth. They smuggled some of them to school to share with their closest girlfriends, and Julie pressed one upon her mother.

Sandra had never tasted anything like it. Despite a dominant strain of treacle, powerful barbs of nutrition jagged out here and there into her taste buds. There were hints of salt mingled with a sugar so pure its taste made her eyes glisten with tears of joy.

Paul Gilbert reaped his reward that night when Sandra slipped into bed beside him, peeled off his pajama bottoms with her teeth, and spent the next five hours lining her stomach with his outpourings of love. Sandra had always blanched at the very notion of oral sex, which was one reason her husband spent three lunch hours each week with Debbie Travers, a woman who loved to lick and be licked, though she refused to let him come in her mouth.

From that night, Paul swore off Debbie and stayed faithful to his wife ever after. Karen, Julie, and Jane, as well as their friends who had partaken of the special candycanes, grew to be skilled milkers of men, and even the plainest of them, once her talents became known, never lacked for dates.

The third time the Tooth Fairy crossed his path, Santa thought he was ready for her. Anya's image he kept close to his heart, catechizing in mid-flight the richness of their lives together, all the blessings they had shared. He devised devastating rebuffs for the temptress should she reappear.

But his strongest defense, he believed, was his clearsighted assessment of the sex act itself. Devoid of love, did it amount to anything more than a poke and a squirt, the thrust of a fleshy banana into a squishy doughnut for the momentary excitation of both? Surely he could quell his sensual urges, acknowledge them yet not act on them, if the dreaded third visitation occurred.

The Townsend residence on K Street in Sacramento was a well-preserved, three-story Victorian, slate-gray with white trim. The house kept a stately watch over its occupants: Harold Townsend, a dealer in used cars, his wife Patricia, and their children Rachel and Billy. Santa had just read Rachel's note to him and taken a crisp bite out of an Oreo.

The sudden pressure of a hand coming to rest upon his shoulder nearly made him choke.

It was her, pantied in red this time, the same fire-engine red as his suit. The savage beauty of her body was as breathtaking as before, but no lust shone in her eyes, nothing of the huntress hung about her.

That caught Santa off guard.

"It's me again," she said.

He swallowed the cookie as best he could, pretending nonchalance. "So I see."

She brought her lips to his fingers and took the last bite of Oreo out of them as if it were a communion wafer. Then she lifted the glass of milk from the table and drank it down.

The not-Santa crept back into him, peering hungrily at the long sweep of her neck and its inviting resolution in the thrust and surge of her mammaries.

What's her game this time? And what is this thing inside me, this thing I call not-Santa? Whatever it was, it felt disturbingly comfortable, like easing into a pair of forgotten slippers.

She set the glass down. "I haven't harvested the little girl's tooth yet," she said. "Let's take a peek, shall we?"

Santa sensed a trap. "I don't think that would be a good idea." But the Tooth Fairy insisted, poking his rotund belly and giving a maddening little laugh.

At last he consented ("But no funny business!"). She led

him down the hall to Rachel's room, passing hand in hand with him through the closed door. In her oversized bed, the sleeping child was dwarfed by the stuffed animals that shared her dreams. It had been her gramma and grampa's bed, but they had bought a new one, and, knowing how Rachel loved it so, had given her the giant bed for her own. Now she lay on a thin sliver of mattress at the rightmost edge, one arm around the neck of a large teddy bear.

"There's the little dear," the Tooth Fairy whispered, closer to Santa's ear than she really needed to be. "Wait here. I'll only be a moment."

She glided to the bed. Rachel's head lolled toward her, her mouth open in the innocence of sleep. The Tooth Fairy ran a greedy finger over the exposed enamel of her bottom teeth. There was something menacing, something perverse, in her movements. Santa made an instinctive feint toward the child. Then the Tooth Fairy's hand slid beneath the pillow and found Rachel's tooth.

Turning to Santa, she opened her mouth and placed it, like a small white pill, provocatively on the tip of her tongue. Hunger flared in her eyes.

Oh dear God, it begins again.

As she chewed, the sharp crunch of bone grinding bone sang in Santa's ears.

And it feels so undeniably good.

Deftly she peeled off the red panties and tossed them his way. He caught and pocketed them without taking his eyes from her, fearful lest she vanish as before.

And what is Anya?

She squatted, legs spread wide, and shat dimes.

Anya is but a being torn from her lifespring, denying the undeniable surge.

Dimes dropped like tight silver turds from her anus, shiny in moonlight, ringing upon the bare wooden floor, spinning and rolling hither and yon.

And what is the Tooth Fairy?

With a practiced hand she retrieved them and slid them beneath the pillow.

Pure body, pure need, pure demand. That which must be caressed and covered and filled.

Then she lay down amongst the stuffed animals and harshly ordered Santa to make love to her.

Her skin shone flawless as a stone madonna's.

When he ran halfheartedly through his poor litany of objections, she stretched most provocatively, her body the body of a cat. And when he protested further, she merely smiled upon him, opened wide her thighs, and massaged with slow fingers the blushing wound of her love. Her breasts, mounded by the narrowing V of her downthrust arms, nippled into the night air. At the sight of them, Santa fell speechless. There were no more words in him. They had played out like line shooting madly off the spool of a fishing rod before a high-spirited bonefish that refuses to be landed.

Now there was only heat in Rachel's room. Heat that made Santa's suit a heavy obscenity, heat rising from the Tooth Fairy's splayed body, heat churning deep in Santa's groin where Santa and not-Santa conjoined most inseparably together. As quick as a nod, he unbooted and unsocked his feet, uncapped his head, unbelted, unsuited, and un-red-flannel-underweared his demanding flesh.

Feels right. Right? By God, it feels perfect!

Massive, all-giving, and generously endowed, Santa Claus went to the Tooth Fairy and lay with her for hour after hour of magic time, sharing the delights of illicit love.

Magic time allows beings benevolent and malevolent to move unseen among humanity, distributing gifts to billions of children in one night, for example, or bartering coins for teeth. Without magic time, the pale hand that guides the planchette would become disquietingly visible. Without magic time, scoffers at superstition would sniff the vile shades that hover beneath ladders and know better than to defy the ancient wisdom. Without magic time, the limitless vistas hidden in the mirror's depths would leap into view, as would the Sandman's wizened visage and the cottontailed hindquarters of a departing Easter Bunny.

For a short while, this same magic time kept what passed between Santa and his lover from Rachel's senses. But then, as sometimes happens, there was a seepage, a commingling of their world with hers. Her brain tingling still with the numbing touch of sleep, Rachel opened wide her eyes and ears and let come to her what would, out of the tremulous darkness of her bedroom.

What came to her were two unclothed grown-ups moving against one another beyond her teddy bear, their heads pillowed on Elmer the Elephant. The glow that outlined them, as well as the numbness that held sway in her body, meant of course that she was dreaming.

Of that she was sure.

Nor was there any question who these grown-ups were. She felt blessed by their presence in her dream, looming large as gods in her bed, even though they seemed to be fighting about something or other. All their grunting and groaning seemed strange to her, hardly what one would expect from Santa Claus and the Tooth Fairy. But then it looked less like fighting than wrestling. Every so often, they would stop and take up a new position, then move and rub against one another again, just like the junior high kids in that boring wrestling match Daddy had dragged her and Billy to the week before.

She couldn't get over how wonderful Santa looked, how kind his face shone even through his sweat. She loved the vastness of him and the soft sweep of his pure white hair, playing about his face. Santa was white-haired too, she noticed, below his astounding belly. And out of that wild riot of white curls, he had grown an extra finger, long and fat and upright. Santa kept hiding it inside the Tooth Fairy, sometimes in her mouth, sometimes down where she went tinkle. The Tooth Fairy seemed to like having it hidden in her.

Rachel was awestruck by the fury of the Tooth Fairy's thrashings, how hungrily she feasted upon Santa's aura of kindness, taking in more and more yet never depleting his stock, then flinging it back into his face, her passion as tossed and distressed as a thunderstorm. She was ghastly. And yet there was something extremely beautiful about her, something that made Rachel want to kiss her.

On occasion, Santa would match the sounds his partner made deep in her throat, savage guttural noises which were transformed, by his echoing voice, into psalms of wisdom and benevolence. It thrilled Rachel's ears to hear the two of them like that. She felt she might almost explode with the joy of it. Her breath quickened but she kept as quiet as she could, lest she be noticed and denied further witness.

Hour after hour it went on, as dreams often do. She pleaded with God to let her remember every bit of it when she awoke the next morning.

Her prayers, however, went unanswered. For Rachel tumbled out of magic time and into normal sleep long before Santa uncoupled from the Tooth Fairy, grabbed his clothes, and staggered spent from her room. And though brief snatches of that night's witnessing flashed before her as she grew to womanhood, not for twenty years or more did the entire scene come rushing back full-bore into Rachel's memory.

And that would occur precisely one year before the Tooth Fairy devoured her at the North Pole.

2.

SANTA'S FIRST LIE

Anya's knitting lay limp upon her lap. Resting her elbows on the curved arms of her rocker, she halted for a moment its mindless movement.

Outside her sewing room window, freshly fallen snow glinted like shattered glass where the sunlight splashed across it. At the edge of the woods, clusters of elves were at play. Some built elaborate snow creatures. Some flung themselves down and made angels. Others leaped and whirled, singly or in pairs, on the skating pond.

It was their day off. The final gift had winked from the workshop shelves, the last home had been graced with a nocturnal visit from Santa Claus, and he was winging his way home. One day each year, *this* day, his helpers got to frolic and cavort to their heart's content. Santa would enjoy a private Christmas celebration with Anya in the morning, followed by the afternoon festivities in and around the elves' quarters. Then it was back to the industrious joy of creating playthings for the world's children.

Anya winced. Pain took a bite out of her left thigh. "Damned sciatica," she muttered, shifting in the rocker and readjusting her skirts.

A face popped up at the window.

Anya started, then she relaxed into a smile.

It was Fritz, her favorite elf: red-haired, gap-toothed, and ageless. Just yesterday he had run up to her, panicked, cradling a squirrel with a broken and bloody leg. It lay still in her hands as she healed its hurts with her tongue. Then it licked her cheek once in gratitude, leaped out of her grasp, and bounded off good as new into the woods. Now Fritz, rapping sharply on the glass, shouted something incomprehensible and beckoned to her. Shaking her head in a play of sadness, she held up her half-finished sweater. Fritz gave her a little-boy grimace and dashed off to join the rest, his cap jouncing this way and that like a buffeted leaf.

Such exuberance, such energy these little men showed. One would hardly guess that they were centuries old. Anya sighed.

Kindhearted though she was, she resented it sometimes that God had waited to grant her immortality until she had grown white-haired, bespectacled, and well past sixty. On those rare occasions when she opened herself to bitterness and regret, it struck Anya as grossly unfair that no rollback clause had been written into the bargain—no divine afflatus that would pull the skin tight over her bones, blow away her aches and pains, and breathe the buoyant winds of rejuvenation through her limbs.

It didn't help matters, she thought, to live with a man whose energies never flagged, who sacrificed sleep for toymaking, often disappearing for days into his workshop and emerging brimful of vitality, a sly hint of marital urgency lighting his eye.

It pained her to remove, night after night, Santa's speculative hand from her flannel thigh. But menopause had claimed Anya way back in the fourth century when they dwelt in Myra and had not yet become immortal. Since then, her carnal urges, never very strong even at their zenith, had dwindled to nearly nothing. It was a banner year if they made love a handful of times between one Christmas and the next.

He was a good man, Claus; the best of men. Sometimes it was a trial being married to him, feeling the need to prove herself worthy of his goodness. Among his many fine qualities, she counted his saint's measure of patience with her; the way he treated his helpers, paternal yet not patronizing; his wholehearted dedication to the children.

In the distance, a silent ruckus began. Flurries of snowballs flew in wide white arcs between two impromptu armies.

"Land sakes, where do they get all that energy?" With a shake of her head and a cluck of her tongue, she resumed her knitting and lost herself once more in the rhythm of the rocking and the clicking of the needles.

Fritz dashed across the commons toward the skating pond, kicking up powdered snow as he went. He wished, just once, that Mrs. Claus would leave the cozy confines of her cottage and join in the festivities.

"Fritz! Look out!"

Knecht Rupert's high-pitched shout rang out too late. The *whoosh* of a snowball—the smack of it against his forehead like the blow of a frost giant's fist—came out of nowhere. Down he tumbled, backward into the snow, and the gleeful taunts of the others washed over him.

He felt his face redden. Johann the Elder and Gustav, Rupert's perennial sidekicks, gave Fritz resounding backslaps of encouragement and bent to the business of turning the gifts of nature into weapons. Then Rupert's strong arms helped him up and the battle was joined.

His allies loped about him, scooping up handfuls of snow and packing them tight, then letting fly toward the porcelain doll contingent which swooped in on the right. So many years had the dollmakers worked together at their specialty that they were almost identical sextuplets. Though their faces were blunt as bulls and they sported long black beards, their lips were bowed like the painted lips of the dolls they made and their voices strained high and tight in their throats.

Everyone called them Heinrich. It was the name they all answered to, and none of them had ever tried in any way to distinguish himself from the others.

Heinrich, then, a twelve-armed wonder, lobbed his battery of snowballs into Fritz's beleaguered group, downing Gustav and smacking Fritz on the ear. Fritz raised his fists to the skies, howling. He stooped and threw like a madman, shaming the restraint of Knecht Rupert and his companions. After an initial flurry of misses, Fritz's canny arm remembered trajectory, adjusting for wind speed, anticipating moving targets. The ensuing barrage turned Heinrich's unstoppable onslaught into first a standoff and then a rout.

"After them!" shouted Fritz, heading for the woods. But as he and his comrades-in-arms pounded closer to the snow-laden firs, reinforcements for Heinrich popped up from behind a great outcropping of rock. Fritz identified the two instigators of this new assault as his bunkmates: Karlheinz, he of the rolling-thunder snore, and Max, whose occasional bedwetting had consigned him, by a two-to-one vote, to the lower bunk. These turncoats descended upon him, flanked by elves from the rocking horse contingent, tubby little men with arms that flailed as they ran and wide eyes that flashed fire.

Now it was Fritz's turn to feel the brunt of attack everywhere on his body. First on face, chest, and arms. Then, as he fled, against his shoulders, hard upon his back, and dripping slow and cold down his neck. Elves swooped in from all directions to gang up on him and his cohorts.

At his heels, Gustav shouted, "For the love of God, Fritz, can't you run any faster?"

No time to answer. The attackers drew closer, their volley of snowballs filling the air like some giant ski shushing to a stop.

Ahead, Mrs. Claus bent to her knitting, framed by the wide rectangle of her sewing room window. How lovely she was. So kind and gentle a woman. The sort Fritz would be glad to spend his life with in holy matrimony, if God had intended elves to marry or entertain thoughts of intimacy.

It occurred to him, as his legs carried him toward Santa's cottage, that many centuries past there had been wild times indeed, intimacies as commonplace as they were scandalous. But memories of those days—before God had conjured them out of nothing to work with Santa—were so hard to dredge up, and so evanescent when you succeeded, that it was scarcely worth the effort.

Another volley of blows hammered against his back. Snowballs whistling overhead fell just short of Santa's cottage. The huge one that finally hit swept rudely past his right ear and boomed against the sewing room window, blotting out Mrs. Claus's matronly bosom.

It came straight out of the blue. One moment, the rhythmic ticking of cuckoo clocks above the low, steady swing of their grandfather clock's gold pendulum; the next, a sudden whump, the heart-clenching report of balled snow smacking glass. Anya rose sharply, threw her knitting into the rocking chair, and glared out at the halted hordes of helpers.

Dear God, how many times must she warn them not to play so close to the cottage? At least once more, that was clear. She made her way out of the sewing room to the front door, muttering all the way.

Outside, two score elves stood chastened in the snow, eyes downcast, shoulders slumped. Some held their caps over their crotches or let them hang listlessly from their hands. Bald pates glistened in the sun. Karlheinz moped forward and made a shamefaced confession.

In her kindest voice, Anya said, "It hardly matters who threw the snowball, does it?"

They shook their heads.

"I'm old. My system doesn't take kindly to shocks. It's fine to let loose on your day off. But please. Not so close to the cottage. You've got that whole expanse out there to play in." She pulled her shawl about her shoulders and gestured to the commons and beyond. Her hand, she noticed, was frail and arthritic, its dexterity lost in the passage of years.

It was cold out here. Her cheeks tingled. Her ears rang with the faint whine of fresh snow in still air.

But no. The sounds she heard came and went. Not the steady throb of winter but high discrete pulses, like the tremolo of distant violins, like zephyrs wafting over harpstrings.

Like sleighbells.

She lifted her eyes. Out past the skating pond, out beyond the elves' quarters, above the tops of the tallest trees that tickled the sky's underbelly, a black dot hung in the distance, growing imperceptibly larger.

Love swelled warm within her.

As effortlessly as a morning glory opens to the sun, Anya smiled.

Fritz raised his eyes to Mrs. Claus. Her left hand gripped the porch railing. Her right froze in mid-gesture as she gazed into the sky.

He was the first to notice her radiance, the first to divine the reason for it. But the others quickly caught fire. Bright green caps, buoyed by whoops and shouts, pancaked into the air. Fritz endured with good humor the sixfold embrace of Heinrich the dollmaker. On all sides, his bearded brethren leaped and hopped about or attempted cartwheels in the snow. Mostly, they jumped for joy, pointing ecstatically to the heavens and rolling out shouts of welcome for their returning master.

Fritz turned about and looked up at the long brown insect struggling through the sky. Santa's whip was an eyelash, his team the third part of a centipede, himself not much larger than a ladybug rearing on her hind legs.

The elf's eyes brimmed with joy.

Santa felt soiled.

And cleansed.

Coursing across the arctic sky, brutal winds above, frozen tundra below, he marveled how these two feelings, so violently opposed, could take root and thrive in his breast, entwined like old friends. Not-Santa had butted his way in, and the Santa Claus he had been before—pure goodness, all giving—stood there in shock, incapable of tossing the intruder out.

He felt deep shame.

Shame for betraying his wife, for reveling in the flesh of another woman. Shame for having befouled the bed of little Rachel

Townsend while the darling girl dozed innocently beside them. Shame for the desecration he had visited upon one dwelling after another thereafter, his mind fixated on copulations past and to come, while it ought to have been fully on the task at hand.

But he also felt delight.

More precisely, the not-Santa, that vile intruder lured out of his depths by the Tooth Fairy—*this* creature felt delight. Delight in the hot savagery of his lover's supple body, in the way she opened herself to his hunger. Santa was shocked to realize that the perverse divinity of their coupling inspired in this not-Santa a feeling that could only be called reverence.

Ahead, a glow on the horizon.

The mild bubble of winter God had given him and his little community so many centuries before.

Home.

"Almost there, my lovelies," Santa bellowed into the deafening wind. "Straight on between Lucifer's antlers. There await warm elfin hands to rub you down, young aspen shoots and willow buds and berries in abundance to satisfy your hunger, and a cozy stall to rest yourselves in."

Santa grimaced. *There await the purest beings God had the good grace to set upon this gentle earth, and the purest of them all—my dear sweet wife Anya.*

He longed to be with Anya.

Yet, God help him, he dreaded it.

Would she sense the change in him? Would she catch the musky aroma of the Tooth Fairy on his clothes, in his whiskers, hanging thick about his sex?

The bubble arched up bit by bit, stretching wider along the horizon and taking on a thin bristle of trees.

He shifted in his seat, eager to entrust the sleigh to Gregor and his brothers for a wax and polish, a new paint job, careful storage until next year. What a relief it would be to roam the woods again after being gone so long, to cast a benign eye upon his elves' labors, to sit by the fire, of an evening, puffing on his pipe and watching Anya knit and rock, rock and knit.

God grant it be so.

Now the tree stubble took on stature, rising majestic from the snow-clad wilds ahead. The sub-zero temperatures of the polar icecap abruptly yielded to the milder weather within. Ahead, like miniatures in a model train set, he saw the tiny workshop and stables, the mica shine of the skating pond, and dead on, his and Anya's cottage, green with touches of red and white. He wept to see their home, floating upon a sea of snow, smoke skirling up from its chimneytop.

And waiting on the porch, his darling Anya.

But fear tainted his joy. Fear that she would slip away, turn her back on his betrayal and vanish forever.

One thing was clear. His unwelcome guest must be locked away, given no chance to show himself before the polar community.

As he began the slow descent, Santa did his best to put on his prelapsarian face.

He was beautiful up there, her man. If anything could rekindle the fires of her infrequent passion, it was watching him sail in over the treetops, cherry-red and rotund, a radiant smile playing upon his lips. The sight always made her stand taller, breathe deeper, go as moist as a lusty young bride.

He urged his team onward, sweeping in ever narrowing circles overhead. The insistent jingle of sleighbells slapping at the haunches of the reindeer made her feel all saucy inside. Part of her wanted him right then in mid-descent with all the elves watching. But the rest of her was more than content to prolong the wait, to savor every moment that stretched from right now to the delicious suspension of time beneath their blankets after the day's festivities were done.

She couldn't be sure, afterward, when she had first begun to feel unsettled. Without question, the feeling was heavy in her by the time hoof and runner touched snow. Before that, its stages were impossible to define. It seemed much more an accretion of small noticings: the way he held back his descent, the angle at which he cocked his head, a hint of tension in his upraised arm, an unsettling disharmony in the team, the unmistakable impression that he was at once avoiding her eyes and forcing himself to smile in her direction.

The elves appeared to notice nothing. They swarmed over him as always, lifted him high on their shoulders, carried him (according to tradition) once, twice, thrice around the sleigh, then wrestled him to the snow and fell to tickling him and mauling him until, through the boom and roll of his laughter, he begged for mercy. When at last they calmed down, the elves set Santa back on his feet, brushed him off, and led him up to the porch where his wife stood waiting.

Without knowing why, Anya felt sick inside.

No, that wasn't true. She knew this feeling well. She understood precisely what was going on. A name flashed inside her head. *Pitys.* Spoken in a voice that belonged and did not belong to Santa, thick with crushed grape and guile and eternal boyishness. Then the voice and the name it had spoken were gone, and all that remained were a hard knot in her stomach and a wife's unerring instinct for betrayal.

Shiny black boots crunched the snow on the steps to the porch. An alien face loomed over her. A chill white beard brushed soft and swirly against her cheek. Around her body, bearish arms wrapped an embrace.

She watched herself return a kiss, heard the roar of the elves, felt the fire's warmth reaching out to claim her as they stepped inside and closed the door.

As Santa stood beside Anya at the fireplace, the crackling flames seemed neither as bright nor as warm as memory claimed they should be. Home didn't feel like home. It felt like some painted replica, a stage set waiting to be struck at the ringing down of some final curtain.

(That's cuz we don't belong here, Santa old buddy. This place is too perfect, not enough blemish, no room for passion, you catch my drift?)

Oh fine, thought Santa. Now his intruder had found a voice. Raspy as a hacksaw, biting as a freshly opened can of shellac, as dark as three coats of walnut stain.

"I must have snow in my ears, Anya dear," he joked. "Couldn't quite hear what you said."

She grimaced. "I said it's good to have you home." Tension lined her face.

(Sexless bitch is on to us. Best we should—)

I won't have her talked about that way.

"Is . . . is something wrong?" Santa gasped out. His scalp beaded with sweat. A fist clenched deep in his gut, down where truths hide unspoken. Her unwavering gaze unnerved him, and unworthy thoughts—seeds of resentment toward his wife—came upon him. Looking away, he fished for his pipe, his pouch, busying himself with them.

(That's it, chum. Evasive action's always good. And we've got lots of evading to do, all that fine humping—)

She took his face in her hands, searched his eyes for oddity. "Something happened to you out there, didn't it? Something you're keeping from me."

(Oooh doggies, we're in for it now, fat boy!)

Santa froze. How could he just blurt out the truth? It felt so bitter on his tongue, this blunt admission of adultery. Yet even if he were successful in putting her off with vague denials, his unspoken misdeed would stand there solid but invisible between them. Better to lay it before her, he thought, come what may.

(Hold it right there, chubbynums. This situation calls for a bit of good old husbandly deception. I—)

That's enough. I'm telling her.

(Heh-heh-heh. Guess some folks gotta learn the hard way. It's your funeral, bub.)

Santa sat beside Anya on the couch by the fire, looking down at the plush throw rug and holding her hands. And as the grandfather clock's great pendulum knocked aside every other second, he began to tell her what had happened, leaving nothing out.

***

Fritz loved the reindeer so. While Gregor and his brothers led them to the stables, Fritz walked beside his beloved Cupid, smoothing his chestnut pelt and fondling the intricate branchwork of his antlers. But as Gregor decoupled team and sleigh, Fritz's enthusiasm made him more hindrance than help. After two unheeded warnings Gregor dismissed him, telling him to come back the next morning when Cupid and the others were rested.

On his way across the commons, heading for the elves' quarters, Fritz heard voices raised and the slamming of doors inside Santa's cottage.

He froze.

His pale blue shadow stretched across the drifts as he strained to distinguish words. Elusive shapes moved from room to room. The muffle of window and wallboard stripped away all consonants, leaving only naked vowels that traced the unfamiliar sounds of marital strife.

A chill slipped into Fritz's bones and held. He raised his hands against the sights and sounds. When he put a finger to his lips, they were dry, hard, tight, the painted lips of a ventriloquist's dummy. He faced about then and ran, kicking up snowy waves of panic and denial as he closed the distance between himself and the dormitory.

Midway through Santa's narrative, Anya startled him with a mangled cry. Santa looked at her for the first time since he had begun. Her rage hit him before he could piece together the face it flared from. She slapped him, hard and stinging. Then she bolted from the couch.

"Anya, wait!" he shouted, his jaw awkward and gangly from being struck. He took off after her, deflecting doors slammed at his nose, begging her to be reasonable, to hear him out. At last he found himself kneeling beside their bed. Her steamed spectacles she protected by propping herself up on her elbows and bending her forehead to the pillow.

"Bastard!" she hissed. Tears curved along her lenses and hit the pillowcase. "Didn't you for one moment stop to think how I'd feel?"

"Anya, she seduced me," protested Santa. "She came up to me and started rubbing against me. Not that it's her fault, that's not what I mean. You don't know what that does to a man, to have a beautiful barely-clad woman drool all over him. I know, I know. I'm as much to blame as she is."

She fisted the pillow and glared up at him. "How dare you make excuses for that fairy slut. Just look at yourself. Big saintly man, brimful of love and presents for the little ones. Ah but put down the pack, strip off the red suit? You're nothing but a rutting animal, just another overweight hog with a twinkle in his eye, sniffing at the hindquarters of any sow that trots across his path."

"Anya—"

"Don't you touch me!" she screamed. "You touched *her* with those hands, didn't you? I know your way. Get a woman all fired up under those incredible hands of yours. Dear God, I'm going to—"

She bolted for the bathroom and slammed the door. Santa heard the sharp report of the toilet lid striking the tank, then the sudden uprush of vomit and a splash as of diarrhea into the bowl.

He went to the door and called her name.

"Don't you come in here!" she threatened. He heard her spit into the water, wad up lengths of toilet paper, flush them away. The water ran as she rinsed her mouth.

Then, eyes watery, white strands of hair gone astray, Anya walked past him and collapsed on the bed, staring up at the ceiling. She had left her glasses in the bathroom. Without them she looked older.

Santa, weak-willed as a dreamer, felt the mattress yield to his weight as he sat upon the edge of the bed, careful to avoid all contact with his wife. Words came into his mouth, words not of his own choosing, the wily intruder's words. Powerless to stop them, not even sure he'd want to if he could, he heard them fall from his lips.

"Dearest Anya," they began, "I never wanted to hurt you. Far better to sink into the earth than hurt you, my perfect mate, my beloved friend. As much love as God has given me for the boys and girls of this world, never have I loved any of them with one scintilla of the love I hold in my heart for you."

It sounded so stilted to him, this speech. It amazed and appalled him. The sentiments were undeniably true, but the words felt absolutely false in the speaking—as they must, he thought, in the hearing.

"You're the only woman for me, Anya," he assured her, blinking back tears, fighting against the raw hurt in his throat. "That's the way it's always been. That's the way it will always be."

Santa dug into his pockets for a handkerchief. Just as his right hand found one, the fingers of his left hand closed on silk. Red silk.

(Ah, that's it, now you've laid hold of a piece of reality, the good stuff, a sweet reminder of the breached gates of heaven.)

Enough. No more. Leave me alone.

Clutching the panties, he felt the tingle of flesh-memory woven into them and became aware of his manhood's demand for stiffening blood. Later, he thought, he would discard them, toss them into the fire while Anya slept.

(Oooh, don't even joke *about such a thing. Lord o' mercy, you gonna make me keel over and die with talk like that. You keep those babies around, hear me, Santa?)*

Yes . . . yes I think I must. It made him ill to picture the red silk falling upon the fire, catching slowly at first, then quicker, seething into oblivion. They were too precious for that; an icon, a totem. He could never bring himself to destroy them.

"Please believe me, my beloved," Santa's false voice continued, "the Tooth Fairy means nothing to me, nothing at all. It was a mistake, a terrible mistake. I'm sorry for the pain I've caused you. If you could see your way clear to trust me, I give you my word it will never happen again."

He was sobbing now, but only partially in repentance. The rest were tears of rage, tears shed for what he seemed to have become. For he knew, even as the words reeled out and honestly begged Anya's forgiveness, that any promise he made to stay away from the luscious body of the Tooth Fairy was an empty one.

The lies lay like spoiled meat in his mouth.

And yet (heaven help him, was he going mad?) he felt good about lying to Anya, liberated somehow, reveling in hidden guile, tasting the fruits of a newfound freedom. Or was it new? At the fringes of his memory, forgotten images, tantalizing and elusive, teased his senses—forest smells, the thick richness of moss beneath his back, the feel of nymph tongue on genital.

"If she appears again next Christmas, I swear to God I'll stand strong against her wiles. I'll send her packing." Anya lay there looking at the ceiling, but her breathing had slowed. "I know that the memory of this terrible time will never fade entirely, not for either of us." The tingle of silk made visions of nudity dance in Santa's head. "But I want to try to get through this with you in a way that, hard as it may seem now, strengthens our love for each other."

Anya had calmed considerably. She looked at him. "All right, Claus. Let's see how things go. I believe we're strong enough to weather this. But don't expect me to want to . . . to engage in intimacies any time soon. It's going to take some time, some adjustment."

Santa nodded. "Take all the time you need."

"I don't know about you," said Anya, attempting a half-smile, "but I'm exhausted." She touched a hand to his knee. "The elves are probably wondering what's keeping us. Go take your shower and let's do what we can to survive the rest of today. We'll start fresh in the morning."

Thank God, he thought, I haven't destroyed it. Not yet.

But in the depths of his coat pocket, Santa's left hand luxuriated in lust.

3.
TWENTY YEARS OF SECRECY

Throughout much of the following year, caught up in the invention of a softer teddy bear, a whizzier gyroscope, a more meticulously detailed dollhouse, Santa was certain he had conquered his lust completely. The intruder's voice had fallen away. Santa hoped he was gone for good.

But alas, in elf as in mortal man, concupiscence is not so easily quelled. Despite his honorable intentions, despite the ardency with which he nightly knelt and prayed beside his bed, despite the endless stream of cold showers he shivered under as Christmas Eve approached, Santa fell and fell hard for the Tooth Fairy. The mere sight of her naked flesh—lying open for him the following Christmas beneath the frosted spruce of George and Bertha Watkins of Augusta, Maine—swept aside all resolve and brought his alter ego fully awake and panting. Into the wanton profusion of her limbs he plunged with all the abandon of some parched wayfarer, desert bound and nigh unto death, who, stumbling upon an oasis, tumbles headlong laughing into its lake of living water.

That Christmas she seduced him once in each of the fifty states, letting him anticipate her presence in every dwelling he gifted, then looming up under his nose when he least expected it and drawing him down into a maelstrom of desire. She had him in hovels, in palatial mansions, on worn runners in dark apartment buildings. She had him in dens, in basement playrooms, in cramped attics thick with time where their oozings left heart-shaped stains in the dust. She lured him into hall closets, where, as she knelt among snowboots, Santa clung to the thick dowelling overhead. And there, his face flushed among the hangers, his breath tightening, urgent love leapt out of him like a surge of panthers into the darkness below.

After their fifth such encounter, Santa, feeling soiled by his infidelity, resolved to call a halt, to plead with the Tooth Fairy to save him from himself.

Sweeping down Broadway in the midst of a blizzard, past Columbia University on his left, Santa banked over Barnard until his team pounded against flurries of snow above West End Avenue. They touched down at last on the tarred roof of a four-story brownstone on West 91st, its black surface aswirl with driving snow. Drifts washed off like capped waves in all directions, their shifting crests blue in the moonlight. And there she lay, upon a soft mound of white near the roof edge— the Tooth Fairy, sleek, round, and ready, her breasts stiff-nippled and flecked with flakes.

She twisted toward him as he stepped down from the sleigh, the wind fanning his beard out around his face. Her arms reached up. "Take me," she whispered, more to groin than ear. Although her voice was low, Santa could hear what she said as plainly as if the boom and moan of the blizzard were no more than a deaf man's dream.

(You heard the lady, bunkie. Have at her.)

That's enough. It's time to call it quits.

(It's never enough, fat boy, never. You know that. We both know that.)

Santa stroked Dancer's flank and lifted his eyes to his team, whose heads were turned every one to take in the naked fairy banked in snow. Lucifer's antlers pulsed in what Santa took to be disapproval but which was really arousal. Santa gave them a comradely shrug, as if to say, "What's a fellow to do?"

Beneath his boots, packed snow squeaked and crunched. Santa crouched beside her. "Listen," he shouted into the storm. "We can't go on like this."

Her only answer? A mock pout. She traced with thumb and forefinger the long fat arc of his erection. Then she unbuckled his wide black belt. In the fury of the wind, her crimson hair blew all about, trapping snowflakes like stubborn gems.

Feeling his saintly goodness crumble once more—far too easily, he thought, for one who had been selfless for centuries—Santa closed his eyes momentarily against the force of her charms. Then, in a last grasp at purity, he snapped them open and grabbed her wrists in a tight grip.

"Don't you hear me, woman?" he pleaded. "I've got a wife. I love her. I've vowed by all that's holy to be faithful to her."

(Don't be a chump, fat boy. Take her.)

You've had your say. Now shut up, whoever you are.

The Tooth Fairy smiled and stretched. Her thighs parted. Santa saw, with sinking heart and rising petard, the hot fluid of her lust pooling there, demanding intimacy. She drew her mouth up past his cheek and gasped, "Fuck fidelity, you fucking stud! Fuck *me*!"

The feel of her lips against his ear, her hot breath, the carnality of her fricatives were too overwhelming to be denied. Sobbing against his fate, Santa fumbled at his suit—*(That's the ticket, Nick old buddy; you and me, we're halfway home, oh yes indeedy, and what an inviting little dwelling place it is)*—stripping himself bare against the blizzard.

And there, with his faithful team looking on, blowing and snorting impatience and arousal, Santa dug his toes into frozen slush and brought them both to the heights of ecstasy, he feeling the chill winds of winter blasting along his spine and freezing his buttocks, she opening her lips wide to orgasm and choking with delight upon the deluge of snowflakes that swirled down into the depths of her throat.

That night, after Manhattan, Santa found it less and less difficult to give in to lust. His pleas to God to steel his will, his regrets that at his creation there had not been included some small inoculative mix of baseness, if only to remove the element of surprise which befuddled him now—these diminished as his prayers for a stronger back and finer taste buds increased.

And beyond that night, other Christmases saw the two of them scheming to cross paths with increasing frequency. Santa's first stop, and his last, became always his fairy lover's wind-whipped island. There upon the rocky shore, beneath the blasted cypress—its twisted limbs decked in shells and seaweed, a dead starfish nailed aloft—the two of them humped and plotted, plotted and humped, bringing into precise and satisfying conjunction their bodies and their evening's itineraries.

Santa preferred things that way. Once he knew where she'd be when, he could give his giftgiving the attention it deserved. The blessed children, after all, had first claim always on his love. Lifting aloft drained and happy from her island, Santa pictured the uncountable millions of sleepy wee ones, nightie'd and pajama'd. The special dreams of Christmas wrapped them round snug and warm. But it was his visitation, the nocturnal touch of Santa Claus, which brought the magic of selfless giving into their homes.

And if, at times, he turned away from the holly and the ivy, set aside his pack, and pressed the lurch and lunge of his gotta-have-it desire up against that of the fairy with the ravenous eyes and the necklace of teeth, where was the harm in that? There was enough of him, by heaven, to go around. He could be Anya's loving mate; he could be the Tooth Fairy's hump-and-grunt of a fuckfriend; and he could be Santa Claus, jovial, roly-poly bestower of gifts and goodies upon children young and old.

Only in the minds of the pinched and narrow, he assured himself, did these roles conflict.

Santa's elves are sturdy creatures. Never growing older, always in the best of health, they laugh and toil year in, year out, free from the vicissitudes of change.

However.

Sometimes, whether it be in the gruff and grumble of a snowball fight, or in the misjuggle of a fistful of ball peen hammers, or in some other such hapless circumstance, sometimes an elf loses a tooth.

In the fifth year of Santa's affair with the Tooth Fairy, Friedrich the globemaker, whose head was as oblate as the earth he modeled, lost his right lateral incisor to a doorframe that didn't look where it was going.

He placed it beneath his pillow.

And the Tooth Fairy, welcomed thus to Santa's domain, ate the elf's tooth, replaced it with one thousand newly-shat shiny copper pfennigs, drifted across the commons, passed through the door of Santa's cottage, hovered over her lover's bed, glared at the dozing Anya, kissed Santa out of slumber and into magic time, lured him across the snow to his workshop, and fucked out his lights amid pinwheels and piccolos, race cars and rockets, gizmos and gadgets galore. The glazed eyes of countless stuffed dolls and animals looked down upon their maker as he brought adultery most foul to the North Pole.

Truth be told, Santa grew uneasy there in the near-darkness with all those unblinking eyes staring at him. But where else could they go? Up here, in this tight little community, no ideal place existed for them to have at each other with complete abandon.

So when the Tooth Fairy drank him spermless one last time and slipped away, Santa remained in magic time and built them a cozy hut way off in the woods where no one had ventured before.

It was the perfect locus for love. Concealed in a copse of ash trees, its stones rose from snow, solid and inviting. Inside, a great stone fireplace roared its paean to love. Blazing Yule logs splashed into every crevice and corner waves of liquid light. Down across surfaces of fur and quilting they went and up over a huge four-poster built of ashwood, its large mattress awash with pillows and stuffed with swan's down. At each side of the bed, wide windows looked out on moonlit snowdrifts and the silhouettes of trees.

Despite his pride in its workmanship, Santa knew that this hut represented a sharp departure from his old ways. Pure selfishness. An absolute concealment from those he had always been open with. Yet the trees themselves seemed to conspire with him, to remind him of some former life he had forgotten utterly, a life his sly intruder had played a leading role in. Names came to him from their swaying limbs: Syce, Crania; Ptelea, Morea, Carya; Ampelus, Balanus, Aeiginus; and repeatedly and with peculiar urgency, Pitys. Names meaningless to him, yet freighted with meaning.

The next night Santa couldn't sleep. He lay awake beside Anya, staring into the darkness, imagining the Tooth Fairy's return, how he would take her to their new-minted hideaway and have her there.

But she didn't come that night.

Nor the following night.

The third night, Santa got smart. First he went to the stables and, one by one, woke the reindeer. No, each of them shook his antlered head, blearing up at him. None of my teeth are loose, none need pulling. Nine times he asked the question. Nine times he took denial, kissed the soft tufted fur between the reindeer's eyes, and let him lapse into sleep.

Next, cloaked in magic time, he visited each of his multitude of dozing elves. His fingers probed their tiny mouths, testing the seating of every molar, every cuspid and bicuspid, every incisor both central and lateral. For hour upon hour, he searched in vain for that one loose tooth which, wrenched free and placed twixt sheet and pillow, would summon his paramour to his side.

Then the lightbulb went on.

To his workshop he went, cursing himself for a fool all the way. Feverishly he snapped on his worklights, gathered materials and tools. His seasoned hands flew among them. Out of the chaos scattered across his workbench, he whipped together a child's bed. Simple, functional, inviting. The sort of bed an eight-year-old would dream wonders in after a trying day battling giants and ogres at school.

Another swatch of chaos, another miracle: a doll so lifelike that in the dimness of a room lit by fire, one would swear she was a real little girl, eyes gently closed, lips parted in sleep. Inside the lips? Teeth. Just a few, made of soft wood with a thick coating of ivory from a store of cast-off piano keys. Teeth that snapped firmly into place in the girl's plastic gums, teeth that snapped out just as easily.

Santa prayed it would do.

To the hut he carried her, bed balanced on his back. He brought the fire to a fine blaze, then turned away to decide where to position the little girl, whom he had begun to call Thea. He settled on one corner of the room, just past the window on the far left side. Thea's bed fit to perfection there. She looked as if she'd been sleeping for eons. Santa bent, like a protective parent, to kiss her forehead. With fingers that shook, he brushed past Thea's lips, took hold of one of her two front teeth just at the gumline, and drew it from her mouth. Scarcely had he slipped it beneath Thea's pillow when two fairy arms enwrapped him from behind and the Tooth Fairy's hot breath thrilled his ear.

"What a lovely gesture," she said, turning him about and tugging his workshirt out of his pants. "And what a lovely little love-nest."

"You like it?"

"I do." Her eyes took the place in as she caressed his clothed erection. "Such industriousness deserves its reward."

Santa's heart pounded. As why should it not? The old ticker had a lot of work to do over the ensuing hours, keeping up with his lover's demands. Just as a tomcat, settling into new surroundings, sprays urine here, there, and everywhere to establish his territorial rights, so the Tooth Fairy, delighting in the romantic rusticity of the woodland hut, brought herself and her fat lover to a boil anywhichwhere she could. Upon every couch and quilt, sprawled over pelt and pillow, pressed to every square inch of Santa's deft handiwork, they oozed love.

Once, she caught him off-balance and they tumbled straight into the fireplace. "What are you—?" he said. Then the flames engulfed them.

She lay upon the logs, burning.

Santa's flesh was afire too. But instead of searing torment, he felt the gentle brush of sunlight on skin. Though his eyes were goggled in flame, he could look down upon her, watch her hair crimp and crinkle yet defy the fire's insatiable hunger. For as fast as it entwined among her flowing tresses, consuming them, so fast did those tresses grow out. Flames licked at her nipples like the tongues of greedy lovers.

Below, her juices stewed.

Santa's manhood flamed from testicles to tip. Everywhere, his hair crisped and tickled like seething centipedes. Closed round by a wall of restless flame, Santa pressed his burning flesh to hers, breathed fire, giggled sparks and cinders. Like a smith's beaten iron plunged hissing into water, Santa drove his fiery rod into his lover's boiling stewpit, so that their flesh seethed and sizzled there.

That night, in the matter of consuming passion, the god of fire took lessons from them.

One morning, in the third year of his affair, Santa fished his master weaver Ludwig out from under a riotous sea of patterned bolts and took him aside. "Ludwig," he said, "we've known one another a long time, haven't we? We respect each other. I'm sure we've gone beyond having to sugarcoat a bitter pill when it's time to take our medicine."

"Medicine, Santa?" Recumbent question marks curled above the elf's puffy eyelids.

"Tell me, my friend. And please be candid." Santa draped an arm round his helper's shoulders. "Has my work been up to snuff lately?"

Ludwig wheezed out a long, slow, painful breath. His fingers worked the corners of his mouth. He cocked his head. "Truthfully?" he asked.

Santa nodded.

Ludwig looked with great deliberation into Santa's beard, pursed his lips, and squinted up into Santa's eyes. "I'd have to say, without the slightest hesitation, that your work is—as it has always been and shall, no doubt, ever remain—exemplary, superlative, without peer, if I may be so bold, among elfhood and humankind alike." The color drained from him as he spoke, and his voice dwindled in firmness from strong coffee to weak tea.

"Thank you, Ludwig," said Santa, shaken to the core. "I prize your good opinion, more than I. . . ." Santa's throat tightened.

Ludwig gave a curt smile and a nod, then ambled off as one scattered in his wits.

Santa watched him go. He felt a tangle of emotions. Deep sadness. Amusement over the elf's eccentricities. A feeling of superiority, which disturbed him greatly. And a fear that he had betrayed the love of the young people of this world.

But beneath all of those feelings throbbed the steady hum of desire. Santa marveled at it. He wondered if he had been this way as a mortal in Myra long ago. Perhaps the Heavenly Father had sanitized his memories, washing the worst of his urges out of him. Now, spurred on by a chance encounter with the Tooth Fairy, they were flooding back full force.

Which was as it should be.

Far better, he thought, to embrace his every side, damned and blessed alike, than to live on in ignorance.

Reaching into the depths of his left pocket, he fingered the cool silk of the Tooth Fairy's red panties. Pictures danced in his head, pictures of scenes lived, scenes imagined, scenes hoped for.

Yes, he thought. Far far better.

Santa dwelt much upon Anya, whom he dearly loved yet could no longer fully confide in. More was the pity. As with his toymaking, so with his marriage: The indefinable something at its core had turned strange or melted away over the years.

Yet she seemed not to notice. She appeared, trusting soul, to have taken him at his word. The day after her blowup that first Christmas morn, she had gone about her affairs as before. A homebody always, Anya strayed rarely from the bright confines of the cottage. Her days she spent in the kitchen or at her crafts, her evenings in the ebony rocker beside the hearth, sharing his delight in the letters he slit open at his writing desk and rushed out of his study to read to her. And when she lay beside him in bed and signaled, by backing up against him, that she was that night receptive, Anya was as earth-moist as the richest silt, chthonic and cavernous as a queen's tomb.

But, God forgive him, her subdued drives maddened him. Months would go by. There she would lie, nightgowned in the fire-toasty bedroom, a book propped open on her breasts—reading, page after page, while he tentatively touched her thigh and fantasized himself erect or fell asleep in the solitary envelope of his unmet needs.

It spawned dark thoughts about her. It made him want to hurt her, to shake the complacency out of her bones, to wrench open the sexless creature she had become and pull out the hidden body of the lusty wench she had once been.

Instead he resorted more and more to the hut.

"I'll tell you what it is," he confided to the head of a marionette one day after painting the tan curves of its ears and its bright blue saucer eyes. "The Good Lord never intended man to be monogamous." A question swam up from the paint drying on the wooden face. "Sure I'm an elf. But before that I was a man. I know what it's like."

He dipped a fresh horsehair brush into a jar of crimson and swept a smile across the shiny sphere cradled in his hand. "Grin all you like, little one. Your body, when I get to it, will be all wood and joints. No sex added because none needed. But the bodies of men are thrown on God's wheel, slapped together from blood and bone, flesh and fire, gristle and gland, then glazed with liquid lust and baked to a frenzy in the kiln of desire. A man's member hangs there between his legs like a dark talisman, directing his life, driving him hither and yon, distracting him from the uninterrupted enjoyment of other than sensual delights."

Santa turned the head this way and that, trying to read its enigmatic expression. He loved crafting dolls, puppets, figurines of every kind. Especially the faces. Their prevailing emotion—joy, anger, sorrow, grief—was usually bold and transparent. But this face, emerging now from the wet womb of his imagination, troubled him with its uncertain mix of emotions. It grinned stupidly up at him. He wished it could talk. Then he quickly changed his mind about that, chuckled wryly, and set it upon a heap of rags to dry.

The Tooth Fairy's island looked, from the stormclouds above, like a gray-green gash knifed into the wet flesh of the sea. Where the waves washed against it, jutting rock alternated with stretches of strand. The sand was finest, the tough dune vegetation least choked together, at the gash's two jagged extremities. From the sparse beaches and ocean-dashed rocks, the island rose abruptly into steep wooded slopes, as though God had placed His hands to either side of a flatland forest and bunched the earth together between them. Save for the blasted cedar at the north tip of the island, the trees were exclusively ash.

When she was in residence, the mistress of the island preferred either to squat upon the shore near the cedar, brooding into the ceaseless storm, or to take refuge up among the ash trees in a grim cavern punched into the mountainside and decked out with bone-furniture. She sat now at the cave entrance on a bleached-white armchair, munching on a bowl of molars and staring past the wind-tossed treetops. Incessant rain beat at her breasts and belly. But her mind was fixed on the fat fellow with the generous cock and the sensitive hands.

These days he called himself Santa Claus. But she knew who he really was, who he had been before the Christers had wrested control from their pagan predecessors.

A rough wind set the tops of the trees to rioting. Vacant now, every one of them, despite their animation. She could still hear, as if it were yesterday, the shriek and moan of her sister nymphs as they perished. She could feel the jaws of death close over her. She recalled how the rescuing hand of Almighty Zeus—in the midst of his own self-transformation—sealed a pact with her and infused her with life.

Bitter pact. Grim life. Sundered from the ecstatic community of nymphs and satyrs—constant byplay, constant sensual delight, life lived to the full. Set down alone on this island, given a craving for bone which could never match, marvelous though it was, her old cravings for wine and fruit and the frenzies of the flesh.

Their god, the One-and-Only-God, he who sometimes glared at her in patriarchal admonishment through swirls of stormclouds, had obliterated Santa's memories of those days, slipping more convenient myths into his head. But whenever she tried to speak of these things, her words would not come.

"You really don't remember," she'd say.

"Remember what?" he would ask.

"The time before you were . . . the time he who calls himself God was . . . back before you were . . ." The hut walls shook with her frustration.

"There, there, don't trouble yourself over it."

But she did trouble herself, and greatly. She wanted Santa to know. Together, they would conspire against the big blowhard in the sky; they'd topple the turncoat whose betrayal had led, in spite of his rescue of her, to the slaughter of her sisters and their goatish lovers.

At times, it was hard to see the old satyr in Santa. From time to time she caught hints, a special stance, a casual scratch behind an ear. But he looked so different. The hornless forehead, the kind eye, the impossibly white curls. They thrilled and disgusted her.

Desolation blew through the dripping forest before her now. A curious feeling harried her heart these days when she thought of Santa. In the beginning her lust had been pure, her desires wholly selfish. She had wanted the jolly fat man because he, of all beings, could best cater to her insatiate whims, could give give give until there was no giving left—and then give some more.

But of late, his selfless giving had seeded her gut, had sent out runners from her viscera to her every soul and limb. More often than not, to her astonishment, she found herself mouthing her lover for the sheer pleasure of hearing him moan, without a thought to the payback to come when he turned her about, as he invariably did, to feast on her fairyhood.

She wondered—perverse thought—if it could be love she felt. "Love. Love for the fat man. Love for Santa," she said. She liked the way that sounded. It made her skin shiver, that word. Seeing him turned her ravenous; she wanted desperately to devour him. But then, fighting that urge had always been the most harrowing part of the copulations of nymphs and satyrs. She recalled the old community, roused by the smell of blood, circling about and egging on a thrusting couple who had lapsed into total anarchy and died feasting on one another's innards, the green moss beneath them drenched red.

She sighed. Tears of rain, rolling down her cheeks, depended from her nipples. She knew, because he'd told her so often enough, that Santa Claus did not love her, not in that way. No, it was lust alone, he assured her, full-throttle lust and nothing more, that tore him from the side of his wife. More rhizome than root, his feelings for her.

A chill rippled through her.

Her eyes clamped down upon a glare.

There had to be a way, she thought. A way to unseat Mrs. Claus, to swivel Santa's head forever away from her, from his elves and reindeer and his blasted beloved brats.

A way to claim him exclusively for herself.

Good Friday, 1990. St. Mary's Cemetery and Mausoleum on 21st Street in Sacramento. A young woman in black held her daughter's hand and watched her husband's coffin sink into the earth.

Time had not stood still for Rachel Townsend. Now nearly thirty, she had lived a full mortal life, joyous and painful, zesty and bland by turns. Of that special night twenty years past, when Santa Claus and the Tooth Fairy tussled naked upon her bed, she remembered nothing.

"Mommy?" Wendy looked sadly up at her. "My legs are getting tired."

Rachel stroked her daughter's braided hair. An image came and went of Frank holding a baby spoon in his hand, bending intently toward the high chair, his eyes smiling in disbelief at his daughter's loveliness. That loving look stayed with him through the years since, and Wendy had loved her father as fiercely. It was a shame Easter had been spoiled for her this year.

So few years, so quickly lived.

"Be patient," Rachel told her. "It won't be much longer."

"Can you lift me up?"

"Later," she assured. Rachel rested her hands on Wendy's shoulders and listened to Father Doyle intone the words of the burial service.

She liked Father Doyle, though she felt nothing but indifference for his Church. But Frank—or Francis Xavier McGinnis, as the reverend father now referred to him—had been raised a Catholic and had remained devout to the end. Frank would have wanted Father Doyle to give him the complete Catholic sendoff.

A light breeze stirred the treetops. Her husband had been a huge man, with a love of life and a sense of humor as expansive as his girth. He'd brought joy to everyone he touched in his fifty-seven years. Little wonder, then, that the funeral party numbered nearly three hundred, and that its mood was not so much funereal as celebratory—of Frank himself, of his caring heart, of the privilege they had shared in knowing him.

Rachel expected that Frank's friends would drop away. The lecherous ones—George Seacrest of the wayward wife, and Harold Stamm who sported a gold tooth—would hit on her once or twice, then take the hint and be gone. The others might hang on a bit longer but she'd be glad to see them go. It was time for her to think about a new life, and that was easier to do without the flotsam of the old floating past.

The sole exception was Mrs. Fredericks from next door, dear old Ellie Fredericks, eighty years young and still full of fire. She couldn't imagine that feisty old woman ever giving up the ghost, let alone abandoning her "little Rachel." She'd been Rachel's pretend granny for as long as Rachel could recall, and now she was Wendy's as well.

She glanced down at her daughter. It had been a rough year for both of them, a year full of death. First Frank's parents. Then Rachel's, a boating accident out on Folsom Lake that also claimed her brother Billy and his wife. Frank had questioned the wisdom of moving into her parents' house on K Street, but they'd been looking for an old house anyway and Rachel's girlhood had been a time of magic, rich memories woven into every room. Rachel hadn't regretted the move for a moment, and Frank and Wendy quickly fell in love with the place.

Now she and her daughter would be alone there. Her husband of seven years—that rarest of all breeds, a truly compassionate underwriter of life and health—had cared more for his clients' well-being than his own. High blood pressure, ignored to the point of disdain, had felled him while Rachel retrieved Wendy from school and stopped at Corti Brothers for groceries. Wendy cried for days. So did Rachel.

She bent over and kissed her daughter on the top of the head, pausing long enough to breathe the sweet scent of Wendy's scalp. Wendy gave her a look of disapproval that was pure Frank.

Funny how they'd met. At nineteen, she had come home from Chico for the holidays, happy to divert her thoughts for a few weeks from the study of bits and bytes, pixels and Pascal, semaphores and CPUs. Her intense flirtation with lesbian love was a year behind her, she was a junior now, between boyfriends, and happy to be home for the holidays. She had gone to Macy's on the corner of 5th and K to hunt for Christmas gifts.

Rachel usually avoided large department stores. She much preferred out-of-the-way places: bookstores, toystores, stores filled with exotic foods or given over entirely to puzzles and games. But Macy's was different. Macy's laid claim to Santa Claus in a way no other store could match. She had seen *Miracle on 34th Street* many times on TV. Once she had even seen it downtown at the Crest Theatre.

Though she'd stopped believing in him around age ten, the figure of Santa Claus held an eerie fascination for her. That year, she lingered at Santa's Workshop, watching him dandle kids on his knee, pose for Polaroids with them, hand them candycanes. In that lingering, the man wearing the red suit captured her heart. She stood transfixed; he noticed her; when closing time came, he changed clothes, met her at the doors, and took her to dinner at his favorite restaurant, Fat City in Old Sacramento.

Six months later, she and Frank were wed. He urged her to complete her degree, then look for work in the Sacramento area. Every few weeks, he'd drive up to spend time with her, inner-tubing down the river (quite a sight, Frank at fifty, floating among the youngsters), or taking long walks through Bidwell Park (where Errol Flynn had once played Robin Hood), or indulging in an endless night of marital bliss locked away in her apartment off the Esplanade six blocks north of campus. Her pregnancy ran neck and neck with her studies that year. She graduated in mid-May of 1984, gave birth to Wendy the following week, and began work three months later as a software engineer for HP in Roseville, some thirty miles east of Sacramento.

"Mommy?"

"We'll be going home soon, honey."

"Where did you say the Easter Bunny lives?"

"Underground in a big burrow. Just show a little more patience, Wendy. You've been very good."

Graveyard grass swayed long and green in the breeze. Father Doyle's lilting voice caressed the words he held in his hands. Opposite Rachel and Wendy, old Mrs. Fredericks coughed into her hand and shifted her feet. Tears welled in her eyes.

"Mommy?" Wendy whispered.

"Not now, dear."

"Is Daddy going down there to be friends with the Easter Bunny?"

PART 2
DISCOVERY

The rabbit has a charming face;
Its private life is a disgrace.
I really dare not name to you
The awful things that rabbits do.
　　　—anonymous

Adultery is a meanness and a stealing, a taking away from
someone what should be theirs, a great selfishness, and
surrounded and guarded by lies lest it should be found out.
And out of the meanness and selfishness and lying flow love
and joy and peace beyond anything that can be imagined.
　　　—Dame Rose Macauley

4.

WHAT THE EASTER BUNNY SAW

Up from the perpetual ice and snow of the North Pole his hind legs rose, invisible as the body they supported. His front paws rested on the sash of the bedroom window, his nose twitched, his eyes sizzled into the writhing pair of lovers upon Santa's bed. He had chanced, the Easter Bunny had, upon far better entertainment than befriending corpses.

'Twas the night, you see, before Easter. And in this cottage, at the tail end of his rounds, two creatures were stirring it up quite nicely. Beside them, a white-haired woman, beautiful beyond describing, slept the sleep of the dead. The Easter Bunny's eyes darted betwixt her and the humping couple. The contrast between their carnal frenzy and her innocent oblivion excited him no end. His heart pounded lubba-di-lubba-di-lub in an odd mix of envy, love, and outrage. Like erratic brushes riding a cymbal, his whiskers skritched against the glass.

How he adored peering in upon nocturnal copulations. Petunia'd once asked him why. She'd stared at him out of those vacuous, shit-brown eyes of hers as he lay spent on the burrow floor, peering up through the dimness. *Why do you peep?* he heard her say.

He shrugged. "Forgive me, dear Petunia, but I like seeing love happen. I like to pretend I'm the man who's making the happy lady even happier. Even though I feel quite sad, suicidal even, right after my genitalia spurt, when the bubble of my fantasy pops and I'm not that man, it's worth it to feel like I'm giving someone my love—someone alive and responsive— even for a few seconds."

She didn't speak to him for days after that. Just sat in her room and sulked.

Usually he had to slip out of magic time to animate the lovers he caught. No problem, most nights. But on Easter Eve, that was an extravagance he could ill afford. He simply had to get on with the business of distributing baskets and hiding brightly colored eggs in grass. There was his schedule to contend with, not to mention the Father's stern face glaring out of the night if he dared dawdle. Whenever he chanced upon pudendal play, he was forced to limit himself to witnessing two seconds, tops.

But these lovers were different.

These lovers were themselves wrapped in magic time, though their beautiful companion languished in the real time of an open-mouthed snore. That meant he could stay and watch for as long as he liked, particularly since his invisibility, God bless it, hid him from immortals as well as mortals. He grew hot with desire at what he witnessed. Hot too with envy. Love for the adorable white-haired woman thumped in his heart; and in his head, a righteous anger at Santa's adultery mixed with strange new thoughts indeed—disquieting thoughts that whispered around the corners of an obliterated past, whispered of powers lost and of divine betrayal.

Nonsense, he thought, shaking such notions out of his head and concentrating on the scene within. His scent glands drooled exudate down his chin and into the snow. His claws unsheathed against the sash. His penis poked out, red and hard, into the chill arctic air.

At the window, soundlessly, he chittered.

Earlier that evening, the elves' quarters had been unusually noisy, what with the anticipation of Easter candy on the morrow. They jostled one another at the sinks, each elf jamming his face close to the mirror, holding his beard free of the water with one hand and working his toothbrush with the other. Hans and Dieter had an argument over whose nightshirt was whose. Pillow fights broke out spontaneously at the east and west ends of the vast dormitory, spreading like two waves toward the middle until a great surge of shouts and feathers whitened the air with happy violence. When at last the ruckus died down, general exhaustion settled upon them like a comforter and they tucked themselves in for the night.

Each elf had his own bed except for Heinrich, the six dollmaking elves who went by one name. In the forgotten reaches of time, they had made one large bed for themselves. Therein they slept, tightly packed, their stubby arms and longish black beards sticking out over the covers.

That night, soon after falling asleep, Heinrich had a dream. In Heinrich's dream, only five Easter baskets lay waiting by his bedside the next morning. One mouth, the dreamer's, went without; one pair of fists, the dreamer's, pummeled five grinning mouths that munched smugly on jelly beans. Heinrich opened his twelve sleeping eyes to find himself embroiled in a bloody brawl, fists flying, sheets and pillows tossed hither and yon. When things wound down, the six sat there bewildered, looking out at a moonlit sea of snoozing elves and consoling each other.

In cleaning up, one of them spat a tooth into the sink. Should Santa be told? Should Knecht Rupert? No. Both were asleep. They positioned their injured brother at the east edge of the bed, placed the tooth beneath his pillow, soothed him, and eased back into sleep.

Hovering voluptuous over Heinrich, the Tooth Fairy smiled to see where she was. She drew her toothsome treat from beneath the pillow, bit into it, savored its elfin sweetness, and replaced it with coins from her anus.

Gold doubloons, six of them.

"One for each of you," she said, planting a kiss on Heinrich's foreheads, hungering for the thick flat bone beneath. She ran greedy fingers in and out of his mouths, reading the raised runes of ancient molars.

As swift as thought, she drifted the familiar path to Santa's bed. The blankets bulked huge as a bear over his rotundity. Behind him, Anya's blip of blanket seemed an annoying afterthought. With a gesture, she paid out her invisible net of magic time until it compassed round both herself and her dozing lover.

For a moment, she watched his untroubled breathing and felt again that odd love she had felt on her island. How giving he seemed, even in sleep. His great mane of white hair spilled like a gift of blizzards from beneath his red stocking cap onto his pillow. His face, bearded and wise with age, was yet the face of a cherub.

His mouth stopped her heart.

She pictured those lips nursing on her, bringing her nipples up high and hard. She was tantalized by a nearly overpowering urge to dig her teeth into his ruddy cheeks and rip them free. She shuddered and shut her eyes. Down below, there came the swell and flush of arousal. Dipping a finger inside, she eased her eyes open and anointed the rims of her lover's large nostrils with divine fluid.

"Santa," she murmured.

A sharp intake of breath, a noisy yawn, the rubbing of hands at eyes, and he was awake. He looked about the room in confusion. Then he brought her into focus. "What in heaven's name are you—?"

"Call it a surprise. For both of us. One of your elves offered up a tooth. I took it and paid him off."

Santa chuckled. He glanced at Anya, then made as if to rise. "Let me put some clothes on and we'll be on our—"

She restrained him, firm hand on shoulder. "No need to go anywhere. I want you here. Right now."

"But Anya—"

"She can't see or hear us. She won't know what's going on."

Santa shook his head. "I will not make love to you lying beside Anya and that's final."

She tried coaxing. "Come on, Santa, it turns me on so, the thought of sucking you off while your frumpy old wife just lies there." She nuzzled his neck. "Don't you want to see what it's like, just once, to rock your dull Anya in the rhythms of our lovemaking?"

Again he refused.

The Tooth Fairy exploded with rage. She tore back Santa's sheets and blankets, exposing him and Anya in their nightclothes. She stood over Santa, straddling him. "Foolish elf, look at my body. Take it all in. Think about the taste of my breasts, how you love to cradle your head here and finger the sweetness between my legs."

Santa was, for the moment, stunned.

"Now look at your wife." Her hands swirled over the sleeping woman, as smart and sharp as fans snapping open. Anya's nightgown went transparent. "Look at this wretched excuse for a woman. Her face a map of wrinkles; two tired old dugs as ugly as they are flaccid; nipples that would shame a sow; a flabby belly that looks more like cottage cheese than flesh; a few spare wisps of crotch hair, dull as flax; an old crone's cunt, as tired and sexless as the lady herself; legs veined and thick; feet grown old and idiosyncratic from years of pointless ambling. Good God, what do you see in her?"

Santa's face burned red during this outrage. Now he grabbed her wrists, pulled her atop him, and drilled into her face with his eyes. "Cover my wife."

"Just tell me—"

He shook her hard. "Do as I say."

Her necklace rattled above him, her breasts swaying with the force of his ire. She glared at him, then shot a scornful glance at Anya, whose nightgown regained its bulk, pattern, and opacity. She snapped back into Santa's anger, writhing upon him. "I've been naughty, haven't I? Maybe you'd like to punish me. Slap me around some. Give me a good spanking."

When Santa opened his mouth to speak, the Tooth Fairy spat into it. His lips flecked white with spittle. She darted forward and pressed her mouth to his, tonguing deep as though to retrieve her saliva. Through the nightshirt, her labia found his rod and rocked upon it like a hen upon an egg. By Zeus, she'd fuck the bastard into loving her if she had to!

He clamped his huge hands tight around her head and pushed her lips away. "Not next to my wife!" he shouted. "Not here!" Her skull strained toward buckling under his grip.

Still she rocked upon his hard-on, crying out at the bone-bending pressure of his hands, laughing her defiance. Her hands yanked at his nightshirt, pulling it above his waist. She straddled him then and her flesh closed about him.

Throwing aside all consequence, he gave off hurting his mistress and hugged her as tight as he could, raining kisses on her face and arching up to meet her as she rode him. And ride him she did, skillfully, as a moth flits and flirts for hours near a flame, swooping near, tempting the heat, singeing a wing, until at last it dips and plunges to a perfect death.

After six hours of bug-eyed voyeurism, the Easter Bunny lost track of how many penile anointings he had graced Santa's cottage with. Enough anyway to turn the snow at his feet to slush.

No matter.

Satiety had come at last. He had wearied of watching these two inexhaustible fornicators and the lovely woman caught in mid-snore beside them. Tired too he became of fending off recurring notions of some long-forgotten role in the world's creation. Whatever he might have been in the past, he was the Easter Bunny now. Time to get in there, do his job, and move on.

He hopped away from the cottage in a zigzag through the snow. Then he sprang up, twisted about so that he once again faced the window, and bounded toward it with the full thrust of his back legs.

Silent as moonlight, the Easter Bunny tumbled through the glass onto the bare wood floor at the foot of Santa's bed. Warm air wrapped him round. The sounds of sucking, no longer muffled by glass, filled his ears. Soundlessly, he padded toward the naked lovers, nearly indifferent in the face of their umpteenth variation on mutual orality. Yet he felt compelled to move in for closer inspection.

It was the glow about them that drew him now. That and the rich aroma of lust fulfilled. He was stunned by the tightly packed beauty of the Tooth Fairy, her hands leaning upon the fat inner thighs of her lover, her lips moving up and down in slow undulation. This close to her, he felt an abrupt rush of danger, a violence in his groin that made him shy off, avert his eyes from her, and fix them on her lover.

God damn your jolly old soul, Santa Claus, he thought, surprised at the depth of his anger. Not only do kids love you more, but your penis is lots bigger, easily twice the size of mine. You enjoy such wonderful repute, yet now I find you're nothing but an adulterer, betraying your adorable mate by allowing this fairy slut to . . . to. . . .

A chill coursed up his spine. Would anyone, he wonder, ever do that amazing thing to him? Or was he forever confined to merely imagining its delights, a furtive witness to the fellating of others?

At the pillow, Santa *mmmm*'d into the Tooth Fairy's vulva. The Easter Bunny's troubled eyes sought the elf's face above his matted beard. Fancy house, fine wife, a voracious lover, the untainted adoration of human beings of every stripe and color, a huge longlasting loveshaft. To top it off, a sickening excess of generosity oozed from every pore. It made him burn with envy, this Clausean outpouring of good will and gratitude, gift after gift after gift.

His eyes narrowed. He reached a paw into the void and pulled out the most pitiful Easter basket he could find. A wretched affair it was, with a handle on the verge of breaking, one tired clump of grass, a chocolate bunny staved in on one side and tan-crumbled with age, and nothing but red jelly beans.

Santa, he knew, despised red jelly beans.

Setting it down by the rutting elf's slippers, he hopped

soundlessly around the bed and raised his head to study Santa's wife.

Anya was her name. Until this night, he had never really paused to appreciate her. She was a vision, this Anya. For all the tug and tussle of Santa and the Tooth Fairy, Anya in the pristine calm of slumber struck him as far more erotic than they. The shape of her head was so like a rabbit's, her hair so like soft white fur.

For the longest time, the Easter Bunny found himself staring at the top button of her nightgown. How breathtaking it would be, he thought, if she were to open those innocent eyes and, fixing him with a fathomless look of purity, undo that one blue button.

At last he looked away, a frenzy inside. The basket he pulled out of the void this time was usually reserved for spoiled starlets and the children of the filthy rich. Obscenely large and bound in gold cellophane, this Easter basket, whose crafted handweaving was itself a work of art, boasted all manner of fruit and nuts, in and out of chocolate coatings both light and dark; an extended family of bunnies, solid milk chocolate through and through save for hearts of marzipan; rich caches of jelly beans waiting to be discovered among the hand-painted Easter eggs and spun-gold chicks of marshmallow; and all of it bedded in the finest, most delicate strands of emerald green grass his machines could manufacture. This he set on the floor where Anya would be certain to see it on waking.

Then, rising to his full height and drinking in one last time the lovely Anya, radiant against the loathsome backdrop of jolly old Saint Nick locked in his fairy lover's embrace, the Easter Bunny turned to the window and leaped out into the night.

When finally she rose to leave, Santa grabbed her to him, kissed her long and hard, and said, one finger raised to admonish: "Next time, our love-nest in the woods."

She took his finger between her lips, tasted herself there,

then cradled her face in his palm. "All right, my big fat fucker. But one request."

He raised a bushy eyebrow.

"Think about dumping her."

Santa scowled. "Incorrigible, aren't you?" He gave her a smart slap on the rump. "Now for the love of God, let me get some sleep."

She threw him a look of pure chaos and, with a toss of her head, vanished into the night air.

For the longest time, Santa propped himself up in bed and pondered the duplicitous life he'd been leading. He ached for the simplicity and goodness of his life before Christmas '69. But he couldn't imagine abandoning his trysts with the Tooth Fairy. Finally, he cast a troubled glance at Anya, turned his back on her, and surrendered himself to sleep.

5.
MOUNTING FRUSTRATIONS

Your typical rabbit—if asked and capable of giving intelligible reply—would choose a temperate habitat, an ideal mix of grassland and woodland, affording plenty of good grazing in tandem with dry, quickly accessible cover. But the Easter Bunny was not your typical rabbit, neither in size, nor in longevity, nor in his taste in living arrangements.

Save for Easter Eve and his nocturnal prowlings at bedroom windows, the Easter Bunny kept almost exclusively to his burrow, as dark and dank a hole in the ground as his Easter leavings were light and airy. He was there now, some six months after watching Santa betray his wife with the Tooth Fairy. Through the dimness of the low archway that separated Petunia's sleeping quarters from his, the metallic gleam of her eyes peered back at him.

"I know, I know, dearest," he said in answer to her weary look. "It's the end of October and I've been going on and on about this since April. So maybe you're right, maybe I am just a teensy bit obsessed. But God bless the jolly old bastard, Petunia, it isn't fair. The simpering Coke-drinker's got two mates, one for his lust, one for his love. I'm not even going to mention the countless copulatrixes he no doubt encounters on his rounds, wanton flibbertigibbets with too much eggnog in their noggins, waiting undraped by their fireplaces and dangling sprigs of mistletoe from their bellybuttons; I'm not even going to mention them. Let's confine ourselves, for the sake of my sanity, to the ones I *know* about. My point is, Santa's got two luscious ladies and I've got nobody."

Mistake. He glanced in at her and immediately wished he

hadn't been so blunt. "Sorry, dearest. But we've been over this before. I love you, indeed I do. You're a good listener, you're compliant, you don't eat much, and you're no small consolation in a pinch. But let's face it, love, you just don't have what it takes when it comes to getting down and dirty. Both of us know that, though we like to pretend otherwise. I'm not blaming you, sweetheart. That's just the way things are."

No sense in being subtle. He squinted at her through the dimness. Clever little creature. If he didn't know better, he'd swear she was weeping. Fine, that was just hunky-dory with him. But if she was going to sulk about it, she could damn well sulk in private. Let her cry all the crocodile tears she wanted. "I'm off to survey my domain, Petunia," he said, trying to keep the anger out of his voice, "to look in perchance on the poultry." Now there were some females who knew how to move it. Petunia could do worse than take lessons.

If the archway had boasted a door, the Easter Bunny would have slammed it. Instead he turned tail, skritched some loose dirt in her direction with his back claws, and dashed from his quarters into the exercise area. There, with all the embittered zeal of one who works at having fun, he ran to and fro in the wide expanse of darkness, stopping on occasion to gnaw on scraps of bark or throw himself down and roll in the dirt, then leaping up again to resume his mad career about the perimeter. When he'd had enough, he sat in the dead middle and thrust his huge ears up to catch and amplify the burrow's activity.

Dull. Boring. Downright soporific.

His eyes pinched with envy. He pictured the North Pole as a place rich in sound: the prancing and snorting of reindeer; the shouts and laughter of elves at work and play; the chill night wind whistling in the chimney; the feathering of snow upon snow; the honeyed voice of Anya calling her husband home to supper; and then . . . the sounds of the bedroom. No! He pressed his paws to his temples and clamped his eyelids shut, refusing to upset himself again with that.

But here in his burrow, what sort of soundscape greeted him? From the sleeping quarters on the right, the sound of worms eating earth, of straw settling, of Petunia in silent pout. Ahead of him, where motes of dust drifted in the dim tunnel leading upward, the faint buzz of forest life, too far removed to distinguish its strands. At his back, the rhythmic weave and tumble of baskets being assembled, the gush and cut of colored grass, the counting-house clatter of jelly beans spilling into bins and hoppers, the dull hum of row upon row of candy-making machines: all of it set in motion by the Creator on the day He had made him the Easter Bunny, running unattended since.

And to his left, the sounds of the laying house.

The distant brooding of innumerable hens. That was the first sound that fired his ears when God created him. Crouched upon this very spot, his eyes not yet opened, he heard God resume a thought, speaking above a comforting wash of hen-sound.

"This burrow shall be your home, a place of rest and solace. And men shall call you the Easter Bunny . . ."

His lids opened to effulgent light. His eyes were bathed in blessedness. He knew that, moments before, he had been something other than what he was, a scaly thing, a thing of wind and bruises, a brutish sinuosity inlaid with pride, a reveler in . . . in what? The otherness slipped away faster than he could grasp it. Pure Easter Bunny filled the gaps.

"After the New Zealand White, a feisty breed and fair, have I modeled you. Yet, though your natural bent be rabbitlike, I have given you the stature and speech of men . . ."

He leaped joyously into the air, feeling the surge of immortality in his veins. About his new-created home he flew, pausing to groom his coat or lie on his side in the straw with his hind legs stretched to their limit.

God laughed, a sound that made him weep with ecstasy. Then God walked with him, blessing with His presence every inch of the burrow. He enlightened room after room: the living quarters; the ever-replenishing food supply; the machines that ran by themselves; the exercise area; and, flinging back its doors, the laying house.

***

How easily impressed he had been then, he thought, slipping in now to observe the production of eggs. When he first beheld these thousands of hens, roosted tier upon tier, easing multicolored eggs from their nether regions, he had nearly fainted in awe.

But now, all that splendor looked prosaic and washed out. Not nearly as impressive as Santa's setup, he brooded. God's favorite saint had engaging elves to enliven his workshop with conversation and antics, a more opulent patch of real estate, and far greater freedom to vary his product lines.

Then there was the question of who, or what, he had been before God had stolen away his memories and awakened him in this burrow.

Since April, the Easter Bunny had come to suspect that in all probability he had once been very important in the scheme of things; that just maybe he, and not God, had created the universe; that God—Whoever He really was—had filched his memories and now forced him to slave eternally in the bowels of the earth. Hurt feelings were not out of place, that much was clear.

He glared at the endless ovoids of color rolling and rumping along narrow troughs, at the gaping back fluff of countless hens, at the confused, quirky heads of Leghorns and Wyandottes, Dorkings and Orpingtons, Plymouth Rocks and Jersey Black Giants, Rhode Island Reds and Whites. At times he loved these creatures very much. But now, in the gloom of envy and resentment, they seemed little more than cogs in a machine.

Sometimes the fetid chicken-stench disgusted him. Sometimes it soothed him. And sometimes it turned him on. Even now, despite the depths of his emptiness, the close air and the seductive knock-and-roll of eggs brought his groin to life. He became aware of his testicles filling their scrotal purse. The vision of a dozing white-haired woman, a woman whose beauty made his heart hurt, floated among the feathers in the air before him.

No! Why waste time thinking about her? Anya was unattainable, a pointless fantasy.

Who then? He had tried one of the Leghorns once. Snatching her one night from the bottom tier, he had carried her through the exercise area into his quarters. A sorry farce, that. Grunting low in his nose, he'd made to mount her. But she kept flapping out from under him. Despite the mismatch of parts, he tried time and again to jam himself into her. But whenever the tiniest bit of dicktip began to wedge its way upward, another emergent Easter egg would push it out. At last he released her in disgust, watched her meander back to the laying house—dropping eggs of red and green and orange as she went—and proceeded to lick himself all the way off.

Once, just once, he had tried a human female. Twenty years before, this eager young doe sat cross-legged on her mattress sucking dark-blue blotter squares with her boyfriend. Through the window of some dreary old brick dorm in Ithaca, New York, he had watched them. Before long, they were saying and doing odd things and laughing a lot over very little. His head buzzed with warm, fuzzy bees, his penis began to straighten up and poke out, and he found himself suddenly feeling amorous toward the young lady, very amorous indeed. After more inane jabber, the humans stripped, she opened herself up on the bed, her boyfriend wiggled into her and spent himself—"Cosmic!" he kept wowing—then he stumbled into the hallway looking for the john while she lay sprawled on the bed, one arm flung over her forehead and an endless string of feathery moans issuing from her lips.

He'd been overcome by the mood of the moment, knowing it was foolhardy in the extreme (not in the least like his customary meek and mild self) and not caring one whit for the consequences. Passing through the window, he stole across the scuffed linoleum to the door and eased its lock shut. When, still invisible, he lowered his furry bulk onto her, she instinctively wrapped her legs around him. She had her eyes closed. A huge grin swam on the surface of her face. His back claws digging holes in her sheets, he gently licked her forehead, poised to thrust into her.

Then everything went wrong. Her stoned mate began to mewl in the hallway, jiggling the doorknob. When her hand brushed against his wet, quivering nose, she snapped open her eyes and discovered that she seemed to be embracing air only. She began to whimper and struggle. Worse than that, in the throes of impending orgasm, he lost his hold on invisibility. When he materialized—all three hundred pounds of him chittering and dripping like some Wonderland nightmare— she paid out scream after scream, plastering the walls with them. He leaped from the bed and zoomed about the room, displacing desks and chairs, bunching up throw rugs, and upsetting metal wastebaskets. Then he vanished through the window.

For weeks on end, he had cowered in his quarters, hearing nothing but screams. He lived in dread of a visit from God that never came. His heart shuddered to recall that time. He never found out what became of her, nor did he want to know. No, he wasn't about to attempt a human female any time soon.

Visions of Anya rekindled inside him. Dear sainted wife of a saint, betrayed in her own bed while she slept. If only there were some way to wrest her from Santa Claus, if only she would consent to live with him here in his burrow, go down on all fours, spread wide her knees, and graciously beg the inthrust of his bunnyhood.

"Wait," he said. A Wyandotte in mid-lay craned its neck around and blinked at him. "Who do you think *you're* staring at?" The hen turned away, looking perturbed, and laid a chartreuse egg. "Stupid chicken," he muttered.

Of course. There was nothing to stop him from paying a visit to the North Pole right now. Fairy-fornicator'd be in his workshop this time of day. He would hop boldly up the cottage steps, rap once, accept Anya's kind invitation to enter, and tell her—haltingly and with much feigned regret—what he had witnessed. Perfect. Expose the big blowhard, put Anya ever in his debt, then whisk her away, assuming she would have him.

Ah but that was pure fantasy. She would never have him, never love him as he loved her.

He would bring flowers. Peonies were nice. Perhaps mums or snapdragons on the side. He pictured his precious Anya puttering about the burrow, bringing a woman's touch to it, making it more appealing. She would sidle up to him here in the laying house, stroke his ears or playfully twist his tail as they watched the hens, then go with him hand in paw, her eyes demurely downturned, to their quarters.

His back foot thumped excitedly on the ground.

Abruptly he stopped. His face twisted into a scowl. Bad plan. What proof could he offer of Santa's treachery? Who would believe his word against the word of Santa Claus? No one. Certainly not Santa's wife.

Envy lit a cauldron in his belly. He wanted to boil that fat little goody-twoshoes in it, singe his whiskers, make his balls swell and burst. God had made Santa Claus almost a god himself. He'd given him a winning smile, a wry wink, and an outsized erection. He'd set him atop the world and tied him to the birth of Christ. And who did he stick with the death of Christ? Oh sure, he knew, all of that culminated in the resurrection. But let's face it, for pure appeal, no empty tomb, no death-defying corpse with a pierced side and wounded hands and feet, could hold a candle to Baby Jesus in the manger. What else had God given him? One lousy burrow, one huge bunny body, one night's horrendous delivery schedule each year. And one raging confluence of hormones. No mate to share his love with, no stimulating companions of any kind to keep him from going crazy, and nothing to do during the rest of the year but peep in at bedroom windows.

Nothing to do . . . but peep in . . . at bedroom windows.

Watch Santa Claus fuck the Tooth Fairy.

Rouse the lovely Anya from oblivion.

Yes! He sprang six feet in the air, provoking a startled flurry of wings in the lower tiers. He dashed out into the exercise area and rolled back and forth in the dry earth, chittering wildly.

That's what he'd do. He'd camp out at the North Pole. He'd watch Santa sleep, all night, every night, studying his every toss and turn. And when he winked his lickerish eyes open, peeled back his blankets, and stole from his sleeping wife, there'd be invisible bunny paws following right behind him, tracking him right to that little love-nest the two of them had joked about. The rest was easy. Draw Anya into magic time, lead her to the hut, and stand beside her watching her husband's elfhood slide in and out of fairy flesh.

Goodbye Santa, hello Easter Bunny. That's what Anya would say. Then he'd have her. He'd have something that used to belong to jolly old Saint Nick. He'd have Santa's ex-wife. But would she love him? Would she have him? Oh yes, she would, she would! He scampered excitedly around the perimeter, drawing the thick woodsy air deep down into his lungs. Then he scurried into his quarters and poked his head around the archway.

"Petunia honey, I've got to have you now!" he said. She gleamed back at him like sex absolute. As usual, all was forgiven, they loved one another so. He hopped toward her, doing his best to hide the vision he was conjuring of Anya in his mind, a vision so vivid he was certain it splashed across the twin screens of his pupils. Not that he could fool dear Petunia, who knew of course his every mood and desire. Things just worked out better if they pretended they felt something genuine for each other.

Nuzzling her gently, he licked her about the neck and ears and forehead. She tasted so-so. No, wait. He shut his eyes and now it was Anya's forehead, wise with age and smelling as close and rich as a smooth block of cedar. He lingered there, exuding droplets of scent from the glands on his chin, letting them moisten her.

Time to move behind her. Turned on though he was, he

paused to admire her great brown tail. There it was, upthrust and fluffed out above her lovehole. That tail had taken him months to get right, months more to perfect so that it would enhance their lovemaking.

He placed his front paws on her shoulders, readying himself to mount her. His left paw drew back sharply as though shocked. She was cold there. He saw, beneath her shoulderblade, the naked gleam of wire winking at him.

"Easily fixed, my girl," he said. Swiftly he bent his head between his legs, everted his anus, and voided a soft pellet into his mouth. Righting himself, he worked it flat with tongue and saliva and smoothed it into the upper edge of Petunia's wound. Instinctively he licked his mouth clean. Then down he dipped again. Up he came and jawed a second pellet into paste, working patiently at his mate's repair. It took thirty pellets to patch her up, but she looked grand when he was finished.

Now for his reward.

He ran in circles about her and pretended she was doing the same. What a dark beauty she was, all in all. There she crouched, hindquarters lifted, her chest and forelegs pressed eternally to the ground. He pawed away the dimness that separated them, mounted sweet Petunia, and closed his eyes to replace her with Anya.

It was Anya under him. It was dear white-haired Anya at his service, taking his bunnyhood inside her holy body and gasping thank-you's at every thrust. Upon her perfect back he drooled, imagining his dribble stepping down her skintight old-lady vertebrae one by one.

And then the great need came upon him.

In an instant, all thought dispersed. A chaos of feelings swept together and tightened into joy. And the buildup that could build no higher reached up one final inch and trembled there, poised to topple. With a thrust so vehement it brought his back feet off the ground, the Easter Bunny shot Anya full of seed and toppled over on his side, chittering and snorting in a delirium of joy.

6.

SPILLING THE BEANS

The dead middle of the night at the North Pole. She dozed like alabaster perfection in the moonlight. One arm lying outside the bedclothes contoured the comforter to her curves. The other had draped itself idly across her breasts.

The Easter Bunny's eyes widened. A soundless chitter passed over his mouth. For an instant, that face made the image of a goddess flare up behind his eyes: before time began, a lone goddess standing—no, not standing, dancing, swaying, weaving—upon nothingness, her undraped contours fanning up a wind, fanning him up behind her, creating him out of chaos. But then his memory blinked away from that, and the bedroom was before him again, the big bed where lovely Anya slept.

He sighed. She would never be his. His fantasy would never come to pass. But if she couldn't be his, then she wouldn't be Santa's either.

When he passed his paw over her and twitched his nose twice to bring her into magic time, the breath flowed into her and turned her sculpted features to living flesh. She was stunning in her loveliness. "Anya," he said, gazing down at her.

Her forehead wrinkled and her face flinched, but she slept on. He had spoken too loud. Would she think him brazen, using her first name?

Softer then: "Mrs. Claus."

Her pupils glistened as her lids began to open. She inhaled sharply. The hand flung across her chest went to her face. With thumb and middle finger, she stroked her temples. Then, noticing him, she startled.

"Don't be frightened," he said.

Hugging the bedclothes to her chin, Anya shrank back against her headboard.

"It's all right," he soothed. "I'm not going to hurt you. It's me, the Easter Bunny. You know. Colored eggs and Easter baskets. I leave yours right here every year."

He pointed to the spot near her night table where he had set down the large basket on his last visit. But she was still only half awake. Her right arm shot out toward her husband, connected with bedding.

"Santa's gone for a little walk," he said. "In fact, that's what I've come to talk to you about."

Her breathing slowed and she squinted at him through the moonlight. "The Easter Bunny," she said, as though answering a child's riddle.

She snatched up the gold-rimmed spectacles from her night table and put them on.

His breath caught at her beauty.

Smiling, she shook her head. "You know you gave me quite a turn, you naughty creature. Old women are frail. We shock easily. And you're quite an imposing figure."

"Forgive me if I frightened you," he said.

She laughed and put a hand to her mouth. "The worst of it is seeing you talk. A six-foot-tall white rabbit is bad enough—"

"Eight, counting the ears," he corrected.

Again she laughed, then abruptly stopped, dipping her fingers into the collapsed comforter on her right. "Where did you say my husband was?"

The Easter Bunny worried his lip and looked out the window. Part of the workshop was visible, its bright red facade turned black by the night. Buttressed against it was the stable where Santa's reindeer now slept.

He felt an urge to go no further, to restore Anya to normal time so her husband could materialize next to her from one eyeblink to the next. Anya would, with the power of her husband's persuasion, be convinced his visit had been a dream.

Of course, if he did that, he would never be able to meet her again. There would be no chance for affection to blossom between them, no possibility that that gentle hand of hers would go roving through his fur. His mating would forever be confined to a doleful doe slapped together from shit and saliva. Enough of that, he thought. She was too good for him, she'd never go with him. But oh how precious she was and what pity she roused in him, lying abed in wifely ignorance, knowing not what dark deeds her husband was about. He owed Anya the truth. And he owed himself the satisfaction of seeing Santa toppled.

Anya was amazed how expressive the Easter Bunny's face could be. Her initial fear had swiftly given way to delight at his ability to talk, followed by astonishment at the emotional range his features commanded. At the moment, he was the very image of anguish and remorse, even to the downturn of his whiskers.

"Mrs. Claus," he said. There was a frown about his eyes and an inability to look directly at her for long that she found alarming. "Your beloved husband, whom all the world holds dear for his unbounded generosity, his irrepressible joviality, is, I regret to say, at this moment in the arms of another woman."

Anya felt a clench in her gut. Then it flew out into a dismissive gesture. "Stuff and nonsense." She hugged the blankets to her chest and laughed. "Not that it's any of your business, but Santa and I aired this issue twenty years ago and he vowed to be faithful. You may not know the value of a saint's vow, but I do."

"Long ago, deep in the woods beyond the skating pond, Saint Nicholas built a cozy little hut." It was as if he hadn't heard her, as if he had only paused for breath as she spoke.

"There's no hut in the woods—"

"A hut whose sole purpose is to conceal from you his adulterous goings-on."

There was something else in his eyes, something she couldn't quite read. It was alien, distancing, and cold. His assertions, absurd though they were, revived memories of the emotional devastation she endured when the whole Tooth Fairy business had surfaced. Thank God all of that was behind them.

"Santa Claus does not lie," she insisted.

"He's there now. Both of them are there now. They are . . ."—he raised a furry eyebrow, shrugged as one ashamed, stared at the floor—" . . . having sex." The Easter Bunny's words struck hard at her heart.

"What kind of cruel joke is this?" she said.

"It's no joke, I assure—"

"I think you'd better leave. I don't recall inviting you in and I'm not even sure you're who—"

"If you'll be so good as to come with me, I'll take you to their trysting place so you can see for yourself." There was a false note to his solicitude, an undercurrent that made her feel uneasy.

"Now what could possibly induce me to leave my warm bed and go hiking through the woods in the dead of night with a six-foot rabb—"

"Eight—"

"—with an eight-foot rabbit who claims to be the Easter Bunny but who might be something else entirely, for all I know, and whose motives may be less than honorable?"

To this, the creature raised one paw and gave a wry smile. Then he hopped—monstrous hops—over to Santa's closet, slid it open, and took out a pair of workpants. He reached a paw into one pocket after another, fishing for something. At last he stopped, drew forth a piece of dark cloth, sniffed at it, and flung it across the room. It landed on Santa's pillow, part of it spilling into the depression where his head belonged. Moonlight caught the red silk, the ribbons, the betraying shape of the thing. Anya's fingertips, reaching reluctantly to touch it, confirmed what her eyes had guessed.

Devastation claimed her heart.

"Fine," said Anya, clutching the red panties and tossing them away from her. They landed on Santa's side and slithered to the floor. She threw back the covers, anger flaring against her furry messenger. "I'll just put a few things on over my nightgown and we'll be off."

The whiff of Tooth Fairy, still potent after twenty years, nearly drove the Easter Bunny wild. He had to hold Santa's pants in front of him to conceal his arousal from Anya. She had flounced out of bed and now stood by her closet in a wash of moonlight. Feeling his right foot readying to thump against the hardwood floor, he crossed his left over it and jammed down firmly. His free paw he pressed to his mouth to keep from chittering. Then he tore the sexual thoughts from his mind and replaced them with forest images, as bland as he could conjure.

She was rebuking him, something about not believing for a moment his wild accusations and warning him not to try any funny business in the woods.

"You'll be perfectly safe in my company," he said. "I'm here to prevent your being taken advantage of. A woman of your caliber should not have to . . . let me say no more. By the way, if you prefer, feel free to change out of your nightgown rather than piling layers of cloth on top of it. I'm impervious to the charms of the female human form, you know. Doesn't do a thing for me."

"Forget it," she snapped back, delightful even in her anger. She moved like some rag doll, double-jointed and comical, reaching up for a woolen cap and jamming it over her ears, fumbling with the buttons of her fleece-lined coat, collapsing on the bed to reach down and zip up her snowboots. She tugged on thick mittens and stood up, her face flushed with defiance. "All right, rabbit," she said. "If we're going, let's go. I want to get this stupid little farce over with, throw you the hell off my property, and go back to bed."

Swallowing hard, he raised a paw to the bedroom door. "After you, lovely lady."

***

Anya stepped off the front porch and followed the Easter Bunny across the commons. Stars hung overhead, stipples of cold fire on a black backdrop. Underfoot, the snow squeaked and crunched in raucous cacophony. They headed toward the pond, scored with the stubborn scars of skate blades. Beyond it lay the elves' quarters.

Skirting the pond, they veered right and headed into the woods. Anya sensed a dread holiness about the place, as though the arching trees formed the ribs and splayed ceiling of some great cathedral whose white-vested prelate now guided her to its corrupt inner sanctum.

Endlessly they worked their way through the snow, he hopping and pausing to wait for her, she moving one tired foot in front of the other. She wanted to believe he was lying, but the bootprints they followed engraved a message of betrayal on her heart.

When it seemed she couldn't walk another step, a wicked patch of orange light winked at her through the trees. The Easter Bunny took her mittened hand and led her into the clearing toward the hut he had spoken of.

His pink nose twitched. "I have the power to become invisible as the wind," he told her. "I've made us both so, though not to one another. They can neither see nor hear us."

He led her straight up to the blazing window.

The first thing she noticed, oddly enough, were his shiny black boots standing at attention by the fireplace. Beneath the bootheels, a pool of melted snow twisted with reflected firelight. Anya had never seen Yule logs burn so feverishly. They lay thick and numerous in the inner hearth, falling all over one another and flaming high and savage in the heat of consumption.

A vision invaded her head. *Darting through sunwash, him hot on her heels, her fir tree in sight, putting on a burst of speed, sweet balsam flaring in her nostrils, diving into the smooth gray bark, yanking her hair free of his fists as he sent up a volley of yowls outside.* Then the vision was gone, abruptly lost to memory.

Anya swallowed. She did not want to look at the bed. The corner of her eye had caught shapes moving there that confirmed all.

"See that little girl there?" He placed one paw on her shoulder, pointing into the hut with the other.

Involuntarily she followed it, saw for one instant her naked mate plunging into naked fairy, and beyond him, against the far wall, a tiny bed in which a little girl lay sleeping.

Anya let out a cry.

"She's not real." A whiff of bunny breath wafted against her left cheek. "I checked. She's just a doll with detachable teeth. It's how he summons her."

She shrugged off his paw and leaned into the window. Her beloved husband lay upon the four-poster, his knees and toes dug into the mattress between the splayed thighs of his lover.

Again the elusive vision swept in and out of her. *His lustspurt splashing her branches, that brute forehead pounding madly against her trunk until two conical gouges spilled drops of resin where his horns sank into her.* Again gone, again elusive, again a rollback.

When she could focus once more on the interior of the hut, Anya's eyes began to tear.

She remembered how it had been for them centuries ago when they were living hand to mouth, giving from their bones to prolong or brighten the lives of others. How God stepped down from the sky, enfolded them, and carried them to the North Pole. How He birthed each elf and reindeer out of the snowbanks in the commons, explored the grounds and buildings with her and Santa, and blessed their new home with effulgent grace. And she remembered how, with one all-giving sweep of His arm, God had granted them eternal life.

That first night of immortality had been so sweet. She had stood on the porch with Santa, listening to him address the elves, basking in their answering enthusiasm. Then he winked at her, ushered her inside, and, to the all-night warbling of elfin choirs, she and Santa made immortal love for the first time.

But now, he topped the Tooth Fairy, covering her fairy face with kisses and performing pushups with his pelvis. Anya lowered her head and wept.

"Shameful, isn't it," said the Easter Bunny, standing close beside her. "A man like that, with his reputation for kindness, for selfless giving—"

She looked at him through the steam on her glasses. "Why would he do something like this? I've been a good wife to him, I know I have." As her lenses cleared, the blur of his face resolved into furry eagerness. His stare chilled her, made her step away.

"Of course you have," he soothed. "Santa must be out of his mind to deceive a good decent beautiful woman like you with a wanton harlot like her."

Anya whipped her head about and again the horrendous sight assailed her.

A flood of vision consumed her, clearer than before. *Sapwood oozing for him, even her heartwood moistening at his heartache, relenting throughout her xylem and phloem, taking back flesh and blood, untreeing herself, extending her arms along her branches, rejoicing in the hot savagery of his delight, feeling his shaggy limbs engulf her, snake inside her, swirl her up into the sweep and surge of his ravening hunger.* It took longer to leave, ungraspable still, but her body tingled inside with a vitality that stayed with her. There was anger there too and a new restlessness in her belly.

"He's not going to get away with this."

"I wouldn't let him."

"I swear I'll get even. I'll show him what it feels like to hurt this way."

"Goose and gander, Anya," he said. "Tit for tat. *Sic semper tyrannis.*" He brushed his wet nose tentatively against an exposed earlobe.

Savagely she wheeled on him. "Don't touch me!" she said. Then she jammed her face against the pane, saw the flex of her husband's buttocks, heard his muffled screams of release.

An unstoppable surge of youth flooded her body *his meaty breath in her face, his holy sweat* and she couldn't understand it. The sight mortified her, yes, *the animal fullness of him thrusting at her loins* but it also shot hot life through her veins. Something was digging at her skull like a claw, raising all sorts of memories or ghosts of *his tongue licking her chin, licking her lips, filling her mouth with tickles of wine* memories flickering in her. It was obscene, that the sight of Santa's rutting could sweep away her bodily ailments and start wicked thoughts of her own spinning in her head, thoughts even of *a taste of nymph* she knew not what.

"I didn't mean to—"

Anya cast a contemptuous glance at the Easter Bunny, who had retreated a few feet but craned now to see past her head. He had one paw over his erection, trying, or was he, to conceal it from her.

"I've seen enough," she said. She plunged into the bleak forest, tracking along their snowprints. The Easter Bunny hopped after, offering thinly disguised propositions veiled as mewls of apology. But her eyes saw only snowy depressions and her mind entertained nothing but wild and terrible revenge.

Halloween, 1990. Late Wednesday afternoon. Rachel McGinnis had taken the day off from work. She sat now at the kitchen table, hunched over her mom's reliable old Singer, putting the finishing touches to Wendy's costume.

She glanced at the clock over the sink. Almost time to pick up Wendy at school. Where do the hours go? she wondered.

Concentrating into the hum of the sewing machine, Rachel gathered net tulle onto a ribbon of baby-blue satin. She couldn't imagine why, but this costume made her nervous. Her daughter had seen the Disney version of *Peter Pan* recently and still remembered vividly her last viewing of *The Wizard of Oz*. She wanted to be a good fairy "with wings and a magic wand and pretty Tinkerbell eyes, Mommy."

Rachel raised the presser foot, pulled the material free, snipped the thread with her orange-handled Fiskars, and switched off the sewing machine light. She needed to apologize to Wendy, she thought. "Fairies don't have wings and they don't have wands," she had insisted, amazed at her own vehemence. She kept pressing the point, as if it were arguable, until Wendy burst into tears and Rachel regained a semblance of self-control.

But six-year-olds, thank goodness, forgive and forget with blessed ease. By the time Rachel arrived at the Montessori school her daughter attended, Wendy fairly leaped into her mother's arms. In the living room now, having pulled on her new ballet tutu over her sky-blue leotard and tights, Wendy stood patiently while Rachel made up her eyes.

"Kim lost a tooth today."

"Kim Rogers?"

"Uh-huh. I can move this front one a little I think with my tongue."

"That's nice, honey. Close your eyes. Okay, now let's tie those wings on." Rachel brought them out, crisscrossing the ribbons on Wendy's chest and tying them in back. Not bad, she thought, admiring her daughter's loveliness as she adjusted the wingtips. But beneath her calm, a dark premonition hummed. Absurd, she thought. It was as if she were afraid she might invoke some savage fairy by dressing Wendy this way. Yet everyone knew that fairies were creatures of myth, no more substantial than Santa Claus or the Easter Bunny.

"There." Rachel smiled. "Now stand right here and don't turn around."

"Why, Mommy?"

"You'll see." She went past Wendy to the tall hutch that had been her mother's, opened the middle drawer, and drew out the wand.

Wendy gasped and reached for it. It was nothing more

than a dowel with a cardboard star taped to it and covered with aluminum foil, but Wendy loved it. Rachel delighted in her daughter's reaction, wishing that Frank were here to share it. His death had happened more than six months before, but she still woke in the night expecting to find his huge bearlike body beside her.

Wendy tugged her outside then and Rachel escorted her winged wonder from house to house, standing on the sidewalk while Wendy strode boldly up porch stairs to demand her due. The eerie feeling stayed with her during their hour on the streets. The shadows of bushes and dumpsters and alley-ways concealed not so much the human terrors she might dread on a normal night in Sacramento, as something unnameable that touched the nape of her neck with a cool hand.

"Look, Mommy," said Wendy, tearing down the steps of a house with a dozen blazing pumpkins grinning from the porch. "The funny lady let me reach into her bowl of steam and take two handfuls of candy."

"Did you say thank you?"

"Uh-huh," said Wendy, then raced to the next house. A heavyset man stood on the porch, watching what Rachel guessed was his son—a cowboy of perhaps four—hold out a pillowcase for a Tootsie Roll Pop. When they passed her on the sidewalk, the heavyset man smiled at her.

Rachel liked the conspiratorial camaraderie that bonded Halloween parents. Except for single mothers like herself, it seemed that mostly fathers escorted their young ghouls and goblins about. There was something very attractive about a man who displayed his love for a son or daughter in this way.

It was even better when he was large and bearded like Frank. Her girlhood friends had watched *Batman* or *The Fugitive* and swooned over the Beatles. But Rachel's favorite shows had been *A Family Affair* with Sebastian Cabot and the short-lived *The Bold Ones* with Burl Ives, whose records she bought exclusively for two years solid. More recently, she had been drawn to William Conrad and Dom DeLuise and

Luciano Pavarotti. Nothing thrilled her—indeed inflamed her with desire—like the sight and sound of the huge tuxedo'd singer, absurd handkerchief in hand, caressing those liquid Italian syllables with all the love in his expansive heart.

"Mommy, my arms are getting tired."

"It's time to head home anyway," said Rachel. "Do you want to hit one more side street?"

"No, I'm getting cold. Mommy?"

"Yes, honey."

"Can I have a Snickers when we get home? I got three of them."

"Yes, but I'll need to look them over first. And then, lovely lady, we'll get you out of that fairy outfit and into a nice warm bath. Sound good?"

Wendy gave an enthusiastic yes. As they walked home hand in hand, Rachel had a sudden urge to hide the fairy costume in the hall closet during Wendy's bath and bury it in the trash the next day.

And though she kept telling herself as she ran the bathwater that the idea was absurd, that's precisely what she did.

PART 3
CONSEQUENCES

God sends meat and the devil sends cooks.
　　—Thomas Deloney

The prerequisite for a good marriage is the license to be unfaithful.
　　—Carl Gustav Jung

Jealousy is the greatest of all evils.
　　—La Rochefoucauld

7.
ANYA CONFRONTS
HER HUSBAND

When Anya woke the next morning, her world had been transformed. She distinctly recalled the long trek back to the cottage. She had glared at the Easter Bunny as he sniffed the red panties and shoved them back into Santa's workpants. But once he had leaped through the window, all was a morass of vague thrashings and feverish dreams.

Her nightgown clung now to her back. She lay there stunned, her eyes roving, cataloging all things drab and diminished.

A dull stirring on her right. Something bulky rolled toward her, its arm heavy across her belly. A hairy upper lip brushed her cheek, a voice babbled alien words: "Good morning, Anya my love."

Whatever she replied seemed to amuse the creature beside her, for his eyes wrinkled up wet and demonic, and intermittent bursts of noise erupted from his lips like genuine laughter. She remembered laughter—what it felt like, what it meant. She wondered why this creature thought it necessary to perform such a pale imitation of it for her.

The bed shuddered when he rose. Then she was alone under the blankets, watching him move here and there, into the bathroom and out again, to the window for a hands-on-hips appraisal of the day, to the closet—Santa's closet, where red panties lay concealed in pants pockets. She fielded sound blips from him, tossed back blips of her own.

Thus it went that morning.

Over the weeks that followed, Anya walked about in a daze. She felt no great urge to re-embrace the myth of free will nor to begin making conscious choices. In fact she was moderately surprised—though she didn't show it—when she heard herself lie to Santa and knew at that precise moment that it was a lie.

"While you and the elves are busy in the workshop this morning," she said, "I think I'll drop in on their quarters and clean up a bit, maybe leave them a surprise."

"Wonderful, dearest," he said. "I'm sure they'll appreciate your thoughtfulness." He raised a bottle of Coke and smiled fatuously at her.

In the empty dorm, she straightened the sheets on a few beds, those belonging to the more voluble elves whose jabber would corroborate her story. Then she opened the windows to let in fresh air and set a potpourri beneath each pillow. When she was done, their quarters smelled like herb heaven.

To avoid being seen from the workshop, she slipped out the back, weaving in and out of the towering fir trees, deep into the woods. Not once did she falter in her steps, nor did the clearing where the lofty trees were thickest fail to appear as expected, nor did the dark stone hut refuse to rise from new-fallen snow like a rotten molar jutting up out of healthy gums.

She pulled off a mitten and touched the pane. *The kingdom and the power.* It was smooth and cold. *The glory and the ecstasy.* In the dim interior she made out the blackened fireplace, the four-poster dusky with shadows, the tiny bed with its dozing doll tucked snug under her coverlets. *The grape and the grope, the wild abandon.* Holding her fingers to the hut, Anya walked once around it, reading the rough stone of Santa's betrayal with her fingertips. *Encirclement by satyrs, goat hoofs in clover, their needy hands touching her breasts, their eyes transfixed by her vulva.* She tried the front door, opened it, felt the pull of youth and . . . something else tempting her inside. She closed it again, leaning against it until her head cleared. *Skin breathing on skin, polyrhythmic grunting, she being slowly spun and spindled, they like four rich flavors alternately sipped.* But when she returned to her original spot by the window, Anya, tears in her eyes, rapped sharply, slowly, repeatedly on the glass as if to rouse the little girl lost in slumber beneath the far window.

Fritz grinned into the mirror, turning his head this way and that to admire himself. His bunkmates Karlheinz and Max on either side of him fluffed their beards up around the red and green ribbons they had tied into them and flashed killer smiles into the glass. At the door to the washroom, envious faces, stacked like cordwood clear to the top of the doorframe, glared at them and shouted taunts.

"Simpering sycophants," growled one.

"Dumb luck for dumb clucks," sneered another.

"May you choke on a drumstick," cursed a third.

Fritz chuckled. Every year it was the same. The chosen three would elbow their way through a barrage of insult and invective to the dormitory entrance, link arms and stroll proudly across the commons to the jeers of their fellow elves, and be welcomed into the cottage to share Thanksgiving dinner with Santa and Mrs. Claus.

At first it was all they had dreamed.

"Max, Fritz, Karlheinz, my dear friends," boomed Santa. "Come in, come in, come in." Slaps on the back, warm hugs, and glad hands all round. The vestibule glowed with candlelight. The inviting aroma of roast turkey and honey-baked ham wafted in from the dining room. Then, a tinkling bell sounded in the next room and Mrs. Claus's melodious grandma-words: "Dinner's on the table!"

Karlheinz and Max, squealing with delight, dashed under Santa's arms and disappeared through the archway. Santa broke into a belly laugh. "Your bunkmates always were eager little devils, Fritz."

Fritz tried to look arch and disapproving. "Thank God some of us know our manners. Shall we in?"

"After you," said Santa, sweeping as low as his bulk would allow, and Fritz passed at a measured pace through the archway, hoping that Santa's laughter was not at his expense. But when the dining room opened out before him in all its splendor, Fritz forgot his misgivings.

In the fireplace, subdued flames sizzled along three neatly stacked logs. From the large beam that stretched across the dark wood ceiling depended a simple but elegant chandelier. Two dozen beeswax candles rose slim and tapered from their holders, spilling soft light onto the great oak table below.

Fritz knew this table well. Long ago, he had been one of a score of elves who had helped Santa apply the finishing touches to it, planing and sanding and staining and polishing and buffing deep into the night so that Anya would have it in time for Christmas that year. Tonight, of course, the craft that had gone into its manufacture—the turnings, the friezes, the knees, the stretchers, the fluted edges—was covered, splendidly, in the finest damask.

But as beautiful as the tablecloth was from where he now paused, it paled in comparison to the spread of food that covered it. Mrs. Claus stood at the head of the table, a carving knife in her hand, a plump roast turkey on the platter before her. Steam rose tantalizingly from its gleaming brown body. The rich aroma that permeated the air nearly made Fritz swoon, it was so warm and full and inviting. Spilling out as though from Mrs. Claus's bountiful bosom were dish upon dish of cranberry sauce, fresh piping-hot peas and carrots, white whipped potatoes, fanned rolls and firm dewy pats of butter, breaded dressing barely contained by the rim of its serving dish, brimming gravy boats, and pumpkin stewed in maple sap.

"Don't stand there gaping, Fritz," said Santa with a chuckle. "Come, sit beside me."

Santa placed himself at the far end facing Mrs. Claus and seated Fritz on his left. Fritz noted the empty chair across from him and its place setting. It was Santa's way of remembering the homeless and hungry. As he stood with his head bowed and his generous hands folded over the back of his chair,

Santa asked the Good Lord to open the hearts of those blest with abundance so that they might know the joy of serving those less fortunate.

They fell then to eating and talking and laughing, to sharing precious memories, to hearing Santa regale them with stories of his nocturnal travels.

And yet throughout the evening, it seemed to Fritz that Mrs. Claus held back. She appeared at times to be observing them through an invisible sheen. Then she would interject a witty comment or a homily, or ask if anyone wanted another slice of breast meat, and Fritz dismissed his fancies.

The strangeness came on full force, however, when they had stuffed themselves fit to bursting and were all—the menfolk anyway—sitting back and letting escape exaggerated sighs of satiety. Santa held the sides of his belly and *ho-ho-ho*'d in sweet pain, then suggested they retire to the sitting room for a pipe.

"Gonna regale us wid yer exploits, Santa?" asked Max. He winked hawkishly at his bunkmates.

Karlheinz giggled, making fire with his fingers. "Oooh Max, you naughty elf, can you be suggesting that our innocent master—he's a saint, don't you know?—after spending all night reaching into his sack, might be so bold as to climb *into* the sack with some sweet single mom? Is that what you're implying, you little scamp?"

Fritz chimed in over them, feeling uncomfortable with the turn their conversation had taken. "Now, now, lads, no need to get indecent. There's a lady present. Let's do as Santa suggests and retire to the sitting room."

It seemed to Fritz that at this moment a sudden blast of air frosted his left cheek. When he turned his head, Mrs. Claus sat hunched over the picked bones of the turkey, her bloodless knuckles dug taut into the damask, her eyes fixed on her husband. "No," she said, "I think it's time for Santa and me to have a little talk, just the two of us."

Santa faltered, then laughed. "But Anya," he said, an index

finger raised in gentle rebuke, "I always share a pipe with my co-workers after Thanksgiving dinner. You know that. It's a fine old tradition."

"Yes, dear," she countered, "and tonight we're going to break with tradition. Tonight you're going to see your guests to the door and then you and I are going to sit at this table and discuss our future together."

What Fritz saw in Mrs. Claus's eyes frightened him.

Max, sucking on a breadstick, seemed oblivious. He took it out of his mouth, screwed up his eyes, and said, "Pipe ud sure hit the spot."

Across from Max, Karlheinz stared down at his plate and said nothing. His hands were hidden in his lap like a little boy's.

Fritz folded his napkin and set it down. "Well," he said, "it's late and we really ought to be running along, thank you for a lovely evening, I haven't eaten this well in ages." He felt like he was fluttering too much, urging his companions out of their chairs, avoiding their hosts' eyes, moving his co-workers and himself awkwardly toward the vestibule.

"Fritz?"

"Yes, Santa?" Fritz had never seen him look less jovial.

"I enjoyed your company tonight, all three of you. It's a powerful pleasure working with you."

Fritz nodded. He ushered Karlheinz and Max to the door and together they started across the snow, stunned into silence at the strange turn the evening had taken. Halfway home, Fritz sent the others ahead and looked back at the cottage.

It sat there, thrusting up warm and fire-lit from the winterscape.

So cozy, so inviting.

But inside, something was happening that made Fritz want to shrivel up and die.

Santa waited for the front door to click shut. He wiped his mouth twice lightly with his napkin, then gazed down the table where Anya sat, her face buried in her hands. "Wife," he said gently, "would you mind telling me what that was all about?"

(Oh, shit, we're in for it now.) The intruder was back. *(The sexless crone is on to us.)*

Anya looked up, her forehead resting on the palm of one elbowed arm, and gave a wisp of a smile. "I'm sorry, I just can't keep up the ruse one moment more. You see," she said, straightening up, "I know."

"You know?"

She nodded.

(What'd I tell you. Can I call 'em or what?)

Yes. Yes I'm afraid you can.

Santa stared at the crossed knife and fork on his plate, at the congealing pool of gravy out of which his fork tines arched. "How long have you known?" His initial flash of panic had yielded almost at once to shame. He also felt, oddly enough, a nearly irrepressible urge to break into a broad grin.

"Since October." She told him of her trek through the woods with the Easter Bunny. She told him about finding the hut and standing in the snow outside.

Santa listened with a growing sense of horror as she described what she had seen. "You watched us make . . . you watched us?"

Anya nodded, unable to look at him, her face fisted into a sob which she quickly stifled.

"Oh my Anya," he said, starting to rise and go to her. "My dear wife, how that must have hurt you."

(Go ahead. Try it. What've we got to lose?)

Oh, shut up. Isn't there any decency in you?

Her right hand shot out, palm pressed to the air. "Stay there," she commanded. "Don't you move from that chair." Then she brought her hand to her chest and asked softly, "How long have you been seeing her?"

Santa shrugged. "Not long. Maybe twenty years."

"I see," said Anya, fingering the ebony of her napkin ring. "In other words, when you swore twenty years ago that you would never sleep with the Tooth Fairy again, you were lying."

"I didn't mean to—"

"You broke a solemn oath."

"I tried to prevent—"

"Didn't you?"

"Now wait!" Santa slammed his hand on the table. Dishes rattled before him. "You've got to understand my position. I had been seduced, you were going all to pieces over something I had no control over—all right, very little control over—and I really meant to stop. But you don't know what it's like to be a man, to have all this . . . this copulatory energy building up inside all the time, and then to be set upon by the most ravishing seductress imaginable. My God, Anya, she's pure appetite. She wore my resolve down as if it were the thinnest veneer, and I swear to you it wasn't. My will was granite, thick and firm. But hers was diamond."

(That's telling her, that's laying it on the line. Give it to her straight. Real men need pussy. She's got no right to keep you away from an open one if she plans to keep hers tightly sealed.)

I told you to shut up, you vile piece of filth.

(Ooh, hurt me, Santa. Hurt me with the truth.)

"You lied to me, didn't you?"

Thoughts swirled in Santa's head, memories of those first encounters, of the Tooth Fairy's singlemindedness, of the overwhelming flood of carnality he willingly let wash through the calm landscape of his life. In the midst of the swirl, a golden ribbon of truth shone like sun through stormclouds. He grasped it now, felt it in his hand. "Yes, I did. I lied to you. In a moment of panic, seeing how much pain you were in, I vowed to be faithful even though I knew it was a lie. I'm sorry."

(Wrong move, fat boy. Don't budge an inch.)

Anya smiled at her hands, which lay before her on the table as if cupped over some prize. "I'm glad to hear you're repentant." Still looking at her hands, reasoning with them: "We could, of course, try to find out why you did what you did. We could poison our bliss by endlessly bickering about it. But I'm content, if you are, to let the whole sorry business recede into the past." Looking up at him now, attempting a conciliatory smile: "Maybe we can work together this time to fortify your vow, maybe we can confront the Tooth Fairy together, maybe—"

"Wait." Santa didn't like the way Anya was racing along the track of her own scenario. "I didn't say I was sorry for sleeping with the Tooth Fairy. In fact I'm not sorry for that. And I don't intend to give her up."

Anya's smile withered.

(Yes! That's my man!)

His vehemence startled him. "Not taking anything away from us, I quite enjoy the time I spend with the Tooth Fairy."

"But you just said she seduced you."

"At first," said Santa. "But I set aside my misgivings pretty quickly—all but one, deceiving you—and came to love the sheer carnality of what she offered. You know, in a way I'm glad we're bringing this out in the open. It feels so cleansing to talk about it." He was going to say more but caught sight of Anya's eyes.

"Cleansing? I'll cleanse your arse, you pitiful tub of guts." A hand went to her mouth. "Heavens, listen to me, I promised myself I wouldn't get mad, but oh you lying saint, you philandering shitwad, you . . . jellybellied slutfucker." Each phrase dealt Santa a roundhouse blow. "God forgive my language, how dare you speak of continuing to carry on with that whore?"

"Now, Anya."

(What's with this 'Now, Anya' crap? Slam into her. She's just a dumb fir nymph—)

A what?

(—she's got no right—the gall of her—to lord it over he who rules the—who rules her and the others—give one of them exclusivity and she turns possessive.)

"How dare you assume I'd put up for one second with

115

such an arrangement? Oh sure. Old worn-out Anya's going to stand on the sidelines, wiping her hands on her apron and grinning good-naturedly, while her husband shucks off his suit and pokes away at some sleek young immortal with the sex drive of a rabbit and the morals of a rutabaga."

"Anya, you're not worn out," Santa protested.

"What chance do I have against someone with a body like hers?" Her eyes were glistening, her voice locked down tight.

(None, sweetheart. Less than zero, you white-haired old bag of used-up gut and gristle, you dusty tunnel, you inflexible sleeve.)

"It's not a contest."

"What does she give you that I don't?"

"Nothing!" he said. "It's just different, that's all. I've got enough energy for both of you. I need both of you."

(Jesus, man, will you listen to yourself? What a wimp. You don't need this sack o' shit, tubby. You need to dump her's what you need.)

Enough!

Her face pruned up at him. "Don't try to fool me, because I can't be fooled. You don't need me. I'm just a tired old woman who'd rather sleep most nights than give you the love you used to deserve. I notice you fondling yourself under the blankets while I read, don't think I don't. You want me to do that more for you, I will. You want me to mouth you more often than once a year—that's what men like best isn't it?— just say so, I'll do it."

(Ooh, maybe dumping her's not something we want to rush into.)

"Anya, please—"

"Only you've got to promise me you'll give up that homewrecking fairy slut of yours."

(Oops. Dump away, Santa babes.)

She folded her glasses and sobbed into her hands. It tore at Santa to see her go to pieces this way. But he couldn't let his love for Anya compromise his own integrity. Strange word to use, but it was right. The Tooth Fairy meant nothing to him, but she had taught him this much at least: that confining his sexual love to one woman was a betrayal of his deepest impulses, would make him less than he was meant to be. "Look," he said, "let me talk this out with her on Christmas Eve, find out how she feels."

"No, you've got to promise me you'll put a stop to it the next time you see her." Her tone grew insistent.

"I'm not going to promise that."

"Promise me right now." Her eyes pierced the air as she rose imperious from her chair.

"Don't give me orders, Anya," countered Santa with a patriarch's calm resolve.

"Promise!" she bellowed.

Anya's eyes burned into his face. Her hands groped the tablecloth. Abruptly the carving knife lifted into the air, slicing through the acrimony hanging between them. Along the table the sharp knife sailed, a flash of silver in the firelight. In the gold turnings of the chandelier above, its swift progress across bowls and dishes crusted with remnants of their feast was reflected fiftyfold.

Santa heard the *thunk* long after he felt the blade rape his chest, and it seemed to him—though surely he was wrong—that Anya turned pale and fled the room long before the steel point lodged in his heart. Through his tears he took in the bolster and web and the dark wooden handle with its three gold rivets. He gripped the handle with both hands and wrenched it out. Then he stared at his ruddy complexion in the blade, burnished red with blood.

His face seemed ancient, petulant, not jolly at all.

(Getting closer, fat boy. Looking more like me all the time. Need a few more hints?)

Had he cared to, he might have noticed the closing of the wound, the swift healing of his heart, the reweaving of immortal tissue carried on effortlessly in his body.

But Santa had other things on his mind.

He shut his eyes and wept.

***

Couples on the outs with one another tend to confine their bickering to hostility's natural habitat, the home. To the outer world, they display the cosmeticized face of marital harmony and bliss.

Such was the case with Anya and her husband.

In her public functions—of which there were admittedly few—Anya had nothing but admiring looks for Santa and affectionate little pecks on the cheek, which drew the cheers and whistles of his helpers. But behind closed doors, all was ice and fire, tempest and inferno, badly cooked meals shared in stony silence, and nights of troubled sleep in separate beds.

For the first two weeks, Anya tried—as did Santa—to come to some resolution of their problem through a round of early evening discussions. But as much as he professed to care for her, to love her deeply and devotedly, Santa refused to commit to giving up his affair with the Tooth Fairy. He sat at the far end of the couch looking stunned or smug by turns. While the fire hissed and popped on the inner hearth, she wept and raged and cajoled and pleaded, but Santa budged not one inch from his fortress of lust.

As often as not, Anya punctuated their evenings by bludgeoning her husband or by taking razors or knives or knitting needles to him. Her violence surprised her at first, but she quickly became inured to it. Santa's acquiescence in her mayhem—thinking, she could tell, that perhaps she would work off her anger that way and come to accept his affair—enraged her beyond endurance, so that at last she threw down her weapons, stomped off to her room, and slammed the door against him.

Then came the two-week, pre-Christmas rush. Santa spent long hours at the workshop and Anya had time alone to think. And the things she thought made her blush with the wickedness of them. More and more, she grew toward a certainty that she was capable of it, particularly given her newfound surge of youth. It was so unlike her, so naughty, it took her breath away. Yet there was a connection between what she now contemplated and her past, the past she couldn't quite recall; a connection that made it natural and (dared she say it) right. Worse, she knew in her heart that the elves—as devoted to Santa as they were—would take to her proposition as if it were second nature.

By the time of her husband's departure, Anya was in a welter of confusion about what to do.

After that peculiar Thanksgiving dinner, the elves kept a wary eye on Santa and his wife. At night, Fritz listened to his bearded co-workers trade gossip, craning over the ends of their beds to feed this or that twig of conjecture into the raging fire of rumor which swept through their quarters.

The work suffered. It wasn't so much a matter of not being industrious as it was a general enervation of the troops, the slightest surrender of spirit to the conqueror uncertainty. But at last, to Fritz's relief, the work came to a satisfying end and they found themselves once more in the commons, cheering as Gregor and his brothers led the caparisoned team from the stables and harnessed them to Santa's sleigh.

Santa seemed in high spirits. He gave each reindeer a hug around the neck and a cube of sugar. Then he made a rousing speech about giving freely of oneself, about the virtues of self-sacrifice, about respecting the core of one's beliefs and particularly that which makes each of us unique and peculiar and idiosyncratic, about not yielding one iota on issues that defined one's very nature, about how love always triumphs in the end. Fritz laughed and cried and cheered along with his compatriots, though he thought it odd that Santa strayed so far from his usual themes.

More fuel for the midnight fires.

Santa and his wife came into one another's arms and kissed long and lingering for the crowd. The elves went wild, as always, but wilder than they really needed to and longer in leaving off their cheers. Then Santa strode to the sleigh, pulled himself into it, picked up the weighty reins, chucked them across the backs of the team, and rose into the air, waving and laughing down at them like life irrepressible.

As always, Fritz and the others watched and waved until the diminishing spot in the sky winked out and the high jingle of sleighbells was but the memory of a memory. Hands dropped here and there in the crowd and heads turned from the sky. Fritz heard the general gasp first. Then he registered the drawn faces of Johann, of Friedrich, of Gustav and Knecht Rupert.

He followed their eyes.

There on the front porch stood Mrs. Claus.

Her peasant blouse—red and white and shot through with stitched green ivy—was unlaced and ripped open to expose the pink-tipped mounds of her breasts. Her skirts she had hiked up and tucked into her wide black belt. Below, she was naked as truth. While one hand teased her left nipple hard, the other moved in slow deliberate circles, rounding upon her sex like the fist of a yawning child at one puffy eye.

And when Fritz brought his gaze to her face, God help them she was looking out over the shocked multitudes with the hungriest old-lady eyes he had ever seen in his life.

8.

VENGEANCE AND LUST

Gregor stood at the stable door, an eternal humph of disapproval stuck to his face. Arms folded tight upon his chest, he gazed out through the buttercup light of magic time at an elfsnake whose long green body stretched deep into the forest, its restless tail tapering off at the middle of the skating pond. He refused to imagine the tomfoolery its head was engaged in. Every few minutes, another green-clad figure with his fly unzipped and his penis flapping right-to-left-to-right dashed out of the woods, kicking up snowdust in his eagerness to rejoin the line for another turn at Santa's wife.

"Disgusting," muttered Gregor. But as he said it, he wondered why he alone, of all the elves, had been able to summon up the willpower to refuse Mrs. Claus's outrageous proposal. Even his brothers, shy by nature, shifted under their clothing at the sight of her—as if a darkness long suppressed slithered up out of their bellies.

The whole wretched mob had grinned and nodded at her words, stamping and whistling their encouragement, until at last they stormed the porch and hefted her, half-naked, high above their heads. Gregor had just stood there by the stable, mouth agape, feeling as though he'd tumbled into a bad dream. Then into the woods they dashed, Mrs. Claus—acting suddenly as young and irrepressible as a schoolgirl—jouncing above and pointing the way.

Gregor missed his reindeer, their clear brown eyes, their animal honesty. He didn't much like these wild new elves with their demented looks and their taunts, these demonic doppelgangers. Some of them, before they rejoined the queue, dashed across the commons and waggled their willies at him.

They laughed. They called him names. Albert did this, and so did Wilhelm, two of his dearest friends. He shut his eyes to stifle a sob.

What Gregor missed most was watching the elves wink in and out. Usually, at the moment Santa's sleigh passed through the protective bubble around his domain, those inside reverted to normal time. Every few minutes thereafter, a handful of elves would "wink out" of normal time into magic time, vanishing from their midst and reappearing soon after, exhausted and ready for sleep. It was no easy task, so they told him, to spend six straight hours transporting gift after gift from storage to loading where they had to be to replenish Santa's pack as he went from house to house. But now that Mrs. Claus, in her fury at Santa, had sustained the wrap of magic time about the entire North Pole, there was no need to wink in and out. There was only this ever-renewing queue of elves stretched into the woods, the now unbearable glowlight of magic time over all, and Gregor's interminable wait for the return of reason.

He rested his hairy forearms on the half-door of the stable. "A sorry time," he muttered. He watched Fritz, Mrs. Claus's appointed pander, march out of the woods with an air of self-importance, barking orders up and down the line.

A sorry time indeed.

From the shadows, the Tooth Fairy watched her lover pull presents from his pack and arrange them beneath the tree. As golden as her memory was of their time together, the reality never failed to outshine it. He was a better lover now—better because more giving—than in the old times, and he had been superb then.

"Santa," she said, low and husky. Her paramour gave the slightest start. Still on his knees, he turned to her. "Do you recognize the place?" she asked. She said nothing about his failure, for the first time in twenty years, to show up at her island; said nothing, though it stung deep.

"Of course." She didn't like the blank look on his face. "Our first time together," he said. "Twenty years ago, red lace panties, little Rachel Townsend's bed. I thought you might show up here so I scheduled California early."

"Like the way I look?"

"Radiant as ever." His eyes never strayed from her face.

"Aren't we the cool one tonight?" she teased, hiding her upset. "There's another little girl sleeping in that same bedroom tonight, Rachel's daughter Wendy." She clung to him and fingered his lower lip. "There's a delectable upper right lateral incisor lying beneath her pillow. Why don't we go in and . . . see what happens?"

"Anya knows," he said.

Ah. Things began to make sense.

"How?" she asked, searching his eyes.

"The Easter Bunny. He brought her to the hut. They watched us through the window."

She laughed. "Well, well. So good old Anya knows what we're up to."

"Yes. And it means we've got to stop."

Reluctance. She hadn't felt that from Santa for years. It unsettled her. "No need for hasty judgments, lover. Let's go in and look at Wendy, shall we?"

He hesitated, then agreed. "But no bedding down next to her." He raised an index finger. "We'll peek in at her. Then I'm off to the next house."

"Of course," she said, cozying up to him and making sure her right breast pressed against his upper arm.

Fritz did his best to seem in control. But inwardly he was a mass of conflicts, all of them bitter and none of them anywhere near resolution.

His penis. That lay at the heart of his problems. Before now, he had hardly been aware of it. It was just something you held onto so you didn't pee on your slippers. Funny soft droopy tubes of flesh, peripheral to their lives; they all had one, no big deal. But now this thing—all of their things—had stirred at Anya's words and deeds up on that porch. (She had insisted they call her Anya, not Mrs. Claus.) Suddenly, this hitherto inconsequential appendage had taken on great pitch and moment, nagging for female completion, refusing to let him think about anything else.

"Stay in line, men," he shouted to those nearest the hut. "Dicks at the ready. And warm them with your hands. Anya's orders." He stopped before a dole-eyed elf whose mittened fists hovered uncertainly at his belt. "Albert, for the last time, will you get your goddamn dick out?"

"Aw gee whiz Fritz, it's too cold," Albert grumbled. But he unbuttoned his pants and did as he was told.

Never before had Fritz's loyalty to Santa been at odds with his loyalty to Anya. "Fritz," she had told him after his first time, "I swear to you the next elf who fucks me deferentially gets tossed out on his ear. I want you diminutive cockwielders to wallow in my flesh like piglets in mud. Spread the word."

Lordy, lordy, why, he wondered, was he taking it all in stride? Why had all of them adapted so quickly to what they would rightly have seen as scandalous behavior scant hours ago?

And what would Santa think of all this?

But the horror—and the humor of it—was that, deep down, Fritz didn't really give a shit *what* Santa thought. In her porch ramblings, Anya had spoken right to the heart of some depraved creature hidden inside him, hidden in all of them. It was rude and rowdy. It refused to be ruled. It stamped, it bellowed, it raged, and it craved precisely what Anya was offering.

Who, it demanded, was Santa Claus anyway? They had a new master now, a new mistress rather, a lusty old woman who seemed suddenly not so old at all, who had taken it upon herself to envaginate them, to bring them to a boil, to strip from them the sweet veneer of elfdom and wrench into focus a wilderness that surged unchecked within.

Wendy's room silvered in moonlight.

As he gazed upon the little girl's beauty, Santa felt its mild reproach. Anya had been right all along. He had been bullheaded about the Tooth Fairy. One glance at the sleeping child was all it took to bring him to his senses. "Aren't they astounding?" he said.

"Mm." The Tooth Fairy's agreement was perfunctory. She was too busy munching on Wendy's baby tooth to say more. Swallowing it, she cupped a palm over her anus.

Santa kept his eyes fixed on Wendy's angelic face. His cheeks were burning. "Are you finished yet?"

"What's the matter, stud?" she taunted. "Afraid to see my cunt pucker?"

"You're being a little childish," he said. He saw her thrust a hand beneath the pillow, heard the muffled clink of coins. Her every curve and concavity was pantherish and provoking.

Without straightening up, she brought her fingers to her nipples and teased them out into hard tight nubs. Her eyes probed Santa's face. "Childish?" she said. With a sinking heart, Santa watched her right hand move down her belly into a thicket of curls whose every twist and turn he had by heart. "Is this the body of a child, Santa?"

In an instant he was behind her, gripping her wrist. He intended to scold her, to plead with her to honor the innocence of the child's sleep and leave him be. But she whirled about, planting a kiss deep in his mouth as she cupped and caressed his burgeoning desire.

And Santa let it happen, neither horrified nor elated, watching his body expend its lust, knowing that this time he had the strength to end it, and the resolve, and the best of reasons—his undying love for his wife.

Anya lay beneath Fritz, out of her mind with rage and desire. His prick was lodged up inside her. His balding head with its wisps of red hair rotated now at her breast, working like a horny babe at her nipple. His long bushy beard tickled her belly.

She couldn't believe how youthful she felt. What she was doing scared and exhilarated her. It seemed precisely counter to anything the wife of Saint Nicholas ought to be doing, yet it felt like something she had done countless times in some forgotten past—done and enjoyed, as now she enjoyed Fritz.

"You're improving, Fritz," she said. "Your first go was wretched, your second only so-so, but honey you've hit your stride with number three. Oh shit Fritz yes keep it up keep doing that don't stop don't break that rhythm."

In Anya's mind, each surge of pleasure Fritz evoked drew a razorline across Santa's face or scored a random whipwelt upon his bare back. Though she had thus far bled the jolly old son of a bitch dry thousands of times, she had thousands more to go before her vengeance would begin to approach anything like completion.

Anya gripped the sheets to either side of her, the same sheets that Santa had slaked his lust upon. Fisting them tight, she arched up to meet the moaning elf-body that pounded down on her. Wide-eyed faces packed tight the windows. Then orgasm bulleted through her and sent her screaming like a newborn, drawing Fritz along as well. He bucked and humped like joy and sorrow combined as she tightened about him.

"Anya, dear Anya," he gasped at his breath's end. He seemed, this detumescing elf, impatient to say something. For a moment Anya couldn't recall his name. "This isn't right," he blurted out, "what we're doing out here in the woods. We've got to start thinking about—"

Abruptly she raised herself on her elbows and glared at him. Then she hauled back and struck him, three hard blows. Fritz scrabbled off the bed and slumped, hands collapsed over his head, in a disarray of green clothing. "Don't you talk to me, you little shit, about right and wrong. We make the rules out here, me and my quim. Not you. Not any of you. Your job is to obey me. Mine is to hurt my sainted husband and to keep on hurting him until there's no more hurt left."

"But—"

"Enough!" she yelled. In an instant she was off the bed, her fingernails dug deep into Fritz's hairy shoulder. He clutched his clothing and winced, slunk in silence.

Anya rushed him to the door and swung it wide. Out he sprawled, naked in the snow.

"You! Inside!" she said, grabbing an elf at random. Then she slammed the heavy oak door on the unending line of little men stretched through the winterscape and fell to her knees, sucking fiercely at the new member, trying to identify its owner not by his face but by the taste and shape of him and by the feel of his buttocks through the chill green seat of his pants.

"It was awful when she found out. Plenty of bickering and hurt pride. Lick a little lower, would you? The knives came out too. Of course my feelings hurt more than my flesh. I stuck to my guns. You would have been proud of me. I tried to insist on having you both. But that's not going to happen, clearly. This has got to be our last time together so—oh Jesus God—so let's—"

The Tooth Fairy poked her head up. "Would you mind not talking so much?" She ducked down and went on with her work.

"No, wait," said Santa, sitting up. "That's lovely, as always, sweetheart, what you're doing. But we've got to come to an agreement about this. Please stop for a moment and talk to me."

With a look of impatience, the Tooth Fairy shifted on his thighs. "What about?" She rubbed the head of his arousal along the soft line of her jawbone.

"About not seeing each other again." Row upon row of toys and books and stuffed animals climbed the wall next to Wendy's bed. Nearby lay Wendy herself, thralled in normal time and looking beautiful as only six-and-a-half can.

"Don't talk nonsense," she said.

"My resolve hasn't been worth much lately," he said, "but things have to change." He tried to sound forceful, but all he felt was ineffectual. The strength of Santa's resistance seemed to ebb and flow in counterpoint to the tides of not-Santa's passion, and just now his tidepools were rapidly filling.

"Tell you what," she replied, leaning her cheek and temple along his erection and running her index finger around its tip, "I want you to remember what it's like to spend Christmas

Eve without me. So you go about your giftgiving tonight, and me about my toothtaking. I'll wait for you to summon me. I'm betting your fidgety little hand will be shoved into Thea's mouth before the week is out."

Santa frowned. "You're not giving me the kind of cooperation I need."

"That's my best offer, big boy. Now shut up and give me that amazing snow-white head of yours." With that, she mouthed him again as deep as she could go, spun about like a noisemaker on his fat fleshy spindle, and smothered his face in fuzzy wet womanflesh.

During round five, emptiness began to tinge Anya's raging desires. She had as yet no name for the feeling. She knew only that it threatened her vengeance and that only copulation frequent and feverish would keep it at bay. The bleeding Santa she beheld in her mind's eye was weeping, yet he also grinned at her antics, grinned as if he had ordered them.

Gripping stray wisps of black hair that swirled about a bald spot, she wrenched up and peered into the bleary eyes of Wolfram, the workshop's master miniaturist with a cock to match. "Not bad, pindick. Now get off me and go. On your way out, send in the next two."

His jowls fell and the ovals of his eyes lengthened like soggy Cheerios. "Did you say two, milady?"

Anya lit into him then, snatching an andiron from the fireplace and whipping Wolfram's baboon buttocks out the door with its long hard length. Flinging it into the snow in spangles of sunlight, she reached out and tight-fisted two elfin erections. "You and you," she said, her eyes locking on the carnal gaze of Gregor's brothers. "Get in here and put these things to their proper use."

They complied.

Doubt bedeviled Santa.

For years he had lost himself in fairy flesh, first by way of

128

seduction, then by design. It was elemental giving, this licking and stroking, this probing and enclosing. It stripped away his Santahood, yes. But it brought out a deeper urge to give, an urge beyond ego and tradition. And it brought out an urge to take as well, a grasping grope at exposed flesh and the joyous oblivion it offered.

But now that Anya knew all, now that he had spent a hellish month watching misery dwell in her, the reminders that he was Santa Claus would not be stilled. They nagged at him no matter how unbearably rhythmic his lover's hips rose and fell about him.

Santa he remained through it all.

The intruder—Santa's dark twin—had been eyeing him sullenly during this struggle, upset with his host's less-than-wholehearted attention to the pleasures of the bed. At the first hint of impending orgasm, he engaged him.

(Okay, friend, the time for introspection is past. We're entering the homestretch here and I want your full attention on maximizing my pleasure.)

What you want no longer concerns me. This, I swear, will be the last time I sleep with the Tooth Fairy.

Her fingernails tensed like claws at his back.

(Swear and be damned. You and I understand the value of a saint's vow. We've heard enough of them. We've seen them broken like twigs. Pay attention, damn it. She's starting to peak and so are we.)

He took in the tumble of her hair, the switch and sway of her head as it tossed to the rhythm of their sex.

Anya is my salvation, my anchor, my love. To her and her alone I hereby pledge my fidelity.

(What a wuss you are!)

Then there are the children. Sweet Wendy here, sleeping so soundly, shames me with her innocence.

The blood throbbed in his head. His heart pounded to the surge of his lover beneath him.

(Where's the shame? Humping is good. More humping is better. It's where kids come *from, in case you've—)*

They deserve better from Santa Claus.

(So be better. Be the best. Cease all this chatter and delve into the delicacy that lies before us—Tooth Fairy tenderloin en brochette.)

The upward thrust of her hips came faster now, less controlled.

To the boys and girls of the world, I vow no longer to dishonor them thus. And to my elves—

(Oh come now, you're going much too—)

—to my elves, faithful to me in all things, I owe this promise as well—to pull myself out of the foul mire of lust and regain my God-given purpose.

Below, she gripped tight along the length of him. He began to tingle all over, inside and out.

I'm rid of the Tooth Fairy. And I'm rid of you.

(Of me!?)

That's right. I'm putting you down, whoever you are. I don't need you anymore.

Santa gave a sharp inward thrust that made the Tooth Fairy cry out.

(Now wait just one—)

No need to wait! You're out of my life!

A second thrust and a third. They pushed her over the edge, ramping and rioting into sweet oblivion.

But Santa's dark twin was less easily defeated. The battle raged fierce and furious right up to the moment of climax. And when it came time to scale the great orgastic peak, they bickered and fought like brothers all the way up the sheer face of the mountain. For every piton his dark twin's sinning prick drove into a rocky cleft, Santa snatched a dozen more from him and hurled them clattering down the mountainside.

At last, the saint gathered his resolve, put firm hands upon the intruder's shoulders, and shoved him screaming down the steep slope. Bleating a cry of triumph, Santa Claus reached one hand, then the other, over the topmost crag and pulled his huge bulk up onto the gasping heights of elemental orgasm.

***

In the frenzied feeding of Anya's revenge, two lovers became three, three became four, and four grew in kind. She dimly recalled Heinrich huddled about her, two of him taking turns at her mouth, two moving against her nipples, one each shoved into bunghole and cunt. But that memory lost its precision in the swirl of so many like it.

Long afterward, when she tried to focus on her bouts of passion, the recollection that shone most clearly was of every last elf packing the tiny hut to the rafters, though by any rational measure that could not have been. Yet there they were in memory—a host of Cupids grown old and bearded, leers of lust or bewilderment in their eyes; and loveshafts everywhere, thick and thin, lengthy and stubby, circumcised and un-. And somehow their slit pricktips all reached her as she lay there on the bed. Every pore was an orifice open to them, and their seed spilled forth rich and viscous, turning the mad swell of her vengeful flesh everywhere deeper, redder, wetter, until— while the Santa Claus that looked on and suffered in her mind's eye grew hardly distinguishable from the flayed carcass of some butchered porker—Anya grabbed all about her for love, bucking and ramping toward absolute forgetfulness.

Thousands of miles distant from one another, Santa and Anya came. Their climaxes were not joyous by any means, not the sort one is wont to replay to heighten the solitary delights of masturbation. Powerful as these orgasms were, they brought with them a terrible ambivalence and the first tentative turnings toward reconciliation.

Santa, pumping and gasping beneath his paramour, looked up and saw pure harpy, pure siren, pure succubus. If this creature, into whose womb tunnel the long arc of his arousal now curved, had anything more to her than insatiable desire, he failed to see it, now nor in the twenty years of their adultery. In the instant his flesh lunged into what it craved, the scales fell from his eyes and he knew that, unlike so many times before, he had the strength to keep them from growing back. For as much pleasure as he shared with this faery daemon, so much pain he now realized would his dear wife endure.

And that was intolerable.

As for Anya, there came a time when the lust she surrounded herself with transmogrified into some bizarre and meaningless flesh-machine and her ire against Santa turned to dust and blew away. Beneath mounds of humping elves, Anya found a certain stillness, in the midst of which stood her husband, whole and pristine and loving as always. There were roses in his cheeks and a twinkle in his eye. Smoke curled in white wisps from the bowl of his pipe, wreathing about his face like the fingers of a loving wife.

When she had come to herself, Anya rose from the bed and hurried two score bare-assed elves out the door like mice before a broom. The last of them—Helmut the clockmaker, whose mind, before this intriguing night, had been preoccupied with springs and flywheels—she collared.

"Send Fritz," she said, and Helmut nodded.

Fritz found her sitting on the side of the bed, staring into the flames. Uncertain of her mood, he wondered if he should tuck his engorged elfhood back inside his trousers.

"Mrs. Claus?" he ventured.

"Fritz," she said, glancing peripherally at him, "please help me into my dress."

"Yes, ma'am." He turned away, working with both hands to maneuver his stiff member beneath the fold of green cloth that fell from belt buckle to crotch. Given his tumescence, he abandoned the buttoning itself as a lost cause. It was all he could do to retrieve the torn peasant dress Mrs. Claus had tossed over the sleeping doll so long ago, carry it like a dead woman draped across his arms, and hold it out to her.

When she was dressed, he ushered her to the door and watched her take her silent way through a gaping sea of faces.

In bewildered silence, the other elves followed Fritz out of the woods, past the skating pond, and across the commons to the porch. Those, like Fritz, who busied their giddy minds with renewed hopes of carnal easement, lingered there in the snow, watching the object of their obsession move from room to room, closing curtains. They heard her turn the shower on. Still they stood there in the snow, the lustful pure, in silent devotion. And when at last the distant hiss of the shower cut abruptly off, they took the occasion—all except Fritz—to disperse like whipped dogs to their kennel of calm, where elfdom damped down the satyr in them and all was right again with the world.

Sexlessness reclaimed them.

But it did not reclaim Fritz.

He stood there in the etched light of magic time, his clasped hands pressed against his erection, waiting for Anya to uncurtain her windows, to re-emerge on the porch, to give him some sign that his priapic adoration of her was not misplaced, that it had its parallel in the urgings of her own lovely sex.

On the long walk home, Anya felt nothing.

In the shower, nothing.

Beneath the comforter staring up at the ceiling, still nothing. The close of her eyelids and her swift drop into sleep came as casually and as unlooked for as a shift in the wind.

In dream, her naked body sprawled across the snowy commons. Her right thigh rested upon the roof of the cottage, her left upon the workshop. Both buildings were weather-beaten, broken-windowed, abandoned and badly in need of repair. So too the elves' quarters along whose ragged front eaves she ran an idle finger.

The winter cloudcover broke. The Lord God's hands parted the firmament. His face showered beatitudes upon her. Then, touching His foot to the earth, He crouched between her legs like the lowliest of His creation. His vestments were of rough bronze and leather. His beard, always feather-white before, had turned a mischievous brown shot with bolts of silver. His eyes rioted with typhoons. With the easy contrariety of dreams, Anya knew that this was how God the Father had come to them at the beginning of Santa's realm, even as He manifested Himself in robe and crown, fingers bejeweled and beard beribboned, with hosts of angels singing His praises.

Along the folds of her flesh, His tongue traced a path of healing. He flicked and swirled blessing upon blessing there until her soul felt so full of passion she wondered the wood didn't blaze up about them nor the snow sizzle into steam.

At first when He moved to cover her, she protested, craving more mouth. But where His divine flesh touched hers, He was all tongue. His private hair was a writhe of tongues, teasing, urgent, intelligent. And His unending organ of generation eased past the swollen petals of her womanhood and gloried inside. Ever deeper His divinity probed, absorbing heartache and radiating epiphany.

And when He kissed Anya's eyelids, she knew for one blinding instant what she had once been. The heady scent of mountain groves in moonlight came to her. Her chaotic queenship over the fir nymphs. Pitys, her name. After elusive chase she had turned to fir, felt Pan peel off a low branch and wear it as a chaplet, watched him kneel in supplication at the base of her trunk, suffered blinding white splashes of devotion against her bark, and at long last metamorphosed back and let him prick her to his heart's content. Thus to Pan and his satyr offspring did Pitys's fir nymphs thenceforth behave, eternally open to poking, giving back better than they got and falling upon each other when the males were spent.

God's love made Anya young again, locked that youth into place. The barbs and burrs of old age softened and fell away. And when His climax came, it was oblivion as sweet as it gets, all-embracing, with a pleasure bearable only because her flesh had become divine.

When Anya's eyes opened, she lay in bed, the hushed light of magic time gilding the lace curtains. A gentle rapping sounded at the front door. A calm lay upon her, and a sadness.

Her dream had evaporated—something about God and fir trees and copulation, something about how life had been for them in earlier times.

No matter.

Dreams were that way: elusive, tantalizing. Anya rose, a spring in her step, and wrapped her bright green robe about her.

She opened the door. "Yes, Fritz?"

He stood on the porch, bent slightly at the waist, hands behind his back, one toe sweeping an arc of shyness across the porch snow. "Um . . . I was wondering . . . that is I was hoping. . . ." Looking up from beneath a mop of red hair, he blushed.

"Come in," she said, opening the door for him, then closing it firmly behind, feeling a whoosh of cold air at her ankles.

Fritz crushed his cap to his breast. "The others, they all drifted away, they don't remember what happened in the woods, they can't understand why everything's in magic time. They look at me standing there in the snow with this bulge in my pants and call me crazy."

Anya shook her head and smiled. "My faithful Fritz," she said, "always so eager to please. It makes me wonder what you were in the other life."

"Other life?"

"No matter. Something I dreamed."

"Oh. Anyway I was wondering if you'd like to go back to the hut and—"

"It's over, Fritz."

"—and you and me, we could . . . what did you say?"

"Things are returning to normal. I'm Santa's wife again and only Santa's."

"Oh, no, don't say that. Please."

"You were there at the beginning, with the others. You saw God resanctify our marriage."

"But doesn't this count for anything?" Fritz took out his penis and held it as though it were a priceless treasure he'd found in his pockets.

Anya contemplated the ruddy column of flesh, its squinty

135

eye, its wrinkled wrap of veins. Men were such children when it came to sex. All of their passion rushed to this hidden finger, the creature they kept in their pants whose primary function seemed to be to turn love into plumbing.

Now here was Fritz in her vestibule, surrounded by wreaths, spare overshoes, a pipe rack, and a dozen other reminders of his beloved master, and all he could think about was his elfin erection. She went to her knees and cupped him in her hands. Moaning, he caressed her face.

"This counts for much," she said tenderly. "These past many days, I've handled lots of these, Fritz, but none so beautiful as yours."

"Yes, yes, ooooooh that's nice."

"But this is what you gave up to be one of Santa's helpers. Surely the sacrifice was worth it."

"Never. Oh, Anya, please?"

Anya looked at the stiff rod she kneaded. Its tip glistened to Fritz's plea, like a lowly petitioner, naked and disarming. "You'll tell no one?"

"Not a soul." His head blurred with shaking.

"I'll drain you so dry, not a memory of any of this will be left in you."

"Fine, fine, just do it. Please." The way he said it, she knew he didn't believe her. The poor dear thought his newfound bliss would go on forever, that he would unseat Santa in her heart.

Anya bent then to the task of obliterating Fritz's memory, giving free license to her mouth to bob and weave as it would. But her thoughts were elsewhere. She scarcely gave ear to the increased volume and urgency of his groans, barely tasted the mucoid surge of his seed. She gave but passing notice to the confused look on Fritz's face as she buttoned him up, showed him the door, and waved the entire North Pole back into normal time.

Steadying herself at the porch railing, she watched Fritz stroll across the commons while elves here and there began to wink in and out. She wondered what her husband was doing at this very moment—and what would happen between them when he returned.

"Well."

"Well?"

"Well, it's over."

"Oh, fuck you, Santa. And fuck your precious Anya too. You're telling me you're never going to want to kiss these nipples, never feel the tickle of my breath on your balls, never again sail your longboat into the saline port of my sex?"

Santa gulped hard. Moonlight accentuated her lithe, lean, perfectly proportioned body. Spent as he was, the demon of desire raced about Santa's heart whenever his senses drank her in. He began once more to doubt his resolve.

"No reflection on you. It's just that I've got to get my life in order, and lust pure and simple is one emotion I've resolved never to act on again."

She seized him. "You see this meat? It's mine. I own it. In twenty years my tongue has given more life to this thing than Anya's whole body in the centuries you've known her. Admit it. See? It's stiffening up again. It knows what's best for it better than you do."

Santa removed her hand. "No more. We're finished." There, it was out, and it felt good. "You have to leave now. There's work to do."

At that, she swirled into a rage, hovering above the bed. "You dare deny me, fat boy? You'll pay for that. Next time you want me—and fuck the Christ child in the manger if it won't be before the year is out—I'm going to make you squirm and beg on your chubby little knees. I'm going to roll back the lips of my cunt like a baboon's mouth and turn my womb inside out right in your jolly old face, and all you'll be allowed to do with my glistening pink flesh is watch it, itching with all your heart and soul to touch it and stroke it and lick it and fuck it. You hear me, fat boy?"

Santa, softly: "If you want your panties back, look in my left pants pocket."

The Tooth Fairy's renewed display of fury took Santa's breath away. She spun in the air like a cat chasing its tail, giving a banshee wail. The enraged fairy whipped up storms of immortal anger, earsplitting peals of thunder, and clouds dark beyond ominous, from which forked lightning split apart Santa's skin and fried his innards. Then she was gone. Abrupt calm fell and Santa healed at once, though his body still tingled and thrilled at her outpouring of rage.

He pictured Anya, knitting and rocking by the sewing room window, and prayed to God it wasn't too late to save his marriage.

Santa looked down at Wendy, tiny fists poking out of the nightgown to either side of her body. "God keep you and all children from such furies," he said, bending to kiss her cheek. The sleeping child made him think of Rachel lying in this same bed twenty years before. And now Rachel had a darling girl of her own. Now she played at being mommy, asleep upstairs in her parents' bedroom.

On a whim, Santa gathered his clothes, tucked them under his arm, and headed upstairs. Rachel would provide closure. His affair would end with one loving glimpse at the girl who had been there beside them at the beginning.

From the door the sight of her, alone in the double bed, made her seem smaller than she was.

Santa entered her bedroom, taking in the nightstands of dark laminate, a matching dresser, a blond wood desk used as a catch-all for bills and stationery. Then he gazed again at Rachel asleep in the bed.

She was stunning in her loveliness.

Santa sat beside her, staring down in awe at the simple summation of humanity in her face.

"Dear, dear Rachel," said Santa. "How lovely you've grown since your first Christmas in this house."

And, God help him, Rachel's large hazel eyes opened just wide enough for Santa to fall into them.

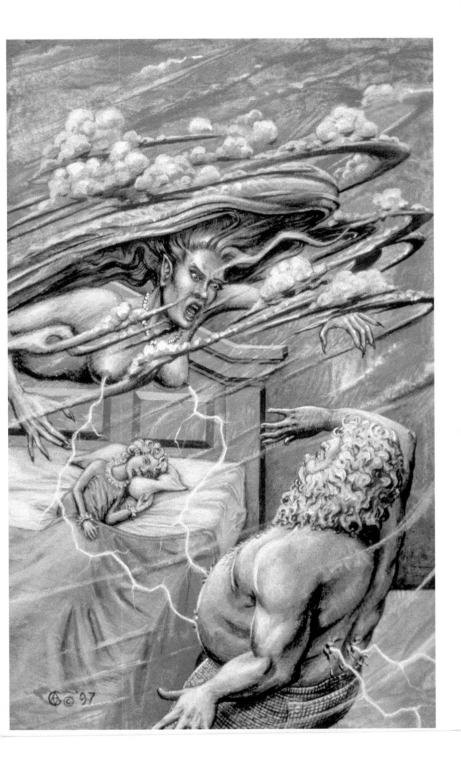

9.
RACHEL ALL GROWN UP

Santa was so astonished at seeing a mortal—let alone this mortal—open her eyes, that he quite forgot to snatch back the stray bit of magic time that had seeped out to claim her. Whether that straying occurred because Santa grew careless or because the events of Christmas twenty years before had opened Rachel to magic time, as the seconds ticked by and Santa ignored God's injunction to maintain the barrier that hid him from mortal eyes, any justification for vanishing from her sight grew less and less compelling.

It was the look she gave him.

A look that silenced his intruder, laid him in a box, and buried him deeper than profundity itself. New love, God help him, flowered among the blossoms of his love for Anya—a flora that complemented that love, not the choking riot of weeds his lust for the Tooth Fairy had given rise to.

The air in Rachel's bedroom seemed as heady as pure oxygen. He breathed it, and so did she. She looked radiant against the pastel columbines of her pillow. In the midst of panic at these new freshets of feeling, Santa's heart basked in a glow of peace.

"Santa Claus?" said Rachel. Part of her wanted to scream in terror, but the rest of her was remembering the details of Christmas Eve twenty years before as she took in the roly-poly phantasm sitting there naked, beaming down at her.

He gave a perfect nod and opened his perfect mouth. "Yes, Rachel," came his words, and their purity speared through her like sunlight.

"Jesus!" she gasped. "Turn down the gain!" She tried to sit up but it was difficult. Her skin tingled beneath her nightgown as though she had become one great heatlamp filament. Her womanflesh swelled and fretted, and a series of soothing orgasms giggled inside her like champagne bubbles.

"What's wrong?" said Santa. His caring voice set off a new round of climaxes, continuous as wavelets lapping at a shore.

"Not a thing," Rachel laughed, holding out her hands to deflect him. "It's just that you're a bit . . . overwhelming."

Santa touched his chest. He looked down at himself. "Oh dear, I'd better put something on."

"Don't," she said, touching his thigh with one hand, then snatching it back as though stung. His words she had begun to adjust to. But touching him had slipped her at once into a cauldron of climaxes. Had it not been so shudderingly delicious, the rush of them would have been painful. "You look fine the way you are."

"Are you sure you're all right?"

"Oh yes," she said, the sweat of delirium at every pore. She laughed. "Now I know how Leda felt."

Santa Claus looked away and repeated the name, trying to place it.

"Yes, Zeus came to earth as a swan and . . . and he slept with Leda, who gave birth to Helen of Troy."

"Oh, please don't think—"

"Of course not, I—"

"You're a beautiful woman, but—"

"It's just that you make me feel . . ."

"I make you feel how?"

"Well, very physical. You take some getting used to. Everything you do feels like a caress." God, was she out of line? She lowered her eyes, though not looking at him was a torture. "An intimate caress."

"Really?" Santa seemed at a loss. "It's not too unpleasant, I hope?"

"Oh, no. Not at all."

"You see there's a reason, not one I'm very proud of, for

my state of undress."

"You don't have to explain."

"I'd like to anyway. I need to tell someone." A moment's hesitation. "I want to tell *you*, Rachel."

And he did.

Reluctantly at first, fearing she would fault him for his adultery. Then, once he had gotten over the hump of telling her about his wife (her smile dimmed at that), he plowed straight ahead, relating more than he intended to about his sins these past twenty years, about the not-Santa that had plagued him and the lust that had tainted his giving.

Rachel was the perfect listener, condemning him for nothing, accepting him completely and returning unconditional love—in her encouraging nods, in the softness of her questions, in every gesture of head and hand. The impact of her presence amazed him. He wondered if an encounter with any mortal woman might tend the same way. Then he understood that Rachel was indeed special: free of guile, open, caring, lovely in her bones.

"Did Wendy see you with the Tooth Fairy?" Rachel's face registered alarm.

"Of course not," Santa assured her. "We kept the magic time strictly to ourselves, just as we did with you twenty years ago."

Rachel smirked. "I saw everything then."

"You didn't!"

She nodded. "Of course I had a child's understanding of what went on. And no recollection of it afterward, none. But now, I see it again as clear as can be." And she proved it, giving an exhaustive blow-by-blow of what she had witnessed as a child.

Santa felt odd listening to her. It was as if her account sanctified the lustful acts he had performed with the Tooth Fairy, honeyed over their vileness, and recreated them as acts of love. Beneath the clothing bunched upon his lap, there burgeoned an erection, and it felt good and pure and brimming with righteousness. When she was done, he said, "You were awake all right, though I don't understand how that could have happened. All I can say is that I think Wendy remained in normal time. You could always ask her in the morning."

Rachel chuckled and shook her head. "Unless she brings it up, I'll just let it slide. Didn't do *me* any harm."

"You're sure about that?"

Rachel shrugged. The way she did it made Santa break into laughter.

"Ooh, I like the way you laugh," said Rachel.

"It's my stock-in-trade," he replied, chuckling again at his own joke.

She had propped her pillows up and was leaning against the headboard, knees bent before her. Now she smiled at him and a sigh escaped her lips. A hand picked absently at the buttons that held her nightgown closed. Santa's flesh stirred again in his lap. Hackles rose at the back of his neck.

"Well, I suppose I ought to be going."

Her smile never faltered. She continued to toy with her buttons as if she hadn't heard him. When the top one popped open, her hand drifted lazily to the next.

God in heaven, thought Santa, this will never do. He had enough explaining ahead of him as it was. "Maybe next Christmas we can talk again."

Another button gave way.

"I want you, Santa," she said, "and I don't. Stop me if you like. I'll understand. But I feel so much love for you. And from you. This seems right as can be. I know I should be thinking about Anya, but the rules seem so pointless with you here. And me here."

Santa saw the smoky gleam in Rachel's eye, her moist tongue moving in her mouth, a moonlit V of skin at her sternum, her breasts straining at cloth, a tantalizing hint of nipple beneath.

Her fingers moved lower, ever working.

Rachel was in love. She had known mortal love, the hurt, the longing, the fulfillment. She had known puppy love, adolescent gropings, a full range of relationships. And with Frank she had known the mingled joys of marital love. But everything paled beside Santa Claus. Santa beguiled, provoked, warmed her and completed her.

Had she stopped to reflect, her seductive ways would have seemed uncharacteristic. But with Santa before her, reflection was pointless. And so, her hands moved to free her breasts, fingers dallying there to entice this elf-man who had so swiftly captured her heart. "Help me undo this button?"

"Really we shouldn't."

"Put your hand here. Please."

"But, Rachel. What will I tell my wife?"

"I am your wife and you are my husband," she said, seeing clearly how things stood between them. "Tell your wife you love her. Do it right now. And do it again when you return to the North Pole."

He started to speak, then smiled and leaned toward her. When his fingers touched her throat and glided along the open flaps of her nightgown to finish the unbuttoning, Rachel closed her eyes and shuddered.

Like a sunbather watching her eyelids redden and feeling upon her skin the wholesome heatlight of a cloud-emergent sun, so Rachel felt Saint Nicholas's face draw nearer. When she opened her eyes, his heavenly visage filled her sight. He was all there for her. There were no dark corners or ulterior motives as there always were with even the best of mortal men.

"I love you, Rachel," he said.

She gave a slight cry at that and gasped out that she loved him too. His hand slid beneath the cloth and found her left breast. Her nipple grew hard and urgent beneath his fingers. She cupped the back of his neck and drew his lips down to hers.

It amazed her—the part of her mind that had room for amazement—that when she thought she had reached the height of sensuality, another plateau waited just above. Their kiss made her body surge up and explode anew. Yet every moment they prolonged it, the last explosion was but prologue to the next. Santa guided her through a land of ever-renewing orgasms, each more wondrous than the one before.

He tossed back the covers. His hands flew up the sides of her body and the nightgown vanished. Then he laid her down and she eased her legs open. Even with Frank, there had always been a residue of fear in that vulnerable position. But Santa was as gentle and all-caressing as a warm breeze, as loving as sunlight itself. Rachel opened everywhere, a flower heavy with dew.

He touched her first with his hands, those great expressive hands that gave without stint and gilded her every pore and orifice with the smooth and supple surety of a craftsman's love. Then he wrapped his hand about the barrel of his loveshaft and touched its hot moist tip to her, beginning at her toes and traveling by degrees up her supine body, lingering at her nipples, warming her neck with its radiant warmth, caressing her cheeks and chin and forehead, and at last brushing it to and fro over her mouth until its heady taste and aroma made her lips fall open around it. He lingered there to please her, stiff and undemanding; and when her jaws ached with the giving and she was ready to move on to new pleasures, he withdrew and brought his tongue into play. The gossamer of his beard acted as thrilling harbinger to his tongue, which darted down and licked her as if he painted her in healing and immortality. And when all of her had been licked clean of the mundane save her vulva, Santa swooped down upon it and made a divine meal of that drenched pouch of flesh, tonguing the folds of her labia and licking like life itself at her clitoris. Wave upon wave of divine love rolled through her until at last her hands insisted him up and around and he was inside her with his hot stiff goodness and she could taste herself on his lips and his heavenly flesh quite covered hers and they rocked and rolled and bucked and heaved their way into the shared joys of concupiscent release.

"Rachel, darling, you're so lovely," Santa said, lying beside her, unwilling to lift his hands from the evanescence of her skin. So delicate, so smooth. Hard to believe he and Anya had been like this once, possessed of a heart that must one day stop, lungs whose allotment of breath was recorded in God's logbook.

She touched his cheek. "You're crying."

He pressed a knuckle to his eyes and wiped his vision clear. "It's because you make me so happy," he said.

"Ohhh," she said. Moving full against him, she rested her arm along his back and snuggled her nose into his beard.

With one finger, he traced a line along the daring curve of her hip. He knew one thing only. He wanted the nightscape of that hip beside him in his bed always; not just here and intermittently, but back home in his cottage every night of every year for all eternity. He wanted to bend down and tongue the elemental epicenter of her lower depths whenever the urge took him after a long day in the workshop with his colleagues, a look-in at his reindeer, and a fine dinner prepared by Anya.

Yes. Anya. That was the sticking point. He loved her no less than before. He loved her fully and deeply, with all the love and affection a husband ought to feel for his helpmate. But he loved Rachel now as well, and he loved her just as much as Anya, though Rachel's uniqueness called forth that love in a different way, as the twist of a kaleidoscope tumbles the same bits of colored glass into new patterns of brilliance.

He despaired of Anya's ever understanding that, she whose reaction to his affair with the Tooth Fairy had been so unreasonable. But this love was different. The Tooth Fairy had been the antithesis of Anya. She drove all thought of Anya out of his mind, and when he did think of Anya, it was in a resentful way. But Rachel, lying warm in his arms and redolent of sex, paradoxically sanctified and made stronger his love for his wife. They were, these two women, multifaceted gems which juxtaposed reflect one another's beauty and so become more beautiful themselves.

"Rachel." He had to chance it.

"Mmm?" She toyed with the curls at his ears.

"I want you and Wendy to come live with me at the North Pole."

Good lord, what are you doing?

I'm asking the woman I love to live with me, that's what I'm doing. Any complaints?

Can't think of a one, except her name be Anya.

Yes. Anya. A formidable bridge to cross. But this felt right to him, just as Rachel had said it felt right to her. She was his wife indeed and he would not live without her. This time, he would be totally above board. And Anya would simply have to come around to his way of thinking.

A stiffening of Rachel's spine, an intake of breath, a still finger encurled. Then she pulled back to look him square on. "You're not serious."

"Never more."

A thousand thoughts raced through Rachel's mind. To give up her home, her job, all her friends was out of the question. She had no winter clothes. She hated cold weather with a passion. What of Wendy's school, the car payments and the mortgage, all the things she owned and loved? Then there was the question of Santa's wife. The image of a wronged woman clutching a carving knife loomed before her, red-eyed hordes of faithful elves glaring out from behind the woman's skirts at Rachel and a terrified Wendy.

"Does your silence mean yes?"

She rested her head upon her hand. "I need . . . it's not an easy decision, you know . . . I need some time to think." She laughed. "God, I can't believe I said that. Santa Claus invites me to the North Pole and my mind spins off into fear, uncertainty, and doubt. But what about Anya? How will she react to this?"

Santa lowered his eyelids in thought, then looked up at her. "I don't know. There could be some difficulty at first. But I think, once she meets you and has a chance to adjust to the idea, everything may work out fine. We can hope so, anyway."

Rachel read serious doubt on his face. She let her eyes laze and glide over the fantastic fat man in her bed, knowing from the sheer corporeality of his flesh that she wasn't dreaming. *Or if I am*, she prayed, *let me never wake.* Her senses, gently orgasmic still at the look and feel and sound and smell and taste of Santa, trumpeted like red brass their Yes and Yes and Three Times Yes I Will. But there were other considerations: the thousands of annoying encumbrances that went with modern life, the call of her profession, the ties of friendship reluctantly broken; but over all, there loomed the face of Wendy, whose love sustained her like no other love she had known and whose welfare was her chief concern. This was not a decision Rachel could in good conscience make on her own.

"You're beautiful when you ponder." Santa softly chuckled. His hand moved on her arm as he bent his great white head to kiss her shoulder. His soft beard brushed her left breast. Inside, the light of passion brightened by a lumen or two.

Touching a hand to his neck, she said, "I'm already taking next week off from work, and Wendy has no school until January third. Could we try it for a week? See how it goes? Subject, of course, to Wendy's approval."

He kissed her throat, her cheek, her lips, which opened to welcome his tongue. She curved a hand along Santa's rotundity, knuckling the riotous curls of his private hair and taking in hand the thick rod of his love. Caressing it, she broke their kiss and pulled back to murmur her question once more. "Just for a week?"

Santa's fingers nippled her left breast. "I think," he said, "that a one-week trial period is a great idea."

She sensed that his thoughts were more complex than his words, but for the moment none of that mattered. There were rising urgencies in both of them that called for their immediate attention.

And attend to them they did.

Perched not at all precariously on the second-story ledge outside Rachel's window, the Easter Bunny drooled invisible drool down the windowpane. Below on a modest patch of front lawn, Santa's reindeer stood stolidly in the Sacramento night, snorting and stamping on the grass, eager to resume their night-journey. He wondered what Lucifer and his antlered friends would think if they could witness their beloved master in action, betraying Mrs. Claus first with the Tooth Fairy in the bed of an innocent child and now upstairs with the child's mother. Hours of magic time the jolly old bastard had spent in this house, a juicy two or three with the Tooth Fairy, twice that much with Rachel McGinnis. If his count was correct, Santa had climaxed three times with the immortal, seven so far with the mortal woman, and the rutting swine showed no signs of letting up.

The Easter Bunny's pride still smarted from Anya's rebuff two weeks before. He had opened her eyes and she had treated him like slime, not even offering a word of thanks. He'd gone back to his burrow and stared at the walls, feeling emptier and emptier, eaten up with envy at the thought of Santa enjoying two lovers while he bore his lonely lot with the likes of Petunia.

Now Santa had added a third woman to his stable of lovers. He appraised her, as much of her as he could see beneath Santa's fat frame. A compact little slip of a thing, tawny and lithe and fully into the rhythm of the hump. This Rachel wasn't some passive Petunia suffering fleshly intrusion. She welcomed Santa into her body as if she needed him for completion. Her hands roved freely.

He liked that in a woman.

He liked it very much.

A dangerous confluence of concupiscence and anger swept his thoughts in bizarre directions. And out of those swiftly flowing waters surfaced an idea, fully formed, that bobbed and held and rode the thudding rapids through the black night. The idea caught hold of him, thrilled his heart, made him turn unthinkably away from the sacred acts of copulation unfolding before his eyes and hie himself westward out of Sacramento, moving swift as darkness out over the ocean.

10.
INVITATIONS ACCEPTED

\Needling his way in and out of an immense gloom-gray blanket of cloudcover, the Easter Bunny strained to pick out the tiny island from the vast wash of ocean. It had to be close by. There was no mistaking the ill winds weaving fiercely for miles now, nor the blind rage that shot through those winds, a rage whose precise counterpart he had seen spill out of Wendy's bedroom when the Tooth Fairy reared up and blasted Santa Claus above the child's bed. Banking low out of the clouds, he saw, no more than a mile ahead, the unmistakable sliver of land rising like a rude welt on the bare buttocks of the ocean.

She squatted upon the sand at the island's northern extremity. Near her hunched a cedar tree. Tattered strands of seaweed hung from the twists of its limbs; broken seashells lay like shattered bone about its base. At its top he saw the torn half of a starfish, as blue and lifeless as the hand of a dead Morlock. The Tooth Fairy's elbows locked her knees rigidly together. Her arms shot straight out, ending in tight claws turned up to the sky. Her eyes, shooting dread far out to sea, burned into a wall of gray that seemed continually to be thudding down upon the horizon.

With caution and cowardice, the Easter Bunny touched paw to sand fifty yards off and hopped closer on a zigzag, pretending to sniff curiously at the stiff dune plants, at driftwood, at strewn clumps of seaweed which marked the limits of the last tide. Her stillness spooked him. Were it not for the nearly imperceptible rise and fall of her necklace of teeth and the dreadful in-out-in-out of her belly, he might have thought her transfixed into statuary.

But despite her apparent calm, there was something unsettling about this ravishing creature's vital signs. Being near her had set up resonances in him, echoes from some dim time, the time before God made him the Easter Bunny, the old time when he had been more in control of his life, and perhaps of the universe itself. His brain hummed dangerously. He suddenly wished himself safe and snug in his burrow with Petunia, whose passivity covered not some smoldering fireball of fury but more passivity, passivity pure and simple.

His heart nearly gave out when she turned her head and demanded: "What do *you* want?" Leaping straight up, he collapsed into a heap of confusion and cowered in the sand, emitting a faint high-pitched squeal like a cornered piglet. She watched him with cobra eyes, waiting for an answer.

Swallowing his fear, the Easter Bunny hopped closer and sat back on his haunches. "I watch at windows," he began. "I watch acts of copulation. It excites me." He fell silent, though his jaws twitched, wanting to go on.

"Is there a point to this?"

He shut his eyes for a moment and forced his neck to bend forward. When he opened them, he was looking at the animal perfection of her midriff, tight and smooth-haired and kissable where it disappeared behind a muscled arc of upper thigh. "I watched you tonight with Santa Claus. After you—"

"You did?" Rising inflection and a razor-thin edge to her voice.

"Well," he said, losing air, "yes I suppose I did. It's harmless really. Just something I do. At windows. But when you—"

"And did you like what you saw?"

"When you left, he—"

"Answer me, you little shit!"

His glance shot to her eyes, then darted off. Why had he come? Things were always easier in the planning. Reality always tumbled out whichever way it liked, wild and out of control. He swallowed with difficulty. "Yes, I did. I liked what

I saw, very much. But I don't think *you're* going to—"

"What in particular did you like?" He was sure she had not yet blinked. Her eyebeams bored like lasers through his left cheek.

"Well uh, I guess when, when you uh, crouched over his face and, you know, moved your hips real slow so he could see your, your fairyhood all wet and swollen, and you fingered yourself until your juices gathered and grew into shiny droplets and splashed onto his beard. That was, that was really"—(*Good God, stay on track!*)—"but as I was saying, after you left, Santa went—"

Her voice cut in like acid. "And what specifically did you like about that?"

"Well . . . you know."

"I'd like you to tell me."

"It's obvious."

"Not to me it isn't."

Some hot hard thing spread upon his mind, twisting his words: "Well uh, I don't know, the glisten, the slickness, the openness of it, it's hard to say, maybe it's seeing it move and shift, knowing he's watching it and taking the abrupt fall of your fluid on his lips and running his tongue over them and reaching out for you and pulling you down onto his mouth, feasting on all those gathering juices, maybe that's it; but— (*Duck out from under!*)—Santa went upstairs and spent twice as much time in bed with Rachel McGinnis—"

"You—"

"—and he told her he loves her and wants her to come live with him at the North Pole." He rode the last tumble of words out over her, pitching them louder and faster and feeling feverish and tight-chested beneath the oppressive cloudcover.

Pure stun beside him.

He became aware of the waves schussing at the shore, at the shore, the shore, shore. Overhead a seagull flew, high and white. The sand felt cold and gritty beneath his haunches.

He took a deep calming breath.

153

When at last she spoke, her voice was low and flat, but full of points and edges. "Tell me everything they did and said, Mister Rabbit. All of it, right down to the last detail."

And that's what he did. He chattered every bit of it out before her like a pagan worshiper laying the fruits of his labor at the feet of an idol. He not only reported every word and deed, but also volunteered precise contrasts between Santa's interaction with her downstairs and with Rachel upstairs. He scattered before her there on the beach the exact words of love Santa had murmured to the mortal woman. These he lingered over like a jeweler contemplating a velvet of diamonds, then set beside them the dead sheen and roughcut facets of Santa's endearments to *her*. Upstairs, he told her, every thrust, every caress, every lick, clip, and cuddle carried special meaning, special caring. Downstairs, all was, by his account, an impressive display of divine animality, a slickening into sweat, a desperate feasting on body parts—a feasting with its own sensual integrity, to be sure, but one which paled beside identical acts done out of the love Santa had come quickly to share with Rachel McGinnis.

As he spoke, the Easter Bunny's eyes grew bold. They drifted over the Tooth Fairy's flawless body, settling in to linger upon cheek or chin, nape or nipple, thigh or cunt or rump-lovely buttock. She was daunting in her ways, this fairy woman. But he wanted her more than he had ever wanted anything. His verbal recounting of her intercourse with Santa brought back into his groin all the passion that had typhooned out of Wendy's bed and washed over him as he watched them. His erection now rose thick and red, right out in front of the Tooth Fairy. He felt no need to conceal it.

"The longer I watched, the more indignant I grew on your behalf," he said. "So when they'd got in their last licks at one another and said goodbye, I took to the sky and crossed the ocean to inform you of Santa's perfidy, knowing that vengeance might interest you, and, if I may be frank, hoping that your sense of gratitude would allow you to . . . to see your way clear to . . . well to—"

But before he could weasel out his oily proposition, his innards began to rumble and pound like thunder. He glanced over in alarm at the Tooth Fairy, who remained in her impassive squat on the strand, staring out to sea. A fist of fury seized on his guts, twisted there with an anger not his own, and splayed open its fingers. He quickly yielded to it, letting it own him and move him, feeling it entwine so with his lust for the Tooth Fairy that it turned into a monstrous meld of emotions, which stood his fur up with rage and sexual need.

"Vengeance?" she said. "The world of men and elves does not yet understand the meaning of the word. But I understand it. And I can see you do too."

"Yes, yes I do. Now please—"

"We feel it in our bones, don't we, you and I?"

"I'm possessed by it, oh believe me I am. But I also need to, to possess, to be possessed by you. Look at the state I'm in and pity me." His head throbbed. His brain felt near to bursting with desire. It didn't help matters to touch a paw to his erection; that felt like the closing of yet another high-voltage circuit in his body.

The Tooth Fairy fell to her knees, her back arched as if to bay at the moon. Her breasts were magnificently pendent. Her fingers dug deep into the sand like gnarled tree roots. At his words, she glanced his way: first a flash of contempt, then a longer look at his privates, a mix of bemusement and loathing and curiosity and some perverse form of reverence. "You want me to give this prick," she reached out and wrapped a rough hand around it, "what it so richly deserves?"

Colors deepened at her touch. Sounds too. "Oh God, yes, anything you say. Please, make me your slave."

"On your back, bunny." She pushed him down onto the sand, leaping upon him like some savage panther and skewering herself on his stiffness. She was dry and harsh there, coarse sandpaper against his tender dickskin.

"Wait, oh Christ, that hurts," he yelped, tearing her thighs to ribbons with his back claws. Splashes of blood spattered the sand behind her.

"Shut the fuck up!" A backhand seared across his face. Never letting up on the bone-dry coitus below, she thrust her hands into his mouth and wrenched his jaw open, straining his facial muscles to their limit. He gave a series of high-pitched squeals and opened deep wounds in her flesh with front claws and back, lacerating her breasts and buttocks until they streamed with gore. But his attacks only turned her on. Her face fisted smack into his mouth and she bit into his huge front teeth, punching through the enamel to the pulp and wrenching at them like a dog worrying a rag, until at last their roots could hold no longer and they broke free of their sockets, drawing fountains of blood after them. She grabbed his front paws and pressed them down into the sand, munching, cheeks full, glaring at him and flaying his dick with her dry tight vagina. Bunny blood embittered his mouth. His jaw muscles throbbed in agony, but shoots of tooth grew back where she had taken her bloody harvest. Down below, sprung sperm coiled up like whomps of flame through his erection, defining it in his mind as one raging column of torment. Every spasm opened a raw wound. Each wrenching spurt dug another barbed hook into his balls. And then she was off him. Blessed healing visited him as he reeled there and her anus opened and dropped gold-foiled coins of chocolate onto the blood-stained beach.

"Did you enjoy that, Mister Rabbit?"

"No, I mean yes, that is I . . ." He was overwhelmed and tingling everywhere.

"Now listen," she said, gripping his testicles and squeezing hard, "I don't give a shit whether you enjoyed it or not, but you'd better get used to it because that's going to be what it's like as long as we work together. And we are going to work together, you and me, aren't we?"

"Yes, ma'am," he gasped. His claws unsheathed into the sand. He hurt everywhere. But by God the pain proved he existed, and my how she thrilled his senses even as she drove them beyond their limits. No, he would gladly give up a bazillion nights with Petunia for one eviscerating evening with the Tooth Fairy.

"Be my eyes and ears, bunny rabbit," she said. "I give the fat elf one year to wise up and reclaim my love. I want to know his every move, what he says and where he goes, who he shares his bed with. I want to know every eyeblink, every wink, every sigh. You'll do that for me, won't you? You'll spy on Santa Claus for me?"

Slowly nodding, his eyes wide with pain: "Whatever pleases you." One raised paw. "But what if he doesn't want you back?"

"Why then, my friend," she said, twisting his balls until he beat the sand with his back feet and screamed for mercy, "you and I are going to hurt the fat little bastard like he's never been hurt before."

Rachel hugged Santa tight, not wanting to let him go, but understanding that she had to share him with the rest of the world. "I'm going to miss you."

"You won't wake Wendy until I return?" he said.

"No," she agreed.

Santa told her he'd be thinking about her everywhere he went. Over and over he said he loved her. She echoed his words. The glow of his presence remained with Rachel long after he withdrew the magic time from her and vanished like pixie dust into the night. But depression also claimed her. The bedroom seemed empty without him, as if the sun had blinked out and plunged the earth into unending pitch. It took a middle-of-the-night walk downstairs and a silent vigil at her daughter's bedside to restore her spirits.

As for Santa, his rounds that night took on renewed meaning. These sweet children of earth, as dear as they'd been to him before, seemed more precious than ever. His and Anya's mortal lives lay so far back in the past that humanity had come to seem almost a race apart. Rachel had reestablished a lost link.

Having reached one last time into his pack and set the last gift beneath the last Christmas tree of the night, Santa bounded off the front porch of the Hansen household on Maisonneuve in Montreal, leaped to his sleigh, took up the reins, and shouted, "No Tooth Fairy's island this year, my patient steeds! One last stop to pick up a dear friend and her daughter, and then we're homeward bound!"

At this, the team sprang into the sky with unflagging zest, galloping through miles of winter to set down once more on the lawn of the old Victorian on K Street. Santa wrapped Rachel round with magic time and roused her from sleep with a kiss. She embraced him, and when they broke their kiss, she sighed and said, "If it was a dream, I guess I'm at it again."

"No dream, dear Rachel. I'm here, my sleigh awaits, and all that remains is to obtain Wendy's consent and hop aboard."

Worry marks crimped her forehead. "Oh, my love, you make it sound so simple. But there's Anya to think about and you know it. Let's not gloss over the problems we're going to face."

"One step at a time," said Santa, soothing with his gentle hand her troubled brow. "Let's live our life together day by day, and let the future unfold as it will. Do you still want to come?"

She pursed her lips, looked down, nodded.

"One week's trial?" he asked.

"Yes. Subject to Wendy's approval."

Memories of the sleeping child came to him as he had last seen her, oblivious in normal time, her light-brown braids framing her face, the flowered, ruffed sleeves of her nightgown lapped over the backs of her hands. A good little girl, he knew; one he would be proud to call daughter, if she'd have him as a father. "Shall we wake her?"

Rachel smiled and said yes.

Wendy lay deep in dream. It was a warm cozy dream with Mommy and Daddy and Mrs. Fredericks and Wendy's best friends from school all holding hands and staring up in awe at a Christmas tree that climbed like a beanstalk beyond the clouds. Then Mommy's voice spoke from outside the dream (because her dream mommy's lips didn't move). Wendy, she said, Wendy, Wendy; and her voice was soothing and solid, as solid as the ears of a chocolate bunny at Easter.

"Are you awake, dear?"

Wendy groaned and rubbed her eyes in protest against the harsh light spilling in from the hall. Her mother's comforting shape sat beside her, her loving hand along the side of Wendy's face.

"I have a surprise for you."

"Wanna sleep s'more, Mommy," she said through a yawn. Then she remembered it was Christmas and the sleep drained from her like darkness fleeing light. "Has Santa Claus come yet?"

"Yes, honey. That's part of the surprise."

Raising herself, Wendy saw the sharp outline of someone standing behind her mother, someone large like Daddy. For a moment she thought it might *be* her daddy come down from heaven, but this man walked in a different way and pure beams of happiness came rushing into her like fresh breezes from the fat black hole he made in her room. Then he moved closer. Moonlight painted his face and the bright red and white of his outfit, and Wendy was at once scared out of her wits and giddy with excitement. Such joy filled her as he approached that she threw herself without hesitation into his encircling arms. "Santa!" she said. Above her hug, his beard softened against her forehead.

Santa's voice tickled her insides: "I'm delighted to meet you, Wendy."

"Santa has asked us both to the North Pole for a week's visit. I told him that all depended on how you felt about it." It seemed as if her mother was trying to hold back her own glee but not succeeding very well.

"When would we leave?" Wendy asked.

"Right away, dear one," said Santa. "My sleigh is waiting on the front lawn and my reindeer are eager to reach home."

"Goody! Oh, but when will we open presents?" She didn't

think she could stand waiting a whole week until they got back, no matter how wonderful their visit to the North Pole was. The whole time, she would picture the packages waiting under the tree, aching to lay her hands on them and tear off the wrappings.

"Well," her mother began tentatively, "we could—"

"We'll take them with us," said Santa, laughing. "My pack is empty. There's plenty of room for gifts."

Wendy's tongue knocked against the blank space in her front teeth. "Oh, I nearly forgot." Breaking free of Santa's arms, she pressed her pillow against the headboard. Five dark discs swam up out of the dim gray sheets. Wendy closed a fist around them. "Look, Mommy, the Tooth Fairy was here too!"

"Yes, she was." There was something odd in her mother's voice.

Santa crossed through the moonlight to her shelves and returned with Mister Piggy. "Better bank those dimes, young lady." She dropped them in carefully, hearing the clatter of metal against ceramic.

"Well then, Wendy," said Santa, sitting back down and giving her another astounding hug, "shall we be off?"

"I . . . I guess so."

"You guess so?"

"I'm worried about Mrs. Fredericks. Won't she miss us at Christmas dinner? And what about the potholders I made for her at school?" She pictured the floppy package under the tree, wrapped in pale yellow paper that showed kittens clawing balls of yarn.

"Tell you what," said Santa. "While the two of you pack your things, I'll put your gift under her tree and leave her a long letter explaining where you've gone and when to expect you back. Then you can bring her something extra special from the North Pole, how does that sound?"

It sounded fine and Wendy said so, though she still missed Mrs. Fredericks and was sure that Mrs. Fredericks would miss her and Mommy.

The rest of the night was a dream Wendy never wanted to wake from. She bundled into her warmest clothes while her mother packed a bag for her and Santa gathered up the presents. Then it was downstairs into the night-smell of pine needles and out the front door. She laid a wondering mitten on the huge gentle head of each reindeer as Santa introduced them. Then he lifted her into his shiny black sleigh. And when the nine great beasts pounded silently the cold night air, raising the sleigh effortlessly into the sky, Wendy giggled at the flutter in her stomach and held on tight. Cities passed beneath them in miniature and cirrus clouds wisped by, but Wendy felt not the least bit cold. Even when they sleighed into the far north and snowflakes danced upon her cheeks—the first snow she had ever seen—and, further still, the icy wind howled in her ears and thick frost formed on the team's bobbing antlers, even then, Wendy felt nothing but warmth and comfort as she sat beside Santa.

Across frozen tundra they flew. In the distance, poking out of endless ice and snow, Wendy saw tiny points of green which, as they drew nearer, shot up into tall trees that kissed the sky. The sleigh's runners brushed the tops of them, leaving a wake of powdered snow that swirled up into the air and drifted down onto the woods below. Ahead, Wendy saw a clearing with bright angular juttings of red and blue and green—buildings out of which now swarmed, like herds of caribou, tiny green figures who Wendy guessed had to be Santa's helpers. Clearer and clearer they became as the sleigh spiraled slowly downward. They were shouting something, but their voices were swallowed by the raucous jingle of sleighbells.

"That's my workshop, Wendy," said Santa, pointing with a child's pride. "And the blue building next to it? That's the reindeer stable." His voice went weird for a moment, then returned to normal: "And look, there's Mrs. Claus in front of our cottage. That's where you and your mommy will be staying."

Wendy clung to Santa's arm and nodded happily. On the porch of the bright green cottage stood a white-haired woman waving up at them. She had on a festive red dress frilled in green and yellow. It reminded Wendy of Shirley Temple's dress in *Heidi*.

The clamor of the elves mingled with the *tzing-tzing-tzing* of sleighbells as down they drifted, spiraling clockwise into a counterspiral of little men. Many of them pointed excitedly at her and Mommy. They waved up at her and she waved right back at them. She had a feeling she was going to like the North Pole a whole bunch.

In the master bedroom, Santa marveled at how lovely Anya looked, despite her upset. "Would you mind telling me who these people are and why they're here?"

Anya's fingers lay rigid and cold against his palms. He was robed in red terrycloth, fresh from the shower. Through the walls came the sounds of Wendy and Rachel settling into their quarters: a closet door rumbling along its track, the muffled piping of Wendy's voice rising in question, Rachel's soothing alto answering her.

Santa led Anya to the bed, seated her there, sat beside her.

"First," he said, "you'll be relieved to know I've broken it off with the Tooth Fairy."

"No backsliding?" Her eyes were cool.

"Well, we slept together one last time," he admitted reluctantly, "but I put my foot down at last. She's out of my life for good."

Exasperation sharpened Anya's eyes. She looked away, then suddenly back, like the steel tips of a cat-o'-nine-tails stinging him across the face. Then her eyes grew soft and a smile glimmered on her lips. "It hardly matters," she said quietly. "I took my revenge while you were gone."

"What do you mean?"

"I slept with all of your elves. Many times over. All but Gregor. They've reverted since then for some reason. They don't remember a thing. But I did it and I'm glad I did it and now I just want things back the way they were. Now will you tell me who this McGinnis person is and why she's here?"

Santa had begun to laugh, but his laughter dissolved when he realized Anya was serious. She really *had* opened her loins to his elves. "Well, in the process of breaking up—" he faltered. "You couldn't have. Surely they would have stopped you."

"They didn't and I did. But that's ages ago and all my demons are exorcised," she said dismissively. "Now get off that subject. You can agonize over it later all you want, but right now you're going to tell me about this McGinnis woman."

Air seemed suddenly in short supply. Santa was sure his face had gone pale, even unto his rosy cheeks. "How dare you boss me around?" he muttered, knowing it was a mistake to let his anger show, but not caring.

"What was that?"

"I said how dare you boss me around? And how dare you take advantage of my elves that way?"

"Keep your voice down."

"I won't," he shouted. Then lower: "Yes I will, but for their sake, not yours." He sprang from the bed and paced before her. "All right, it was a mistake to carry on for so long with the Tooth Fairy without your knowing about it and it was a mistake to sleep with her tonight, though you've got to believe me I did try to resist her, I really did. I got to thinking about you out there and how much you mean to me and so I vowed to end it and by God I did end it. It was a relief to rid myself of her and it was . . . it was comforting to picture you waiting by the fire, rocking and knitting and glancing out the window at the elves cavorting on the commons."

"Tell me who she is."

"Instead I discover you stripped yourself naked and fucked the living daylights out of my co-workers. My God, Anya, what did you expect me to do? Nod sagely, give a sly wink, and say, That's nice, dear?" He caught sight of himself in the mirror over Anya's dressing table, pacing back and forth with his huge bear-like feet ankling out of his robe while his wife sat sad and defiant on the bed. "Oh Anya, my precious one, listen to me carry on. So much pain, so much anger. It feels wrong. But all of that we can let go of. We're husband and wife. We can renew our vows. I love you, after all, and that's all that matters. And you love me, don't you?"

"Tell me who she is, Claus."

He sat beside her once more, feeling frantic and elated and talking much too fast. "Yes, as I was about to say: When the Tooth Fairy stormed off—Lord, she was in a towering rage, you should have seen her!—I went upstairs to look in on Rachel. It was her house you see and she'd been an exceptionally well-behaved child in years gone by. But I guess I got sloppy with my magic time because her eyes opened and she caught me. And she was so . . . so fascinating that I let it continue and got to know her and—now I know you're going to be tempted to take this the wrong way, but please try not to—I fell in love with her. Not that I love you any less, because of course I don't. No, it's just a different kind of love. But anyway the upshot was, I asked her to come live with us at the North Pole and I really think you two will hit it off. We're going to give it a week's trial and then she'll decide whether to stay or not." He paused for breath, feeling like he'd been jabbering for hours. Anya sat next to him, head bent, hands picking at each other on her lap. "I mean it will be a group decision of course, whether she goes or stays. She and little Wendy and . . . and all of us will decide."

"She'll go." Anya spoke with a quiet finality, not looking up. "I'll make it clear to her she's not welcome and she'll go."

Wonderful, thought Santa. Now she's playing the long-suffering wife. "There, you see? You *are* taking it the wrong way," he said, his voice as winning as he could make it. "Look, I know this will take some getting used to, but give it a chance, won't you? At least promise me you'll be on your

164

best behavior when Wendy unwraps her Christmas gifts and takes the grand tour."

She looked up at him, her eyes red and moist. But he guessed it was too hard for her, because she looked away, rested her hand on his shoulder, and stared into the back of it. "Claus, my big little boy," she sighed, "when are you going to grow up? It seems we were once creatures of questionable morality. That much I learned while you were away. But we're the Clauses now and this world depends on our being faithful to each other, on foregoing lust—however lovely the feeling—for the sake of love."

"Anya, it's true I felt lust and nothing but lust for the Tooth Fairy," said Santa. "But what I feel for Rachel is different. It's love I feel, a love as right and good as the love I hold in my heart for you, and the two loves can co-exist, I know they can, if you'll let them."

A tiny knock came at the door and then Wendy's voice called his name.

"Yes, Wendy?"

The handle turned. The little girl's head poked in, brown braids flying. "Hi. We're all unpacked and Mommy says I should ask you if it's time to open the presents yet."

"Give me five minutes to dress," he said. "You and your mother make yourselves at home by the Christmas tree. We'll be right along."

Wendy agreed excitedly and vanished.

Santa rose from the bed. He pulled a comfortable cambric shirt and a pair of pants from his closet and tossed them over a chair. Long red flannel underwear and two thick red woolen socks joined them out of his dresser drawer. He sighed audibly, unable to look at the silent figure of his wife on the bed. He hung his robe in the closet, pushing his shirts aside so it could dry properly.

Santa paused naked by the chair. One hand rested on the red shirt draped over the chairback. "Are you . . . are you all right?"

"Oh yes," she said slowly, not looking up. "Never better."

"Just try," Santa pleaded, feeling strange in his nakedness but standing there anyway, exposing himself to her, hoping the undeniability of his flesh would turn her around and sweep her along to his conclusion. "Try just a little. That's all I ask. Will you do that for me? Will you give it a try?"

PART FOUR
TRYING TIMES

Even in civilized mankind faint traces of monogamous instinct can be perceived.
> —Bertrand Russell

Here's to our wives and sweethearts—may they never meet.
> —John Bunny

So heavy is the chain of wedlock that it needs two to carry it, and sometimes three.
> —Alexandre Dumas

11.

MODUS VIVENENDH

Fritz had never been happier.

The exchange of gifts between Santa and Mrs. Claus on Christmas morning was traditionally a private affair. But now, on top of the arrival of Wendy and her mother—an event which spun Santa's helpers into a leaping tizzy of joy—Fritz had been one of a handful of elves singled out to join them on this special occasion.

The Christmas tree dominated the living room. It had to be the tallest, greenest, branchiest tree Fritz could recall, riotous with ornaments and icicles, colored lights and unending strings of popcorn.

On the floor to Fritz's right sat Gregor and his brothers, friends again, though the reason they had fallen out in the first place escaped him. Indeed all the elves were somewhat hazy about what had occurred during Anya's magic sway over them. What remained from that time were vague stabs of pleasure and guilt, a sudden waking on the commons, and delight at Mrs. Claus's newfound exuberance.

Upon the couch, somewhat obscured by branches and stepped towers of gift, sat Wilhelm and Siegmund and Karl, specialists in the subtleties of kiln and glaze and brushwork on plateware or piggybank. Their excitement at being in Santa's living room was palpable. Fritz felt it himself, a joy radiating from the pit of his stomach. He needed suddenly to hug somebody, so he latched onto fat Josef, Gregor's younger brother, and squeezed a tight *oomph!* out of him. Then a door clicked open down the hallway and a young girl's high excited whisper filled the air. At once, they shrank back tight and eager-eyed into their best behavior.

Wendy, puffed-sleeved and lovely in white, appeared in the archway. She gazed at them, her wide eyes unsure at first. Then she crinkled into a broad grin, reached back for her mother's hand, and pulled her into the room.

Fritz liked Rachel McGinnis lots. Her face was fresh and open, and there was something bouncy in the way she moved. But now, despite the glee with which she took them in, she seemed to be holding back an essential store of treasure. She dropped into a chair and gave them all a warm smile.

Her daughter homed in on the couch and thrust out her hand—"Hi, I'm Wendy!"—to an astonished Wilhelm. His hand seemed to rise on its own like a seed-puff in the wind, but he sat there, mouth ajar, saying nothing, until Siegmund knuckled him on the shoulder and began the introductions. Then the others on the couch chimed in, followed by Fritz and Josef and Gregor and Englebert sitting on the floor, and suddenly the room was alive with cheery banter.

At first it focused on Wendy. But when Fritz sensed that Rachel was feeling left out, he spoke up: "That's a lovely dress Wendy's wearing, Mrs. McGinnis. Did you make it, by chance?"

"Yes, I did," she said, "last week in fact. Oh and please call me Rachel." Fritz could tell she appreciated his gesture. Her smile generated a warm, baked-bread glow in his heart.

Everyone reached out to finger the cloth and admire the hemstitches, telling Wendy, who beamed, how fortunate she was to have such a skilled seamstress for a mother. "Yes and she writes very fine computer programs too," Wendy said, and they at once praised Rachel for that talent as well.

Then Santa burst into the room, trailing Mrs. Claus behind him. "Merry Christmas, everybody!" He swooped Wendy up and charged about the room, gladhanding and hugging each elf in turn. Fritz noticed, as Santa descended upon the crowded couch, that Mrs. Claus slipped silently into her rocking chair by the fire.

Her hands clung tight to its arms.

"Fritz, old friend!" Santa's booming voice washed like goodness into his ear, warming him inside and out with the spirit of giving. The jolly old elf's strong red right arm hugged Fritz to the bulge of his belly and to Wendy's thin bony legs where she rode in the crook of his left arm. Hasty kisses to his cheeks, a glimpse into Santa's animated face (but was there something false in that animation?), and Fritz watched him hurry past his wife and deposit Wendy on her mother's lap. Then he sank with a sigh of pleasure into the far end of the couch, lit a long thin white ceramic pipe, and enjoined his elves one by one to retrieve and deliver gifts.

The ensuing orgy of dissemination swept them all into a sweet oblivion of wrappings torn asunder, boxes unlidded, and tissue paper parted; of squeals of delight and unending thank-yous and you're-welcomes; and beneath it all, like the bowel-stirring pedal point of a Bach passacaglia, the hearty boom of Santa's laughter thundered forth. Fritz found most of his deliveries going to Rachel or Wendy—they had, after all, brought their cache of presents with them—but some he held out to Santa, and others to Mrs. Claus, who, while decidedly less old-ladyish in her movements than at past celebrations, looked at him with the fretted eyes of the elderly. But it was hard to focus on Anya for long, what with the level of excitement whirling about the room and the wonder of having actual mortals sitting here in the same room with them.

And when the last gift had added its contribution to the colorful mountain of torn wrappings and ribbons, a sly grin spread across Santa's face. "Dear me," he said, "I nearly forgot the best present of all." Fritz saw the slightest flicker about Santa, the telltale discontinuity of magic time kicking in. Leaning forward, he brought forth from behind his back two mewling kittens, one black and one white. They hugged two or three of his fingers with their front paws and let their back legs splay, claws out, to either side of his wrists.

"Oh, they're so cute," said Wendy. "What are their names?"

"That's up to you, Wendy," replied Santa. "They're yours."

From the look on Wendy's face, Fritz understood for the first time why they were in the business of delighting children. Nothing in his experience could compare with watching Wendy's eyes light up. "This one has got to be Snowball," she said. "And this one I'll call Nightwind."

"Snowball and Nightwind," said Santa, holding the kittens to his rosy cheeks. "Say hello to Wendy." With that, he placed them carefully in her lap and knelt beside Rachel's chair watching the little girl glide her hands in wonder along the fur of their tiny bodies.

When Fritz chanced to look up, Mrs. Claus's rocker, now empty, was rocking back and forth on its own.

A timid knock sounded at Anya's sewing room door. Setting down her knitting, she removed her glasses and wiped her eyes with the back of her hand. Then she put them on again and picked up the knitting needles. "Come in," she called.

It was the little girl, alone, her hand lingering at the brass doorknob. "Can I talk to you for a minute?"

"Of course, my dear. Close the door and come sit by me." Anya gestured to the footstool with the embroidered reindeer on top. She felt ashamed. Part of her—a small but vile part—wanted to strike Wendy with such violence that her hated mother would keel over and die. The rest of her wanted to take this dear young child to her heart and hold her there forever, tight and warm and loving. It surprised her that there could be any mitigation to her rejection of Santa's latest folly, yet the little girl filled a vacancy in her life she hadn't been aware of.

Wendy sat down. "This is a pretty room."

"Thank you, child."

"My mommy is teaching me to knit."

"That's nice. Do you like knitting?"

"Oh yes," said Wendy. "Um, can I ask you something?" Her voice took on a conspiratorial air.

Anya smiled tightly as her hands danced before her through the clicking of needles and the slow sweatering of

172

yarn. Somehow her bout with the elves—as crazy as it had been in other ways—had instilled new youth in her, right down to her now nimble fingers. More precisely, it had taught her that the illusion of age had been her choice all along. "Yes, my dear," said Anya, "you may ask me anything you like."

Wendy stood beside the rocker, her white dress pressed against its arm. When she put her hand on Anya's shoulder and leaned in, Anya, delighting in her touch, turned an ear to receive the girl's confidence. "Mrs. Claus," Wendy whispered, "why don't you like me?"

Anya pulled back at this, noting the deep runnels of concern on Wendy's forehead. "Where did you ever get such a silly notion?"

"I'm very observant," Wendy said, a trace of pride in among her concern. "Just like Nancy Drew and Miss Marple. I guess it was mostly how you looked up at us when we flew in. The way you hugged me when Santa lifted me down from the sleigh, like your shawl was doing most of the hugging for you. And the way you sat by the fire and watched me. Stuff like that."

Anya felt her temples pounding. She set her knitting down on the basket beside her and patted her lap. "Young lady, be so good as to sit here," she said. And when the child had allowed herself to be lifted up and was nestled comfortably against Anya's bosom: "I want you to listen very carefully to me. Will you do that?"

Wendy said she would.

"Good girl," said Anya, gently rocking and placing her hand upon Wendy's nape. She did not at all like the streak of jealousy that urged her to do violence to this innocent creature. As she told Wendy how she and Santa sat here on top of the world with their hearts full of love for every boy and girl on earth, how they felt like special godparents to them all, the savagery of the green-eyed monster made her throat seize up. But for the child's sake, she narrowed her attention to herself and Wendy, two orphans with no connection to anyone else in the world.

And Anya's core of benevolence triumphed. Her love touched the child's love and she found herself sobbing and hugging her and kissing her, this frail mortal creature on her lap whose beauty was as the beauty of fresh meadow grass. Once more she welcomed Wendy to the North Pole and this time she meant it. She promised to teach her all the tricks she had learned about knitting and needlepoint and crochet and macramé, and how to coax culinary magic out of grains and vegetables.

"You mean just like my mommy does?"

Anya smiled. "Maybe even better than your mommy does."

Deep in the dark recesses of the workshop, with the smell of manufacture all about and the firm give of foam beneath them, Rachel felt Santa's lips upon her cheek, the thick goodness of his penis nestled like an infant inside her. Her eyes, drifting into the darkness above, could make out only the dim outlines of lighting fixtures and an impression of laddered shelves lofting upward. Cavernous yet comforting this place was, even in the dead of night.

Santa sighed. "That was beautiful," he said. "You couldn't begin to guess how much I've needed you."

Rachel ran her fingers idly through his soft white beard and smiled. "Mr. Claus, you are the most amazing lover I've ever had."

"So glad you enjoyed it, Ms. McGinnis."

Then it was time to be serious with him.

"We need to talk," she said. "About Anya." There. It was out. She hated being the other woman, particularly when Santa's wife had been so kind and loving to Wendy and was clearly as dear and sweet and attractive in her own way as Santa was in his. There were oblique reminders—in the sway of her hips, in certain vocal inflections and turns of phrase—of Rachel's fling at college with Rhonda Williamson, whom she still remembered fondly. "You and I have been exchanging looks for three days now, hoping things would improve. But they haven't. You know they haven't."

"You're right," Santa admitted. "When she deigns to look my way at all, she gives me that withering stare. It's worse for you, isn't it?"

"Yes. It's like a blast of winter licking at my heart." She laughed. "That sounds a bit melodramatic, but it's the truth. Yet when I'm with you or your elves, everything is wonderful again."

Santa, thoughtful behind the sparkle of his eyes, soothed her brow. "Thank goodness she's not taking it out on Wendy."

"She's the only reason I've held on this long. I've never seen her happier or more continuously excited about anything. She grows wiser and more mature and more beautiful every hour she's up here. But we've really got to go home. Tomorrow."

"Give it time," he pleaded. "I love you so much. Wendy too. I don't want to lose you. You've been my salvation. I haven't thought once about the Tooth Fairy since we met, not a whisper of illicit lust."

His warmth enwrapped her. "You're such a dear kind soul," she said as though it were a complaint, and hugged him as tight as she could. Suddenly she was sobbing with her whole body, freely like a betrayed child, making the moonlit workshop ring with wailing. Santa kissed her and comforted her and promised he'd talk to Anya first thing in the morning. With his words he assured her, with his kisses, with his caresses, and, down below, with the gentle movement of his manhood, which eased like a mage's healing touch along the troubled walls of Rachel's vagina, soothing and arousing her.

And for a time, Rachel knew nothing but the joyful oblivion of their makeshift bed.

After kissing Rachel goodnight at her bedroom door, Santa stole into his bedroom, doffed his clothing, and slipped beneath the covers. He lay there wide awake for hours, idly listening to the paced breathing of his wife lying as far away from him as she could. Down the hall, he heard the low muffled beat of the grandfather clock he had built eternities ago. It patterned his thoughts, granting them an orderliness they otherwise lacked.

But that sense of order wasn't enough. He felt no optimism about the coming confrontation. While his dear adversary slept and rested, Santa fretted the night away until dawn began to engray the black, gradually wedging under its oppression and easing it aside.

When Anya rose into the pale morning, Santa feigned sleep. His eyes followed her to her closet. She put on a robe over her nightgown, cinched it tight, and headed for the bathroom.

"Anya?" he spoke up.

She stopped. "You're awake."

"We need to talk things over."

She blinked once, then nodded. "Not here. In the woods. I need a shower first." She paused, her face still impassive. "Why don't you join me?"

Before he could stop himself, he said yes. In the past, sharing the shower had usually meant lovely sudsy sex, but there was no such intent in Anya's eyes now, none at all. She smothered his rotundity in suds, lathering him with the rough hands of a mother grim-set against grime. And he let her treat him so, like a little boy guilty of one too many wallows in mud. She stopped soaping at his belly, glanced at his drooping manhood, thrust the bar of soap into his hand, and said, "You can clean that yourself." Then she turned away from him and bathed her breasts with sperm-white, sperm-thick liquid soap, rubbing it into a rich lather, moving handfuls of foam down her belly and working them through the white wonderland he loved to rove in. When he moved to touch her, her eyes warned him to keep away.

Later, he followed her into the forest just beyond the workshop. The snow lay thin there and the evergreens, though full and lofty, grew far enough apart to let in lots of sunlight. When they reached the clearing the elves called the Chapel,

Anya half-sat against a long flat outcropping of granite known as the Altar, and said in a voice carefully expunged of emotion, "You have something to say?"

Santa groped for words. "Are you . . . are you still dead set against . . . I mean are you feeling any better about our guests than you did a few days ago?" A rotten way to start, but those damned eyes of hers were locked on him as he paced before her.

"I can't stand the presence of that woman in my home. It makes me ill, knowing what you've done with her and how you claim to feel toward her. It's all I can do to keep from flaying her face with my fingernails."

Her reply seemed measured, as if rehearsed, as if she only half-believed it. "Anya," he said, "as messed up as our lives seem to be at the moment, I know in my heart that bringing Rachel here was the right thing to do. And meeting her seems to have put to rest, finally, the lust that drove me to the Tooth Fairy."

Anya laughed. "There doesn't seem to me a whole hell of a lot of difference between them. Birds of a feather. And both of them have driven a solid wedge between us."

"It doesn't have to be that way."

She looked up archly. "It surely doesn't."

"That's not what I meant. I need Rachel, dammit. And I need you."

"Oh? Whatever for? What could you possibly need me for when you've found yourself a sexy young widow eager to fall at your feet and worship the great Santa Claus?"

"You're being unfair to her. She's a mortal—"

"She's a mortal homewrecker is what she is," Anya broke in, "and far worse than most—she has the gall to ride in, arm in arm, with my philandering husband and peddle her wares right under my nose." The woodland hung dreadfully still around Anya's rising passion. "Don't go talking to me about fairness, Mister Tell-Anya-It's-Over-But-Screw-The-Tooth-Fairy-Anyway."

"Anya, must we dredge that up again?" he pleaded. His

wife's arms were tense, right down to the mittened hands poised against the rocktop of the Altar. "Who slept with a thousand elves while I was out on my yearly rounds, picturing my loving wife rocking and knitting by the fire when all the while she had her skirts hoisted, her legs parted, and her womanhood splayed open for the delectation of my helpers?"

"I did, that's who. And I'm glad I did it, not that I had much choice in the matter. It cleared things up for me, or seemed to until you . . . you. . . ." Anya broke off, blinking back tears. In that instant, Santa wanted to take her in his arms, kiss her tears away, and assure her of his love by doing precisely what she wanted. But Rachel rose to mind, so perfect, so full of love, and it was impossible.

"So," he said, "we've reached an impasse. I want Rachel and Wendy to stay, to blend in, to become part of our family. You want them to leave."

Then, for the first time, Santa saw the hardness in Anya's eyes soften. "Well," she said, staring down at her boots and thrusting her hands deep into her coat pockets, "I'm quite taken with the little girl. I don't know if I could bear to see her go."

It stunned him. "What are you saying, Anya?"

"That there's room for compromise." She attempted a smile. "A few days ago, I would never have said such a thing. But Wendy's so precious. I love watching her with the elves. I love teaching her things. She brightens my life."

An image came to Santa: Wendy beside Anya in the kitchen, stirring a pale-green bowl of cake batter with a large wooden spoon, Anya steadying the bowl with one hand and resting the other on the little girl's shoulder. They looked wonderful together.

"So it's not hopeless?" he ventured.

Anya glared at him. "Not in the way you mean, you old satyr." Santa had never seen her this touchy about anything. "I will never welcome Wendy's mother into our home, and you and she had better get used to that. That's not about to change.

No, if she's not comfortable around me, you'll have to put her up somewhere else."

"Where?"

"That's your problem, not mine. Build her another cottage if you like. You seem fond of new buildings for your paramours. All I know is I plan to avoid her and I hope she'll have the good sense to do likewise."

Santa wondered why he still felt defeated, despite Anya's assent to their staying. "There are bound to be times when you two are together, holiday gatherings, that sort of thing."

"We can work around them. I'll promise not to look daggers at her if you two promise not to make a public spectacle of your affection for each other. Oh God in heaven, listen to me. It makes my throat hurt just to think of it!" She slapped the flat rock silently with her mittened palm and gritted back tears. "And don't expect me to . . . there won't be any relations between us as long as she's here. None."

"Are you sure you'll be able to live with that?" he said, feeling a chill inside.

"The question is, can you live with it?" A pause, then quieter, "I always thought you were such a kind and generous soul. Now you've chosen another woman over me."

"I'm making no such choice," he protested. "I love both of you. Why can't you accept that? No, don't bother snapping back at me. It's obvious you can't. And I guess I've got to honor your feelings and accept you as you are. All right, then. I'll tell Rachel what we've talked about and see what she thinks."

Anya nodded. Her eyes were moist.

"Shall we walk back?" he asked.

"You go," she said. "I want to stay here a while and collect my thoughts."

"All right," said Santa. He raised a hand to touch her sleeve, then thought better of it. White head bent, he turned away and trudged back through the woods. The glare of sun on snow made everything red when he blinked: fallen branches, rocks dusted white, Anya's bootprints pointed off determinedly in the opposite direction from the fresh tracks he now made.

It was a wonderful year for Wendy. Midway through their first week at the North Pole, Rachel, tucking her in, had asked whether she would mind staying longer. Wendy flung her arms around her mother's waist and said she wanted to stay forever, going on and on about the reindeer and the elves and Snowball and Nightwind and Mrs. Claus and dear dear Santa. Her mother seemed both happy and unhappy, but she hugged Wendy and cried tears of joy, and the next morning Wendy woke to find that Santa had built them their own cottage.

Wendy came awake knowing that Santa stood beside the bed looking at her. Nightwind and Snowball raised their heads from the blankets. Santa lifted a finger to his lips and said, "Can you keep a secret?" Wendy nodded and he took her hand and led her to the living room window and pointed across the commons. Santa's workshop made its usual bright red sprint across the snow, but now, beside it, stood the dearest little cottage she had ever seen. She clapped her hands in delight and promptly dubbed it the gingerbread house, and so it was called ever after.

It had a kitchen and a sewing room, just like Santa's cottage, its own Christmas tree in the living room, and the best bedroom a girl could wish for, with plenty of shelves, a workbench for her art projects, a lovely bed that precisely fitted her, and a huge picture window opening out onto the commons. Her mom's bedroom, at the back of the house, had a perfect view of the wooded hills rising from the far side of the workshop. For days, the gingerbread house was the talk of the community. There was a lot of tramping in and out, much elvish gawking and grinning in at windows, and that first night a ceremonial toast shared by Santa and Wendy and her mother and a few dozen lucky elves. But Mrs. Claus did not come, nor did she ever visit the house afterward. Whenever Wendy asked her why, she pretended not to hear, or she changed the subject, or she told her she would surely have to do that some day—and Wendy soon accepted it as how things were.

Wendy's life that year was filled with wonder and instruction. From Mrs. Claus she learned and perfected the arts of handstitching and macramé, tie-dying and stained glass, quilting and needlepoint and cream etching on glass. She became her helper in the kitchen, growing intimate with spices and spatulas and the magic of putting together meals that brought rare smiles to her mother's lips. Most of the time Wendy ate at the dinner table with Santa and her mother, carrying out each course when Mrs. Claus called from the kitchen that it was ready. But sometimes, and more often as the year advanced, she ate with Mrs. Claus at the old oak table in the kitchen, sharing the day's experiences and waiting to see if Mrs. Claus would wink at her and reach into the pantry for some special chocolate treat she had prepared just for them.

Once when a fox darted from behind a tree and nearly tore poor Nightwind's throat out, the elf who responded to Wendy's cries of alarm chased off the attacker and rushed the broken kitten to Mrs. Claus. She swept Nightwind up into her arms and licked at the bloody flesh and fur until he was whole and purring again. "It's a special talent I have, dear," she said, and Wendy was suitably impressed.

Santa and the elves taught her, more by example than explanation, the intricacies of toymaking. Their simple love and respect for the tools and materials they used were abundantly clear. Every task they put their hand to they carried out with sensual joy, and this approach Wendy learned and applied as diligently as she could to her own tasks.

But what she liked best was to climb up on Santa's lap each evening in the living room of the gingerbread house, feeling on her scalp the warm glow of the lamp beside them and listening to his deep voice thunder forth stories of dragons and kings and monumental quests from a heavy leather-bound book he held open in front of them. And when her eyes grew heavy and the thundering images took on distance, Santa carried her to her bed, tucked her in warm and snug, and touched his lips to her cheek.

Still, from the way the grown-ups acted, her visit to the North Pole did not feel at all like forever. So she was disappointed but not surprised when her mother took her aside a few weeks past Thanksgiving to tell her that they would be leaving after Christmas. Wendy acted as brave as she could, giving her mother gigantic hugs and assuring her that things would be all right (though just once, late at night, she cried her eyes out on her giant teddy bear's shoulder and felt better for it).

"Besides," she added, "Mrs. Fredericks has probably missed us a whole bunch."

"That's my big girl," her mother said, giving her a squeeze. Wendy had smiled back and worried her loose front tooth with her tongue.

Despite the happy times, Wendy had noticed her mommy's growing sadness. She had been okay at Easter, standing beside Santa watching Wendy and the elves hunt for eggs in the snowy commons while the cats sniffed curiously at the Easter baskets, batting at bits of grass. But by Independence Day, a chronic anguish lay upon her face. Despite the fireworks Santa set off above a skating pond full of whirling elves, sadness lifted in waves from her mother as they watched from the porch of the elves' dormitory.

Even Santa couldn't lift her mother's spirits when she was sad. Wendy noticed his unusual way of trying, though. She would sometimes waken in the night and hear Santa groaning at the back of the house; then her mother, higher pitched, joined in. When she asked them about it, they smirked at one another and mumbled something about making love, assuring her she would understand when she was older. But it didn't sound much like love to her—she had never heard anything remotely like it when Daddy was alive, and he had certainly loved Mommy. No, Wendy was convinced they were just trying to make the sadness go away by bringing it out in the open and sharing it with each other. But she knew it wasn't working because of the way they kept at it and the way the groans never seemed to ease up; they were, if anything, louder and more insistent. By the time autumn came, her mother had begun to sob quietly afterward. It made Wendy sob too and feel cold inside her skin, despite the thick blankets that covered her.

So she accepted Rachel's announcement with all the stoicism of a maturing seven-year-old and felt pleased at her mother's relieved look. When Santa came in and hugged them both, Wendy brightened at his promise: he vowed to bring her back to the North Pole for a visit every Christmas thereafter.

She knew better than to ask if her mother would be coming with them.

"Please try to understand," Rachel pleaded. "It's nothing you've said or done." Through the window, she watched her daughter, scarfed and mittened and booted, being pulled on her sled by Fritz and Heinrich from one end of the commons to the other.

"Then why are you leaving?"

"Because I don't want to be your mistress. I want to be your wife."

"But dear one, you *are* my wife."

"You say that, and I know you mean it, and we both know it's true. But as long as I'm a problem for Anya, I don't fit in here the way I want to. She's been fine. I'm not faulting her. But all she can do is avoid me and expect me to avoid her. Your helpers feel that tension. So do the reindeer. Even my own daughter treats me like the outsider I am."

Santa chuckled bitterly and ran his fingers through her hair. "You're not an outsider, *liebchen*. Or if you are, it's only because you worry yourself into that role."

"The reason's not important," she said, kissing his free hand. "When we're together, just you and me, it's wonderful. But that can't make up for the rest of it."

"Please reconsider." There was pain in his throat. "I need you. You saved me from my own weakness—"

"You did that—"

"No, Rachel, it was you. I could never have stayed away from the Tooth Fairy if I hadn't met you. If you go away, I'm afraid the not-Santa will return and drive me back to Thea's mouth."

"Don't you see, that can have nothing to do with my decision. Fight him if he returns, and triumph over him. But Wendy and I have to go."

Santa held her for a long time without saying a word. Closing her eyes, she let the touch and the smell of him invade her senses.

The first indication she had of Santa's heartache was the sting of a tear, cold and shocking, tumbling down his cheek where their faces touched. Then he began to shake and Rachel opened her eyes to find Santa Claus sobbing in her arms. The sight was heartrending. From the surprise on his face, she doubted that Santa had ever had occasion to cry before.

At her ear: "Shall I . . . visit you at Christmas?" What he was asking was clear.

"No," she choked out. "I couldn't bear it. Take Wendy with you if you like, but let me sleep."

He nodded against her shoulder, then made to pull away.

"No. Come with me," she said. "Wrap us in magic time." And Rachel led Santa, wet-faced, to her bedroom, where— while Wendy and her friends froze in frolic—they made the most dolorous love the world will ever know.

"They're going then?" she said.

"It seems so, yes."

"I'll miss Wendy."

"So will I." He paused. Anya said nothing. She stared into the fire, mindlessly rocking. "At least," he said, "we can look forward to her visit at Christmas."

"Yes, there's that."

"Anya, I'm scared."

"I know you are."

"I'm afraid about what may lie ahead. About our future."

"I am too, Claus."

"We've grown apart, haven't we?"

"There seems far less common ground between us. It's sad."

"I'd like you to hold me."

Nothing. Just the soft steady protest of the rocker.

"Will you hold me, Anya?"

"Not yet. Not now. Give me time. Let it heal."

Anya had triumphed. But as she stood at the counter kneading dough, hands white with flour, she wondered why she felt defeated. Less than a hour before, her husband had lifted off into the sky and his wave had seemed empty, mere ceremony. She punched the dough and pursed her lips, feeling that the world would never be right again.

She no longer blamed Rachel for that. She didn't even blame Santa. A goodness had fled from their lives, and it seemed as though it might just be a symptom of the world's decay, not subject to reversal no matter what they did.

Footsteps sounded in the dining room. A light knock tapped at the doorframe to soften an entrance. Anya turned and saw Rachel.

"Where's Wendy?" Anya asked.

"She went to help Gregor and his brothers freshen up the stables I think."

Anya turned back to the cutting board. The dough was nearly ready for the rolling-pin.

"What are you doing?" asked Rachel.

"Making gingerbread men with raisin eyes. It's Santa's favorite cookie."

"More of a favorite than Oreos?"

Anya smiled over her shoulder. "Oreos don't even come close. Want to help?"

"Sure." She went to the sink and washed her hands,

drying them with an embroidered dishtowel hanging by the refrigerator.

A comfortable truce had grown up between the women since Rachel's decision to go, even though Santa continued to spend his nights in the arms of his mortal lover. Anya was glad she and Rachel were ending things on a positive note. Although she hadn't the least desire to visit the gingerbread house, she had pretty much opened her doors to Rachel, and Rachel now spent most of her daylight hours there. Something about being nearer the heart of things, she had said.

"The cookie cutters are in that bottom drawer there," said Anya, nodding. "Trays are under the stove."

"Right."

While she rolled out the brown dough, Anya gave half an eye to Rachel. Her light blond tresses curved like wraps of sunlight about her face. Her breasts and hips Anya found disarmingly lovely beneath her heavy wool sweater and long skirt. No wonder Santa had been taken with her. Indeed in these final weeks, while they had tiptoed about one another, Anya had noticed how engaging Rachel was in her own quirky way. It was unfortunate, she thought, that Santa's having cast them as rivals for his affection had precluded their getting to know one another better.

She would sorely miss Wendy. But in an odd way, she would miss Wendy's mother too.

"All right," said Anya as Rachel finished waxing a cookie tray, "I think it's thin enough to—"

A sharp rap fell upon the front door, loud and not at all like the knock of any elf. "Good lord, who could that be, and me with my hands all doughy?"

"Don't bother, I'll get it," said Rachel. In an instant she was out of the kitchen and moving through the house, Snowball and Nightwind at her heels.

"I'll be right there," called Anya.

She plunged her hands under the faucet and grabbed at a towel. She was still wiping them off when, shouldering her way through the kitchen door into the dining room, she heard Rachel scream with terror, and saw, looming in the doorway at the end of the hall, the furry white figure of the Easter Bunny holding in one paw an enormous bouquet of red roses and pink carnations.

12.

BLOOD AND PASSION

The Easter Bunny strode in, unasked, and kicked the door shut behind him. He stared hard as nails at Santa's new fuckmate, clothed for a change, cringing back against the hall mirror, shock splashed across her face. A sweet morsel she'd be, this Rachel woman, once she calmed down and extended freely the warm sleeve of friendship to him. Santa's wife, a feisty old biddy full of dark fire, was drying her hands on a dishtowel and frowning at him from the archway.

"Ladies," he protested, "is this any way to greet a gentleman caller?" He clutched the bouquet tight to his chest, keeping his other paw concealed behind him.

Anya glared. "I don't recall inviting you in. What are you doing here with your eyes shot red and your fur bristling out in all directions? You look a fright."

"Just dropped by to give this lovely bouquet to the fair Ms. McGinnis"—he thrust a pawful of flowers under Rachel's nose and she fumblingly took them, holding them in both hands like frozen fire—"and to offer you, my peppery Anya, this exquisite treasure."

Here he brought forth his prize, feeling its burning luster fuck and refuck his paw, the tiny orgasms coursing up his arm like wavelets lapping at a golden shore.

"An egg?" She was mesmerized. Her arms fell to her sides, the dishtowel dropped to the floor.

"Not just any egg, Anya. From the way you gaze upon it, I can see you appreciate that. Yes, Rachel, you too. Come closer, there's nothing to fear." As they stared in wonder at the pulsing pink ovoid, he skittered his lust over the soft curves and

188

concavities of their bodies and told them how, one thousand Easters after Christ rose from the dead, while he (the Easter Bunny) was out making his rounds, his most lackadaisical layer (a Wyandotte who was the butt and scorn of the other hens) blinked open her astonished eyes and, protesting every inch of the way, brought forth from her nether regions four divine eggs, blood-pink and perfect, dropped to form the corners of a square, and a fifth egg, this one, at their center. With the fires of heaven they throbbed, and God had stepped down from His high throne upon the Easter Bunny's return and adjured him to keep their quincunxial pattern unbroken until the last trump sounded.

"But for you, sweet Anya, to buy your carnal favors, I now break the pattern. Go ahead, touch it. As amazing as it looks, a thousand times more wonderful is the feel of it upon your flesh."

Anya's hand rose, hesitant. How lovely her elderly fingers were to his eyes, those fingers he'd seen fondle into full flower so many elfin genitals the year before. As irresistible as the Tooth Fairy was, the prospect of yet another bout of knock-down, bone-dry sex had lost much of its perverse charm. And when he'd stood in the snow at the rear of the gingerbread house, watching Santa plunge into the wide-open meat of a soft, wet, yielding Rachel, he ached beyond the ache of gonads. How soothing that moist warm tunnel of flesh was going to feel hugging his abraded organ, which now rose painfully to full tilt. His nose twitched. He sniffed the interwoven womanstench of Santa's lovely wives, who drifted ever closer under the unrelenting lure of the quintessential egg.

Anya's scalp tingled. The hallway had grown suddenly dark, as if night seeped through its walls to cup the precious egg in its palms. And the egg? It gave off a glow, pink and powerful as sunset across a howling tundra. Rising to a gentle dome above the two clutching paws, it looked like the unslit tip of the perfect lover's penis, the pink and perfect skin of its

189

glans waiting, tight as a drumhead, for her fingers, her lips, the opening flower of her womanhood. Now the hallway closed around her like a hothouse, rich with the aroma of warm damp earth. Longing to loosen her garments, she let the fingers of her left hand move upon her breasts, toying with the cross-lacing there, as her right hand floated closer to the egg.

She watched Rachel reach out and finger the eggtip, then heard a spike split open her throat and unholy orgasm seize the mortal woman. Anya broke from the egg and jerked her head up to gaze into the mad reddish whorls of the Easter Bunny's eyes.

For the first time, Anya saw him clearly. This was a rogue bunny now. Something had gotten to him since they had last met, eating away at his restraint until there was nothing left but death and madness.

She snatched the egg from the Easter Bunny's grasp. "Here's what I think of your gift, Mister Rabbit!" she said, and hurled it hard toward the hall mirror. As lights once again flared in the hallway, the egg's pink twin came rushing to meet it, kissing with a loud crack its cracking double and dribbling yolk and bits of shell down the glass. The cats grew wide-eyed and raced out of the hallway.

But before she could turn back and throw her unwanted guest out, the Easter Bunny slammed into her and she fell hard upon the floor, buried beneath white fur and raking claws. "Stupid cunt," he screamed, his bunny breath rank as weeds, "I'll teach you!" Her spectacles flew off and clattered across the floor. Razors seared her face. Then he was grinding her skull into the carpet. Her neck strained from the twisting and she saw out of the corner of an eye the hard pink pads of his paw, and her blood dripping from the curve of his claws. His long bristling ears whipped furiously above her. He rent her bodice with his teeth, taking skin as well as cloth. Below, his back claws tore her dress to tatters. He wrapped his powerful legs tight around her lacerated thighs, prying them apart and doing his best to thrust his huge red erection into her. Past

190

his shoulder, Rachel was pummeling his furry back, her face knotted in anger, her mouth hurling harsh words.

Now shock gave way to rage, and Anya's fury knew no bounds. Strength surged back into her arms and legs and she bit into his paw, tasting bunny blood. She twisted a knuckled fist into his underbelly. When the swiftness of it made him momentarily loose his hold, Anya pressed her attack, digging into his throat with one hand and twisting mercilessly at the pinched tip of his prick with the other. Rachel, she saw, was tugging on his long upright ears, wrenching at them and making them stretch. Good for her!

"Jesus Christ!" yowled the Easter Bunny. Suddenly he was out of Anya's grasp and off her. The cool air of the hallway slapped at her wounded body. She raised herself on her elbows, looked about, and swore. Rachel, full of useless protest, had fallen victim to his attack. Bits of bloody sweater flew free of her torso. Her skirt hung in tatters about her hips. Long thin slashes cut across her inner thighs and burbled over with blood. Then their attacker was inside her, thrusting and chittering, and Rachel, screaming and struggling, clutched her bleeding breasts, dark red dripping from a deep gash across one cheek.

Anya staggered to her feet. She had to act quickly or the mortal woman would die. But time hung heavy about her. She waded knee-deep in it. The crazed rabbit drove himself home again and again as Rachel's blood-laced arms flailed helplessly at the air. Between the Easter Bunny's hind legs, translucent brown skin cupped his pink kidney-shaped testicles. Anya hauled back with her right foot and slammed her shoetip into his crotch. He fell with a shocked yelp onto the carpet, glared at Anya through his pain, snarled, made a weak swipe at her with one claw, and vanished.

Gone into magic time, Anya supposed. But pursuit was the furthest thing from her mind. Though Anya's wounds had healed completely, Rachel would be dead in minutes if she didn't act swiftly to save her.

Without a thought regarding their late rivalry, she began at the deep gash on Rachel's face, tonguing around the ragged edges of it, making her way lick by lick to its harsh red center. If she tasted its bitter tang, she paid it no heed. Rachel had lost a great deal of blood. Her wounds had to be closed at once.

Face looks fine now, thought Anya. Thank God he left her neck alone. Ugly lacerations across the chest. She straddled the unconscious woman and licked in haste at the torn left breast, taking the aureole and nipple and skin into her mouth and tonguing it all back into shape. Then one by one she soothed and erased with her healing saliva every bloody clawtrail the Easter Bunny had blazed across Rachel's torso. The victim, she noted, though still unconscious, was breathing easier.

But there was no time to let up, no time for Anya to give a care to the ruins of her own clothing, which fell away as she ministered to Rachel. Worse mayhem lay below and Rachel was hemorrhaging badly. The fiend's back claws had shredded her skin, laid bare the muscles of her inner thighs, de-lipped the very organ he proceeded to violate. Anya plunged her face into the carnage and licked to save Rachel's life. Though the taste of gore filled her mouth, she shut her eyes and let instinct guide her, keeping her tongue moving back and forth over the mortal woman's belly and thighs, ministering to her, healing where hurt had sundered flesh.

Soon the taste of fresh blood no longer met her lips and Anya opened her eyes to behold the smooth expanse of Rachel's flawless white body, no wounds anywhere, not even a scar, her blond private hair mottled now with shades of russet under Anya's fingers where the blood had tinted it. There was a new taste on Anya's tongue, a taste she very much liked. But mingled with it was a vile drop of rabbit semen, and she knew that one task remained if Rachel were to be truly healed. Down she dipped, her mouth against the mortal woman's sex, tonguing deep inside her, as deep as she could probe, and sucking with all her might. The rapist's bitter seed halted its mad hurtle wombward, beaded protesting backward down the walls of his victim's vagina, and passed out of her labia into Anya's mouth. Resisting the impulse to gag, Anya leaned aside and spat out as much of the rank fluid as she could. It puddled like pale pus on the blood-soaked rug.

A gentle hand touched her leg. Anya gazed up from where she crouched over Rachel, past the riotous blond curls shining like angel hair in the lamplight of the hallway, and saw her large hazel eyes open and glowing. "How are you feeling?" Anya asked.

"Don't stop," whispered Rachel and reached out with her other hand to urge Anya's head gently back down.

Throughout the attack, it seemed to Rachel that she had fallen into a tangled mix of her worst nightmares: smotherings, helplessness, unbearable cold, monstrous clawed beings invading her and stretching out her death through an eternity of pain. Then it no longer boasted even the soft ameliorating edges of a nightmare. It felt everywhere hard and sharp, and she knew she was bleeding to death.

But abruptly the relentless slashings and impalings ceased and a benign goddess began pasting her face back together. Rachel's eyes fixed idly upon a rectangular lake: a chandelier hanging sideways above it in the walled sky found its double beneath the ice, which shone mirror-clear save for translucent skids of yolk and egg white and scattered shards of eggshell.

Then the goddess's mouth went to her chest, her teeth tearing away wrappings of pain. Her swift tongue stanched the bloodflow, replacing throbs of hurt with the pulse of healing. The lake resolved into a mirror indeed, the goddess into Anya. Rachel felt her kind lips, insistent with life, close upon a nipple. Through half-shut eyes, she pictured Santa's wife wrestling with death, who now conceded Rachel's torso but shifted his firepower to her loins, a wide battlefield of trauma and devastation.

Letting her eyelids fall, Rachel saw a distant light, alluring beyond this earthly plain of suffering and sadness. She drifted toward it, feeling the hooks lift free of her body. It would be so easy to cut loose of the torment, so much nicer to go into the light, to join Frank there. But down below, the waves lapped against the shore of her thighs, thudding down insistent beneath the moon that hung like a huge breast in the night sky. That moon opened its mouth in a sad O and spoke to her of womanly matters—of childbirth, of tides, of desires long kept under. The rhythmic slap of waves sounded below. Foam fizzed and sizzled against the shore, glistening silver in the moonlight.

Rachel opened her eyes to Anya's naked flanks where she knelt beside her, one knee resting warm against her ribs. The older woman's arms angled along either side of Rachel's hips. Her head was lowered to Rachel's parted thighs, the bun of her hair tightly curled and circling. Inside, the unbearable pain of violation still seared. But now, it felt as if Anya's healing tongue stretched clear up into Rachel's womb, licking away all traces of suffering.

Life surged anew into Rachel's veins. Life, yes, and something more: an impelling desire for physical love, to affirm life, to tie her more completely to it after nearly losing it. She rested a hand upon Anya, below the rounded curve of one buttock.

"How are you feeling?" Anya's glasses were gone and she looked ancient and beautiful. Her face was rusty with blood, Rachel's blood.

"Don't stop," she whispered. She felt whole again and glowing, and her vagina throbbed now for completion. She caressed Anya's neck, gently coaxing her back down between her legs as she had often done with Santa when he teased her with stopping. Down went the tight white head and again Rachel felt the amazing gift of Anya's tongue on her sex.

Rachel felt doubly weak, from loss of blood and from her gathering arousal. Yet it was as if Anya's healing tongue were speeding the manufacture of new blood as well as stimulating the old. Life surged through her from her moistening nexus.

Running her fingers along her savior's lovelips, Rachel coaxed Anya's parted thighs down over her mouth and feasted on the fluids that flowed there. Dark and rich their flavor, like blended herbs steeped on stone hearths, an elixir for all the world's ills.

For an eternity, naught existed but licking and being licked. Anya's moans mumbled upon her labia. When climax claimed them, it brought with it for Rachel the sweet painful wrack of rebirth. Stretching every limb beyond its limits and gasping gloriously for air, she felt at once born out of her own birth canal and out of Anya's, washed head to toe in a glow of sweat and lovejuice.

At last, they rose and threaded their way past dark puddles of gore and torn tufts of fur, washing the blood off one another in the shower, and spending hours of magic time in bed. Rachel apologized over and over for the suffering she had caused Anya, to which Anya tearfully regretted her own stubborn jealousy. Then both of them praised to the stars Santa's exquisite taste in women and dove into one another's arms for more.

"You know what I can't wait to see?" Anya asked as she fondled Rachel's right breast.

"What?" said Rachel, offering up a silent blessing to God for inventing nipples.

"The look on Santa's face when he finds out."

As Santa neared the Pole, his sleigh passed abruptly from the blizzard that whipped furiously about him into the mild winter of his domain. But he paid the transition no mind. His shouts to Lucifer and the others, his *pro forma* whipsmacks over their heads, unfolded on automatic.

There was far too much else to think about.

For one thing, the Tooth Fairy had not shown up once on his rounds. He had braced himself for his worst trial yet, certain that this time he would withstand her wiles. It unnerved him, her not attempting to seduce him along his route. The Tooth Fairy was not, he knew, the sort of creature to give up easily.

Then there was the sorry situation awaiting him at home, his two lovely wives who ought to adore one another but did not.

It hurt Santa's heart, the sadness of it all.

Wendy and Rachel's impending absence shrouded him in gloom. God knew how long it would last, that gloom, and how Anya would respond to it. Would their marriage ever be whole again? Did it matter?

The sleigh's runners skimmed the tops of snowy pines, throwing up clouds of mist that sparkled like diamond dust in the sunlight. Out from the elves' dormitory swarmed hundreds of dark dots. The dark dots did a slow curl around the skating pond, then scattered everywhichway across the commons. As Santa swooped lower, they grew greener and sprouted distinguishable legs and heads. More came tumbling out of workshop and stable, all of them headed for the expanse of snow before his cottage.

There on the porch was Wendy in a bright red dress, waving wildly up at him. Beside her on the railing sat Snowball and Nightwind, legs tucked under, patient black and white pods.

Behind them stood Anya and Rachel, holding hands and waving like twins, broad smiles lighting up their faces. Santa dropped the reins in shock, then groped forward and grabbed them again.

When Wendy leaped into the roil of elves that swarmed the sleigh, Santa lifted his radiant stepchild out of the turmoil—as though he plucked a holly berry from a cluster of leaves—and squeezed her tight. Her kisses warmed his cheek. Then his helpers closed in and one beloved face after another came into focus. Hearty handclasps and hugs besieged Santa on all sides. Wendy laughed in his arms and clasped him round the neck.

"We're staying!" she shouted.

When the green sea finally parted, Santa's wives were waiting on the porch. He bounded up and hugged them both, Wendy giggling as he crushed her against her mother. Anya he kissed first, tasting a new flavor of frisk and frolic there that pleased him greatly. Then, still puzzled, he bent to Rachel; her full lips parted and her lovely scent captivated him anew.

In the commons, the crowd went wild with cheering.

Later, in the living room, Santa heard the laundered version of what had happened. "Mommy got attacked by a giant animal," Wendy blurted out. Then, skirting around the details they later provided, Anya and Rachel painted the broad picture of what had occurred and how it had brought them together. Santa had noticed the bare floor in the hallway and the dried trail of egg running down the mirror. "Several of the elves have volunteered to weave us a new carpet," Anya told him, which left the larger question unanswered, "and the egg residue simply refuses to yield to conventional methods of cleaning, so we're leaving it there for now. More on that later."

When he had showered and was robed in red, soft black slippers hugging his feet and a long thin clay pipe wreathing aromatic wisps of smoke about his lips, Santa sat back in his easy chair and let Christmas unfold before him. On his return trip, he had dreaded this final round of giftgiving, the funereal mood that would surely pall every attempt at merriment. Now it was all he could do to keep from laughing out loud, things having fallen out as he had always dreamed they would. There was Wendy in a beautiful gingham dress Anya had sewn for her, once more assuming responsibility for delivering the gifts, pausing before him once to stick out her lower jaw and wiggle her first loose tooth in more than a year. ("Be sure to let someone know the instant it comes out," he cautioned.) There was his dear wife Anya, rocking and knitting and beaming as he hadn't seen her beam in ages. And there was Rachel, young and zesty and full-breasted, an arm draped over Heinrich's nearest shoulder where he sat, all six of him, bunched up on the couch, barely able to contain his glee.

At long last, after the eggnog had vanished but for a filmy residue at the bottom of the cut-glass bowl, and the large plates piled high with gingerbread men held only a stray crumb or two, Santa put on his holiday best and they adjourned to the elves' dormitory for festivities and giftgiving that lasted until dusk.

By nightfall, Wendy began to nod and Santa brimmed with a delicious mix of curiosity and lust. She drifted asleep in his arms as they watched elf after elf whiz by on the ice. With a twinkle of his eye, Santa summoned Fritz to his side.

"Fritz, I think you understand how much Wendy and her mother mean to me."

"Of course, Santa," Fritz assured him, watching the sleeping girl's head loll against the crook of Santa's arm as they made their way across the commons. "All of us, to the last elf, feel the same way."

"Good. That's good, Fritz. Now I want to tell you something. Get the door, will you?"

Fritz opened the front door of the gingerbread house, turned on the hall light, and stepped aside to let Santa through with his precious burden.

"Now, Fritz," said Santa while the sleepy girl was in the bathroom brushing her teeth, "Wendy and Rachel are not like us. They can be hurt. They can be killed."

"But Santa," Fritz scoffed, "who'd want to hurt—"

Santa held up a finger. "Never mind who. I'm afraid they may be in danger of further attack. You saw the rug. You heard what happened."

"Yes, but—"

"Then you know as much as you need to know. Keep an eye on Wendy tonight. Don't relax your vigilance for an instant. Will you do that?"

Fritz, puzzled and frustrated, stood by the picture window and looked out across the commons at the skating revelers. "She'll be safe with me, Santa."

"Thank you, Fritz."

Tucking Wendy in, Santa laid a fatherly hand upon her brow. "Go back to sleep now, darling. Fritz is here to look over you, and I'll see you in the morning." He bent down and kissed her.

"I love you, Santa," said Wendy with a yawn.

"I love you too, Wendy," Santa replied. "Sleep well, dear one."

Wendy smiled and her eyelids closed.

Santa paused at the door, his face soft but fearful. "Remember," he whispered to Fritz.

Fritz mouthed renewed assurance, and Santa headed back to his wives.

Hours later, when the festivities were over, Anya took one of Santa's hands and Rachel took the other and they led him beguilingly to his bed, stripped him naked, and demonstrated beyond the power of words how much love they had in their hearts for him and for one another. Hour after hour they dallied, these three, exploring with delight the new instance of matrimony they had become. Three hours shy of dawn, his arms full of contented woman, Santa drifted off at last into sleep, feeling safe and cozy and warm, drained and happy and, by any measure, complete.

"G'night, Fritz," Wendy said. The next moment her eyes blinked open and everything was dark and silent except for the soft glow of her nightlight and the breezy snores of her guardian elf curled up in a chair by the window. Snowball and Nightwind lumped dim and immobile at the foot of her bed. Outside, snow stretched in a silent blue roll across the commons past the gleam of the skating pond.

Too much hot apple cider. She needed to go tinkle. She had to leave her warm cozy bed and lift her nightgown above her waist and sit on the cold potty seat. Yes, but then she would get to nestle back under the covers again and that would feel wonderful. Nothing to be done. Wendy angled back her blankets and stepped down, chill air upon her ankles. She eased open her bedroom door so as not to disturb Fritz, crossed the hallway, and snapped on the bathroom light.

Loud knock of potty cover against the bright white tank; white seat cold on the backs of her legs; a sudden spray of tinkle hitting the water, and the easing of her discomfort within. Nightwind craned his head around the door and yawned up at her. Wendy worried the loose tooth with her tongue. She felt it give. Raising a hand from the seat, she brought it out.

It glistened between thumb and forefinger, jutting up thin and white and almost smooth, a pinched drop of red at its root end.

In her mouth she tasted blood.

She wiped herself and flushed the potty, then stood at the sink. Santa had said to let someone know if it came out. Should she wake Fritz? She set the tooth on the countertop and stared at it. No need. She was fast approaching eight, a big girl. What had Mommy done the last time in their old house? Stood next to her, an arm around her shoulder. Suggested she rinse her mouth out. Set the tooth beneath her pillow and tucked her in.

Anya told her often what an independent young lady she was becoming. They would be proud of her the next morning when she told them she had taken care of things herself. There might even be more dimes in it, assuming the Tooth Fairy rewarded such efforts. It was worth a try, anyway.

Wendy sloshed warm water about in her mouth and spat out the pink fluid, washing it down the drain. She did it a second and third time. Then she closed her palm around the tiny tooth, flicked off the bathroom light, and ushered Nightwind back into her room, shutting the door as quietly as she could behind them.

Fritz snored. He looked cold, Wendy thought. She tipped up the pillow and centered her prize beneath it, then pressed it firmly down around the tooth. She lifted a confused Snowball off the bed and set her on the floor. "Sorry, Snowball," she said. Her top blanket, light blue and pilled with age, she took off, draping it around Fritz and tucking it behind his shoulders so that he looked as if he had fallen asleep in a barber chair. A smile came to his lips. At last, Wendy crawled beneath the covers, savoring the mommy-like warmth that wrapped her in its arms, and drifted down into deep slumber.

13.
THE TOOTH FAIRY TAKES HER REVENGE

When immortals dream, death and disfigurement come surprisingly often into play. And yet not so surprising when one considers their indestructibility in waking life. Upon the deadly playground of a dreamscape, the agonies of separation and irrevocable loss are theirs at last to claim and be claimed by.

Because God had given Santa and Anya memories of past mortality, their dreams frequently took up these themes. In a typical scenario, God reached down in displeasure to peel away the veneer of immortal life from this or that inhabitant of the North Pole. There followed many tearful visits to the victim's deathbed, an elaborate burial scene in the woods, and after a heartrending period of gloom and mourning, at last a reversal: God forgave all, the grave belched forth its victim amidst a rain of flowers, and joy returned tenfold to every heart.

This night, however, Santa's dreams took an atypical turn. He floated blimplike above the world, an earth made not of rock and soil but of mattress, white with feathery blankets and pillows of snowdrift. Lying legs akimbo in every direction were vast expanses of women, naked and swollen-lipped. Down he drifted into the embrace of each of them, dipping into her ready flesh and leaving liquid gifts inside her. Glancing back, Santa watched them belly up and birth out girl babies, who blossomed swiftly into womanhood, their limpid gaze inviting his return.

But when he closed his eyes to savor his bliss, a blast of chill air suddenly assaulted him. Peeling his lids back against the wind, Santa found himself falling precipitously toward an island engulfed in flame. One twisted cypress burned, as did the ash trees racing up a mountain slope. Beaches of sand and rock roared with the ferocity of a furnace. Into this inferno he fell, skin scorched, lungs scandalized. And this isle—which was somehow the Tooth Fairy herself—rose to seize him. She held out inflaming arms, hugged him to her fiery bosom, sucked his prick into her pit of love, and pressed it to white coals until it sizzled and blistered like a hotdog on a grill.

"Santa." Her demonhood gripped him. "Look into my face. Behold what once you were, what realms of bliss you lorded over in days past." Through the wash of flame, her skin cleared like a pool and he witnessed scenes of forest abandon, heard reed-pipes endlessly rippling. His head fell forward into hers and the goatishness surged within him, wild and gamy, clever in chase, rough in capture, rude in ravage. Raising a hairy arm, he splashed wine down his throat and the spirit of pressed grape filled him. "Nymphs," came his command, "pleasure me!" At once, out from the trees—ash and oak and lofty pine—they flew to him. Lips moistened, grandly flush between the thighs, they grabbed at him, smothering him in tongue and cunt, nippling his lips with full milk-yielding breasts.

She thrust him up from her flaming face, tearing the vision away. Pain seized his limbs and worse pain gripped his sex. "But you gave that up long ago, fearing to die. Hoodwinked by God into a life of selfless giving, you are no longer worthy to wield such a lovely weapon as this." The blazing pit of her vulva, sprouting teeth and tongue, parted its jaws and inched around the tight pouch of his testicles. Then her teeth dug deep and incisive, severing his genitals with one savage chomp. As he screamed, her vaginal jaws munched away at their prize. Then she tossed him upon the hissing sea, straddled his head, and irised open her anus. Out fluttered flurries of currency, all colors, shapes, and sizes. Engraved presidents and kings and queens slapped across his face. Monetary excrement blinded him. So thick and furious came the defecation of banknotes that no air was left for breathing. With his last gasp, he found enough breath to scream, scream for his life . . .

. . . but suddenly he was awake. And it wasn't his scream he heard but Rachel's. There by the bedroom door in the moonlight stood the Tooth Fairy, her strong right arm thrown savagely across the shoulders of Wendy's torn nightgown. Wendy's head whipped from side to side in protest. Ringed in a ghastly red, her torn and toothless mouth sobbed open.

When Rachel saw the look on the intruder's face, she knew at once why this hellspawn stood at Santa's bedroom door, hurting her daughter. In the same instant, she saw Wendy's terror, her face a fist of pain, and Rachel's love for her took over.

"Let her go!" Flinging back the bedsheets, she leaped at the vengeful demon before her.

"With pleasure," said the intruder, hurling Wendy with a loud smack against the wall and turning to embrace the charging mortal.

"Mommy, a big bunny rabbit took Thnowball," she heard her daughter cry out, but then Rachel's ribcage snapped like a rack of twigs in the Tooth Fairy's brutal hug and the creature's jaws suddenly gaped far wider than seemed possible. Rachel inhaled sharply, astonished at how much pain went with the puncture and crush of internal organs. Then the Tooth Fairy's head sprang forward and her teeth lit into Rachel's face, and Rachel knew no more.

Blond bitch tastes halfway decent, came the thought. But there was no time for thinking, no time to savor the woman's flesh; time only to bolt it down. First the head, face and teeth and tongue, shove the skull in, crush it, gulp down bones, brain, and all. Then the torso, ripping into it like a hungry shredder pulping a treetrunk, taking in shoulderflesh and clavicle, arms and elbows, wrists and fingers, breasts and breadbasket. Finally she heaved the rest of the woman up into the air (a swirl of motherblood slapping across the whimpering girl's nightgown), ate away at innards and cunt and buttocks, stuffed down thighs and legs and feet, gulped flesh and bone and blood in quick triumph.

She was in high spirits, the Tooth Fairy. She'd been in the room ten seconds tops, her feast had taken no more than three, and Santa and his wife lay wrapped in shock. Already she could feel her insides working over her meal. Her belly bulged and she rose into the moonlight, hugging her knees to her breasts, ready to mint the mortal bitch.

She screamed at the pain.

Her anus gaped wide, straining at all sides. The milled edges of the coin came first, accordioned over three or four widths' worth. It fanned out as it emerged, gleaming golden. Faster and faster the impacted metal issued from her, hurting her even as it fed her pride. Like a flat balloon it filled out huge and round and golden. On the upturned side, she made out the mortal woman's breasts and hands and anguished face. When its last serration had been shat, the huge disc stiffened in the air like swiftly tempering steel and clattered to the hardwood floor, digging deep dents in it.

The sound roused Santa to action, but the Tooth Fairy rocketed over to Wendy and swooped her up, screaming and kicking, by the waist.

"In the name of God, put her down!" Santa shouted as he leaped from the bed.

She threw him one last look, then folded herself and her victim into magic time and was gone.

Still cocooned in shock, Anya watched Santa race to grapple with the Tooth Fairy.

Too late.

The moment his moon-white arms began to close on her, she winked out, Wendy with her. Santa slammed full force into the wall. A long, wounded howl issued from him. He struck it with his fist and crumbled against it, weeping.

Anya went to Santa. Turning at her touch, he hugged her. "Good God," he sobbed, "what have I done?"

"There, there, Nicholas." He blubbered in her arms. Anya fought away her tears, shutting out the terrible images of her loved ones bloody and dying, so as to tend to her husband.

"I could have stopped it. I could have held Rachel back. Don't you see, Anya, I could have gone into magic time and saved her."

"That's enough," she replied, looking him straight in the eye. "It happened much too fast for either of us to stop it. Now pull yourself together. You've got a child to save."

"Yes, I must think of Wendy." The catch in his voice tore at Anya's heart. "But how will I ever find them in time? They could be anywhere. Wendy might already—"

"Wendy is not dead," said Anya with more conviction than she felt. "But she's out there somewhere, hurting, and you've got to find her and rescue her." An image of Lucifer sprang to Anya's mind, his antlers glowing bright as neon.

"Claus, do you still have those red panties?"

Back in his burrow, the Easter Bunny's brain was buzzing. The Tooth Fairy had tossed him a sop for his conscience, this vigorous young she-cat, this Snowball. An insult to his dignity, a blatant bribe. And a prize worth having. It didn't by any means erase the sight of that little girl's mouth being savaged. He had almost leaped in to stop it, screeching at the Tooth Fairy to quit hurting her. But she had looked death at him and shouted, "If you value your balls, you'll stay the fuck where you are and shut up!" And he, God help his wormy soul, had prized his accursed genitals above the well-being of a child in trouble. Where had his virtue—what little there had been—gone in the last year? He grimaced. He knew the answer. Right into the Tooth Fairy's quim, that's where. She had sucked it clean out of him. Yes, he thought bitterly, casting a baleful eye along the walls of the exercise area; and he hadn't lifted a claw to stop her.

He hung his head and felt chills of regret course along his spine for the degenerative spiral he had hopped down since last Christmas.

Snowball meowed up at him.

"What's that, my pet?" he said. "You'd like to see the rest of the burrow?" He stroked her smooth white fur, at which she lifted against his paw and piano'd upon his chest in approval.

At his groin, a stirring.

"All right, my precious little Snowball. First I'll show you where the candy is made and where the baskets are assembled. Then we'll go watch the hens lay Easter eggs, won't that be fun?"

She purred.

"And then I'll show you my bedroom."

Lucifer was dreaming about Bambi's girlfriend Faline again: her gangly legs, her white wiggly paintbrush tail, and below—what Disney dared not draw—her puckered anus and the sweet wet furrow along which Lucifer eased the tip of his buckhood.

But then the stable door's sharp creak and the harsh gleam of Gregor's lantern robbed him of his cartoon lover. He looked up in annoyance to see Santa all suited up; Mrs. Claus in bathrobe and slippers; Prancer and Blitzen poking their heads over the sides of their stalls, blinking in curiosity; Fritz standing alone, looking stunned; yonder, Gregor lifting a saddle out of an old trunk and wiping the dust off it. All of them were bathed in the soft glow of magic time.

What in blazes was going on?

"Lucifer, old friend," came Santa's voice, with an edge of desperation that frightened him. "I need your help."

At once, new vigor came into the lead reindeer's limbs. He rose from his straw bed and cocked his head.

In the glow of Lucifer's antlers, Santa's face shone like a violent blush. "The Tooth Fairy has taken Wendy. We've got to find them and get her back, and it must be done quickly." Fumbling in his pocket, Santa brought out a bunched handful of red silk and lifted it to Lucifer's nose. "Can you track her from this?"

The reindeer shut his eyes and inhaled.

He had once thought it strange when Wendy carried her kittens into the stable one morning, teasing them with a catnip mouse Mrs. Claus had stitched together from scraps of calico. It had amused him, how they dizzied about their prize, sniffing it and batting it and pouncing upon it. Now he understood. Now, with the aroma of the immortal seductress rising in his flared nostrils, by God he understood.

"Easy, Lucifer!"

Great Christ, his antlers flared at once into aflame, straight out to the tips. Down below (Jesus in a manger, how embarrassing) his sex suddenly stiffened, her fairy hand stroking him there. His hoofs beat out a tattoo on the stable floor and seed shot from him in gleeful jets and spurts.

"Gregor, for God's sake, help me hold him! Anya, stay where you are!"

Strong elfin arms steadied him. His brain felt energized, as if there were networks of bright white Christmas lights everywhere agleam along its folds and runnels. He shook his great antlers and snorted. Then, looking at Santa, he nodded sharply.

Santa smiled. "Good boy! All right, Gregor, saddle him up. Make haste. Watch where you step." While Gregor placed a blanket across his back and cinched him into the jingling saddle, Lucifer watched Santa exchange a parting word and an embrace with Mrs. Claus by the door.

Then they led him outside into the sleeping snowscape, where he caught her scent, faint but unmistakable, in the air by the cottage.

With Santa riding him, he bounded away, speeding southward, tracking his prey on her zigzag path through the night, down across the frozen reaches of the Yukon, swooping low over sleeping cities sprawled the length of British Columbia and Washington and Oregon, straight on toward the gleaming heart of the Sacramento Valley.

***

Wendy had no more tears and very little fight left in her. Her gums throbbed and it hurt something fierce when her jaws accidentally jarred shut. But the images in her mind hurt much more—the sudden appearance of the hard-faced fairy in whose grip she now flew, jolting her out of sleep and digging her fingers again and again into Wendy's mouth; Nightwind's mewls of protest; Fritz frozen in normal time; the gigantic white rabbit who just stood there and Snowball's sharp yowl when she was snatched up and tossed to him; and worst of all, her mother vanishing in a sweep of blood down the Tooth Fairy's throat.

She bleared down at the frosted lights of yet another city. So many cities she had passed over, so many homes strung with color, full of warm beds and dozing children.

But this city, wet with rain, they began to descend toward. Twin pinpoints of light inched along ribbons of highway, enlarging into small circles that threw before them glittering scoops of yellow.

They banked sharply and her nemesis pointed down. "That's where we're headed, right there. Recognize it?"

Wendy saw a wrought-iron gate in a tall dark fence that ran for several blocks. A dimly lit road branched out from the gate, meandering along wide patches of earth. Here and there, trees gloomed up like glistening broccoli. The only sign of life was a lone lit windowpane in a tiny building near the gate. The place nagged at her, as if she had seen it in a dream. But she shook her head.

"You will soon enough," came the harsh voice. "Keep your eyes open."

Wendy looked. Below them, black teeth thrust up through the earth in serried rows. A certain stand of oak trees moved into place about a rise in the landscape, and it dawned on her. She moaned anew as they circled in on her buried father.

"That's more like it," said the Tooth Fairy, pausing in the air above Frank McGinnis's grave. "Now I want you to read the words on this tombstone." She fingered the wet cold stone along the engraved X in XAVIER. "My spies tell me you like to read. Be a good girl and tell me what it says."

"Read it yourthelf!" said Wendy defiantly.

But the Tooth Fairy's fingers clenched like steel calipers around her cheeks and bore down. "Do I have to tear the words out of your mouth, young lady, or will you do as I say?" Wendy nearly fainted, but she managed to hang on until the hurtful fingers withdrew at last. "Now read!"

She lisped painfully through her father's name and the numerals engraved beneath. Born 1933. Died 1990. Knuckles of rain beat upon her skull. She wished Daddy were alive to rescue her. Or that she could die now, escape this cold and rain and torment, and be held by his strong arms forever.

"Now this part, the phrase below."

Wendy didn't need to look but she wiped her eyes with the back of her hand. "Beloved huthband and father," she muttered, choking on the last word.

"Good girl," said the Tooth Fairy, who flew Wendy to the grave opposite her daddy's and sat her atop a fat blocky marker. "You understand what 'beloved father' means, I suppose? Well now, I'm going to show you why your mother called him 'beloved husband.'"

As Wendy watched, the Tooth Fairy beckoned toward the carefully tended mound with outstretched arms. The moist earth rumbled. Wendy heard slow scraping sounds that grew stronger and faster. Then a sharp wrenching. The earth sifted like dark wet flour beneath the incantatory hands of the Tooth Fairy, who cackled in triumph as she lifted free one gnarled grasping remnant of a hand, then another.

By the time her father's head emerged from the mound and his muddy eyes blinked open, Wendy had retreated far far inside.

"And this," he said, "is where I sleep. Do you like the pretty straw?"

Snowball meowed.

"Yes, of course you could share all this—if you treat me right. Oh and just beyond my nice soft bed is the opening to the sleeping quarters of a very special friend of mine. Let's knock, shall we? Oh Petunia, we have guests. Are you decent? She says she is."

He stroked the pure white cat from head to raised rump. Petunia's room, as always, was dim and dank. But he sensed something new in the air. A whiff of jealousy, perhaps? He hoped not.

"Petunia, I'd like you to meet Snowball. Snowball, Petunia. That's right. Give her a good sniffing. She likes that. Now Snowball, I have a question to ask you."

The cat looked up quizzically.

"Do you think you could get into that same position for me?" He licked his lips. "Right now?"

One moment Frank's mind was one with the Eternal Hum. The next, a strong pull from somewhere grabbed him off the line and stuffed him back into bones.

Like an angry surge of bees, a superhuman strength rushed through him. The pine lid splintered in his hands. Rising through churning clods of earth, he shut his eyes against the yielding mud and clawed upward until he felt . . . a hand. Two hands. They helped him rise. At last his head crowned out of the soil, and his shoulders followed. Cold sweet air. He tried to breathe it. In vain. Then he opened his eyes and saw his benefactress: naked but for a necklace of large white teeth; white of skin but muddied where she had touched him; pure-breasted and pure-thighed, pure everywhere.

A face that bewitched.

She had been talking to him for some time, but until she swam into focus all he heard was a soup of sound. As he regained language, he understood and obeyed. "That's right, lover boy. Lie back and let momma attend to your needs. My, my, you were a chubby one, weren't you?"

He managed a loud prolonged vowel, which he paid for in

vicious hurt inside.

"Still plenty of you left, though. And I'm delighted to see you're mostly intact down here. Let me help you stiffen this right up. Will you do that for your lover? Will you go all hard, Frank darling?"

She smiled sardonically at him, kneading him where he couldn't see. But the ghost of old thickenings arose. He had forgotten what it was called, that piece of flesh her fingers sculpted. But its name didn't matter. Only the feeling of life resurgent mattered.

"Yes, that's the way momma likes it, Frank. Thick and juicy."

She mounted him. She closed around his muddy member and rode him, looming full-breasted and red-haired above. It pleased Frank immensely, despite the voracious hunger in her eyes.

But in an instant, all of that changed.

That was the moment when a high-pitched filament of sound, faint at first, grew louder and resolved itself into the insistent jingle of bells.

That was also the moment when Frank saw the wounded figure of a little girl seated upon a tombstone and knew at once that it was his Wendy, that she had been watching him, and that she was in terrible pain.

The Easter Bunny held Snowball's front paws together and wrapped them tight round with baling wire. She tugged hard against it and *mrrrrrowl*'d up at him.

"Now, now, little one," he muttered. "You'll only hurt yourself that way. And that's my job, wouldn't you say? Just a little joke, precious. I want you to enjoy yourself too, stick around awhile, make this a habit for both of us." He found a gnarled branch he liked at times to whet his teeth on and wired her back legs far apart at its opposite ends.

Snowball's claws curved full out. But as she had no room to maneuver, he felt quite safe. Her yowls were loud and incessant now, the way his lazy Wyandotte might sound laying an abrupt succession of angular eggs.

Stooping, he placed her upon his bed of straw. Her hindquarters waggled violently back and forth. Her saucy target made "pay-me, pay-me" movements beneath her puffed-up tail. "Take it easy, sweetie pie. I'll try to make this as pleasant as I can for both of us."

His paws floated down his belly and found plenty to grab onto, lots of stuff to stiffen there.

As they flew in over I-80, Santa brought them out of magic time. The stuck traffic below resumed its dark hurtle east and west. He assumed that Lucifer would alight at Rachel's home. To his surprise, they passed it by and headed south. From his mount's angle of descent, Santa sensed their journey was nearly over. He prayed to God they weren't too late.

(He-he-he, you can pray to God all you want, big brother, but you're the one who's responsible for this mess, and you're the who has to clean it up.)

So. You're back.

(Never left, really. Just laid low.)

Rachel told me I should fight you if you returned, fight you and triumph.

(That's crazy, bubba. I'm part of you. Hell, I am you. What you used to be before the big man in the sky turned you into Santa Claus. You know who I am, don't you? Why not just out and say it?)

Santa, staring down at the shiny roofs below, heard wet tires peel back pavement. *Pan*, he thought simply, letting it out for the first time.

(Ooh yes, that's right, that felt good. Let me hear it again.)

Pan. I used to be Pan. His head felt strangely airy all of a sudden.

(Feel that rush? That's yours truly, the old goat-god himself, feeling his oats. Trust me, bro, all right? Don't deny your deepest self.)

214

You got me into this mess, you and your lust!

(Hey, mea culpa, okay? What can I say? I like to fuck. We both do. Couple of old rutters from way back. But listen, I got the goods. You can feel the power knocking against your ribcage, right? Pounding in your pecker? Beating at your skull? I can give you the strength to best the bitch.)

I'll do that on my own, no help from you.

(Shit, man, you're trembling like a leaf. You want to fight fire you use fire, not milk and cookies.)

Santa was on a cusp. He knew it. He ought to refuse the intruder, to deny his Pan side. But doubt clouded his judgment, and: *So be it, then. Do your worst.* And the thing slipped into his heart, hardening it like a cock and turning his thoughts dark.

As they banked over tall trees, Wendy came first into view, pale and thin and white, a ghost perched upon a tombstone. Then, her father's gaping grave and Frank McGinnis's muddied corpse writhing under the Tooth Fairy, who glared defiance at Santa as he descended.

When Lucifer set hoof to ground not ten yards away, Santa bounded off and made for Wendy.

"Not so fast!" The Tooth Fairy pointed a finger at Wendy, who cried out in pain. Recalling how she had split open his skin in just this way, Santa halted. The dead man, a fat rotting caricature of Santa himself, pleaded for his daughter from the muddy depths of his throat.

"If you know what's good for you," boomed Santa, "you'll give me the girl." His tone struck him as odd indeed. Stentorian, commanding, ruthless, threatening mayhem. He didn't like it one bit.

(Good one! That got her goat!)

The Tooth Fairy looked momentarily stunned. Then she laughed, her buttocks thick with mud where she straddled the dead man's lower body. "Idle threats? That doesn't suit you, lover."

"Why are you doing this?" said Santa.

(Oh, come on, man. Let me through. Tell her you don't make idle threats, tell her you're going to whup her ass.)

"That's not at all like Santa Claus. He's so kind and generous. Everybody knows that."

"Please," he said. Lucifer gave a troubled whinny of protest. Santa took a step toward the awful copulation. "In the name of all that's decent, let me take Wendy away from this."

(Please and decent, right. Sure got her on the run now, don't ya? Must be time to break out those Pat Boone records, pound the last nail into her coffin.)

"And interrupt her lessons in lovemaking?" She cast a steely glance at Lucifer, then hurled it into Santa. "Would that be fair? To show our little lovely the joys a man and woman can share and not allow her to indulge in them herself?"

"You're insane."

She tossed her head back. "You betrayed me, you jolly bastard. I'm going back to my dear wife Anya, you said, be faithful, and fuck nobody else. Then you went upstairs and latched onto another tasty piece. Did you really believe I'd let you get away with that?"

"We fell in love," he pleaded. "What you and I had was never love. It was animal lust pure and simple. But that's over now. You've murdered my Rachel. Now you're killing her daughter, my daughter. Please. She's hurt. She's in shock. She's freezing to death. At least let me cover her with my coat." Santa tugged at his top button and took another step toward Wendy.

In a flash, the Tooth Fairy was upon him, twisting muddy fingers into the clean cloth of his suit, grinding her groin against his belly. "You want the girl, you can have her." With a wicked grin, she ground her cheekbones into Santa's face and tore at his beard. "You can have *her*—if I can have Lucifer."

"What?"

"You heard me. I want that large studly buck over there, the one with the big stiff furry handle poking up beneath his belly. Yes, that's what this bad little girl wants for Christmas,

Santa. She wants Lucifer, the jolly old elf's favorite reindeer, ready to do her bidding for a year."

Santa pried her off and hurled her into the air. She floated like a wind-wraith before him. "That's out of the—" he began.

Enraged at his rebuff, the Tooth Fairy hauled back and blasted Santa's mouth with a thick gout of flame. It scoured the flesh off his upper palate and charbroiled his tongue.

At once, Santa gave Pan free rein. The goat-god pumped up Santa's body into a fighting machine, planting his boots like hoofs in the grave-ground, feeling the chthonic solidity root him deep in the earth.

He gave a blast of sound so bellicose that it ripped straight down the Tooth Fairy's front, whipped the skin off her like a winding sheet, and sent it flapping and fluttering into the night sky like an albino bat hellbent for heaven.

Undaunted, she oozed new covering out of her bloody flesh. Her necklace clacked as the skin re-wrapped her, clattering like mini-blinds. "So you want to play rough, eh?"

Her fingers danced about her head, pointing this way and that. Flowers lifted from grave after grave, flying straight into Santa's face. Into his lungs they flooded. They filled his belly, made it swell up. A button popped. Another.

Gathering his rage, Pan-Santa puked out the impacted petals and thorns, shaping the projectile with his mouth. It shot forth thin and hard and sharp as wire.

The weapon speared straight through her. It claimed several vertebrae, leaving her lower body dangling until self-healing regenerated what was missing or damaged. But she was too full of fight to wait for that. She flew to Frank's tombstone and grappled it from the earth, lifting the thick slab of granite and hurling it at Santa with all her might.

Frank's marker whumped into his body, driving him to the ground, snapping bones. Then healing erased the trauma, reshaped and knit his broken bones. Pan-Santa shoved the stone away and went for another, this one twice the size, twice the thickness, of Frank's.

By Zeus, he thought, he'd beat her at her own game.

Then Santa saw the inscription: TO THE MEMORY OF MY BELOVED WIFE, ELLIE MARSH JEFFRIES. 1914-1987. MAY SHE REST IN PEACE.

Good God, what am I doing? This is sacred ground.

(Can it, Santa. We're doing what needs to be done.)

But this isn't right, I—

(Shut up and grab the fucking tombstone!)

But a loud whinny, close by, cut him short.

Lucifer nosed Santa's armpit from behind and threw him off-balance. Turning, he saw the eager eyes of his lead reindeer; the fiery filaments of his fur; his antlers swaying with the high winds of desire.

The Tooth Fairy laughed. "Out of the question, is it?" she said. "So do we strike a bargain, or do you feel like ripping the whole goddamn cemetery apart?"

Santa turned to his nemesis. There was no time to argue the point. Lucifer was willing. And Wendy might die if he didn't spirit her away quickly.

"He must be back at the North Pole one week before Christmas."

"Done."

"In perfect condition."

"Spanking clean and ready for action."

"So be it," said Santa. "He'll arrive on your island before daybreak. And Wendy—?"

"She's yours." The Tooth Fairy gave Lucifer a wicked look and twisted about to delve into her dead lover.

"One thing more," Santa said.

"What?" Impatience thundered in her face.

Santa tugged off his coat, wrapped it snug around Wendy, lifted her from the tombstone, thrust a hand into his pocket, and took out his prize. "You can have these back. I'm finished with them."

Hissing at him, the Tooth Fairy snatched the red lace panties from his fingers and pussied down onto her lover's aroused putrescence, twisting the wispy garment about his exposed neckbone in a grim parody of sexual strangulation. Santa's last glimpse of her, as he settled his precious, unresponsive burden before him on Lucifer's back and lifted into the air, was of her necklace knocking like a rattle of dice against the screaming corpse's chest as she bent to bury her teeth in his skull.

Between his paws his bunnyhood grew rigid. His back right foot had begun to pound the packed earth of his burrow. The sharp high-pitched *meowl*s coming from the bed wove a stirring counterrhythm across the boom and thud of his thumps.

He felt good, very good indeed.

But just as he bent to touch the fat red tip of his sex to Snowball's pink privates, the earth rumbled. At once he straightened, perking up his ears. A ringing sang in his head, a jangling that made him slightly nauseous.

Then thunder sounded and the burrow shook. Giving out with a high treble squeal, he dashed wildly about, making for the door, hoping to reach open air before an earthquake swallowed his home. But as the archway gaped to let him into the exercise area, a flash of brilliance flared at the mouth of the burrow, growing in intensity as the jangle of sleighbells shrilled louder.

Through a pulsing ring of light burst the figure of a fat red rider on an antlered steed. Light swept in with them, swirling about them. And he saw that it was Santa Claus glowering down from Lucifer's back and looking like no Santa he had ever seen—harsh, shifty, full of muscle and meanness, not the soft and fuzzy elf he'd grown used to. The pale unseeing face of Wendy McGinnis poked up out of Santa's coat.

Terrified, he skittered backward into his bedroom. But the bells started up again with a raucous jangle and the solid wall of earth which kept him from his invaders dropped away like a curtain of dust. Lucifer charged through glowing motes of earth, bringing his master and the little girl through without a spot. The Easter Bunny cowered against the outer wall, trying to stay out of the vast corona of light which splashed through the bedroom, trying to avoid the fat elf's piercing glare.

Santa's eyes swept the room and whipped back to sting him with righteous wrath. The great hands lightly flicked the reins they held. Then Lucifer dashed into the air. Flattening himself against the wall, the Easter Bunny felt the sharp tip of an antler sear a line of fire across his face and the quick vicious punch of hoofs—front, back—pounding at his belly, bringing blood and pain welling up there. Santa swiped across the bed and lifted Snowball, unrestrained, up into his lap.

Holding his belly as the blood burbled from between his paws, the Easter Bunny sobbed bitter tears. "I'm sorry," he blubbered. "She made me do it. I'll be good from now on, I promise."

Santa reined in, hanging in mid-air, and looked back in scorn. "Shame on you! May you roast in hell for this!" Then he put bootheels to the sides of his mount and he and the girl and her still-protesting pet dashed away in a blur of color.

Gloom descended then upon the Easter Bunny. Dread, despair, emptiness. For hours he stood against the wall, sobbing and chittering as his flesh—but not his spirit, no never his spirit—healed. When at last he moved, it was beneath a weight of misery that would not be shaken off. He looked upon his hens with indifference, upon Petunia with loathing.

For weeks, guilt and shame filled his heart. He ate little and slept less. Thus his life limped along until Valentine's Day, when the Lord God Almighty Himself paid him a long-overdue second visit and relieved the Easter Bunny of his torment forever.

PART FIVE
AFTER THE STORM

Sex is nobody's business except the three people involved.
—anonymous

Faith is under the left nipple.
—Martin Luther

The marriage supper of the Lamb is a feast at which every dish is free to every guest. . . . In a holy community, there is no more reason why sexual intercourse should be restricted by law, than why eating and drinking should be—and there is as little occasion for shame in the one case as in the other.
—John Humphrey Noyes

14.
A TIME TO MOURN

The weeks which followed were the saddest ever spent at the North Pole.

When Santa streaked out of the night, his elves were out in force, their faces turned upward to catch the distant *chin-chin-chin* of sleighbells. Pacing the porch in fret over his failed watch, Fritz was the first to spy the bright light of Lucifer's antlers parting the darkness above the trees.

"Here they come!" he shouted.

Anya threw up the sash of her sewing room window and leaned out. Wendy's pale face shone above Santa's folded hands. Her husband's features seemed gaunt and drawn, his hair wild and unruly.

Those nearest the landing swarmed about, reaching to steady Santa's mount. Some helped unclaw Snowball from Santa's pocket and set her down in the snow; she scampered off with Nightwind toward the skating pond. Others lifted Santa's red-and-white bundle down from the reindeer's back and conveyed her to Anya's arms. "Easy with her," Santa snapped. "She's had a terrible shock."

Wondering murmurs arose at this, and again when Santa whispered in Lucifer's ear, reached down to uncinch his saddle, and slapped his lead reindeer briskly on the rump, sending him bounding skyward again. Santa's shout rose up like a stern whipsmack: "And God help you if you're a day late in returning!"

Then Santa elbowed aside elf after elf, disappearing into the cottage with Anya and Wendy. Inside, Fritz drew a hot bath and heated some broth. The others stood in the commons, feeling relief at Wendy's safe return, horror at rumors of Rachel's death, and shock at the harsh demeanor that had overtaken their master. When Fritz reappeared on the porch, his features were drawn, his manner distracted. Choking back tears, he confirmed the rumors, saying only that the Tooth Fairy had killed Rachel and turned her to gold. "Wendy will live," he said, "but her condition is uncertain. She focuses on no one, says not a word, hears nothing, takes food sparingly. Santa and Mrs. Claus ask that we pray for her, and for her mother."

And so, with long faces and leaden hearts, Santa's helpers returned to their quarters. There they knelt by their beds, hands clasped, eyelids shut tight, lips moving in their beards. And when they had poured out to God all the love and concern they felt for Wendy and commended Rachel's soul to His keeping, they added a special prayer for the restoration of Santa's spirits and crawled beneath the covers, seeking in vain the solace that sleep brings.

Santa leaned against the jamb of the bathroom door, arms folded, watching Anya bathe Wendy. The child's eyes stared straight ahead. Her arms and shoulders shivered as they had done throughout the return trip, though she was immersed, her head only excepted, in steaming bathwater. "So how long's the little—?" Stopping himself, Santa softened, let his arms unfold. "I mean, will she be all right?"

"We're going to be just fine," said Anya, a tinge of anxiety in her voice, "aren't we, Wendy?"

Wendy remained silent.

"Of course we are."

"Don't patronize her, Anya. Wendy's a strong girl, strong enough to deal with her own grief, surely."

With a wrung washcloth, Anya gently daubed away the streaks of blood around the little girl's mouth. When she asked if she might use her tongue on Wendy's wounded gums, the girl made no reply. But when Anya lifted her fingers to her chin to ease open her mouth, Wendy screamed and lashed out at her with such frenzy that Santa was forced to rush into the chaotic slosh and outfling of bathwater to help his wife soothe the girl.

Anya dried her and wrapped her in a warm robe. Santa carried her to the bed in the guest room and watched while Anya stood over her and kissed her and caressed her brow and wished her a good night. Then it was time to close Wendy's door, return to their bedroom, confront the blood-spattered walls and the huge gold coin lying atilt on the hardwood floor.

Since Santa's departure, Anya had avoided the bedroom. She wept anew in her husband's arms when she saw the pained engraving of Rachel's face howling up through the moonlight, her golden hands tensed to fend off death. "Oh Claus," she sobbed, "her pain hurts to look at." The object's obscene clarity rattled her, the shoulders and breasts and belly thrust into prominence, yet receding at the same time into the coin's artificial depths.

"I'll turn it away."

Santa righted it to vertical on its thick milled edge and slowly rotated the offending sight about; caught the obscenity of the obverse side; quickly turned it back to heads and rolled it like a warped cymbal against the wall, where he tossed Anya's blue knit shawl over it. But the cruel depiction of Rachel's lower body—the wrinkled soles of her feet, the splayed legs, the taut buttocks, and the wide golden gape of her vulva—burned into Anya's brain and caused her to weep the night away.

Santa alternately wept and scowled, confused by the oceanic struggle within. He did his best to soothe his wife *(the simpering bitch!)* beneath the covers, turning to stare for long stretches at the shrouded shape propped against the wall.

Strange ideas percolated in his head.

Lacking Rachel's body, they buried the coin.

"It may help Wendy," Santa confided to Fritz the next morning. A large ledger lay open on the rolltop desk's ink-stained blotter. Santa's quill pen rested slantwise across one page. He had been making notes in an odd hand—not his usual florid script but one that looked runic, ancient, unwholesome. "It might help focus her grief if we hold a funeral, all of us gathered in the Chapel." Santa's voice had a rasp to it. "Along with that wretched coin, we can bury a good deal of Wendy's pain. It might snap her out of it sooner. What do you think?"

"Sounds like a good idea," said Fritz. He disliked the hard glare Santa sometimes fixed him with, as though he found him—found all of them—utterly despicable. Worse, he disliked the preoccupation that often claimed his master, his massive thumbs massaging erratic circles into the skin of his clasped hands, the corners of his mouth struggling against a smirk. Fritz noticed patches of coarse hair sprouting on the backs of Santa's hands.

"Fine!" Santa hunched over in his swivel chair and ticked off funeral preparations, drawing Fritz into what felt like a dark plot.

Fritz went at once to the workshop, where the elves sat glumly at empty workbenches, awaiting Santa's traditional opening speech to inaugurate another year of toymaking. He walked to the podium from which Santa usually spoke. In his piping voice, he gave them Santa's orders concerning the funeral.

Then, while a team of woodworkers bent to the manufacture of a pine coffin lined with red velvet, four feet and a tad more square, and the others queued up for armbands snipped from bolts of black-dyed muslin, four of the burliest elves—Knecht Rupert, Johann, Gustav, and flaxen-haired Franz the watchmaker—followed Fritz to the toolshed by the stable and broke out pickaxes and shovels. Silently through the snow they trudged, tools slung over their shoulders.

At the Chapel, Fritz paused and picked out a smooth patch of ground near the Altar. It was dappled now in sun and shade, but Fritz calculated it would be bathed in sunlight two hours hence. "We'll dig here," he said.

Johann and Gustav measured out the plot. Then Fritz

watched his four friends swing their pickaxes through the air and break open the earth.

Anya shrouded herself in magic time. For a time, she allowed nothing to exist but moving vistas of black cloth, her own nimble fingers, and the mind-numbing *mmmmmmmm* and *shutch-shutch-shutch* of her sewing machine. No thoughts or memories. Just the easy reliable thrust and withdrawal of a sharp silver needle. With the embracing slowness of eternal solitude, two black dresses and one black Santa suit furred in funereal gray took shape under her hands.

When they were completed, lying across her lap like three boneless bodies, she allowed normal time to surge back into her life. She put on one of the dresses and carried the other garments to Wendy's room, where Santa sat gazing at the sleeping girl.

Despite the depth of Wendy's slumber, she woke easily at Anya's touch. No discernible improvement. Anya helped her use the potty, washed her face, and brushed her hair, speaking softly to her all the while. While Nightwind and Snowball watched wide-eyed from the blankets, she removed Wendy's nightgown and buttoned her into the black dress. Then she told her that they would have a light breakfast before burying her mother in the woods near the Chapel.

Anya held spoonfuls of porridge to Wendy's mouth, cupping her other hand beneath the spoon to catch drips but being careful not to touch Wendy's chin. Wendy took apple juice in small sips the same way, and Anya lightly patted her lips with a napkin.

At a knock on the front door, Santa rose to let Fritz in. Since his return, there was a roll to her husband's walk, a hint of swagger. He had changed. He looked less chubby in the face, smiled rarely, spoke less often and sounded earthy and rough when he did. But then he wasn't alone, she thought. They had all changed. Odd how grief wore one down.

Low whispers sounded in the hallway. Fritz and a number

of elves carried something angular and white, the coffin, past the archway and beyond. Some minutes later, they returned, slower now and struggling with the plain brass handles, the bells they wore on their caps and slippers sounding heavier as they paced.

Santa glanced in. "It's time," he said, and Anya, rising, helped Wendy to her feet.

It was peaceful in the Chapel, thought Fritz; silent and lovely and full of woe. Now that the dreadful dead-march of thousands of elfin bells on thousands of elfin slippers had died away, the only sounds were the forlorn dripping of leaves in the trees and Santa's solemn voice raised in prayer.

"We commend to You the soul of Your servant Rachel," he intoned, standing at the head of the lowered coffin in his black suit. Anya, head bowed, stood at Santa's right with one arm draped round Wendy's shoulder. "Take her to Your bosom, Lord, and grant her eternal rest.

"Rachel Townsend was a good girl as she grew, and a kind and good-hearted woman when grown. To Frank McGinnis she was a faithful and loving wife; to her daughter Wendy, a mother full of love, and caring, and compassion without stint. Those who knew her, those who called her 'friend,' were blest indeed.

"In her last year of life, Rachel brought new light to our community. That light dims at her passing; never again shall it burn as bright.

"My helpers took her to their hearts at once, and as they loved her, so she loved them, every one. Anya, my wife and helpmate, whom I cherish and adore beyond the telling, ever patient, longsuffering in the face of her husband's blundering ways, came in the last days to prize Rachel as I did and as I do yet: I loved Rachel and I will always love her. She . . ."

Here Santa faltered. His eyelids closed and Fritz saw a tear tremble down his cheek. When he opened them again, his eyes darted about, seeking something or someone. He tugged at his beard. His lips quivered. Fritz pictured his master in the study, the ledger lying open on his desk, the thick angular calligraphy, fibrous hair on the backs of his hands.

All around, the forest dripped.

In harsh tones, heavy with woe: "*She was my second wife. Yes, she was! She served me! She serviced me well, she did!*" Santa seemed to catch himself, shook his head to clear it. "Rachel McGinnis was bright, buoyant, quick with cheerful thoughts, and words, and deeds, a stranger to all things mean and ugly.

"Failing her mortal remains, we bury now a distorted image of her, wrought out of gold and jealousy by her fairy enemy." He paused, seemed to bunch together at the shoulders. "*Her enemy and ours, yes, a sleek, sexy, simpering—!*" Again the catch, the release. "But no quantity of—" Fritz noted with alarm the strain in his master's voice. Then, calmer: "No quantity of gold, my friends, can ever match Rachel's precious love. And no hatred, however vast and dreadful, shall ever tarnish our sacred memory of her, which will live forever in our hearts.

"Ashes to ashes, dust to dust. If indeed our Rachel must remain dead, may she find peace in the cradle of Your arms."

In the days that followed, Wendy showed little improvement. Her care had fallen to Anya and Fritz, though all the elves pitched in. They sledded their bright red bundle to and fro across the commons, Snowball and Nightwind perched upon her lap. Some tried to joke with her, pretending that she joked right back at them. Others peered in at the kitchen window awaiting a chance to help feed her, to spoon up blendered food and hold it under her nose and watch her slotted mouth open to take it in. It was a difficult time.

What made it rougher was Santa's absence.

Not that he had left the North Pole.

But he might as well have.

They saw him at meals, wearing his black Santa suit long

after the others had put off their mourning, toying with his food, tucking it into his mouth like so much fodder, responding only when a question was repeated. They watched him slink through shadows in obscure corners of the workshop, claiming stray scraps of something or other and carrying them back to his locked workroom, a strange hobble to his walk.

Anya awoke each morning aware that sometime between midnight and dawn her husband had slipped away. From all appearances, he was losing weight, taking on muscle, growing hairier about the thighs and shanks. He left a peculiar odor on the sheets, not exactly unpleasant, not unpleasant at all, but not the most civilized of smells either.

Fritz made bold once to lay aside his tools, climb down from his wooden stool, walk like Oliver Twist along a corridor of craned necks, and knock on the workroom door.

No response.

Again his knuckles fell.

No response.

Yet a third time, louder, longer, more insistent. All heads turned his way and elves from every part of the workshop stood in curious clusters a cautious distance behind.

Impatient footsteps, the snap of a deadbolt thrown back, the large ornate knob turning. A crack opened in the door and Santa's eye peered out, bloodshot, slightly crazed. Fritz took in the punishing gleam of worklights behind, wild unkempt hair, half a slit of mouth, and the master's yellowed fingernails where his hand gripped the door. "What is it?"

Fritz faltered. "Some of us, sir—"

"I'm busy, Fritz, very busy."

"We're worried that you—"

"Surely this can wait." The fingers vanished. The eye pulled away.

"But Santa—"

"I have no time for this foolishness. Now get back"—(the door closed)—"to work!" The bolt slammed home and Santa's footsteps retreated.

"Please!" Fritz shouted. He raised his fist but opened it and let his hand drop to his side. The walk back to his workbench—amidst murmurs of "Nice try" and "We're with you, Fritz"—was the longest walk the brave little elf had ever taken.

The third of February, just shy of midnight, she was complete. Santa snaked his hands behind her earlobes and toggled her on, pressing his fingertips firmly up toward the brain, above where the jawbone hinged. She blinked, fixed her hazel eyes on him, and spoke.

"Santa," she whispered.

And Santa nearly crumbled.

(Perfect. She's perfect. Get a lot of mileage out of this toy, yes indeedy.)

You're mad, Pan. Totally out of your mind.

(Dare to dream, Santa baby. Dream big. This is gonna work like gangbusters.)

For a few hours, he put her through her paces. She performed beautifully. She bantered easily, laughed at his jokes, did all the things that pleased him in bed.

He grew to despise her.

Her skin was Rachel-soft. Her long blond hair felt utterly convincing. Every curve and angle evoked anew the feelings that had first brought them into being. But she brought out other feelings too, now that Pan took charge more often. She made him feel filthy inside, like snowbanks black with soot.

With a shudder of disgust, he switched her off and withdrew his flaccidity from the manufactured warmth of her lips. His long black fly he buttoned up. Then he closed her mouth, laid her across the makeshift bed, and pondered his next move.

It occurred to him that perhaps he was too close to this thing. Perhaps, because he knew the mechanics of her so well, it spoiled the effect. Things might go smoother if the pleasure she offered weren't a hidden one. If he could somehow integrate her into the community, convincing Anya and the others that she had returned, he might come to love her as he had the real Rachel.

Delusion billowed in his brain. Ten minutes later he swept her inert form up into his arms, left his workroom, and carried her across the commons to the cottage.

Anya was snoring lightly. Santa set his creation down in an old armchair and stripped. He caught a glimpse of himself in the full-length mirror by the bathroom and paused to admire the growing definition of his deltoids, his biceps, his pectorals, the rough tufts of hair upon his chest. The days of roly-poly appeared to be on the wane. Hard inside, hard outside.

(Getting to be quite a hunk, Santa old buddy.)

Yes, but at what price?

(Always one Gloomy Gus in the crowd. What price? Try free, my friend. Free and easy and unfettered and unrestrained. Let's get to it, shall we?)

Peeling back the bedclothes, he maneuvered her beneath them, climbed in beside her, and pulled the blankets up around them. With trembling hands he activated her, heard her take breath, watched her head shift this way and that as one suddenly waking in the night. She gave a soft *mmmmm* and draped a loving hand across his chest. Her left leg moved against his thigh, bending so that her toes flexed at his knee and a delicate crush of curls brushed his hip.

"Rachel?" he spoke softly.

"Ummm?" the thing replied, feigning sleepiness.

His breath caught. Then: "Make love to Anya."

"But she's sleeping." The false note of concern struck him as obscene.

"She loves being wakened that way."

"All right, Santa. If you'll promise to join in." Playfully she kissed his cheek, then shifted off him and turned to snuggle up against Anya.

Anya's sleep was dreamless. Slowly she rose out of it, luxuriating in the lips at her nipple and the fingers working between her thighs. When she opened her eyes, everything she saw told her the impossible. She blinked a question at her husband, but he said nothing. Anya touched Rachel's blond locks, felt Rachel's lips swirl in sensuous circles at her chest. "But how—?"

The golden hair twirled aside and Rachel's beautiful face beamed up at her. Anya gasped in delight. There was an aura of beatitude about her revived lover that nearly undid the horrors of Christmas night. "Not now," Rachel whispered. "Lie back and let me pleasure you."

And Anya obeyed her, running one hand along Rachel's back and taking into the other the hanging fullness of her right breast. The nipple stiffened under her thumb. Then Rachel cast off the covers and kissed her downward. She dipped between Anya's parted thighs, her hands snaking up under Anya's splayed legs to take between thumb and forefinger the hard nubs atop her breasts and worry them toward ecstasy.

Anya grew aware, through the dizzying haze of her bliss, that Santa now towered up behind Rachel, a dark fat shade whose large hands curved and turned in the moonlight to define Rachel's naked hips. His head was bent like a bull goat poised to charge. From the rising tones of Rachel's *mmmmm* and the gaspaceous accelerando of her tongueflick and the shud and judder rhythming through her body, Anya guessed that Santa had sunk his erection deep inside their beloved and was thrilling her clitoris with his skilled fingers.

The splash of moonlight across Anya's belly, Rachel's writhing body, Santa's clamped hand at her hip, Rachel's merciless tonguetip, the rising sounds of Rachel readying to explode, the guttural moans of their musky, humping husband—all these swam deliciously before Anya as she reached down through Rachel's hair and moved her fingers firmly along the flare of her ears, down past the lobes, caressing inward as her orgasm began.

And Rachel died.

Her tongue lay still against Anya's womanhood. Her fingers became as the fingers of a corpse, cold and hard, at

Anya's nipples. Her moans abruptly cut off.

Orgasm and terror seized Anya.

As she climaxed, Anya wriggled out from under her lover, casting the dead woman off in horror and hugging the warmth of her blankets about her. The pleasure that still coursed through her turned her stomach. She felt violated.

"Anya," said Santa, moving to her side of the bed. His erection parted the moonlight.

"What in the name of heaven is that . . . that thing?"

"An experiment. I wanted to—"

She spat in his face. "What sort of filth have you turned into?" she said. "Take that disgusting thing out of here and get rid of it."

"But Anya—"

"Now!" She pulled the blankets around her and buried her face in her pillow. She heard Santa throw on his clothes, muttering darkly. Then the weight lifted off the foot of the bed and he was out the door and down the hall, the front door slamming behind him like the short sharp blast of Gabriel's horn.

What woke Wendy were the muffled duet of sounds Santa and Mommy made being sad together, the sounds Mommy had told her were part of grown-up love.

Wendy loved the night. Being alone in her bed with Snowball and Nightwind curled against her brought her cautiously back into her body.

Darkness helped. Silence did too.

When others were around, she observed as through a telescope the elves' antics, the loving face of Mrs. Claus as she bathed her, the automatic workings of her mouth and throat and innards as someone spooned egg custard or cream of tomato soup into her. But the black comfort of night backed them all off and gave her space to breathe.

Now the sounds of her mother's love drew her further out. She blinked awake and turned her head on the pillow to listen.

Different walls, a greater distance: but the pitch and rhythm thrilled her. Then her mother's high-pitched noises vanished and Santa's low moans choked off. A new voice, Mrs. Claus angry, stabbed through the walls like a mouthless woman shouting.

When the front door slammed, Wendy arose. Peering out the sewing room window, she watched Santa's bent form trudge toward the stable. Something heavy was slung over his shoulder, something wrapped in a floppy blanket. By the time Wendy had dressed, he was halfway across the commons, a shovel propped on his other shoulder. His boots left deep black pits in the snow.

Wendy eased out of her room, tiptoed through the darkness to the front door, and slipped into the night. She was afraid that the squeak of her boots against the snow-packed porch would turn Santa's head or bring on all the lights. But the buildings remained dark and Santa, now a tiny dot near the skating pond, kept on across the moonlit snow. Wendy lost him in the sliver of moon and the evergreens. But his bootprints, large teardrops in the snow, guided her up into the hills.

Santa's path skirted the drip and trickle of a creek to cut abruptly through towering pines and outcroppings of rock. Wendy pressed on. At times, she stopped to listen. When at last she heard not the silence of the forest but what sounded like the short sharp huff and chug of a train surging to life every few seconds, she took more careful steps, slow and silent.

Wendy set a hand against the bark of a thick ash. She made out a dark hut through the trees, and Santa bent to his digging. The flat patch of earth he had chosen was slapped with a blaze of moonlight. Propping the shovel against the hut's outer wall, he dropped the blanketed shape into a shallow hole. Looking more serious than Wendy had ever seen him, he took up the shovel again and began covering his burden.

Then Santa stopped and stood up, peering about. He turned his back to her and his pants loosened and fell about his boots. His legs were muscled and hairy. When he peeled back the dirt-clotted blanket, it seemed to Wendy that the woman he unwrapped, whoever she was, was dead. But then Santa touched her neck and she came at once to life, kissing him and wrapping her legs about his waist, and Wendy had at last a clear view of her mother's face—*her mother's face!*—her lips pressed to Santa's, her long blond hair spilling across the blanket.

Santa knew his mind was diseased. That it had been so at least since the incident in the graveyard when Pan had taken over. And that things had steadily deteriorated since then.

While slogging out to bury the doll, he had cursed Anya many times over. But she was right. This contrivance slung over his shoulder was an outrage, a madman's fantasy. He must have been insane to imagine for one moment its successful incorporation into the community.

By the time he broke open the earth, Santa thought he had regained control.

But then the shape of the doll, the remembered heft of it, its womanliness, its vulnerability to violation, brought the intruder rushing to the fore. Horrified, he fell upon her. He plunged into her, groped for her lobes, felt her surge into a ghastly parody of love beneath him.

No, he thought, *this is wrong, this is vile, I can't be doing this.*

(That's right, pal, disassociate. It's not you, after all. It's me. A convenient fiction, this split between us. I get to wallow like pigs in shit, you get to be as appalled as a priest pulling his pud, and your star hitter slides into home plate.)

The doll writhed under him. *Must gain control, must put you under.*

(Fine, fine. Just let me fuck in peace, okay? Go off somewhere and count daisies, why don't you.)

Then the doll moaned at his mouth and whispered depravities in his ear.

Revulsion seized him. He rebelled. He saw Rachel mocked by his hands, the memory of Rachel dishonored by his selfish acts. It was enough to make the virtue well up in him and topple the intruder.

(Now hold on here—)

Enough! Santa swiped at him with all the goodness in his heart. And in a flush of anger, with more ease than Santa thought possible, the goat-god was gone.

Santa gave a cry of rage and horror, a cry that cut into Wendy's heart. Leaping off her mother, he pulled up his pants, took up the shovel, and began throwing clods of dirt on her.

She tried to rise, looking hurt and confused, saying "What's wrong?" and "Where are we?" and "Stop that!" but Santa brought his shovel down hard upon her head and she fell forward. Then Santa shouted "Die, damn you, die!" and his shovel whipped through the air again and again until she lay still.

The chug of the train began anew, picking up steam, and Wendy's eyes watched a weeping Santa bury her mother under a deep mound of earth. But Wendy herself climbed aboard the warm embracing train and let it take her, one painful puff after another, farther and farther from the hut.

She didn't notice Santa walk away, head bowed, when he was done.

Nor the falling snow that flaked and clumped against her cheeks.

Nor winter's icy fingers moving in to touch her skin, to press upon her skin, to sink beneath her skin.

Not until seven the next morning, when Anya brought in porridge, was Wendy's absence discovered. The cats glared up at her from an empty bed. Ten minutes later, Santa, dressed at last in something other than black, stormed into the elves' quarters. Quickly they were out in force, combing the countryside.

239

Santa cast a wide net of magic time about his lands and took to the air in his sleigh, tightly spiraling out into the woodlands, skimming as close to the treetops as he dared. Two hours into the search, a dreadful thought seized him and he flew at once toward the hut. On the first pass, he caught the bright red of Wendy's down jacket. She was standing, dear God, in a copse of ash trees not a hundred feet from where he had buried the Rachel doll.

When the elves in that sector of Santa's domain saw his sleigh zoom overhead on its way to the commons, they guessed the reason and raced for home. Others heard the rumor shouted through the trees but kept on until the lifting of magic time confirmed it. Then they too broke off the search.

Santa's sleigh stood empty outside the cottage, the reindeer restless and neglected in their traces. Growing clusters of elves crowded about the porch, waiting.

Inside, Anya feverishly tongued Wendy's frostbitten fingers and toes while Santa knelt beside the little girl, chafing her hands and pleading with her not to die. But Wendy opened her eyes just once and made a soughing sound low in her throat. She raised a hand to him. And then, as all mortals do in time, little Wendy slipped down the rabbithole of death and was gone.

Santa wept. He crushed the dead girl to his chest.

Anya stroked her forehead, then turned away, wanting to dole out her grief bit by bit. With two small safety pins, she fastened a black armband around Santa's arm. Then she draped a shawl of black knit about her shoulders.

"It's time we told the others," Anya said, touching her husband's head. He rose and sobbed upon her shoulder. Then he released her and nodded. Turning back to the bed, he lifted Wendy's lifeless body into his arms.

Someone saw movement in the cottage and someone else caught a glimpse of Wendy being carried by Santa. Wasn't certain, he said, but it looked as though she was beaming up at him. Mrs. Claus appeared at the door and rumors of full recovery flew backward through the crowd.

Santa stepped out onto the porch.

And the rumors fell to the snow.

"Our beloved Wendy," he announced, "is dead." He stood there for the longest time and displayed the bald fact of it. No one spoke. No one moved.

Then Anya touched her husband's elbow. He gazed at her, confused. Nodding like one bumped awake in travel, he looked over the crowd toward the gingerbread house to his right. Like a green sea they parted to let him pass. Those in back glimpsed only Santa's bare head moving and Mrs. Claus's white bun bobbing at his far side. But the front ranks saw it all: Wendy, skin white as porcelain, her long auburn hair waving unbraided as they walked, her patent-leather shoes giving a ghastly carefree bounce; Mrs. Claus with one hand at her husband's arm, the other clutching an embroidered handkerchief to her lips; and Santa, face drawn, the color drained from his cheeks.

Wilhelm and Fritz helped bring Wendy's bed away from the far wall of her bedroom and prop it up by her picture window. Then they joined the others outside. The crowd watched Santa lay Wendy down and bend a slow kiss to her forehead. Mrs. Claus knelt beside her, cradling the dead girl's face in one hand and smoothing her hair against the pillow with the other. She folded Wendy's hands across her waist, fussing with her clothing until Santa stepped in and raised his wife.

Then began a parade of elves past Wendy's corpse, a parade that stretched across three days and nights. The line hugged the perimeter of the commons, running the length of the workshop and veering at the stable, then going past Santa's cottage and making a wide bulge out, which twisted back to the elves' quarters, curved round the skating pond, and hugged the hills almost to the gingerbread house again.

Those who, cap in hand, had said one farewell to Wendy wanted to say another. They rejoined the line. Soon the far bulge flattened out, the end of the line met its beginning, and the visitation became continuous.

Midafternoon of the first day, Englebert and Josef retrieved the black armbands from the recycling bins in the workshop and passed them out. Over their protests, they were thrust forward to the front of the line.

At sunrise on the second day, Knecht Rupert disappeared into the woods and returned with an armload of snow crocus. Until Anya called a halt to it, there was a brief incursion into the hills and hordes of elves returned with the purple and yellow flowers clutched to their chests. Soon a blanket of soft petals covered Wendy from chin to ankles, filling her bedroom with fragrance.

And on the following night, Heinrich, heartsick at the happy sound his half-dozen bells made dangling from his half-dozen caps, not to mention the bells jangling at the tips of his dozen slippers—Heinrich closed his fists around the cold silver X-cut spheres, wrenched them with a muffled *clk-clk-clk* off his clothing, and placed them, shiny with candlelight, above Wendy's folded hands on the crocus blossoms. Those that followed saw. And seeing, did likewise. Anya's sewing scissors were passed round the circle of mourners until, to an elf, they held their bells clutched tight in their hands and moved solemnly through the silent night, contributing, when it was their turn, to the shimmering coat of moonlight that silvered and grew about Wendy's corpse.

Such were the rituals that developed in the course of their three-day vigil. But none so simple nor so moving as the ritual approach to the body, the kneeling, the gaze upon Wendy's face, the kiss upon her brow, the reluctant rise, the slow nod to Santa and his wife, and the stoop-shouldered departure.

Mrs. Claus held together well.

But Santa looked worse at each pass.

The first day, he avoided their eyes. He stood there without a word, looking down at Wendy and letting her death assault him full in the face.

The second day, he stared at them as though they were unearthly beings that angered and appalled him. Late afternoon, he seemed like a fat old man with no home, no food, no one to love.

By the third day, the strangeness he had shown of late began to dominate. Above his forehead, twin bulges rose at the hairline as if inch-thick brass rings pressed his flesh outward in torment. And his grief grew, all that day and into the night and on into the dawn that followed.

The odd thing about their visits to Wendy's side was that no one expected them to last more than a few hours, a day at most. They thought their shared grief would peak, that the flow of elves across the threshold would cease and Santa would lead them back to the Chapel to bury Wendy beside her mother. But even as the cloud cover grew darker and more oppressive during those three days, just so did Santa's sorrow feed the communal woe, wrapping them in ever more unbearable layers of woe. Death coaxed them hour by hour—none more so than Santa—toward some awful orgastic brink. But, like a cruel lover, he withheld release, letting the torment build and build in them.

When Santa could stand it no more, he broke from the house with a roar of agony, sending Friedrich and Helmut tumbling into the snow. Anya followed, her mouth red and wet, her tears streaming free. Clouds churned above him like blankets of pitch. Trembling before the weeping elves, Santa ran his fingers through his beard in a gesture of supplication. Then the buttons from chin to belt popped like cherries into the snow and his red suit peeled open under his hands.

"Help me Lord!" he supplicated, in a voice that tried their hearts. Then abruptly, full of gall and grapeshot: "*Show yourself, you god of scum and shit!*" Santa shouted this aloft, rending his garments, tearing off his boots, and hurling his belt away from him like a shiny black snake twisting through the air. Patches of red and puffballs of white filled the air about him and fell in fury to the snow. He stood there naked, his body wavering between two extremes: one was the round soft Santa they had always known; the other had horns and hoofs and hair, eyes that burned, and a shout that hurt their eardrums.

"Heal me, oh my God! *Bully pantheon tyrant, I spit in your face!* Let me vomit my soul into oblivion, let me fling away all trace of Santa, for Santa is a sack full of sin and ashes, a fraud, a fiend, and I must be rid of him or my heart will burst! *I defy you! I hurl figs at you out of my arse! May you choke on them, you slayer of the innocent!*"

And his wife wept and tore her dress and let her hair tumble down, as she knelt naked in the snow beside her husband and opened her hands to the heavens. When he was penitent, she was the sweet-faced old woman they knew; but when Santa raged and shook his fist, she swayed toward him and her body appeared to tuck and smooth and firm and tighten, fir-green tresses flowing down her back, her eyes reflecting—as the moon the sun—her mate's outrage.

Santa's alternating rage and self-loathing washed against the rapt circle of elves. And though they were mightily confused, they too stripped and knelt, joining hands, holding them high. They keened into the clouds, weeping and swaying with the buffet of Santa's words, but giving vent to a delicious defiance when Santa veered that way.

"Dear God," implored Saint Nicholas, "hollow me out, scoop me clean of presumption and lust." But Pan surged forth and bellowed, "*Forget what the wimp says! Physician heal thyself!*"

The split raged in him, first one side of him holding high ground, then the other. "Mercy I pray. Give me, if such be Thy will, the gift of nullity. *Go ahead, blast me! You scared to? Do it! Annihilate the fuck out of me!* The immortal blood pounds in my skull. Naught passes before my eyes but cascades of boys and girls falling, endlessly, into the grave. They die. We live. Dear Lord, the burden crushes. *Get the fuck down here! Get the fuck down here right now! We got things to duke out, you and me, and I'm raring to take you on!*"

Then it happened.

Those in front of Santa saw the shaft of light fall upon him and strip away the rage and pain, salving his visage with soothing. They saw the body come back full and Clausean, the droll little mouth, the twinkling eyes, the rosy cheeks, the bowlful of jelly—all there in the wink of an eye. Gone the horned bellicosity. Gone the defiant fist, the goat-god's savage eyes.

The elves gazed along the bright chute of light, up into the firmament, and their deepest pain fell from them like a mere mood, as the hand of God swept aside a thick batting of cloud: Pure love beamed down upon them from the beatitude that was the Creator's face.

15.

A TIME TO REJOICE

And God carried on many conversations in that hour, as many as there were creatures to hear and be heard. Every deer and elf He took aside, off from the others, addressing his inmost hopes and fears and refreshing his parched soul with the waters of divinity.

And each of them felt singled out and loved for his unique qualities.

And so it was.

But Santa and his wife, kneeling naked in foot-deep snow, He held in thrall. For He wanted all to witness the wonders in store for them.

And when the elves had been newly dressed, inside and out, God unbound the beloved pair and spake thus to them: "Santa, Anya, do you not know how precious to Me is the least mote of your being? Can you not feel within you the pulse of My continuous creation? Does your faith falter so, is your charity turned so inward, are your hopes so blighted by misfortune, that you have grown insensible to truth?"

Santa took Anya's hand in his. "Forgive us, Lord, our unfaith," said he. "Though immortal by Your grace, we share with all humanity feelings of love and loss, the—"

With a flick of His fingernail, God silenced him. Then, though it was barely dawn, He suffered the sun to top the sky, moving like a mole behind the clouds. When it reached its zenith, a precise circle of cumulus irised open. Golden light coned down around Santa and his wife, so that the snow cover melted away in a wide radius about them. Beneath their knees thick grass sprouted. Around them the earth turned verdant. Soft breezes warmed their bodies. Beyond that radius, all remained ice and snow and rapt elves, and a fresh descent of snowflakes, large and clumped and fragile as puffs of dandelion.

Now there rose up four saplings, reaching toward the heavens and thickening as they reached, resolving at last into palm trees stretched thin as Chinese handcuffs and arching out, broad-leafed, thirty feet overhead. Beneath the unclothed couple the earth rumbled and warped. Like bread rising in a rectangular tin, it plumped up and out. And the grass upon this uplifted bed, with its bedposts of palm, split and twisted into moss, luxuriant and spongy to the touch.

Then God stretched forth His hand and beckoned past the gingerbread house into the woods. A faint snap was heard by all. Then they saw the coin, thick and clean and solid gold, rolling through the trees. Out of the hills it came, leaving a deep milled track of snow in its wake. Heinrich split apart to let it pass, and it rolled through him as feathers of snow fell and melted upon it. Onto the bed of moss it rolled, coming to rest against the palm tree at Santa's left. Rachel's face agonized out of sun-gleamed gold.

And God said, "Though you hate the means by which it was made, love the coin. Only love the coin and all will be well."

And He began to withdraw behind the cloud cover.

"But Lord," Santa said, "what will become of the Tooth Fairy?"

Anya chimed in, "And the Easter Bunny?"

Their hearts thrilled to see God smile. And He said unto them, "Leave those two to Me."

"But our dear Wendy—" Santa said.

And God's smile turned enigmatic and He repeated, as He faded, His injunction: "Only love the coin." But they could scarcely hear His last word, and then He was gone.

Fritz was struck heart-sore at God's disappearance. To judge from the groans that rose from his brethren, he was not alone. But the Father, as He had done at their first creation, inlaid

His healing hand and toyed with their emotions, turning wretchedness to regret and, by degrees, to blessedness.

God's departure drew all eyes to Santa's bower, where divine love infused the brilliant cone of light, the bed of moss it fell upon, the gleaming coin upon that bed, and the immortal pair who now laid hands upon that coin.

Santa rolled the golden disc between them and set his hands at ten and two o'clock. Below him were Rachel's nether parts, down to the sculpted soles of her feet. "Only love the coin," he said.

Anya placed her hands between his. "Oh, Claus, she seems in such agony." Rachel's face howled, twisted rivulets of hair streaming past her ears, her neck bent sharply back, her nipples thrust forward. The arms, mere suggestion, resolved into hands taut with vain rebuff.

"Close your eyes, Anya," Santa suggested, doing likewise. "Close your eyes and explore her features with your fingers." His right hand moved to Rachel's rump, tracing the familiar curves of her buttocks. Touching this mockery brought back at once the self-loathing he had felt making love to the doll he had created. But those feelings he now put by, bringing to the fore all his love for the mortal woman. As he caressed her hindquarters—the golden buttocks and the gaping labia of gold between them—their year together flashed before him and he almost fancied that the cold metal warmed beneath his touch.

"It's astonishing," Anya said, "how something made in such an awful way could capture so precisely the softness of Rachel's cheek."

Santa felt Anya's right hand beside his left, still clutching the striated edge of the coin. "Use both hands, Anya. I've got it." Anya's fingers slipped away.

"The breasts are simply breathtaking."

"Are your eyes closed?" he asked.

"Yes."

"Touch your face to hers," Santa said. "Make her suffering

your own." He ran his index and middle fingers past the gold nub of her clitoris to the inverted V of private hair, fine and curly, etched in gold. Then, defying the coin's abrupt angle there, Santa strove to push further.

"Yes, I can feel it. Oh, Claus, she's so cold. And her mouth is stretched so wide."

"Press your mouth to hers, Anya. Lick about her lips. Breathe into her. I think I'm starting to sense some give back here."

"Yes. Her nipples seem to be softening. I can feel the tension leaving her hands."

"Her mouth, Anya. Look to her mouth." The coin edge beneath his left hand no longer curved hard about. When he opened his eyes, he saw that the edges all round were pulling inward little by little. His fingers inched along Rachel's right buttock as though he were a sculptor working tough clay. He felt resistance at his fingernails but pushed on until he rounded her hip. "It's yielding, Anya!"

"Mmmmm."

Now Santa brought his other hand down and pushed his way through gold until he had her other hip, bone-hard at its turn but covered now with something less than metal and more than skin. His belly pressed against her buttocks as he reached around her and, fighting the stubborn metal, felt his fingers meet at her navel. He ran his hands down the flat of her tummy and found a stiff yield of hair and the start of her thighs.

Her toes flexed against his legs.

And something of Santa's flexed too.

He was turned on by joy. His blood pulsed and he laughed as his growing member throbbed with love for the reviving Rachel. Into the golden gape of her vulva he eased, feeling her flesh yield and grow warm at his entry. Closing his eyes again, he leaned forcefully into the upper reaches of the coin, willing his powerful chest down along her back, willing with all his heart that his lips would not crush against flat hard metal but come to rest upon Rachel's soft neck, his beard pressed playfully into endless billows of blond hair.

***

Anya's eyes were shut. Over her head, palm leaves rustled. Tropic breezes caressed her skin. Astonished murmurs came to her from some far-off dream world.

What was reality? Hands pilloried in gold, now flexing, now responding to her hands. Rigid ropes of hair that had begun as faint suggestion, passed into a cabled mass, and now frayed and separated under Anya's touch into fibrous strands. Stiff jaw relaxing shut. A tongue losing its metallic taste, softening at the lick of Anya's tongue. The flutter of golden eyelashes against her cheek.

Anya cried for joy. Into the moving taffy of the coin she sank her eager hands, finding there the dead woman's arms, straight down to the elbows. Her fingers explored the length of the softening torso, the ribs and midriff. Kissing her crimped lips, she sobbed along one gilt cheek.

When Anya opened her eyes, Rachel was kneeling upon the moss, but a Rachel gilded and trembling, twisting her neck like a wild mare. Santa had her by the flanks and was moving within her. "Claus, she's not breathing!"

"Keep loving her," he gasped, eyes on fire. "She's almost free."

Anya lay on her back and brought her lips to Rachel's left nipple. The right one she tormented with thumb and forefinger. Bringing her free hand to Rachel's sex, she found there the glistening gold nub of flesh and danced her fingertips over it.

Rachel arched up and stiffened.

"Anya, we've lost her!"

Rage.

Bound across bedroom.

A sharp intake of breath.

Then pain everywhere, swift and slashing, a pain like the swift chill of a winter's dive.

She had dropped out at once, preferring the peace of the

void. Now something coaxed her back. Hands of love pulled her toward pain.

Suddenly she had returned. The hands, though they adored her, coaxed her into cruelty and raw hurt. Yet she craved their touch. She knew them. Through the agony, she struggled to put faces to them, caught them, lost them, saw a little girl, *her* little girl. Wendy!

There came suddenly a remembrance of stretch and pressure below: Wendy emerging, coated with vernix, milking her, sleeping, raising her head, turning over, crawling, toddling, struggling with words, waving forlornly from a pre-school window, learning to read and being read to, writing notes to Mommy and Daddy and Santa Claus, playing with elves in snow, standing with her mouth ravaged and the Tooth Fairy's arms grappled about her.

Rachel's body throbbed. Though her eyelids raised and lowered, she saw nothing. She needed to exhale, but her lungs burned at the impossible task.

Then the pain zoomed upward and peaked. Riding her scream, it paid out bit by bit until a divine point of inflection twisted it up into pure pleasure. And death tumbled away empty-fisted. A gush of immortality shot through her and held at her center.

Through her howls, she heard sobs upon her throat. Anya's sobs. Rachel's vision cleared and there was Anya's radiant face, and upon her shoulders Santa's kisses, and in her quim Santa's cock. And Anya was sobbing "You've come back to us, you've come back" over and over again. Rachel hugged the dear soul and kissed her, the memories flooding into her now.

Then Santa, disengaging, fell to the moss and clipped and cuddled her like a man starved for love.

A surge of green, shrieking with delight, descended upon them and a sweep of tiny hands lifted them into the air.

***

Pandemonium broke out in the commons.

Fritz dove in with the others to touch the trio of lovers, to hoist them high and fling from his throat the joy that had built up as he watched God's miracle unfold. Green caps, skyrocketed above, were caught in midfall and catapulted back into the sky.

Then someone dashed into Santa's cottage and brought out three robes, red for Santa, green for Anya, and blue for Rachel. They put them on and stood beneath the palm trees, trading hug after hug with the elves until they felt their spines would never again straighten for stooping.

But the sun burrowed back down to the horizon and the clouds sealed up again. Moss became grass. The palm trees shrank into the earth. Fritz expected snow to reflocculate in the circle but that didn't happen. Even so, the ground seemed hungry for snowfall.

Then Fritz saw Rachel, radiant in immortality, turn toward the gingerbread house. In the midst of recinching her robe, her fingers froze. Fritz, tugging at Gregor's sleeve, nodded discreetly in her direction.

The crowd fell silent.

Rachel sat on the edge of Wendy's bed, resting a hand upon her daughter's folded hands.

"How did it happen?" she asked.

Santa told her. She was spared the gruesome details of her late husband's resurrection. Santa felt it prudent as well to omit any mention of the Rachel doll, lest acts he had committed out of desperation be misconstrued.

As he spoke, her eyes remained fixed on Wendy. Santa and Anya glanced from mother and daughter to the drawn faces outside the picture window. New snow fell like somnolent feathers. It looked like midnight outside.

Rachel bent to her daughter and kissed her cheeks.

They were cold.

Bloodless as marble.

She pressed her lips to Wendy's lips. Held them there, remembering. Sobbed without breaking the seal, keening softly into Wendy's mouth. Her tears fell warm upon the little girl's face.

A jinglebell clattered to the carpet. Then another, and another.

Anya gasped.

Wendy's right hand fell to her side, sending a cascade of bells jangling to the floor.

Rachel, disbelieving, brought a hand to her mouth. Wendy's cheeks flushed out, turning from waxy white to carnation pink and at last to full fleshtones. She yawned and stretched, setting off splashes of tintinnabulation.

She blinked. "Mommy, why's it so noisy in here?" she asked.

Then Rachel hugged her fiercely and kissed her over and over, despite Wendy's protest. So tight were mother and daughter intertwined that Santa and Anya embraced them as a unit, kissing ear or cheek or wave of hair.

Wendy was smothered in bodies. Three pairs of feet waltzed her about the bedroom, skating gingerly over a floorful of jinglebells. Snowball and Nightwind, perched on the sill of the picture window, looked absolutely appalled.

In the commons, ecstatic elves leaped and pranced and hugged one another silly. Fritz shouted, "Look, she's got her teeth back!" but only Gregor, hugging him and breaking into an atypical grin, heard what he said.

The snowfall stopped and the black clouds turned pure white and dispersed and the fat round godlike flaring sun burst apart over all eternity, scattering rays of joy and sunshine everywhere.

Santa, in close consultation with his Maker, proposed to wed his wives in the Chapel on Valentine's Day, God presiding. Anya and Rachel willingly accepted and Wendy clapped her hands.

The week leading up to the ceremony saw everyone in a frenzy of activity. With Wendy's help, Rachel pieced together two beautiful white-lace wedding gowns and a powder-blue bridesmaid's dress. Anya gave the dollhouse contingent a crash course in clothing construction. Under her direction, they turned their skilled hands to the manufacture of tuxedos: a Pavarotti-sized red one for the groom and hundreds and hundreds of tiny green ones for the guests. To Fritz fell the preparations for the wedding feast, and none could recall in sheer cornucopial splendor any meal to match it. Knecht Rupert, with Johann and Gustav taking turns at the bellows, practiced the pump organ way off in the woods and when the happy day arrived, he swung to and fro upon his bench beside the Altar, note-perfect and in harmony with the world.

"Are we really immortal now, Mommy?" asked Wendy, stroking Nightwind as Rachel fastened a lace collar to Anya's dress.

"Yes, dear. No one can ever harm us again."

"And we'll never die again?"

"That's right, honey." She pulled Wendy close and kissed her forehead. "Do me a favor and bring me my sewing basket. Right behind you on the bookshelf. We have lots to do before tomorrow."

And tomorrow dawned pure and brilliant. The Chapel was flooded with winter sunlight. Two towering oak trees bent in toward one another, and from them a natural aisle led outward. Down that aisle the wedding party (which is to say everyone) marched, belting out a wedding song that Fritz and Gregor had cobbled together while preparing garnishes in Anya's kitchen. It was long on enthusiasm, their song, if short on merit, and its first verse went thus:

> Here come the brides,
> A day past the ides;
> Here comes their hubby,
> All jolly and chubby.

To nature's bowers
'Midst hearts and flowers
We march and dance and sing;
We'll see them wedded
And stripped and bedded.
We wish them everything.

When at last they attained the Chapel, the Perfect Light of God hovered and gleamed before the great oaks at the end of the aisle, just in front of the long flat rock of the Altar. Anya and Rachel paced hand in hand between blocks of bearded ecstatic elves, Wendy following after, clutching a nosegay and beaming with pride. Behind them came Santa, looking serenely debonair and stifling a belly laugh; and Fritz, his best man.

Fritz stood to Santa's left. To Santa's right stood Anya, then Rachel, and Wendy breaking into a full-toothed grin beside her mother. Someone tapped Knecht Rupert on the shoulder, and he came out of an inspired improvisation on the march theme and brought it to a sweeping finish on the tonic, tearing his hands away at last so that the final chord's thrilling affirmation echoed through the trees.

Now the Light transformed. And God the Father stood revealed before them, white of robe, white of beard, twice Santa's height and holding an open book in His hands.

"Dearly beloved," He said, "we are gathered together in this beautiful setting to join three blessed souls in wedlock.

"Some souls might wonder at this, saying one wife to one husband is God's way. But I say unto you (and who better should know), let threesomes and more flourish upon this planet. Let men and women seek for love where they may, and let them unloose the grasping hand of jealousy, rejoicing instead in the righteous unfolding of a spouse's holy lust. For lust built upon love and caring is divine lust; and wedlock, like all useful locks, must at times be unlocked to welcome in beloved friends.

"My servant Martin Luther, though guilt-ridden to a fault, glimpsed something of the truth when he approved the bigamy of Philip, Landgrave of Hesse. But he closed himself off.

"My servants John Humphrey Noyes and Brigham Young reached beyond monogamy for a time. But they too closed themselves off—the Oneidan, by fishing in the murky waters of stirpiculture and copulation by committee; the Mormon, by prizing procreation over pleasure, by denying women their natural urges toward multiplicity, and by rousing the nosy-parker anxieties of an America in the throes of a Victorian intolerance from which it has yet to recover.

"Adam himself, at the beginning of time, could have enjoyed Lilith as well as Eve. But he imposed a duality upon them, projecting his own poor judgment onto Me and casting aside the 'wicked' wife in favor of the 'good.' Foolish one! He chose exclusion in a universe I created expressly to favor inclusion. Adam, the first man, closed himself off.

"But My dearly sainted Nicholas and his dear saintly wife Anya now open themselves to embrace and clasp to their hearts My beloved Rachel. She is to serve as their helpmate and they as hers and one another's. I say that it is good, good beyond exceeding good. Henceforth, let the word go forth and let it be known and celebrated through all the world that humankind was shaped for polyfidelity, that elves and mortals and all creatures great and small are polymorphously perverse, and that from this time polygamous and polyandrous urges shall be heeded and revered. No more shall husband or wife skulk in shame to the bed of a second beloved, but wife or husband shall with open arms embrace the new and worthy lover, even as Anya now embraces Santa's Rachel. For just as your God is a triune God, so shall trinitarian love flourish on this planet."

Anya stole a glance across Santa's belly at Fritz. He had never looked happier, and it did Anya's heart good to see him so. Then she turned the other way and cast an admiring eye upon her new bride. It felt funny—and wonderful—to be taking a wife, to be taking this wife. She thrilled to see Rachel standing there, whole and lovely, her hand resting on Wendy's shoulder.

God turned to Fritz. "You bear the rings?"

Fritz nodded serenely. He fetched an oblong jewelry box from his coat pocket and opened it to reveal six gold bands, holding them up proudly for all to see. Hermann the goldsmith, standing tall and thin-faced in the third row, blushed furiously and ran a giddy hand in circles over his face.

Then God led them through the exchange of rings and vows. Santa kissed Rachel, and Rachel kissed Anya, and Anya kissed Santa. God laid His hand upon each of them in turn, blessing them. Then He did likewise to Wendy—who gasped at the sheer ecstasy of it—and said, "Blessed be Wendy, type of all good children everywhere. She shall brighten the hearts of all who know her and be a light henceforth unto the children of the world."

He raised His eyes out over the crowd, back toward the distant commons. And all knew, without knowing what, that another miracle awaited them at home, something that involved Wendy.

But Wendy, God's hand resting upon her head, saw clearly the new life He had brought into being. She knew also what her mission was to be, and how God's gift fit into it. And, hearing His words issue from His mouth in every human tongue, Wendy was instantly fluent in them all, knowing that she would eventually need each of them.

Then God stretched His arms over the crowd and spoke the benediction. "Go now all ye who are here assembled. Love thyself; love one another; love this world and those who dwell therein. Live well, make toys, and be at peace, now and forevermore. Amen."

God vanished back into Everything, where He had always been, and universal hugging and kissing filled the Chapel. A figure in red and two in white were swirled and spun through a roiling mass of green, while over the elftops, buoyed by crafty hands, rode a giggling, grinning, happy-as-could-be Wendy, shouting out "Happy Valentine's Day!" in all the languages of the world.

***

If, during the festivities that followed in and about the commons, a few elves here and there went missing, neither Santa nor his wives took any notice of it. So their surprise was indeed genuine when, as things wound down, the elves raised them up and ran with them into the woods.

If Santa felt any misgiving about the direction they took, he was too drunk with happiness to reveal it. When they reached the hut which had once concealed his trysts with the Tooth Fairy, he relaxed into delight and joined his brides in admiration for what he saw.

For the elves had completely made the place over. Karlheinz and Max had laid toothsome little Thea to rest beside Santa's buried Rachel doll; her bed had been broken up and burned. The ashwood four-poster was gone too, as was every scrap of quilting and fur, all the blankets and bedding, every remembrance of that sorry time of grasping lust.

New skylights peeled back the darkness. A fire blazed upon the hearth and stacks of fresh-cut pinewood climbed halfway up the stone wall. A kitchen nook and a bath had been added, and a large bed spoke boldly from one wall. It had room and to spare for marital gymnastics, but it also felt perfect for napping or lazing upon.

After a flurry of thanks and good wishes, the elves discreetly withdrew. And here the three newlyweds spent untold months of magic time—more than two days of normal time—in honeymoon retreat.

Upon their return, Rachel resettled herself and her daughter in Santa's cottage, and she and Anya moved their sewing and craftwork into the gingerbread house. She helped Anya manage the domestic side of things at the North Pole. She introduced the more technically minded elves to the joys of computing and helped design tasteful toys that took advantage of electronic smarts. She delighted too in teaching Santa's helpers, most of whom were stone-cold illiterate, to read. Many were the times that an excited student would rush up to her, bursting to share some choice passage he had found in the book he held open before her.

And what of Wendy? Of the acts she had witnessed at the hut, Santa was relieved to find she had no memory; but he spoke to her, just in case, of having missed her mother so much that he had done many foolish and much regretted deeds. During the week of her parents' honeymoon, Wendy spent most of her time at the stable. For when they had returned from the Chapel, God's new gift poked its head over the half-door and watched wide-eyed their return.

As a Shetland is to an Arabian, so was this reindeer to the least of Santa's team. She had a delicate filigree of antlers atop her head and a nose that glowed green as a traffic light through night fog. Her fur was milk-white and fine, her eyes an engaging shade of gray. At first Wendy called her Ivory, but later, when Santa read to her out of Ovid, Ivory became Galatea. "Galatea means white as milk in Greek, Daddy," she explained to a bemused Santa. "Besides, I think Galatea the green-nosed reindeer sounds better than Ivory the green-nosed reindeer, don't you?"

Santa laughed and said he did.

When Wendy shared her mission with Gregor, he fashioned a miniature sleigh for her, modeled on her stepfather's. Every Christmas Eve thereafter, she hitched up Galatea and followed Santa into the sky. Then, splitting off from him, she went one by one to the homes of children on her list. For Santa had taught her how to turn her gaze to the world, watching boys and girls carve out their lives, second by second, from the limitless possibilities before them. And each year, she chose a hundred who were very well behaved (but not of course in a priggish sort of way) or who tended toward kindheartedness but needed one small miracle to tip the scales. These she kissed awake and led by the hand to her sleigh. Through the night sky they sailed, sharing the wonders of the world which passed below.

The children she so honored woke on Christmas morning with the certainty that something wonderful (but what it was they could not say) had happened to them, that they had been blest beyond measure. It gave thereafter a focus to their lives; they developed low-voiced but persistent obsessions, one in music, another in medicine, this one in public service, that one in private enterprise. And each excelled and carried an aura about him or her, an aura of hope and goodwill that inspired everyone they touched and, when at last their lives ended, brought masses of grief-stricken mourners to their graves.

Wendy reserved a special time for Mrs. Fredericks, whom she visited each year until the old woman died, sitting on her lap and telling her teary-eyed listener of the wonders of living at the North Pole. After her death, Wendy placed a snow crocus upon her grave each Christmas Eve, missing her to tears.

The rest of the year, she helped inspire the elves. She served as a focus-group-of-one for new toy ideas and tested every prototype. Praise came quickly to her lips, and she learned to soften her criticisms with suggestions for improvement. She came to know all the workers, their quirks and foibles, their strengths at the workbench and their weaknesses, the secret gifts she could spring on them to brighten their faces. And she took it upon herself to learn what she could about every aspect of Santa's operation: she dabbled in wood and clay and metals, in fabrics and typography and printed circuitry, in dolls and board games and stuffed animals; she learned the ways of wrenches and hammers, looms and presses, lathes and sanders and bandsaws; and for a time she disappeared into the incestuous circle of clockmakers, emerging weeks later with a new cuckoo clock of her own design.

But the time Wendy loved best was night time. For Santa Claus would lift her onto his generous lap in the big armchair, and she would watch her mommies rock and knit by the fire and listen to her daddy's booming voice give life to the story he held before them.

Santa loved those times too.

The coming of Rachel and Wendy had turned him into a family man. He swore off long nights at the workshop, excepting only the December crunch; but even that he did his best to minimize by using the tools Rachel introduced him to: Gantt charts and PERTs and Hoshins, top-down design and prototyping, focus groups and usability testing and post mortems, TQC and QFD and FLURPS, along with huge doses of TLC, her own addition to the acronymic broth of best business practices.

He took Wendy and his wives for long walks in the woods, sometimes together, sometimes one at a time. He pitched in with the cooking and cleaning. He stretched out on the rug before the fire and played card games with Wendy or wrestled playfully with Snowball and Nightwind. As close as he had been to the children before, he felt umpteenfold closer having Wendy to watch and talk with and love. His Christmas deliveries became more precious to him, and he thanked God every day for bringing her into his life.

His elves became as sons and brothers to him. He gave them more free time and often joined them when they pulled Wendy on her sled. He even laced up iceskates (something he hadn't done for centuries) and joined in the post-Christmas ice-a-thon on the skating pond. It soon became a tradition, at that event's climax, to link arms, speedskate round and round faster and faster, and whip Santa off—his loud booming whoops of jollity filling the snow-flecked air—into the commons, where he would roll and tumble and come up halfway to the cottage, staggering like a drunken snowman.

But Santa's favorite moments were those he shared with Anya and Rachel in the intimate heartspace of the marriage bed. He loved his wives, especially when the three of them came together like a swirl of wind and fire under the down comforter.

Even now, as you read these words, the jolly old elf lies delirious beneath them, enjoying the give and take of their favorite triadic practice, 969. The bedclothes have been flung to the floor and moonlight spills boldly across their sheets. Anya and Rachel murmur words of love to Santa and to one another. From the waist down, his body lies in normal time, his thighs spread wide to welcome the kisses of his wives, his sex tight and hard and veined in silver beneath their fingers. Above, he moves through magic time, the better to serve and observe them.

Part of the time, Santa's head rests pillowed between two sets of feet. Rachel's right leg warms the heartside of his torso, Anya's left the other. He contemplates with holy rapture the curves and folds of their loins. His fingers work their flesh like a friar telling his beads. When his head flutters in and out of magic time, their bodies seem to strobe in the steady light of the moon. He feels as if he's flying through the night. Their flanks rock to the rhythm of his hands like the soft white haunches of Donner and Blitzen twitching under the gentle slap of leather across their backs. Their long beautiful bodies move like his team in harness, supple, articulate. Down below, where Lucifer's gleam might light up the night sky, the glistening blood-purple tip of his penis emerges from the mouth of this wife or that. Rachel favors tight lips and the suck and swirl of salivation. Anya, going wider and deeper, brings her tongue into it. Together, they give him heaven.

And when his head is not pillowed and marveling, he does his best to return the favor. Bifurcating at the waist, he arcs beneath them, giving each wife in turn his full attention. He hums as he licks, something they've told him excites them immensely.

Moving in and out of magic time, Santa's brain plays strange games. He sees Superman standing behind a seated Clark Kent in his Daily Planet office, fooling Lois Lane by changing clothes so fast she can't detect the flicker. Santa watches him repeat the trick with his new now-savvy bride at the Fortress of Solitude, splitting into two, then four, then as many ardent supermen as he can sustain without distracting himself, crowding around his wide-eyed Lois and loving her with the multiplicity of his manhood.

Had Santa a hand free, he would slap his forehead for not having the idea sooner. Time enough for that, he tells himself; and time enough for Anya and Rachel, if they like, to please him in the same way. He imagines them riding him everywhere in blurred overlap, opening to him like blooms in time-lapse photography the infinite variety of their love. Just picturing it makes Santa's pillowed head burst apart at the beard and split the night with a rousing *ho-ho-ho*. His delight spills into the hum of his cunnilingus. That familiar feeling starts to rise in him like the unspeakable wonder of life itself, and he readies himself to give his beloved women the whitest Christmas they have ever enjoyed.

God bless us, comes his last coherent thought before sweet oblivion claims him. God bless us every one!

EPILOGUE
TOOTH AND CLAW

*Fear not the flesh nor love it. If you fear it, it will gain
mastery over you. If you love it, it will swallow and
paralyze you.*
　　　　—the Gospel of Philip

*Subduction leads inevitably to orogeny. And the earth
moves.*
　　　　—anonymous

Underground. Valentine's Day. For weeks, anxiety unrelenting had shattered the Easter Bunny's nerves. He had hopped about his room, sniffing aimlessly at the dirt, staring for hours at a bent piece of straw. Once he had peeked in at Petunia, only to pull back in disgust. He hadn't dared venture into the rest of his domain.

Upon waking that morning, however, anxiety had given way to calm. It was a calm as deep as sadness. He left his room at last but kept to the confines of the burrow. Everything, down to his hens and the blush-colored eggs they laid, seemed glazed with a patina of resignation and regret. He knew what was coming and welcomed it.

When God's footsteps first shook the earth, he went to his room, found its precise centerpoint, and hunkered down with as much humility as he could muster. Trees toppled. God's approaching tread matched the steady dead-march of his heart.

The Easter Bunny glanced up at the domed roof. A dark crack opened along the arc of the outer wall. Then the roof lifted from the burrow like an earthen shield. He blinked away a thin trickle of dirt that fell as the roof rose and daylight flooded in. Shafts of sun streaked through settling dust. But what captured his eye was the towering figure of God the Father, Who propped the giant disc of earth against an oak tree and, turning His gaze on him, sadly shook His head. "What, Mister Ophion, am I to do with you?"

"I beg your—?"

"This I believe is yours." God gestured north and the Easter Bunny could see dried egg remains lift from a distant mirror, defy space and time, and come together at God's fingertips like a jellybean. God stooped and laid it at the Easter Bunny's feet. "To voyeurism, which I shut My eyes to, you have added rape, an act intolerable in mortal men, let alone in an immortal entrusted with spreading happiness on the anniversary of My Son's resurrection."

"But I can expl—"

"Further, you have seen fit to lend aid and comfort to the Tooth Fairy. Sinning by omission, you have helped her mutilate and torment a child, devour that child's mother before her eyes, and dishonor her father's corpse."

"It was her fault. The Tooth Fairy. She forced me into it."

The tip of God's index finger stopped his lips. It stung like iodine on a cut. "No more lies, Mister Ophion, Mister Boreas, Mister North Wind. Pause a moment. Pause and think about your misdeeds. Then you may confess your sins and beg, if you will, for mercy."

His lips were free again.

God sat upon the lip of earth, His feet resting inside the burrow near where Santa Claus had burst in. The Easter Bunny began to ask Him why He had called him such peculiar names, but the stern look in the Father's eyes stopped him.

He paused. He pondered. One by one, he named his sins and humbly begged God's pardon for them. Then he raised his head. "But it's just not fair. Really it isn't."

"What's not fair, My beloved?"

The sweetness in God's voice broke his heart, but he went on. "When You created me, Lord, You chose to make me a rabbit. If You'd only kept to scale—please forgive my presumption—I might have mated with mortal rabbits and been content. Instead, You made me an order of magnitude larger than normal. Even that wouldn't be a problem if I had a mate, a real Petunia just my size to love and honor and fill with seed. Instead I roam the world alone. And, dear Lord, as You well know, my sex drive, like everything else about me, is ten times that of a normal rabbit's. Lately, I fear, it has overwhelmed my better judgment."

"Go on."

"And also, well," he looked away, embarrassed, "this may sound funny, but I've had the feeling lately that You may have made me forget things about myself, that there's more to my past than You've let on, that maybe I—dear God forgive me, it seems so absurd now that You're here—that maybe *I* was the true creator of the world way back when and somehow You snatched that position from me."

"Interesting. Very interesting."

"Of course it's all nonsense. I see that now. You needn't say a word about it. But this mate thing, oh dear Father, it's that that drives me buggy."

God reached down and lifted the Easter Bunny into His lap. The folds of His robe felt like a soft patch of pure heaven against his underbelly. The hand that stroked him made tears of joy start in his eyes. "I understand," said God. "And I see how to make things right."

Yes! thought the Easter Bunny. God's going to bring my Petunia to life, just like Pinocchio. Or He'll scrap her and fashion from His infinite love a fresh new mate, white and soft and fluffy, always eager for me to top her. Or maybe He'll fill the burrow with dozens of does. Hell, I can handle scores of the twitchy-tailed beauties. Nay, hundred, thousands. Bring them on. Let legions of lovers smother me in kissyfur.

But God's hand covered his eyes and at once he saw straight back to the dawn of creation. "All begins in Chaos," said God. "But soon the goddess Eurynome rises out of it like naked love, full-thighed, full-breasted, her hair tumbling in wanton ringlets about her shoulders. She tries to rest her feet but finds nothing save herself and Chaos. Look there, her long lithe hands part sky and sea. She dances lonely upon the waves."

The Easter Bunny thumped against God's palm, snared by the image's fleshy perfection. "And there you are, the north wind she stirs up as she moves. She wheels about and snatches you up in her hands, rubbing you thick and tight until, behold, you become the serpent Ophion. See, she holds you close, dancing, ever dancing. Coiling about her limbs, you copulate with her."

He saw it all and remembered, even as God spoke it. He saw Eurynome, goddess of all things, turn herself into a dove, brood upon the waves, lay the universal egg. He saw himself coil sevenfold about the egg and hatch it and stare in amazement as all of creation, all the stars and planets, everything upon the earth and under the sea and in the firmament, leapt forth and took its place, pushing Chaos all atumble into oblivion. He saw too how it had gone bad: his boast that he alone had created all things, the heel she planted upon his head, the loss of his fangs, and his banishment to the dark places beneath the earth.

Now God brought the vision forward to the point of his rebirth as the Easter Bunny. The distant brooding of innumerable hens. The sound of his Creator's voice instructing him, his leaps into the air—all of it as he had always remembered it. But then there befell a memory splice: God paused in the past, as He had never done before, and looked about the burrow, His eyes full of prescience. He stretched out His hand, set a finger between the Easter Bunny's back legs, and—like a cartoonist erasing a smudge—massaged away the genitals, leaving only one small hole to pee with. Then the splice was over, and it wasn't a splice at all but the Easter Bunny's sole memory of his creation.

God lifted His hand from His creature's eyes and set him down in the burrow. "Does that clear up our little problem?"

"Yes," he said, confused. He couldn't begin to guess what problem the Father was talking about.

"Good," said God. "By the way, you've been doing a wonderful job with your Easter deliveries and a wonderful job managing things here. Keep up the good work."

Exhilaration filled his heart. "I do it all," he said, "to please You and to make the children happy."

"Bless you, My beloved," said God, and blest he felt. "Now be at peace. It's time I paid a visit to another of My servants, one not so contrite and cooperative, I fear, as you have been."

The Easter Bunny knew He was talking about the Tooth Fairy, though he had no idea how he knew. But he beamed up at the Lord and watched the roof close out the sunshine and the crack reseal itself, wondering what on earth the thing made of pellets over wire mesh was doing in the room next to his. When he had hauled it outside, crushed it with heavy stones, and skritched dirt over it, he headed back to the laying house to see how things were going with the hens.

Easter was little more than a month away and he was determined it would be the best Easter ever.

Rain pelted the Tooth Fairy's face.

The storm, at its height, billowed out of control. Lucifer

lay exhausted on the beach. His antlers blushed pale pink from the abuse he had suffered since Christmas. Gripping his penis, she waited for signs of renewal.

As the wind whipped up her hair, the teeth of her necklace rattled upon her breasts. She forced her eyelids not to blink. Sheets of rain beat against the whites of her eyes and washed across her irises, flowing like sorrow down her cheeks. Squatting beside the blasted cedar, she awaited with relish the final showdown.

Where wails of typhoon fury had filled her ears, there now abruptly sounded the *Sanctus Dominus!* of angel choirs. The roiling sky turned blue and filled with billows. Angel faces beamed upon them, psalms of heavenly praise blasting in triumph from their throats.

Then God parted the clouds, sitting in state upon His golden throne, and glowered down at her. Lucifer's feeble head rose from the sand to stare in wonder. Letting go of his limp lovehandle, she stood defiant before the Lord.

"Call off your minions!" she shouted. "You're not about to overwhelm *me* with your heavenly bullshit!"

A flick of God's hand and the angels vanished. Pointing at Lucifer, He gestured north. Instantly, the reindeer sprang into the air and flew off, his antlers as bright, his gait as sure, as ever.

"Santa and I had a bargain—!" she protested.

"Do you want to continue to be the Tooth Fairy?" He asked quietly, resting His hands upon His throne and fixing her with His worst glower.

"Listen, just cut the—"

"Do you want to continue to be the Tooth Fairy?" If anything, the question came at her lower and more simply inflected than before. It chilled her to the marrow.

"Fuck you, all right? All right? You and the other shitheads of this world want to call me the Tooth Fairy, that's your lookout. My real name, as you well know, is Adrasteia. If I harvest molars and bicuspids and canines, it's because I damn well choose to."

"It's the position I gave you."

"Sure, okay sure, I pretended to kowtow to you back then.

But I never lost myself. I never forgot who I was. An ash nymph I was from the beginning—proud sister to the Furies, born from the blood spilled when Kronos castrated Ouranos—and an ash nymph I remain. That gives me an integrity that Santa Claus and the Easter Bunny and you, you big blowhard, lost long ago."

"Let's not stray from the point. You've engaged in practices which—"

"And what makes you so high and mighty? Where do you get off sitting in judgment? You trying to come on like some *deus ex machina* and bring me to heel, you holier-than-thou son of a bitch?"

"I warn you. Don't provoke Me."

Something flared about His head. The sharp sting of ozone filled her nostrils. "You remember who you used to be, don't you?" she taunted. "When your mother Rhea gave birth to you and spirited you away from your child-eating father, your care fell to me and my sister Io and the goat-nymph Amaltheia, whose milk you shared with baby Pan and from whose horn you fashioned Cornucopia, the horn of plenty. Don't you recall how I pressed your infant lips to these nipples and let the maddening suck of your gums moisten me below?"

"You will cease this idle—"

"How I toyed with your baby penis, how I licked you down there and made you break out in a smile provoked by something other than gas? And when you matured beyond boyhood, how all three of us taught you lust? Look here, little fellow, long before you violated your mother and went on your libidinous rampage through the likes of Leda and Io and Europa, I was your first lover as well as the nurse of your babyhood. But when the old ways died and the Christers came in, you caved in with the rest of them, took on the Grand Persona they demanded of you, and forgot your true godhood, your triumph over Kronos, forgot, by God, that you were none other than almighty Zeus!"

"Enough!" He said. His fingers fastened upon her throat, though He remained where He was. "If Zeus you crave, foolish nymph, then Zeus you shall have!"

As He rose to His feet, the Tooth Fairy felt His other hand pin her to the gritty sand and splay her legs wide. The placidity of God's visage split apart and out peered the face of old: Zeus's face, with its full salt-and-pepper beard, its wild corona of curly hair, and its ruddy-cheeked rage.

His white robe he tore asunder. Beneath it lay the old armor it thrilled her to see. His body was muscled and hairy where it emerged from his chiton. Medallions and weapons hung about him everywhere.

Without looking away from her, Zeus shot a hand into the heavens and filled his fist with fire. Heavy bolts of burning light into the swollen wound of her womanhood he hurled. Thirteen times the fire struck. Thirteen times it singed her flesh, burrowing deep inside her womb.

"You shall leave Santa Claus and Anya and Rachel and Wendy and those they love forever in peace. From this day forth, the North Pole is off limits to you.

"You shall avoid the Easter Bunny at all costs. He has been reformed.

"Never again shall you dare to harm one hair on a child's head. The mere thought of doing so I disallow.

"These my words you shall heed, or I swear by the God I have become, I will return and annihilate you. Slowly. The pain I have visited upon you now shall be, I promise you, as the tenth part of a fleabite when set against the torments I shall mete out on that day!"

Then he vanished from the sky. The sizzle of her flesh filled her nostrils. Her belly was one flaring pit of pain. Healing, when it came, was horrendous and slow. Still, she thought, she would survive it. She would endure the expulsion of mortal hurts and let immortality make her whole again.

A smile, despite her agony, appeared on her lips.

But then something caught inside her, a thing of claws and scales. Her smile rounded into a howl. Her screams split the sky. Through pain immense, she watched her belly stretch and swell like some demon had flexed his thorned fist deep inside her womb. Then, when her flayed insides hung in ribbons and the ribbons frayed to crimson fuzz, he began to pull his invisible arm out of her, the claws delving deep red furrows in the blistered flesh of her birth canal.

But what emerged from the bubbling froth was far worse than a demon's hand. It was squat and fat, her infant, and when its girth stuck halfway and her straining labia refused to stretch further, it blinked its bloody eyes at her. "Muzzer," it buzzed with murderous hate. Then it twisted about, teeth flashing like razors, and episiotomized her perineum all the way to her anus and beyond. The fat thing tumbled out, dragged its bloody afterbirth down to where the breakers thudded in, and battened on it.

Thank God that's over, she thought, lying spent and sweaty on the beach. But then, as one who having vomited feels an instant of well-being but is immediately seized by renewed wrack, she suffered the thrust of the giant's fist again into the bleeding wreckage of her womb. Her belly ballooned up, as did her agony, redoubling the torment that had gone before.

There on the beach beneath a slate-gray sky, the Tooth Fairy gave birth to thirteen impossible imps, each fatter and uglier than the one before. Thirteen times her belly ballooned. Thirteen times her vulva blurted out a brat. Each dropped goblin took longer than the one before, stretching torment beyond itself. Many times she screamed for death to take her.

Deaf ears.

When the last one spilled out, the universe was one solid throb. Clotted sand stretched from her sex to the sea. From belly to thighs, she was nothing but bruise and blood. Her lungs hurt from howling.

Then they attacked her breasts. One fat whelp waddled up, sniffed at her torso, and, having found his prize, put two three-fingered hands around her right breast and opened his head about her nipple. His suck staggered her. A second one dragged himself up from the waves and, seeing what his brother was about, took a pull at her left teat. One by one, the others crowded around and reached their heads in, snuffling at the blue-veined bulges that held the stores of milk they craved. "Wait your turn," she said, and three heads lifted as one and glared.

Then the first one bit her. She whacked him on his large flat head and said, "No!" His eyes rolled toward her. He growled over his meal and bit into her so hard that rivulets of milky blood trickled down the sides of her breast. A tongue came out of the crowd and licked up the spill. Its owner, baring his teeth, sank them into her, seeking milk ducts in the most direct way he could. Then thirteen heads tore into her and made mincemeat of her chest, finding the lactation they demanded in the bloody ruins of her breasts.

Her hands tore helplessly at their hunched backs as they fed. But eventually she gave it up, embracing the pain as her lot. For her baker's dozen bastards she even felt a mother's love. No question they were wicked and selfish and nearly impossible to control. But they were hers. Even through the agony of birth and first feeding, part of her understood what wonders she could work with them.

And that's what she did.

Her nights she spent as usual going from bed to bed collecting teeth and leaving coins; and despite her every intent, her thoughts turned benign in those bedrooms and left her furious afterward. But the rest of the time she spent with her brood, suffering anew their feeding frenzies and then, as her bloody chest healed, sitting them down on the shore and filling their eager hearts with hatred.

Hatred of God.

Hatred of Santa Claus and his kiss-ass crowd of sycophants.

Hatred of mortals of every stripe, especially children.

She mapped out a mission for them and for ten months drilled every detail into their heads. She made little Santa suits for them, taught them world geography, gave them lessons in flight and magic time, showed them how to scan the earth for likely victims.

They learned fast, her brood, demonstrating a marked precocity for all things vengeful. When Christmas was but two weeks away, she sent them out, one each day. Her firstborn went first, Gronk of the piercing eye and the tight fist. He slouched and slavered down to the sea, then lifted off and bumblebee'd eastward away from his brothers' envious taunts. They turned then and savaged her for milk. But she only grimaced, looking ahead to Christmas Day when they'd be gone for twenty-four hours, wreaking havoc on the world and leaving her in peace.

And so it was. Her imps went forth and made the holiday season less joyous. Food and water they randomly polluted with their undetectable urine and feces, bringing on cramps and stitches, dizziness and fainting spells, nightmares that induced deep despair. They smothered family pets in their sleep, withered the branches of Christmas trees, and stole benevolent thoughts from sleepy heads. But their favorite task was to roam the streets on those nights leading up to Christmas, hunting for bad boys and girls to feed upon. Their screams they drank with glee, gobbling down their sinful little bodies to augment their own stores of wickedness.

Thus was a new tradition established. And the Tooth Fairy saw that it was good.

But her boys had one more tradition they'd long been scheming to institute. For they were precocious in more ways than one.

When, on the day after Christmas, they came swarming back to the island, they fell, full of spunk and vinegar, upon their mother. The vinegar of their misdeeds they waited until evening to recount. But the spunk homed in at their groins and made them stiff, with which stiffness they penetrated mommy dearest, unleashing upon her the unholy force of their desires.

And the Tooth Fairy laughed and saw that this too was good.

And when they were spent at last and she lay drenched in imp spunk, she hugged her loathsome brood to her and said unto them: "Thus shall you go forth into the world every Christmas hence, my boys, spreading evil cheer. And thus shall you return to your mother's arms.

"God damn us, my blasted little boys. God damn us every one!"

AFTERWARD
MAKING LIGHT OF SANTA CLAUS

---

by Robert Devereaux

Montaigne once said, "There is no man so good, who, were he to submit all his thoughts and actions to the laws, would not deserve hanging ten times in his life." Saint Jerome warned, "A fat paunch never breeds fine thoughts." More to the point, Goethe had this to say: "The ideal goat is one that eats hay and shits diamonds."

Born in 1947, I was brought up in a modest three-bedroom home on Long Island. Here's what I remember about Santa Claus. I remember being too excited to fall asleep right away on Christmas Eve. More than likely, I keened my ears into the stillness, knowing it was too early for Santa's visit but caring not in the least. In the crisp morning, I woke to the astounding realization that Santa Claus had been by. My three-years-younger sister Margie and I raced down the hall, skidding on our pajama'd knees before a rain-festooned tree topped by a lighted star and anchored with a green striated bulb we called the Toilet Plunger for its resemblance to a float ball. "Presents!" we exclaimed, re-racing and re-exclaiming until we tired of the game. No gifts were ever unwrapped in our house before breakfast, and our parents were unbearably slow in waking on Christmas morning. Still, the bracing aroma of pine needles pervaded the air amid the certainty that we had indeed been visited by the jolly old elf.

I wasn't much of a visual child. Not even before my mind's eye did I spin notions about where Santa stood and what he looked like as he bent to our tree. Neither did I much wonder how he gained access to our chimneyless house. My images

279

of him were culled from magazine ads, black and white TV, Christmas songs, and a ViewMaster disc that told Rudolph's story in dioramas I can summon forty years later with near-total recall.

As for the Easter Bunny and the Tooth Fairy, I had no images of them at all. Yet their unquestioned visits made our house feel and smell special indeed.

I wrote the initial version of *Santa Steps Out* in 1988 and 1989. Why did I do that?

First, I had after long gestation brought to light my initial attempt at a novel, *Oedipus Aroused* (a clever botch never published, though it landed me a mediocre New York agent). That book had taken two years of research into 13th century B.C. Delphi, Corinth, and Thebes, into Minoan and Mycenaean quirks, customs, clothing, weaponry, roadwork, abortifacients, bull-leaping, the vast network of oracles of which Delphi was only the most famous, and so forth, and nearly another two years to weave all of it into a novel. I promised myself that my next effort would require as close to zero research as possible (true except for bunny behaviors, which are drawn from Marshal Merton's *A Complete Introduction to Rabbits* and especially from R. M. Lockley's delightful *The Private Life of the Rabbit*).

Second was the emergence of the basic imaginative material. Precisely how that happened is lost to memory, but here's the gist: Suppose the all-giving Santa Claus had once been the all-grasping Pan? Suppose further that the creatures of our common childhood fancy—that magical triumvirate we accepted without question, who slipped into our homes to leave us money and candy and gifts—shared a forgotten, forbidden, pagan past? And that a crossing of paths which never ought to have happened did, by dint of heavenly bumble, happen?

Greek mythology had been an enduring love of mine since, at age nine, I played Zeus in a dramatization of *The*

Iliad, twice performed in the school auditorium at Newbridge Road School—with a different Hera each time, I note with delight and curiosity. Here was a way to bring into renewed existence the chaos, the daring, the sheer exuberance of that treasure trove of myth, to celebrate the vastness and majesty of our Dionysian impulses while having great heaps of fun.

We never really lose our younger selves. Rather, we accrete new selves about them. The spellbound child at our core remains, I believe, as emotionally attached to these three beloved nocturnal visitors as it always was. (For a study of precisely this topic from the perspective of a child psychologist, see Cindy Dell Clark's *Flights of Fancy, Leaps of Faith*, University of Chicago Press, 1995.)

Moreover, all three, unlike say Batman or Superman, are in the public domain. This, I'm sorry to say, is not true of Rudolph the Red-Nosed Reindeer, nor was I able to persuade the holders of Rudolph's copyright to license him to my use, which is why Santa Claus has a different lead reindeer in this novel.

What cinched it for me, though, was realizing where the Tooth Fairy's coins came from. Goethe's goat.

Santa Steps Out has had a tangled time finding its way into print.

In 1989, David Hartwell at William Morrow & Company held the manuscript for many months, eventually sending me a brief rejection. Meanwhile, I had squeaked my way into the Clarion West Writers Workshop for 1990. My primary reason for wanting to attend was David's presence on the roster of instructors. When upon his arrival one Sunday in July I introduced myself, he carried on about *Santa* in a way that astonished and delighted me, going so far as to buy me dinner at a Mongolian restaurant a short walk from our dorm and generally acting as if the work of a pretty-much-unpublished writer mattered.

At the end of that week, during which David had given

me, in private conference, a detailed criticism of *Santa Steps Out* (six months after his last glimpse of it, the man a natural-born editor), he took me aside. "Now that I've seen the range of your short fiction," he said, "I want you to revise *Santa* along the lines we talked about and submit it again."

I did so. After another period of deliberation, yet another rejection came in. David, it seems, was ready to buy the book this time, but no one at Morrow would support him.

I had since signed with a second agent on the basis of her love for *Santa*. Alas, that love could not be translated into a sale. She did however sell *Deadweight*, my first published novel, to Jeanne Cavelos for the Dell Abyss line of horror novels. Jeanne had seen and rejected *Santa* a year earlier. She too wanted eventually to publish it, "after your readership has grown," she said. Jeanne, bless her twisted little heart, left publishing to pursue teaching and her own writing career. In any case, it's unlikely that Dell would have gone along with her, any more than Morrow had with David Hartwell, unless my career had skyrocketed into the realms of bestsellerdom.

For years, my favorite brainchild lay dormant. Then at the 1996 Pikes Peak Writers Conference, I had the good fortune to meet Pat LoBrutto. Years before, when I had been sending my Santa synopsis to agents and editors, Pat had been working for Meredith Bernstein. He urged her, in vain, to request the manuscript. Said Pat at Pikes Peak over a microbrew: "You mean nobody's bought it yet? Send me a copy!"

I did. Pat loved it, vowing to do what he could to usher it into print, saying indeed that he wanted to be able to tell his grandchildren that he was the one who had edited my odd little Santa novel.

Pat brought it to TOR Books, where, as it happened (did I think the gods were smiling on me, you bet I did), David Hartwell was senior editor. For the longest time, it seemed as if a TOR *Santa* would fly. The manuscript had the advantage of Pat LoBrutto's editing expertise, David stood foursquare behind the purchase, and the head of the company had bought in as well. *Santa Steps Out* came as close as a book can come to a yes without quite getting there. Then the marketing weenies, from what I gather, killed it. In his rejection letter, David assured my agent that if he ever returned to small press publishing, he would publish the book himself.

There's a bit more, and in all fairness writers are rarely privy to what really goes on inside a publishing house, but that will suffice.

So what's the problem here? Why do so many benighted souls run screaming from *Santa Steps Out*? And why is it that others, saints and angels every one of them, embrace my jolly old elf with such enthusiasm?

Turning down my request for a blurb, Peter Straub, in all good humor and based solely on the synopsis, wrote me as follows:

"My work load is so impossible at the moment that I have to pass on reading the extraordinary tale outlined in the pages you sent me. If good old Dark Highway is looking for the hideous, the blasphemous, and the prurient, Jason Bovberg ought to show up at your house every day to shine your shoes, make breakfast, and wash your dishes. Clearly, we all missed a great many educational experiences by sleeping through the Tooth Fairy's visits to our bedrooms, and we underestimated Santa *tremendously*. Me, I always had my doubts about the Easter Bunny, and it's nice to see them confirmed.

Well—wow! Of course, anything so deliberately provocative depends *completely* on the writing—on the second-by-second delivery of its effects. That you came so close to getting what would be ordinarily unpublishable accepted by trade houses in New York must mean that you have found a way to give weight to your transgressions.

Even though I have no time to provide a blurb, I do want to see the finished book—and I'm not begging for a free copy here, I mean only that I'll look for a way to order the book—

but even more, I want to see the reviews. After all, you're not just throwing down the gauntlet, you're using it to slap them in the face."

I quote Peter at length because (1) I like him, (2) it's prose from a master's pen after all, (3) I promised him an inscribed copy in exchange for permission to quote him and I like to get value for money, and (4) his words hint, tongue in cheek to be sure, at outrage and offense, at transgression and blasphemy.

But again I ask, where is the outrage in this novel? My three protagonists aren't, after all, religious icons. One might, to stretch a point, claim that status for Saint Nicholas, but surely not since the transformations wrought upon him by Thomas Nast, Clement Moore, and the ad men at The Coca-Cola Company.

God? He's treated with the utmost respect, he swears only in incomprehensible foreign tongues, he plays a cameo role (Marlon Brando, if you please, to Jack Nicholson's Santa Claus). In any event, he turns out to be Zeus, so his appearance should hardly count as a slap in the face of true believers.

In fact, the most twisted offshoots of Christianity would, I believe, be thoroughly in my camp. Just as some fundie lunatics want to ban Halloween, others lobby to be rid of Santa Claus. During my near-zero research, I came across a pamphlet by Sheldon Emry entitled "Is Christmas Christian?" (Lord's Covenant Church, 1976).

Here are three brief passages:

"[S]ecret Baal worshipers have foisted upon us their "Santa," their counterfeit "God," who appears to do "good," even as God, and they have presented him to us with white hair and beard, sparkling eyes, and a deep, low laugh. . . . Do you need still more proof that "Christmas" has its origins in Baal worship? Read on. We will "take apart" more of this strange "festival."

[M]ost of Christendom, even professing Christians, have been deceived by the forces of darkness into acting out the rituals of Baal worship which are an abomination to our God.

[Most men in Church pulpits] ignore or ridicule such information as you have read in these last pages. Could the reason be that many are not followers of Jesus Christ, but instead are secret priests of the false messiah of Babylon and they only profess to be Christians so they can get in Church pulpits and lead God's sheep into the 'ways of Baal worship?'"

As a longstanding Baal worshiper, I am astounded at how uncannily, though his head be full of muddle, Pastor Emry has set his wagging finger so squarely on the truth. Brothers and sisters, we must complexify our efforts at obfuscation. The Freemasons, the Illuminati, and those sly purveyors of the lone-gunman theory must surely heap scorn upon us for our ineptitude.

But I digress. . . .

In pondering the question of *Santa*'s reception by the affronted, I have come to the tentative conclusion that it won't be the loonies who regard *Santa Steps Out* as blasphemous (body-haters that they are, they'll slam as usual my explicit sexual descriptions, but the religious content shouldn't faze them)—no, it will outrage, if it outrages anyone at all, the mainstream Christian with an imperfect understanding of storytelling.

How dare I cast dirt upon the image of their beloved Santa Claus, the gentle Tooth Fairy, the generous Easter Bunny? That's what I hear them asking. For in many ways, these three secular creatures touch the hearts of children far earlier, far deeper, and far more effectively than God or Jesus or Mary ever could. It is *they* who carry the weight that more traditional religious icons may once have carried for the average American youngster.

A dear friend of mine, a psychotherapist who has not

yet read the book, suggests another reason. Santa Claus, she notes, is a grandfather figure, a friend to children. Eroticize him and he becomes at once disquieting, a figure of potential incest and child abuse. I think at once of Jean Hersholt from the Shirley Temple *Heidi* film, no more perfect a grandfather than he. Were he to be sexualized, would he appear as a threat to Heidi? I don't think so, as long as he manifests no sexual interest in children (which is decidedly the case with my characters). Yet I find this theory intriguing and I'll be curious to see if it figures at all in reader response to the book.

Why then do I judge this work to be not offensive in the least?

Because it's a vivid and heartfelt dream. Only nuts of the medievally monkish sort whip, hairshirt, castrate, or otherwise do injury to themselves over the contents of a dream. In dreams, anything goes; they follow their own logic, wending where Psyche's whim takes them.

Because it tells the truth, it does so joyously, and it is no more outrageous in its way than *Salome* or *Titus Andronicus* or *The Bacchae*, three classic literary works which dabble expertly in excess.

Because the multiform emotion known as passion is a godsend. By no means are all of its forms pretty. Some have the capacity to kill or cripple relationships. But the erotic form of passion is as divine as all the rest, the stuff souls are made of.

Because sacred cows often deserve a vigorous milking, a swift kick to their fly-encircled rumps, a one-way trip down the chutes of the slaughterhouse, a fall beneath the butcher's knife. Besides, it's always useful to discover that gods and goddesses have feet of clay, that they too suffer temptation and a measure of imperfection; it eases the burden of being human.

Offense, I have found, is far more often taken than given in this world. Each venture into a new narrative opens up new avenues into yourself. If you are reading these words after having taken your way through *Santa Steps Out*, I trust that the journey both enriched and entertained you. If beforehand (one of my vices, I must confess), may your upcoming trip be a safe and pleasant one, a turn-on and a treat.

And if my good-hearted reader finds aught in these pages tart to the taste, or bitter:

Think but this, and all is mended—
That you have but slumber'd here
While these visions did appear.
And this weak and idle theme,
No more yielding but a dream,
Gentles, do not reprehend.
If you pardon, we will mend.

—Fort Collins, October 1997

FAR FAR AFTERWARDS: AN ADDENDUM

by Robert Devereaux

Somehow, fourteen years have sped by.

First publication of *Santa Steps Out* occurred in 1998 in the Dark Highway Press hardcover, though it had been kicking around for a good ten years prior. Two years later, thanks to Don D'Auria, Leisure Books brought it out in mass market format.

Now, as the spirited wonder-workers at Eraserhead/ Deadite Press—eternal gratitude to Carlton Mellick III for his initial email—rebirth my fondest brainchild as a trade paperback, please allow me to add a few more words.

I've left the first Afterword intact. Since writing it, Marlon Brando has gone to his reward without playing the part of God the Father. And for reasons unknown Jack Nicholson hasn't called or written. No matter. I'm a man of infinite patience, though not alas infinite in the number of years granted me on God's green earth. Besides, there are many worthy potential Saint Nicks out there among the ever-shifting roster of film actors. No need to name them. They'll be obvious to you, I'm sure.

What has amazed me about *Santa Steps Out* is how widely varied the reactions to it have been. Some readers loathe it, grow bored at its frequent depictions of in-and-out, project their own sexual peculiarities and fears onto its harmless little plot, or throw it across various rooms for reasons never to be known. Others adore it with a passion, wear out their copies rereading it, dig, grok, and groove on the erotic goings-on, and understand that when one is dealing with Pan, king of the satyrs, there are very few boundaries that cannot be breached. Publishing such a book vividly reveals how wide the spectrum of reader response can be when childhood icons, which so many have envisioned in their own way and at such a young

288

age, are toyed with for fictive purposes.

In the course of time, along came an unexpected sequel, *Santa Claus Conquers the Homophobes*. This book too I had problems placing with mainstream publishers. So, determined to see it languish no more on my PC, I signed on with booklocker.com and ushered it into the world of readers myself. Bless their thrice-blessed hearts, the spirited lovers and producers of books at Deadite Press are bringing *Santa Claus Conquers the Homophobes* out as well, late in 2011, along with [TITLE HERE], the third and possibly final Santa novel I'll write.

May you find abundant joy, my brothers and sisters, in these tales of the good and sometimes-not-so-good Santa Claus.

And may all your Christmases be as white, bright, light, and as void of fright, blight, shite, plight, and spite as you desire.

Now and forevermore, amen!

—Fort Collins, April 2011

ABOUT THE AUTHOR

Robert Devereaux made his professional debut in Pulphouse Magazine in the late 1980's, attended the 1990 Clarion West Writers Workshop, and soon placed stories in such major venues as Crank!, Weird Tales, and Dennis Etchison's anthology MetaHorror. Two of his stories made the final ballot for the Bram Stoker and World Fantasy Awards.

His novels include Slaughterhouse High, A Flight of Storks and Angels, Deadweight, Walking Wounded, Caliban, Santa Steps Out, and Santa Claus Conquers the Homophobes. Also not to be missed is his new short story collection with Deadite Press, Baby's First Book of Seriously Fucked-Up Shit.

Robert has a well-deserved reputation as an author who pushes every envelope, though he would claim, with a stage actor's assurance, that as long as one's writing illuminates characters in all their kinks, quirks, kindnesses, and extremes, the imagination must be free to explore nasty places as well as nice, or what's the point?

Robert lives in sunny northern Colorado with the delightful Victoria, making up stuff that tickles his fancy and, he hopes, those of his readers.

You can find him online at Facebook or at www.robertdevereaux.com.

deadite press

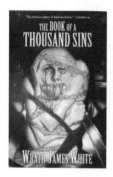

"The Book of a Thousand Sins" Wrath James White - Welcome to a world of Zombie nymphomaniacs, psychopathic deities, voodoo surgery, and murderous priests. Where mutilation sex clubs are in vogue and torture machines are sex toys. No one makes it out alive – not even God himself.

"If Wrath James White doesn't make you cringe, you must be riding in the wrong end of a hearse."
                                        -Jack Ketchum

"Highways to Hell" Bryan Smith - The road to hell is paved with angels and demons. Brain worms and dead prostitutes. Serial killers and frustrated writers. Zombies and Rock 'n Roll. And once you start down this path, there is no going back. Collecting thirteen tales of shock and terror from Bryan Smith, Highways to Hell is a non-stop road-trip of cruelty, pain, and death. Grab a seat, Smith has such sights to show you.

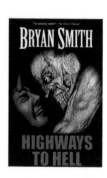

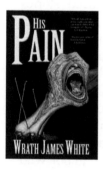

"His Pain" Wrath James White - Life is pain . . . . . . or at least it is for Jason. Born with a rare central nervous disorder, every sensation is pain. Every sound, scent, texture, flavor, even every breath, brings nothing but mind-numbing pain. Until the arrival of Yogi Arjunda of the Temple of Physical Enlightenment. He claims to be able to help Jason, to be able to give him a life of more than agony. But the treatment leaves Jason changed and he wants to share what he learned. He wants to share his pain . . . A novella of pain, pleasure, and transcendental splatter.

"Bullet Through Your Face" Edward Lee - No writer is more extreme, perverted, or gross than Edward Lee. His world is one of psychopathic redneck rapists, sex addicted demons, and semen stealing aliens. Brace yourself, the king of splatterspunk is guaranteed to shock, offend, and make you laugh until you vomit.
"Lee pulls no punches."
        - Fangoria

"Whargoul" Dave Brockie - It is a beast born in bullets and shrapnel, feeding off of pain, misery, and hard drugs. Cursed to wander the Earth without the hope of death, it is reborn again and again to spread the gospel of hate, abuse, and genocide. But what if it's not the only monster out there? What if there's something worse? From Dave Brockie, the twisted genius behind GWAR, comes a novel about the darkest days of the twentieth century.

"Super Fetus" Adam Pepper - Try to abort this fetus and he'll kick your ass!

"The story of a self-aware fetus whose morally bankrupt mother is desperately trying to abort him. This darkly humorous novella will surely appall and upset a sizable percentage of people who read it . . . In-your-face, allegorical social commentary."

- BarnesandNoble.com

"Slaughterhouse High" Robert Devereaux - It's prom night in the Demented States of America. A place where schools are built with secret passageways, rebellious teens get zippers installed in their mouths and genitals, and once a year one couple is slaughtered and the bits of their bodies are kept as souvenirs. But something's gone terribly wrong when the secret killer starts claiming a far higher body count than usual . . .

"A major talent!" - Poppy Z. Brite

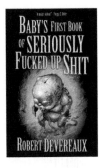

"Baby's First Book of Seriously Fucked-Up Shit" Robert Devereaux - From an orgy between God, Satan, Adam and Eve to beauty pageants for fetuses. From a giant human-absorbing tongue to a place where God is in the eyes of the psychopathic. This is a party at the furthest limits of human decency and cruelty. Robert Devereaux is your host but watch out, he's spiked the punch with drugs, sex, and dismemberment. Deadite Press is proud to present nine stories of the strange, the gross, and the just plain fucked up.

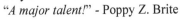

THE VERY BEST IN CULT HORROR

Lightning Source UK Ltd.
Milton Keynes UK
UKHW022058110621
385359UK00005B/288

VICTORY
OF THE
WEST

Born and raised in Florence, Niccolò Capponi is a historian special-
izing in military history. After earning his Ph.D. at the University of
Padua, he was for three years a fellow at the Medici Archive Project
and has published extensively in Italian as well as English.

NICCOLÒ CAPPONI

VICTORY
OF THE
WEST

*The Story
of the
Battle of Lepanto*

PAN BOOKS

First published 2006 by Macmillan

First published in paperback 2007 by Pan Books
an imprint of Pan Macmillan Ltd
Pan Macmillan, 20 New Wharf Road, London N1 9RR
Basingstoke and Oxford
Associated companies throughout the world
www.panmacmillan.com

ISBN 978-0-330-43158-3

1 3 5 7 9 8 6 4 2

A CIP catalogue record for this book is available from
the British Library.

Typeset by SetSystems Ltd, Saffron Walden, Essex
Maps designed by Raymond Turvey
Printed and bound in Great Britain by
Mackays of Chatham plc, Chatham, Kent

Visit **www.panmacmillan.com** to read more about all our books
and to buy them. You will also find features, author interviews and
news of any author events, and you can sign up for e-newsletters
so that you're always first to hear about our new releases.

For Francesca and Ludovica,
whose ancestors fought on both sides

PREFACE

~

'The most noble and memorable event that past centuries have seen or future generations can ever hope to witness': Miguel de Cervantes would thus sum up in a sentence the battle of Lepanto. He could speak with first-hand knowledge, having lost there the use of his left hand. Later, the philosopher Voltaire – with a keener eye for belittlement than historical truth – would dismiss the battle as inconsequential, living as he did in an age which measured a successful war by the amount of captured territory. The nineteenth century would exalt the battle as a victory of Western Civilization over oriental barbarism. Latter-day 'politically correct' historians have reversed these parameters, it being now fashionable to consider Islamic civilizations equal, if not superior, to those based on Christian principles. For these reasons this book's title has been chosen with provocation in mind, *pour épatur les incultes*.

Lepanto was not so much a victory of Western technology, but of the world that had developed it from the so-called Middle Ages onward. This is not intended as a statement of qualitative superiority: Western thinking may be at the root of democratic representation and scientific advancement, but has also fathered biological racism and weapons of mass destruction. I don't intend to go into complicated explanations of the hows and the whys of this situation

– others have already done so, and better than I could ever hope to do. More simply, for the last 300 years a speculative approach to knowledge has allowed the West to impose its own vision of reality on the rest of the world.

As a result, determinism (whether economic, technological, philosophical or any other) can be an irresistible temptation for any historian dealing with East–West relations. Historical anachronism is also an ever-present trap for those studying the Early Modern age, and so is the habit of dividing the world into 'us' and 'them', as if an insurmountable barrier existed between the two. At the same time it is difficult for those used to a Western view of reality to understand how a polity could be built on religious beliefs, and how much these tenets shaped the life of the average citizen. So while it would be wrong, for instance, to draw parallels between the religiously inspired Ottoman empire and the atheistic former Soviet Union, one must also not forget that the division between East and West in the sixteenth century did follow sacred lines. Individuals were prepared to fight for their beliefs, which were the foundations of their way of life and affected both their physical and metaphysical worlds. The struggles between Muslims and Christians in the Mediterranean were not so much wars of religion as wars fought by religious people.

I don't expect this book to be the ultimate work on the battle of Lepanto, for nothing is definitive in the historical field. Yet, just going back to the original sources, whether printed or archival, has made me rethink a whole set of acquired truths. For one, there was never a battle of Lepanto on 7 October 1571; Lepanto, the modern Nafpaktos, is some forty nautical miles from the site of the clash, and more accuratley the Venetians called the battle after the Curzolaris, a group of islands at the mouth of the Gulf of Patras. For this reason, in the present text Curzolaris has been used instead of Lepanto when referring to the battle. The circumstances surrounding the fight have also been coloured by writers wishing to promote their own version of events, following national and/or political allegiances. After reading some contemporary accounts one is left doubting what and whom to believe, so cross-checking became a necessity as much as a historical duty. Some anecdotes, however, were too good to be left out, even if based on only one source. Like the apocryphal story of George Washington and the cherry tree, they provide spice to what could otherwise become a dull sequence of facts and figures.

Over the last few years I have come to know many of the protagonists in this book through personal letters, direct accounts, related stories or historical hearsay. I have tried to give the Ottomans their due, regretting not being able to use as many Turkish sources as I would have liked. I also admit to having something of a soft spot for the Turks as fighters, my great-great-grandfather, a Crimean War veteran, describing them as the best soldiers in the world. Still, my unstinted admiration goes to the men on every side who fought and suffered in the wars fought in the Mediterranean during the sixteenth century. *Requiescant in pace.*

~

During the research and writing of this book I have been helped by many people, too many in fact for me to give all of them the credit they deserve. My first and foremost thanks go to Dr Marco Morin, for his constant and tireless help in finding Venetian documents, as well as for correcting some of my most glaring mistakes in technological matters. Dr Luca Lo Basso was likewise precious for his advice on galleys and oarsmen, not to mention the many documents he sent by post or email. Admiral Tiberio Moro clarified a number of crucial nautical matters as well as sharing with me his deep knowledge of the Cyprus war of 1570–3. My deepest thanks go to Professor Christine Woodhead for her generous translations of Turkish sources, and for the many valuable exchanges of ideas. Professor Erendiz Özbayoğlu and Dr Sinan Çuluk helped me in no little way with archival sources in Istanbul, allowing me a better understanding of Ottoman politics at the time. Dr Giulia Semenza's help in the Archivo General de Simancas (Valladolid) was priceless. The late Dr Carlo De Vita was particularly generous in sharing his knowledge about archives in Rome. My gratitude goes also to the director and staff of the state archives of Florence and Venice, to my friends and former colleagues at the Medici Archive Project, and Dr Anna Evangelista for her understanding of logistics.

For books, rare printed matter and manuscripts, I can't thank enough the director and staff of the Biblioteca Casanatense (Rome), the Biblioteca dell'Istituto Nazionale degli Studi sul Rinascimento (Florence), the Biblioteca Marucelliana (Florence), the Biblioteca Moreniana (Florence), the Biblioteca Nazionale Centrale (Florence), the Biblioteca Nazionale Marciana (Venice), the Biblioteca Riccardiana (Florence), the British Institute Library (Florence), the British Library (London) and the Kunsthistorisches Institut (Florence), and the Bernard Berenson Library of the Harvard University Center for Italian Renaissance Studies, Villa I Tatti (Florence). In particular, Dr Silvia Castelli of the Biblioteca Marucelliana bent over backwards to find otherwise unavailable printed sources.

My special thanks go to Prince Jonathan Doria-Pamphilij for allowing me to use his family archive, and to Dr Allessandra Mercantini for guiding me through Giovanni Andrea Doria's papers. Countess Floriani Compagnoni and Count Piero Guicciardini kindly permitted me to browse through their ancestors' fascinating documents. I am most grateful to the town hall of Noventa Vicentina, and especially to Dr Cristina Zanaica for allowing me to photograph the frescoes in the Villa Barbarigo.

Among others who helped in no little way with suggestions, references, support or simply by sharing ideas, I would like to thank the titular grand duke of Tuscany HRIH Sigmund v. Habsburg-Lothringen, Professor Gabor Ágoston, Don Nino Allaria Olivieri, Professor Nancy Bisah, Dr Maurizio Arfaioli, Dr Pinar Artiran, Brandon Barker, Professor Jeremy Black, Professor Palmira Brummet, Professor Franco Cardini, Professor William J. Connell, Dr Mary Davidson, Professor Domenico Del Nero, Dr Brooke Ettle, Captain Robert E. Ettle, Melinda Ettle, Dr Roberta Ferrazza, Leonie Frieda, Leticia Frutos, Madeleine Gera, Father Michele Ghisleri OP, Professor John Gooch, Professor John F. Guilmartin Jr., Thomas Harris, Dr Mark Hutchings, Professor Colin Imber, the unforgettable late Professor Patricia Labalme, Professor Thomas Madden, Christine Moritz, Dr Bruno Mugnai, Dr Rosemarie Mulcahy, Dr Rhoads Murphey, Dr Alana O'Brien, Dr Ciro Paoletti, Dr Susanne Probst, Douglas Preston, Dr Gianni Ridella, Andrew Roberts, Dr Brian Sandberg, Professor Richard Talbert, Professor Bruce Vandervort, Professor Roger Vella Bonavita and Dr Marino Zorzi.

My infinite gratitude goes to my agent Georgina Capel and to my editor Georgina Morley. Kate Harvey at Macmillan showed incredible patience in putting up with my mundane questions on minor details ('Do you think Don Juan of Austria's photo should be in black and white?') as well as kindly providing me with some very useful books. I can't thank enough Georgina Difford and Hugh Davis for their help in editing the original manuscript. My gratitude goes to all those who have written before on the subject of the battle of Lepanto, no matter the quality of their work; if in every tenth-rate film there is a shot worth a Rembrandt, then even in the lousiest of history books there might be an intuition worthy of Ranke.

Finally I would like to thank my family for their support during the difficulties I have had to face over these last two years, especially my darling daughters Francesca and Ludovica; just their 'Hello, Papa' after a long day is enough to dispel all troubles.

Florence, 30 April, 2006

CONTENTS

AUTHOR'S NOTE

~

MEASURES

In the sixteenth century no uniform system of weights and measures existed in the Mediterranean, or in the world at large for that matter. For this reason, when possible I have converted all weights into imperial (British) pounds. For linear measures, yards and sometimes metres have been used in the text. Miles at sea are the standard nautical miles.

TIME

In 1571 there were two systems for calculating time: the French, derived from the earth's rotation, and the Italian, based instead on the hours of daylight. The latter system was particularly inaccurate as sunrise and sunset vary according to the seasons. It should also be remembered that the Julian calendar used at the time had caused over the centuries a discrepancy between the astronomical and legal dates. Thus, 7 October in 1571 was actually the 17th, the sun rising at 06.40 and setting at 17.35.

OTTOMAN SURNAMES

Until the 1920s the Turks used nicknames instead of surnames to distinguish one another. Thus Müezzinzâde Ali means Ali son of the prayer caller (muezzin); Sokollu Mehmed, Mehmed from Sokol; and Sari Selim, Selim the Sallow.

LANGUAGE

For Turkish terms I have used the modern spelling, with the exclusion of those words like, for instance, 'muezzin' that have an accepted English form. The spelling of 'Pasha' has also been anglicised, except when part of a proper name or title (Salihpaşazâde; Kapudan Paşa). Place names are usually in their modern form (for example, Zakynthos instead of Zante) unless there is a universally accepted alternative (for instance, Lepanto instead of Nafpaktos). Where an English equivalent exists, it has been retained (Rome and not Roma). I have also tried to use 'Ottoman' instead of 'Turk' (unless for the sake of variety), the latter being a misleading term since by 1571 the Ottoman empire had ceased being ethnically Turkish. I employ the terms 'Muslim' and 'Islamic' as viable alternatives to 'Ottoman', not so much to indicate people's faith (the Greeks serving on the Ottoman fleet were usually Christians), but as a reference to the Porte's political philosophy.

CURRENCY

Until the French Revolution, European countries as a rule followed the old Carolingian monetary system, based on the *libra* (£), the *solidus* (s.) and the *denarius* (d.): £1 = s.20; s1. = 12 d. The names of these currencies varied from country to country, but the subdivisions remained the same. Higher denominations such as the ducat (*ducado, ducato*), or the *scudo* (*escudo* in Spanish) could be worth anything from £3 to £20. The Ottomans used a different system, based on the silver *akçe*. For the sake of clarity, whenever possible I have converted everything in Spanish 'pieces of eight'.

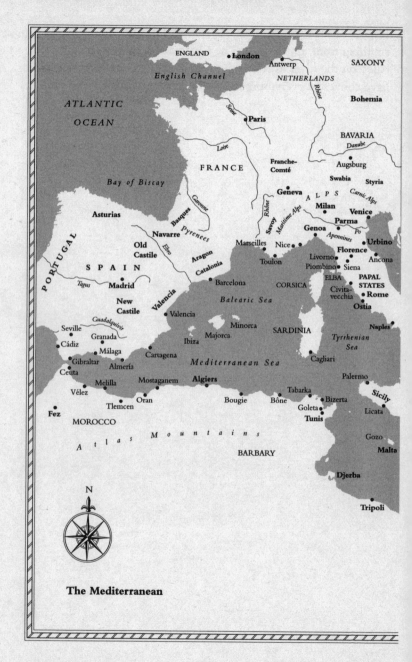

The Mediterranean

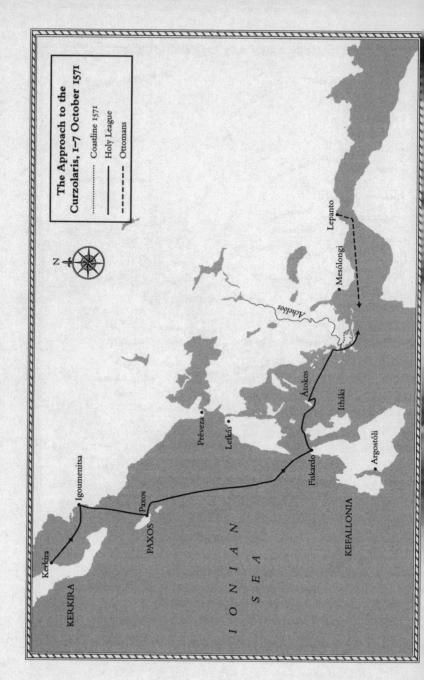

The Approach to the
Curzolaris, 1–7 October 1571

········· Coastline 1571
———— Holy League
– – – – Ottomans

N

KERKIRA

Kerkira

Igoumenitsa

PAXOS

Paxos

Préveza

Lefkás

IONIAN
SEA

Fiskardo

Itháki

KEFALLONIA

Argostóli

Átokos

Achelóos

Mesólongi

Lepanto

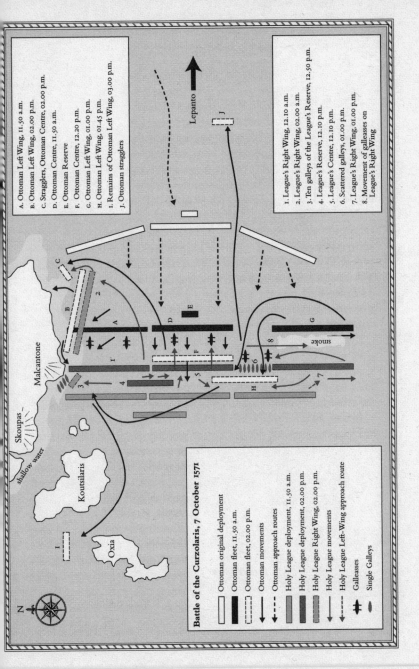

Battle of the Curzolaris, 7 October 1571

Legend:
- ▭ Ottoman original deployment
- ▬ Ottoman fleet, 11.50 a.m.
- ▭ Ottoman fleet, 02.00 p.m.
- ↓ Ottoman movements
- ⇣ Ottoman approach routes
- ▬ Holy League deployment, 11.50 a.m.
- ▬ Holy League deployment, 02.00 p.m.
- ▬ Holy League Right Wing, 02.00 p.m.
- ↑ Holy League movements
- ⇡ Holy League Left-Wing approach route
- ⚓ Galleasses
- ◆ Single Galleys

A. Ottoman Left Wing, 11.50 a.m.
B. Ottoman Left Wing, 02.00 p.m.
C. Stragglers, Ottoman Centre, 02.00 p.m.
D. Ottoman Centre, 11.50 a.m.
E. Ottoman Reserve
F. Ottoman Centre, 12.20 p.m.
G. Ottoman Left Wing, 01.00 p.m.
H. Ottoman Left Wing, 01.45 p.m.
I. Remains of Ottoman Left Wing, 03.00 p.m.
J. Ottoman stragglers

1. League's Right Wing, 12.10 a.m.
2. League's Right Wing, 02.00 a.m.
3. Ten galleys of the League's Reserve, 12.50 p.m.
4. League's Reserve, 12.10 p.m.
5. League's Centre, 12.10 p.m.
6. Scattered galleys, 01.00 p.m.
7. League's Right Wing, 01.00 p.m.
8. Movement of galleasses on League's Right Wing

Lepanto

Malcantone

Skoupas

shallow water

Koutsilaris

Oxia

smoke

N

XXI

DRAMATIS PERSONAE

~

Abd-el Malik Moroccan prince. Fought at the Curzolaris, later ruler of Fez.

Abu Humeya (Hernando de Cordoba y Valor) Leader of the Morisco revolt in Spain 1568–70.

Adrian VI (Adrian of Utrecht) Pope 1522–3. Tried unsuccessfully to unite Europe's rulers to fight the Ottomans.

Ahmed ben Sinan Helmsman of the *Sultana* at the Curzolaris. Later promoted to galley captain as a reward for his bravery during the battle.

Alticozzi, Muzio Captain of an Italian infantry company in Spanish service. Executed by the Venetians for revolt at Igoumenitsa.

Alva, Fernando Àlvarez de Toledo, duke of Viceroy of Naples in the late 1550s and later governor of Flanders. Opposed Philip II's Mediterranean policy.

Álvarez de Toledo, Garcia Viceroy of Sicily 1565–6. Gave advice to Don Juan of Austria about sea battles during the Holy League's campaign of 1571.

Álvarez de Toledo Osorio, Pedro Viceroy of Naples, 1532–3. Father-in-law of Cosimo I de' Medici.

Andrada, Gil de Knight of Malta and captain of the *Real* in 1571. Conducted scouting missions for Don Juan of Austria in the weeks preceding the battle of the Curzolaris.

Antinori, Bernardino Knight of St Stephen. Fought at the Curzolaris. Executed by Francesco I de' Medici in 1575.

Aruj Reis Corsair captain and elder brother of Hayreddin Barbarossa, ruler of Algiers 1516–18. Killed fighting the Spanish at Tlemcen.

Ashkenazi, Solomon Personal doctor of Grand Vizier Sokollu Mehmed Pasha. Sworn enemy of Joseph Nassi and supporter of a peaceful settlement between Venice and the Porte over Cyprus.

Austria, (Don) Juan of Illegitimate son of the Holy Roman Emperor Charles V. Commander-in-chief of the Holy League 1571–3.

Ávalos Aquino, Francisco Fernando d' Marquis of Pescara and viceroy of Sicily 1568–71. Responsible for providing supplies to the Holy League's fleet.

Ávalos Aquino-Gonzaga, Isabella d' Wife of the above, took over her husband's duties during his last illness.

Badoer, Alvise Venetian politician sent to Constantinople in 1540 to discuss peace term between Venice and the Porte.

Badoer, Andrea Venetian politician sent as ambassador to Constantinople in 1573 after the end of the Cyprus war.

Badoer, Giovan Andrea *Provveditore* of the Venetian arsenal, responsible with Marcantonio Pisani for the creation of galleasses.

Baffo, Dimo Christian renegade corsair in Ottoman service, captured and executed by the Venetians at the Curzolaris.

Baglioni, Astorre Military governor of Famagusta, executed by Lala Mustafa Pasha after the city's surrender.

Balbi, Antonio Venetian governor of Korcula. Repulsed an Ottoman attack in 1571.

Barbarigo, Agostino Deputy captain-general of the Venetian fleet in 1571. Mortally wounded at the Curzolaris.

Barbarigo, Antonio Venice's permanent ambassador in Constantinople 1556–8.

Barbaro, Marcantonio Venice's permanent ambassador in Constantinople, 1568–74. Imprisoned by the Ottomans at the beginning of the Cyprus war.

Barbaroszâde Hasan Pasha Son of Hayreddin Barbarossa. Fought at the Curzolaris and later became governor of Algiers.

Barbaroszâde Mehmed Pasha Son of Hayreddin Barbarossa. Fought at the Curzolaris.

Bayezid Süleyman I's second son. Revolted against his father but was defeated by his brother Selim. Taking refuge among the Persians, his hosts eventually handed him over to the Ottomans for execution.

Bayezid I Known as the Thunderbolt. Crushed a crusading army at Nicopolis in 1396, but in turn defeated and captured by Tamerlane at Ankara in 1402.

Bayezid II Sultan 1480–1512. Bested the Venetians in the 1499–1502 war. Deposed by his son Selim I in 1512 and died soon after.

Berardi, Alfonso Florentine *bailo* in Constantinople in the 1540s.

Biffoli, Agnolo Knight of St Stephen. At the Curzolaris he commanded the Tuscan galley *San Giovanni*, suffering severe wounds in the battle.

Bonelli, Michele Cardinal, nephew and adviser of Pius V.

Bonelli, Michele Soldier and nephew of Pius V. Fought at the Curzolaris and later became general of the pope's infantry.

Bourg de Guérines, Claude du French diplomat in Constantinople in 1570 and negotiator of a treaty between France and the Porte.

Bragadin, Marcantonio Governor general of Famagusta. Flayed alive by Lala Mustafa Pasha after the city's surrender.

Bressan, Francesco Master builder of the Venetian arsenal. Transformed a dozen large galleys into the first galleasses.

Caetani, Niccolò Known as Cardinal Sermoneta. Uncle and sponsor of Onorato Caetani.

Caetani, Onorato Duke of Sermoneta. Commander of the papal infantry contingent at the Curzolaris.

Canal, Antonio da *Provveditore* of the Venetian fleet in 1571. Distinguished himself at the Curzolaris.

Canal, Cristoforo da Venetian politician, author of *Della Milizia Marittima* and reformer of the Venetian navy in the 1550s.

Caracciolo, Ferrante Count of Biccari, fought at the Curzolaris and later published an account of the Holy League's exploits.

Carafa, Carlo Cardinal and nephew of Paul IV. Tried to gain Ottoman military support during the war of the papacy against the Colonna. Executed by Pius IV.

Cardenas, Bernardino de Spanish nobleman, killed at the Curzolaris.

Cardona, Juan de Leader of the advance party during the Holy League fleet's approach to the Curzolaris. Later commander of Sicily's galley squadron.

Caur Ali Reis Genoese renegade in Ottoman service. Captured at the Curzolaris.

Cavalli, Giovanni Antonio Brescian nobleman and veteran of the battle of Mühlberg. One of the two *sopracomiti* designated in 1570 to command the galleys armed for Venice by the city of Brescia.

Cavalli, Marino *Provveditore generale* of Crete in 1571. Sent a frigate to inform the Christian fleet of the fall of Famagusta.

Cecco Pisano Mariner in the service of Marcantonio Colonna.

Cervantes Saavedra, Miguel de Spanish soldier, administrator and author. Wounded at the Curzolaris.

Charles V of Habsburg Holy Roman Emperor 1519–56.

Charles VIII of Valois King of France. His invasion of Italy in 1494 triggered off the so-called Italian Wars lasting until 1559.

Charles IX of Valois Son of Henry II and Catherine de' Medici. Opposed to the Holy League.

Clement VII (Giulio de' Medici) Pope 1523–34. His bad political judgement caused Rome to be sacked by Charles V's troops in 1527.

Colonna, Marcantonio Cardinal, cousin and namesake of the papal commander at the Curzolaris.

Colonna, Marcantonio Duke of Tagliacozzo and Paliano. Papal commander at the Curzolaris and later viceroy of Sicily.

Cosimo I de' Medici Duke of Florence and Siena, and from 1569 grand duke of Tuscany. Twelve of his galleys, loaned to Pius V, fought at the Curzolaris.

Dandolo, Nicolò Venetian governor of Cyprus. Killed at the fall of Nicosia.

Dax, François de Noailles, bishop of French envoy in Constantinople 1571–3.

Dervis Pasha Ottoman governor of Aleppo, Syria. Distinguished himself at the storming of Nicosia.

Diedo, Girolamo Venetian officer and writer. Fought at the Curzolaris and later wrote a lengthy account of the 1571 campaign.

Donà, Leonardo Venetian ambassador in Madrid 1570–3. Elected doge of Venice in 1604.

Doria, Andrea Prince of Melfi and knight of the Golden Fleece. From 1529 admiral of Emperor Charles V. Bested by Hayreddin Barbarossa at the battle of Preveza in 1537.

Doria, Giovanni Andrea Knight commander of Santiago, marquis of Tursi and later prince of Melfi. General at sea of Philip II in 1571. Led the Christian right wing at the Curzolaris.

Doria, Pagano Knight of Malta and brother of Giovanni Andrea. Wounded at the Curzolaris.

Dragut *See* Thorgud Reis.

Duodo, Francesco Commander of the Venetian galleasses at the Curzolaris. Later governor of Brescia and *procuratore di San Marco*.

Ebu's-su'ud Chief mufti under Süleyman I and Selim II. Upheld the legitimacy of the Porte's claim over Cyprus.

Elizabeth I Tudor Queen of England 1559–1603. One of the main supporters of the anti-Spanish rebellion in the Netherlands.

Emmanuel Philibert of Savoy Duke of Savoy. Won the battle of St-Quentin against the French in 1557. Sent three galleys to fight at the Curzolaris.

Esdey Mustafa Paymaster-general of the Ottoman fleet in 1571. Fought at the Curzolaris.

Espinosa, Diego Cardinal and bishop of Siguenza. One of the main advocates of the repressive measures enacted by the Spanish crown against the Moriscos, 1567–71.

Facchinetti, Giovanni Antonio Papal nuncio in Venice 1570–3. Later elected pope with the name of Innocent IX.

Farnese, Alessandro Son of Ottavio Farnese, duke of Parma. Fought at the Curzolaris and later became governor of the Spanish Netherlands.

Ferdinand I of Habsburg King of Hungary, king of the Romans and Holy Roman Emperor. Opposed Ottoman expansion in Hungary.

Figueroa, Lope de Commander of the Spanish troops embarked on the *Real* during the 1571 campaign. Wounded at the Curzolaris. Gave detailed report of the battle to Philip II of Spain.

Fisogni, Orazio Brescian nobleman. One of the two *sopracomiti* designated in 1570 to command the galleys armed for Venice by the city of Brescia.

Floriani, Pompeo Military architect and engineer. Fought against the Huguenots in France and against the Ottomans at the Curzolaris. Wrote a number of treatises on strategy and fortifications.

Foscarini, Giacomo Venetian *provveditore generale* of Dalmatia. Took over from Sebastiano Venier as commander of the Venetian fleet in 1572.

Francesco I de' Medici Crown prince and later grand duke of Tuscany. Sent by his father Cosimo I to Genoa to appease Don Juan of Austria.

Francesco Maria II della Rovere Son of Guidobaldo II, duke of Urbino. Fought at the Curzolaris and succeeded his father in 1574. Left a rich correspondence on the 1571 campaign.

Gatto, Angelo One of the defenders of Famagusta 1570–1. Left an account of the siege.

Gianfigliazzi, Bongianni Knight of Malta. Fought at Montechiaro in 1570 and was captured at the Curzolaris the following year. Appointed Florentine ambassador to the Porte in 1578.

Giustiniani, Pietro Knight commander of the Order of Malta. Severely wounded at the Curzolaris.

Giustiniani, Vincenzo Genoese governor of Chios in 1566. Taken prisoner by Piyale Pasha after the island's surrender.

Gómez de Silva, Ruy Prince of Eboli and duke of Pastrana, secretary to Philip II of Spain.

Granvelle, Antoine Perrenot de Cardinal and bishop of Arras, enemy of Marcantonio Colonna. Spanish plenipotentiary in Rome, 1570–1. Later viceroy of Naples and president of Philip II's *Consejo de Italia*.

Gregory XIII (Ugo Boncompagni) Successor of Pius V in 1572. Reformer of the Western calendar in 1583.

Guasto, Paolo dal Venetian officer. Defended Nicosia in 1570.

Habsburg, (Don) Carlos of Son of Philip II of Spain. Given to bizarre behaviour, he was imprisoned by his father in 1568 and died in confinement.

Hasan Bey Commander of the *capitana* of Rhodes at the Curzolaris.

Hayreddin Barbarossa (Hizir Reis) Turkish corsair. Ottoman governor of Algiers in 1519. Commander-in-chief of Süleyman I's navy 1533–46.

Hindī Mahmūd Judge and member of Selim II's household. Taken prisoner at the Curzolaris.

Hürrem Sultan Former slave of Slavic (possibly Russian) origin. Wife of Süleyman I and mother of Selim II.

Ibn 'Ulayyan Leader of the anti-Ottoman revolt in Mesopotamia in 1567. Later Ottoman governor of the region.

Isfendiari Mustafa Pasha Cousin of Süleyman I and commander of the Ottoman army at the siege of Malta in 1565.

János Szapolyai King of Hungary 1526–40. Ally of Süleyman I against Ferdinand I of Habsburg.

Jem Brother of Bayezid II. Escaped to Europe after his unsuccessful bid for the Ottoman throne.

Kara Hodja Bey Ottoman *sancak bey* of Avlona, corsair and former Dominican friar. Killed at the Curzolaris.

Kılıç Ali Pasha Algerian corsair, born Luca (or Giovanni) Galeni. Governor of Algiers in the late 1560s. Commanded Ottoman left wing at the Curzolaris. Became *kapudan paşa* in 1571. Retook Tunis from the Spanish in 1574.

Lala Mustafa Pasha Former tutor of Selim II and commander of the Ottoman army in Cyprus 1570–1. Famous for his savage treatment of Venetian prisoners after the fall of Famagusta. Grand vizier in 1580, following the death of Sokollu Mehmed Pasha.

Landriano, Giuseppe Francesco Count of Landriano and viceroy of Sicily 1571–6.

Loredan, Pietro Doge of Venice at the outbreak of the Cyprus war.

Marignano, Giangiacomo de' Medici, marquis of Milanese nobleman, commander of the Holy Roman Empire's forces during the war of Siena.

Mawlay Hamida Spanish-backed lord of Tunis. Evicted by the Ottomans in 1569.

Maximilian II of Habsburg Holy Roman Emperor from 1564. Refused to join the Holy League.

Mazzinghi, Luigi Florentine knight of Malta. Fought at the Curzolaris and left an account of the battle.

Medici, Catherine de' Widow of Henry II of Valois and regent of France.

Medici, Tommaso de' Commander of the Florentine galley *Fiorenza* at the Curzolaris. Severely wounded in the battle.

Mehmed II Ottoman sultan and conqueror of Constantinople in 1453.

Mihirimah Daughter of Süleyman I and wife of Grand Vizier Rüstem Pasha.

Mocenigo, Alvise Doge of Venice 1570–8.

Monte, Piero del Grand master of the Order of Malta at the time of the battle of the Curzolaris.

Moretto, Ottaviano Captain of the Savoyard galley *Piemontesa*. Killed at the Curzolaris.

Mudazzo, Zaccaria Venetian governor of Kyrenia in Cyprus. Surrendered without a fight to the Ottomans in 1570. Arrested by the Venetian authorities and died in prison.

Müezzinzâde Ali Pasha *Kapudan-i deryâ* from 1567 in place of Piyale Pasha. Killed at the Curzolaris.

Mustafa First son of Süleyman I. Executed by his father on suspicions of treason.

Nani, Federico Agostino Barbarigo's deputy at the Curzolaris. Took command when the former was mortally wounded.

Nassi, Joseph Jewish merchant, duke of Naxos and adviser to Selim II. One of those responsible for the Cyprus war.

Negroni, Alessandro Commander of the Tuscan galley *Grifona* at the Curzolaris.

Noailles *See* Dax.

Nobili, Leonardo de' Florentine ambassador in Spain in 1569.

Odescalchi, Giulio Maria Papal nuncio with the Holy League fleet in 1571.

Orange, William of Nassau, prince of Leader of the Netherlands revolt in 1568. Murdered in 1584.

Orsini, Paolo Commander of Venice's infantry contingent at the Curzolaris. Badly wounded in the battle.

Orsini, Paolo Giordano Son-in-law of Cosimo I de' Medici. Fought at the Curzolaris on the *capitana* of the Lomellini.

Pacheco, Francisco Cardinal and archbishop of Burgos. Spanish plenipotentiary in Rome 1570–1.

Parma, Margaret of Habsburg, duchess of Natural daughter of Charles V and mother of Alessandro Farnese. Governor of the Netherlands 1559–67.

Paruta, Girolamo Venetian governor of Tinos in 1571. Repelled the Ottomans under Piyale Pasha.

Paul III (Alessandro Farnese) Pope 1534–9. Convened the Council of Trent in 1545.

Paul IV (Gianpietro Carafa) Pope 1555–9. Went to war with Charles V and Philip II for their support of Marcantonio Colonna.

Pertev Pasha Second vizier and *serdar* during the in 1571 campaign. Opposed attacking the Christian fleet but was overruled. Wounded at the Curzolaris, he was forced to retire in disgrace after the battle.

Philip II of Habsburg King of Spain 1556–8.

Piyale Pasha *Kapudan-ı deryâ* 1558–67. Commanded Ottoman fleet at Djerba, Malta and Chios. Created vizier by Selim II, he was put in charge of Ottoman naval operations in 1570. Forced to retire for failing to stop Venetian reinforcements from reaching Famagusta.

Pius IV (Giovanni Angelo de' Medici) Pope 1559–65. Closed the Council of Trent.

Pius V (Antonio Ghisleri) Pope 1565–72. The main force behind the creation of the Holy League.

Podocattaro, Ettore Venetian defender of Nicosia. Executed by Lala Mustafa Pasha after the fall of the city.

Porcia, Silvio da Commander of a Venetian infantry regiment at the Curzolaris.

Provana de Leynì, Andrea Savoyard admiral. Fought at the Curzolaris and left a report of the battle.

Querini, Marco Venetian *provveditore generale* of Crete in 1570. Commanded the relief expedition sent to Famagusta in the winter of 1571. One of the deputy commanders of the Venetian fleet at the Curzolaris.

Ragazzoni, Giacomo Venetian merchant, unofficially sent on a peace mission to Constantinople in spring 1571.

Requesens y Zúñiga, Luis de *Comendador mayor* of Castile of the Order of Santiago. One of Don Juan of Austria's advisers during the 1571 campaign. Later became governor of Milan and of Flanders.

Romegas, Mathurin Lescaut dit Knight of Malta and corsair. Captain of Marcantonio Colonna's galley at the Curzolaris. Left an account of the battle.

Roxelane *See* Khürrem.

Rüstem Pasha Grand vizier and son-in-law of Süleyman I.

Saint Clément, François de Commander of the Maltese galley fleet in 1570. Defeated by Uluç Ali at Montechiaro and subsequently executed by his brethren for dereliction of duty.

Salihpaşazâde Mehmed Bey Governor of Evvoia. Captured at the Curzolaris and released a few years after the battle.

Santa Cruz, Alvaro de Bazan, marquis of Commander of the

Christian reserve at the Curzolaris. Later defeated an Anglo-French fleet at the Azores.

Scetti, Aurelio Tuscan musician sent to the galleys for murdering his wife. Left an account of the battle of the Curzolaris.

Selim I Known as the Grim. Deposed his father Bayezid II in 1512. Conquered Egypt in 1517.

Selim II Known as the Sallow. Sultan 1566–74. Declared war on Venice over Cyprus.

Sereno, Bartolomeo Papal officer. Fought at the Curzolaris, and later wrote an account of the Cyprus war.

Sermoneta *See* Caetani.

Shah Ismail Founder of the Safavid dynasty and promoter of Shia Islam in the Middle East.

Sokollu Mehmed Pasha Grand vizier under Süleyman I and Selim II. Opposed the latter's decision to go to war with Venice. Murdered in 1579.

Soranzo, Giovanni Venetian plenipotentiary in Rome 1570–1.

Spinola, Ettore Commander of Genoa's state galleys at the Curzolaris. Left a report of the battle.

Strozzi, Piero Florentine exile, arch-enemy of Cosimo I de' Medici. Fought for the French in the Siena war, and later for Paul IV.

Süleyman I Known as the Lawgiver. Sultan 1520–66. Reorganizer of the Ottoman legal system. Fought successfully the Persians, the Habsburgs and the Venetians. Failed to take Malta in 1565. Died on campaign in Hungary in 1566.

Şuluç Mehmed Pasha Governor of Alexandria in 1571. Commanded the Ottoman right at the Curzolaris. Captured by the Venetians, he died of his wounds soon after.

Surian, Michele Venetian plenipotentiary in Rome 1570–1.

Thorgud Reis Turkish corsair, known in Europe as Dragut. An associate of Hayreddin Barbarossa. Conquered Tripoli for the Ottomans in 1551. Killed at the siege of Malta in 1565.

Toledo *See* Álvarez de Toledo Osorio.

Uluç Ali Pasha *See* Kılıç Ali Pasha.

Vallette, Jean Parissot de La Grand master of the Order of Malta. Defeated the Ottoman attempt to take Malta in 1565.

Venier, Sebastiano Commander-in-chief of the Venetian fleet in 1571. Fought at the Curzolaris in the central squadron. Elected doge of Venice in 1578.

Zane, Gerolamo Commander-in-chief of the Venetian fleet in 1570. Disgraced and imprisoned for his failure to relieve Cyprus.

Zaydi Imam Leader of the anti-Ottoman rebellion in the Yemen 1566–7.

Zuñiga, Juan de Venetian plenipotentiary in Rome 1570–1. Later viceroy of Naples.

PROLOGUE

~

On the morning of 7 October 1571 a long procession exited Constantinople, capital of the Ottoman empire, heading west in the direction of the town of Edirne. Forbidding-looking soldiers marched, or rode, alongside turbaned officials, veiled ladies, doctors, pages, clerks, cooks and all the other individuals necessary for the running of a court. In the middle of this human snake, protected by his bodyguard of janissaries and Sipahis of the Porte, rode the flushed, swollen figure of Sultan Selim II, 'Emperor of Rome, Constantinople, Romania, Africa, Asia, Trebisond, Cyprus, Capadocia, Paphlagonia, Cylicia, Panphilia, Licia, Frigia, Archanania, Armenia; Lord of the Greater and Lesser Tartary, with all its provinces of Arabia, Turkey and Russia; Sultan of Babylon, Persia, and of Greater India, with everything that the seven branches of the river Ganges touch; Universal Lord of everything that surrounds the Sun; descendant from Divine Lineage; destructor of the Christian Faith; and dominator of the Universe'. The forty-seven-year-old sultan could feel satisfied as he travelled to his winter palace in Edirne, anticipating a rewarding hunting season. He had reasons to be pleased. After nearly two years of war with the republic of Venice his army had finally conquered the last enemy stronghold on the island of Cyprus, while the Ottoman navy had harassed Venetian-held territories along the Adriatic coast. It was true that

1

now he was facing an alliance of many Western states, but it was common opinion that the league would soon collapse due to internal dissent. This year he had added Cyprus to his empire; the next would see Crete, Corfu, Kotor and – Allah willing – Venice itself.[1]

~

Several hundred miles away in the Gulf of Patras a swift-moving frigate approached a large galley immobile in the water. On the frigate the twenty-four-year-old Don Juan of Austria, illegitimate son of the Holy Roman Emperor Charles V and half-brother of the king of Spain Philip II, scanned the galley's stern searching for someone: Sebastiano Venier, captain-general at sea of the republic of Venice and a very difficult character. Don Juan and Venier had not been on speaking terms for some days, ever since the Venetian had arbitrarily hanged some rebellious soldiers in Spanish pay; but the present situation demanded personal and national pride be swallowed. 'Must we fight?' shouted Don Juan at the seventy-five-year-old, thick-bearded Venetian leaning over his galley's railing. Venier, turning towards the Ottoman fleet slowly deploying into battle order eight miles to the east, answered with steely determination, 'We must, and can't avoid it.'[2]

~

From his station on the poop deck of his galley, Müezzinzâde Ali Pasha, the grand admiral of the Ottoman fleet, beheld the Christian array in the distance. Early reports that the enemy was on the run had been disproved, and it appeared that the Christians intended to fight. Müezzinzâde Ali, confident of victory only a few hours before, was having misgivings. Admittedly, the Ottomans enjoyed a numerical superiority over the allies, but the latter's fleet was bigger than expected. Everything pointed to a tough battle ahead, but despite everything the *kapudan-ı deryâ* believed that his plan would be successful – provided everyone worked in unison. Of his captains and soldiers he was sure, and even of the Greek volunteer rowers, but what about the Christian slaves? Had not one of his subordinates expressed suspicions that they would rebel at the first opportunity? 'Friends,' said Müezzinzâde Ali, turning towards the oarsmen chained to his galley's rowing benches, 'I expect you do your duty today, in return for how I have treated you. If I win, I promise you your liberty. Should the day be yours, then Allah will have given it to you.'[3]

~

In the allied fleet others were also hoping that victory would give them freedom. On 9 August 1565 the musician and convicted murderer Aurelio Scetti had laid his head on the executioner's block in the city of Arezzo. But instead of feeling on his neck the cold steel of the axe, Scetti was pulled to his feet by the hangman amidst shouts of 'Pardon!' His sentence commuted to life servitude and the confiscation of his property, the musician had since lived with the other criminals condemned to row on the galleys of His Most Serene Highness Cosimo I de' Medici, grand duke of Tuscany. Many a time had Scetti petitioned the Florentine authorities for a reprieve, but to no avail. Now his hopes of being liberated were revived as news of the general amnesty proclaimed by Don Juan of Austria for all those convicts prepared to fight spread through the fleet like wildfire. Dragging himself to his battle station, the lame Scetti could only wish to survive the day without ending up chained to an Ottoman rowing bench.[4]

~

Like many of his colleagues Salihpaşazâde Mehmed Bey, governor general of the province of Negropont (the present-day Evvoia) was puzzled by the Christians' behaviour. What did they think they were doing towing to the front of their battle line what appeared to be six large transport galleys? According to intelligence reports the Venetians had modified some *mavna* (as the Ottomans called such vessels) to carry guns, and prisoners taken a few days earlier had confirmed this. But the captives had only admitted to three artillery pieces at the bow and stern – not much in the way of ordnance, and hardly capable of stopping the Ottoman advance. The Christians' move looked like an act of sheer desperation, and as the Ottoman fleet started moving forward the forty-year-old, squint-eyed Salihpaşazâde Mehmed could only assume that the allies were behaving like sheep ready to be slaughtered.[5]

~

From the forecastle of his heavily armed galleass Captain Francesco Duodo watched the Turkish galleys as they loomed ever larger on the horizon, approaching steadily at a speed of about 100 yards a minute. The Venetian commander and his crew welcomed the enemy's arrival. Less than three days had passed since the Christian fleet had received word of the brutal murders in the Cypriot port of Famagusta. Word had circulated of the Turks' treachery after they reneged on their promise of safe conduct for their Venetian prisoners. Among Duodo's crew anger toward the Ottomans ran at fever pitch. Now, in the waters off the western coast of Greece, the Venetians had the chance to exact revenge; their six galleasses, rowing ships of a novel design never before tested in battle, would strike the first blow at the Turkish fleet. Venice had placed all its hopes in these unusually heavy vessels, laden with six times the ordnance of a conventional galley. In a significant tactical and technological shift, the Venetians would rely first on the overwhelming force of their artillery before resorting to hand-to-hand combat at close quarters. Taking in the approaching ships with the eye of an expert mariner, the captain coolly waited until they were only half a mile away.

~

The glow of the early afternoon sun hovered over the city of Rome, shining through the windows of the Vatican palace as Pope Pius V conversed with a group of close collaborators. The sixty-seven-year-old pontiff had many worries: Protestants were busy spreading their heresies all over Europe and the Ottomans' advance in the Mediterranean seemed unstoppable. Pius had done much to

4

counter both perils, even managing to create a league of quarrelsome Christian princes to fight the Muslims. He knew that an allied fleet had been operating for some weeks in the Levant, and all this time the gaunt, deeply religious pope had been fasting and praying for divine aid against the Islamic menace. Suddenly Pius walked towards a window, opened it and stood for some time looking at the sky. At length closing the shutters, he turned towards his treasurer Bartolomeo Busotti. 'It is no time for business,' he exclaimed, his face lit with joy. 'Let us go and thank God, for this very moment our fleet has defeated the Turks.'[6]

1. THE WAXING CRESCENT

~

In early February 1545 Duke Cosimo I de' Medici was busy inspecting the new fortifications of Prato, twelve miles to the north-east of Florence. With him travelled his wife Eleanor Álvarez de Toledo, who being in the final stages of a pregnancy would have wanted to pay a visit to the Sacro Cingolo (Girdle of the Virgin) in the local cathedral. This sacred relic was believed to be especially beneficial to women who were unable to conceive, or who feared complications in childbirth. Since February was also carnival time the ducal couple managed to combine military and pious duties with the pleasures of the season, including attending a theatrical presentation in the old castle of Prato which involved a mock battle between Christians and Turks. At one tumultuous moment of the show an actor portraying a Turk accidentally exposed his 'larger that usual' privates, which caused everyone in the audience to laugh with great gusto.[1]

But in the circumstances the ducal guffaw rang hollow, for in 1545 the Turks were no laughing matter. Anybody travelling along the coasts of the western Mediterranean could have witnessed the havoc caused a few months before by the Muslim fleet under the command of the redoubtable corsair and Ottoman high admiral, Hayreddin Barbarossa: villages torched, crops and livestock destroyed, thousands of people killed or enslaved. In a Venetian atlas of the same year six Turkish galleys can be seen cruising off the Tuscan coast, ready to strike at the Italian mainland, or at anybody unfortunate enough to cross their path. 'Do you think the Turks will invade this year?' asks one of the protagonists of Niccolò Machiavelli's ribald play *The Mandrake*. 'Yes, if you do not pray,' answers a friar.[2] Machiavelli was poking fun at credulous people and corrupt clergymen, but nobody in his day would have denied that the Muslim menace was very real. Indeed, for many it must have seemed only a matter of time before a final onslaught brought the whole of Europe under the rule of Islam.

By the standards of the time, the speed of the Ottoman expansion in Europe and Asia had been stunning. At the beginning of the fourteenth century a petty Turkish warlord called Osman had controlled some land in the north-west of Byzantine Bithynia; 200 years later his descendants, known as the Ottomans, ruled over territories stretching from Durazzo on the Adriatic to Erzurum in eastern Anatolia. In the following decades the Ottomans would conquer the whole of Egypt, large swathes of North Africa, more than half of Hungary, nearly all the Aegean, a big chunk of the Caucasus, the Crimean peninsula and Mesopotamia down to modern-day Basra. In addition, the Sublime Porte,★ as the Ottoman empire was commonly known, extended its rule to the Yemen and the Muslim holy cities of Mecca and Medina, also holding sway over a number of tributary territories, including the whole of Arabia plus the principalities of Moldavia and Wallachia in the Balkans. Through war and treaty, skilfully exploiting the weaknesses of their enemies, the Ottomans had gobbled up piecemeal the Byzantine empire and many other sovereign entities in the Mediterranean. When compelled to

---

★ A translation of the Turkish *kapi* or *dergah-ı-ali*, which originally indicated the place where the Sultan heard legal suits and engaged in law-making activities. The term eventually became the common way to describe the Ottoman government, very much as the White House is synonymous with the executive of the United States of America.

give battle, the Ottoman armies usually prevailed thanks to their superior tactics and discipline. A crippling blow was inflicted on the Serbian kingdom at the first battle of Kosovo in 1389, and the Serbs were forced thereafter to accept the Ottomans as overlords before being finally conquered in 1458. At the battle of Nicopolis in 1396, Sultan Bayezid I crushed a crusading army sent to aid the beleaguered kingdom of Hungary.[3] The flower of European chivalry was either killed or taken prisoner, and Bayezid followed up his victory by annexing the whole of Bulgaria.

The Ottoman expansion was not, however, without its setbacks. The death of Sultan Murad I on the field of Kosovo prevented the Turks exploiting their victory in full, while thirteen years later the famous Mongol warlord Tamerlane delivered a nearly fatal blow to the budding empire. In a series of whirlwind campaigns Tamerlane managed to carve out a huge state in central-west Asia, eventually overwhelming and capturing Bayezid I at the battle of Ankara in 1402. The sultan died in captivity a year later, and everybody reckoned that this was the Ottoman state's death knell. But Tamerlane did not manage to consolidate his conquests, and when his empire collapsed after his death in 1405 Bayezid's heirs took the opportunity to reclaim their inheritance. A civil war amongst the former Sultan's offspring ended with Mehmed I (1413–21) as the sole victor and ruler, allowing his successor Murad II (1421–51) to resume the Ottoman expansionist drive.

But the title of 'conqueror' would appropriately be bestowed on Murad's son, Mehmed II (1444–46, 1451–81), although his first experience as a ruler was well nigh disastrous.[4] His father abdicated in 1444, only to be recalled from retirement by his former viziers when the twelve-year-old Mehmed hesitated in the face of a devastating offensive led by the king of Hungary, Vladislav I, against the Ottoman territories in the Balkans. In a show of daring, Murad crossed the Bosporus with his army – mainly thanks to the active collaboration of the Genoese fleet – and inflicted a crushing defeat on the Hungarians at Varna, killing Vladislav and restoring Ottoman dominance in the region. He then proceeded to suppress a number of internal revolts before overpowering the Hungarians once more at the second battle of Kosovo (October 1448). By the time Murad died three years later, Mehmed had more than learnt his lesson.

From the very beginning of his reign Mehmed's fixed idea was the conquest of Constantinople.[5] The Byzantine empire under the rule of Constantine XI had been reduced to a shadow and a few scattered territories in Greece and Asia Minor. However the sultan undertook the war methodically, first by securing his borders through treaty and military force. He then proceeded to block the Bosporus with fortresses, artillery and ships, before laying siege to Constantinople from the land side. The garrison of the city counted 7,000 men, of which 2,000 were foreigners, and thus vastly inferior to the approximately 150,000 Ottoman attackers. Nonetheless, the Byzantines were prepared to fight to the bitter end, and had the advantage of Constantinople's triple circuit of massive walls. For this very reason Mehmed's army had in its train two colossal bombards designed specifically for the destruction of heavy masonry. The city fell after a two-month siege, thanks to intense artillery pounding and incessant assaults. There followed an orgy of rape and pillage, until Mehmed put a stop to it. The fall of Constantinople not only sent shock waves through the Western world, but also provided the Ottomans with a legal and psychological basis for their wars of conquest: by possessing Constantinople they could claim sovereignty over all the lands of the former Roman empire − of which the Byzantines considered themselves the heirs.

Mehmed followed up his victory by conquering the Genoese colonies on the Black Sea, the Greek–Florentine duchy of Athens, the kingdom of Serbia, most of the Peloponnese, and the last Byzantine enclaves in Anatolia. He next turned against the rebel ruler of Wallachia, Vlad III Drakul (whose favourite pastime was impaling Turkish prisoners of war), forcing him to submit to Ottoman rule. Then, after taking over the Genoese island of Lesvos,

Mehmed turned his attention to the kingdom of Bosnia and the duchy of Hercegovina. By 1466 both territories were completely under Turkish rule, resulting in a wave of conversion to Islam among the native populations. While still engaged in Bosnia Mehmed's aggressive policies in Greece and the Balkans caused him to become embroiled in a war with Venice over the latter's colonies in Greece, as well as having to fight the troublesome Albanian lord George Kastriote 'Skanderbeg'. Kastriote was beaten, although not without considerable effort, and driven into exile. The war with Venice lasted until 1479 when the Venetians were forced to relinquish to the sultan a number of important locations, including the islands of Zakynthos and Kefallonia, as well as the strategic port of Avlona at the mouth of the Adriatic. Even more serious for Venice was the fact that from their bases in Bosnia the Turks had been able to make a number of devastating inroads into the Venetian home territories, exposing not only their vulnerability but also that of the whole Italian peninsula to a determined attack. Although the European powers would not become aware of Italy's weakness until the French invasion of 1494, Mehmed had already grasped it. While planning his offensive into the heart of the Mediterranean, he was determined to rid himself of a foe nearer home: the Christian-held island of Rhodes – this to be followed by a deep probe into Apulia, the heel of Italy.

Since the beginning of the fourteenth century Rhodes had been the headquarters of the monastic–chivalric order of the Hospital of St John of Jerusalem. Its members, known as Johannites, Hospitallers or Knights of Rhodes, had over the years transformed the island into one of the finest fortresses in Europe.[6] On 23 May 1480 the Turkish army, 70,000 strong with a powerful artillery train, landed on the island under the command of Mesic Pasha, a Greek renegade and kinsman of the last Byzantine emperor. The siege lasted until the end of July, but bombardment and mass assaults did not manage to overcome the defences. Mesic Pasha re-embarked his army, having lost at least 25,000 men killed or wounded, plus enormous quantities of materiel, against a few hundred defenders. Rhodes had been a disaster for the Ottomans, and now Mehmed looked to his Italian campaign to redress the balance.

On 28 July a Turkish expeditionary force of 18,000 men under the command of the redoubtable *sancak* of Avlona Gedik Ahmed Pasha landed in front of the town of Otranto.[7] The ostensible reasons for this invasion were Mehmed's vague claim to Apulia as heir of the Byzantine empire, plus his desire to punish the king of Naples for his military assistance to Skanderbeg. In reality, the expedition's objective was to probe the defences of the kingdom of Naples and, or at least it was rumoured so at the time, even attempt the conquest of Rome.* Otranto was taken, the Ottomans executing about 800 male prisoners who refused to convert to Islam and enslaving the women and children. But very soon Gedik discovered there was not enough plunder in the area to sustain his army and, in the face of stiffening Neapolitan resistance, the following October he retired across the Adriatic, leaving 800 foot and 500 horse to garrison Otranto. His intention was to come back the following year, and for the whole winter rumours abounded in Italy about the pope being about to leave Rome for fear of a Turkish raid. But Mehmed II's death in May 1481 and his successor's desire for peace after thirty years of constant warfare – leaving the state coffers empty – resulted in Gedik's downfall and subsequent execution. The Ottoman troops in Otranto quickly surrendered to the Neapolitans, some of them even joining the ranks of their vanquishers. Italy was saved, at least for the time being.

~

* While Mehmed's plans may seem overambitious, it has to be remembered that at the time the south of Italy and the Papal States were seriously depleted of military forces, the king of Naples and the pope being engaged in central Italy against a joint Florentine–Venetian army – the so-called War of the Pazzi Conspiracy. The sultan's decision to strike indicates an awareness of the Italian situation, a tribute to Ottoman espionage.

The speed of Ottoman conquest had been possible thanks to superior tactics, organization and cunning, all augmented by Islamic doctrine. The relevant tenet of this was the notion of jihad, meaning effort, struggle or fight, but implying in general holy war on behalf of Islam. Akin to jihad is *gaza*, meaning a raid (against infidels), and the fact that from the beginning Ottoman rulers adopted for themselves the title of *gazi* shows their commitment as fighters in a religious war. Sharia, Islamic law, in fact stresses jihad against non-Muslims as a specific duty for Muslims as a group; thus a continuous state of conflict is believed to exist between the *darülislam*, the abode of those who have embraced the true faith, and the *darülharb* (literally 'house of war'), the dwelling of the unbelievers. Jihad against infidels is a perpetual obligation until the universal domination of Islam is attained, so peace with non-Muslim polities is but a provisional state of affairs, justified by peculiar circumstances. Given the permanence of holy war, only truces, not authentic peace treaties, are possible with non-Islamic political entities; at the same time any truce may be repudiated unilaterally before its expiration should it be profitable for Muslims to resume the conflict, although notice should be given to the infidel party together with a request to accept Islam. Technically only the 'people with holy books' – Christians and Jews – can refuse to embrace Islam once subjugated; anybody else who rejects conversion may be freely killed or enslaved. However, Trinitarian Christians may be seen as polytheists and thus not protected by the sharia law – the massacre at Otranto being a case in point. Similarly, incursions conducted by Muslim border raiders and corsairs, even in times of peace, may be justified by the legal–religious obligation to wage *gaza* as stated in sharia law.[8]

Gaza, as described above, is taught by the Hanafi Islamic school of religious law, the one followed by the Ottomans.* Thus, by

---

* The other three schools of law within Sunni Islam are the Shafi, the Maliki and the Hanbali.

fighting the Christians the sultans were not only following God's command, but also legitimizing their role as rulers of the faithful. However, although the tenets of Islam did pervade Turkish society and institutions, it would be wrong to see the Ottoman empire as a conquest machine single-mindedly driven by religious beliefs. It had come together by force, but also thanks to the tacit, and often open, acceptance of Ottoman rule by the various conquered populations. This meant that the empire's make-up – indeed its military forces – comprised not just orthodox Sunni Muslims, but Christians and Jews as well. Also important were the more or less heterodox Islamic cults: for example, the *Bektaşi* dervish sect, which combined elements of Islam, Christianity, Buddhism and pre-Muslim Turkish paganism, was particularly popular amongst the elite janissary troops. While it would be wrong to describe this as tolerance in the modern sense, it is however true that the teachings of the Hanafi school – stressing political harmony and the rights of the 'people with holy books' – in general favoured a live-and-let-live policy. As a result, the sultans allowed the various religious communities to run their own affairs, provided this did not lead to unrest. Islamic law thus allowed the Ottomans an opportunistic approach to international politics, but also provided them with an ideological framework to justify their expansionist policy.

The Ottoman advance had been possible mainly thanks to their army and the administrative system created to support it. The early Ottoman army had consisted mainly of mounted raiders gathered around their leader, conducting a highly mobile and unsystematic type of warfare.[9] As the expanding Ottoman state started developing its own internal organization, it also adopted a more stable and efficient military structure. This process owed as much to specific martial necessities as to the need of the central government to exercise an efficient form of territorial control throughout the empire. Ottoman troops were essentially of four types: 'feudal', permanent, militia and volunteer.

The army derived most of its quantitative strength from the feudal *timar* system,[10] which involved the sultan granting land to individuals in exchange for cavalry service. By the mid-sixteenth century this system had been adopted throughout the empire, with the exclusion of a few places such as Egypt and Algeria. Of the military fiefs the smallest was the *timar* proper, considered to be worth up to 20,000 *akçe* per year (the *akçe* being the standard silver monetary unit), followed by the bigger *zeamet*, with a value of up to 100,000 *akçe*; any fief worth more than 100,000 *akçe* was known as a *hass* and reserved for district and provincial governors.

A typical *timar* would consist of a village or a number of villages, with adjoining fields, ruled by a cavalryman, or *sipahi*, who had the right to collect taxes from the local peasants, and exercise 'low justice' – imposing and collecting fines for misdemeanours. Part of the taxes collected in a *timar* went to the imperial treasury, while the remaininder paid for the *sipahi*'s upkeep. The *sipahi* had to maintain his own horse, carry a fixed set of weapons (bow, sword, shield, lance and mace), plus armour if he could afford it, and for every 3,000 *akçe* of revenue provide also a fully armed *cebelü* horseman. At the beginning of the sixteenth century a *sipahi* running a *timar* worth 5,000 *akçe* would bring on campaign a suit of armour, one *cebelü* and a tent.[11] The *timars* of a certain district, or *sancak*, would come under the control of an appointed official known as a *sancak bey*. *Sancak*s were grouped together to form a province (*beylerbeik*) under a *beylerbey*. With the exception of a few hereditary *sancak*s, the sultan appointed district and provincial governors, and the same was true for most *timar* holders.

The *timar* system was possible for two reasons. For one, the vast majority of the land was *miri*, crown property. Second, the sultan's subjects owed their allegiance to him only, prompting Machiavelli's famous comment, 'The Turkish empire is ruled by one man; all the others are his servants,' a sweeping statement, perhaps, but containing a lot of truth.[12] Comprehensive lists indicating *timar* holders, as well as all others enjoying in some way the revenues of a *sancak*, allowed the central government to create accurate muster rolls for campaigns, and enforce when necessary the statutory penalties against unjustified absences. However, the system needed tight control from the centre since only a strong executive could intimidate the fief holders to obey the rules. Luckily for the Ottomans, during the sixteenth century they never lacked strong leaders.

Failure to appear at musters could cause a *sipahi* to lose his *timar*, while the sons of fief holders only inherited the right to acquire one, not their father's actual holding. It could take years of military service for someone to obtain a fief in the first place, and one of the reasons behind the Ottomans' expansionism was the never-ending need to find more land to allocate to the many aspiring *timar* holders, especially those who came from the ranks of the imperial bureaucracy or professional military. By 1525 there were nearly 28,000 such holders, a number that would increase in the following years with the empire's territorial expansion. At the beginning of the seventeenth century such contingents amounted to a paper strength of 100,000 men, albeit not all of them serving at any one time. Thanks to the *timar* system, the sultan could plan a military expedition with a precise idea of the number of feudal cavalrymen at his disposal.[13]

The Ottoman permanent standing army, the *kapıkulu* troops, followed a different pattern. For one, its members were recruited in the same way as top government officials, which many, not just in the West, found repugnant. Nonetheless, the system guaranteed professionalism and total loyalty to the Ottoman dynasty, if not to the sultan as an individual. From the beginning the ranks of the sultans' army and administration had been augmented by slaves, captured in war or bought at market. The practice of using slaves as soldiers and administrators was not new in the Islamic world: the *ghulam* or *kul* system, emphasizing the training of slaves in order to make them loyal government agents or soldiers, had allowed the rise of centralized military regimes like that of the Mamluks of Egypt. But even at the acme of Ottoman expansion the captured or purchased slaves did not cover the state's needs. Alternative ways had to be found to solve the manpower problem, and starting in the mid-fourteenth century the sultans started employing the *devşirme* (literally collection), which meant nothing less than the enslavement of their Christian subjects. This practice went against Islamic law, since non-Muslims living under Muslim sovereignty who pay the prescribed taxes may not be enslaved or have their property confiscated. Nevertheless, the sultans found the *devşirme* too useful a tool, and although certain scholars debated its lawfulness it would survive until the eighteenth century.[14] For the majority of those subjected to it, the *devşirme* was an odious practice; and even if it catapulted some people from impoverished backgrounds 'into arguably the most powerful and refined polity in the world',[15] for most this was hardly a consolation. It was not simply that parents lost their beloved sons; the prospect of the collected youths becoming Muslims was appalling for all Christians.

The *devşirme* appears not to have been applied on a regular basis, but rather when need arose. Once a collection was decreed, officials visited Christian villages, and also by the Bosnians' own request the Muslim ones in Bosnia, where they would select boys between the ages of eight and eighteen at the rate of one every forty households, being careful not to pick only sons, craftsmen, married individuals, people of good social standing or anyone with unacceptable physical or personality traits. The youths thus chosen were sent to Constantinople, where they were inspected by the ağa, or commander-in-chief, of the janissaries, circumcised★ and then, according to their physique, intelligence or other qualities, sent off to their final destination: one of the palace schools, the royal gardens or, for the majority, a farm in Anatolia. From now on the boys' careers, indeed their very lives, depended on the sultan's will, and each of them, from the future vizier to the lowest of soldiers, became a *kapıkulu*, a slave of the Porte. Those selected for the military were 'sold' to Muslim farmers, eventually being recalled to

★ Circumcision was not practised by the Christians but is a mandatory condition for a Muslim. Thus, the removal of the foreskin, if not technically a forced conversion, was at least from a psychological point of view a powerful way to give the collected youths an Islamic imprint, forcing on them a sense of being separated for good from their original family and religious community.

the capital to train for one of the most formidable military corps of all time, the janissaries.

Founded probably by Sultan Orhan in the mid-fourteenth century by recruiting prisoners of war, a practice that was never fully abandoned even after the introduction of the *devşirme*, the *yeniçeri* (new troops, hence janissaries) were educated for several years in spartan conditions. During this period they exercised with every type of infantry weapon and tactics, besides performing a series of manual jobs for the sultan. Some of them were also trained as artillerymen or engineers. Once their schooling ended the recruits were accepted into one of the *kapıkulu* units. The years of hardship and rigorous training, enhanced by legally imposed celibacy and the soldiers' religious commitment, contributed to the creation of the janissaries' esprit de corps. On more than one occasion battles were won thanks to the determination and resilience of the janissaries, and foreign observers were right to consider them the core of the Turkish army. Tough, disciplined, highly professional and often brutal, the janissaries were amongst the finest troops the world has ever seen.

The janissaries' fame was originally enhanced by their small numbers, which however would markedly increase as the Ottomans found themselves embroiled on more fronts: 10,156 in 1514; 11,439 regulars and apprentices in 1527; 20,543 in 1567, more than a third of them novices; 21,094 seven years later; and finally a grand total of 45,000 in 1597. During this period the proportion of cadets was between a third and a fourth of the total. This allowed for a steady stream of replacements, as the regulars either died or retired, without burdening excessively the Sultan's treasury, given that all *kapıkulu* troops were permanently on the payroll. This said, the janissaries could be very costly in other ways, their habit of meddling with the internal politics of the empire often forcing the Ottoman rulers to appease them with monetary or other gratifications. On the other hand, the idea of the worthy receiving generous rewards was widespread, and woe betide any Ottoman army commander not displaying the appropriate degree of largesse.[16]

The sultans' permanent household troops also included the Six Cavalry Divisions (the Sipahis of the Porte), numbering 5–6,000 men in the sixteenth century, and the 2,000-odd gunners of the artillery, all *devşirme* individuals not selected for administrative duties. Outside the *kapikulu* corps were the less glamorous but nonetheless useful *azab*s, militiamen from the towns, by the 1500s used mostly for garrison duties. In addition, there were the roughly 40,000-strong *akincis*, or Raiders, light cavalrymen from Rumelia (Ottoman-held Europe) who served for booty on a semi-voluntary basis, conducting a sort of permanent warfare along the Habsburg–Ottoman frontier in the Balkans. The corps of sappers, organized in a manner similar to the *timar* system, in 1521 could send on campaign something like 50,000 men out of a pool of 300,000.

Although the sultan could field armies of more than 150,000 combatants the main strength of the Ottoman war machine in the sixteenth century lay in its organizational structure, superior battle tactics and the employment of up-to-date military technology. The individual soldier's direct allegiance to the central government played a part in this, for as the Venetian envoy Daniello de' Ludovisi would report in 1534, 'The Lord Turk can count on good soldiers because they are not mercenaries . . . nor given to him for aid by other princes . . . instead, the troops of the Lord Turk are but his own.'[17] Although Ludovisi was speaking specifically of the sultan's standing army, the same could be said of the rest of his forces including the upper levels of the military. *Sancak bey*s, *beylerbeyk*s, *ağa*s of the janissaries and viziers overwhelmingly came from the ranks of the *kapıkulu* and thus owed their loyalty to none but the state. A centralized administrative structure coupled with an efficient road network also guaranteed that armies on campaign received sufficient supplies. The system's major drawback was the need of a firm and efficient controlling hand, and disaster could occur if a top official, for whatever motive, decided to withhold provisions from an army on campaign. Infighting among Ottoman commanders or administrators would be the cause of numerous military failures.

Until the end of the sixteenth century, and despite a few setbacks, the Ottomans ruled supreme on the battlefield. This was partly due to their numbers, a factor emphasized time and time again by European observers, but also their skilful use of technology. Indeed, until after the Peace of Passarowitz (1718) the Turks could boast comparable military know-how to their Western opponents, showing a remarkable capacity to adopt new discoveries.* From the beginning the Ottomans had perceived the importance of firearms, and by the mid-fifteenth century had an impressive artillery park, employing also some of the best cannon makers and artillerymen of the day.† Technological developments tended to spread quickly in the Mediterranean area, but the Turks demonstrated great ingenuity and flexibility in applying them to battlefield situations. For example, they adopted the *wagenburg* from the Hungarians once they had seen it in action, creating a train of mule-drawn carts equipped with hand gunners and light cannons. Despite the fact that Ottoman artillery is usually associated with big siege guns, the sultans' armies made extensive use of easily transportable pieces weighing about 125 pounds. These guns used in coordination with infantry and cavalry were to prove a great tactical asset, real battle-winning instruments, according to some observers.[18]

The main weakness of the Ottoman military machine lay somewhat paradoxically in the fact that in many ways it was still very much a medieval institution, each soldier fighting in formation but always as an individual. The janissaries chose their own weapons,

* The Peace of Passarowitz between the Ottomans, Venice and the Holy Roman Empire provided for a twenty-four-year peace and gave to the Habsburgs what remained of Turkish Hungary, Lesser Wallachia and Belgrade with parts of northern Serbia. Venice retained a few of the territorial gains it had acquired in the previous years. Although this is considered to mark the end of Ottoman western expansion, it must be remembered that Belgrade and Lesser Wallachia were recovered once more by Turkey after the Treaty of Belgrade in 1739.

† Mehmed II employed a number of German and Hungarian gunners, lured to Constantinople by high wages. During the 1480 siege of Rhodes a German engineer and artillery expert in Ottoman service by the name of Maister Georg defected to the Knights of St John, only to be executed by them when they discovered that he was passing information to the besiegers about the position of the defenders' guns.

were superb marksmen and unbeatable in a man-to-man situation, but it took years and much expense to train them properly. By the mid-sixteenth century the West was perfecting the musket and pike system, allowing masses of men to be trained for battle in a relatively short period of time. Even more important, these men were easy to replace, but most Ottoman soldiers, in particular the household troops, were not. Europe adopted the opposite view to that of Grand Vizier Lufti Pasha, that troops should be few but excellent, and in the end the Western system of warfare would emerge victorious. To be fair, the Ottoman attitude was not simply blind conservatism, being instead the result of a pragmatic approach to warfare. During the sixteenth and seventeenth centuries the Porte faced simultaneously a number of enemies employing different fighting techniques. Adopting exclusively Western tactics would have put the Ottomans at a disadvantage when facing their easterly foes, and vice versa.

~

Mehmed II's death caused a civil war between his two sons Jem and Bayezid. When the former lose and had to flee, he sought asylum first with the Knights of St John and then with the pope. The following fifteen years would see Jem playing an important, if passive, role in all Mediterranean diplomatic manoeuvrings, with Bayezid always concerned about his exiled brother being exploited by some European state. This situation benefited the Sultan's neighbours: from the very beginning Bayezid was eager to conclude treaties with his former adversaries or ratify existing ones. Until the mid-1490s the Ottoman empire did not attempt any major war against a Western power, this being as much due to Jem's presence as to Bayezid's need to reorganize the state and settle its finances. It is often believed that the Ottoman empire was a 'gunpowder state', not interested in commerce; but the Porte recognized the importance of trade, the treaty with the the Dalmatian city of Dubrovnik (Ragusa) being a case in point. For a token annual tribute of 3,000 ducats the Ragusans obtained extensive commercial privileges in the Levant and the assurance that their territory would not be subjected to the peacetime raids launched by the Turks as part of *gaza*. Moreover, like every Early Modern polity much of the empire's revenue came from custom duties, an inflow of money that could dry-up dramatically in time of war.[19] Bayezid needed peace in order to rebuild the state's financial assets, and places like Dubrovnik were the gates through which strategically important goods and new discoveries, military technology in particular, made their way into the Ottoman empire.

Despite Bayezid's essentially peaceful nature, during the early years of his reign there was no lack of war. The first target was the prince of Wallachia, Karabogdan, attacked for refusing to pay the tribute due to Constantinople, and in the following years the Ottomans slowly brought the lower Danube area under their control. Temporarily distracted by a six-year war against the Mamluks of Egypt, Bayezid had to wait until 1495 before resuming his father's expansionist policy. Jem's death in the February of that year freed the sultan's hands, allowing him to attack Hungary, fight Poland over the control of Moldavia, and finally go to war with Venice. The change from a low-conflict policy, for the sake of which even border raiding was kept to the minimum, to one of open warfare was not only the result of Jem's death; for some years there had been no major campaign and the army, the *kapıkulu* corps in particular, was getting restless. After major riots in Constantinople in the summer of 1496 the government realized that it could no longer keep its professional troops from pursuing glory, booty and rewards.[20] Bayezid needed new *timar* land, and to secure his frontiers in Greece and the Balkans. The war with Venice in 1499 was a direct result of this, although the ostensible motive was the Franco-Venetian alliance – Charles VIII of France having proclaimed an anti-Ottoman crusade – and Venice's financial support for the Sultan's enemies in the Balkans.

The conflict had been brewing for some time, and from 1496 onward the Ottomans subjected the Venetians to continuous provocations in the Balkans and the Adriatic. The Republic of St Mark swallowed one humiliation after the other with little protest, considering the safeguarding of her Levantine trade more important. Partly for this reason war did not erupt immediately, and in any case between 1496 and 1498 Bayezid was too busy fighting in Poland to pay much attention to his western frontiers. However, by the summer of 1498 Venetian merchants in Constantinople were reporting with alarm the Sultan's extensive shipbuilding programme, suggesting there could be only one target for such preparations.[21] These fears became reality the following spring, when, after some further desultory diplomatic exchanges, the Ottomans suddenly attacked and quickly overran most of Venice's territories in Greece with the exception of a few coastal cities. Then a Venetian fleet was roundly defeated at Zonchio, sending the message that not only had the Ottoman navy come into its own but, was also a force to be reckoned with. The Ottomans followed up their victory by taking the key fortress of Lepanto and fortifying the entrance to the Gulf of Corinth. From now on the main Venetian trade route to the Levant could be closed at the sultan's whim. Disastrous as the situation might have appeared in Greece, the rudest shock for the Venetians came from another front. In June a rapidly moving army under Iskender Pasha departed from its bases in Bosnia and proceeded to conduct a massive raid deep into Friuli, with cavalry units arriving at Venice's very doorstep. From the lagoon the terrified citizens could see the flames of the torched hamlets.

In the course of the war the Venetians lost the majority of their coastal cities, managing to hold on only to Nafplio, Monemvasia and Corfu. Their only real success was the capture of the Adriatic port of Levkás. Venice could not throw all of her resources into the conflict, as the republic was also fighting in Italy and desperately seeking allies elsewhere. Eventually, following France's example, the papacy, Hungary and Spain also agreed to join the fray, but Venice had to pay the Hungarians a subsidy of 100,000 ducats for their support. Hungary's contribution was half-hearted, and never really a threat for the Ottomans. Venice's other allies also proved a disappointment: in 1501 a joint French–Hospitaller–Venetian expedition against Mytilene (Lesvos) ended in fiasco, mainly because of the indecision of the French commander. In the end Venice had to give up most of her few conquests, retaining Zakynthos and Kefallonia plus a small number of footholds on the Greek mainland. For Bayezid the war had been a triumph; not only had he managed to consolidate his European borders, but now many trade routes between east and west were under Ottoman control. This not only resulted in an increase in revenue but also boosted the sultan's international standing.

From 1503 until 1521 the Ottomans paid little attention to Europe, having to face a new threat that had arisen in the east.[22] The new enemy, and the Ottomans' bane for the next two centuries, was the Persian Safavi dynasty, which in less than ten years, from 1501 to 1510, managed to conquer not only most of Mesopotamia and the whole of modern Iran, but also Azerbaijan and a number of territories around the Caspian Sea. A clash between the Ottomans and the Safavis was pretty much inevitable, not only due to the latter's claim to Turkish lands in eastern Anatolia but also because of their religious beliefs. The Safavis were Shia, considered a heterodox branch of Islam by the Sunni Ottomans, and their leader Shah Ismail was soon actively promoting Shi'ism in Anatolia, thus suborning the allegiance of many of the sultan's subjects, especially the Turcomans of the border regions, ever resentful of Constantinople's rule. Worrying as this might have been, even worse from Bayezid's point of view was Ismail's membership of the dervish *Bektaşi* order. Since the latter was traditionally associated with the janissaries, the sultan risked seeing his standing army going over to the Safavis literally lock, stock and barrel.[23]

Bayezid at first approached the problem with great caution, trying unsuccessfully to close his eastern borders to Shia missionaries and exiling to the Peloponnese a number of Safavi sympathizers. Otherwise he limited himself to sending an army to keep watch on his eastern frontiers, and studiously tried to avoid hostilities with his powerful new neighbour. The sultan's prudence was largely motivated by the desertion rate among Ottoman soldiers in the east, many going over to Ismail, attracted by his religion, ideology and generosity.[24] The sultan watched with apprehension the growth of Ismail's power and Safavis' diplomatic overtures towards Venice and his other potential enemies. From this date the Ottomans would be constantly concerned about possible alliances between Persia and one of the Western powers.

Things came to a head in 1511 when a massive Safavi-sponsored rebellion erupted in western Anatolia. Led by the charismatic Shah Kulu (the shah's slave), the rebels marched north, defeated an Ottoman army, stormed Kütahya and proceeded to advance towards Bursa. News of these events threw Constantinople into a panic, but the government reacted quickly: 4,000 *sipahi*s and *kapıkulu* troops were sent to Asia from Rumelia under the command of Prince Ahmed and Grand Vizir Hadim Ali Pasha. The rebels defeated this force near Sivas, killing Hadim; but Shah Kulu also lost his life, leaving his leaderless followers to seek asylum in Persia.[25] The rebellion discredited Bayezid's regime, causing Prince Selim, who from the beginning had advocated strong measures against Ismail, to revolt against his father. Obtaining the janissaries' support, he forced Bayezid to abdicate in his favour on 24 May 1512. Broken in spirit, the old sultan died two months later.

Despite its sad ending, Bayezid's reign marked a period of great economic growth and administrative consolidation for the Ottoman empire. The war with the Egyptian Mamluks resulted in improved weapons for the *kapıkulu* troops, in particular the janissaries, and during this period the Ottomans adopted smaller field guns. The Mytilene campaign of 1501 taught them also some lessons about the use of naval artillery in amphibious operations, and indeed Bayezid's greatest achievement was the creation of a fleet equal to that of Venice. Although he conquered few territories, these were nevertheless strategically important, and the strengthening of the Ottoman state and its military organization would pay enormous dividends under his successors.

Selim I showed immediately that he came from a different mould than his father, and it is with some justification that he is known as Yavuz (the Grim). After eliminating his brothers Kurkud and Ahmed he proceeded to launch a mopping-up campaign in Anatolia, executing Ismail's followers in their thousands and removing disloyal fief holders. He then attacked the Shah himself since Ismail's religious beliefs ran contrary to orthodox *Sunni* Islam, being careful first to obtain a *fatwa** declaring that it was just and mandatory to destroy the heretical Ismail and his followers. At the battle of Chaldiran, in August 1514, the *Safavi* cavalry was brought down by the entrenched Ottoman artillery and handgun-armed janissaries, and Selim followed up his victory by annexing the mountainous area from Erzurum to Diyarbakir, bringing under his control the local warlike Kurdish tribes. However, at the same time Turcoman tribes from Anatolia emigrated en masse to Persia, where they enlisted to fight for the Safavis.

Selim's next move, and his military masterpiece, was the subjugation of Egypt, one of the biggest grain producers in the Mediterranean basin.[26] Having received intelligence of a possible anti-Ottoman alliance between the Egyptians and the Persians, Selim struck first and, in a two-stage campaign lasting from the beginning of August 1516 to the end of January 1517, conquered the whole of Syria and Egypt. The Turkish takeover of the Mamluk state meant that nearly all the commercial routes to the Levant were under Ottoman control, and now, thanks also to his powerful navy, the sultan could dominate the grain trade of the area. For the rest of the century the resources of defeated Egypt would sustain the Ottomans' expansionism, while many European countries used to tapping into the Mamluks' grain supply found Egypt's new rulers disinclined to grant them such facilities.

Selim would have liked to continue campaigning in the east but discovered that his exhausted troops would follow him no further. Not one to be deterred from new conquests, the sultan turned his attention to the improvement of his arsenal and fleet with the objec-

---

* A fatwa is a legal opinion based on the Sharia law and is issued by an individual or a body of spiritual standing within the Islamic world.

tive of capturing Rhodes. This was as much a matter of necessity as of prestige, since while Rhodes remained under the control of the Knights of St John the sea routes between Egypt and Istanbul would never be secure. Besides, the conquest of Rhodes fitted very well with Ottoman expansionist strategy, which stressed, according to one writer, a policy of 'one step eastwards, one step westwards'.[27] By the end of Selim's reign the Ottomans would be able to pursue at the same time extensive maritime and land campaigns against Europe, not just thanks to an extensive shipbuilding programme, but also because by 1519 they had managed to establish their suzerainty over the cities of Tunis and Algiers. On a map the Ottoman empire now resembled the gaping maw of a prehistoric beast, poised to devour the whole of the Western world.

Selim died in 1520, bestowing to his son Süleyman an empire doubled in size. He also left a legacy of war with Persia and plans for future conquests in Europe, and for this reason Süleyman's reign has been described as having a 'crisis of orientation'.[28] Süleyman is justly known in the West as the Magnificent as under him the Ottoman state would reach its apex of splendour and power, but it was also during his reign that the first cracks in the edifice of the empire started to appear.* Selim I may have warded off the Safavi threat, but already a new foe had appeared in the south. Ever since Vasco de Gama had rounded the Cape of Good Hope in 1497, the Portuguese had been threatening Muslim commerce in the Indian Ocean. In 1507 they captured the stronghold of Hormuz, all but closing down the route from Basra to Aleppo. In 1517 they attempted the same in the strategically important Red Sea, only to be rebuffed after a sharp fight off Jiddah, forty miles west of Mecca. But in the long run the Portuguese maritime advance to the east, followed later by the Dutch and the English, would contribute to the disruption of the Mediterranean trade system, of which the Ottomans were one of the greatest beneficiaries.

---

* For the Turks he is *Kânûni*, the Lawgiver, since it was during his reign that Ottoman civil law was given an organic and permanent structure.

Likewise, the sultan's aggressive stance towards the West turned him into something of a bogey man and effectively stifled the possibility of trustworthy relations between the Ottomans and most European countries. But right from his accession Süleyman was faced with the compelling need to keep his standing army occupied and find new *timar* land for the ever-growing list of postulants from the military and administrative classes, the ultimate buttress of his power. Since the one way for somebody to obtain a fief was to prove his worth on campaign, for the Ottomans war-fed expansionism was almost inevitable. To this should be added the ideology of conquest developed by the Ottomans over two centuries, summarized by Süleyman himself as 'not fighting for gold and treasures, but for victory, glory, renown and the increase of the empire'.[29] For the Ottomans war was as much a political and social necessity as the result of a powerful ideological drive.

Süleyman started his reign by crushing a rebellion in Damascus, before turning his attention to Hungary on the pretext that King Lajos II had imprisoned the Ottoman ambassador. It appears that the Porte had been planning an attack for some time, having decided that of all the possible targets Hungary was the weakest,[30] and in the course of a brief if not totally successful campaign captured the important fortress of Belgrade. His next move involved using Selim I's navy against Rhodes, and at the end of June 1522 a gigantic expeditionary force of 300,000 men, including soldiers, support units and sappers, landed on the Hospitallers' island. After six months of relentless bombardment and assaults, the few surviving defenders, lacking food and munitions, surrendered on the condition they could be allowed to leave the island with their treasure and records. Süleyman could afford to be generous; and as the grand master and his surviving knights set sail from the island on the first day of the following January, the sultan commented gravely, 'Truly I cannot but grieve to see this unfortunate old man, driven out of his dwelling, to depart hence so heavily.'[31] He would soon be cursing his chivalrous attitude.

It took Süleyman a couple of years to make good the losses in men and materiel sustained at Rhodes, giving his neighbours a brief respite while the sultan chose his next objective. He had a number of choices, including a naval campaign against the Portuguese in the Red Sea to protect the spice trade routes. For a number of reasons, mostly logistic, this plan proved difficult to implement, the Porte preferring instead to obtain the same result by striking a deal with the Persians. Thus the only military option left to Süleyman was to advance westward – a decision helped by a revolt of the war-hungry janissaries in 1525 – and specifically once more against the kingdom of Hungary, having first taken care to isolate it politically. The campaign not only succeeded in subjugating the kingdom and satisfying the *kapıkulu* troops, but also secured safer borders. Thus, after attempting to obtain King Lajos' surrender by diplomatic means, an Ottoman army invaded Hungary in the summer of 1526 and on 29 August won a resounding victory at Mohács. Intense fire from the Turkish artillery and the janissaries' muskets broke the badly coordinated Hungarian attacks, killing Lajos and 15,000 of his men. Süleyman followed up his victory by sacking and burning the Hungarian capital of Buda; however, with overstretched supply lines and in the face of reorganizing enemy forces, he decided not to occupy the whole kingdom, preferring instead to retain only the strategically important southern part of the country and retiring his army to its winter quarters in Belgrade.[32]

For the next two years serious troubles in Anatolia kept Süleyman busy, allowing a political crisis to develop in Hungary which would engage him for the rest of his reign. The death of King Lajos at Mohács had produced a power vacuum that the Hungarian Estates attempted to fill by electing the magnate János Szapolyai, a decision contested by the late sovereign's Habsburg brother-in-law Ferdinand who had himself crowned king of Hungary in December 1526. Süleyman decided to throw his weight behind Szapolyai, and in 1529 the disgruntled Ferdinand invaded Hungary and took its capital, provoking the Porte's immediate response. Moving swiftly, Süleyman retook Buda and reinstated Szapolyai, but now as an Ottoman vassal and with a janissary garrison. Keeping up the momentum of his advance, the sultan marched deep into Austria and proceeded to besiege Ferdinand's capital Vienna. Although forced to retreat due to Austrian resistance and the approaching winter, Süleyman's feat sent shock waves through Europe. Nonetheless, Ferdinand's appearance on the scene had considerably complicated the Ottomans' position in Hungary. Now they were facing a serious opponent, the king of Bohemia and brother of the Holy Roman Emperor Charles V, not simply a weak and politically isolated country.

The Habsburg–Ottoman war ground on for another two years until Ferdinand and Süleyman agreed to a truce in 1533, leaving the Hungarian question largely unresolved. The sultan was having troubles with the Safavis, and thus unwilling to fight on two fronts at the same time. The Ottoman campaign in the east lasted until 1536, bringing to the empire Bitlis, Tabriz, Erzurum and the plum city of Baghdad. But Süleyman's Western adversaries were not idle; in 1535 a Spanish amphibious expedition led in person by Emperor Charles V managed to capture the Ottoman vassal city of Tunis. Süleyman realized that despite his considerable fleet, to gain supremacy at sea he needed a skilful strategist and tactician. As a result in 1533 the *beylerbey* of Algiers Hayreddin Barbarossa was summoned to Constantinople and made *kapudan-ı deryâ*, grand admiral of the Ottoman navy.

The choice could not have been better. Born in Mytilene around 1466 to a family of Albanian origin, Hayreddin, then called Hizir, had become a corsair with his older brother Arouj at an early age. The two brothers, known as Barbarossa allegedly because of their red beards, enjoyed a certain amount of success as pirates in the eastern Mediterranean, operating partially with the support of Bayezid II's son Kurkud. With the advent of Selim I and the death of their sponsor, Arouj and Hizir decided to take their business to healthier North African waters. Arouj quickly established himself as ruler of Algiers and on his death in 1518 power passed to Hizir, who by now had taken the nomme de guerre of Hayreddin.[33] Faced with the growing power of the Spanish, the surviving Barbarossa understood that if he was going to survive he needed a patron. In 1519 he submitted to the sultan in exchange for the title of *beylerbey*, and from his base in Algiers became the scourge of the Mediterranean. By choosing him as grand admiral Süleyman was entrusting his fleet to one of the most distinguished sailors Islam has ever produced, while Barbarossa could now count on the immense resources of the Ottoman empire.

Hayreddin wasted no time. In 1534 he launched raids on the Italian coast, leaving a trail of destruction from Latium to Calabria. On the night of 8 August he stormed the town of Fondi, near Rome, intent on kidnapping the internationally renowned beauty Giulia Gonzaga as a gift for the sultan. Warned in time of the impending peril, Giulia escaped in her nightgown, leaving a thwarted Barbarossa to vent his fury on the town. The next year, in revenge for a Spanish expedition against Tunis, he attacked the Balearic Islands, netting 6,000 slaves. In the meantime, to resist growing Habsburg power Süleyman had become an ally of the French king Francis I. The two rulers hatched a plan involving a French attack on the north of Italy, while Barbarossa executed an amphibious assault in the south. In February 1537 a French army crossed the Alps, the sultan waiting with his army in Avlona for the right moment to strike. In mid-July the advance party of Süleyman's army under Lufti Pasha landed on the heel of Italy and, avoiding the strongholds of Brindisi and Otranto, began to advance towards Naples. But the military situation was very different from what it had been in 1480, the south of Italy being now part of the Habsburg Mediterranean system. The Turks only managed to conduct a raid in depth, and in the meantime Francis signed a ten-year truce with Charles V. Faced with the risk of his communication being cut by a joint Venetian–papal–Habsburg naval force, Süleyman was forced to withdraw his forces after only two weeks.[34]

Francis had assured the Porte that the Venetians would remain neutral in the event of a war against Charles V, but for the safety of his communication and supply lines the sultan had to be sure that no surprise would come from Venice's remaining bases in Greece. When the Republic of St Mark hesitated to join the Franco-Turkish alliance, Süleyman initiated hostilities in August 1537 by besieging unsuccessfully the Venetian fortresses of Corfu and Nafplio. The sultan's decision was made after it became clear that the French were not going to invade Italy after all, but Süleyman needed to give his booty-deprived war hounds something to chew on. Predictably, the Ottoman move pushed the Venetians into the arms of the Habsburgs, Venice, Charles V and Pope Paul III creating the first anti-Ottoman Holy League. The following year the league's naval forces were mauled by Hayreddin's fleet at Preveza. Dissent among the allies had hampered coordinated action against the Ottomans, and for the next thirty years the naval initiative in the Mediterranean would be in Muslim hands.

The Ottomans had started out as a land-based power, and it had taken them some time to develop an interest in the sea. During the fourteenth century and the first half of the fifteenth Venice had been the undisputed hegemonic maritime power in the Levant, using the dozens of independent political entities in the Aegean Sea as buffers against the Ottomans' advance. Only after the war of 1479 had the Ottomans managed to push the Venetians back towards the western Mediterranean, and by capturing the city of Avlona in Albania they had gained an important post at the entry to the Adriatic for monitoring Venetian, and later Spanish, naval movements.[35]

Ottoman sea policy was to an extent conditioned by Islamic legal thinking. From the earliest days Muslim scholars had distinguished between the high seas, coastal and inland waters, the former being somewhat of a free zone and the others falling under the jurisdiction of whoever controlled the adjacent land. However, according to some Islamic theorists the Mediterranean was not really an open sea, but, as the twentieth-century French historian Fernand Braudel aptly put it, a series of watery plains united by channels of varying width. Thus the Adriatic, the Sea of Marmara, the Black and Red Seas were treated as inland waters, the property of the states that controlled the nearby coasts. This idea gained strength with the taking of Constantinople, since the city was the pivot between Asia and Europe, the Black Sea and the Mediterranean. It was in this same period that Rome took the place of Constantinople as the mythical Red Apple, the capital of the world to be conquered by Osman's descendants, a city that could be taken only by crossing the Adriatic.[36] Still, until Selim I the Ottomans had limited their maritime claims to the eastern seas, an Ottoman Mediterranean vision developing only after the conquest of Egypt and Algiers. According to Selim I, since the 'White Sea' (Mediterranean) was but one big gulf, it was logical that it should belong to one and not many. Süleyman I would claim to be 'Sultan and padişa (roughly emperor) of the White and Black Seas', to which his successors added also the Red Sea.[37]

Starting in the fifteenth century, the Ottoman maritime advance proceeded from east to west, gaining territory piecemeal by the apparently unsystematic conquest of the various islands of the Aegean. However, this was actually the result of a sound strategic scheme, which aimed to isolate major potential objectives, such as Crete, Cyprus and Rhodes, by creating around them a cordon sanitaire of Turkish-held islands. Moreover, the fragmentation of Venetian and to a lesser extent Genoese possessions in the Levant allowed the sultans to occupy one by one the less well-defended islands. Since the Ottomans' ultimate objective was the conquest of the whole West, it was more important to open wide enough gaps in the liquid frontier to allow large forces to pass through without hindrance than to conquer all the islands.

Although not originally a seafaring power, the Ottoman empire could rely on a pre-existing naval tradition. The Seljuk conquest of a substantial portion of Anatolia in the eleventh century had brought the Turks into contact with the sea, and very soon they had a fleet large enough to threaten Constantinople.* But the Byzantine

* The Seljuks were the Turkish dynasty which from the eleventh to the fourteenth century ruled in Anatolia, Syria, Persia and Mesopotamia. From the mid-1200s the Seljuks were reduced to the status of Mongol tributaries and it was the definitive collapse of their rule after 1302 that permitted the rise of the Ottomans, who considered themselves the Seljuks' heirs.

empire was then still a force to be reckoned with, and in a series of campaigns it managed to push the Turks back inland. Following the turmoil that engulfed the Byzantine state after the Fourth Crusade, the Seljuks occupied once more the southern Anatolian coastline around Antalya and quickly took to the sea. Their subsequent capture of Alanya, where they built a superb arsenal, allowed them to extend their range of naval activities down into Egyptian waters. The Mongol invasion of the Middle East in the mid-thirteenth century and the consequent destruction of the Seljuk state favoured the rise of a number of maritime *gazi* emirates. The capture of these polities by Bayezid I did not curb the actions of the sea *ghazi*; instead, by allowing them to enjoy the resources of the empire, the sultans channelled their energies into Ottoman expansionism. In addition, Mehmed II's conquest of Constantinople, Greece and the Balkans had provided the Ottomans with further maritime knowhow. Naval entrepreneurship was supported, and to an extent financed, by the state, allowing the creation of a pool of experienced captains – the Barbarossa brothers being the most famous products of this system. More important, the Ottomans could substantially increase their fleet at the drop of a hat by simply commandeering corsair vessels.[38]

The navy's command structure took longer to develop. After 1453 the fleet was usually entrusted to the *sancak* of Gallipoli, probably because the main Ottoman naval base came under his jurisdiction. This, however, was not a fixed rule and on more than one occasion the sultan appointed commanders according to the requirements of a specific situation. During the Otranto expedition of 1480 Gedik Pasha was in charge of both land and sea forces. The position of the naval commander-in-chief, the *kapudan-ı deryâ*, better known after 1567 as the *kapudan paşa*,[39] increased in importance with Hayreddin Barbarossa, Süleyman adding to the title the newly created *beylerbeik* of the Archipelago, carved from the coastal *sancaks* of Greece and western Anatolia. High admirals did not always come from similar backgrounds, by-products of the *devşirme* alternating with Muslim-born professionals. Privateers were a permanent and important feature of the Ottoman fleet, Katib Çelebi maintaining that if the admiral was not one of them he should seek their advice 'and not act on his own initiative'. On the other hand, it would appear that in the sixteenth century some Ottoman commanders considered corsairs a somewhat unsavoury lot, the Venetian ambassador Bartolomeo Cavalli stating in 1560 that 'they don't trust them much and employ them in the same way doctors use poison, that is in small doses and intermixed with the rest of the fleet'.[40]

The Ottoman conquest of the eastern and southern Mediterranean meant that their fleet had to face an increasing number of challenges. Since these often required a quick response without recourse to the main fleet in Constantinople, a number of autonomous naval commands were established in the course of the sixteenth century. The northern Aegean was under the responsibility of the captain of Kavala, whose main duty was to escort grain ships from northern Greece to the capital; more to the south, the *sancak* of Lesvos patrolled the waters in the vicinity of his island. After the conquest of Rhodes by Süleyman I a substantial flotilla operated from the former Hospitaller base, guarding the sea routes between Egypt, Turkey and Syria. To this purpose the Rhodes *sancak* was to collaborate closely with the Alexandria squadron, the second Egyptian unit, based in Suez, being responsible for security in the Red Sea. Other flotillas could be found on the Danube and in the Black Sea, while after 1519 the sultan could count, albeit never easily, on the experienced men and fine ships of the North African maritime cities. In addition, the various coastal *sancak*s could be ordered to patrol the seas under their jurisdiction with one or more galleys, and after 1566 it became customary for the eight *sancak beys* of the Archipelago to provide a certain number of vessels for the imperial navy. Thus the sultan had at his disposal a rapidly deployable fleet unequalled in the Mediterranean.[41]

A large navy required a well-tuned organization to function properly, and that meant arsenals. Bayezid I built a large one at Gallipoli in the 1390s, placed in such a position as to control the

Sea of Marmara and facilitate the passage of Ottoman troops from Anatolia to Rumelia. In addition it provided a base for raids on enemy islands in the Aegean and controlled the shipping routes to and from the Black Sea. Despite the construction of a new arsenal at Galata by Mehmed II immediately after the taking of Constantinople, Gallipoli remained the main Ottoman naval base until the beginning of the sixteenth century. Later Selim I and Süleyman considerably enlarged the Galata arsenal, diminishing Gallipoli's importance. Other permanent shipbuilding sites were at Sinop on the Black Sea, Alexandria in Egypt, Suez on the Red Sea, Izmit near Galata and, after 1538, Basra. However, the nature of most sixteen-century Ottoman shipbuilding meant that vessels could be built at ad hoc sites along the coast. This appears to have been standard practice when the sultan needed a large fleet at a short notice.[42]

The Ottomans started probing at Western defences in the Aegean in the 1390s, alternating *gazi* forays with major naval operations, their initial lack of experience resulting in some very hard knocks. In 1416 and 1429 the Venetians trounced them in two battles at the mouth of the Dardanelles. Despite their successes on land, it took the Ottomans most of the fifteenth century to build up confidence in naval matters, and in 1466 they still considered a superiority of at least four to one necessary to tackle the Venetians. The real increase in Turkish naval power came with their territorial conquests during the 1463–79 war. By denying the Venetians and other Western states a number of key havens in Greece and the Aegean, they reduced their enemies' capacity to conduct major operations in the Levant. Likewise, the Ottomans' occupation of certain islands allowed them to control the main sea lanes in the eastern Mediterranean, casting an ominous shadow over the whole region. Even before the battle of Zonchio there was no doubt that the sultans' fleet had become a force not to be dismissed.[43]

The 1499–1503 war also demonstrated an improvement in the Ottomans' ability to launch amphibious operations, and following the French expedition against Mytilene the Turks learnt the use of galley artillery fire to cover the advance of troops on shore. Most of the Greek islands were within striking distance of their bases, allowing the Ottomans to execute surprise attacks against targets vulnerable to gunpowder weapons. But if the Ottoman conquest of most of the Aegean allowed them to push their frontier to the west, the fragmentation of this maritime border also put them in a vulnerable position. It was now impossible for the sultans' fleet to control the thousands of nooks and crannies dotting the eastern Mediterranean, making it an ideal hunting ground for pirates and corsairs. This situation could result in disruption to the trade routes linking Egypt to Anatolia and was one of the main reasons prompting Süleyman to conquer Rhodes, and his son Selim II to do the same with Cyprus.

At the beginning of the sixteenth century the Turks were attempting to protect the main trade routes in the Levant by a system of naval patrols, but it soon became evident that Christian pirates and corsairs still had access to the fresh-water resources of the Greek islands. An extensive control system was impossible to implement except at crippling cost, since small enemy fleets operating from Italy or the centre of the Mediterranean could sneak up nearly to the mouth of the Dardanelles and ambush Ottoman shipping before the local naval defences had time to react.[44] The only way to stop this menace was to push into the western Mediterranean, forcing the Christian states of the area to employ their resources to defend their own coasts. But by concentrating their attention on Europe, the Ottomans were losing a different contest in another part of their empire. By the time of Selim I's conquest of Egypt the existence of the world beyond the Mediterranean was a known fact, and some of the sultan's advisers were pushing for the conquest of India or even China. This would have called for the development of a significant navy in the Red Sea and a consistent policy to sustain it. However, the internal dynamics of the Ottoman regime caused Süleyman I to focus on the conquest of Europe, thus inhibiting the possibility of an Ottoman expansion in the Indian Ocean. Although the sultan was fully aware that the

Portuguese presence in the Red Sea had diverted much of the local tax-producing trade once directed to Egypt towards the Iberian peninsula, faced with a fief-hungry army he preferred to concentrate his attention on *timar* holdings as a source of revenue than engage in a more long-term expansion policy through the control of oceanic trade routes.[45] Besides, land conquests fitted better psychologically with an expanding *darülislam* – always a major concern for the Ottomans – even if Grand Vizier Lufti Pasha warned the sultan that 'however important may be the business of land affairs, those of the sea are far more important'.[46] To the Ottomans' credit, up to the very end of the sixteenth century nobody could have predicted the huge developments in the field of oceanic shipbuilding. In the mid-1520s it made perfect sense to think that, should need require it, the Red Sea fleet could easily grow big enough to tackle the Portuguese with success.

Süleyman was nevertheless forced to act when the slump in the Mediterranean spice trade became too serious to be ignored, although this decision was also influenced by the Portuguese threat to Muslim pilgrims travelling to the holy city of Mecca. Ottoman naval commitments in the Mediterranean caused further delay, and it was only in 1538 that a fleet finally sailed from Suez and circumnavigated the Arabian peninsula, trying unsuccessfully to capture the Portuguese fort of Diu on the north-west coast of India. The Portuguese retaliated by attempting to take Suez three years later, and their control of Hormuz in the Persian Gulf effectively stunted the development of Basra as both an Ottoman military base and commercial centre. In 1552 the Turkish admiral and cartographer Piri Reis tried in vain to take Hormuz, a failure that cost him his life, and despite a number of territorial acquisitions in the region over the next few years, including part of the Abyssinian coast, the Ottomans by now understood that evicting the Portuguese from the Gulf area was impossible without huge human and material investments.[47] But Süleyman had already too many problems to deal with in Europe and the Middle East and never pursued victory in a war fought at the fringes of his empire. It would also appear that at this point expanding the navy was not among Constantinople's top priorities, prompting a Venetian diplomat to comment that luckily the Ottomans were less powerful on sea than on land.[48] The strategic choices made by the Ottoman empire meant that it was destined to lose the race for world domination, as more European countries joined the Portuguese in the struggle for the eastern trade routes, while at the same time the Ottomans were unable to exploit the vast riches of the New World.

~

But this was all in the unforeseeable future, and in the meantime the Ottoman juggernaut continued to press forward. Barbarossa's victory at Preveza caused the Holy League to collapse, and from the subsequent peace treaty between Venice and Constantinople the Ottomans obtained among other things the important bases of Monemvasia and Nafplio in the Peloponnese. Süleyman also managed to annex the south-eastern part of Moldavia, before turning his attention once more to Hungary. The Habsburg–Ottoman arrangement of 1533 had left everyone dissatisfied, and despite Süleyman bestowing the Hungarian kingship on János Szapolyai it was clear that the Porte was just waiting for the right moment to bring the whole country under its direct control. In the meantime the Ottomans slowly increased their military presence in the area, much to Szapolyai's chagrin. As a result, in 1538 the Hungarian ruler and Ferdinand I agreed that on János's death his lands would pass to the Habsburgs, and when this happened in 1540 Ferdinand lost no time making good his claim. Dissent within the Hungarian ruling elite thwarted Ferdinand's attempts to capture Buda, giving Süleyman sufficient time to assemble a strong enough army to defeat the Habsburgs in the field. The sultan annexed the whole of Szapolyai's former lands, as a sop to Hungarian pride nominating János's infant son king of Transylvania, the eastern portion of the old kingdom.[49]

While busy in Hungary, Süleyman was having to face another Habsburg threat. In the late summer of 1541 Charles V launched an attack against Algiers, and the renewal of full hostilities in the Mediterranean brought to the fore the tensions existing within the Ottoman government between those, like Grand Vizier Lufti Pasha, who advocated a more incisive maritime policy, and others committed to land conquest. Süleyman dismissed Lufti Pasha from his post for opposing the Hungarian venture, believing that in order to keep the Habsburgs at bay he had to confront them on their own turf. Besides, such a move would also test the ground for a possible Ottoman expansion in the western Mediterranean. Conveniently, Francis I now decided that the time had come to break the truce he had signed earlier with Charles V and employ Ottoman naval power to try and recapture strategic positions in Italy. Backed by French logistical support, in the summer of 1542 Barbarossa laid waste the coastal regions of northern Italy and Spain, even taking the town, although not the castle, of Nice. He wintered his fleet in Toulon as the guest of Francis I, and then proceeded to raid all the way down the Italian coast before making a triumphant return to Constantinople.[50] This was to be Barbarossa's last campaign, the old admiral dying peacefully in the magnificent palace he had built overlooking the Dardanelles. For years to come Muslim ships sailing through the Bosporus would fire a gun in salute as they passed in front of his mausoleum.*

The peace of 1544 between France and the Holy Roman Empire deprived Süleyman of an ally, but in the meantime both Charles V – who was having trouble with his Lutheran subjects – and Ferdinand were willing to come to an agreement with the sultan over the Hungarian question. A formal five-year treaty was concluded in 1547 confirming the territorial status quo in Hungary, with Ferdinand agreeing to pay a tribute of 30,000 ducats a year for the land under his control. For the sultan the treaty had an added value, since Charles, who did not wish to sign as Holy Roman Emperor, was mentioned in the agreement simply as 'King of

---

* A rather less flattering legend states that he jumped out of his tomb various times, until a necromancer found the solution of burying him with a black dog.

Spain'. Süleyman believed that the document sanctioned for good his right to style himself Emperor of the Romans or Caesar.[51] In addition, Ottoman jurists could now argue that by paying tribute to the Porte Ferdinand had become Süleyman's subject. Even if only psychologically, the horns of the Ottoman crescent had penetrated deep into the heart of Europe.

Peace with the Habsburgs left Süleyman free to deal with the Safavis, returning to the western theatre only in 1550. By then the situation in Hungary had once more erupted into war, this time the struggle being over the control of Transylvania. The Ottomans managed to conquer part of the kingdom including Temesvár (Timişoara), but as usual the sultan had also to deal with the Mediterranean front. In 1550 Charles V's Genoese admiral Andrea Doria conducted a series of operations against Tunisia, capturing a number of strongholds from Thorgud (or Dragut) Reis, Barbarossa's heir as foremost Muslim corsair. The fact that at the same time the Spanish were trying to take over the city state of Siena in the south of Tuscany alarmed the French, who were afraid that the western Mediterranean was fast becoming a Habsburg lake. The new Franco-Ottoman alliance initially resulted in very little, partly because Süleyman was more interested in his Persian campaign, although in 1551 the Turks managed to capture the city of Tripoli, held by the Knights Hospitallers since 1530. By the time peace was signed with the Safavis in 1555, the Ottomans had lost a golden opportunity to take their offensive against the Habsburgs onto the Italian mainland.

At this point Süleyman's anti-Habsburg offensive was not confined to military action. Ever since the Reformation had started in central Europe the Ottomans had followed its progress with interest. Advised by the French, the sultan wrote to the German Lutheran princes, urging them to continue to fight the pope and Charles V and pointing out beliefs shared by Protestantism and Islam. This move was only partially successful, since the reality of the Turkish menace was apparent to both Catholics and Protestants. Moreover, Charles V's need to obtain the financial and military support of the imperial estates for his wars in the end compelled him to grant a certain amount of tolerance to Lutheranism. Thus, while the wars of the first half of the sixteenth century favoured the rise of Protestantism, it is also true that for Charles V France was as dangerous as the Porte. A more serious threat to the Habsburgs was the Ottomans' backing of Calvinism in Europe, since this represented an authentic revolutionary force, hostile to Lutheranism nearly as strongly as it was to Catholicism and not averse to striking a Faustian pact with Islam. For this reason the Calvinist populations of Hungary and Transylvania increasingly looked to the Porte as an ally against the Catholic Habsburgs. Needless to say, the Ottomans were only too happy to oblige.[52]

But religious divisions in France soon deprived Süleyman of his best ally in Europe. The abdication of Charles V as Holy Roman Emperor, and the division of his territorial possessions between his brother Ferdinand and his son Philip, was initially good news for the Porte; the Habsburgs were no longer a united front. But the following year Philip, now king of Spain as Philip II, inflicted a crushing defeat on the French at the battle of Saint-Quentin in Flanders, and for some time it was expected that the Spanish would march on Paris. Faced with the Spanish threat and having to deal at home with the unrest caused by the Calvinist Huguenots, the French king Henry II started peace talks with Philip. In the ensuing treaty of Cateau-Cambrésis France recognized Spain's claims in Italy and Flanders, ratifying what is commonly know as the fifty years of the Pax Hispanica in southern Europe. Philip II then took the war to North Africa, sending an expeditionary force which included contingents from the pope, Malta, Tuscany, Monaco and Savoy to fortify the island of Djerba, halfway between Tunis and Tripoli. In Philip's plan Djerba would together with Hospitaller-held Malta effectively block the sea route from Algiers to Constantinople.

In the event the Djerba expedition was a complete fiasco. The Spanish did indeed manage to capture the island and build a fort, but on 6 May 1560 the Ottoman fleet under the command of Grand Admiral Piyale Pasha caught them as they were re-embarking. Piyale may have been a man of no great intelligence, at least according to the Venetians,[53] but in this action he showed both ability and daring. Running a considerable risk, the grand admiral launched his fleet against the scattered enemy vessels, capturing or sinking thirty of them and killing or capturing around 8,000 men. The beleaguered fort at Djerba resisted until the end of the following July, when lack of munitions and supplies forced the garrison to surrender. While most of Spain's allies had their fleets wiped out by Piyale's exploit, more serious for Philip were his considerable losses in skilled naval personnel, hampering Spain's ability to launch any major naval operations for years to come.[54] Piyale's triumph was crowned by his solemn arrival in Constantinople with the captured galleys in tow on 27 September 1560. Their success at Djerba had offered the Ottomans a vision of future victory, and it appeared only a matter of time before they attempted the conquest of the remaining Habsburg territories in the Mediterranean. But without French support it would have been logistically impossible for Süleyman to launch such an ambitious operation, unless some suitable advance base could be found between Constantinople and Gibraltar. The ideal stepping stone was the island of Malta, between Tunis and Sicily, boasted some excellent havens where a large fleet could find shelter. For the Ottomans the island was a ripe fruit ready to be plucked, provided they could first defeat its masters: old acquaintances of Süleyman and not likely to give up without a fight, the Knights Hospitaller.

Seven years after it had been ousted from Rhodes, the Order of St John had found refuge on the island of Malta. Its new home was a gift from Charles V, who, already burdened with too many commitments, also thought well to saddle the knights with the defence of the recently conquered city of Tripoli on the North African coast. Although initially not happy with the bequest, the Hospitallers, now known as the Knights of Malta, quickly resumed preying on Ottoman shipping routes in the eastern Mediterranean. For the sultan the knights represented a constant source of irritation, and while it may be true that it was the insistence of Mihirimah,

Süleyman's daughter, and other members of the Ottoman administration which tipped the Sultan's decision, he hardly needed their
prodding to realize that Malta was a problem that urgently needed
solving. In October 1564 the *dîvân-ı hümâyûn* (imperial council)
debated a possible expedition against Malta. Not everybody agreed
on the venture, but in the end the sultan's will prevailed and it was
decided to attack the island the following spring.

News of Ottoman preparations quickly reached Hospitaller
headquarters, but the order's grand master, Jean Parissot de La
Vallette, had no intention of repeating the experience of Rhodes.
Determined to make the most of the island's defences, he resolved
to resist until the arrival of the Spanish relief force promised by the
viceroy of Sicily, Don Garcia de Toledo. La Vallette and Toledo
were counting on time, the latter not wishing to risk another Djerba
by facing the Ottoman fleet at the height of its strength. The
Ottoman commander, on the other hand, hoped to capture the
island before autumn weather forced a return to Constantinople.

The Ottomans landed on Malta in the second half of May 1565
with a force of roughly 35,000 fighting men, including about 10,000
timar holders and 6,500 janissaries. To put together the force some
two dozen *sancak*s had been milked dry of their manpower,[55] extra
soldiers being provided by volunteers, plus North African and
Anatolian corsairs. A substantial number of artillerymen handled
a siege train of nearly sixty guns, some of them huge masonry
destroyers. By contrast, La Vallette could count initially on less than
600 members of the order, 400 Spanish troops, 4,000–5,000 Maltese
capable of bearing arms and nearly fifty artillery pieces of various
sizes. The Ottomans first tried to take Fort St Elmo, but to their
chagrin it held out until 24 June, when the remaining defenders
were overwhelmed in a massive assault. But in the meantime the
Christians had inflicted on the invaders something like 6,000 casualties, many of them *sipahis* and janissaries, against losses of 1,500.
The most illustrious victim was the famous corsair Dragut, killed by
a cannon shot while directing artillery fire.

As the weeks drew on the Ottoman losses in men and materiel

started to tell, fatigue and diminishing gunpowder stocks lessening the besiegers' efforts and bombardment by the day. It was just the moment that the viceroy of Sicily had been waiting for since May. On 9 September a relief force of 11,000 men engaged the Muslims as they retreated towards their ships. In vain the Ottoman commander Isfendiari Mustafa Pasha tried to rally his troops but nothing could stop the Ottomans after months 'of fighting devils, not men'.[56] As La Vallette led his brethren to give thanks to the Blessed Virgin for her miraculous aid in lifting the siege, the whole of Europe breathed a sigh of relief. But although the Ottomans had suffered a serious defeat they still remained a formidable threat.

2. A HOUSE DIVIDED

~

Grand Master La Vallette was not a man to mince his words. As he watched the construction of the new fortified city which eventually would take his name – he could not but feel a sense of uneasiness. True, the Hospitallers' popularity after the siege had meant the arrival of new recruits and an influx of much-needed cash, but with the Ottoman threat still real it was necessary to build fortifications capable of withstanding another attack. Yet the grand master had constantly to plead and cajole to get the necessary assistance from European sovereigns, venting his anger in a letter to the Duke of Anjou, brother of the king of France, Charles IX. Stressing the risk of an Ottoman onslaught against Malta, La Vallette reminded the duke, 'After what we have passed, we are still weak.' For this reason he was writing to all the Catholic rulers and especially to the king of France, asking for help, stating bluntly that he foresaw 'great trouble against which we cannot hope to preserve ourselves unless we are aided'. He concluded by begging the king and his councillors not to refuse assistance, for the Turkish threat was not directed solely at the order 'but against Christendom'.[1]

The grand master had reasons for concern. At the time of the siege the French, because of their alliance with the Turks, had been reluctant to help the Knights of St John, King Charles IX even preventing a force of French volunteers from joining the beleaguered Maltese. Valois hostility towards the order came from the fact that Malta was a Spanish fief, and there were others in Europe who would have been happy to see the Hospitallers destroyed. Many Venetians, despite some of their fellow citizens being members of the order, were furious that the knights' corsair activities disrupted commerce in the Levant. Undismayed by the Ottoman retreat, the knights' enemies were sure that the following year the sultan would come back with a more powerful fleet to finish the job.[2]

~

This sort of attitude was no novelty; it could be described as standard in Christian Europe. For centuries its various states had been busier fighting each other than trying to stop the Muslim advance. In some cases they had even actively helped it, wittingly or otherwise. To make matters worse, the one force potentially capable of uniting the warring polities was no longer able to do so. The pope, while still considered rather more than just another head of state, was nevertheless often treated as such, and the very secular behaviour of many clergymen did not help. Admittedly the papacy was not in an easy position, needing to be not just a spiritual but also a temporal power in order to maintain its independence. In many ways it was difficult for the pope not to get deeply (sometimes too deeply) involved in the European political game. It should also be remembered that clergymen are part of the same cultural milieu as their lay counterparts, and in this sense the Church has always mirrored the secular world.

By the beginning of the sixteenth century Christendom was in a very sorry state. Gone were the crusading ideals of old; people turned deaf ears to the alarmed utterances of preachers and popes about the necessity of stopping the Turkish advance. For most European governments the Ottoman threat was low on their list of concerns – being more interested in maintaining their positions in the rich eastern markets – while a few states were quite ready to abet, or at least not hinder, the sultans' expansionist policies for the sake of their own commercial interests. Both the Venetians and the

Genoese on different occasions provided the Ottomans with technology and ships for their campaigns. Some Europeans were even prepared to admire the efficiency of the more centralized Ottoman state, especially when contrasted with the situation in most of western Europe. As much as the Ottoman political and legal system smacked of arbitrary rule, not everyone saw this as a drawback. Indeed, somebody as distinguished as the Florentine jurist and historian Francesco Guicciardini considered it beneficial in more than one way:

> I do not wholly condemn the Turkish method of administering the law in civil matters, though it is sudden rather than summary. For he who determines with his eyes shut may likely enough decide half his cases justly, while he saves the parties time and expense. Our own tribunals move so slowly, that often it were better for him who has right on his side to have the cause given against him on the first hearing, than to win it after all the cost and trouble he is put to. Besides, because of our judges ignorance and dishonesty, as well as from obscurity in our laws, even with us black is too often made to appear white.[3]

On the other hand, Niccolò Machiavelli in *The Prince* emphasized how the main strength of the Porte was, in the long run, in fact its main weakness. By stating that it was 'difficult to win control of the Turkish Empire' but that once it had been conquered it could be 'held with ease',[4] Machiavelli underscored the fact that the Ottoman state could only function effectively with strong leadership. For once, Machiavelli was right in his analysis. Although administratively less efficient in the short term, the decentralized states of western Europe were much more capable of sustaining the sort of political, military and social blows that nearly brought the Ottoman empire to its knees in the course of the seventeenth century.

In the meantime the West watched with indifference Mehmed II's conquest of Constantinople, although only a few years before the Eastern and Western Churches had decided to end the schism that had divided them since 1055. The effects of this reconciliation were, however, largely nominal; the vast majority of Byzantines hated the very idea of Rome and, according to one source, 'preferred to be ruled by the Sultan's turban than the Pope's tiara'.[5] Many Westerners reciprocated the feeling. One of them after a lengthy stay in the east came to the conclusion that the stories about Ottoman cruelty were nothing but malicious gossip: 'I have found the Turks to be much more friendly than the Greeks,' wrote the Frenchman Bertrandon de La Broquière.[6] In any case, the Ottoman conquest of Constantinople nullified the attempts at a permanent rapprochement between the Churches, the sultan, with the support of his Greek Orthodox subjects, preferring to rule over Christians whose leaders he could control and, following the old Byzantine practice, appoint himself.

Not everybody in Europe was passive in the face of the Turkish onslaught. Aeneas Sylvius Piccolomini, one of the foremost scholars of his day, while convinced that the negative image of the Turk was exaggerated and that some Christians were second to none in committing atrocities, also had a very clear perception of the Ottoman peril.[7] Once elected pope as Pius II in 1458 he immediately tried to unite the rulers of Italy and other parts of Europe for a military expedition in the Balkans. Pius's anti-Ottoman international conference, held in Mantua in 1459, failed miserably, the various European governments studiously avoiding committing themselves. The failure of the conference prompted Pius to write his famous 'Letter to Mehmed II' in which he suggested the sultan become a Christian in exchange for Papal recognition of his present and future conquests. By offering to Mehmed in effect nothing less than the crown of the Holy Roman Empire, Pius was sending a message to European rulers that the only thing the sultan lacked was baptism to be a legitimate sovereign with the material and spiritual means to rule the whole of the Western world. But, as historian Nancy Bisaha has convincingly demonstrated, the letter was never intended for Mehmed, since Pius's lambasting of Islam would have turned the missive into a huge diplomatic faux pas, making it largely useless as an instrument for Mehmed's conversion. The text was probably intended for the edification of Western readers, and indeed it circulated widely in Europe even before being put into print a few years after the pope's death.[8]

Pius's efforts to launch a crusade continued unabated for the rest of his pontificate, and when war erupted in 1463 between the Ottomans and the Venetians he jumped at the opportunity. Wishing to set an example, he declared his intention of leading himself an anti-Ottoman expedition. Faced with such commitment, many rulers promised to send money and troops, the king of Hungary and the duke of Burgundy even expressing the desire to join in person. One head of state who actually did participate was the neo-pagan lord of Rimini, Sigismondo Pandolfo Malatesta, anxious to regain papal favour after Pius had hounded him with sword and pen into submission. Encouraged by all this, the pontiff left Rome for Ancona, where the whole army was supposed to embark on ships provided by the Venetians. But neither the king of Hungary nor the duke of Burgundy appeared, the Venetians sent just a few galleys, and only a handful of soldiers eventually arrived in Ancona. An ailing Pius was still hoping for the promised troops when he died on 14 August 1464, being spared the ultimate disappointment of seeing his crusade fall apart.

As soon as news of the pope's death became public, every government discovered more pressing priorities nearer to home, Philip the Good of Burgundy for one preferring to wage war against the French than the Ottomans. Many historians have belittled Pius's crusading attempts as inane, forgetting that the pontiff did actually manage to put together the skeleton of an expeditionary force, something that many of his predecessors had failed to do.[9] It is legitimate to ask what would have happened if the pope had not died and instead departed for the east. Given the mentality of the time, it would have been difficult for Europe's rulers to avoid supporting the spiritual head of Christendom in his crusading efforts. After Pius II the papacy continued to advocate military expeditions against the Ottomans, but without Aeneas Sylvius's dedication; the popes became too entangled in Italian politics to seriously consider launching crusades. In any case the cosy world of fifteenth-century Italy, with its crafty political games, was soon to be shattered in a dramatic way.

~

The French invasion of 1494 triggered off what are known as the Italian Wars, destined to last until 1559. The term is actually misleading, since the Valois' initiative produced a domino effect that set the whole of Europe aflame. Still, up to 1530 much of the fighting involved Italy, the Spanish opposed France's attempts to gain control of the kingdom of Sicily and the duchy of Milan. The game immediately involved all the other Italian states, the Holy Roman Empire, the Swiss Confederation and, albeit on the side, the Ottomans. In a whirlwind of uncertainty, the various participants played a deadly diplomatic and military game, alliances being made or undone yearly.

By 1520 the situation was somewhat clearer: southern Italy was more or less under Spanish control; the Venetians had been humiliated; the Swiss were out of the game; while both Spain and the empire were under the rule of Charles V of Habsburg. Five years later the French suffered a crushing defeat at the battle of Pavia, and in 1527 the Habsburgs brought the papacy to its knees by taking and sacking Rome. After 1530 Florence also fell within Charles's sphere of control, as did most other Italian states.[10] However, the struggle for Italy between the Habsburgs and the Valois would continue for another twenty years, although the actual fighting was somewhat reduced in intensity. Yet there was always the risk for Charles that the French could regain the upper hand, in particular after the alliance between Francis I and Süleyman I. The alliance between the 'Most Christian King' and the heathen Turk may have shocked many at the time, but this would not be the only occasion when political expediency prevailed over religious division.

Religion was one of the main factors at play in sixteenth-century Europe, the struggle between Islam and Christianity overlapping with the latter's internal split. The papacy was a major player in both disputes, although often in an ambiguous manner and sometimes in contrast with basic Christian principles, inevitable for something that was at the same time a metaphysical institution and a political entity. To this should be added the theological confusion characteristic of the period. Since the mid-fourteenth century the intellectual movement known as Humanism had been growing in Europe, emphasizing the importance of the classical world at the expense of the so-called Middle Ages. By stressing the importance of textual analysis the humanists, at the beginning unwittingly, were undermining the very foundations of Catholic tradition. Taken to extremes, humanism bred secularism and scepticism, but most scholars were simply happy that ancient Roman and Greek culture was reborn (hence the term Renaissance). As Europe struggled to find a balance between antiquity and Christianity, few at the time realized that the continent was a religious time bomb ready to explode at any moment.

By now almost everybody in Catholic Europe agreed that a reform of the Church was badly needed. The poor behaviour of the clergy was no novelty – the corruption of clerical mores being as old as the Church itself – and down the centuries ecumenical councils, forceful emperors and reforming popes had often performed drastic religious house cleaning. The corruption of the clergy had always created scandal, but in the past this had been seen as a consequence of churchmen being imperfect human beings, not the fault of the Church as a divine institution. Paradoxically, ecclesiastical vices could even be an instrument of eternal salvation. In Giovanni Boccaccio's *Decameron* the Jew Abraham becomes a Christian after visiting Rome and witnessing every single vice in the world. Abraham's logic is that God must really be upholding the Church, since all clergymen, from the pope downwards, 'are devoting all their care, all their intelligence and skill to expunging the Christian religion and ridding the world of it, whereas they are supposed to be its bedrock and mainstay.'[11]

But many Renaissance thinkers spurned such niceties, convinced that the metaphysical beliefs of centuries were less important than the truths to be found by studying ancient texts. Since humanistic ideas and ideals permeated most of the culture of the time, it was logical that many cultivated people, clergymen included, should abide by them. Christianity, paganism, erudition and superstition lived side by side, as Plato, Aristotle, Cicero and the astrologists of old were put on the same level as the Bible and the Church fathers. Pope Alexander VI in his Vatican apartment had a painting with Moses conversing with the third century AD mage Hermes Trismegistus (considered a contemporary of Moses and thus as authoritative) and the Egyptian goddess Isis. Salvation, it was felt, could be obtained through knowledge as well as faith. Yet humanism and classical culture were causing theological confusion. For instance, the philosopher Pietro Pomponazzi, basing his arguments on Aristotle, could happily deny the immortality of the soul and argue the impossibility of miracles. Using textual criticism a humanist like Lorenzo Valla argued that the temporal power of the popes was based on a forgery. By editing, albeit in a rather cavalier manner, and publishing a Greek version of the New Testament, Erasmus of Rotterdam cast doubts on the textual veracity of the Gospels as originally translated into Latin by St Jerome in the fourth century AD. The movement stressing the importance of original texts spilt over into religion, many advocating not just ecclesiastical reform but also a return to the Church's original purity. The Dominican friar Girolamo Savonarola would thunder from Florentine pulpits against vanities and clerical corruption, targeting in particular Pope Alexander VI. The novelty of his preaching was that it advocated the creation of a world based on Christian humanistic values, Savonarola being a biblical scholar who filled his sermons with references to themes dear to the humanists.[12]

It was these factors coupled with the political ambitions of rulers that triggered off the Protestant Reformation in Germany. Started by an Augustinian friar by the name of Martin Luther in 1517, the Reformation quickly took hold thanks to the fact that many German princes considered it a useful way to gain control over the

Church in their domains. Luther's arguments asserting the superiority of sacred scripture over apostolic tradition owed much to the cultural milieu of the time, and so did his selective use of the Church fathers. Also – giving a theological justification to a well-established attitude – Luther upheld the interference of secular rulers in ecclesiastical matters. At the beginning Rome reacted with indifference towards the new movement; it was used to crackpot theologians. Emperor Charles V's approach to Lutheranism was more ambiguous. Although he rightly considered himself the protector of religious orthodoxy, he also saw Lutheranism as a way to enhance his own authority and force the Church to clean itself up.

At the beginning both the reformers and the papacy shared a common fear of the Muslim peril – Pope Leo X (reigned 1513–19) was genuinely concerned with the threat posed by Selim I, in particular after the latter's conquest of Egypt – although the answer of the religious reformers of northern Europe to the Ottoman problem was somewhat uncertain. Erasmus of Rotterdam in his *De Bello Turcico*, whilst recognizing the existence of the Ottoman military threat, maintained that even against the Turks 'war must never be undertaken unless, as a last resort, it cannot be avoided'.[13] Luther initially thought that fighting the Turks was like resisting God, who had sent the Ottomans to punish the Christians for their sins. Later, after the scare of Süleyman's siege of Vienna, Luther would urge the princes of the empire to fight the Turks under the leadership of Charles V.[14] However religious reformers in Germany were now starting to look on Rome and not Constantinople as the main evil threatening Christianity. As Luther himself would write, 'Is there nothing more corrupt, more pestilential, more offensive than the Roman Curia? It surpasses beyond all comparison the godlessness of the Turks.'[15]

Pope Adrian VI, Leo X's successor, would have agreed. Adrian was a pious, stern and thorough man, bent on extirpating clerical abuses, checking Lutheranism, bringing peace to Europe and stopping the Turkish advance. In all these fields he was to be singularly unsuccessful. King Francis I, who considered Adrian a puppet of the emperor, threatened schism; the Roman Curia, jealous of its privileges, stonewalled the pope in every possible way; and Lutheranism continued to spread like wildfire, with Adrian's own utterances against the papal court bolstering the reformers' case. Italians thought him a miser and a barbarian. His frantic appeals to Christian rulers to defend Rhodes fell on deaf ears, and the fall of the island hastened Adrian's earthly demise.[16] He died on 14 September 1523, nineteen months after his election. The Roman Curia sighed with relief, and predictably the next conclave elected the Florentine Giulio de' Medici, Leo X's first cousin, as Clement VII. For many it seemed that, after an unfortunate pause, it was business as usual.

Alas, this was not to be the case, not least because Clement proved himself a very bad politician. Although in the past he had been admired as a skilled negotiator, he showed little diplomatic ability after his election to the papacy. He was much disliked in his native Florence, then under Medici control, because of the high-handed attitude of his henchmen. By mismanaging the dispute over the marriage between Catherine of Aragon and Henry VIII, he caused the religious split between England and Rome. To cap this bleak picture, his dealings with France and the Habsburgs would prove disastrous for the papacy. Convinced that Charles V represented a threat to papal freedom, Clement allied himself with the Valois king. It was a huge miscalculation. The French proved unreliable and in the spring of 1527 an imperial army 30,000 strong, comprising Germans, Spaniards and Italians, marched through Italy against scant opposition, when not actively aided by local rulers. On 6 May the Habsburg troops stormed the walls of Rome, Clement having barely the time to take refuge in the fortress of Castel Sant Angelo. What followed was a savage sack of the city, 'as if done by Turks',[17] which lasted days, while the pope watched impotently the scenes of rape, pillage and murder from the walls of his shelter.* At the beginning of June he threw in the towel, regaining his liberty

---

* As sacks went, that of Rome was no worse than others. What shocked people was that Rome was not only the spiritual centre of Christendom, but also one of the great cultural hubs of the time.

with a promise to pay a huge ransom. In exchange for the restoration of Medici rule in Florence – the city having revolted against the pope's relatives at the time of the sack – he agreed to crown Charles as Holy Roman Emperor.* With the Turks at the gates of Vienna, Charles was more than willing to reach an agreement with the pope, at the same time trying to convince Clement to call a general council. Yet, despite some timid attempts in the direction of reform, the pope was unwilling to bow to Charles's request, fearing that the council might turn against him.[18]

It was left to Clement's successor to make the first step in this direction. Paul III (reigned 1534–49) was no saint; originally made a cardinal thanks to his sister Giulia being Alexander VI's lover, as Cardinal Alessandro Farnese he had fathered several illegitimate children. Pope 'Fregnese' (thus satirized by distorting his surname into the vulgar term for vagina) would prove to be an unrepentant nepotist, loading his relatives with honours and riches, even carving out independent states for them.† But he was also aware of the need to reform the Church and stop the Ottomans. After many years of preparation and a number of failed attempts at reconciliation with the Lutherans, in 1545 Paul declared the opening of a general council in Trent. It would last for nearly twenty years, on and off, and dramatically change the face of the entire Church.

The pope was not the only one having problems with the Protestants. Charles had managed to stop the Ottomans in front of Vienna by granting concessions to the Lutheran princes of the empire, receiving in exchange money and troops. But Lutheranism had taken on a definite militant and military aspect, a number of powerful German princes in 1531 creating the Schmalkaldic Bund.[19]

---

* Charles until then was only the emperor-elect, although his imperial authority was undisputed even before his coronation.

† Papal nepotism stemmed largely from the popes' need to appoint people they could trust in key administrative positions. While in itself not a negative thing, nepotism was prone to abuse in the hands of pontiffs more interested in the good of their families than of the Church.

Officially a pact of mutual defence, in reality its goal was to consolidate the reformed religion throughout the empire. The Bund had created a substantial military force – 10,000 foot and 2,000 horse – and was openly defiant of the emperor's authority. To make matters worse, the following year it allied itself with France. Since Charles could not afford, militarily or financially, to stop this, he was forced to tolerate the spread of Lutheranism, often by force, in the Schmalkaldic-controlled territories. The creation of a Catholic Bund in 1538 appeared to many the prelude to a showdown between Charles and the Protestant princes, but at the Diet of Frankfurt the following year the two sides agreed to a temporary and uneasy peace since Charles was still busy fighting the allied Franco-Ottoman forces.

Charles bided his time while trying to undermine the Schmalkaldic Bund by exploiting its internal rivalries. By 1546 he had won over the dukes of Saxony and Bavaria, signed the Peace of Crépy with France, agreed to a truce with the Ottomans – once more distracted by war with Persia – and was busy raising troops to fight his Lutheran enemies. Paul III, also convinced that Protestantism needed to be crushed, sent money and troops. The Bund was slow to react, its army marred by a divided leadership. In April 1547 Charles smashed the Schmalkaldic forces at Mühlberg in Saxony, but his desire to consolidate his victory by restoring Catholicism throughout the empire or alternatively reach some sort of advantageous settlement with the Lutherans was thwarted by Paul III's fear of him becoming too powerful. The papal troops were withdrawn from Germany, and Paul started considering the possibility of a French alliance. The situation was exacerbated by the murder by imperialist-backed conspirators of the lord of Piacenza, Pier Luigi Farnese, Paul's son, who with the rest of his family, including the pope, had backed a number of anti-Habsburg plots in various parts of Italy. Charles V's decision to retain Piacenza threw the pope into the arms of Henry II of Valois, Francis I's successor, and by the time of Paul's death in November 1549 negotiations for a league between Rome and France had reached an advanced stage.[20] Paul III had been committed to reforming the Church, but like many of his predecessors his interest in worldly matters made him forget the common good of Christendom. In this sense, the Renaissance papacy had only itself to blame for the spread of Protestantism in Germany.

The German Lutherans had suffered a severe blow at Mühlberg, but once more received aid from the French, the Ottomans and ultimately the pope. Julius III, who succeeded Paul III, was initially well disposed towards the family of his predecessor, confirming its various members in the possessions they had managed to acquire, including the duchy of Parma. In spite of this, relations between the pope and the Farnese soured quickly when the latter got embroiled in a dispute with the Habsburg governor of Milan, Ferrante Gonzaga, who insisted that he needed to control Parma for the defence of his master's territories against the French. As a result, the Farnese appealed to the king of France for protection, much to Julius's chagrin and concern; by placing themselves under Henry II's suzerainty the Farnese were not just committing an act of rebellion against their feudal overlord, but also threatened to cause another war in Italy. Reluctantly the pope was forced to side with the emperor, fearing that otherwise the papal territories would be in jeopardy.

Military operations initially went well for the joint papal–imperial army, and by August 1551 it appeared that the city of Parma was about to capitulate, but a French attack through the Alps forced Gonzaga to rush to Piedmont, leaving the pope to fend for himself. Meanwhile, a Turkish fleet under Dragut raided the coast of Sicily, sacked the Maltese island of Gozo, before swinging south and capturing Tripoli from the Hospitallers. By now Charles V had not only to deal with the French and the Ottomans, but also with the Lutherans. Exploiting the emperor's difficulties, the German Protestants led by Maurice of Saxony unexpectedly attacked the imperial forces, while Henry II occupied the imperial cities of Metz, Toul and Verdun. Charles was forced to conclude the Treaty of Passau with the insurgents in April 1552, agreeing to a high degree of religious freedom for the German princes. With the main theatre of war now in the Low Countries and Charles fully occupied with the French and Turks, Julius, his coffers empty, was happy to make peace with the Farnese, allowing them to keep Parma and all their other territories. The Renaissance papacy had run its course, burnt out by the world it had helped create.

3. MEDITERRANEAN MEDLEY

~

It was cold in Rome in mid-January 1557, and inside the Vatican His Holiness Pope Paul IV's mood only increased the winter bitterness. Less than two months before he had been forced to agree to a humiliating truce with the Spanish commander Fernando Alvarez de Toledo, duke of Alva, whose army was encamped a few miles from the city. The ease of Alva's advance, brushing aside the troops sent to stop him and capturing stronghold after stronghold, had only increased the pope's shame. To add insult to injury, mingled with Alva's forces were those of the hated Colonna family, against which Paul had waged incessant warfare. Individual Colonna had been imprisoned or excommunicated and their property in the papal states confiscated and redistributed among the pope's nephews. Now the soldiers of the rebel Marcantonio Colonna had reoccupied many of these lands, sending the papal protégés running.

Since the expiry of the truce, on 8 January, Paul's forces, reinforced with contingents sent by Henry II of France, had managed to retake the fortress of Ostia, and a French army under the duke of Guise was about to invade the Spanish-held kingdom of Naples. But this was not enough for the eighty-year-old firebrand pontiff, doggedly determined to remove the Colonnna from their inheritance and the Habsburgs from Italy's soil. Thus, on that cold winter day while conversing with Cardinal Giovanni Morone, the pope declared emphatically that he was prepared to seek every possible ally in his just war against Philip II of Spain, even from Protestant Germany if necessary. Morone, who knew the Lutherans well from first-hand experience, cautioned Paul that the Germans hated the papacy. The aged former inquisitor glared at the cardinal, whom he suspected of Lutheran leanings, and hissed, 'The Turks will not fail us!'[1]

Paul IV's comment may come as a shock (and Cardinal Morone was indeed shocked), especially since we imagine St Peter's successors to be unwavering champions of Christianity and not prepared to sell their souls to their worst enemy for political reasons. However, when it came to striking deals with the infidels, Paul was very much of a latecomer.

~

Although by the sixteenth century the Venetians remained the only consistent Christian bulwark left in the east, they had never been happy fighting the Ottomans, preferring commerce to crusading activities. According to Paolo Preto, between 1453 and 1797 the Venetians and the Turks were at war with each other only for a total of 61 years, against 273 during which they were on peaceful terms. With pragmatic realism, the Republic of St Mark would pursue war ferociously — often with the help of other powers — to defend its Levantine possessions against Ottoman attacks, but for the sake of its commercial interests would be as determined to stay at peace with the Ottomans once hostilities ended. For this reason, after the end of the 1463–79 war the Venetians steadfastly refused to join the other Italian states in an anti-Ottoman league, prompting accusations of an unholy alliance between Venice and Constantinople. Given the scare provoked by the Turkish occupation of Otranto, the accusations were understandable, but there was another side to the coin: the Levantine trade was what allowed the republic to maintain a fleet large enough to counter the Ottomans' maritime expansion. Venice's dealings with Constantinople coupled with its growing power on the Italian mainland caused considerable concern and hostility in European diplomatic circles; Louis XI of France is said to have once commented that if the sultan agreed to be baptized, he would gladly help him against the Venetians.

Venice's expansionism set her on a collision course with her neighbours and also with some rather more powerful enemies. By the late 1490s the Republic of St Mark had managed to acquire a number of key ports at the heel of the Italian peninsula, fighting Florence and Milan with French backing. Meanwhile, Sultan Bayezid II feared a possible Franco-Venetian attack against Constantinople, especially after King Charles VIII of France trumpeted his intention of launching a crusade. To make matters worse, the Venetians had been giving support to a number of Balkan petty lords hostile to the Ottomans. The Milanese and Florentine ambassadors in Istanbul were busy poisoning Bayezid's ear against the Venetians, counting on the Turks to distract Venice from pursuing further territorial conquests in Italy.[2] A series of incidents at sea involving Venetian corsairs and Turkish merchantmen gave the sultan an excuse to attack, although ostensibly his military preparations were directed against Rhodes.

The war of 1499–1503 was disastrous for the Venetians. Not only were they defeated at sea, but the Ottomans also managed to capture the key fortress of Methoni on the southwest coast of the Peloponnese. The sultan's orders to give no quarter resulted in the massacre of Methoni's soldiers and adult males: they died on the impaling stakes, at the flaying posts or after having witnessed their internal organs thrown to dogs. These grisly details may be exaggerated, but it is certain that between 800 and 1,000 men were executed in the presence of Bayezid and his court. The strongholds of Koroni and Zonchio (near Navarino) then surrendered without a fight, and despite French support when the war ended in 1503 Venice was left with precious few possessions on the Greek mainland.[3]

A few years later all the pieces on the political chessboard had moved. By 1507 Venice's expansion in the Romagna region, traditionally claimed by the papacy, had aroused the ire of the warlike Pope Julius II. To counter the Venetians, the pontiff found allies in France, the Holy Roman Empire and Spain, all of which considered the republic a dangerous competitor in Italy. In the 1509 War of the League of Cambrai, Venice suffered a major defeat at Agnadello, and in the wake of the battle lost nearly all its territorial possessions on the Italian mainland. With the Republic's very existence in peril, the Venetian government took the dramatic step of seeking a military alliance with the Ottomans, a decision which did not come easily. More than one heated debate took place in the council chambers between those who could not swallow the idea of such an impious treaty, fearing it would bring destruction to Italy and the whole of Christendom, and those who were quite prepared to see 'the infidels in Italy' to save Venice. Eventually the hawks prevailed, and secret talks took place with the sultan's envoys for the dispatch of a Turkish expeditionary force. Bayezid, however, was unwilling to get embroiled in a war in Italy, since his truce with Hungary was about to expire, and the Venetians only managed to obtain a few consignments of grain and permission to recruit some units of Ottoman–Albanian cavalry. These troops were actually employed for military operations, but Venetian public opinion was aghast about involving the sultan in an anti-papal campaign. Moreover, Venice had once more regained the initiative in the field, as well as most of the territory it had previously lost, making the Ottoman presence unnecessary. When Venice signed an anti-French treaty with the pope in 1510 the planned alliance with Bayezid was quickly forgotten and the republic attempted a historiographical cover-up on the whole matter.[4]

This volte-face was typical of the Italian wars of the first half of the sixteenth century; to survive Venice had to play a very tricky diplomatic game. After the French defeat at the battle of Pavia in 1525 the Venetians became alarmed about the Habsburg presence on their borders, since it was known that Charles V's brother Ferdinand had set his eyes on Hungary. To counter the threat of encirclement by the Habsburgs, Venice encouraged Süleyman I to invade Hungary, and a formal embassy was sent by the republic to the sultan to congratulate him after his victory at Mohács. Charles V fumed at what he considered this betrayal of the common Christian cause, Venice being a 'poisonous plant' capable only of sowing discord amongst Christian princes and constantly in alliance with the sultan. Charles's ire was more than just a rhetorical outburst, since it was clear to everyone that the Ottomans were fighting Venice's battle against the Habsburgs.[5]

~

As much as the Venetians feared his retaliation, the emperor preferred to wait. The chance to repay Venice came a decade later, at the time of the 1537 Franco-Ottoman operation against Italy. Süleyman was concerned about the vulnerability of his communications between Apulia and Albania, fearing they could be cut by a hostile fleet. A few accidental skirmishes between Venetian and Ottoman ships convinced the sultan that the republic was indeed playing a double game, and these fears were adroitly exploited by Charles V's admiral, Andrea Doria, who started attacking Ottoman shipping in Venetian waters. In vain Venice's envoy in Constantinople protested that his fellow citizens were not responsible. Having failed to conquer southern Italy, Süleyman was unwilling to face the embarrassment of having to go home empty-handed, and war with Venice was exactly what he needed. The sultan also understood that before launching any future expedition against Italy he would first have to take the Venetian island of Corfu, considered the key to the Adriatic, Italy, Dalmatia and north-western Greece. For Süleyman war with Venice was necessary for the advance of the *darülislam*.

The Ottoman attack against the Venetian possessions in Greece was not unexpected, but executed swiftly. The fortress of Butrint was taken by surprise, and Corfu resisted only because the local commander, warned of the impending attack at the eleventh hour, managed to put together an effective defence. As soon as news of these events reached Venice, the republic mobilized its troops, seeking allies in the emperor and the pope with the hope of putting together an army 50,000 strong and a fleet of more than two hundred galleys. Paul III immediately sent his fleet, but Doria, originally from Venice's traditional rival Genoa, replied that he could not move without explicit orders from Charles V. In the meantime Ferdinand of Habsburg started new military operations in Hungary, while Venice managed to take a few coastal towns in Dalmatia. Süleyman's siege of Corfu was leading nowhere, the fortress being state-of-the-art and too hard a nut to crack even for the skilful Ottoman engineers. The same thing was true for the other Venetian strongholds of Monemvasia and Nafplio. After months of assaults and heavy losses, the Sultan decided to throw in the towel. He informed Venice that he was prepared to discuss peace terms provided the republic paid compensation for his losses, threatening otherwise to attack Friuli and Crete. In the face of such effrontery the Venetians decided to continue fighting, although the resolution passed by only one vote in the senate and the doge himself opposed it.

Venice joined the Holy League with the pope and the emperor on 8 February 1538, agreeing to pay two-sixths of its total expenses and contribute eighty-two galleys to the war effort. The Venetians were unhappy that the league's naval forces should be under the command of Andrea Doria, a manifestation of the mutual mistrust which plagued the league from the beginning. Venice feared that the Habsburgs would exploit the alliance for their own hegemonic interests, while the pope and the emperor suspected the Venetians of planning a separate peace with the Ottomans. The continual bickering among the allies meant that the league's fleet did not come together until September. It was late in the campaign season, and Doria was willing to postpone all military operations to the following spring. When the Venetians protested, he agreed to move towards the Muslim fleet under Barbarossa anchored at the entrance to the gulf of Preveza. Doria tried to lure the *kapudan-ı deryă* out of his protected haven, but the wily corsair bided his time, waiting for the allies to exhaust their provisions. At the right moment he struck, catching the league's fleet as it was retreating towards its supply bases. The allies' losses were light – seven vessels in all – but Doria's caution aroused a storm of criticism, the Venetians accusing him of having deliberately snatched defeat from the jaws of victory for the sake of weakening Venice's position vis-à-vis Charles V. Even more sinister was the accusation that Doria was engaged in secret negotiations with Barbarossa, a charge substantiated by more than just circumstantial evidence.[6] Partly to quash such allegations, the following October Doria captured the fortress of Castelnuovo in Dalmatia, which he proceeded to garrison with Spanish troops. Once more Venice protested, stating that according to the league's terms any conquered territory in Greece previously owned by the Venetians should revert to them. Doria ignored these remonstrations; he was following Charles V's agenda of diminishing Venice's power, and he also needed to disembark thousands of mutinous soldiers. These troops disappeared permanently from the scene when the following year Barbarossa retook Castelnuovo after a siege lasting from March to September, and which Doria made no effort to lift. Indeed, the behaviour of the Genoese admiral proved so desultory that the Venetians became convinced the only option was to seek terms with Constantinople.

This humiliating course of action was forced on the Venetians not only by Doria but also by France. The French ambassador in Constantinople had encouraged the sultan to prolong the war unless Venice agreed to give up Napflio, Kotor and Corfu, hoping thus to force the republic to seek help from the Valois and sever the Habsburg alliance. French envoys were sent to Venice offering substantial aid against the Ottomans, but the Venetians soon discovered these promises to be hollow. Now completely alone, Venice decided to pursue peace talks, sending to Constantinople Alvise Badoer with instructions to secure terms without if possible ceding Kotor, Corfu, Nafplio or Monemvasia. Badoer was given authority to agree to an annual tribute of up to 6,000 ducats and war indemnities up to a maximum of 300,000 ducats.

The Venetian ambassador arrived in Constantinople in April

1540, but to his dismay found the Turks adamantly committed to obtaining Nafplio and Monemvasia as well as an indemnity of 300,000 ducats. What Badoer ignored was that the French envoy in Venice had managed through bribery to obtain copies of the ambassador's instructions delivering them to the Ottomans. The Venetians were forced to give in, only managing to obtain the evacuation from Nafplio and Monemvasia of all those unwilling to live under Ottoman rule. In 1542 the Valois spy ring in Venice was uncovered and the Venetians did not hesitate to besiege the French embassy where a number of those involved had taken refuge, threatening to attack the building if they were not handed over. France complied with the request, having also the decency not to protest at the violation of its ambassador's diplomatic immunity.[7] As for Venice, until the Ottoman invasion of Cyprus it would bend over backwards to stay at peace with the Porte.

~

The Venetians had every reason to be suspicious that Doria was playing a double game; he had a remarkable record for duplicity. It had been the admiral who in 1528 had set Genoa firmly in the Habsburg camp, after decades of the city switching alliances between France and her enemies. Just a few months before finally throwing in its lot with the emperor Genoa had actively assisted the French in their final bid to conquer Naples. A mixed Venetian–Genoese fleet had been providing support to the advancing Valois troops, the Genoese under Andrea Doria's son Filippino even defeating a Spanish naval force off Capo d'Orso on 28 May. But the high-handed behaviour of the French, which included territorial encroachment in Liguria, provoked Genoa's bitter resentment. Protests having no effect, Andrea Doria negotiated for his fellow citizens an alliance with Charles V. Thus, on 4 July the Genoese vessels abandoned Neapolitan waters, leaving their erstwhile allies in the lurch. Doria profited considerably from the deal, obtaining from Charles V, in addition to the Order of the Golden Fleece, 60,000 florins a year for the rent of twelve galleys.[8] Henceforth, a large part of Charles V's Mediterranean fleet included vessels managed by Genoese *condottieri* families. Genoese bankers would also become the major moneylenders to the Spanish crown between the sixteenth and the seventeenth centuries, benefiting greatly from the riches of the Iberian empire.

Given these events, the Venetian mistrust of the Genoese and Doria in particular was understandable. But there were also other factors behind the lack of Genoese military commitment against the Turks. Most of Genoa's overseas empire had been gobbled up by the Ottomans in the course of the fifteenth century with the notable exception of the island of Chios, and for a number of reasons both the Genoese and the Ottomans had an interest in maintaining the status quo. The Porte received a yearly tribute of 12,000 ducats from the Genoese corporation, the *Maona*, ruling Chios, but also had other motives for tolerating an independent and potentially hostile territory near its coasts. The thought of a Habsburg–Genoese fleet using Chios as a base for operations against Ottoman territory in the Levant must have given nightmares to the sultan's admirals; but the Genoese understood that they held Chios on sufferance, and tried in every possible way not to irritate the sultan. The Genoese diplomats in Constantinople were always at pains to justify the actions of the 'citizen' Andrea Doria, and even asked the latter to nominally relinquish the command of his fleet to his great-grandson Giovanni Andrea, so as to deprive the French representatives in Constantinople of any excuse to poison the sultan's ear against Genoa. Because of its alliance with the Habsburgs, by the 1520s the Ottomans' main adversaries in the Mediterranean, Genoa was now one of the Porte's potential enemies. Relations between the two states became even more strained after the Franco-Ottoman alliance, which, among other things, contemplated punishing the 'treacherous' Genoese.[9]

This was easier said than done. Although by the beginning of the sixteenth century Chios was no longer the trade centre it had once been, it still played a significant role in the commercial exchanges between Genoa and Constantinople. By controlling the bulk of tin imports into the Ottoman empire, the *Maona* was in a position to impose severe limitations on the sultan's war effort. The cannon foundries of Constantinople's arsenal depended heavily on English tin, the Mediterranean trade in which was virtually monopolized by the Genoese. The English also benefited from the commerce, keeping a resident consul in Chios until the reign of Mary I, despite the occasional protest over the high taxes imposed by the *Maona*. Merchandise also flowed in the opposite direction, many Genoese having an interest in the Chios trade in gum mastic, alum, salt, pitch and aromatic resin, 'God's gift to the *Maonesi*' according to a contemporary.[10]

How much Andrea Doria was involved in Chios's commerce is unclear, but in any case, as befitted a good Genoese, he must have been concerned with the island's safety. Apart from its economic value, it was considered the republic's 'right eye' in the Levant[11]. Since it would have been very difficult and costly for Genoa to send a relief force to Chios in the event of an Ottoman attack, Doria preferred to safeguard the island by striking a deal with Barbarossa. The Genoese admiral's duplicitous behaviour before, during and after the battle of Preveza, was motivated by pragmatism and economic convenience. A few years later such considerations would cause the Genoese to liberate Dragut, one of the most famous Muslim corsairs of the time, in exchange for the coral-rich island of Tabarka off the Tunisian coast.[12] In addition, it should not be forgotten that at Preveza many of the 'Spanish' galleys were actually the private property of Genoese entrepreneurs on loan to Charles V. In no way could Doria have risked investments worth thousands of ducats unless absolutely sure of a return. Charles V would have agreed, considering also the repercussions of any major damage to Doria's fleet on his Mediterranean strategy. At the time of Preveza a gap existed between the emperor's objectives and those of the Venetians wide enough for someone like Doria to behave with the political adroitness his fellow citizens expected from him. As often the case in the history of the Mediterranean, fighting and friendship went hand in hand.

~

For Charles V the 1537–8 war was part of a greater strategy aimed at containing the Muslim, not just Ottoman, onslaught in the Mediterranean. By the time of Preveza the Habsburgs' southern maritime frontier was porous to say the least. The coasts of Spain, southern Italy and Sicily were especially exposed to the raids of Muslim corsairs, not to mention full-scale Ottoman invasions. This represented a serious challenge for the 'Catholic kings' – as the rulers of Spain styled themselves – even before the advent of the Habsburgs on the thrones of Castile and Aragon in 1516, a challenge destined to consume considerable quantities of Spain's military and financial resources.

By capturing Granada in 1492 Ferdinand VII of Aragon and Isabelle II of Castile had brought an end to the last independent Muslim state in the Iberian peninsula, everything possible being done to ensure that this situation remained permanent. The fall of Granada in no way ruled out another Islamic invasion. Twice before, the *Reconquista* – the reconquest of Iberia from the Moors, starting in the eighth century AD – had been stopped in its tracks by an influx of Muslim warriors from North Africa. No one could guarantee such a thing not happening again. This fear strengthened a very particular Spanish attitude which had taken shape during the centuries of the *Reconquista*, namely the feeling that Spain had a unique and exclusive role in the defence of the Christian faith. For this reason the Catholic kings would always be as much concerned with threats from abroad as with those lurking within their borders. In pursuing their enemies the kings were hampered by Spain at the time being politically and administratively divided – indeed, it was referred to as 'Spains' – the various kingdoms, political bodies and communities of the peninsula being fully conscious of their traditions, rights and privileges. Any failure by the central authorities to recognize these could trigger uprisings, and indeed in 1520 Castile was shaken to its roots by the widespread rebellion of the kingdom's communities, the revolt of the *Comuneros*.[13] Painfully aware of their weakness, the Catholic kings reacted with aggression, both at home and abroad, in order to guarantee the safety of their kingdoms.

Given this situation, it was almost inevitable that all those hostile to the Catholic faith should be perceived as potential enemies, to be dealt with accordingly. The first blow fell on the Jews, who were given the choice between conversion and expulsion soon after the fall of Granada. Next came the Moriscos, the Islamic population of Moorish ancestry left behind by the *Reconquista*. Mainly concentrated in Andalusia but strong also in Castile and Aragon, they made up large and economically important communities. Expelling such a substantial number of people would have been well-nigh impossible for the Spanish rulers of the time, the country's political divisions not allowing the sovereign to muster enough support for such a radical course of action. The alternative was forced conversion, the hope being that the converted Muslims would soon be absorbed into the Christian environment.

By 1502 Islam had been proscribed throughout Castile, although Granada was spared for a few years after 1492 thanks to the moderation of its Christian administrators. However, the archbishop of Toledo Cardinal Ximenes de Cisneros had been heavy-handed with the Granadan Moriscos. This had produced a rebellion in 1499–1501, put down only with great difficulty. A lull followed until 1525, when Charles V extended the policy of compulsory Christianity to Aragon. The Moriscos in Valencia promptly revolted, but were swiftly suppressed by royal troops. After each uprising many Moriscos agreed to be baptized, but many more escaped to North Africa nourishing a burning hatred towards all Christians. Those who remained in Spain as Muslims were subject to a growing number of restrictions, more in the kingdom of Castile than in Aragon, where for a time they were allowed to exercise their religion in private. All these measures were motivated by fear of a Morisco fifth column, capable of giving active aid to a Muslim expedition launched from Africa against the Spanish mainland.[14]

This was not paranoia. The frequent *gazi* expeditions launched by Barbary corsairs against the Spanish coast were actively aided by the Moriscos living in exile in North Africa but still in contact with their brethren across the sea. For the Spanish authorities stopping this sort of exchange was virtually impossible, lacking as they did the necessary forces to control, let alone repress, the large Morisco population in Andalusia. A viable alternative was denying the corsairs use of their African naval bases. As early as 1302 the Spanish had established a presence in Algiers by occupying for some time the Peñon, the island at the mouth of the city's harbour. In 1505 at Ximenes's instigation the stronghold of Mers-el-Kebir was taken, followed in 1508 by the Peñon de la Gomera. In May 1509 Oran fell, and many of its inhabitants were slaughtered. These conquests were followed by those of Bejaia, Tlemcen and Tripoli, and in 1510 the Spanish reoccupied the Peñon of Algiers. This series of victories came to an abrupt end when, the same year, an over-bold Spanish army was ambushed and cut to pieces on the island of Djerba off the Tunisian coast. Over the following years, distracted by the Italian wars, the Spanish were to lose much ground in North Africa.

Unable to challenge the Spanish effectively, the North African rulers looked abroad for aid. Desperate for help, in 1515 the emir of Algiers Selim al-Toumi sent for the Turkish corsair Arouj Reis Barbarossa, who with his brother Hizir, later more famous as Hayreddin, was operating successfully off the Tunisian coast, preying on Christian shipping and ferrying Moriscos to North Africa. Arouj expelled the Spanish from the vicinity of Algiers, although not from the Peñon, had the emir strangled and himself proclaimed ruler of the city. Turning it into a corsair haven, he quickly extended his control over the adjacent region, regaining much of the territory previously conquered by the Spanish. In 1518 Arouj was killed in battle at Tlemcen, and his brother then submitted to Sultan Selim I in exchange for an Ottoman garrison in Algiers. Hayreddin continued Arouj's work, retaking Bône (Annaba) in 1522 and the Peñon of Algiers seven years later after a siege lasting only three weeks. In 1534 he captured Tunis, throwing out its Spanish-backed ruler. Spain's bid for security had paradoxically resulted in Ottoman rule being extended over the greater part of North Africa.

By this date, however, Charles V felt secure enough in Italy to direct his energies against the Muslims in the Mediterranean. His granting of Malta and Tripoli to the Hospitallers in 1530 freed him of the necessity of guarding these two strategically important places, allowing him also to tap into the military and financial strength of the foremost chivalric order of Europe. At the end of May 1535 a joint Spanish, papal, Genoese and Maltese fleet of seventy-four galleys and 330 other ships descended on Tunis. After taking the key fortress of La Goleta, six miles from the city, the expeditionary force marched towards its main objective. Barbarossa's troops were routed, and the former ruler of Tunis, Muley Hassan, restored to his throne. Charles capped his victory by taking also Bône and Bizerte before returning in triumph to Sicily. Six years later, having covered his back by agreeing to a truce with France in 1538, the emperor decided it was high time to deal with Algiers. In the autumn of 1541 an expeditionary force of fifty galleys, 150 transport ships and 24,000 soldiers sailed for North Africa, confident of overpowering Algiers' garrison of 6,000 men. As fate would have it, however, in late October the armada was hit by a devastating storm that wrecked two thirds of the ships and killed thousands.[15] For the next quarter of a century the North African theatre witnessed once more a gradual Muslim resurgence. Despite the small Habsburg success against the Tunisian fort of Africa, north of Sfax, in 1550, Tripoli was retaken by Dragut from the Hospitallers the following year, and Bejaia in 1555.[16] In both cases the Habsburgs did not react, having more serious and pressing problems to deal with.

~

Once more France and the Ottomans were to prove the main source of trouble for the emperor. What Charles probably had not envisaged, despite the vagaries of Italian politics, was the possibility of an alliance between the papacy and the Porte. No sooner had the Parma war ended than on 3 August 1552 the city of Siena, a Habsburg protectorate, expelled the garrison from the Spanish-built fortress, proceeded to demolish it, and immediately sought the protection of France. For Charles V this was a serious blow; it threatened to create a French-controlled state in the heart of the Italian peninsula and had come when he already had his hands full in Germany, Flanders and Hungary. To make matters worse, a French-backed Ottoman armada under Dragut had been spotted off the Roman coast sailing in the direction of Naples. The Habsburg viceroy of Naples Don Pedro de Toledo had very few men at his disposal to face the expected invasion and sent frantic requests for help to Andrea Doria. The Genoese immediately put to sea a mixed Spanish–Italian fleet, but one contingent under Don Juan de Mendoza was ambushed and destroyed by Dragut off the isle of Ponza on 5 August. Too distant to give any help, Doria preferred to withdraw his ships to Sardinia. Emboldened by their victory, the Ottomans laid siege to the town of Gaeta, but finally decided to sail for Constantinople after waiting for twenty days for the French galleys to arrive. The French fleet eventually appeared in Constantinople a few weeks later, but despite the insistence of Admiral Antoine d'Escalin the Ottomans adamantly refused to resume operations until the following spring.

Charles V, however, was not prepared to wait, and in the winter of 1552–3 started operations in earnest against Sienese territory laying siege to the town of Montalcino, having previously obtained from the pope authorization to march through the papal states. With memories of the sack of Rome still fresh, Julius III was not in a position to refuse. By May it seemed that nothing could save Montalcino, when suddenly the imperialists lifted the siege and departed towards Naples, recalled by the threat of another Franco-Ottoman invasion. The Valois–Ottoman fleet, 150 sails strong, did materialize in the lower Tyrrhenian Sea, but after a few raids on the Neapolitan coast sailed north to the Sienese coastal stronghold of

Porto Ercole in the south of Tuscany. Having embarked there some 4,000 French troops previously been sent to aid Siena, this armada went on a devastating rampage through the Tuscan islands before swinging west towards Corsica. The island was weakly defended, and in addition the population was in a chronic state of revolt against its Genoese overlords. In little more than a month the Franco-Ottomans had occupied the whole of Corsica with the exception of Calvi, being unable to overcome the spirited resistance of the local Spanish garrison.

When the Ottomans retired towards the Levant at the beginning of October the French remained in sole control of the island and proceeded to impose terms: in exchange for Corsica, the Genoese were to abandon Charles V and become allies of Henry II. But the Franco-Turkish military alliance had sent shock waves down the length of Italy, bringing into the Habsburg camp many states until then cool towards Charles V's policies. Cosimo I de' Medici, duke of Florence, was worried that if Genoa fell to the Valois the French would then try to conquer Naples and dominate the Mediterranean together with their Ottoman allies. Although Cosimo had always tried to remain neutral in the fight between the Valois and the Habsburgs, his wife was Don Pedro de Toledo's daughter and the duke also owed his position to Spanish backing. In addition, Cosimo wanted Siena for himself, particularly after in early January 1554 Henry II put the city's defences under Marshal Piero Strozzi, a ferociously anti-Medici Florentine exile. Cosimo played his hand carefully, asking Charles V to be allowed to make war on Siena in the emperor's name, both sides agreeing on the number of troops and the expenses necessary to bring the city back into the Habsburg fold. At this stage Cosimo was not asking for Siena, but only the reimbursement of his expenses.[17]

The duke struck immediately, three columns of Florentine–imperial troops crossing the Sienese border on 26 January under the command of Giangiacomo de' Medici, marquis of Marignano, a Milanese nobleman unrelated to the duke. But despite the capture of a few strongholds in the countryside the invaders failed to take

Siena by storm and were forced to settle down for what promised to be a long siege. Marignano's difficulties were increased by Piero Strozzi's military ability, the Franco-Sienese commander conducting hit-and-run raids deep into Florentine territory. These forced the besiegers to detach forces to engage him and relieve the pressure on Siena. But Strozzi's strategy could ultimately succeed only with substantial French reinforcements, and these did not materialize in time for the marshal to deliver Marignano a knock-out blow. Instead, the Florentine commander caught and soundly defeated Strozzi with a numerically superior army at Marciano, south of Siena, on 2 August 1554. Siena was forced to surrender on terms the following 21 April. A number of exiles from the city joined together in Montalcino, and with French help resisted for another two years.

The Siena war was bitterly fought, both sides committing atrocities seldom seen during the Italian wars. Much of the latter part of the conflict was fought in southern Tuscany, the Franco-Sienese forcing their enemies to capture each stronghold in turn, sometimes more than once. In addition the Florentines had always to contend with the possibility of an Ottoman raid, this threat materializing in July 1555 when a naval force of 104 sail under Dragut attempted a two-pronged attack against Piombino. Luckily for the Florentines their commander in the area, Chiappino Vitelli, intercepted the Ottomans just after they had landed, forcing them back to their ships. The invaders lost 550 killed out of a force of 3,500, all Ottoman prisoners being summarily dispatched by their captors. Dragut then tried to take Portoferraio on the island of Elba, but finding it too tough a target sailed towards Corsica.[18]

By now another front was about to open up in Italy. Pope Julius III died at the end of March 1555, was succeeded briefly by Marcellus II (twenty days) and then by Paul IV. The new pontiff, born Gian Pietro Carafa, a stern and devout man of unbending principles, was nearly eighty when elected. From the early part of his ecclesiastical career he had shown himself zealous in fighting heresy, and had even been entrusted by Paul III with reorganizing the Roman inquisition. During his sojourn in Spain as papal nuncio under Leo X he had also developed a burning hatred of the Habsburgs, the latter fully reciprocating the sentiment. Paul's priorities were the defence of Catholic orthodoxy and diminishing the power and prestige of the Habsburgs, his loathing of Charles V becoming even more pronounced when the emperor, through his brother Ferdinand, yielded to the Lutherans' demands at the Diet of Augsburg (February–September 1555): from then on in Germany it would be up to the local authorities to determine the official religion of their subjects, thus introducing the concept of *cuius regio, eius religio*. By now, Charles, tired and ailing, had lost the will to fight, and between October and August 1556 he abdicated to his son Philip (Philip II) his domains in Spain, Italy, the Netherlands and the Indies, while his brother Ferdinand received the imperial title together with Germany and Hungary.

For Paul, Charles's behaviour towards the Lutherans was nothing less than an open betrayal of those same Catholic principles the emperor was supposed to uphold. Determined to destroy the Habsburgs once and for all, on 15 December 1555 he signed a treaty with Henry II of France – although somewhat uneasy about the Valois alliance with the Porte[19] – for the creation of a Franco-papal army of 20,000 to conquer Milan, Naples and Siena. The French were to keep the conquered territories, minus a large chunk of the Neapolitan kingdom to be incorporated into the papal states, and Siena, which was to go to one of the Pope's nephews. If Venice and Ferrara should decide to join, then they too were to receive territorial compensation, with Sicily being reserved for the Republic of St Mark.[20] The proviso on Siena was probably the most striking element of the treaty; despite all his reforming zeal, Paul IV was very much a chip off the nepotistic Renaissance block. For advice he relied on his pushy nephews, in particular the ambitious and unscrupulous former soldier Cardinal Carlo Carafa. In many ways Paul was a man of the fifteenth century and was fond of recalling the days of his youth, when Italy was 'a musical instrument with four strings' – the Church, Venice, Naples and Milan, Florence not then being part of this idyllic picture – until the French invasion of 1494 had put an end to this 'ancient harmony' and to Italy's liberty.[21]

Paul's plans nearly fell through when in February 1556 the Valois and the Habsburgs agreed on a five-year truce at Vaucelles, near Cambrai, which in essence allowed the French to keep all their conquests in Savoy and the empire. The agreement left the pope to face alone the Spanish army in Italy, but Cardinal Carafa effectively managed to destroy the truce by convincing Henry II to assist the pope in the event of a war with Spain. Strengthened by the promise of French aid, the pope started persecuting all of his subjects with Habsburg sympathies. A number of prominent cardinals and Roman citizens were either imprisoned or put under house arrest, but the full force of the pope's fury was reserved for the Colonna family, their lands in the papal states being confiscated and redistributed among Paul's nephews. When Philip II welcomed Marcantonio Colonna and others of his kin into the kingdom of Naples, the pope excommunicated him with his father Charles V, placing their domains under interdict and absolving their subjects from the oath of fealty. It was tantamount to a declaration of war.

Paul's actions proved costly.[22] Philip II acted rapidly, obtaining Venice's neutrality and securing the support of Florence and Parma by promising Siena to the Medici and Piacenza to the Farnese. When attempts to reach an agreement with the pope met with Paul's stubborn refusal, war became inevitable. On 1 September the duke of Alva, viceroy of Naples after the death of Don Pedro de Toledo, invaded the papal states from the south with an army of 12,000 foot and 1,800 horse, 300 of them provided by Marcantonio Colonna. Advancing through the Roman countryside and occupying a number of strategic places against little resistance, Alva thwarted all attempts to stop him. As the Spanish approached Rome the populace, mindful of the sack of twenty years before, flew into a panic: citizens, priests and friars were sent to work on the walls and additional troops hastily raised. Alva, however, was not interested in taking the Holy City as much as in denying the pope the chance of receiving French reinforcements from the sea. On 18 November, shadowed by Piero Strozzi's forces, he took the fortress of Ostia, at the mouth of the Tiber. Having put a stranglehold on Rome's supply routes, Alva was willing to negotiate from a position of strength.

Alva and Cardinal Carafa, acting in the pope's name, met near Ostia on 28 November, but with the exception of a forty-day truce the parties did not manage to reach an agreement. The pope steadfastly refused to give in to Alva's demands, which included restoring to the Colonna their confiscated possessions. Carafa himself was willing to exchange these lands for the lordship of Siena, but this was something that Philip II was not prepared to concede.[23] Alva returned to Naples, leaving behind Marcantonio Colonna with 7,000 men. Both contestants needed the respite to reorganize and augment their forces for the next campaign season; the viceroy was also concerned about a possible French inroad into the kingdom of Naples. Cardinal Carafa departed for Venice in an attempt to convince the republic to enter the fray on the pope's side, but the Venetians refused to relinquish their neutrality despite Carafa's offer of a substantial chunk of Neapolitan territory in the event of a papal–French victory. The pope's nephew hinted darkly that should the Venetians refuse their support then Paul IV would be forced not only to bring into Italy so many French troops that it would then be very difficult to get rid of them, but also, lacking a navy of his own, the pontiff would have to avail himself of the Turkish fleet.[24] Carafa was invoking the spectre of an Ottoman invasion of Apulia, something ultimately capable of putting Venice's very existence at risk.

The cardinal would later state that this had been but a ploy to convince the Venetians, but this assertion is disingenuous. Already in September 1556 he had concocted a plan to employ the Ottoman fleet against Spain's domains in Italy. The following March he would write directly to Süleyman – probably with the pope's blessing – asking him to stop waging war in Hungary and instead concentrate on building a great fleet to attack the kingdom of

Naples. Carafa had already been in correspondence with the sultan some months before, and the cardinal would later defend himself by stating that he had acted on papal orders. Although we may doubt the veracity of Carafa's account, there is no doubt that Paul IV knew about his nephew's dealings. In any case the pontiff's hatred of the Habsburgs overcame any scruples he may have had when it came to choosing his allies.[25]

In the meantime the French had intervened in force, an army of 12,000 foot and 1,200 horse under the duke of Guise marching from Piedmont down the Adriatic coast. Skirting the borders of the duchy of Florence it entered Umbria, although both Guise and Cardinal Carafa would have preferred to attack Cosimo I: the pope's nephew still had his eye on Siena. As a result, Cosimo, who in order to obtain Siena had been toying with the idea of a French alliance, threw his lot with Philip II. The pope, encouraged also by the progress of his own forces against Marcantonio Colonna, was adamant that the main objective should be the kingdom of Naples. Colonna had weakened his position by dispersing his soldiers in a number of garrisons, and Piero Strozzi was quick to exploit the situation. Upon the expiry of the forty-day truce he pounced on Colonna, forcing him to abandon Ostia and retreat towards the south, losing a third of his troops in the process. With the supply routes to Rome reopened and Colonna on the run, the papal army could manoeuvre freely in the Roman countryside, and very soon Vicovaro, Palestrina, Frascati, Grottaferrata, Castel Gandolfo, Marino and Tivoli had been recovered for the Holy See. With the French army approaching fast, the Spanish faced the real risk that Strozzi and Guise would unite their forces, something that in conjunction with the feared arrival of an Ottoman fleet could have put an end to Habsburg domination in the south of Italy. The Ottomans, however, did not materialize, and Guise instead of moving towards Rome entered the Abruzzi region, occupying a few towns and laying siege to the fortress of Civitella del Tronto. The stronghold proved impregnable and in mid-May Guise lifted the siege, unwilling to face Alva's superior forces approaching fast from the south. With the situation under control in the Abruzzi, Alva dispatched 3,000 men to help Marcantonio Colonna. Strengthened by these reinforcements Colonna rapidly went on the offensive, regaining much of the ground lost to Strozzi the previous winter. On 15 August he stormed Segni, sacking the city and putting the garrison and many civilians to the sword. In the meantime Guise remained inactive, the French having become increasingly dissatisfied with the pope since he had not provided the promised troops or the necessary funds. Alva exploited the situation by once more invading the papal states, but acting on strict orders from Philip II limited himself to raiding the Roman countryside up to the walls of the Holy City.

Paul was losing ground fast. On 10 August – the feast of St Laurence, a saint to whom Philip II was particularly devoted – the French under Constable Anne de Montmorency were roundly defeated in Flanders at the battle of St Quentin by a Habsburg army led by Duke Emmanuel Philibert of Savoy, who previously had been evicted by the Valois from his domains. France lay open to invasion, and Guise was hastily recalled from Italy. Philip II had also finally managed to corner Cosimo I by giving him Siena as a Spanish fief, thus making the slippery Medici his vassal.[26] To everyone except the pope it seemed high time for peace. Paul, now completely isolated and desperately short of funds, grudgingly accepted Venetian and Florentine mediation, and on 12 September 1557 signed the Treaty of Cave. The terms were extremely generous for the pontiff: all papal lands were to be restored, in exchange for the lifting of the temporal and spiritual sanctions against the Habsburgs and their followers. Excepted from this pardon were confirmed rebels such as Marcantonio Colonna, the latter getting the muddy end of the stick, since both Alva and Cardinal Carafa had reasons for leaving him high and dry. The pope's nephew knew that Paul would never agree to pardon Marcantonio, and in any case Carafa had benefited greatly from the confiscation of Colonna lands. The viceroy of Naples, meanwhile, was hoping that the Colonna possessions, including the important fief and fortress of

Paliano, would go to his kinsman Don Garcia de Toledo, married to Marcantonio's elder sister, Vittoria.[27] In any case, both Alva and Philip II, always uneasy about waging war against the Holy See, were eager to strike a deal with the pope in order to tackle the Valois undisturbed.

The French were in no condition to continue fighting. Most of their former allies in Italy had opted for neutrality or chosen the Habsburg camp. In Hungary, Ferdinand and Süleyman had agreed some time before on a temporary peace, which, despite a number of border clashes over several disputed fortresses, seemed to be holding. The Ottomans, of course, remained a viable option for Henry II, and indeed in the early summer of 1558 a large Turkish fleet conducted extensive raids on the coast of southern Italy and across the western Mediterranean. As had happened before, lack of coordination meant that the Ottomans never managed to link up with their French allies, who waited in Corsica while the Turks plundered the isle of Minorca. In any case, Süleyman was now facing problems at home, having to deal with the rebellion of his son Bayezid, and thus in no position to aid his Valois ally in any way. Henry II had no choice but to agree in April 1559 to the Peace of Cateau-Cambrésis with Philip II.[28]

By the treaty, France was forced to give back practically the whole of Savoy to Duke Emmanuel Philibert and Corsica to the Genoese, and withdraw all its troops from Italy. The Habsburgs kept for good the southern Italian kingdoms of Naples and Sicily, the duchy of Milan, and Siena. The latter had already been enfeoffed to Cosimo I de' Medici with the exclusion of a few fortresses in the south of Tuscany retained by Spain, although the treaty actually called for the restoration of the Sienese republic. Cosimo got round this through a *fictio juris*: allowing the old Sienese magistracies to survive, but adding others staffed with his henchmen. The Valois retained the imperial cities of Metz, Toul and Verdun, plus regaining certain territories in north-eastern France. In addition, it was agreed that French and Genoese merchants should have free access to each other's ports. All these agreements were to be cemented with a series of dynastic marriages. Finally the parties agreed to employ all means to help reform and reunite the Church, a clause filled with unintended irony since the French by allying themselves with the Lutheran princes in Germany had done everything possible to shatter for good the religious unity of western Europe. They were already being repaid in kind. The Huguenots, Protestants of extreme Calvinist persuasion, had grown to alarming numbers within France itself. The Huguenots included in their ranks commoners as well as a substantial portion of France's nobility, and were rapidly becoming a vociferous, compact and militant force, soon to challenge the very existence of the Valois dynasty. For nearly forty years after Cateau-Cambrésis France would not be able to play any sort of significant military role in Europe, being crippled by religiously inspired civil unrest and war. Having sown the Lutheran wind, the Valois were now reaping the Huguenot whirlwind.

~

Cateau-Cambrésis not only confirmed Spain's hegemony in Italy, it also inserted most of the Italian states, albeit in different degrees, within the framework of the Habsburgs' Mediterranean strategy. This did not mean absolute control on Spain's part. Venice pursued its interests as before; the papacy had its own, variable, agenda; and both Savoy and Florence were, at best, very opportunistic allies. Duke Emmanuel Philibert of Savoy, the victor of St Quentin, had recovered his duchy from the French thanks to Philip II, but continually tried to escape from his patron's suffocating embrace. Nearly completely landlocked, Nice being its only port of significance, and wary of its troublesome French and Swiss neighbours, Savoy preferred to concentrate on its army rather than its navy. Florence was in a different position.

With Siena, Cosimo I de' Medici acquired a coastline extending the length of the upper Tyrrhenian Sea, together with the burden of protecting this watery frontier. It was an unenviable task, Florence having no fleet at the start of the Medici dukedom in 1532, the Florentine republic for financial reasons doing away with its galley squadron at the end of the fifteenth century.[29] The low priority given to naval matters by the Florentines was also due to the fact that up to the 1530s they were little affected by Ottoman expansion in the Mediterranean. This had taken place mostly at the expense of Venice, with whom Florence had a somewhat antagonistic relationship. What changed the Florentines' attitude towards the Porte was the Franco-Ottoman alliance of 1536 and Hayreddin Barbarossa's victory at Preveza two years later, events leading to a series of Muslim raids on the Italian coasts. The situation worsened with Barbarossa's massive raiding expedition across the western Mediterranean in 1543–4, and Florence became seriously alarmed by the possibility of a Franco-Ottoman attack.[30] By 1547 Cosimo I had started reorganizing his state's coastal defences, basing them on watchtowers, galleys and mounted units. This system was intended only for local protection, and until 1550 there were no more than a couple of Florentine galleys cruising the upper Tyrrhenian Sea between the port of Livorno and the island of Elba. It was the war for Siena in 1554–5 that precipitated a dramatic increase of the Medicean fleet – from two to six galleys – after the Florentines were forced to confront a Franco-Ottoman amphibious expeditionary force in southern Tuscany. In addition, the acquisition of Siena by Cosimo meant not only the Florentines having to protect a longer coastline, but also the inclusion of the Medici fleet in the Habsburgs' Mediterranean defences, the enfeoffment agreement stipulating that the Florentine galleys be at the disposal of the Spanish crown in times of need.[31] However, in dealing with the Ottoman problem the military option was but one of a number at Cosimo's disposal, diplomacy being for a long time a viable alternative. Besides, as befitted the descendant of merchants, the duke was interested in establishing strong commercial links with the Levant.

The republic of Florence had a long tradition of economic relations with Constantinople, the first trade concessions being granted by Mehmed II around 1455 and reconfirmed by Bayezid II in 1488. However, Florence's political turmoil after 1494, together with the wars of the sixteenth century, had not allowed the city to establish a stable commercial partnership with the Ottomans. Only with the advent of the Medici dukedom in 1532, coinciding with a more stable political and economic situation, were attempts made to reverse this situation. Despite what has been written by some,[32] the death of the Florentine *bailo*★ in 1530 did not imply the end of diplomatic relations between Florence and Constantinople, the presence of other *baili* being recorded at the beginning of the 1540s. Certainly by 1543, ten years after the accession of Cosimo I, the Florentines were trading actively in Constantinople as well as in Alexandria. The Medici representative in Constantinople, Alfonso Berardi, was instructed to do everything possible to cultivate the powerful Grand Vizier Rüstem Pasha so as to encourage Ottoman merchants to trade with Florence as they had once done. Cosimo was prepared to go to any length and expense: Berardi was ordered to discover what sort of gifts the grand vizier might appreciate.[33] The greatest expansion of Florentine trade with the Ottoman empire took place in the 1550s, and a Florentine diplomat was present in Pera until the middle of the next decade. By then direct commercial links between Tuscany and the Near East had been all but severed, trade giving way to an endemic state of war between the Medici and the Porte destined to last until the eighteenth century. What happened?

The culprit is usually identified as Counter-Reformation religious zeal, which resuscitated the apparently moribund crusading spirits of the Medici and their subjects. While evidence of such a revival can't be ignored, it is also true that beliefs were but one of many factors at play. Cosimo had some very strong dynastic ambitions, entwined with a compelling need to bring under control Tuscany's ruling elites. Immediately after the conquest of Siena, the duke had started to toy with creating a new maritime chivalric

★ *Bailo*, a word of Venetian origin, indicated a state's permanent resident at the Porte.

order, with himself in the role of grand master. Cosimo's objective was twofold: provide himself with an experienced pool of naval personnel and create a socio-political patronage system firmly in Medici hands. The order could also channel the energies of potentially unruly members of society towards the noble goal of protecting Christendom against the Muslim onslaught.[34] Cosimo chose to name the institution after St Stephen, pope and martyr (not to be confused with the more famous St Stephen, the first martyr), whose feast fell on 2 August, a date the duke considered particularly auspicious since it coincided with two of his most important military victories, including that of Marciano.

According to Cosimo's intentions, the order was to be self-sufficient, and thanks to its revenues capable of maintaining up to twelve galleys. But the grand duke's dream of the knights having their own fleet quickly foundered in the face of the order's unwillingness to use its considerable fortune to fight the infidels. As a result, the Tuscan fleet, while manned by the knights of St Stephen, was invariably financed by the Medici purse. Only in the 1620s would the order agree to pay a token yearly sum towards the upkeep of the fleet, at a time when the galleys were costing the Medici on average 15 per cent of Tuscany's yearly revenue.[35] Large numbers of Italian, and not just Tuscan, aristocrats swelled the ranks of the order immediately after its creation, and soon vessels flying the red eight-pointed cross of St Stephen became a common and feared sight in the Mediterranean. Even more important, the Medici became firmly associated with the order, a thing that would ultimately condition the Florentine dynasty's foreign policy.

Still occupied fighting the Valois, Philip II decided it was high time to reach some sort of agreement with the Porte, concerned that his uncle Ferdinand's agreement with Süleyman over Hungary would leave him to face alone a possible Franco-Ottoman offensive. Around the middle of 1558 Philip sent the Genoese Francesco Franchis to Constantinople to sound out the sultan on the matter, the king's choice of agent motivated by his desire to save face by not appearing to be making the first move. Franchis was also entrusted with the task of establishing an intelligence network in the Ottoman capital.[36] But in Constantinople there were doubts about the Genoese's real mission, Grand Vizier Rüstem Pasha openly accusing him of spying. Only after much persuasion did Franchis manage to convince the Ottoman authorities of the sincerity of his intentions. Like Philip, Rüstem was unwilling to take the initiative, but was prepared to consider informal talks with his Spanish counterparts. Following up on this, the king's secretary Gonzalo Pérez drafted a truce proposal to be submitted to the sultan: it was to last at least ten years, include 'tributaries, subjects and allies' of the two parties, and also contemplated an exchange of prisoners of war reduced to slavery. The following 6 March Philip informed Gonzalo Fernández de Córdoba, duke of Sessa and governor of Milan, that he had decided to send Niccolò Secco to Constantinople as his envoy since he knew well the local situation, having spent many years in the Levant. The instructions to Secco included bribing the grand vizier to obtain the truce from the sultan and also to stop the Ottoman fleet from sailing west that year.[37] Eventually, nothing came of these initiatives, both sides being unwilling to commit themselves to a treaty that might result in a loss of political prestige.

As was often the case, negotiations went hand in hand with military activities. The Peace of Cateau-Cambrésis effectively prevented the Turkish fleet from using French ports during their forays into the western Mediterranean, but for the Spanish the North African corsair bases remained a source of deep concern. Muslim sea *gazi* were an incessant threat to shipping routes, and regularly raided Christian shores. Even more worrying for Philip II was the fact that these bases could be used as logistical stepping stones for a major Ottoman attack on Spain or the Habsburg domains in Italy. Following an established pattern, in June 1559 it was decided to strike at the Muslim corsair bases in North Africa, but the expedition against Tripoli ended in disaster at Djerba the following year. For

Spain and her allies this was a dramatic defeat, the losses in men and equipment being equivalent, if not worse, to those suffered by Charles V at the time of his expedition against Algiers in 1541. More setbacks were to follow. In 1561 the Muslims captured three galleys under Visconte Cigala, one of the few squadrons to have survived Djerba. A few weeks later, Dragut with seven vessels captured the whole Sicilian war fleet of eight galleys. This litany of woes reached its climax a year later when a force of thirty-two galleys under Juan de Mendoza foundered off Malaga, with the loss of twenty-nine ships and 4,000 men.[38]

Ships could be replaced, but to rebuild a significant pool of experienced naval personnel took years. It would be some time before the Spanish could again tackle the Ottomans at sea, and inexperienced crews made amphibious operations very risky. For this reason, when the Ottoman host descended on Malta in 1565, the viceroy of Sicily, Don Garcia de Toledo, did everything he could to safeguard the meagre resources at his disposal, biding his time until it was safe to send a relief force to the island. For Don Garcia, and indeed the Spanish crown, the relief of Malta was as much a matter of sound military strategy as of prestige. By capturing the island the Ottomans would not only have imposed a stranglehold on shipping routes across the Mediterranean, but from Malta and their bases in the Balkans could also threaten the whole of southern Italy. Besides, Philip II was the Hospitallers' feudal overlord, and thus had a compelling duty to give them assistance. Yet Don Garcia knew perfectly well that any hasty move on his part could result in disaster, and preferred to deal with the situation using Fabian tactics. The viceroy knew that the Knights of St John would put up a stiff fight, allowing him to buy time while the Ottomans exhausted themselves in a prolonged and costly siege. Malta's location also meant that the Ottomans had dangerously extended their supply lines, making them vulnerable to a counterstroke delivered at the right moment. But this was not so easy to determine, Don Garcia having to judge exactly when the Ottomans were at their weakest. For this reason he was careful to send enough reinforcements before and during the siege to stiffen the knights' resolve, but not too many to seriously affect his own capabilities should Malta fall. The viceroy was taking a calculated risk, but his strategy ultimately proved successful.

Don Garcia's tactics provoked a storm of criticism from the Hospitallers and their followers, the viceroy's prudence going as far as forbidding a number of knights gathered in Messina to join their besieged companions. He also ordered that the reinforcements sent in the middle of June should not land in the event of Fort St Elmo having already fallen, there being no way the troop-carrying ships could enter Malta's Grand Harbour without being intercepted by the Ottomans. As it happened, the reinforcements arrived the very day St Elmo's defenders were overwhelmed, but the knights leading the relief force managed to conceal this from the Spanish commanders on board the galleys and make their way to the town of Birgu from the south, passing undetected through Ottoman siege lines – a feat little less than miraculous. But Don Garcia was not being excessively cautious, as the loss of the relief force would not only cause Malta to fall, but also put Sicily at grave risk. The island's vulnerability to an enemy invasion would be graphically described a few years later by another viceroy, the duke of Terranova: no money, few soldiers, even less sailors for the galleys, lack of provisions and undermanned fortresses.[39]

Don Garcia received continuous news on the progress of the siege from Maltese boats that time after time managed to elude Ottoman patrols. The viceroy also placed lookouts on Capo Passero, Sicily's southernmost tip, to listen to the distant boom of the great Ottoman siege guns. He knew that St Elmo had fallen when the sound ceased, since it would take the Ottomans several days to relocate their artillery and resume firing against the next objective.[40] The slackening rumbles from Malta gave Don Garcia the clue that the Turks were running short of gunpowder, meaning that they would not be able to continue the pounding for long. But even at this point, by deciding to send a large relief force to Malta the viceroy was stretching his luck, for there was always the risk of encountering a numerically superior Ottoman army. Nevertheless the viceroy arrived just at the right moment to inflict the coup de grâce on the Ottoman expeditionary force, although the historians of the Order of St John would like us to believe otherwise.[41] Don Garcia's strategy had certainly paid off, but prudence and procrastination would not always work with the Ottomans.

4. BUILD-UP TO DRAMA

~

On Easter Sunday 1566 there was a palpable sense of uneasiness among the inhabitants of Chios. The day before an Ottoman fleet numbering eighty galleys with 7,000 men on board had dropped anchor just outside their port; and whilst the *kapudan-ı deryâ* Piyale Pasha had refrained from entering the harbour – ostensibly for fear that his presence would disturb the Easter celebrations – this show of sensitivity only increased the Chians' apprehension. The island's governors were perfectly aware that they were personae non gratae with the Ottoman government, and especially with Grand Vizier Sokollu Mehmed Pasha. The latter had more than one reason to be irate with the Genoese rulers of Chios: Genoa was now firmly in the Habsburg camp, while the island was perceived by the Porte as a nest of spies – the Chians constantly keeping Genoa, and thus Spain, informed about the movements of the Ottoman fleet – and a haven for fugitive Christian slaves. In addition, the Maona in control of Chios was always in arrears with the tribute it was supposed to pay to the Sultan.[1]

Visits from large Ottoman fleets were no novelty for the Chians. Given the island's proximity to the Anatolian mainland, Turkish ships often stopping for water and victuals. When Piyale entered the harbour the following Monday he was received with the customary greeting salvos from the fortresses' artillery. The next morning the admiral, having expressed his desire to relax for a few days in the island's orchards, took a boat to the shore in the company of a number of high-ranking officers, *sancaks* and engineers. Piyale enjoyed a pleasant day observing fortifications and gardens. The following day he announced his departure, adding that before going he wished to discuss an important matter with the Chian government. Presently six of the twelve *signori governatori* arrived on Piyale's flagship but he, claiming that this constituted a breach of etiquette, stated adamantly that he would only speak to the whole governing board. The *podestà*, the governor of Chios appointed by Genoa, Vincenzo Giustiniani and the *signori governatori* were in a quandary. Although suspicious of Piyale's motives, they could not afford to offend the admiral by refusing to meet him, fearing that this could lead to a military confrontation. Chios's extensive fortifications would have allowed the city to resist for a short while – given also that the Ottoman army was busy fighting in Hungary and still making good the losses sustained at Malta – but in the long run the distance between the island and Genoa made relief a very unlikely eventuality. Besides, the Genoese were busy putting down yet another revolt on Corsica, and the Spanish had their own problems trying to defend their Mediterranean possessions.

The fates of Chios and Corsica were actually more closely linked than may appear, Corsican rebels, backed by the French, attempting to obtain the Porte's aid in their fight for independence. The Ottomans, unwilling to help directly, knowing that they could not count on the Valois' active support, had provided some undercover aid to the leader of the rebellion Sampietro di Bastelica. When the latter landed on his native island in June 1564, triggering off a revolt that would last until 1569, it had been the Ottomans who had provided the transport for him and his followers, a number of Muslim vessels also helping him in the taking of Porto Vecchio.[2] To the acute embarrassment of the Maona, the notorious Sampietro had stopped for three days in Chios harbour, under the protection of the sultan's banner, when returning from his diplomatic mission to Constantinople.[3] Since the Genoese proved unable to crush the

Corsicans themselves, they had to turn to the Spanish for aid, the rebellion thus having the effect of tying down both Habsburg and Genoese naval forces in the western Mediterranean. As far as Chios was concerned, the Ottomans' hands were free.

With the deepest reluctance the island's governors went to Piyale's galley, where they were courteously received by the admiral. His politeness, however, was short-lived. Piyale proceeded to accuse the Maonesi of espionage, giving aid to fugitive slaves and Christian corsairs, failing to pay tribute to the Porte, and providing information to the sultan's enemies. He then informed the governors that it was the sultan's will that they be punished accordingly, arrested them and threatened to torch the city of Chios if the tribute, together with an extra sum of money for himself, was not paid within three days. The Chians quickly got word of what had happened, but Piyale moved swiftly. Thousand of Turks with weapons concealed under their robes had already infiltrated the city over the previous two days, under the guise of buying clothes and other items.[4] As soon as they received the admiral's signal they quickly moved to occupy the fortress, while the populace could only watch in dismay and fear the hoisting of the crescent standard. Piyale disembarked with the rest of his troops, took over the city gates and ordered that under pain of death no injury should be done to the Christians, hanging two soldiers guilty of disobeying his command. But the next day, the admiral had the interiors of the cathedral and of other churches destroyed, seizing the gold and silver vessels, destroying the altars and removing the bells. The cathedral was left to the Christians, but two other churches were turned into mosques, the Chians observing all this vandalism with tearful eyes.

On Friday 19 April Piyale summoned all the Giustiniani – the family whose members ran the Maona – to the government palace, and played a cat-and-mouse game. He promised them his protection but demanded they hand over all the diplomatic documentation between them and the Porte over the possession of Chios. The Maonesi agreed, despite knowing only too well that by doing so they were losing any chance of future legal redress. Next, Piyale announced that anyone wronged by the Maonesi should come forward and receive justice. No one appeared, although the Maona was notoriously corrupt, and over the years tensions had existed between the Catholic and Greek Orthodox communities. Indeed, many Chians asked Piyale to intercede with the sultan on behalf of the Giustiniani. But the admiral's answer came as a shock: an order had arrived from Süleyman to execute the leading Maonesi and exile the others to Caffa on the Black Sea. Frantically, the Chians dipped into their purses to pay for a frigate to carry an appeal to Constantinople. When the ship returned (if it was ever sent – there was a strong suspicion that Piyale had been lying the whole time) the admiral announced that the sultan had decided to exile the *podestà* and the *signori governatori*, while the other Maonesi were to buy their freedom for between 500 and 1,000 ducats ahead. In order to raise this money – which included also the tribute to the Porte – the Giustiniani were forced to 'sell' their property to Piyale. The island's erstwhile governors were then shipped to Caffa together with their families, excluding twenty-one of their children sent instead as *kapıkulu* to Constantinople. Eighteen were put to death a few months later for refusing to embrace Islam, while the remaining three accepted circumcision but eventually managed to escape back to Genoa, where they reverted to Catholicism.

On the sultan's order Chios was turned into a *sancak* governed by the Hungarian renegade Gazanfer Bey. Piyale left a force of five galleys, 500 janissaries and 200 *sipahi*s to guard the island, forbidding anyone to leave without permission or suffer severe penalties.

Piyale followed up his success by sailing across the Aegean Sea towards the western Mediterranean. On 24 June the Turkish armada was sighted by two Spanish galleys some thirty miles south of the isle of Zakynthos. The Ottomans gave chase, but their quarry managed to escape. Both in Madrid and Rome it was feared that Malta would be Piyale's objective, and hastily raised troops were sent to man the island's yet unfinished fortifications. Instead, the sultan's admiral skirted Italy's heel and moved up the Adriatic, dropping anchor in front of Dubrovnik. The Ragusei had already received news of Chios's fate, and, fearing that Piyale would try something similar with them – Dubrovnik, despite being one of the Porte's tributary states, always maintained extensive relations with the Habsburgs and other Western powers – adamantly refused Piyale entrance into the city's fortified harbour, for good measure pointing their guns towards the Ottoman ships. Whether because of this show of force or because he had never planned to take Ragusa in the first place, Piyale limited himself to collecting the sultan's yearly tribute before sailing north towards the Gulf of Trieste. After trying unsuccessfully to deal with some Albanian rebels and raiding the eastern coast of southern Italy, he turned back to Constantinople. On the return voyage he occupied the islands of Naxos, Andros, Kea and Sifnos – all independent states held by Venetian families since the thirteenth century.[5] By the end of the year very few islands in the Aegean Sea were not in Ottoman hands, Venetian-held Cyprus and Tinos being among the exceptions.

As in the case of Chios, all these takeovers went smoothly, and the Porte could be satisfied that it had managed to remove a number of troublesome thorns in its side. Yet Piyale's escapades were not without consequences: Chios may have been a source of irritation to the Ottomans, but while it was in the hands of the Maonesi Constantinople could be sure that the Genoese would be reluctant to aid the Habsburgs should the latter decide to launch a major offensive in the eastern Mediterranean. Worse, Piyale's rapacity destroyed an important commercial community and effectively severed a number of important economic links between the Ottoman empire and the rest of Europe. Chios, as we have seen, was the sultan's main source of English tin, and until the establishment in Constantinople of the English Company of the Levant in the early 1580s the Ottomans suffered from a shortage of this metal.[6] Since tin was essential for the manufacture of artillery, one can argue that the losses incurred by the Ottomans in conquering Chios by far outweighed the gains.

Chios was to be Süleyman's last victory. The seventy-two-year-old sultan had aged considerably, battered by lingering ailments and private misfortunes. His beloved wife Hürrem, known in the west as Roxelane, had died a few years before, and family upheavals only increased Süleyman's grief.[7] Suspecting that his first-born, Mustafa, born of the concubine Mahidevran, was plotting to depose him, Süleyman had him executed in 1553. Ottoman historians have long maintained that the flames of the sultan's suspicions had been adroitly fanned by his wife, his daughter Mihirimah, and the latter's husband, Grand Vizier Rüstem Pasha. Indeed, rumours circulating at the time pointed to Rüstem as the main instigator of the prince's downfall, the grand vizier allegedly forging a letter from Mustafa to the shah of Persia. Hürrem had every reason to want Mustafa out of the way, wishing one of her offspring to be the next sultan and knowing all too well that if Mustafa came to the throne he would immediately execute his half-brothers together with their male descendants.* Perhaps Süleyman's bad health made the hatching of palace plots inevitable – by custom, from the mid-fourteenth century all sons of the ruler were equally entitled to succeed their father, making the Ottoman throne 'occupative', rather than hereditary or elective.[8] Mustafa's popularity with the janissaries and other sections of the army made him a very dangerous player. Mindful that his grandfather Bayezid I had been ousted by a conspiracy spearheaded by the janissaries, Süleyman opted for a pre-emptive strike against his son for both his throne and his life's sake.

The death soon after Mustafa of Hürrem's third son Jihangir left only two other candidates, Selim and Bayezid. Hürrem's own demise in 1558 spared her further tragedies, for the two princes, until then kept in check by their mother, were immediately at each other's throats like a pair of Kilkenny cats, with Süleyman unable to

---

* Fratricide was customary within the Ottoman royal family. Introduced by Mehmed II, it was justified by the need to eliminate any potential pretenders to the throne. The practice of the new sultan killing his brothers and their male offspring was discontinued in the seventeenth century, although this did not stop Ottoman rulers from occasionally executing their siblings.

make up his mind about the succession, the sultan favouring in turn Selim and Bayezid. Their incessant squabbling irritated Süleyman to the point that he threatened to break with all law and custom by bestowing the throne on his sister's son, Osmanşa. He also tried to separate the two brothers as much as possible, dispatching Selim to Konya and Bayezid to Amasya.

Bayezid was not at all happy with this decision, accompanying his departure from his governor's seat in Kütahya with threats of rebellion and calling Selim a coward. His decision to raise an army from discontented *timar* holders, country people and border tribesmen, took him further down the slippery slope to civil war. Selim, on the other hand, showed himself totally submissive to his father's wishes, thus earning Süleyman's favour. The sultan not only provided Selim with troops, artillery and commanders, but also managed to obtain from Chief Mufti Ebu's-su'ud, a fatwa ruling that it was rightful for Süleyman to fight his rebellious son's followers.[9] As it happened, when the two brothers' forces clashed near Konya, Bayezid's 12,000 men were utterly routed. The defeated prince managed to flee to Persia, throwing himself on the mercy of the Safavid Shah Tahmasb. Süleyman embarked on a concerted diplomatic campaign to convince the shah to hand over his guest. Tahmasb procrastinated until he had managed to squeeze the most favourable concessions from the sultan, including a peace treaty, a hefty sum of money and a number of gifts for his family. The hapless Bayezid was then delivered to Ottoman officials, and executed together with his sons.

Selim was now the only heir to the throne but in many ways far from being an ideal candidate for the succession. Despite having a certain amount of experience as a provincial governor, he preferred wine to statecraft. Süleyman could do nothing to correct this situation, only behold the ruin of what had once been his family. As a result the embittered sultan retreated more and more into the privacy of his palace, leaving the day-to-day running of the empire to his ministers, in particular the able Grand Vizier Sokollu Mehmed Pasha. Yet, despite increasing bouts of senility, Süleyman was still the recognized, respected and feared Ottoman leader, and a force to be reckoned with.

The Austrian Habsburgs realized this very soon. The Holy Roman Emperor Ferdinand I died in 1564, and his son Maximilian had initially been willing to renew the truce agreed by his father with the Porte a few years before. But Maximilian still claimed suzerainty over Transylvania, and in 1565, exploiting the fact that the Turks were occupied in the Mediterranean, took the border towns of Tokaj and Szerencs. Süleyman ordered the governor of Buda to make a raid in reprisal, but it was not until the following year that a serious campaign could be undertaken against Maximilian, who was now suing for peace. Unfortunately the grand vizier intended to teach the Habsburgs a lesson, anxious also for a success to eclipse the Malta debacle. Operations started in June 1566, and the following month a huge Ottoman army – 300,000 strong according to one source,[10] and with Süleyman himself in command – crossed the Danube, penetrating into Habsburg-held territory and laying siege to the fortress of Szigetvár. The town finally fell to a determined assault on 8 September, but not before the defenders had blown up the walls burying many of the enemy with them.[11] Süleyman could not rejoice over the victory or grieve at his losses: the aged sultan had died two days before, possibly from a stroke, with the grand vizier at his side.

Sokollu Mehmed acted quickly.[12] Süleyman's entrails were removed and buried on the spot and his death kept hidden from the army, lest turmoil should ensue. For good measure, all those of low rank privy to the secret were quietly executed. The grand vizier immediately sent a message with the news to Selim, then in Kütahya, telling him to return to Constantinople in haste. Selim wasted no time doing so, securing the allegiance of all the officials in the capital before departing for the Balkans. He arrived in Belgrade in the middle of October and waited for the arrival of the grand vizier. The latter had in the meantime settled the army's pay, and, with the excuse that the campaign season was coming to a close, dismissed the *timar* troops. On 21 September Süleyman's body was placed in a covered litter as if he were still alive, and only when the army approached Belgrade did the grand vizier reveal what had happened, showing the troops their lord's corpse – a grim sight, even for battle-hardened soldiers. Yet, as much as they grieved over Süleyman's death, the troops wasted no time informing his successor that they expected some sort of monetary gratification, and Selim was forced to distribute generous sums and *timar*s to his unruly military to avoid having to deal with a rebellion.

The new sultan was cast from a different mould to that of his father. In Ottoman history he is remembered as Sari Selim, Selim the Sallow, due to his yellowish complexion, or perhaps to the blonde hair inherited from his mother,* but in the West he was universally known as the Sot, because of his love for alcohol. Perhaps it is not surprising that after what he had witnessed while growing up – including the violent death of his brothers – Selim should have sought refuge in drink, much to his father's displeasure; allegedly Süleyman had one of Selim's drinking pals executed, considering him to be his son's evil genius. The Venetian ambassador Andrea Badoer has left us a rather unflattering description of the sultan, confirming his worst excesses:

> This Sultan Selim is fifty-three years of age, small in size and weak of health. This is due to his intemperance, with women as with wine, drinking great quantities of the latter. He is very ugly indeed, with all his limbs out of proportion, according to everyone more a monster than a man. His face is burnt and ruined, from too much wine and the spirit he drinks to digest . . . Not only is he ignorant about the arts, but also can barely recognize written characters. He is uncouth in his speech, unversed in state affairs and lazy, leaving all the great weight of government to the Grand

---

* Hürrem was almost certainly of Slavic origin, and some maintain that her original name was Aleksandra Lisowska. However, in Italy there is the tradition that she was the daughter of Nanni Marsili, a Sienese gentleman with possessions in the south of Tuscany, and was kidnapped by Muslim corsairs when little and sold as a slave in Constantinople.

> Vizier. He is miserly, sordid, lecherous, unrestrained and reckless
> in all the decisions he makes . . . What he enjoys doing most is
> drinking and eating, something he does for days on end; I am told
> that His Majesty sometimes spends two or three days constantly at
> the table.[13]

Given that this report was written after the Cyprus War, there
is a legitimate suspicion of bias on Badoer's part. Yet the French
ambassador to Venice, François de Noailles, would describe Selim
as 'the biggest fool ever to run a state',[14] and another Venetian
diplomat, Costantino Garzoni, would comment on the sultan's
stubbornness and lack of character.[15] It is also true that Selim
delegated most government tasks to the grand vizier, but in his
defence it should be noted that his father had never bothered to
train him properly in the art of statecraft. Being the third son, he
had never expected to become sultan, anticipating rather that he
would be executed once Süleyman died. Yet Selim was not devoid
of qualities, being a skilled archer, an accomplished poet and a
discriminating patron of the arts – so much for Badoer's comments.[16] He was also lucky to have some very capable advisers, and
although he looks unimpressive next to Süleyman, many of the
political decisions made during his reign, if ultimately flawed, were
based on sound strategic reasoning.

The advent of Selim II meant a reshuffle within the Ottoman
hierarchy. Sokollu Mehmed remained grand vizier, but would soon
find himself in the imperial council in the unwelcome company of
Selim's old tutor, Lala Mustafa Pasha. An ambitious intriguer, Lala
Mustafa had been relegated by Grand Vizier Rüstem Pasha to the
political backstage, first as a provincial governor and then, with the
object of ruining him for good, as tutor (lala) to the then Prince
Selim. In this position Mustafa had proved himself once more to
be a troublemaker, being one of those responsible for igniting the
rivalry between Selim and Bayezid.[17] Sokollu had little love for Lala
Mustafa, and initially managed to get him transferred once more to
a provincial governorship in what would prove to be a vain attempt

to get him out of the way. In settling other old scores the grand vizier was more successful, for instance convincing Selim to execute the chief treasurer, Yussuf Ağa. Piyale Pasha was also added to the imperial council, being promoted to vizier after having been demoted from the position of *kapudan-ı deryâ*, allegedly for having kept most of the Chios booty for himself. His place as *kapudan paşa*,[18] the title from then onwards bestowed on an Ottoman admiral-in-chief provided with a *beylerbeik*, was taken by one of Sokollu's protégés, the former *ağa* of the janissaries, Müezzinzâde Ali Pasha.[19] Very soon two factions would emerge in the *dîvân*, one headed by Sokullu advocating the continuation of Ottoman expansion in Hungary, and another, its chief proponents being Lala Mustafa and Piyale, insisting instead on pursuing a Mediterranean policy. The latter group could count on the support of an influential person working behind the scenes of the Ottoman power system: Joseph Nassi.

Nassi is an enigmatic figure, his real influence on Ottoman politics being still a matter of debate among historians.[20] He was born João Miquez into a prominent Castilian *marrano*** family who had left Spain for Portugal in 1492, moving then to Antwerp, Venice and Ferrara. Around the mid-1550s, the Nassi made Constantinople their final abode, reverting to the Judaism of their forefathers and engaging in a number of successful business enterprises. Joseph's relocation to the Ottoman capital, however, was as much due to his behaviour as to commerce, having been banished from Venice for the abduction of one of his cousins. His wealth allowed him to live majestically in a palace in the district of Ortakoy, where in a richly furnished library he would discuss politics with the French ambassador, ornithology with the local rabbi and astrology with the Greek Orthodox patriarch. Something of a proto-Zionist, as early as 1563 he tried to establish a Jewish settlement on the banks of Lake Tiberias in Palestine, attempting to obtain the money for the venture from the king of France.[21] Although this

---

* *Marrano* was applied to those Iberian Jews who converted to Christianity.

project failed, by becoming one of Selim II's drinking pals he managed to obtain Naxos, together with the title of duke, as a fief from the sultan, Piyale Pasha obligingly evicting the island's legitimate ruler Giacomo Crispi. Harbouring a deep hatred of Venice, Nassi was considered by the Venetians the evil genius behind the sultan's drive to extend his rule over all the islands of the Aegean Sea.

But the sultan had more compelling problems on his plate before attempting expansionist enterprises. The war in Hungary was occupying the Ottoman army just when its presence was badly needed on other fronts. Zaydi Imam of the Yemen had revolted against the sultan's rule, expelling the Ottomans from most of the province, and to make matters worse the Arabs living in the marshes north of Basra had also rebelled. In order to avoid getting bogged down – literally – in Mesopotamia, Sokollu employed carrot-and-stick tactics to deal with the Arab uprising. In 1567 Ottoman troops launched a river-borne expedition against the rebels' bases, forcing their leader Ibn 'Ulayyan to submit. This show of force was immediately followed up by the sultan bestowing on the defeated Arab the title of governor, thus securing his loyalty in a key region on the border of Safavid Persia. In Hungary, after Süleyman's death there had been some desultory fighting, but by and large the two sides were happy to play a waiting game. Maximilian wanted peace and so did Sokollu; the former because the war was draining his financial resources, while the latter needed a free hand to deal with the Yemen problem. In September 1567 three Habsburg ambassadors arrived in Constantinople and were treated to an amicable audience with the sultan. The next five months witnessed much hard bargaining between the two parties, the ambassadors trying to win the grand vizier's favour, as well as that of other important officials, with rich monetary and material gifts. Finally, on 21 February 1568, an eight-year peace treaty between Maximilian and Selim was signed, apparently more or less restoring the situation in Hungary to the status quo ante; in reality, by recognizing Maximilian's rights to certain parts of Hungary, the pact turned out to be more favourable to the Habsburgs. Three days after the agreement the grand vizier made some extra requests, in particular asking that France be included in the treaty. This was a result of the French ambassador in Constantinople's attempt to put a spanner in the diplomatic works, fearful that peace between Maximilan and the Porte would encourage the former to try to recover Metz.[22] The Habsburg envoys politely refused Sokollu's demands, and the grand vizier gave in without insisting further. Both parties were satisfied with the pact, no one at this stage wanting to upset the apple cart.

With his hands free in Europe and Mesopotamia, Sokollu could now tackle the Yemen problem, also with an eye to palace politics. He skilfully managed to get Lala Mustafa appointed commander of the expedition, hoping he would discredit himself. Sure enough, no sooner had Lala Mustafa arrived in Egypt than he managed to get into a fight with the local governor-general, Koja Sinan Pasha, over the provisioning of the army. Lala Mustafa was dismissed from his post, returning to Constantinople apparently in disgrace, and Sinan appointed in his stead. Selim, however, continued to favour his old tutor, saving him from execution and appointing him vizier in 1569, thus thwarting Sokollu's plans.[23] Meanwhile, Sinan conducted a successful campaign in the Yemen, in 1568 capturing Taiz, and then Aden with a brilliant amphibious and overland attack. The following year he took Zaydi Imam's fortress of Sana'a and by 1570 the whole of Yemen was once more under the sultan's control. The conquest of this unruly province would shortly have a number of momentous consequences.

~

While the Ottomans were busy fighting in Hungary and in the Arabian peninsula, a new foe had arisen in Europe. On 7 January 1566, following the death of Pius IV the previous December, Cardinal Antonio Ghisleri was elected pope, taking the name Pius V. Destined to become one of the most celebrated pontiffs in the history of the Catholic Church, he was an incredibly strict yet extremely charitable man, born in 1504 of a noble but impoverished family from Alessandria in Piedmont. He joined the Dominican order, taking the name of Michele, and was ordained a priest in 1528. Striving to spread the authentic spirit of St Dominic among his brethren, Father Michele, as he then was, was the first to give an example: he fasted, did penance, meditated and prayed for long hours during the night, matters of God being constantly on his lips. His religious commitment brought him to the attention of Paul IV, who in 1556 made him bishop of Sutri and inquisitor for Lombardy. This promotion was followed in quick succession by a cardinal's hat, the title of inquisitor general and the diocese of Mondovì, where he made a name for not tolerating any breaches in ecclesiastical discipline. He often clashed with Paul IV's successor, Pius IV, not approving of the latter's worldly and nepotistic attitudes. As soon as he was elected pope, a position he accepted with reluctance, he made it known that he did not intend to favour his relatives in any way.[24] Many of his family who arrived in Rome with hopes of preferment were told that, if not really indigent, their connection to the pope was richness enough. Bowing to considerable pressure from the College of Cardinals, who thought it inappropriate that the pope should not create one of his nephews cardinal, he finally elevated to the purple his sister's son, Michele Bonelli. A few other deserving relatives over time were given administrative or military positions within the papal states. However, the pope did not hesitate to demote and banish one of his nephews on discovering his illicit love affairs.

Once elected, and despite the burdens of his office, Pius practised the virtues he had previously displayed as a friar and a bishop, praying constantly, visiting hospitals and tending personally to the needs of the sick. He also strived to impose greater standards of morality on the clergy, no matter the rank. Indeed, bishops now had to prove themselves spiritually, morally and intellectually qualified for the job and were obliged to reside in their dioceses. Pius was a giant in a century of giants.[25]

The pope was actually doing nothing more than putting into practice the dispositions and decrees of the Council of Trent.

Convened originally, as we have seen, by Paul III in 1545, the council had suffered up to 1560 a number of interruptions, postponements and relocations from its original meeting place. Despite this, it had managed to pass some fundamental doctrinal measures, including that on the correct interpretation of Holy Scripture, and one on justification by faith – incorporating some Lutheran elements. The delays which had occurred to the council's work were due mainly to the opposition of the various Catholic rulers of Europe, each of whom had his own political agenda and unwilling to support a reform process – although officially in favour of it – that threatened to remove the Church from the control of secular powers. For instance, when Pius IV reconvened the council in 1560, the Holy Roman Emperor Ferdinand I attempted to have all decisions on matters of dogma deferred in order not to alienate his Protestant subjects. Nonetheless, the council worked with alacrity between 1562 and 1564, issuing proclamations on such matters as clerical celibacy, Holy Communion, relics, sacred images, the intercession of saints, the Church's independence vis-à-vis rulers, catechism, the mass, ecclesiastical benefices and discipline. All these matters were the subject of lively – and often heated – debates within the council. The obligation for bishops to reside in their dioceses was opposed by some members of the Roman Curia, in one case by arguing that the removal of so many bishops from Rome, together with their households, would ruin the city's economy. Many secular rulers opposed through their delegates ecclesiastical independence, and much negotiation was necessary before a document on this matter could be agreed upon. Yet, when Pius IV formally approved the council's decrees on 26 January 1565 nobody could doubt that, finally, the Church had done some very thorough house cleaning.[26] The clear language used in the official documents – something lacking in those of the later Second Vatican Council – meant that from then on Catholics would know where they stood, what they believed, what could be discussed and those articles of faith that could not. As for the Protestants, they were able to develop a clear sense of their own religious identity, the Council of

Trent having done away with the doctrinal ambiguity of the early years of the sixteenth century.

Notwithstanding their force, the Tridentine rulings risked becoming yet another of the many disregarded documents with which the history of the Church is littered. The peril was very real, given that most European states greeted the council's decrees unenthusiastically at best. The Italian states not under direct Spanish rule accepted them, and so did Poland. Spain acknowledged only those decrees that did not affect royal authority. The French crown, wishing to uphold its ecclesiastical privileges and not enrage its numerous Calvinist subjects, declined to accept Trent's rulings, and the Emperor Maximilian I decided that their official adoption would be imprudent. Protestant countries like Sweden, Scotland, England and Lutheran Germany simply ignored them. Yet the Council of Trent, secular opposition notwithstanding, boosted a movement within the Catholic clergy and laity for widespread religious renewal and reform which was destined to yield substantial results in the years to come. While many in the upper echelons of society were aping pagan practices, apparently not interested in the Church's plight, at the grass roots of Catholicism a renewed spirituality was in the making. For some decades the religiosity of orders like the Jesuits, the Theatines and the Capuchins, impeccable for their way of life and theological beliefs, had been progressing silently but steadily within the body of the Church.* By the 1550s an increasing number of high-ranking clergymen, including many of those who would attend the final sessions of the Council of Trent, shared this spiritual outlook. The reform movement within the Church was given a huge boost by Pius V, who in the six years of his pontificate strived incessantly for the implementation of the Tridentine decrees within the Catholic world.

But there were also other tasks facing the pope. In northern Europe and France Calvinism had gained significant footholds; in

---

* This despite the fact that one of the first Capuchin leaders, Bernardino Ochino, turned Protestant and escaped to Calvinist Geneva.

the Mediterranean the Ottomans appeared increasingly menacing. Practically from the day of his election Pius V started to canvass the creation of an anti-Muslim league with the Catholic rulers of Europe. The moment for such an alliance was favourable, the impending war in Hungary seen as a chance to bring together the forces of Spain and the Holy Roman Empire to inflict on the Ottomans a decisive blow.[27] Pius was hoping that France and Venice would also join the fight, but the Valois had too many problems at home – and in any case their alliance with the Porte was not up for discussion – while the Venetians were adamantly opposed to anything that might damage their Levantine trade. Philip II, always with an eye towards North Africa, expressed his interest in the venture, provided he could get enough money to finance an army and a fleet. Pius was only too happy to oblige, granting the king of Spain the renewal of the five-year subsidy, known as the *quinquennio* or *subsidio*, first granted by the Holy See in 1560. This was to be levied on the clergy of Castile and Aragon, and was supposed to finance a combined force of forty Spanish and sixty papal galleys.[28] Since the money ended up being handled by the Spanish treasury, in reality it could be used at Philip's discretion. The measure of Pius V's personal uprightness and sincerity can be seen by the fact that, unlike his predecessor, he did not ask for a single penny for himself or his relatives in exchange for the *subsidio*. As it happened, Sultan Süleyman's death, together with the end of hostilities in Hungary, lessened considerably Philip's interest in an anti-Ottoman crusade, the king considering such an enterprise fruitless and damaging if undertaken by Spain alone. Philip instructed his ambassador in Rome, Luis de Requesens, to obtain as much money possible from the pope, but to adopt a dilatory attitude every time the subject of military alliance against the Ottomans was broached.[29] In any case, Spain was distracted by another matter, which Philip considered far more important than fighting the Ottomans.

For some time trouble had been brewing in Flanders, where high-handed Spanish policies had ignited a general revolt. The causes of the uprising were many, but chief was the attack on the ancient liberties of the Flemish aristocracy. This was closely linked to the huge inroads made by Calvinism among the local population, resulting in widespread attacks on Catholic clergymen, buildings and religious objects. The regent of Flanders Margaret of Parma, illegitimate daughter of Charles V, had managed to restore a modicum of order by playing off the various Flemish factions against each other, but her tolerance of religious dissent did not go down well with Philip. In an attempt to restore royal authority and also implement the Tridentine decrees in the province, the king made the mistake of sending to Flanders the duke of Alva with a large army and extensive military powers. 'I don't know for what purpose,' commented the count of Egmont, a leading dissident noble, to Margaret. 'It is not possible to kill 200,000 people.'[30] Philip, who was planning to visit Flanders in person, was convinced that only by decisive action could bloodshed be averted, and to this purpose he gave Alva instructions to arrest and chastise the rebel leaders before his arrival. Not known for his subtlety, Alva did exactly that. Dissidents, both Catholic and Calvinist, were arrested, tried and executed, including leading nobles like the counts of Egmont and Horne. Another prominent dissident, William of Nassau, prince of Orange, saved his neck by escaping to Germany, where he immediately started organizing anti-Spanish resistance. In all, some 1,700 people lost their lives during the repression, and instead of solving the Flanders problem Alva's ham-fisted behaviour managed only to alienate everyone in the region, including those previously favourable to Habsburg rule. By the end of 1568 armed revolt was widespread in Flanders, Alva's army several times having to fight forces advancing from Germany and France under the sponsorship of William of Orange. Although the Spanish proved victorious on each occasion, they would be stuck fighting in Flanders for the next eighty years. Ultimately, the Flemish revolt, with all its international implications, would prove a ruinous drain on Spain's finances.[31]

The *devşirme* or 'collection':
Christian youths forcibly
enlisted in the Sultan's service

The results of the *devşirme*:
the Vizier Lala Mustafa Pasha
entertaining janissaries

Europe's bogeyman:
Sultan Süleyman I

Unequal to his father:
Sultan Selim II

The backbone of the West: Pius V, Pope and Saint

Able diplomat and foresighted statesman:
Grand Vizier Sokollu Mehmed Pasha

Roman Cardinal and
Habsburg courtier: Antoine
Perrenot de Granvelle

The Papal Admiral Marcantonio
Colonna: charming, if an
inexperienced sailor

Giovanni Andrea Doria:
a skilled mariner
and politician

The Florentine Fox:
Grand Duke Cosimo I
de' Medici

Elegance, looks and chivalry:
Don Juan of Austria

The acme of Venetian patriotism: Captain-General Sebastiano Venier

In charge of Venice's secret weapon: Captain Francesco Duodo

Last of the school of Barbarossa: the Beylerbey of Algiers, Uluç Ali Pasha

Victim of treachery: the Governor-General of Famagusta, Marcantonio Bragadin

Brave, humane and unlucky:
Kapudan-ı deryâ Müezzinzâde
Ali Pasha

Timing and opportunity:
Don Álvaro de Bazan,
Marquis of Santa Cruz

Cold steel more than artillery: Müezzinzâde Ali's *Sultana*

Technological cutting edge in 1571: a gun–bristling Venetian galleass

Knowing from the beginning that Flanders would be a costly enterprise, Philip started pressuring the pope for more money. Pius, however, was initially unwilling to grant any more subsidies, having already authorized the *quinquennio*. What irritated the pope most was that despite all the funds he had managed to collect for the maintenance of the Spanish fleet (500,000 ducats, three-quarters of its costs),[32] the king was delaying sending his galleys to protect the coasts of the papal states, with the excuse that he had to defend his own extensive maritime frontiers.[33] In the end, Pius was forced to yield to the king's requests, concerns about the spread of heresy in Flanders playing a decisive role in the pope's decision. The king was given the right to collect a five-year tax, known as the *excusado*, diverting from the Church's revenues a tithe on every third house of each parish in the Iberian peninsula. The purpose of this levy was not just to help pay the army about to go to Flanders, but also to cover the expenses incurred by Philip in defending Christendom against the Turks.[34] Yet, in the face of Spain's procrastinations over defending the papal territories against Muslims raids, Pius was forced to look elsewhere for protection, his position and prestige allowing him to play at more than one table in the international gaming room. In any case, he had now a willing partner: Cosimo I de' Medici, duke of Florence and Siena.

Philip II's bestowal of Siena on Cosimo I had tied the latter to Spain in an unequivocal manner: not only was Cosimo now a Habsburg vassal, he also had to provide free of charge his galleys and a substantial number of troops (4,000 foot and 400 horse) every time the Spanish-ruled duchy of Milan or the kingdom of Naples came under attack. In addition, the duke was effectively denied the ability to make alliances with other states without Spain's approval.[35] Cosimo had tried to escape the suffocating Habsburg embrace, by upholding the independence of his Florentine territories and then by creating the knightly Order of St Stephen with the open support of Pope Pius IV. Philip disliked the new order,[36] correctly perceiving that by founding a knightly organization, canonically subjected to the Holy See,* the crafty Florentine was attempting to pursue an independent military policy. But Cosimo could not count on Philip for defence – Spain having already too many commitments – and the duke was aware that the security of his states depended on advancing his sea borders to the North African coasts.[37] This ambitious policy involved considerable costs which Cosimo could ill afford, and the duke tried to have it both ways by loaning in the mid-1560s ten galleys to Philip II for a five-year period. The terms of the contract (*asiento*) were heavily stacked against Cosimo, who for all intents and purposes had handed over his entire fleet to the king's discretion.[38] But the duke needed time to build up the Order of St Stephen's strength and reputation, and so for the moment was content for his own sea forces to acquire some useful experience by working with a well-established navy. In any case, at its foundation the Order of St Stephen had received a gift of two galleys from the duke, the *Lupa* and the *Fiorenza Nuova*, thus allowing it to operate independently from the Spanish fleet.

Maritime skill was something not to be acquired overnight, as the duke would learn to his expense. Eager to show his flag, in 1560 Cosimo had sent four galleys to join the Djerba expedition, only to lose two in the ensuing disaster. These losses were somewhat compensated for by the capture a month later of three Muslim galliots,[39] but significant results were to be obtained only through trial and error. In July 1563 a Florentine force was sent to aid the Spanish force engaged in the relief of Oran, then besieged by Dragut. En route the *Lupa* lost its mainmast, forcing the galley to head back alone to the port of Livorno for repairs. No sooner had the *Lupa* distanced herself from the rest of the squadron, than she

---

* The Order of St Stephen was closely modelled on the Spanish Order of Santiago, whose members were not monks but laymen who took vows of chastity within marriage and obedience to the grand master – the king from the end of the fifteenth century. Within the framework of canon law the Order of St Stephen can be conceived as a papal institution 'entrusted' to a ruler for a specific purpose, in this case the defence of Christendom. For the Order of St Stephen as an institution of canon law, see: N[ERI] CAPPONI: 39–54.

was jumped by two Muslim galliots. The *Lupa*'s makeshift crew managed to swim ashore, leaving the knights of St Stephen on board to fend for themselves. Many of them died during the ensuing battle, while others were taken prisoner and enslaved.[40] For the budding order it was a serious blow, and during the following years the knights preferred always to operate in conjunction with the Spanish. Only in 1569 did the order gain its first significant victory, a force of four galleys catching and defeating in a seven-hour battle an enemy squadron of five commanded by the redoubtable corsair Kara Ali. The Florentines managed to capture two of the Muslim vessels, securing 310 prisoners and freeing 220 Christian slaves with the loss of 70 killed and 90 wounded. The Florentine ships also suffered much damage, and on their return to Livorno people commented that they looked more the vanquished than the victors.[41]

Despite their grievous losses, Cosimo could be satisfied with the knights' success, since it gave the Medici some much-needed international prestige. It also allowed the duke to take a more independent stance towards Spain in the Mediterranean. Cosimo resented Philip II's attitude towards him, the king for instance refusing to pay for two Florentine galleys sunk in a storm while transporting Spanish troops from Italy to the south of Spain. The duke tried to corner the king by informing him that in such circumstances it was impossible for him to observe the terms of the *asiento*, and offering to renegotiate it on terms more favourable to himself. In exchange, Cosimo was prepared to arm up to fourteen galleys for Philip's service, but the king answered curtly that the matter would be discussed once the present contract expired. Philip was short of money, and continually pestering the pope for the renewal of the *cruzada*, which, with the *quinquennio* and the *excusado*, formed what were known as the Three Graces. Based on the sale of bulls of indulgence, the *cruzada* had first been granted in 1482, yielding, according to a seventeenth-century source, 800,000 ducats a year.[42] The pope was reluctant to renew the *cruzada*, and not just because he had already subsidized in abundance the always money-starved Spanish crown. One of the decrees of the Council of Trent had clearly stated that indulgences should be granted with moderation, 'less ecclesiastical discipline be too easily weakened'.[43] Since the sale of indulgences had been the spark that had set alight the powder keg of the Reformation, it is more than understandable that Pius V was reluctant to grant the *cruzada*. Cosimo, on the other hand, had every interest in Spain's coffers being full, but at the same time perceived that the pope could give him much more than the Habsburgs.

Cosimo was painfully aware of being a newcomer on the international scene. Not only was his ducal title recent, but also it had been originally bestowed on the Medici by the Florentines themselves. Only later had Charles V confirmed the title, and Cosimo had done much to better his own situation by marrying Eleanor of Toledo, daughter of the viceroy of Naples. But nobody ever allowed the duke to forget his family's merchant origins – his cousin Catherine's marriage to the second son of Francis I was considered by the French very much of a *mésalliance*,[44] – and Cosimo's frustration was increased by the fact that he was from a secondary, impoverished, branch of the Medici. There was also the question of precedence, in European courts the ambassadors of the dukes of Savoy, Ferrara and Mantua always preceding their Florentine colleagues during audiences or official events.* Cosimo's attempts, with the backing of pope Pius IV, to see his dominion elevated to an archduchy were rebuffed by Emperor Maximilian II, his Habsburg relatives having no intention of seeing an Italian upstart become their equal. In the face of this refusal, Pius IV had intended before his death to bestow himself a title on Cosimo.

His successor Pius V was initially much less favourably inclined

---

* While for us such matters may appear trivial, they were hugely important in the sixteenth century. Ambassadorial precedence was not only a matter of prestige, but also determined who would be first to get a ruler's ear. Since at the time in Italy there were no independent kingdoms (the papal states were not considered such, being an exception in every way) the fight for precedence involved duchies, marquisates, counties, lordships and republics.

towards the duke of Florence, since the latter was known to harbour one of the leading Italian Protestants, the former secretary of Clement VII Pietro Carnesecchi. Cosimo had up to then managed to protect Carnesecchi from the inquisition, but now for reasons of political expediency agreed to turn him over to the pope's envoys. Predictably, and notwithstanding his former protector's pleas for clemency, Carnesecchi was found guilty and executed in October 1567. But Cosimo now could count on Pius's benevolence, and the duke repaid this attitude by taking a decisive stand against the reformed religion, to the point of sending an expeditionary force to fight in France against the Huguenots. The pope then gave Cosimo what he most coveted: an elevation in rank by granting him the title of grand duke of Tuscany in September 1569. From a strictly legal point of view Pius was acting beyond the limits of the law – Tuscany being part of the Holy Roman Empire – but since Maximilian had given his tacit consent, although he never formalized it so as not to displease the duke of Ferrara, the pope considered he was acting within his prerogatives, which included conferring titles of sovereignty.[45]

Pius's move provoked uproar in all the European courts. Cosimo immediately tried to distance himself from the quarrel, maintaining that the grand ducal title was nothing but honorific – not desiring for one thing to accept any overlord for what he regarded as his own Florentine territories. Maximilian was furious. Philip II threatened to reclaim Siena for his half-brother Don Juan of Austria. The king of Spain was also miffed by Cosimo's attempts to woo France, something that risked igniting anew the Italian wars. Philip would have been even more enraged if he had known at the time that since 1562 the Medici and the Valois had agreed to a pact of mutual support in the face of the Habsburgs' overbearing presence.[46] Yet Cosimo had no desire to favour a French return to Italy, in September 1570 writing to the dowager queen of France Catherine de' Medici that on the matter of the grand ducal title he did not wish her 'to take on any burden in this affair', adding that the emperor knew that Cosimo was 'the same servant to Him, as my actions have always proved'.[47] Moreover, by this date many things had changed in the Mediterranean theatre, allowing Cosimo greater opportunities for diplomatic manoeuvring.

~

As much as Philip may have desired to punish his disloyal ally, he had plenty of worries in Spain. First there had been the death of his deranged son Don Carlos, whom the king had been forced to lock up because of his bizarre behaviour. To make matters worse, the royal authorities attempted to conceal the whole matter behind a thick veil of secrecy, allowing Philip's enemies to speculate wildly on the circumstances surrounding the unfortunate prince's fate.[48] Philip soon received another blow, his wife Elizabeth of Valois dying a few months later after delivering a stillborn child. The king was stricken with grief, but could ill afford to let sorrow interfere with his duties as head of state. In fact, he was about to face an emergency within the Iberian peninsula requiring his full attention.

Despite attempts by the Spanish authorities over the years to enforce Christianity on the Moriscos, the majority had remained practising Muslims. The decrees of 1526 forbidding their ancient customs had been largely ignored, in particular after the payment of a large sum of money by the communities of Granada and Valencia. In many cases the Moriscos adopted *taqiyya*, or dissimulation – a practice allowed by Islamic law to Muslims living in a religiously unfavourable environment. By the mid-sixteenth century the situation of the Spanish Islamic community was very bad. Restrictions imposed by the central authorities on their traditional silk trade had left many Moriscos impoverished, and in addition they were subject to increasing attentions from the inquisition. Still, many local nobles in Spain favoured a policy of tolerance towards their Islamic subjects, since they were an important source of labour and revenue. However, a number of clergymen, in particular the bishop of Siguenza and future cardinal Diego Espinosa, president of the Council of Castile, adamantly opposed this lenient attitude, demanding that vigorous measures be employed to stamp out Morisco language, customs and dress.

The crown started doing this at the beginning of 1567, despite the protests of a number of Andalusian landlords, headed by the captain-general of Andalusia Iñigo López de Mendoza, count of Tendilla, who correctly foresaw trouble. While religious intolerance undoubtedly played a part in this repression, people like Espinosa feared that differences in belief would lead to social unrest. Espinosa was also closely linked to Pedro de Deza, whose family had a running feud with the Mendozas, and had Deza himself appointed to enforce the ban against Morisco practices. It is also true that the Iberian Muslims were seen as more than just a potential threat to internal security; in the eventuality of a Muslim inroad, in no way could the Spanish be sure that they would not side with the invaders. In 1565 the discovery of an alleged Morisco spy ring revealed a plan to seize the coast of southern Spain while the Ottomans attacked Malta. There was also fear about supposed Huguenot infiltration of Catalonia, and the Catalans' reluctance to pay the *excusado* in the name of their ancient liberties was seen as an indication that the region was about to turn Protestant. With the spectre of an imminent Muslim invasion aided by a Morisco – and maybe also a Huguenot – fifth column looming over their heads the repressive measures of the Spanish authorities were more than an exaggerated manifestation of religious zeal.[49]

Rumours that an uprising was planned for Holy Thursday 1568 provoked increased police measures by the government against its Islamic subjects; but these only served to postpone the rebellion to the following Christmas Eve, when many Muslim communities rose up in arms, sacking Christian houses and churches, and putting many people to the sword. From an estimated 4,000 at the beginning of the uprising, the insurgents' numbers swelled rapidly, reaching a strength of 30,000 by the summer of 1569. Unable to take Granada immediately due to bad timing and inclement weather, the rebellious Muslims retreated into the mountains to conduct a guerrilla war. All the elements of Morisco culture were resurrected, in particular ancient religious and civic practices. Their leader Hernando de Cordoba y Valor, who had reverted to his Muslim name of Abu Humeya, was proclaimed king in the course of an elaborate traditional ceremony. The rebels did not limit themselves to purely exterior manifestations of sovereignty; the capture of a number of small ports in the south of Spain allowed them to establish political and military links with the Islamic states of North Africa, and a request for help was sent to Constantinople.[50] The fear of an Ottoman attack against the south of Spain was a real concern for Philip's officials, at one point the Spanish ambassador in Paris reporting that three Jews from Salonika had arrived in the French capital with the secret news that the Ottomans were putting together a fleet to help the Moriscos. The sultan, as we shall see presently, had other plans, but nonetheless sent orders to the governor of Algiers Uluç Ali Pasha to aid the Spanish rebels with men and materiel, and indeed Muslim volunteers would fight at the side of their beleaguered Iberian brothers. But arms remained always a scarce commodity for the insurgents, to the point that in the Andalusian coastal town of Sorbas a Christian slave could be exchanged for a gun or a few edged weapons.[51]

The Spanish authorities acted quickly, relying on the man on the spot, the count of Tendilla, to crush the revolt. The Habsburg war machine needed time to get moving, and in any case few royal soldiers were available in Spain, most regular troops having been sent to Flanders. Tendilla did the best he could with his meagre forces, managing to obtain some results by using force coupled with diplomacy. In particular he advocated a policy of tolerance and mercy, maintaining that it was the best way to solve the problem quickly. The king, however, fearing that the rebellion could spread to other parts of Morisco Spain, opted for a more muscular approach, replacing Tendilla with his own half-brother Don Juan of Austria.

The change of commander initially did not produce much in the way of military success. Don Juan was young and inexperienced, and in the meantime the Moriscos had reorganized their forces. As a result, the royal troops suffered a number of reverses. On 3 May the marquis of Los Vélez was roundly defeated while trying to capture the port of La Ragua. The war, already displaying all the brutality of a religious struggle, was destined to become more savage as time went by, many atrocities being committed by both sides. In February 1570 royal troops took the town of Galera, putting the whole population of 2,500 to the sword, razing the settlement and pouring salt over the ruins. Massive influxes of soldiers and weapons from Italy helped to turn the tide in favour of the Habsburgs, and by mid-1570 it was clear that the Moriscos could not hold out much longer despite the help of some 4,000 Turks and North African Muslims. In order to whip up support and cash for the crown, Philip himself had made an extensive, and in many cases triumphant, visit to the south of Spain in the winter and spring of the same year. The rebels were left with no other option than to seek terms, and by the end of November the revolt was over. The aftermath was to be more tragic than the war itself. Fearing future uprisings, the authorities deported some 80,000 Moriscos from Granada, scattering them all over the Iberian peninsula. Nearly 15,000 died during the process; others were enslaved under the pretext that, although baptized, they had abandoned Christ for Muhammad.[52]

The period 1568–70 had been *horribilis* for the Spanish Habsburgs, and not just for the Morisco and Flemish rebellions. The rulers of Tunis had for a long time been closely controlled by the Spanish, who held the key fortress of La Goleta at the mouth of the city's harbour. In 1568 the lord of Tunis was Mawlay Hamida, who in his twenty years of rule had managed to alienate practically everybody. With the Spanish fully occupied with revolts in Flanders and at home, Uluç Ali, *beylerbey* of Algiers, decided to act. In October of the same year he led a force of some 5,000 crack troops overland towards Tunis, the ranks of his army augmented during the march by numerous volunteers picked up en route. Mawlay Hamida's regime collapsed practically without a fight, and the deposed ruler saved his skin only by taking refuge with the Spanish in La Goleta. On 19 January 1569 Uluç Ali made his formal entry into Tunis, busying himself over the following two months with the reorganization of the city's administration. When he departed for Algiers at the end of March he left behind a large garrison, paid by the citizenry, under the command of one of his lieutenants.[53] The Spanish presence in North Africa was now confined to a small number of scattered and beleaguered outposts, which could count on little assistance from Philip II in the event of a determined Muslim attack. The Ottomans were indeed about to strike, but luckily for the Habsburgs they were not to be the objective.

5. CYPRUS

~

As Piyale Pasha was preparing to sail for Chios in the spring of 1566, the authorities in Venice received some very alarming news: in a letter of the previous 13 January, the Venetian *bailo* in Constantinople Vettore Bragadin had informed them of the existence of an Ottoman plan to invade Cyprus.[1] Venice and the Porte had been at peace since 1540, and the republic was concerned that after Süleyman's death its possessions in the Levant would be in danger. Now it appeared that the storm would burst even before the aged sultan was lowered into his grave. Luckily for Venice, the losses incurred by the Ottomans at Malta and during the war in Hungary did not allow them to pick a target bigger than Chios. The Venetians watched anxiously the unfolding of events in the months following the transition from Süleyman to Selim II, and were relieved to receive in July 1567 the news that the new sultan had confirmed the previous peace treaty between the two states. Selim, however, had added to the treaty a clause to the effect that all captured Ottoman pirates should be handed over to the Porte for punishment. The Venetians accepted the clause, even if difficult to implement, prompting the papal nuncio in Venice to comment that the sultan had 'an open door to break the treaty should this suit him'.[2]

But the Venetians remained uneasy about the Ottomans'

intentions towards Cyprus, and with good reason. Between 1567 and 1570 Venice's efficient secret services received a series of warnings about Ottoman espionage activities on the island.[3] The number of reports indicates the Ottomans having accomplices among the local population and it was known that many Cypriots were dissatisfied with Venetian rule, some even asking the sultan in writing to take over the isle.[4]

A real scare for Venice came in September 1568, when a fleet of sixty-four galleys under Müezzinzâde Ali Pasha dropped anchor off Cyprus. When the island's officials boarded the Ottoman admiral's galleys for the ritual courtesy visit, Ali proved to be most inquisitive about the new fortress being built at Nicosia. He objected that there was no need for such a fortress, Venice being at peace with the Porte, and in the unlikely event of a Spanish attack – the Habsburgs were always considered potential enemies by the Venetians – the sultan would surely aid his friends. The admiral appeared to be satisfied with the officials' answer that the construction was a way to provide employment for the island's needy inhabitants. The Ottomans then sailed into the harbour of Famagusta and were graciously received by its captain Marco Michel, who, out of courtesy and because there was no viable alternative, showed them the city's fortifications.

The Turks exploited their time on Cyprus to do some thorough spying, even using the excuse of finding ancient columns for one of the sultan's palaces. Müezzinzâde Ali, however, did not attempt the same trick Piyale Pasha had used in Chios, returning instead to Constantinople to report his findings to the sultan.[5] It was too late in the season to start a campaign, and in any case the war in the Yemen was absorbing most of the Ottomans' military potential. But during the course of the following year rumours of an imminent Ottoman attack abounded, although there was much debate over whether the fleet being prepared in Constantinople was intended instead to aid the Moriscos in Spain. But the Venetians knew that Selim's Jewish adviser Joseph Nassi had visited Cyprus with the Ottoman fleet, and by the end of December the Venetian *bailo*

Marcantonio Barbaro was pretty sure that the objective of the Porte's military preparations could only be Cyprus.[6]

The Venetian's deductions were not based on rumours as much as on an understanding of the Ottomans' geo-strategic goals. Cyprus was, even more than Chios, a thorn in their flesh. Not only did its harbours provide havens for Western corsairs and pirates, but the island was also within striking distance of the Anatolian coast. Every time the Ottomans went on campaign, troops and ships had to be left behind against a potential attack from Cyprus. There was also the contraband problem. By the mid-sixteenth century, the Near East, once the granary of the Mediterranean, produced only enough grain to satisfy local consumption. The Porte reacted by repeatedly banning the export of grain, knowing perfectly well that hunger is a ready trigger for social disorder. Cyprus was a nest of grain smugglers and a danger to the commercial route between Constantinople and Alexandria in Egypt.[7] The Ottomans' campaigns in the Yemen after Selim II's accession were motivated by their desire to chastise a rebellious province, but also derived from the need to protect the Red Sea trade routes, the Portuguese by now having become a permanent and aggressive presence in the area as well as in the Indian Ocean. Süleyman's attempts to evict them from Hormuz had ended in failure, and Ottoman vessels soon proved to be no match on the high seas for the square-rigged Lusitanian ships. At the same time all Portuguese attempts to establish bases in the Red Sea had been repulsed, but in order to face any future challenges from this sector it was important for the Ottomans that there should be no obstacle to the transfer of military resources from the north to the south of their empire. Cyprus was one such obstacle, and to make matters more serious it was also a threat to the pilgrims taking the sea route from Constantinople to Mecca and Medina. In 1517 the Ottomans had declared themselves the protectors of Islam's holy cities, and no sultan who wished to be considered a pious Muslim could allow pilgrim ships to come under attack.[8]

Cyprus was also a hindrance to the development of the Porte's grand strategy, which required a coordinated effort in the Mediterranean and in Asia. The need to rapidly switch military resources to curb the activities of their various enemies and the desire to find alternative trade routes had caused the Ottomans to look at the possibility of building canals to unite the rivers Don and Volga, and to connect the Red Sea to the Mediterranean. These two engineering projects would have allowed the Ottomans to bypass the Safavid empire and rapidly deploy military and economic resources as far as the Persian Gulf. For such plans to be implemented in full, Cyprus had to be Ottoman, by treaty or by force. In 1569 the capture by pirates of the ship carrying the *defterdar* (treasurer) of Egypt dispelled any of Selim's residual doubts. On hearing the news he flew into a rage, and from then the conquest of Cyprus became central to the Porte's political agenda.[9]

In November 1569 Selim went hunting, accompanied by the members of the *dîvân*, specifically to discuss the takeover of Cyprus. As the chase proceeded, the various ministers rode up in turn to the sultan's side to give their opinion on the matter. Sokollu Mehmed tried to dissuade Selim from going to war with Venice, pointing out that it would be damaging for the economy, since the Ottomans benefited substantially from trade with the republic. He felt it would be more fruitful in the long run to aid the Moriscos, not only for reasons of religious brotherhood, but also to keep the Spanish busy. Finally, there was always the risk that the invasion of Cyprus could produce an anti-Ottoman alliance, with unpredictable results. Piyale Pasha and Lala Mustafa Pasha, who both hated Sokollu as well as having a vested interest in the Cyprus enterprise, hotly upheld the necessity of war. Piyale was hoping to regain his position as *kapudan paşa*, and Lala Mustafa wanted command of the invasion army in order to restore his tarnished military reputation. The two viziers underscored the military and geographical problems involved in aiding the Moriscos. On the other hand, Cyprus was near and a Venetian relief force would have to cross half the Mediterranean before reaching the island. The divisions among the Western powers made the creation of an anti-Ottoman alliance unlikely in the short run, and Cyprus was expected not to be too hard a nut to crack. Selim was swayed by these arguments, although it is possible that he had already been convinced by Joseph Nassi, who later would be seen as the villain of the piece, the evil genius behind Selim's decision to go to war against Venice.* He certainly played a part in convincing the sultan, and not just out of hatred for the Venetians. He had extensive economic interests in the Aegean wine trade and held the monopoly on the importation of timber for wine barrels. Nassi supported the Cyprus enterprise because the island's large wine production promised considerable profits.[10]

Besides distance, the Ottomans had other reasons to believe that Venice would be incapable of defending Cyprus. On the night of the 13–14 September 1569 the explosion of a powder magazine in the Venetian arsenal ignited a general conflagration. Nearby houses and churches were destroyed or severely damaged, but luckily the lack of wind hindered the spread of flames. In the end, apart from four galleys, in the arsenal only the buildings used to store munitions and a section of the wall surrounding the compound were destroyed – not an excessive loss in monetary terms. The Venetian authorities launched an inquiry to ascertain who could have been responsible for the conflagration. Almost immediately rumours started that Ottoman agents or saboteurs in the pay of Joseph Nassi had caused the explosion, but investigations in this direction proved inconclusive. When news of the blaze reached Constantinople, the Ottomans believed that the Venetians had suffered greater damage than in reality. This gave extra fuel to the arguments of the war party, who declared Venice to be in a state of military paralysis.[11] Even if the real facts had been known, it would probably have not made much of a difference to the warmongers. It would take some time for Venice to replenish its ammunition stocks, and while this was in no way crippling the Venetians in the meantime could react but slowly.

---

* According to von Hammer, Selim promised to make his friend king of Cyprus, and Nassi created for himself a coat of arms with this title (HAMMER: 195).

Sokollu was still trying to stem the tide of war, knowing that the only possible way to do so was to convince the Venetians to cede Cyprus peacefully. At the end of January 1570 he agreed to meet Marcantonio Barbaro, worried about rumours of an imminent Ottoman attack on the island. It was known, for instance, that the previous October Lala Mustafa Pasha had informed the French ambassador in Constantinople about a planned assault on Cyprus. Mustafa had also suggested that maybe the king of France or the duke of Savoy might advance their claims to the island and become tributaries of the Porte, something that the Ottomans would consider economically more convenient than direct rule.[12] As much as we may doubt Mustafa's sincerity, the episode is nonetheless indicative of the attempts of the war party in Istanbul to isolate Venice diplomatically before striking. Both the French kings and the dukes of Savoy possessed ancient claims to Cyprus – a relic of the crusades – but neither were in a position to assert their rights over the island. Still, by dangling Cyprus in front of their noses, the sultan could hope that they would be more reluctant to take up arms against the Porte.

When Barbaro met Sokollu he protested that the Venetians had always been friends with the Porte, having systematically refused in the past to join anti-Ottoman alliances. Sokollu, who previously had told Barbaro that the Ottomans intended to aid the Moriscos, answered that he was sorry about what was happening, but there had been many examples of the Venetians violating the terms of the peace treaty. Now the affair was in the hands of Muslim doctors of divinity, and since it had become a 'matter of religion' there could be no going back. Sokollu then asked the distance between Venice and Cyprus. Slightly baffled by the question, Barbaro answered that it was about 2,000 miles. To which Sokollu retorted, 'What do you think you can do with such a distant island, that gives you no profit and causes only trouble? It will be better off in our hands, since we have so many possessions nearby.' The sultan was determined to have Cyprus, and it would be better not to waste time, men and money defending it. The only comment that Barbaro could offer in response was that 'dignity and reputation' compelled states to defend their possessions.[13]

When Sokollu had spoken about matters of religion he had not been dissembling, for the war party had managed to obtain the support of Chief Mufti Ebu's-su'ud. By this stage the chief mufti, the *şeyhü'l-islam*, had acquired considerable influence in matters of state policy; although not a member of the imperial council, he had obtained the right to nominate candidates for the best-paying professorships and judicial posts, and continually engaged the state administration in struggles over jurisdiction. The grand viziers hotly resented the mufti's meddling, provoking from one of them the outburst that instead of intervening in state affairs, the *şeyhü'l-islam* should keep himself busy by 'seeking answers to religious questions'.[14] Yet it was precisely because of his authority in divinity matters that the mufti had become a permanent presence in Ottoman political life. He was the highest interpreter of divine law, and thus no official, not even the sultan himself, could disregard his opinion. Given the importance of religion in Ottoman and all other cultures any fatwa issued by the *şeyhü'l-islam* carried enormous weight. At the same time, when it came to questions regarding matters of state any mufti with political sense would know exactly what sort of opinion was expected from him. When the sultan delivered to Ebu's-su'ud the question of whether it was legitimate to break a peace treaty in order to restore to the true faith a country that once had been under Muslim rule – Cyprus having been under Arab domination from the seventh to the tenth century – the mufti, quoting Islamic sacred texts, had no problem stating that any treaty with the infidels could be broken should this bring advantage to the universal community of the true believers.[15] This sort of religious carte blanche was exactly what the war party needed, and an invasion became pretty much inevitable.

The mufti's ruling was mainly intended for internal consumption, the Ottomans being too politically savvy to use it in the international arena. Instead, in denouncing the treaty with Venice they protested the many violations of the pact committed by the

Venetians over the years: building castles and villages in border regions; protecting pirates and allowing them to use Cyprus as a logistic base; executing captured Muslim pirates. It was true that during the previous few years there had been a number of violations of the Venetian–Ottoman treaty, but these were not limited to one side. The Venetians had indeed rebuilt the border castles destroyed during the previous war, and worse were using them as raiding bases against Ottoman territory. On the other hand, Muslim corsairs had been attacking ships in the Adriatic with the complicity of the local Ottoman authorities. The commander of the Egyptian squadron Şuluç Mehmed Pasha had captured a Venetian ship, imprisoning the crew, and the same had happened to a number of Spanish soldiers on board two other Venetian vessels arbitrarily taken by the Ottomans. Venice, however, habitually executed any Islamic corsair it managed to catch rather than sending the culprit to Constantinople for punishment.[16] As often happens in history, fault is born an orphan and dies a spinster.

The sultan's representative, the *çavuş* Kubad, brought all his master's grievances to Venice at the end of March 1570, accompanying them with an ultimatum that only by giving up Cyprus peacefully would Venice retain the Porte's friendship. Sokollu Mehmed also sent a letter, repeating the same arguments and inviting the Venetians to be reasonable, given the costs of a war and the difficulty the republic had in finding allies. The Venetians had been expecting this for some time, and over the previous months had quietly strengthened their overseas defences, recruited soldiers and mariners, and built new ships. Doge Pietro Loredan dismissed Kubad, saying that justice would give the Venetians the sword to defend their rights, and God would aid them to defeat the sultan's unjust violence. An official reply in the same tone was sent to Selim, together with a covering letter to Sokollu Mehmed ending with the words, '[the sultan] will be an example to all princes how much they can trust his promises'. [17]

On his way back to Constantinople Kubad stopped in Dubrovnik, divulging the news that Venice had declared war. Immediately, the Ottoman forces in the area launched a series of raids across the border, remaining a menace to Venice for the rest of the conflict. Kubad arrived in Istanbul on 5 May, and informed his master of the doge's decision. Selim may have expected his answer but was apparently irritated by the fact that Loredan addressed him simply as 'The Most Serene and Excellent Lord Emperor of the Turks', omitting all his other titles. What really enraged the sultan, however, was another episode. Two months before Kubad's arrival in Venice the French diplomat Claude Du Bourg de Guérines had arrived in the city accompanied by Mahmud Bey, the sultan's ambassador to the king of France. The two men intended to proceed to Paris to formalize a treaty negotiated between Du Bourg and the Porte, although the former had by now incurred Charles IX's displeasure. Du Bourg left soon after, leaving behind Mahmud Bey as a guest of the French ambassador in Venice. Suspicions soon arose about the Ottoman envoy's real mission, and on 6 March he was arrested and locked up with his entourage by the Venetian authorities. No justification was given for this action, but it was common knowledge that Mahmud had been sent by the sultan to spy on the Venetians. When Selim heard the news, he ordered the arrest of all the Venetian diplomats in the Ottoman empire, Marcantonio Barbaro being consigned to the fortress of Alcasabach. Initially his confinement was not too strict, with only a small number of janissaries to watch him. Later, the Ottoman authorities would tighten the screws, sealing all doors and windows of Barbaro's quarters. Nevertheless, he still managed to send information to Venice by circuitous routes with the aid of Sokollu's Jewish doctor Solomon Ashkenazi, a sworn enemy of Joseph Nassi. Barbaro was aware that Sokollu was intercepting all letters to and from Venice, although reading them was a different matter as they were mostly in code. In any case, the *bailo* and the grand vizier depended on each other: the former to get information to Venice; the latter to keep a diplomatic channel open with the Republic of St Mark.[18]

Military activities picked up in mid-spring with an Ottoman attack on the island of Tinos, south of Evvoia and one of Venice's strategic outposts in the eastern Mediterranean. Piyale Pasha, the vizier senior to the *kapudan paşa* in charge of naval operations, believed the island to be easy prey and its conquest the first step to restore his reputation. But the governor of Tinos, Girolamo Paruta, expected mischief and had taken adequate countermeasures. Piyale moved down the coast of Evvoia, arriving at his objective in the early hours of 5 May. Hoping to catch the Venetians napping, he landed 8,000 men and sent them to assault the island's main stronghold. Paruta, warned of the impending Ottoman arrival, managed to bring most of the inhabitants within the walls and then proceeded to engage the attackers with a brisk cannonade. Frustrated in their attempt at surprise, the Turks brought forward their artillery and opened fire on the fortress, hoping to create a breach in its walls. Getting nowhere, Piyale settled his men down for a siege, in the meantime conducting systematic raiding operations across the island. After ten days, having torched houses, destroyed churches and killed livestock, Piyale left for Rhodes with little more than his losses to show for the attack. The first round had gone to the Venetians, but a long and gruelling match lay ahead.

~

Even before war was formally declared, the states of Europe had had their eyes fixed on the Levant. The Venetians, who until then had snubbed every proposal for an anti-Ottoman alliance, suddenly became very concerned about the Ottoman threat to Christendom. Initially the republic showed some reluctance in joining forces with the Spaniards, fearing not only the Habsburgs' hegemonic designs over Italy, but also that it might be asked to defend Spanish possessions in North Africa.[19] Towards Rome they had a different attitude, everybody knowing Pius V's willingness to create a league to stop the Muslim advance. But the pope was at loggerheads with Philip II, still fuming because of Pius's bestowal of the grand ducal crown of Tuscany on Cosimo I de' Medici. Apart from resenting what he considered to be the pope's unjustifiable interference in matters outside his jurisdiction, Philip's chagrin had been increased by the presence at Cosimo's coronation of Marcantonio Colonna and Paolo Giordano Orsini. That Colonna was the hereditary high constable of the kingdom of Naples was particularly annoying, and the fact that Orsini's family had always been pro-French made the king suspect mischief. Indeed, some of Philip's ministers were convinced that Pius's attempts to create an anti-Ottoman alliance involving the Italian states would weaken the Habsburgs' presence in the peninsula, and were 'the true way to throw us out of Italy'.[20]

It was in this climate of suspicion that Pius met the Spanish ambassador Juan de Zuñiga at the beginning of March. The pope informed Zuñiga of the imminent Ottoman war against the Venetians, adding that the latter would be willing to conclude a defensive alliance with the Spaniards. Zuñiga answered that the Venetians were always out for themselves, and once the Turkish peril had passed would happily resume relations with Constantinople. In any case, any alliance was conditional on the pope's renewal of the *cruzada*, since without it the king could not possibly defend his territories let alone fight the Ottomans. Zuñiga was following Madrid's orders, and in another meeting with Pius a few weeks later he again expressed his scepticism about Venice's real intentions, stating that the Venetians would probably try to strike a deal with the Ottomans. However, he suggested to Philip that it would be better to send his galleys to Sicily, the Ottomans' real objective being still unclear, and that an alliance like the one envisaged by the pope could turn out to Spain's advantage in the long run.[21]

Pius decided to approach Philip in person, and in mid-March sent Monsignor Luis de Torres to the Spanish court. Torres arrived in Cordova on 19 April 1570 and two days later had a long interview with Philip. The king proved not ill-disposed towards the idea of a league between the papacy, Spain and Venice, adding however that since it was a serious matter it needed to be thought through. Two days later Torres dined with Cardinal Espinosa, who informed him that the king was prepared to send all his available galleys to

Sicily and also that he would write to the viceroys of Naples and Sicily ordering them to provide victuals for the Venetian fleet.[22] Philip was willing to do something to 'please the Pope and provide always for Christendom's needs' – as he would write to his naval commander, Giovanni Andrea Doria.[23] The king, as we have seen, had his own reasons for sending his fleet to the south of Italy, and intended to obtain as much ecclesiastical money as possible before formally committing himself to an alliance. Philip was aware that without papal subsidies any Spanish funds spent on the Mediterranean theatre would have to be diverted from Flanders, something the duke of Alva virulently opposed. In any case, as the king himself would write to the pope, there were also the Islamic powers of North Africa to consider, not just the Turks; he therefore had instructed his representatives in Rome – Zuñiga, with Cardinals Granvelle and Pacheco – to discuss the terms of a possible treaty. To these Philip sent word that negotiations had to include some sort of agreement about the subsidies, and in any case Spain was not prepared to send more than sixty galleys.[24]

It was common knowledge that Philip's main targets in the Mediterranean were the Barbary states, and for this reason he would try – as the Venetians feared – to avoid fighting in the Levant. This became immediately apparent when the delegates from Spain and Venice met on 2 July, two days after Pius had delivered a vibrant sermon exhorting them to conclude an agreement to fight the Ottomans. Granvelle and Pacheco presented Pius with the request for subsidies and tried to badger the Venetian ambassador Michele Surian into accepting the inclusion of North Africa among the league's potential targets. Spain's initial proposal in fact included a permanent alliance against all infidels, which for Philip also meant the Protestants. Surian retorted that just saying 'the Turk' would be sufficient, Venice not wanting to be involved in some far-flung venture in the western Mediterranean, let alone Flanders. The cost of the league was another bone of contention, the Spanish being unwilling to pay more than half of the total expenses and the Venetians a quarter. The pope pointed out that his annual revenues amounted to just 400,000 ducats, and the most he could give was 35,000 a month for the upkeep of twelve galleys. Besides, Spain was already drawing funds from ecclesiastical sources, had a large empire, and by using the league's army could save on the cost of garrisons. As for the commander-in-chief of the alliance, Philip, as the main financial contributor, insisted on one of his men. The Venetians, unsurprisingly, wanted one of theirs, since they would be providing most of the ships; besides, the war concerned primarily the republic's possessions. In the end it was agreed that Don Juan of Austria should be the leader of a group made up of Venetian, Spanish and papal generals, with the pope as supreme arbiter. The final agreement, however, would be delayed for many months, due to incessant bickering among the delegates. The suspicion that Venice was trying to strike a deal with the Ottomans was always present, despite the fact that the new doge, Alvise Mocenigo – Loredan having died in April – was considered a hawk.[25]

The Pope was determined to help the Venetians, no matter what. On 11 June he nominated Marcantonio Colonna, duke of Paliano, captain-general of the papal fleet, sending him to Venice to hammer out the details of an agreement between the republic and the Holy See. After the death of his arch-enemy Paul IV and the subsequent downfall of the Carafa, the Roman nobleman had been restored by Pius IV to his former possessions and since then had enjoyed papal favour and protection. But Colonna's promotion was ill received by the Spanish delegates in Rome. Both Zuñiga and Granvelle were his enemies, in part because Colonna was a protégé of their rivals at Philip's court. Besides, despite being a Habsburg subject because of his possessions in the kingdom of Naples, Colonna had accepted the pope's naval commission without first consulting Philip. In addition, Granvelle considered the newly appointed captain-general incompetent in naval matters, Colonna's only real experience at sea being his participation in an anti-corsair expedition a few years before.[26]

The pope did not have a navy worth mentioning, and one of the reasons behind Colonna's mission to Venice was to obtain ships and men for his master. The Republic of St Mark duly obliged, providing Pius with four galleys – albeit not the best of vessels, Venice having her own priorities – to be added to another eight, for which the Venetians had provided the shells, being completed in the papal dockyards of Ancona. Venice also provided a minimum of ordnance for the galleys, their other needs not allowing them to equip Colonna's vessels with full gun batteries. The Venetians were less than satisfied with the pope's choice of Colonna, despite the fact that the latter managed to get on extremely well with his hosts. Venice had agreed to place its own galleys under the pope's command, and while the duke of Paliano may have been a charming person his inexperience was a cause of major concern. For this reason the doge wrote to Venice's captain-general, Girolamo Zane, instructing him to be respectful towards Colonna, but retain his independence in matters of importance.[27]

At this point the Venetians' main worry was money. During the last few years fortifying Cyprus had cost the republic enormous sums, and it was an accepted fact that in wartime military expenses went through the roof. In order to raise cash Venice employed the usual expedients of any money-starved Early Modern state: selling offices, increasing the public debt and extraordinary taxation. Although these methods brought in some funds, they were but a drop in Mars' bucket, and by the time the war ended in 1573 Venice would have spent nearly ten million gold ducats.[28] The Venetians were hoping that the pope would cover some of their expenses, but Pius had his own financial problems, and in order to ameliorate these it was rumoured that he had asked for contributions of 30,000 ducats from sixteen newly created cardinals. The pope also deprived his nephew of the office of chamberlain, bestowing it on Cardinal Alvise Corner in exchange for 68,000 ducats.[29] Pius had never been a nepotist in the first place, and believed that his family should share in full the burden of war.

The king of Spain, as we have seen, was always short of funds, and in serious need of those ecclesiastical subsidies that the pontiff had until then denied him. Philip by now understood that it was useless to try and stop Pius from aiding the Venetians, and endeavoured to turn the situation to his advantage. On 15 July he wrote to Colonna informing him that he had ordered Doria to join him with the galleys gathered in Sicily, adding that the Genoese admiral was to obey the papal commander. A letter to the same effect was sent to Pius, and the delighted pope now expressed his willingness to grant the requested subsidies.[30] Pius would have been less elated if he had known the king's secret orders to Doria. Philip had no intention of risking his galleys in what he considered a rash venture, and instructed his commander to 'preserve the galleys as much as possible' sailing with 'all the prudence necessary'. These directives were deliberately ambiguous, in practice giving the admiral carte blanche to decide the best course of action.[31] Doria was not happy with the king's vagueness, and on 8 August confided to his father-in-law the prince of Melfi, 'The king commands and wishes that I should serve him and guess [his intentions]. Yet the more I read his letter, the less I understand it; and the more I squeeze it, the less juice I pull out of it. Thus, I have no other choice but to go, but slowly and with the expectation that another courier may arrive with clearer orders.'[32]

But Doria would wait in vain, despite all his pleadings. Three days later he would write to the king asking his permission to quit the combined fleet by September, and also for precise instructions on what to do, including disobeying Colonna's orders, to ensure the safety of Spain's galleys. He concluded his letter by stressing the opportunity for a strike in North Africa, adding that the Venetians were probably already trying to reach an agreement with the Ottomans. The possibility of a raid against the Barbary states was always present in the minds of those serving the Spanish crown. On 28 July Philip's ambassador in Genoa had written to his master pointing out that it was the right moment to attack Algiers, its governor-general Uluç Ali having gone to sea leaving only a few troops to guard the place. Only a few years before Don Garcia de Toledo had recaptured the Peñon de la Gomera, and a similar operation against Algiers seemed a more viable option than fighting for distant Cyprus. Doria was as determined as Philip not to hazard the galleys under his command, twelve of them being his own property, just to please Colonna and the Venetians. He intended to procrastinate until the season was too advanced for any sort of military operation in the Levant, and attempt instead to convince the allies to attack Tunis. Doria was also worried about the possibility of encountering Uluç Ali, and with good reason.[33]

Immediately after the siege of 1565 the Knights Hospitallers, which by this point had acquired for good the title of Knights of Malta, had resumed their anti-Muslim naval activities. Piero del Monte, grand master after La Valette's death in 1568, willingly responded to the pope's appeal to send his galleys to join the allied fleet to aid Venice against the Ottomans. On 26 June the Maltese contingent of four galleys under the French knight François de Saint Clément sailed from Malta towards Sicily, where it joined Doria's squadron. It was a small unit, yet highly professional and boasting some of the best fighters in the Mediterranean. However, Saint Clément decided to return to Malta after loading his galley with choice wines and provisions, despite having been warned that Uluç Ali was in the area with a fleet of about twenty galliots. Brushing aside all objections, the Maltese commander set sail from the port of Licata on the evening of 14 July.

Twenty miles off the island of Gozo the Maltese squadron stumbled upon Uluç Ali's ships in the early-morning light. The galleys immediately turned tail, heading for the Sicilian coast. Initially Ali hesitated to act, fearing the four vessels to be the vanguard of Giovanni Andrea Doria's fleet. But once he realized that his enemy was on the run, he gave chase. For many hours the Maltese, aided by a favourable breeze, managed to keep their pursuers at a distance. But the wind suddenly dropped, and the swifter Muslim galliots rapidly gained on their quarry by force of oars. The Maltese squadron now split in two, the *Santa Maria della Vittoria* and the *Sant'Anna* heading for the open sea while the flagship and the *San Giovanni* made for the Sicilian coast. Uluç Ali in turn divided his forces, sending seven galliots to chase one pair of galleys, while he with twelve vessels went after the other. Seeing two of the pursuing galliots struggling to keep up with the rest, the *Santa Maria della Vittoria* and the *Sant'Anna* attempted to take on the remaining five in a daring counter-attack. But during the difficult manoeuvre the *Sant'Anna* was immobilized when her sails got tangled. Separated from her companion, the *Sant'Anna* was surrounded and attacked by the whole pursuing force. The Maltese put up a stiff fight for several hours, and only at sunset did the Muslims manage to board the enemy vessel full of dead and dying men. The *Santa Maria della Vittoria* managed to extricate herself and find refuge in Agrigento.

Meanwhile, disaster had also struck Saint Clément's force. Sensing freedom at hand, the Muslim slaves on the Maltese galleys had deliberately rowed slowly, allowing Uluç Ali to catch up. The first to go was the *San Giovanni*, surrounded and captured after a brief, ferocious fight. The Maltese flagship could have been saved, had Saint Clément not failed to spot the nearby port of Licata. Desperately trying to escape his pursuers, the commander ran his galley aground near the tower of Montechiaro. At this point the Muslim slaves managed to free themselves and attack their erstwhile masters with hatchets. Retreating ashore to the summit of the tower, the Maltese watched impotently as Uluç Ali refloated and towed away the stranded galley, which he subsequently used as his own flagship. Saint Clément also committed the unpardonable crime of trying to save his own gold and silver, forgetting the banner of the Order of St John. A quick-witted galley clerk by the name of Michele Calli with the help of the knight Bongianni Gianfigliazzi managed to pull down the standard and bring it to safety.

Initially Saint Clément intended to commit suicide, and then decided instead to expiate his sin by becoming a hermit. But in Malta they were not prepared to let the matter drop. Sixty knights and hundreds of Maltese soldiers and sailors had been killed or taken prisoner, and popular opinion demanded that the culprits be brought to justice. The Maltese were particularly enraged that the grand master had tried to blame the disaster on the local seamen, hanging the flagship's pilot. To avoid a revolt, Piero del Monte put all the survivors from the flagship on trial. Saint Clément got wind of this and went to Rome to ask the pope to intercede in his favour, but Pius V, scrupulously fair, answered that it was his duty to go back to Malta and face the consequences of his actions. When the reluctant knight landed on the island he was barely saved from being lynched by the irate populace, who greeted him with 'Kill, kill; die, die!' The subsequent inquiry revealed in full Saint Clément's criminal negligence. He was deprived of his habit, tried by a secular court, condemned to death, strangled, and his body cast into the sea at night-time.*

The capture of three galleys by Uluç Ali was a crippling blow for the Hospitallers and a serious loss for the allies. Philip II immediately sent the order two new galleys from Messina and one from Naples, with an extra gift of sixty criminals condemned to the oars. Still the lack of sailors and rowers meant that the knights could fully arm only two ships. By the beginning of September the renewed Maltese squadron was ready to sail, its numbers augmented by the return of the *Santa Maria della Vittoria*.[34] But by now events had taken a turn which would force the allies to reconsider their strategy.

~

The Ottomans had wasted no time putting together their expeditionary force against Cyprus. On 1 July a squadron under Piyale Pasha landed troops near Limassol, intending to sack the town. Thrown back into the sea by an energetic Venetian counter-attack, the Ottomans sailed along the coast to the salt mines south of Nicosia, and undisturbed managed to establish a beachhead of about 10,000 men, mostly infantry. During the following days a

---

* Since Saint Clément was a member of a religious order, he first had to be 'reduced to the state of a layman' before being tried by a secular court, the only ones which could inflict penalties involving loss of life or limb.

number of skirmishes occurred between the invaders and the Venetians, but without the latter attempting seriously to tackle the main enemy force. This was largely due to the overcautious attitude of the *luogotenente generale del regno* Nicolò Dandolo, who, despite the urging of his subordinates, preferred to wait behind the walls of Nicosia for the Ottoman attack.* This allowed Lala Mustafa Pasha to return on the 18th with a fleet of about 400 vessels of various types and sizes. Half of his 160 galleys were modern and well furnished with troops, harquebuses and cannon; the rest were in bad shape, lacking also men and equipment. Many more soldiers were embarked on the scores of vessels, big and small, that made up the armada. Each galley carried two horses, while the remaining equines, including many mules, travelled on a number of transport ships. The mounted troops totalled 4,000; the janissaries 6,000, the remaining soldiers being artillerymen, auxiliary infantry, sappers and support units. In total the army was between 70,000 and 100,000 strong, drawn from half a dozen *beylerbeik* and boasting a train of some 200 artillery pieces.[35]

The Turkish commanders debated whether to attack first Famagusta or Nicosia. With Malta in mind Lala Mustafa decided on Nicosia as the initial objective, being not only the key to Cyprus but also an ideal place to establish winter quarters. During the Malta campaign Isfendiari Mustafa Pasha's failure to take Mdina, in the centre of the island, had forced the Ottomans to withdraw at the end of the summer, and in addition the garrison of Mdina had proved a constant thorn in the besiegers' side.[36]

It took Mustafa some time to disembark his troops, advancing towards Nicosia four days after his arrival. He proceeded slowly and cautiously, fearful that the Venetians' lack of activity was a ruse to lead him into a well-prepared trap. Dandolo, however, was busy

---

* The title 'lieutenant general of the kingdom' derived from the fact that Cyprus had been a realm since the Middle Ages. Caterina Cornaro (or Corner), widow of the last king of the house of Lusignan, had surrendered to Venice her sovereignty over the island in 1489.

strengthening Nicosia's defences, counting on 24,000 men, 250 guns, abundant powder and provisions to withstand the siege. But portable firearms were in short supply – no more than a thousand harquebuses being available – while citizens and militia made up most of the city's garrison. Yet Dandolo, 'a man of weak judgement' – chosen for having previously served in a number of administrative military positions, was confident that Nicosia's state-of-the-art fortifications would more than compensate for any deficiency deriving from his men's inexperience or lack of weapons.[37] The famous military architect and engineer Giulio Savorgnan had completely rebuilt the city walls between 1567 and 1568, although he considered the work of little use since Nicosia could not be relieved from the sea and stood in a valley surrounded by hills.

To strengthen the city's defences he had reduced its perimeter to four miles. The old medieval walls and ditch, being outside the new ramparts, were levelled so as not to provide shelter to an attacking force, and the stones used to build the updated fortifications. Since there was not enough building material for the planned eleven bastions, these had to be constructed with earth and faggots faced with stones. Savorgnan was recalled to Venice before he could finish his project, leaving its completion to Dandolo. Another military engineer, Bonaiuto Lorini, would describe the new fortifications as: 'The best and most intelligent work (although made of earth) . . . that could be found'.[38] Yet even such modern fortifications were inadequate if unsupported by a field army. Relying exclusively on fixed defences was a mistake that the French would repeat four centuries later, when they counted on the concrete forts of the Maginot Line to repel the attacking Germans.

Mustafa arrived within sight of Nicosia on 28 July, pitching his camp to the south-east on high ground. His headquarters boasted Spanish tents taken by Uluç Ali at Tunis a few months before, and captured Habsburg banners were planted in front of his own pavilion.[39] The various *beylerbey* with their military contingents placed their tents in front of the four southern bastions: Davila, Costanzo, Tripoli and Podocattaro. Mustafa immediately ordered the building on the hills of Santa Margherita and San Giorgio of two redoubts surrounded by ditches to house his artillery. From there he commenced firing against Nicosia's walls, ordering also the diversion of the stream that fed the city's moat, sending his sappers to do the work under the cover of darkness and the siege guns. The Ottomans built two other makeshift fortresses to provide more covering fire for their engineers, and shielded by these batteries occupied the half-filled mediaeval ditch. From there the besiegers advanced to within 150 yards of the ramparts, pushing forward zigzag trenches which the defenders could not enfilade. Here the Ottomans set up another line of batteries and engaged in a four-day bombardment of the southern bastions. The walls, however, had been reinforced with further earthworks, and the artillery barrage produced few results except an expenditure of ammunition. More effective were the Ottoman harquebusiers sent forward by Mustafa to protect his engineers. The janissaries were crack shots, and their accurate fire hindered the defenders' attempts to stop the Ottoman sappers.[40] Trenches were pushed up to the counterscarp, protected against enfilade fire with earth and brushwood ramparts nearly as high as the city walls. In this way the Ottomans were able to reach the angles of the bastions and they began to cut away at the masonry in order to prepare a sloping approach for assault troops.

The Venetians attempted countermeasures, at one point building a wooden parapet with loopholes to allow their harquebusiers to fire at the Ottoman sappers without being hit by enemy marksmen. But the besiegers destroyed the device with well-directed artillery fire, killing a number of defenders in the process. Meanwhile, Dandolo, unnecessarily concerned about a shortage of powder, ordered his soldiers not to return fire, his behaviour arousing in many a suspicion that he was working for the enemy. Far from being a traitor, Dandolo was simply unimaginative, although, given the inexperience of many of his soldiers, his caution if excessive was not irrational.

On 5 August Mustafa launched his first assault against Nicosia's defences and nearly managed to capture the Costanzo bastion, the defending troops taking to their heels. Only the timely intervention of Paolo dal Guasto's company averted a major disaster, and the Ottomans were forced to retreat with considerable losses. As the besiegers' bombardment resumed, the frustration of the besieged increased. Since Dandolo refused to allow sorties against the enemy's siege works, some of the defenders took matters into their own hands. On the night of 10 August 300 men rushed the Ottoman trenches facing the Davila bastion, throwing back the enemy in disorder. Informed of the action, Dandolo refused to send reinforcements, allowing the Turks to counter-attack successfully under the cover of their artillery. Undaunted by this failure, a number of officers in Nicosia organized another raid behind Dandolo's back. On 17 August, as the Ottomans were resting in the midday heat, a large force of about 1,000 men silently exited the Famagusta gate and fell on the enemy siege works. Two batteries were captured, but once more Dandolo, having discovered what was happening, stopped other troops from joining the fray by ordering the closure of Nicosia's gates. Left to their fate, the attacking Venetians nevertheless managed to retreat into the city, but with the loss of many officers and men.

The demoralized defenders gave up the idea of future sallies, concentrating instead on building inner lines of defence across the four threatened bastions against the Ottomans managing to gain footholds on the walls. There was still hope that a Venetian relief force would arrive in time to lift the siege, and in any case provisions and munitions allowed for a prolonged resistance. All of Mustafa's proposals for an honourable surrender were rejected, but this show of bravado belied the gravity of the situation. By the beginning of September the defenders' numbers had been dangerously depleted by death and sickness, the professional soldiers being reduced to a few thousand, and many sections of the walls were barely manned. Artisans, hitherto exempted from military service, were forced to stand sentry to relieve the exhausted soldiers.

Mustafa tried to induce the garrison to give up by putting pressure on the civilian population. Arrows with messages urging surrender were shot over the walls while Ottoman gunners targeted the city's houses and, on Sundays, churches. During a truce the besiegers tried to talk the defenders into surrender, mocking their hope of relief from the Venetian fleet. It was still in port, they said, its crews riddled with disease. The garrison ignored the taunts, and Mustafa ordered a renewed artillery barrage followed by an assault against the walls. Once more the attackers were repulsed, but it was clear that the defenders could not hold out much longer. Colonel Podocattaro begged Dandolo to mine the bastions against the possibility of the Turks capturing them. Dandolo refused.

Mustafa had his own problems. Despite the fact that according to the standards of the time the siege was proceeding well, the Ottoman commander could not keep up the pressure against Nicosia indefinitely. Venetian mounted troops from Famagusta had been harrying his rear, and the bombardment was taking its toll on the besiegers' supplies of powder and shot. Manpower was another of Mustafa's concerns. Dandolo may not have shown much imagination, but his policy of relying on fixed defences was causing considerable losses to the besiegers. The janissaries were unhappy about being in the fore of each assault fearing the bastions to be mined as at Szigetvár. In a few weeks the campaign season would be over, and if Nicosia had not been taken by then the whole Ottoman enterprise would be at risk. After another fruitless attempt to convince the Venetians to surrender – threatening to put the stormed city to the sack – and desperately in need of troops, Mustafa sent an urgent request to the Ottoman naval commanders to send him at least 100 men from each of their galleys. Müezzinzâde Ali Pasha and Piyale Pasha were concerned about weakening their ships' strength in case the allied fleet appeared, but also recognized that the success of the campaign hinged on the capture of Nicosia. Müezzinzâde Ali arrived in person at Mustafa's camp on 8 September, bringing with him some 25,000 men. With these reinforcements Mustafa felt confident of success, and to encourage his janissaries he promised abundant rewards to those first over the walls.

By now Dandolo was at the end of his tether, dithering and desperate. The defence of Nicosia fell to his subordinates, who on 6 September tried to execute another sally to dislodge the Ottomans from their siege lines. The timing was bad, the raid a failure, and with less than 3,000 professional soldiers available Nicosia's defenders could not afford to risk any more of their troops, only wait for what appeared to be the inevitable outcome. In the early light of 9 September the Turks crept up to Nicosia's walls, concentrating most of their troops below the much-damaged Podocattaro bastion. At a signal the Ottoman force rushed the walls, engaging the defenders in a furious hand-to-hand struggle. Eventually numbers started to tell, despite the last-minute reinforcements sent by Dandolo to the beleaguered bastion. At this point, having ordered the blowing up of the remaining gunpowder should the Ottomans prevail, the *luogotenente generale* prudently retired to his palace.

By now the Ottomans had captured Podocattaro and were swarming along the walls to attack the remaining defenders from the rear. The Costanzo and Tripoli bastions were taken after desperate fights, the Venetian survivors retreating into the city chased by the victorious Turks. The defenders gathered for a last stand in the square where Dandolo's palace stood, engaging the Ottomans fiercely at close quarters. From the Tripoli bastion Derviş Pasha, the governor general of Aleppo, fired three guns loaded with canister shot into the square, cutting down friend and foe alike. Fumbling for a solution that would save his skin, Dandolo tried to negotiate terms with the assailants. He ordered Tuccio Costanzo, who was leading the resistance, to take a letter to Mustafa offering surrender in exchange for the defenders' lives and property. It was all too late. Costanzo was immediately taken prisoner, and the remaining soldiers retreated into the palace. There Dandolo was confronted by the Venetian patrician Andrea Da Pesaro, who accused him of treason. As Pesaro pulled out his sword, he was slain by two of Dandolo's bodyguards.

Death, confusion and despair held sway in Nicosia. Men,

women and children ran panic-stricken through the streets. Here and there small groups of Venetians attempted last stands, only to be overwhelmed by the enemy. The Ottomans opened the Famagusta gate, allowing their cavalrymen to pour into the city, mercilessly cutting down anyone who stood in their path. Captain Paolo dal Guasto, still holding the bastion of San Luca, turned his guns on the city in a desperate attempt to stem the Ottoman tide. For eight hours the fighting continued, until the last of the garrison had been killed or captured. In the house of the count of Tripoli, Colonel Ettore Podocattaro resisted until nightfall, finally surrendering on condition that all those with him be spared and allowed to buy their freedom, leaving all the goods in the house to Mustafa's discretion. Earlier, the Ottomans had convinced Dandolo to capitulate on terms. The *luogotenente generale* had opened the gates of the palace but unaware of the negotiations a party of janissaries which had managed to enter through a side door attacked and killed Dandolo. Seeing this, the survivors in the building resumed fighting; they were pushed back, resisting room by room. Only a few score were left when the Ottomans broke through the windows, killing all who remained.

Mustafa entered the city in the afternoon and immediately ordered all fighting to cease providing the remaining defenders laid down their weapons. To some extent he managed to restore order, but there was little he could do to stop his battle-maddened troops from engaging in an orgy of murder, rape and pillage. Women, no matter their age or standing, were ravished, churches and houses sacked, and anyone who dared to resist was killed on the spot. This sort of behaviour was not confined to the Ottomans, many other armies throughout history displaying the same brutality.* The

---

* Among a few examples of savage sacks through history one should mention: Brescia (1509), Rome (1527), Antwerp (1576), Magdeburg (1630), Drogheda (1649), Badajoz (1812), Warsaw (1944), Berlin (1945). It should also be remembered that according to sixteenth-century conventions of war if a town was taken after having refused to surrender, the lives and property of its inhabitants were at the victor's mercy.

victorious troops, in particular the janissaries, quarrelled over prisoners and booty, and further bloodshed ensued. The Ottomans captured 160 good artillery pieces, together with much powder and shot, and Mustafa's share of the plunder amounted to 50,000 ducats. Breaking his word, the Ottoman leader also enslaved Colonel Podocattaro with all his family. When the Venetian officer protested, threatening to lodge a formal complaint with the sultan, Mustafa had him beheaded.[41]

The next day the prisoners were auctioned off, while a choice batch of women and boys, together with much treasure, was loaded onto three ships to be sent to Constantinople. Unfortunately, due to the negligence of the crew or, according to Venetian sources, the action of a female prisoner, one of the vessels exploded, engulfing the other two in its flames. Eight hundred young girls perished, and only a few sailors managed to swim ashore.[42] These deaths should be added to the 20,000 Venetians who died during the siege and storming of the city. Ottoman casualties were also high, amounting to perhaps 30,000 men.

Following the capture of Nicosia, Mustafa sent messengers to all the other Venetian strongholds on the island with requests to surrender in exchange for life and liberty for the garrisons. The governor of Kyrenia, Zaccaria Mudazzo, asked for time to make his mind up, adding that no decision could be made without the approval of his superiors. He then sent a letter full of bravado to the governor of Famagusta, Marcantonio Bragadin, who ordered Kyrenia to resist to the last man. But Mudazzo was not made of heroes' stuff, and after consulting with the fortress's military governor surrendered Kyrenia to Mustafa on 14 September, not even waiting for Bragadin's answer. The Venetian authorities were infuriated by this craven behaviour, given that Kyrenia's defences had recently been updated at a cost of 150,000 ducats.[43] True to their word, the Ottomans transported Mudazzo and his men to Crete, but on his arrival in Venice the governor was arrested, ending his days in jail.

Famagusta proved more resilient. Mustafa sent a request of surrender, accompanied by Dandolo's head on a plate, offering generous terms. These included life, freedom and property for all, with the possibility of becoming Ottoman subjects. He added that resistance was useless, since no relief force could arrive in Famagusta without first battling Piyale's fleet. But Bragadin and the military governor Astorre Baglioni were made of stronger stuff than Mudazzo, and sent back a defiant answer. Mustafa had no choice but to settle down for another siege, hoping the city would fall quickly. In this he was to be disappointed.

~

The allied fleet had failed to come to Nicosia's assistance for a number of reasons. When war appeared inevitable Venice had flexed its naval muscles, managing by June 1570 to deploy some 125 galleys, eleven galleasses and twenty-two other vessels. In addition, another fifty galleys, four galleasses and twelve further ships were being built in the Arsenale. The quality of the existing vessels was mixed, some of them being old and not particularly seaworthy. Crews were another problem. Despite the fact that Venice had been busy recruiting troops at home and abroad, by April less than 12,000 soldiers were available for naval service, a meagre seventy-five for each vessel. Their numbers eventually rose to 15,000, still an insufficient force for the task they were supposed to perform.[44] Rowers were also in short supply; Venice, like the Ottomans, relying mostly on free men, not slaves or convicts, to operate its ships' oars.

The Venetian fleet concentrated in the port of Zara (Zadar), sailing for Corfu on 12 June. Its commander Girolamo Zane arrived there on the 23rd with seventy galleys, not bothering to wait for the slower ones. Corfu's *provveditore*, the crusty Sebastiano Venier, asked Zane to provide him with troops to capture the Ottoman-held fortresses of Margariti on the nearby coast. However, the commander of the Venetian naval infantry, Sforza Pallavicino, decided that this was too daring a venture, preferring instead to ravage the enemy countryside. Venier, who with fewer men had captured a few days before the strategically important castle of

Sopot, was incensed by this behaviour, forcing Pallavicino to justify himself to the doge. In any case, the Venetians had more pressing needs than conquering strongholds. Most of the galleys had to be refitted and repaired once they reached Corfu, and moreover the crews had been hit by an epidemic, probably typhoid fever, which was reported to have killed in a few weeks some 20,000 men, 'including many gentlemen, galley owners, and others of the highest condition'.* The lack of proper medical supplies worsened the situation. Those left alive took weeks to recover, preventing Zane from sailing to Cyprus.[45]

Not all the Venetian forces were inactive. The *provveditore* Marco Querini with twenty-one galleys was stationed in Crete to prevent an Ottoman descent on the island. Having received orders to join the main fleet in Corfu, en route he decided to strike the fortress of Mani in the Peloponnese. Managing to hide in a small haven, at nightfall he landed with his men and proceeded to surround the enemy stronghold. The Ottomans managed to retreat to the keep, but their resistance was cut short when Querini brought forward his artillery and bombarded the walls ferociously. The Ottomans surrendered and were immediately sent to the oars. Querini had the fortress razed with mines before sailing for Corfu, reaching his destination on 1 July.[46] It was a small success, but nevertheless an important boost for the Venetians' flagging spirits. Zane immediately sent Querini to recruit men in the nearby islands, whilst he remained in port waiting for his surviving crews and soldiers to get back into fighting shape. Finally, on 23 July he set

---

* Natale Conti would variably impute the disease to 'evil air', 'God's displeasure' or 'someone's carelessness' (CONTI: II, f. 9r). However, Pantero Pantera, an experienced naval commander writing a few decades later, would place the blame squarely on the 'avarice' of those officials who had supplied the fleet with rotten victuals (PANTERA: 95). On 7 April 1571 the Venetian senate would write to the deputy captain-general of the fleet Agostino Barbarigo, accusing the commanders of the 1570 expedition of having kept the galleys in totally unhygienic conditions: 'From which it may be understood the disease and deaths that hit our fleet . . . causing an offence to God our Lord and great damage and misfortune to the public good.' ASV, *SM*, reg. 40, f. 21r.

sail for Crete, where he joined up with Querini in the first days of August.

Meanwhile, Marcantonio Colonna had travelled with his refitted galleys from Ancona to Otranto. His flagship was a great quinquereme, built some forty years before by the humanist naval architect Vettor Fausto.* Arriving in the Apulian port on 6 August, he found a letter from Philip II informing him of the imminent arrival of Giovanni Andrea Doria with a squadron of forty-nine 'Spanish' galleys. The king added that Doria had received instructions to obey the papal admiral's decisions, but the letter's closing lines had an ominous ring for Colonna:

> I trust and pray that in battle you seek Giovanni Andrea's full advice, having been told that it will be most useful. This will contribute to the success of the operation, given his experience and practice in naval matters, and in any case be sure to inform us about any needs you may have. However, if the Turkish armada should pursue a different direction from what it is said to have taken, and should attack our states, then I confide that you will hasten to come to their assistance with all your galleys.[47]

Effectively, Philip was saying that Doria was to obey Colonna at his discretion, and was also reminding the papal admiral of his duties as hereditary constable of the kingdom of Naples.

Colonna had to wait two weeks for Doria, who in a deceitful letter of 16 August blamed the weather for his delay. Eventually the Spanish and papal squadrons were united on the 21st, and the two commanders held a conference to decide what next. The lanky, pointed-featured Doria contrasted starkly with the medium-height, roundish Colonna. The Genoese was not slow to point out the problems facing the allies: the strength of the Ottoman forces, the late season and the poor condition of the Venetian fleet. He suggested to remain in the Adriatic and also recall the Venetians from Crete, reminding the papal commander that his first duty was

---

* A quinquereme is a rowing vessel with five oars to each bench.

to preserve the king's galleys. Colonna was adamant about the need to join Zane, and Doria in the end gave in. In a letter intended for the viceroy of Sicily, the Genoese stated, 'I will try to preserve this fleet, but without some good excuse it will be difficult for me to avoid the accusation of not wanting to fight'.[48] The two squadrons departed slowly from Otranto, Doria not wishing to tire his crews and deliberately neglecting to take advantage of the favourable wind. Ten days later the allies joined forces in Souda, where Zane immediately summoned a war council. He informed his fellow commanders about the urgent need to relieve Nicosia, adding that the Ottomans could field only 150 galleys against the 200 of their enemies; besides, the firepower of the eleven Venetian galleasses was far superior to that of any Ottoman vessel. But Doria had already perceived that Zane was not a man of decision, and adroitly exploited the Venetian's doubts. His arguments for not engaging the enemy were the same he had used with Colonna, adding also that from Crete onward there were no havens where the fleet could find refuge. He asked for a rapid decision on the course of action to take, wanting to be in Sicily by the end of September.[49]

Doria was clearly employing delaying tactics, but had his reasons for doing so. Not only had Philip II ordered him not to put his galleys in harm's way, but the Genoese also had no intention of risking his own fortune in some reckless enterprise. Doria's twelve galleys were leased to the king of Spain for a yearly 72,000 ducats. In theory, Philip was supposed to pay one sixth of this every two months, the interest rate for any delayed payment being 14 per cent;[50] but the Spanish were notoriously cavalier with their debts, and Doria knew that he would have to meet any losses out of his own pocket.* In any case, the allies may have had an advantage in

---

* This situation was in fact more favourable than it may appear. Doria, like many Genoese naval entrepreneurs, exploited the king's lack of cash to get himself repaid in other ways: the concession of lucrative fiefs in southern Italy, enjoyment of custom revenues, commercial advantages and titles. I thank Dr Luca Lo Basso for this information.

ships, but the Ottomans were superior fighters. By recruiting or, as one contemporary put it, chasing men 'like hares'[51] in the Aegean islands, the Venetians had managed somewhat to make good their lack of personnel, but they were still woefully short of infantry. Colonna had 1,100 and Doria roughly 4,000 infantry, each of the Spanish and papal galleys boasting something less than 100 soldiers each, but on the Venetian vessels the fighting contingent numbered only eighty, many of them sailors. The Genoese admiral even accused the Venetians of misleading their allies about their real strength by constantly moving men from one galley to another. Zane was forced to disarm five galleys, distributing the men among the rest of his fleet. The Venetians were still battling with the epidemic that had hit them in Corfu, Zane complaining to his superiors in Venice about the fleet's desperate condition.[52]

The war council was split between those supporting Doria and others determined to seek battle with the Ottomans. Colonna had the support of the leader of the Neapolitan contingent, one of the most distinguished Spanish mariners of all time. Born Álvaro de Bazán in 1526, he had gone to sea at an early age, in 1544 fighting his first battle against a French corsair squadron. An expert in Atlantic as well as Mediterranean warfare, Bazán had participated in every major anti-Muslim expedition, including Malta and the Peñon de la Gomera. Given command of the Neapolitan squadron, in a short time he had made it a model of efficiency, and in 1569 Philip II in reward for his services elevated him to marquis of Santa Cruz.[53] With such support, Colonna had a field day belittling Doria's objections: the allies had numerical superiority, the Ottoman fleet being scattered along the coast of Cyprus; the season might have been advanced but there was still enough time to engage the Turks and return home; the Venetians had made good their losses, and in any case their rowers being free men could participate in a battle; as for havens, there were many in Cyprus, starting with Famagusta; finally, aiding the Venetians was not just obeying the pope and the king's will, but also a matter of honour.[54] The main parties involved in the debate did not limit themselves to spoken words, being also careful to circulate, in manuscript or print, their own version of events.* If not in agreement about how and when to fight the Ottomans, the allies were united in waging propaganda war against each other.

The debate about what to do was still raging in the middle of the month when Marco Querini, who had been sent to seek news of the situation in Cyprus, reported that Nicosia was still resisting and the Ottoman fleet dispersed amongst the island's havens. Forced to agree with his more bellicose colleagues that something had to be done to relieve Nicosia, Doria raved in a letter to Fernando d'Avalos, viceroy of Sicily, that Colonna was behaving 'as if he was born Venetian, and caring little for the king of Spain's fleet'. He added that if something was not accomplished by the end of the month he would return home – God protect him in the meantime – although he feared the weather more than the enemy.[55] On the 17th the allied fleet set sail towards the east, numbering 179 galleys, eleven galleasses, one galleon, and fourteen transport ships.† En route they received the dramatic news that Nicosia had fallen, and immediately a war council was convened to decide what to do. It was clear that with Nicosia taken the Ottomans would have many more soldiers on board their galleys, ruining the allies' chances of an easy victory. The mariners were also fearful of encountering bad weather out of reach of a haven sufficiently large to contain the whole fleet. Overruling Zane, who wished to continue on to Famagusta or at least try to capture some of the Ottoman fortresses in the area, the other commanders unanimously decided to return

---

* For instance, Doria's account dated 16 September on the uselessness of going to Cyprus enjoyed wide circulation. I have used the copy preserved in: AGF, *Miscellanea*, II, n. 24.

† The strength of the allied fleet varies according to source. Santa Cruz estimated that on 5 September the total number of galleys was 187: 126 Venetian, 49 Spanish, 12 Papal. AGS, *SE*, 1058, n. 108 (marquis of Santa Cruz to Philip II, 5 September 1570, from Crete). Yet, by the time the fleet set sail twelve days later, the Venetians had been forced to disarm a number of vessels; some sources also give Doria 45 and not 49 galleys. My estimate follows the breakdown given in: CONTARINI: 16r–19r. Give or take a few vessels, it is safe to say that the armada numbered roughly 200 ships of all kinds.

immediately to Crete.[56] As ill luck would have it, during the return journey the armada was hit by a storm, with the loss of a papal and a Venetian galley. Once again Doria aroused suspicions by insisting on keeping his own ships out at sea, and his colleagues acidly insinuated that he was seeking an excuse to return home. The Genoese retorted that he feared being bottled up, should the Ottoman fleet suddenly appear, but more likely he was concerned about the risk of infection from the Venetian crews.[57]

Doria was not just being difficult, for the Ottomans were well aware of the allies' plight. Around 20 August Piyale Pasha had sent five galliots to find out the Christians' whereabouts, and by interrogating some prisoners captured on the Cretan shore the Ottoman commander learnt of the epidemic that had hit the Venetian crews.[58] At the time the Venetians were still waiting in Corfu for their allies to appear, and on the strength of this intelligence Piyale felt confident enough to provide Lala Mustafa with the necessary troops for the storming of Nicosia. Doria feared a replay of Preveza and Djerba, and during the next war council he made known his intention to return home as soon as possible. When Colonna reminded him who was in command, the Genoese answered that he obeyed the king of Spain. During the subsequent verbal scuffle the Neapolitan Don Carlo d'Avalos insulted Colonna, who answered that henceforth he wanted nothing more to do with the Spanish contingent. Doria, who would later accuse Colonna 'of wanting to acquire honour in Cyprus with my goods',[59] was only too happy to oblige, although careful to keep his ships close to the rest of the fleet to avoid accusations of cowardice. The Genoese was partially vindicated when the allies ran into a violent squall while navigating towards Souda. More than twenty galleys ran aground, four of them belonging to Doria and two from the papal squadron. A number were eventually refloated, but it was clear that the autumn weather prevented any further major naval operations that year.

After spending a few days in Candia (Irakleio) Doria departed for good on 5 October, to everyone's chagrin and relief. Zane met Sebastiano Venier, recently arrived from Corfu, to discuss what to do next. Venier, following his usual bellicose approach, asked for a galley squadron, 4,000 men, equipment and 200 barrels of gunpowder to take to Famagusta. Zane, by now dispirited and sick, showed little inclination to grant his subordinate's requests, restricting himself to sending some ships to gather intelligence before retreating with the rest of his squadron towards Corfu. Marco Querini and Venier were left in Crete to put together the relief of Famagusta. Once in Corfu, Zane reviewed his fleet, disarming some thirty badly damaged galleys. He also sent a report to Venice justifying his actions over the last few months and asking to be relieved due to age and poor health. Venice was notorious for its ruthlessness when dealing with failure. Zane found himself dismissed from his post, arrested with a number of his subordinates, thrown into jail and put on trial for incompetence and corruption. He would die in prison two years later, still awaiting the final sentence.[60]

Piyale Pasha left Cyprus on 26 October in search of the allied fleet, capturing on his way one of the galleys sent by Zane to gather news on the Ottoman whereabouts.[61] Luckily for the allies, Piyale's ships were hit by a fierce north-west wind, forcing him to turn towards Constantinople. Colonna joined Zane in Corfu, where he gave back six of his galleys to the Venetians (now short of ships) before sailing up the Adriatic coast towards Ancona. Bad weather turned the voyage into a nightmare, forcing Colonna to spend weeks in port. Topping everything, while in Kotor his flagship, Fausto's quinquereme, was struck by lightning and blew up. Colonna managed to save his men, including those chained to the rowing benches, the papal standard and his papers, being the last to leave the burning galley. With what remained of his fleet he set sail again, only to be driven ashore by adverse winds three miles from Dubrovnik. The Ragusei helped him and his crew, refusing to turn them over to the Ottomans. Colonna returned to Rome at the beginning of February.[62] Due to indecision, divisions, disease, bad weather and ill luck, 1570 had been disastrous for the Christian cause, and given the discussions still going on in Rome it seemed that 1571 would be no better.

6. A LEAGUE OF MISTRUST

~

The allies' failure to relieve Nicosia produced a stream of bitter recriminations from all sides. Giovanni Andrea Doria was the target of criticism and accusations, Marcantonio Colonna writing to Philip II that the Genoese admiral had purposely distorted for his own personal interest the meaning of the king's orders in order to preserve the Spanish galleys. Pius V refused to receive Marcello Doria, who had arrived in Rome to plead on his relative's behalf. Instead, Pius sent Pompeo Colonna, Marcantonio's cousin, to Madrid to protest with Philip about Doria's behaviour. The king, however, diplomatically chose to approve Marcantonio's handling of the allied fleet, at the same time continuing to place his trust in the Genoese admiral. Colonna had managed to bring back only three of the papal galleys, a fact that his enemies were not slow to exploit. Cardinal Granvelle, for one, did not mince his words. He had been furious when informed about Philip's decision to place Doria under Colonna, 'saying very extravagant and inconsiderate things about the king and his ministers'. Granvelle felt vindicated by Colonna's mismanagement of the papal fleet, and when reminded of Philip's trust in the Roman nobleman, he ironically commented that the king could confide in his own sister but not for this reason entrust her with military affairs.[1]

Doria had also started his own propaganda campaign, his target being not just Colonna but also the Venetians. Although the Genoese felt he had done his duty towards Philip and his native city by behaving with the utmost caution during the campaign, his reputation was now at stake. What rankled with him most were the accusations of cowardice, negligence, self-seeking and ineptitude in naval matters which he suspected originated from Colonna and Santa Cruz. To counter such charges, in letters to various Spanish officials he would stress Colonna's systematic disregard of his advice which had put the Spanish fleet at risk to please the Venetians. Somewhat hypocritically he stated that the latter were to blame for the loss of Nicosia, having wasted time in Crete.[2]

By now it was common knowledge that Doria was the main culprit for the failure of the expedition, but the Venetians received their own share of criticism. An anonymous treatise of the time enumerated the mistakes committed by the Republic of St Mark in handling the war: incompetent diplomacy, disregard of Barbaro's warnings, faulty strategy, bad tactics, awful leadership, inadequate fortifications coupled with an insufficient number of professional soldiers; all these had allowed the Ottomans to take Nicosia and virtually the rest of Cyprus while Venice had lost men, artillery pieces and the substantial revenues from the island's salt pans. The treatise ended on the pessimistic note that the change of Venetian commanders was not likely to solve much, given that both Venier and his deputy Agostino Barbarigo were inexperienced in military and naval matters.[3] The author of this tirade was informed only to a point, but the circulation of such writings did nothing to help the Christian cause.

On the diplomatic front there had been little progress since the summer. The Spanish were still insisting that the pope grant the requested ecclesiastical subsidies before committing themselves to a formal alliance with Venice. They also had other requests, deriving from their suspicions about Venetian trustworthiness. Everyone knew that despite his confinement Marcantonio Barbaro was in contact with the Ottoman authorities, and that the Venetians, worried by the increasing costs of the war and the loss of trade with the east, were ready to reach an agreement with the Ottomans at the drop of a hat. The Spanish therefore asked that the treaty of alliance also stipulate automatic excommunication for any member who should agree to a separate peace with the Turks. The Venetians vigorously rejected this request, arguing that such a clause would give the impression that loyalty to the Christian cause derived only from fear of ecclesiastical censure. They also opposed as unnecessary the Spanish request that fifty galleys be permanently stationed off the Barbary coast to protect Spain's territories, since an attack on one of the allies would cause the others to come to his aid. Finally, the Venetians asked that all grain destined for the allied fleet should be exempt, at least in part, from taxation. Philip's answer to the Venetian points was mixed. He agreed that the excommunication proviso was inappropriate but at the same time insisted that Tunis, Tripoli and Algiers were legitimate targets. After all, the Spanish had sent their galleys to the Levant, so it was only right that now the Venetians should help Spain against the Muslim states of North Africa. As for the grain, the king promised to price it in such a way as to limit his treasury's losses.[4] The negotiations had reached a dead end, and this situation appeared unlikely to change at any time in the near future.

These developments – or the lack of them – in Rome were followed with extreme interest in European diplomatic circles. Ever since receiving his grand ducal title from the pope, Cosimo I de' Medici had been trying to get back in the Habsburgs' graces and have them recognize his new status. Devious as always, Cosimo was playing a risky triangular game between Madrid, Paris and Rome. By using the veiled threat of switching his allegiance from Philip II to the French king Charles IX, he hoped to get the Spanish to intercede in his favour with the Holy Roman Emperor. France's recognition of him as grand duke of Tuscany certainly pleased Cosimo, yet he had to tread carefully so as not to alarm Spain too much, lest Philip should decide to curb by force of arms his recalcitrant vassal's ambitions. The grand duke fully understood France's wish to play once more an active part in Italy's affairs, but was also aware of the perils of a Valois embrace, not least because many in Florence considered his cousin Catherine de' Medici to have a better claim to the city's lordship — something Catherine herself never forgot.[5]

The negotiations to create an anti–Ottoman league provided Cosimo with a golden opportunity to increase his prestige on the international scene by making himself indispensable to one of the parties. But Venice, although eager for allies, was not interested in the Medici. The duke of Savoy was out of the game, Emmanuel Philibert having too many problems with his own Protestant subjects. Besides, the Spanish were concerned that any assertion of the house of Savoy's old claims on Cyprus would upset the Venetians. Emmanuel Philibert, however, denied he wished to assert any such claim and agreed to put his three galleys at the league's disposal. Venice tried to gain the support of the Holy Roman Emperor, since having Maximilian II in the league would force the Ottomans to concentrate their military efforts in Hungary rather than Cyprus. But Maximilian was still fuming over Cosimo's title and had no sympathy for Pius V, whom he described as 'the impertinent bishop of Rome'. Indeed, he was so incensed by the pope's behaviour, considering it an infringement of his rights to contemplate an invasion of Italy with the backing of Germany's Protestant princes, Maximilian himself having an unabashed liking for the reformed religion. He had no intention of going to war with Selim II, having just signed the Peace of Edirne, and knew perfectly well the difficulties involved in raising a sufficiently large army. Besides, he calculated that a league made up of states with such diverse interests would not last long. Still, as the nominal head of Christendom he could not openly refuse to join the alliance without losing face, maintaining nevertheless that it would be unbecoming to renege on the solemn treaty just signed with the infidels.[6] However, in the early months of 1571 the Venetians were still hoping that Maximilian would change his mind, although worried that the inclusion of Tuscany in the alliance would sabotage their efforts at the imperial court.

Cosimo knew that he could not count on Philip II's support, the king being firmly opposed to his presence in the league. But Cosimo was also aware of Philip's need to obtain ecclesiastical subsidies, and that Tuscany possessed a commodity that Pius V desperately needed but had difficulty in obtaining – namely a fleet. The grand duke had been trying to renegotiate with Philip a more favourable *asiento* for his galleys, but now offered them to Pius V. Cosimo was careful to ask for Madrid's approval before agreeing to a deal; and since the pope himself had requested Tuscany's galleys, he could claim he was only acting in the interests of Christendom.[7]

Pius had already tried unsuccessfully to obtain a functioning fleet elsewhere, but with no result. Finding galleys as such was no problem – many states could provide those. But keeping ships running involved considerable logistical capabilities that the papal states did not have. All the pope's attempts to find 'cash-and-carry' galleys had failed thanks to Spain's meddling. Philip needed Pius to depend exclusively on him for his fleet, in order to obtain the *cruzada* and the other subsidies, there being no greedy papal nephews to whom to give pensions in exchange for the pontiff's favour. As a token of goodwill – and to stop anyone else from doing the same – Philip had ordered his half-brother Don Juan of Austria to keep a few galleys at the pontiff's disposal in the papal port of Civitavecchia, north of Rome. Unfortunately, the revolt of the Moriscos and fear of an Ottoman invasion had forced Philip to concentrate his fleet in the western Mediterranean, leaving the Roman coast open to Muslim attacks. Knowing that the pope would look elsewhere for a fleet, the king tried to convince him to conclude an *asiento* with Genoa or the Hospitallers, both firm Spanish allies. But Pius rejected the Genoese, believing that they armed galleys only for commercial reasons; as for the Knights of St John, the distance between Malta and Rome was a serious handicap.[8] For his fleet, the pope now could only turn to Venetians, who had their own problems, or Florence.

It was clear by now that Philip only favoured an alliance which catered to Spain's needs, but the king had to act carefully lest the pope decide to move ahead without the Spanish – Pius being quite capable of doing so – and, God forbid, refuse to concede the renewal of the Three Graces. Philip was trying not to irritate the pope but also buy time so that, should the planned league see the light of day, it would be too late to implement the dreaded 'general enterprise' – as the king called the expedition to the Levant. It would take a long time to prepare the ships and the men for such an expedition, and the protracted delays could eventually result in a military expedition in North Africa. There was also another reason for being cautious: the insistent rumours of peace negotiations between Venice and the Porte.[9]

~

At the start of 1571 the Venetian fleet in Corfu was in a miserable state. Many ships were still under repair, the typhoid epidemic had not yet abated, and to make matters worse the new captain-general Sebastiano Venier was bedridden with phlebitis. But in Crete things were moving, thanks to the energy of the *provveditore* Marco Querini. Discovering that the Ottoman fleet was wintering in Constantinople, with only a dozen galleys remaining to support the army besieging Famagusta, Querini decided that now was the best time to strike. Taking thirteen of the galleys left by Zane to guard Crete the previous year, the *provveditore* set sail for Famagusta on 16 January accompanied by four round-ships loaded with men and munitions. En route one of the galleys had to be sent back because its disease-ridden crew could not keep up with the others, but this did not deter Querini. On the 26th he came in sight of Famagusta, moving his galleys near to the shore before ordering the round-ships to make a dash for the harbour. When eight Ottoman vessels stationed in Costanza, six miles north of Famagusta, tried to intercept them, they were hit in the flank by Querini's galleys. Taken by surprise the Ottomans made for the shore, losing three galleys sent to the bottom, the shot-up survivors seeking refuge under the cover of the guns of a makeshift fort Laca Mustafa had built to protect Costanza. The victorious Querini entered Famagusta harbour with the round-ships in tow, to the rejoicing of the local populace. Not satisfied, the *provveditore* spent the next few days in raids, destroying the fort of Costanza and capturing various enemy vessels. He departed on 16 February, the reinforcements of men, munitions and victuals helping to boost the defenders' morale despite the fact that the quality and quantity (1,319) of the new soldiers left much to be desired. Now Famagusta's garrison numbered 8,000 infantry, including professionals and militia, and 100 horse.[10] With these forces and plentiful supplies Marcantonio Bragadin felt that he could resist until a bigger relief force arrived the following spring.

When news of Querini's exploit reached Constantinople, heads rolled – literally. Like the Venetians, the Ottomans were not inclined to forgive those who had failed. *Pour encourager les autres*, the bey of Chios was beheaded and that of Rhodes deprived of his command. Piyale Pasha shared the latter's fate, although he retained his place in the *dîvân*, and responsibility for all naval operations was assigned to the *kapudan paşa*, Müezzinzâde Ali. The Ottoman admiral, winter notwithstanding, immediately dispatched one of his subordinates with twenty galleys to Cyprus with orders to stop any other Venetian attempt to relieve Famagusta. Ali himself departed a month later, gathering reinforcements for Lala Mustafa. Once in Cypriot waters, he organized a ferry system to transport men and munitions from the Anatolian mainland to the island.[11] Everything was ready for resuming military operations against Famagusta, the Ottoman commanders hoping the city would fall like Nicosia to the sheer weight of their army.

Things were also moving on the diplomatic front. Querini's expedition had proved that the Venetians were not lacking fighting spirit, and with Nicosia in Ottoman hands the grand vizier considered it appropriate to start negotiations. For the Ottomans the war was not proceeding as expected, while for the Venetians it represented a colossal expense. In Constantinople Sokollu did not discount the worrying possibility that the Christian states might set aside their petty quarrels and ally themselves against the Ottomans.

An added risk for the Ottomans was that after the death of the *voivode* of Transylvania John Sigismund, war could erupt again in central Europe. The last thing the grand vizier wanted was another front before the Cyprus question was closed for good. He may also have considered that the peaceful surrender of Famagusta would enhance his prestige and damage that of his rival Lala Mustafa. Sokollu desired peace, and the Venetians needed it. Their fleet lacked rowers, fighting men and victuals. The famine which had plagued the republic's territory for the previous two years was causing serious manpower problems, and forcing Venice to raise the wages of those soldiers destined for the Levant 'so that being able to provide to their needs with greater ease, they will more willingly and readily serve us'.[12]

To attain his objective the grand vizier played his hand skilfully, counting also on his French allies. The Valois had everything to gain by brokering a settlement between the Venetians and the Porte, and much to lose if the pope, Venice and Spain consolidated their alliance. The French, particularly Catherine de' Medici, feared that the league would strengthen the Habsburgs' grip on the Italian peninsula. Many saw Spain as the only real bulwark against the Ottomans, a belief that Philip II had no interest in changing by reducing the Turkish threat. Given that Venice was the only completely independent polity left in Italy – if one excludes the papal states – it was in Spain's interest to see the republic weakened by a prolonged war with the Ottomans. France wanted the exact opposite, and in an effort to separate Venice from her potential allies Charles IX even promised to supply the republic with military aid should the Ottomans refuse to make peace. Predictably, the Venetians were unconvinced, aware of the strong political and commercial ties between Paris and Constantinople.[13]

The grand vizier chose to make the first move, banking on the Venetians' exhaustion and their suspicion that the league Pius so much desired would never come into being. Since the need to save face made it impossible for Sokollu to start direct peace talks, another way had to be found. Conveniently enough, a Jew had arrived in Constantinople from Venice, bringing with him some useful news. At the outbreak of hostilities a number of Ottoman subjects in Venice – Muslims and Jews residing there for commercial reasons – had been rounded up, imprisoned and their merchandise seized. One of the prisoners had managed to escape – perhaps with the help of the Venetian authorities, as skilled as Sokollu in dancing the diplomatic tango – and on his arrival in Constantinople petitioned the sultan to secure the release of his unfortunate colleagues.[14] This was exactly the excuse that Sokollu needed to approach the Venetians, and he acted on it immediately.

Around the end of January Sokollu's envoy, the dragoman Mateca Salvego, arrived in Venice accompanied by Marcantonio Barbaro's personal administrator (*maestro di casa*). Officially his mission was to obtain the liberation of those Ottoman subjects held in custody by the republic in exchange for the Venetians detained in Constantinople, but in reality he had come to start unofficial peace talks. When Mateca in his master's name asked the republic to send a negotiator to the Porte, the Venetians reacted with caution, but like Sokollu wasted no time in sending an envoy to the enemy capital. The man chosen for the job was Giacomo Ragazzoni, who possessed the double advantages of being a merchant and the brother of the bishop of Famagusta. Ragazzoni's task was to negotiate the exchange of the imprisoned subjects of the two states, but he also received instructions to sound out Sokollu about a possible peace treaty. Ragazzoni's mission immediately became the subject of much diplomatic gossip, and even if its real objective was only a matter of speculation, an acute observer like the papal nuncio Facchinetti rightly suspected monkey business on the Venetians' part.[15]

Ragazzoni departed from Venice on 11 March, arriving in Constantinople six weeks later. Sokollu received him on 29 April, the two men engaging in a diplomatic fencing match. The Venetian stated that he had only come to settle the matter of the imprisoned subjects and wished to brief Barbaro about it before negotiations could start. Sokollu, who had been informed by his intelligence service about the true nature of Ragazzoni's mission, answered by reminding him of Venice's mistake in wanting to fight. He added that now the sultan also wanted Crete and Corfu 'since the Muslims believe the prophecy that they must be the lords of Rome, it was necessary for the Turks to conquer Venetian territories that would allow [them] to get nearer [to that city]'. As for an exchange of their respective subjects, some Ottoman Jews had protested that the Venetians had sold their confiscated goods for low prices to finance the war. Sokollu also commented obliquely that for such matters it was not necessary to inform the *bailo*, unless Ragazzoni's real purpose was to seek peace between Venice and the Porte. Should that be the case, the grand vizier would be happy to mention it to Selim.

The Venetian envoy stuck to his guns, insisting that he could decide nothing before speaking to Barbaro, adding also that all Ottoman subjects had been well treated by the republic and that the money gained from the sale of perishable goods (with the owners' approval) was in safe storage. Sokollu then went back to the topic of the war, asking how the Venetians could hope to win against the sultan's military machine. Ragazzoni retorted that the Ottomans had started hostilities with no justifiable reason and that Venice had the means to fight back; besides, the republic was about to sign an alliance with other Christian sovereigns and this united front could very well turn the tide of war against the Ottomans. This was the last thing Sokollu wanted to hear, and he angrily called the Venetians fools to place their trust in a league that would most certainly founder. In any case, he retorted, the Ottomans would win because God was on their side. Diplomatically, the envoy answered that any victory was the Almighty's doing. The conference broke up, apparently without accomplishing anything; but Ragazzoni returned to his lodgings convinced that the grand vizier was 'most inclined to peace'.[16]

On 2 May Ragazzoni went to visit Barbaro in Pera, being treated en route to the sight of the Ottoman fleet in full array. The grand vizier had organized the spectacle in an attempt to cow the

Venetian, but the latter appeared unimpressed by the show of force. Ragazzoni and Barbaro agreed to ask Sokollu for another audience to discuss the exchange of prisoners and, possibly, the preliminaries for a peace agreement. On 7 May the meeting took place, this time with Barbaro in attendance, followed by another on the 16th. On both occasions Sokollu ably alternated honeyed words with threats, while the Venetians adroitly avoided being cornered. It became clear that peace between Venice and Constantinople would not be accomplished easily. Sokollu was adamant in demanding the whole of Cyprus – Ragazzoni having proposed the Venetians keep Famagusta as a trading base – plus an indemnity of 750,000 ducats; otherwise the Venetians should carefully watch their other territories, including their capital, because the Ottomans would surely conquer them.[17]

The grand vizier's obduracy was partially due to Selim's stubbornness and the intrigues of the war faction at court, but also to the Transylvanian crisis having evaporated, and with it the peril of Maximilian II and the Poles siding with the Venetians. The Ottomans now had their hands free to deal with Cyprus. Venice was also in a belligerent mood. On 7 May the senate wrote to Barbaro and Ragazzoni about the developments in Transylvania and the arrival in the city of Marcantonio Colonna to advocate the conclusion of the Christian alliance. The Venetians were also elated by the news of anti-Ottoman revolts in Albania, allowing them to capture Durazzo (Durrës). Given the militarily favourable situation, the two envoys in Constantinople were in no mood to cede Famagusta, nor agree to any sort of peace settlement without Venice's authorization.[18] Ragazzoni would receive such instructions only on 17 June while about to depart for home, but by then events had moved at a quicker pace than diplomatic messengers. Neither the Porte nor Venice now had much interest in a peace settlement, each expecting the situation to change in its favour. As for Ragazzoni, having negotiated the exchange of prisoners there was supposedly nothing more for him to do in Constantinople. In this endeavour at least he had been successful, although the sultan, apparently encouraged by Joseph Nassi, insisted that the Venetians be the first to free their detainees and ship them with their goods to Dubrovnik or Zara. On the 18th Ragazzoni took his final leave of Sokollu, leaving Barbaro to wait out the rest of the war in confinement.

~

While the Venetian envoys were busy negotiating in Constantinople, things had moved ahead in Rome. Philip II had already made sure – should the alliance ever materialize – that the general of the Christian fleet would be Don Juan of Austria, and at the beginning of 1571 the king's half-brother was officially designated commander-in-chief of the coalition's forces. Yet many had reservations about the choice, worried by the appointee's age, inexperience and above all his notorius rashness. The twenty-four-year-old Don Juan, son of Charles V and the Bavarian beauty Barbara Blomberg, was a dashing, almost reckless individual blessed with culture and grace. Educated in Spain on his father's orders, he was a model of sportsmanship and gallantry. He had been received into Philip's court at twelve, growing up with the heir to the throne, the unfortunate Don Carlos, and the future duke of Parma Alessandro Farnese, destined to become one of the greatest military leaders of the sixteenth century. Philip had restrained with difficulty the then eighteen-year-old Don Juan from joining the Malta relief force in 1565, and the king was weary of his relative's energy and audacity. These traits coupled with exceptional good looks made Don Juan a great favourite with the ladies; the prince fathered a number of illegitimate children. Predictably, when Philip appointed him commander of his Mediterranean fleet in 1568, he kept Don Juan on a tight leash. Even now the king would ensure that the new commander of the allied fleet was surrounded by cooler, more experienced heads. After all, Don Juan's military experience was limited to the Morisco campaign, and the Ottomans were a rather more formidable foe.[19]

The selection of a second-in-command proved more problematic. The Spanish representatives tried to impose someone of their king's choosing, but Pius and the Venetians would have none of it. The problem was not just one of national prestige; since the first of the planned league's objectives was ostensibly the relief of Famagusta, the Venetians wanted someone committed to this venture. The pope wanted his trusted Marcantonio Colonna for the job, but this was anathema to Cardinal Granvelle. Philip II, not wishing to alienate Pius, sent to Rome a list of acceptable candidates, including Colonna, topping his roll with Alessandro Farnese, the duke of Urbino, the marquis of Pescara and the duke of Mantua. It was a clear, not to say unsubtle, attempt to force Pius to change his mind, but the aged Pontiff didn't budge: it would be Colonna or nobody. Granvelle and Pacheco, already dragging their heels, slowed down the negotiations to a snail's pace. Determined to have their way, they asked Cardinal Colonna, Marcantonio's cousin and namesake, to convince the pope to be more malleable: if Pius insisted on Marcantonio's candidacy, then the league had no future; the pontiff should agree that his protégé be appointed instead as commander of amphibious operations in the event of Don Juan's absence. Cardinal Colonna politely told his colleagues to get lost, adding that it was not his business to advise Pius on military appointments.[20] The pope's obstinacy was a source of much irritation in Madrid, Cardinal Espinosa acidly commenting that the pontiff should limit himself to prayers and encouragements and not meddle in military matters – a fine example of the pot calling the kettle black. Pius, however, was flexible enough to agree that Philip appoint Colonna as Don Juan's deputy, on condition that the Roman nobleman enjoy the supreme commander's full authority in his absence.[21]

Deciding the chain of command was but one problem, the road towards final agreement being fraught with every kind of difficulty. By mid-March 1571 it even appeared that the league might be stillborn, Granvelle insisting that the Spanish fleet would not be ready for operations in the Levant until the following year. The cardinal's objective was clear: to force the pope and the Venetians to agree to an operation against Tunis some time late that summer, when the Ottoman fleet would not be in a position to interfere. Even more enraging for the other negotiators was the Spanish representatives' brazen proposal that Venice provide and pay for all the ships necessary for the enterprise against subsequent reimbursement.[22] Given Spain's notorious record of insolvency, the Venetians felt insulted and threatened to break off negotiations.

The Spanish representatives' constant duplicity has an immoral ring to it, but one should sympathize with Philip II's reluctance to commit himself to the Cyprus enterprise. Spain considered its Mediterranean frontier to coincide with an imaginary but relatively defensible line running from Corfu to Tripoli; anything east of that mattered little, unless directly affecting southern Italy, Malta or the Iberian peninsula. Besides, as we have already seen, Philip's strategic–religious priorities lay elsewhere, and these were becoming a source of increasing worry to him.

Tensions with England were growing, the English resenting Spain's policy in Flanders for a number of reasons. Elizabeth I had become a champion of Protestantism, giving refuge and assistance to Dutch rebels, and the English trading community considered the Flemish market vital to its interests. In London there was also concern about the rise of a hegemonic power on the other side of the Channel, something England has always resolutely tried to avoid. By the end of the 1560s Elizabeth was already a nuisance, seizing Spanish ships in English waters and attempting to disrupt Habsburg trade in the New World. Retaliation followed, as resentment on both sides grew. But despite Philip commenting in 1570 that England and Spain were 'nearly in a state of war',[23] he was trying not to alienate the English to the point of throwing them into the arms of the French. For this reason he was angered by Pius's decision that same year to excommunicate Elizabeth, although the pope had correctly perceived that by then the queen was committed to the Protestant cause. The troubles brewing in northern Europe were a greater concern to Spain than the war in the eastern Mediterranean, and Philip was all too aware that a prolonged

Levantine campaign would be a serious drain on his military and monetary resources.[24]

However, neither the pope nor the king wanted the alliance negotiations to fail. If Pius was primarily motivated by religious zeal, Philip was anxious not to lose face and, even more important, the long-awaited ecclesiastical revenues. Philip reiterated an old offer to provide 50,000 troops plus the necessary munitions and supplies for the sea expedition, promising also to have some eighty or so galleys ready by the end of May. Venice was asked to provide the greater part of the remaining ships. The Venetians were unconvinced by these proposals, not trusting the king to deliver by the agreed time. The Spanish, for their part, knew about the Venetians' talks with the Ottomans, and the pacifist lobby within the Venetian senate was growing by the day. Unless something concrete was accomplished soon, the only treaty to materialize would be a humiliating deal between the Republic of St Mark and the Porte. Nuncio Facchinetti was doing his best to convince the senate about the perils of an agreement with the Ottomans, fully aware that the Venetians were sitting on the fence. Many senators were convinced that, even if the alliance materialized, the Spanish galleys would not be ready in May. In the meantime a deal could be reached with the Porte, using the league as a bogey; alternatively Venice could threaten an agreement with the Ottomans to obtain better terms in Rome.

To add extra weight to his diplomatic endeavours, in April Pius sent Marcantonio Colonna to Venice. Initially the Roman nobleman's pleadings cut little ice with the senators, to the point where the pope decided he would call his envoy back at the end of the month, 'remitting to the Lord God's will the decisions that the other princes will make'.[25] Undaunted, Colonna pressed on, using his personal connections to bring the senators over to his side one by one. He was also not slow to remind the Venetians that he, unlike Doria, had not abandoned them during the previous campaign. In the end his efforts were rewarded, on 23 April the senate voting to continue negotiations for the league. But the Venetians wanted guarantees before going ahead, telling Colonna that they wished the pope to allow them to tax ecclesiastical property to help their war effort. Philip was, among other things, to provide the promised fully equipped eighty galleys by the end of May and open a surety account somewhere in Italy to contribute to the alliance's financial needs.[26]

The Spanish knew the Venetians would need their support for any major enterprise in the Levant. The same was also true of Pius, and Colonna's mismanagement of the papal galleys meant that the pope would have to rely on someone else for his fleet. This played squarely into the hands of Cosimo I de' Medici. The grand duke was still trying to get involved in the putative league, counting on the support of Cardinal Pacheco to overrule Madrid's objections. But the Spanish were dead set against Cosimo's participation, although Philip wrote to Zuñiga to act prudently and not irritate the Florentine. Instead he should stick to vague promises about allowing Cosimo into the alliance some time later without attempting to prolong the negotiations further. The grand duke was himself anxious that the league should see the light of day, instructing his ambassador in Madrid Leonardo de' Nobili to insist to Philip that he speed things up. Should the Turks get wind of the league, they would react by assembling more troops and ships; and seeing no move coming from the Christians, would use these forces to attack the West. Worse, should the Venetians get tired of Spain's procrastination, they were sure to strike a deal with the Porte, leaving the Muslims to turn their attention to Italy.[27] Cosimo, of course, was trying to convince Philip that since the Ottoman peril threatened everyone, it would be illogical to exclude Tuscany from the league.

Not being able to enter by the front door, the grand duke used the back one. He had already offered his galleys to the pope the year before, obtaining Philip's approval on condition that the ships be employed only in the Levant. Pius, however, wanted them also to guard his coasts – something the Spanish had failed to do – but for prudence's sake Cosimo would initially not agree to this without

Philip's approval. In the end, not receiving any answer on the matter, the grand duke decided to go ahead. The negotiations between Florence and Rome over the galleys took three months, the main discussions between the Tuscan and papal plenipotentiaries concerning the price to be paid per vessel, their captains and the appointment of the squadron's deputy commander. Thanks to the mediation of Marcantonio Colonna it was agreed that Cosimo would nominate ten of the twelve captains and provide all other officers, oarsmen and sailors. Colonna would provide the soldiers, something that the papal admiral, with an eye to his own authority within the fleet, was more than willing to do. The choice of second-in-command proved more difficult, Pius wanting to reserve the decision to himself. In this he was backed by the Spanish and Colonna himself, for different reasons both wishing to diminish as much as possible Cosimo's control over his galleys. The grand duke proved amenable to the pope's request, keen as he was to conclude the *asiento*. Although the main points of the treaty had been settled by the end of April, more weeks would pass before the final agreement. Pius and Cosimo were waiting to see if the negotiations over the league would be fruitful, otherwise Madrid would not approve the leasing to the pope of the Tuscan galleys. Punctilious as always, Pius promised that in such a case he would ask Philip to pay for the Medicean vessels. The *asiento* was finally signed on 11 May, the pope obtaining twelve galleys from Cosimo but with the obligation to pay for only six. Pius still had to meet the cost of the soldiery on board, and certain logistical details took further months of discussion.[28] Still, both parties had gained what they desired: the pope, a fleet costing him only 3,250 ducats a month (500 ducats each for five galleys and 750 for the flagship); Cosimo, an unofficial place in the league.

Pius's acquisition of the Tuscan galleys and Venice's endorsement of the league cornered Philip. The pope had already threatened to revoke all existing concessions on ecclesiastical revenues should the Spanish continue with their delaying tactics – a serious blow, and not just financial, for the king. If losing hundreds of thousands of ducats was a nightmarish prospect, the loss of face for the champion of Christendom would be even worse.[29] The Venetians, however, were stretched to the limit and badly needed Spain's help to protect their remaining Levantine possessions. The Florentine envoy in Rome Piero Usimbardi was convinced that the Venetians had run out of resources and were eager for peace with the Ottomans, fearful of losing Crete as well as Cyprus.[30] There were still to be disagreements, but once the delegates reconvened in Rome at the beginning of May, everyone had the feeling that the league was a done deal. Cardinal Granvelle's absence – in the meantime he had been sent to Naples as viceroy – eased the process considerably. Up to the very end the Venetians haggled over their monetary contribution, while the Spanish moaned that, given their other military commitments in Europe, they were already financially overstretched.[31] By the 19th everything had been settled, and two days later the pope granted the much-desired Three Graces. Although neither Philip II nor the doge would sign it for a couple of months, on 25 May the treaty establishing the Holy League was signed by Pius V for the papacy, Cardinal Pacheco and Don Juan de Zuñiga for Spain, and Michele Surian and Giovanni Soranzo for Venice.

According to the terms of the agreement the league, with its declared aim of fighting the Ottomans and their allies Tripoli, Tunis and Algiers, was to be maintained in perpetuity. Its military forces were to comprise 200 galleys, 100 other ships, 50,000 infantry, 4,500 light cavalrymen, artillery, munitions and other war materiel. Strategic objectives were to be designated each autumn for the following spring, the traditional start of every campaign season. The pope was to provide twelve galleys, 3,300 infantry and horse and one-sixth of all expenses; should the Holy See be unable to meet its bill, this would be divided between Spain (three-fifths), with Venice providing the remaining two-fifths by arming twenty-four galleys. Victuals were to be provided in abundance by each of the participants at an 'honest price'. Articles VIII to XII dealt with the possible use of the league's forces against North Africa or to defend its members' lands against enemy attack. In addition, the Spanish obtained the right, in the absence of any threatening Ottoman naval or land force, to request fifty fully equipped Venetian galleys to use against the Barbary states. As a quid pro quo, Venice could ask for the same support from the Spanish for operations on the Adriatic coast. All strategic and tactical decisions were to be taken by the commanders of the three fleets and executed by the commander-in-chief Don Juan of Austria or, in his absence, by his deputy Marcantonio Colonna. However, 'for any particular enterprise' it would be up to Don Juan to designate the officer in charge. Pius was made arbiter of all future disputes, and the allies promised to uphold Dubrovnik's neutrality 'unless for some reason the pope should judge otherwise'. No member could make a separate peace with the Porte without the knowledge and consent of the others. The last article was an invitation to the kings of France, Poland and Portugal to join the league, together with 'all the Christian princes'.[32]

To a greater or lesser degree the treaty satisfied everyone. The Spanish had obtained the inclusion of North Africa among the league's targets, while the Venetians could be happy that the main effort would be directed against the Ottomans. They also got the pope to grant them 100,000 ducats per year for five years of the tithes owed to the Church by the Venetian clergy. Yet some matters remained vague. For instance, Article V stated that the league's forces should receive priority in the distribution of victuals, but that the king of Spain had the right to look after his own states, plus the needs of the island of Malta and La Goleta. It would be easy for Philip to exploit such a loophole to blackmail the other members, the famine that had hit Italy the previous two years making many states dependent on Spanish and Sicilian grain. As we shall see, the provisioning of the allied navy would be one of the bones of contention.

The ink on the treaty was hardly dry when problems started. Philip had taken badly the pope consorting with the Medici, and as soon as the negotiations for the league were over he delivered an official protest over the concession of the grand ducal title to Cosimo. The Spanish move blighted the enthusiasm and rejoicing that had followed the league's proclamation, creating considerable tension between Madrid and the Holy See as well as arousing Pius's ire. The pope believed that Philip had deceived him, first extorting the ecclesiastical subsidies and only then issuing his protest. Pius even threatened to withdraw from the league, adding that Don Juan's arrival in Italy was probably to wage war on Tuscany and not on the Ottomans. In the end, thanks also to the mediation of Cardinal Ferdinando de' Medici, Cosimo's son, Pius agreed to receive Zuñiga with his sovereign's protest.

The Tuscans clearly had every reason to pour oil on the troubled diplomatic waters, concerned as they were that Philip might wish to reclaim Siena by force. To be on the safe side, an embittered Cosimo fortified his territories, raised professional troops and called up the militia. He even threatened to switch his allegiance from Spain to France, but it was clear to everyone that, given the Valois' internal problems with their Protestant subjects, this was not a real possibility. Cosimo also attempted a more conciliatory approach to Philip through his friend Pacheco. But, when, at the end of July Don Juan arrived in Genoa the Florentines' fear of Spanish invasion reached a feverish pitch, aided by a prophecy circulating at the time about the Medici losing Florence that very year.[33] But Philip had no interest in starting another Italian war, preferring to humiliate his slippery vassal in some other less expensive way and avoid the repercussions that a military action against Tuscany would most certainly provoke.

~

The alliance's immediate ostensible objective was the relief of Famagusta, where the beleaguered Venetian garrison was putting up a stiff fight.[34] The Ottomans had tried to take the city immediately after the fall of Nicosia, but Marcantonio Bragadin and his deputy Astorre Baglioni* were determined to resist. Famagusta's state-of-

* Since in the sources of the time he is also called Baglione, it should be pointed out that individuals were often identified by the singular version of their surnames.

the-art fortifications, designed by the celebrated architect Sammi-cheli, allowed for a prolonged siege. The walls, nearly three miles long, were reinforced with bastions, towers and earthworks, and surmounted by forts known as 'cavaliers' dominating the seafront and the surrounding countryside. In addition, the city was ringed by a deep, water-filled moat. An initial bombardment had produced little effect, the distance of the Ottoman guns from the walls not allowing for concentrated fire. Moreover, since Famagusta was built close to the sea mining proved a difficult task, and turned out in addition the besiegers were constantly harassed by sorties from the garrison. In the first three weeks of October the Venetians executed a number of attacks against the still-incomplete Ottoman siege lines, destroying trenches and redoubts before retreating to Famagusta with minimal casualties. But with the arrival of more enemy troops these sorties became more difficult to perform, forcing the defenders to limit their attacks to Ottoman troops caught in the open. At the beginning of November, having failed to obtain the city's surrender by a show of force, Lala Mustafa decided to postpone any further assault to the following spring, hoping that dwindling supplies would force the defenders to give in without too much fighting.

Provveditore Querini's daring relief expedition in January stiffened the defenders' resolve and subverted Mustafa's plans. He had placed his camp to the south-west of the city, strengthened his siege lines throughout the winter and executed some probing attacks to keep the garrison under pressure. The Venetians stood their ground, on one occasion inflicting considerable losses on the enemy by luring them into a well-prepared trap. The Ottomans were made to believe that the defenders had left en masse with Querini's fleet, only to be subjected to a hail of bullets, coupled with a cavalry charge, when they approached the walls. But everyone was aware that the Turks could easily make good their losses, having the double advantage of practically unlimited supplies of men and the proximity of their supply bases. As for the defenders, they could only hope that the relief force, should there be one, would arrive in time.

At the end of March the Ottomans received considerable reinforcements together with some extra artillery pieces from Nicosia. Preparing for the inevitable, Bragadin and Baglioni did everything they could to husband their meagre forces. Their first move was to expel from the city all 'useless mouths', their number varying, according to the source, from 3,500 to 5,500. The Ottomans, seeking to undermine the resolve of the city's defenders, allowed these people safe passage through their lines after providing them with victuals. The Venetian commanders' decision had been taken mainly for reasons of morale; the suffering of women, children and the aged would have imposed additional psychological strain on the defenders and perhaps hastened capitulation. All foodstuffs were listed and a strict rationing regime introduced.

Mustafa was hoping that the daunting size of his army – 240,000-strong according to Angelo Gatto★ – would induce the garrison to surrender. On 17 April he organized a general review of all his forces some three miles from the city in full view of the defenders. The Ottomans believed to be out of range of Famagusta's artillery, but Mustafa had not reckoned with the Venetian gunners; Baglioni ordered two 120-pound pieces to be loaded and aimed at the enemy mass. Just as the Ottoman commander was riding in front of his arrayed army, the guns fired. A number of shots landed among the packed troops, doing considerable damage and bringing the review to an abrupt end. The biggest loss was Mustafa's face, making him even more determined to solve the Famagusta problem as soon as possible.

This was easier said than done. Over the following months the Venetians displayed an uncanny ability to thwart the Ottomans' attempts to bring the siege to a rapid close. Following standard practice, the Turks dug trenches, built artillery redoubts and slowly advanced towards the walls, harassed by the defenders' sorties and

---

★ An Ottoman hostage gave this number to Gatto at the time of the negotiations for the city's surrender. GATTO: 54–7. The Ottomans were known for their ability to field and supply large forces, so we should be careful not to dismiss the figure as fantasy.

constant shooting. Scores of besiegers died each day, but inexorably the Ottomans advanced to the fortress counterscarp. Under cover of loopholed earthworks they sniped at the Venetians on top of the walls. Gun emplacements were built to house some eighty artillery pieces, including a couple of giant 180-pounder 'basilisks'. On 19 May the Ottomans subjected the city to an intense cannonade, to which the Venetians answered with equally forceful counter-battery fire. Since the attackers were firing over the walls with the intent of sapping the Famagustans' morale by destroying their houses, the defenders were able to direct their fire unimpaired into the enemy redoubts, destroying earthworks, silencing a number of guns and killing many Turks. Yet in the long run the Ottomans' advantage in men and materiel meant that Mustafa was able to rebuild during the night what the Venetians destroyed during the day, while the defenders were rapidly consuming their powder supplies. By the end of the month the shortage of powder had forced Bragadin to slacken his fire. Soon the number of shots per gun was reduced to eight a day, and the Ottomans, sensing the defenders' problems, increased their pounding.

To make the Venetians' plight worse, the attackers had now found that it was possible to dig mines under certain sections of the southern wall. The main Ottoman attack was directed against Fort Andruzzi, below which stood another bastion known as the Rivellin. As the Ottomans advanced above and below ground, they used the earth from their tunnels to fill the city moat and build assault gangways. The Venetians dug counter-mines and targeted the enemy with explosive devices; the Ottomans answered in kind by throwing over the walls lighted sacks full of gunpowder and metal fragments. These tactics, together with cannon and musket fire, daily reduced the number of defenders, as the enemy prepared to deliver the final blow. On 21 June a mine was exploded under the tower of the arsenal, bringing down a large section of the walls. With great shouts the Ottoman army surged forward, attempting to carry the breach before the smoke and dust produced by the mine had settled. For five hours the battle raged, the Venetians trying to contain the enemy attack with enfilading artillery fire. At one point the accidental ignition of an explosive device being carried by a group of soldiers killed or wounded 100 Venetians but the Ottomans hesitated, thinking that the explosion had been caused by a mine placed on the walls. The respite was enough for the defenders to pour reinforcements into the breach, forcing the Turks to retire.

Undaunted, on the 29th Mustafa exploded another mine under the Rivellin. The crumbling masonry filled the moat, and the breach was subjected to an intense cannonade to keep the defenders' heads down. The Turks rushed to the attack, one column charging the ruins of the Rivellin, another the fortifications of the arsenal. As the land troops moved forward Ottoman galleys attempted to force their way into Famagusta harbour, only to be repulsed by Venetian artillery fire. Bragadin and Baglioni sent as many reinforcements as they could spare to contain the enemy attack, and after six hours of fighting once more the Ottomans were pushed back with heavy losses. Feverishly the defenders set to work to repair as best they could the ruined walls, Bragadin even commandeering all the bales of cloth stored in the city's warehouses to make earth-filled sacks. However, seeing the impossibility of mending the Rivellin, he ordered it to be mined. The Ottomans built a redoubt in front of the arsenal, targeting the breaches day and night. By now Venetian numbers were dwindling fast, many infantry companies being reduced to two dozen men at most.

As if all this were not enough, Bragadin now had to face serious internal dissent. Victuals were being used up; what wine was left went for fifty ducats a barrel; poultry, used to feed the wounded, three or four ducats apiece; horse or donkey flesh, four or five ducats a pound. The incessant Ottoman bombardment had also destroyed many of the buildings within the city, forcing the still substantial civilian population to seek refuge within the fortresses, placing an extra strain on the combatants. At last the Famagustans petitioned Bragadin to surrender. Relief was unlikely, the Ottomans were stronger than ever, and if they should take the city by storm everyone would lose their possessions, the men their lives and the women and children their honour. The governor and Baglioni used all their powers of persuasion, begging that resistance continue for another two weeks. There was still hope of relief, duty and honour requiring that every effort be made to hold Famagusta as long as possible.

But the end was arriving fast. On 8 July the Ottomans unleashed a violent artillery barrage, 5,000 shots falling on the unfortunate city. The next day another assault was mounted, the Turks concentrating their efforts against the Rivellin. The intensity of the fighting was such that the Venetian guns overheated and were unable to continue firing. Inexorably, the Ottomans pushed the defenders back, occupying the Rivellin. Captain Luigi Martinengo gave the order to explode the mine previously prepared for just such an eventuality. The whole bastion went up, burying under the falling masonry some 1,500 Turks and a few hundred defenders. Again the Ottomans hesitated, fearing the presence of other mines. The respite allowed the Venetians to bring up reinforcements and once again push back their attackers. This pattern was repeated at every assault, each time the Ottomans losing hundreds of men but inflicting losses that the defenders could ill afford. The savage fighting did not spare those women and children left in the city, many of them being killed while bringing food or munitions to the troops, or, harquebus in hand, trying to repulse the advancing enemy. On the 29th the Ottomans launched a series of massive assaults lasting two days. Again and again they were thrown back, losing, among many others, Mustafa's own son, but by their end the Venetian soldiers left standing numbered only 700, too few to oppose another determined enemy onslaught.

The city had resisted for longer than the two weeks requested by Bragadin, but now the population was determined to give up. Food was virtually finished and powder reduced to just seven barrels. Bragadin and Baglioni could do nothing more, and now risked facing enemies within as well as outside the city. Months before, Bragadin had complained – maybe unfairly – to the doge that Nicosia had been lost thanks to 'the slumbering laziness, and extreme cravenness of the defenders'; he also did not want to behave like those of Kyrenia, 'who without a murmur went over to these dogs having always promised to do the opposite'.[35] One of the biggest problems for the Venetians in Cyprus was the local population, for the greater part Greek Orthodox and opposed to Catholic rule.

Mustafa's spies within the city evidently managed to inform him of what was happening, for the Ottoman commander immediately sent an envoy with a proposal that the garrison surrender on terms. The Ottomans were also exhausted, and Mustafa feared the arrival of an allied fleet. Under popular pressure Bragadin agreed to a parley, but refused to have anything to do with it, delegating all negotiations to Baglioni. Observing the death and destruction around him, the governor exclaimed, 'Oh God, why did I not die on these walls?'[36]

A cry destined to become tragically prophetic.

7. THE CUTTING EDGE

~

Unaware of the situation in Famagusta, the allies were busy preparing their next Levantine expedition. The ports of Barcelona, Genoa, Livorno, Civitavecchia, Naples and Messina were hives of activity, filled with soldiers, artillerymen, slaves, free rowers and mariners – a multitude from all parts of Europe, speaking a babel of tongues, following different religions and, in the words of a near contemporary, 'for the most part lawless and unfriendly to God'.[1] Accompanying them on the expedition would be an army of clerks and sutlers, plus the servants of the many officers on board each vessel. The combination of all these individuals allowed the functioning of the primary weapon system of Mediterranean warfare: the galley.

Powered by wind and – more important – by human muscle, the late-sixteenth-century galley was the descendant of a long line of ships that from the classical age onward had dominated southern European seas. Forty-one metres long, five to six metres broad, displacing approximately 200 tons and with two lateen sails, the standard galley (*galera* or *galea* in Italian, *galia sottile* in Venetian) was an elegant vessel. A narrow central deck, flanked by others at port and starboard, standing above the rowing benches, allowed the men on board to go from bow to stern. Galleys from the western Mediterranean sported at the bow a forecastle (*arrembata* in Italian, *arrumbada*, in Spanish), which also housed the ship's main artillery battery. Venetian galleys sported an elevated fighting platform, lower and less easy to defend than the *arrembata*. At the stern stood the poop deck, often richly decorated and reserved for senior officers.

A galley's main propulsive force were the rowers sitting on twenty-four to twenty-six benches along each side of the ship. Galleys built as flagships (in Italian *capitane*, singular *capitana*) or deputy flagships (*padrone*, singular *padrona*) – known collectively as *lanterne* or *fanò* from the large lamps they carried astern – were usually but not invariably the significantly larger *bastarde*, which in some cases reached fifty-five metres in length, seven across, and sported up to thirty-six benches.* Smaller versions of the galley were the galliot (thirty to thirty-eight metres and sixteen to twenty-three benches), the *fusta* (twelve to fifteen benches) and the *bergantine* (eight to eleven benches). Apart from the size, the main differences between a galley and its smaller cousins consisted in a higher freeboard, greater amount of ordnance and tactical employment.

To say 'galley' is very much like saying 'World War II fighter plane'. In 1940, for instance, the British and the Germans had mainly monoplanes, while the Italians, for political and industrial reasons, by and large fielded biplanes.[2] Likewise, each Mediterranean country of the sixteenth century had its own galley-building philosophy, developed according to its strategic and economic needs. Besides, different building skills meant that no two galleys were alike, the judgement and ability of individual master builders playing a crucial part in the construction of each vessel. Basically, galleys came in two types: the *ponentina*, employed by Genoa, Savoy, Tuscany, the papacy, Malta, Spain and her Italian dependencies, and the *levantina*, used by Venice and the Ottoman empire. North

---

* In modern Italian *bastardo* has taken on the English colloquial meaning of scoundrel or villain. In reality its proper meaning is that of love child, or mongrel. Thus a *galera bastarda* was conceptually a cross between a normal galley and a *galera grossa*, or large galley, the ancestress of the galleass and built for commercial purposes.

African states normally built vessels of the first type, although adapted to the requirements of the hit-and-run warfare practised by Barbary corsairs. The terms *ponentina* and *levantina* indicated also a system of galley management, the former relying more on slave labour. Ottoman and Venetian galleys drew less water than *ponentine*, being also swifter under oars. On the other hand, when it came to sailing *levantine* did not perform as well as their western cousins, the latter also having larger sails.

Until recently it has been fashionable to consider the sixteenth century galley an anachronism, and to assert that by the 1600s the south of Europe had become a technological and military backwater. The survival of galleys in the Mediterranean up to the beginning of the nineteenth century has often been used as evidence of backwardness, ignoring the fact that there were sound strategic, tactical and economic reasons for keeping oar-powered vessels.★ In fact the meteorological and geographical conditions of the Mediterranean favoured galleys much more than sailing ships. In ideal circumstances square-rigged sailing vessels could travel an average of forty or fifty miles in twenty-four hours. In good weather and provided the hull was in reasonable repair, a galley under oars could normally sustain a cruising speed of three to three and a half knots, reaching a maximum of seven to seven and a half for short periods. Although their human engines made galleys far less susceptible than sailing ships to the presence or lack of wind, captains would exploit any favourable breeze to allow their rowing crew to rest. It has been estimated that a galley under sail could reach a top speed of twelve knots, but something in the range of nine or ten appears more reasonable. Sails and oars were often used together, for instance if a galley was giving chase or trying to flee from an enemy. Moreover, until the advent of steam engines, rowing vessels guaranteed that distances could be covered in a fixed

★ For instance, a small state like Tuscany would try in the first half of the seventeenth century to create a sailing fleet akin to those used in the Atlantic, only to find that galleys were better suited, and much less expensive, for waging war in the Mediterranean. N. CAPPONI (2002).

time.[3] The ability to move without wind, their fighting complement and formidable ordnance allowed war galleys to remain an important component of all Mediterranean fleets up to the mid-eighteenth century.

The sixteenth-century galley did have significant drawbacks, and in the end, despite a number of improvements over the next 200 years, these would eventually prove fatal. For one, with a freeboard of only about half a metre amidships the galley could not cope with winter swells, thus limiting its operational season to March–October, at best.[4] This was not invariably true, as demonstrated by Marco Querini's relief expedition to Famagusta in January 1571; but navigating in the winter always involved risk. Even during the summer galley captains preferred to travel with the coast in sight, beaching their ships when hit by inclement weather.

Inactivity during winter months was a straight financial loss for a galley owner. Even if unable to store any cargo of significant size or weight, galleys often transported precious merchandise, such as silk or bullion.[5] They were also used extensively to carry letters of credit, diplomatic dispatches and other mail of importance, a galley being able to make the return trip from Genoa to Barcelona (460 nautical miles) in ten or twelve days. All this was difficult if not impossible in rough seas, while galley rowers always needed to be fed and clothed. The solution, of course, was to build bigger galleys, capable of carrying more freight and navigating all year round. By the mid-seventeenth century galleys were large enough to brave day-long storms without sinking or having to find shelter.[6] However, increased size meant greater overall production and maintenance costs, as well as larger, more expensive, rowing crews.

In the sixteenth century a normal galley was still relatively simple and cheap to produce. Building material and skilled workers permitting, a new vessel could be constructed and outfitted in two months, even if Giovanni Andrea Doria was rumoured to have once done it in the record time of twenty-seven days. The Venetians, on the other hand, considered it took a year to properly build a normal galley, with a squad of twenty men permanently at work.[7] Several types of wood were used, the stern, where the captain's quarters were located, being made of walnut. The deforestation around the western Mediterranean and indeed in the whole of Europe – forcing many governments in the seventeenth century to implement tree-planting programmes – had resulted by the 1550s in a shortage of construction timber. For this reason western Mediterranean galleys were built to last, while the Ottomans, having forests in abundance, appear to have been less concerned with the quality of their construction material.

Overall, Turkish vessels appear to have been cheaper to produce. In 1591, after the Ottoman empire had been hit by a serious economic crisis and the *akçe* dramatically devalued, the average cost of a completely outfitted galley was 30,000 *akçe*, equivalent approximately to 3,750 pieces of eight. By contrast, a Florentine estimate of 1558 calculated that some 4,800 local ducats, or nearly 6,000 pieces of eight, were needed for a galley shell, and more than double that amount for outfitting and arming the vessel. However, it would be dangerous to use exchange rates indiscriminately, other factors such as the costs of living and labour in a given place, the availability of construction materials and the complexity of a specific vessel playing their part. In 1650 a galley shell built in Genoa was sold for 4,565 pieces of eight, the workers' wages amounting to one third of the price; in the same period the cost of labour for a galley built in Istanbul was 80,000–90,000 *akçe* (roughly 1,000 pieces of eight).[8]

Different economic and strategic needs dictated different approaches to galley building. Since the Ottomans pursued war essentially for the sake of territorial conquest, in many ways their fleets functioned as an auxiliary branch of the army. Ottoman galleys, in the words of John Guilmartin, were designed 'to get the siege forces to their objective and to prevent interference with their activities by enemy naval forces once there'.[9] We can thus understand why the Ottomans did not care too much about the quality of their oared vessels. Besides, their many outposts in the Aegean needed to be constantly supplied all year round and the short

distances between the various islands made sailing relatively safe
even in wintertime. It made no economic sense to invest too much
money in high-maintenance galleys, as demonstrated by the fact
that in 1590 the subsidy given by the sultan to a *reis* (captain) for
building a galley was just 400 ducats (48,000 *akçe*).

In 1558 the Venetian *bailo* Antonio Barbarigo reported that the
sultan could easily put 130 galleys to sea every year, since it was
customary to build them with green timber, 'sometimes the construction taking place in the very forest where the trees are felled'.
As a result the life span of a Turkish galley was extremely limited
– 'little more than a year' – Barbarigo adding that at the end of
the sailing season it broke one's heart to see them 'so derelict and
ruined'. Four years later Marcantonio Donini, secretary to the *bailo*,
would report that the Ottomans could deploy 170 galleys 'for long
voyages' and up to 200 'for short ones', plus those privately owned
by corsairs. Donini also noted that the quality of Turkish galleys
had improved markedly 'compared to what happened previously,
and that only because of the slackness of those in charge'. What
really rankled the secretary was that these improvements were due
to the presence of 'Christian' shipbuilders, many of them Venetian
subjects. Be that as it may, it is certain that on the eve of the
Cyprus war Ottoman construction techniques were nearly as good
as those employed by their Western counterparts. In 1580 the
supervisor of the Venetian arsenal Andrea Quirini had in his care
twenty-eight Turkish galleys captured nine years before, of which
he thought only one should be scrapped as useless. Galleys employed by Ottoman or North African corsairs were of good quality,
given the job they had to perform, although an Ottoman captain
relying on state subsidy to build his galley would try to economize
on building materials in order to pocket as much as possible – one
wonders how, given that the subsidy covered only one sixth of the
total building costs. In any case it would be wrong to believe that
the use of unseasoned wood was something unique to the Ottomans, the Spanish also having problems with the quality of their
timber.[10]

By the mid-sixteenth century the development and diffusion of firearms had significantly affected European naval warfare, even if it would take another century for gunfire to become the determining factor in maritime engagements. Artillery had been a permanent feature on war galleys at least since the 1470s, and a century later Western oared vessels mounted an impressive weight of ordnance. A Western galley's main hitting power was concentrated in its bow pieces, capable of delivering a murderous amount of metal. The main gun was a centreline muzzle-loading piece mounted on a recoiling sleigh, weighing between 2,500 and 6,000 pounds and throwing a shot of between fifteen and sixty pounds. By its side stood a pair of seven- to twenty-pounders (1,400–1,800 pounds), usually flanked, at least on Venetian galleys and on *bastarde* in general, by two other shorter pieces of variable calibre. In addition, a galley mounted up to twenty-five smaller breech- or muzzle-loading guns for close-quarters fighting. (See Appendix 2.)

Yet there was never any such thing as standard galley armament, ordnance varying according to tactical necessity or simply what was available. In 1566 the artillery on board one Venetian galley was one fifty-pounder cannon, three six-pounders, two three-pounders, and fourteen smaller breech-loading pieces. Seven years later another Venetian galley deployed one fifty-pounder culverin, three six-pounders, one three-pounder, and twenty smaller guns. In these two cases the armament was respectively completed by twenty-four and sixty-eight *archibusoni* – large muskets placed on fixed stands. By contrast, an inventory of two Spanish galleys dated 1588 lists for the first a 5,400-pound centreline piece, a pair of 1,465-pound *moiane*, four 300-pound *mortarete* swivel guns and five large harquebuses, and for the second a 5,200-pound main gun, a pair of 750-pound *moiane*, and four 300-pound *mortaretes*.[11]

There is evidence that Genoese galleys mounted less ordnance than their Venetian counterparts. In 1582 the vessels of Doria's squadron had on average a 4,500-pound centreline cannon, two 900–1,200-pound *moiane* and four 250–380-pound swivel guns.[12] This relatively light armament can be explained by the need to sacrifice artillery for speed, Doria's galleys travelling continually between Genoa and Barcelona, or Genoa and Messina. The 1575 inventory of the Genoese Lomellini squadron, present at the battle of the Curzolaris, is even more telling in this respect. Like the Doria, the Lomellini, another Genoese family of maritime entrepreneurs, loaned the vessels to Spain as a matter of course.

The names and sizes of the various types of artillery pieces were different across the Mediterranean. The Venetians fielded (in local weight) the one-pounder *moschetto da zuogo*, the three-pounder *falconetto*, the six-pounder *falcone*, the twelve-pounder *aspide* and *sacro* (both having a calibre of 95–100 millimetres, the *sacro* being a foot longer); larger pieces were the fourteen-to-sixty-pounder *cannone* (cannons) and *colubrine* (culverins), the latter being a third longer than the former. Gunpowder produced in the sixteenth century burnt more slowly than its modern equivalent, and as a result the pressure it created in the barrel lasted longer. Thus a shot fired from a culverin would travel a greater distance than one fired from a cannon of the same calibre and loaded with the same amount of powder. Experiments conducted by the Venetians at various times in the sixteenth and seventeenth centuries confirm this: on a straight trajectory a shot from a fifty-pounder culverin would travel for approximately 600 metres, compared to the 480 of a fifty-pounder cannon. A charge three times as big was needed for a cannon to reach the same distance as a culverin and there were

TABLE 1. GUNS OF THE LOMELLINI GALLEYS (1575)[13]

Galleys Guns	*Capitana*	*Padrona*	*Lomellina*	*Furia*
Cannons	1 (46-pdr)	1 (44-pdr)	1 (23-pdr)	1 (21-pdr)
Sacri	2 (1-pdr)	2 (2-pdr)	2 (2-pdr)	2 (2-pdr)
Swivel guns	2	4	2	2

Each galley had twenty-four rowing benches.

TABLE 2. RANGE OF DIFFERENT GUNS AT FIXED MUZZLE
ELEVATIONS (METRES)[14]

Elevation Gun	0°	7.5°	15°	30°	45°
60-pdr culverin	650	3,215	5,465	7,330	7,715
60-pdr cannon	520	2,600	4,430	5,940	6,255
50-pdr culverin	600	3,040	5,170	6,935	7,300
50-pdr cannon	480	2,430	4,135	5,550	5,840
40-pdr culverin	570	2,865	4,875	6,540	6,880
40-pdr cannon	470	2,345	4,000	5,175	5,630
30-pdr culverin	550	2,780	4,725	6,395	6,675
30-pdr cannon	450	2,260	3,930	5,150	5,422
20-pdr culverin	520	2,600	4,430	5,945	6,255
20-pdr cannon	430	2,170	3,690	4,953	5,170

As can be seen, even the slightest muzzle elevation (*un punto di squadra* or one point of the gunner's quadrant) emphasized the clear advantage of culverin over cannon loaded with a thirty-pound powder charge. Interestingly, twenty-pounder culverins appear to perform as well as sixty-pounder cannons. In fact, the Venetians would slowly reduce the weight of their galley artillery, concluding that against a light-framed target a twenty-pounder would do the same damage as a bigger gun.

limits to the amount of powder a gun could take without exploding.[15]

The Spanish used different names for their pieces, such as *medio sacre* instead of *falcone*, while, confusingly *sacro* was sometimes used to denote a cannon. *Ponentine* galleys often carried two *moiane*, shorter versions of the *sacro*.* Finally, there were the stocky ten-to-twenty-pounder *petrieri* (*petreros* in Spanish), so called because

* All the artillery types were named after animals. *Aspide*, for instance, is an asp, while a *sacro* is a kind of falcon.

designed to fire stone balls; they were used with or in lieu of the *falconi*.[16]

Galley guns were not intended to be fired in volleys. Centreline pieces were used for long-range shooting, while for close-quarters engagements the preferred weapons were large calibre *petrieri* loaded with grapeshot.[17] Crewmen employed similarly loaded swivel guns to sweep decks, repulse enemy boarding parties or assist their own. Centreline pieces once fired could slide back on the main deck to the mainmast, but the flanking guns could only recoil the length of the gun platform. Weight and technical constraints dictated the amount of ordnance a galley could carry.

The comparative swiftness under the oars of a well-kept Muslim galley was also due to its light ordnance load; indeed, at least by Venetian standards, Islamic rowing vessels appear to have been undergunned, around the 1580s a normal Ottoman galley (*kadırga*) sporting a maximum of thirteen pieces of all types. Reporting to the Venetian senate after his return from Constantinople in the summer of 1571, Giacomo Ragazzoni stated that Ottoman galleys carried only three artillery pieces, 'and many just one'. This was also true for the galleys employed by North African corsairs, who preferred to employ boarding tactics. A 1573 inventory of a captured Turkish galley lists a main five-piece gun battery equivalent in every way to what one would expect to find on a western Mediterranean vessel: a centreline cannon weighing 4,300 pounds, two *sacri* of 1,830 pounds, and a pair of *falconetti* swivel guns of 870 pounds; additional evidence points to this galley being a thirty-two-bench *bastarda* and lacking the small pieces typical of western Mediterranean vessels.[18]

Apparently Ottoman naval artillery was nothing to write home about, although 'naval' is a misleading term here since at the time most guns could be employed differently on land and at sea. In 1572 the officials of the Venetian arsenal informed the Council of Ten, at the time responsible for managing the republic's ordnance, of the 'bad quality' of 115 captured Turkish pieces. Their suggestion was to recast the lot, adding a certain amount of good metal. Similar reports about the inferior quality of Ottoman guns appear in Venetian documents up to the end of the seventeenth century, and an inventory of eleven Ottoman pieces taken in 1571 shows them to be lighter in weight than Venetian ones of the same calibre.[19] This would appear to disprove Gábor Ágoston's statement that notions of Ottoman technological inferiority 'are hardly tenable',[20] but could also be evidence of sound tactical reasoning. Galley warfare did not call for prolonged artillery duels, ships exchanging only a few shots before engaging in close-quarters fighting. The Venetians recognized this when they decided to mount on their galleys fifty-pounders 'with little metal', weighing between 2,600 and 3,000 pounds, since 'even during important engagements they do not need to shoot so many times and as often as when used in fortresses'.[21] For both the Venetians and the Ottomans it made no sense to risk losing good pieces in maritime operations. Besides, the pool of experienced fighting personnel at the Ottomans' disposal inclinded them to rely more on hand-to-hand fighting than long-range gunfire.

By the time of the Cyprus war naval gunnery, particularly in seafaring states like Venice, had become an art in itself. The importance attached by the Venetians to artillery is underscored by their galleys carrying six bombardiers, compared to the two normally embarked on a *ponentina*.[22] Although the theoretically effective range of smooth-bore pieces of any size was limited to a few hundred metres, in ideal conditions expert artillerymen with intimate knowledge of their weapons could do great damage even at a considerable distance. According to one study, the possibility of a smooth-bore muzzle-loading gun hitting a target was about 10–15 per cent of the range for all shots fired. This meant that at 1,000 metres all shots fell within an area 100–150 metres across. At such a distance the chances of hitting a small target, like a galley bow or stern, were therefore slim, especially when firing from a pitching vessel. But it was a different matter when shooting at an extended line of men or ships.[23] At short or even medium range the destructive power of galley guns could be devastating, especially if directed against light-framed vessels. Paolo Giovio paints a clear picture of the effect of galley artillery on timber and flesh in his description of the battle of Capo d'Orso, fought in 1528 between a Genoese squadron under Filippino Doria and a Spanish one led by Don Ugo de Moncada:

> Count Filippo [Doria] who in this [artillery fire] placed every attention, as well as being a crack shot, discharged against the enemy his large artillery piece called the Basilisk.* The terrible ball, smashing through the ram and the forecastle [of Moncada's galley] with horrible slaughter of men, travelled from bow to the stern across the bridge with such violence that, having already killed more than thirty between soldiers and sailors, it slew many honourable people on the poop deck ... so that the Marquis of Vasto and Don Ugo were spattered with their blood and guts.[24]

Artillery shot was usually made of cast iron or stone, the latter, much favoured by the Ottomans since its shattering on impact produced a shrapnel effect. Most naval gunners employed straight-trajectory firing, but some preferred what in Italian was known as *il tiro di ficco*, i.e. shooting the ball into the sea at a certain angle to make it bounce and hit the enemy vessel at the waterline. It was a method favoured by the Portuguese, although some criticized it by pointing out that bouncing caused the ball to lose too much speed and hitting power to cause much damage to ships of even medium size.[25] However, a ball fired in this way could still inflict considerable punishment on light-framed craft such as a galley, provided the target was reasonably close.

~

Western reliance on firepower would be at the centre of one of the most revolutionary developments in Mediterranean naval warfare.

---

* A basilisk was originally a gun made of wrought-iron hoops. By the 1530s it was a cast piece of the culverin type.

From the 1520s the Venetians had been experimenting with new galley designs in an attempt to create a battle-winning vessel combining manoeuvrability with heavy ordnance. Much ink was spilt in the debate on how to build the perfect oared ship, some arguing that classical examples should be followed, others opting for a less erudite approach. Vettor Fausto's already-mentioned quinquereme was the product of the first school of thought; and while ultimately disappointing it showed that bigger galleys were necessary to carry the desired amount of ordnance. However, the galley's low freeboard meant that artillery could only be placed on the foredeck – excluding a few swivel guns on the gunwales – even if some of the larger vessels carried a few medium-sized pieces at the stern. More artillery meant slower galleys, while there was also an absolute limit to the weight of ordnance a galley could carry; sometimes guns had to be recast into lighter pieces before being taken on board.[26]

On the strength of their experience with Fausto's quinquereme, the Venetians came up with a brilliant solution. Up to the end of the fifteenth century the typical Mediterranean transport ship had been the fifty-metre-long large galley (*galia grossa* in Venetian), known also as a *maona*.* By the 1550s a rise in crew costs had made such ships largely unprofitable, and many were scrapped or left to rot in dock. The Venetians, marrying expediency with scientific theory, realized that they could be turned into excellent gun platforms, and that is precisely what happened. Under the supervision of the *provveditore* of the arsenal Giovan Andrea Badoer and his successor Marcantonio Pisani, the master builder Francesco Bressan between 1568 and 1571 completely refurbished a dozen or so large galleys, turning them into gun-bristling warships. This was done through a feat of engineering genius which involved building a forecastle strong enough to carry half a dozen heavy pieces without

---

* The *maona* (*mavna* in Turkish) is often described as being without oars and having square sails. There is enough evidence, however, to show that *maona* was an alternative name for *galia grossa*. See: ANDERSON (1919): 282.

affecting the vessel's stability. The engineer and inventor Arturo Surian went a step further, devising a system to stop the pieces on the ships' side from recoiling into the rowing benches.[27]

The firepower of these galleasses, as they would soon be called, turned out to be formidable indeed.* A Florentine document of 1572, reporting Venetian practice, gives the following breakdown: forty-four guns in total, including a powerful battery of two fifty-pounder culverins, four thirty-pounder culverins, and four thirty-pounder cannons; there were also twelve cannons or culverins shooting balls weighing between fourteen and twenty pounds, plus twenty-two smaller pieces.[28] About ten large and medium pieces were placed at the prow on an elevated forecastle; fourteen, medium and small, stood on the upper deck at each side of the ship, with the remainder mounted aft. Swivel guns are not mentioned, but their number must have been considerable. Whatever its ordnance, a galleass was able to deliver a devastating artillery barrage from all sides, and in addition its height made it impervious to boarding. The following table gives an idea of the punch these ships could pack.

The galleass sported three tall masts with lateen sails, but like the galley its main propulsive system was provided by a *ciurma* (roughly, rowing crew) of 165 men sitting on twenty-seven benches placed below the upper deck. Given the size of the vessel the number of oarsmen was inadequate to enable galleasses to keep up with the faster galleys, and consequently they had to be towed by smaller vessels. But the Venetian senate had decided that galleass rowers were to be all free men, not slaves or convicts, and the difficulty of finding an adequate number of oarsmen meant having only three men to each bench.[29]

~

* Interestingly enough, for a long time Venetian shipbuilders would refer to galleasses as *galere alla faustina*, thus acknowledging Vettor Fausto's influence in their creation. CONCINA: 152–3.

TABLE 3: ARTILLERY ON BOARD THE VENETIAN GALLEASSES DURING THE 1571 CAMPAIGN[30]

Artillery Captain	60cl	50cl	30cl	20cl	14cl	50cn	30cn	20cn	16cn	12s	6fl	3fn	30p	3p	1mb	1mz	Total
F. Duodo	0	2	0	2	6	0	2	6	0	0	0	2	0	8	0	0	28
J. Guoro	2	0	2	0	4	0	4	6	0	0	0	0	0	5	0	0	23
A. da Pesaro	0	0	0	2	0	2	0	8	0	4	0	0	2	8	0	0	26
An. Bragadin	0	2	2	0	4	0	2	4	1	0	2	6	0	4	6	0	33
Am. Bragadin	0	2	2	0	4	0	4	4	2	0	2	12	0	0	8	0	40
P. Pisani	0	2	2	0	4	0	4	4	2	0	3	0	0	2	8	4	35
Total	2	8	8	4	22	2	16	32	5	4	7	20	2	27	22	4	185

The numbers in the upper row indicate the weight of the shot, and the letters the type of gun; thus 60cl stands for 60-pounder culverin. Legend: culverin (cl), cannon (cn), sacro (s), falcone (fl), falconetto (fn), petriere (p), moschetto da braga (mb), moschetto da zuogo (mz). In 1570, when this list was drawn up, Pietro Pisani's galleass was commanded by Vincenzo Querini. The captain of a galleass was called a governatore.

Finding galley rowers was a problem all over the Mediterranean during the Early Modern period.[31] By the beginning of the sixteenth century rowing, once a respectable profession, had become more and more a socially degrading job. The resulting shortage meant that experienced oarsmen could now command higher wages. In addition, the constant state of war in Europe led to a veritable arms race, each state spending enormous sums on expanding armies, fleets or both. More galleys meant having to find extra rowers, but this was becoming increasingly difficult given the ever-shrinking recruiting pool. To make matters worse, the same period saw a change in rowing methods, producing an even greater demand for manpower.

Around the 1530s maritime states as well as private galley owners started experimenting with rowing *a scaloccio* (a term possibly derived from the Italian word *scala*, ladder) instead of the traditional *alla sensile* (from the Spanish *sencillo*, simple). The latter required each oar to be pulled by one man, each bench accommodating three rowers (but sometimes four or five), a standard trireme galley *alla sensile* having a complement of 144 to 164 rowers. In contrast, *a scaloccio* entailed a single large oar for each bench handled by three to five men. This brought an increase in the number of rowers – to a maximum of 240 for a twenty-five-bench galley. It may appear perverse that with fewer oarsmen available a rowing system requiring more of them should be introduced; yet with the *a scaloccio* method it was possible to crew a galley without large numbers of trained men, as expert rowers could be interspaced with green ones. One reason for this change lay in the lack of shipbuilding timber, another result of the aforesaid arms race. Since a normal galley *a scaloccio* needed approximately fifty oars instead of the 150 of one *alla sensile*, the result was a drastic reduction in wood, resulting in lower fitting-out costs. In addition, the bigger *a scaloccio* oars broke less frequently. On the other hand, at the time of the Cyprus war the Ottomans, having adopted the *a scaloccio* method, had only three men to each bench manning thin oars 'since this tires the crews less'.[32] It took some time for the new rowing method to take hold, and at the beginning of the seventeenth century experts were still arguing about which of the two systems was best.

The increased demand for rowers meant finding an alternative to volunteers, but luckily for galley captains the grim life led by many people coupled with the endemic violence of the age meant that there was no lack of criminals roaming the streets – ideal candidates for a rowing bench. By the mid-sixteenth century all the Mediterranean states, including the Porte, had introduced laws prescribing galley work for a number of felonies and misdemeanours: murder, robbery, theft, sexual offences, fraud, forgery, coinage counterfeiting, blasphemy and vagrancy. In the Ottoman empire drinking alcohol in public was added to the list.[33] Sending convicts to the oars had the twin merits of removing unwanted members of society and allowing galley fleets to function adequately. States without sea coasts habitually sold their convicts to maritime governments or to private individuals in need of a constant influx of muscle. The small republic of Lucca, with no port of any significance, introduced the penalty of the galley in 1532 following a suggestion by Andrea Doria, and from then onwards *Lucchesi* convicts were always present in the Doria fleet. This did not mean that volunteers disappeared entirely from galley benches, many needy individuals – cold and hunger being very effective recruiting agents – or those with a twisted sense of adventure choosing the oars as their trade. In some states like Venice or the Ottoman empire, where rowing on a galley did not carry any sort of social stigma, recruiting volunteer rowers was not too difficult. Still, most governments or private shipowners preferred forced labourers since their maintenance costs were half those of *buonevoglie* (Italian, loosely freewillers) and they were 'on the whole better rowers'.[34] The following tables, which refer to two *ponentine* galley fleets, one private and another state-owned, demonstrate the overwhelming preponderance of forced rowers over volunteers.

From a superficial glance at the numbers, it would seem that Doria's galleys were still being rowed *alla sensile*, the Genoese entrepreneur changing to the *a scaloccio* system starting from around 1562. At that date he had two galleys employing the new rowing

TABLE 4. GIOVANNI ANDREA DORIA'S *CIURME* (EARLY 1560s)[35]

Galley	Oarsmen	Convicts	(%)	Slaves	(%)	Buonevoglie	(%)	Total
Patrona	(27)	81	(42.4)	98	(51.3)	12	(6.3)	191
Monarcha	(23)	67	(44.4)	73	(48.3)	11	(7.3)	151
Temperanza	(22)	63	(40.9)	82	(53.2)	9	(5.9)	154
Donzella	(22)	89	(57.8)	56	(36.4)	9	(5.8)	154
Vittoria	(24)	74	(49.3)	66	(44.0)	10	(6.7)	150
Fortuna	(23)	85	(55.9)	54	(35.5)	13	(8.6)	152
Perla	(23)	69	(44.5)	76	(49.0)	10	(6.5)	155
Doria	(22)	84	(54.5)	63	(40.9)	7	(4.5)	154
Marchesa	(22)	77	(50.3)	65	(42.5)	11	(7.2)	153
Aquila	(23)	63	(40.4)	81	(51.9)	12	(7.7)	156
Signora	(15)	80	(52.3)	73	(47.7)	0	(0.0)	153
Total	(246)	832	(48.3)	787	(45.7)	104	(6.0)	1,723

The numbers in the first column refer to the *uomini de cavo* (*gente de cabo* in Spanish), a term covering the fighting men other than soldiers normally part of a galley complement. Their numbers, like those of the *buonevoglie*, appear suspiciously low, so it is possible that the inventory was done when the galleys were in *scioverno*, winter quarters.

system 'with only three men at each bench'.[36] It should also be underscored that although the overall number of *buonevoglie* in the Tuscan galleys was less than 20 per cent of the total, in the *Elbigina* they represented the largest single group within the *ciurma*. The case of Naples is interesting. In 1571 on thirty Neapolitan galleys out of a total of 5,241 rowers *buonevoglie* were 2,220 (42.5 per cent), convicts 2,469 (47.2 per cent), but slaves a mere 552 (10.3 per cent). Thirteen years later out of 4,310 oarsmen on twenty-four galleys, volunteers numbered just 955 (22.2 per cent), while 2,449 convicts

TABLE 5. *CIURME* OF THE TUSCAN GALLEYS (1570)[37]

Galley	Oarsmen Convicts	(%)	Slaves	(%)	*Buonevoglie*	(%)	Sick	(%)	Total
Capitana	186	(69.1)	83	(30.9)	0	(0.0)	0	(0.0)	269
Padrona	139	(64.4)	54	(25.0)	17	(7.9)	6	(2.7)	216
Fiorenza	106	(52.2)	53	(25.7)	39	(19.2)	5	(2.9)	203
Santa Maria	45	(39.4)	13	(11.4)	42	(36.8)	14	(12.4)	114
Toscana	ND	-	ND	-	ND	-	ND	-	ND
Vittoria	94	(45.8)	47	(22.9)	54	(26.4)	10	(4.9)	205
Elbigina	74	(33.9)	56	(25.6)	82	(37.6)	6	(2.9)	218
Pisana	140	(66.6)	44	(21.0)	20	(9.5)	6	(2.9)	210
Grifona	116	(52.2)	59	(28.0)	27	(12.8)	8	(4.0)	210
Siena	115	(54.2)	53	(25.0)	36	(17.0)	8	(3.8)	212
Pace	59	(40.1)	29	(19.7)	21	(14.2)	38	(26.0)	147
San Giovanni	60	(44.7)	9	(6.7)	28	(20.9)	37	(27.7)	134
Total	1,134	(53.0)	500	(23.4)	366	(17.1)	138	(6.5)	2,138

made up nearly 60 per cent of the total crews; slaves amounted to just 19 per cent.[38] In 1571 one might speculate that the Holy League's religious and material incentives had helped to recruit volunteer oarsmen. The presence of relatively few slaves was typical of those states, like Spain, France, Savoy or the Holy See, that did not conduct corsair activities on a large scale.

Slaves and prisoners of war – often both, although not invariably the same thing – clearly constituted an important source of galley manpower. Muslims captured at sea or during coastal raids were regularly sent to the oars by the Christian powers, and vice versa. Yet religion was not as discriminating a factor as initially may appear. French and Greeks figured among the rowers on board Florentine galleys in 1555: Christians, but subjects of states then at war with the Medici.[39] However, the use of enslaved oarsmen varied across the Mediterranean. The Hospitallers employed them extensively, together with large numbers of *buonevoglie* – an indication both of the predatory activities of the knights, and the sea being the primary economic outlet for the Maltese. Contrary to popular Western belief, the Porte did not make massive use of slaves to man its ships. In 1562 Marcantonio Donini calculated that only forty of the sultan's galleys had slave oarsmen.[40] The situation was different in the galleys of the various maritime *beylerbeik* and those owned by Ottoman corsairs, in this case slave rowers being abundant. The same was true of the Muslim states of North Africa. In July 1560 three 'Turkish'* galliots beached on the Tuscan coast had on board 300 chained Christians.[41] Large numbers of slaves or convicts represented a considerable security risk, and captains had constantly to guard themselves against possible rebellions. For this reason the Ottomans preferred to mix slave crew members with free men taken from the annual maritime levy. The statutes of the Order of St Stephen specifically called for no more than one slave per bench, a rule difficult to implement.[42]

The Porte and Venice were the two states that made most use of conscription to man their galleys. The Venetians had followed this practice since the Middle Ages, and in 1545 created a specific magistracy, the *Milizia da Mar*, for a more efficient handling of the levy, which covered the city of Venice, its immediate hinterland and all subject cities. The system devised by the Venetian authorities called for a general muster roll, and also specified the number of men each community or social body had to contribute to the crewing of fifty galleys. In the mid-sixteenth century the city's guilds were supposed to supply a total of 2,622 rowers, the *Scuole Grandi* (charitable associations, members of which were both merchants and workers) 1,200, the neighbouring communities 2,340. Within the cities of the Venetian dominion the pool of conscript

---

* The adjective 'Turkish' (*Turco* or *Turchesco* in Italian) in the sixteenth and seventeenth centuries was applied to anything Muslim. 'Becoming a Turk' was synonymous with converting to Islam.

rowers amounted to a theoretical 10,062 men, all liable to be called up – names to be chosen by lot, although substitutions were permitted – in times of emergency.[43]

The Ottomans employed a similar system. Every *sancak* was divided into a series of different administrative sub-districts, each of which had to contribute one rower every twenty-three households, together with one-month's wage: 106 *akçe* for Muslims and 80 for Christians. Households could opt to contribute a sum of money (*bedel*) instead of the oarsman, to cover the cost of recruiting and maintaining a substitute. Only people from the *reaya* class (non-military, tax-paying subjects) could be levied, and from existing records it appears that conscript crewmen (*küreçi azab*) came from the most distant provinces of the Balkans and Anatolia. The Ottomans also employed volunteers, known as *mariol* – vagabonds, tavern aficionados, the unemployed, Greeks exiled from Venetian territories, all ready to take on any job for a bit of money. More than just a bit, as a matter of fact: in 1558 the Venetian *bailo* Antonio Barbarigo would complain that Venice's Greek subjects were enlisting in droves as rowers in the Ottoman fleet, 'for they are very well treated and paid'.[44]

Given the available pool of free rowers, conscripts and volunteers, one understands why it took the Venetians longer than anyone else to introduce convict oarsmen. This was mostly done at the instigation of Cristoforo da Canal, who advocated the introduction of the crewing methods used in *ponentine* galleys after seeing them in action during the Preveza campaign. In his work *Della Milizia Marittima* da Canal cited considerable evidence to back his thesis: convicts rowed more efficiently for fear of punishment and cared more about personal hygiene, resulting in a lower mortality rate; nor could they run during sea fights. Galleys could be built to travel efficiently under either oars or sail, and the presence of convicts allowed for more soldiers on board. Finally, non-free oarsmen – being chained to their benches and thus unable to stand erect and move back – could adopt a rowing style known as *a rancata*, which used short, quick strokes that allowed galleys to move at greater speed.[45]

Many historians have accepted da Canal's treatise as a bona fide document, but a comparison with existing archival sources shows he manipulated the evidence to support his case. Firstly the assertion that murderers, thieves and robbers rowed better for fear of the lash is unproven. Secondly, free oarsmen were cleaner than convicts, and were trained to fight. As a matter of fact, convicts and slaves tended to suffer greater battle casualties precisely because they were unable to move from their benches. Thirdly, galleys crewed with forced oarsmen were less efficient under oars, since the rowers tended to do the least work possible. As for embarking more soldiers, galleys, due to their structure, could allow on board only so many men – one wonders where da Canal got his idea about convict galleys having extra space. To top everything, rowing *a rancata* exhausted crews more rapidly than other styles involving slower, longer strokes.★

Despite all these contraindications in 1545 the Venetian Senate introduced *galie sforzate*, rowed exclusively by convicts.† It is doubtful that the senators, many of whom had extensive naval experience, did this because convinced by da Canal's arguments. More likely, the reasons were economic and social. Convict galleys cost 7.5 per cent less than those rowed by free men, and in addition allowed the authorities to empty the jails. Moreover, recourse to criminals put less pressure on the aforementioned social bodies to provide conscripts, always an unpopular solution. However, it became immediately apparent, despite da Canal's opinion to the contrary, that galleys manned by chained oarsmen were not the best fighting machines, and to ameliorate the problem it was suggested to alternate convicts with free men on the benches. Initially da Canal's reform seemed to work, so that on the eve of the Cyprus War Venice had twelve galleys entirely crewed by convicts. Yet it was already evident they were qualitatively inferior to those

★ It should be noted that in modern Italian one of the modern meanings of the verb *arrancare* is trudge.
† The use of the letter 's' in front of certain Italian words can mean different things, depending on the area. For instance, in sixteenth-century Tuscan a galley convict was a *forzato*, while *sforzare* meant to force or even to rape.

manned by free men, not least because their commanders had no interest in running them efficiently. One of the main differences between a Venetian *sopracomito* (captain) and his *ponentine* colleagues consisted in his administrative and not just military responsibilities. Commanding a galley not only brought with it prestige but could also be very profitable.

In theory enlisting for the oars in Venice could be quite remunerative, volunteer *galeotti* (free and non-free rowers – in Venice free ones were known as *galeotti di libertà*) receiving a recruitment bounty of at least twenty-five Venetian ducats – between thirty-two and thirty-five pieces of eight in the late sixteenth century. Sometimes this sum was doubled or even tripled, a considerable incentive for individuals coming from the lower strata of society. In any case, even if rowing was hard work, in Venice it was considered an acceptable profession, no worse and sometimes better than toiling in a mine, a field or a workshop. Moreover, for free men life on a Venetian galley was not as hellish as popular imagination would have it. Volunteers were not chained to their benches; unlike what happened in *ponentine* galleys, they enjoyed legal rights and a considerable amount of freedom when in port. The yearly pay of roughly twelve ducats was comparable to that of an unskilled worker, and supplemented by the assurance of food and clothing. Yet, despite all these incentives, it was never easy for the Venetian authorities to find men willing to enlist for galley work.

To begin with, not all the promised bounty was given to the oarsman, but kept instead by the captain against future expenses. Every galley had an account book recording not only each *galeotto*'s earnings and expenses, but also details of his illnesses, dismissal, desertion or death. From the man's original credit were deducted the costs of clothing, medicines, extra food, any money he might owe to other members of the crew, and so on. In any case the *galeotti*'s earnings were calculated in the virtual and largely devalued *moneta d'armata*; but his expenditures in real money. Galley accountants often would also surreptitiously transfer the debts of the deceased and deserters to the remaining members of the crew. Very soon the original credit nearly always became a debit, turning the free man into an indentured labourer. Galley captains sold their men's debts to colleagues in need of rowers, and whole crews could be transferred by means of legal contracts from one galley to another. On the other hand, a *galeotto*, even if a convict or slave, was usually allowed, despite rules to the contrary, to engage in trade and other economic activities when in port, or work for his captain for extra money. It should also be remembered that in Venice *galeotti di libertà* were supposed to fight alongside the soldiers during sea battles, and thus had the opportunity to acquire enough booty to buy back their freedom and retire with more than a few coins in their pockets. Enlisting for the oars was a game of chance, and in Spain, its Italian dominions and Genoa this was more than just a metaphor. Recruitment officials would put up betting stalls, advancing money to penniless individuals who then would gamble for their freedom; losers were immediately sent to the rowing benches until they had repaid their debts.

The lot of the convict or enslaved oarsman was usually worse than that of his free colleague. Venetian law did not allow anyone to be sentenced to the galleys for life, the maximum being twelve years, although this rule did not apply to those criminals acquired from abroad. But even Venetian *forzati* were forced in to the spiral of debt that afflicted the *galeotti di libertà*, and galley accountants would resort to every possible trick not to liberate unencumbered convicts who had served their terms, often 'accidentally' increasing the length of sentences in their books. Muslim slaves appear to have been used only when Venice was in a state of war with the Porte, and were supposed to be liberated once peace was signed. Since most *ponentine* states in the Mediterranean were always more or less at war with their Islamic neighbours, slaves on western Mediterranean galleys generally rowed for life or until ransomed. Convicts on *ponentine* galleys served from a few months to life, or *a beneplacito* – at the discretion of their governments, a rather vague and sinister concept.

The sort of chained humanity which could be found on a western Mediterranean galley can be understood by the following examples taken from an inventory of the Florentine fleet in 1555.

> Bernardino from Bibbiena for having taken three wives, sent for five years ... Ercole di Benedetto from Pisa, cheese maker, with a three year sentence for sodomy ... Ser Lorenzo di Bernardino Niccolucci from Modigliana, sent by the inquisition for life as a heretic ... Senso di Giusto from Monterchi, sentenced for life for having raped and deflowered a thirteen-year-old girl ... Mustafa, Turk from Anatolia, 45 years of age, tall and white-skinned, branded in the face with His Excellency's [Cosimo I de' Medici] arms, captured in the Gulf of Salerno by Don Pedro de Toledo ... Salem, moor from Tunis, branded on the right cheek with an M, and with an S on the left, lame, bought in Naples ... Abdul of Tripoli, blackamoor, known as *Cazogrosso*, tall and lanky with a mark near the hair, lacking two upper teeth ... Saim, Granadane [now] from Algiers, aged 35, can't row being blind ... [46]

Information like this evokes images of sweating, gaunt men, constantly subjected to the lash of their overseers. But the way the crews were treated depended on the individual captains, and only very foolish ones would unnecessarily overwork their rowers: forced oarsmen, convicts or slaves, were expensive, costing anything from forty pieces of eight upward in the mid-sixteenth century.[47] Likewise, the entrenched belief that galleys stank to high heaven is only partially true. Some captains had little care for hygiene – with potentially disastrous results, as shown by the fate of the Venetian fleet in 1570 – while others insisted on washing men, decks and benches every other day.

Nonetheless, the life of a galley oarsmen was tolerable at best and at worst hellish. When not at the bench non-free oarsmen, and in the western Mediterranean also *buonevoglie*, stayed in special places called *bagni*, corral-like structures with courtyards surrounded by rooms or cells. In Christian ports there was usually only one *bagno*, while in places like Algiers, Tripoli or Tunis there could be several, housing not only oarsmen but also many of the other slaves of which these cities were filled. Rowers could be recognized by their shaved heads – although Muslim slaves had a small knot of hair in the middle of the skull – and the iron ring on their right heels. In Livorno they wore a shirt, baggy trousers and a floppy red cap. A recognized hierarchy based on seniority existed among slaves and convicts, one functioning as spokesman for the others. Many paid their overseers for the right to exercise some sort of commercial activity or avoid being selected for the heaviest tasks – in Algiers, for instance, working in the local stone quarry. Suicide was a regular occurrence among *bagni* inmates, many being unable to withstand the imprisonment and constant bullying. Yet *bagni* were also meeting places with shops and taverns, in Algiers the latter being run by Christians but frequented also by Muslims. Everywhere official or tacit religious tolerance was practised, Christian clergy being allowed to say mass in Algiers, and in Livorno the Islamic slaves had their own mosque inside the *bagno*. Contrary to what is commonly believed, slaves both in Christian and Muslim countries were not under constant pressure to change their religion, although the Algerians would try to convert to Islam prisoners with particular skills in exchange for their freedom.[48]

Given their hard not to say harsh life, it not surprising that many galley convicts, slaves or even *buonevoglie* took to their heels when they had the chance. Those who enjoyed greater freedom and privileges would also attempt to escape, like a certain Maestro Pedro, who after many years in captivity managed to seize a boat and sail to Valencia, despite having in Algiers his own house with a chapel.[49] Escape rings, sometimes run by unscrupulous locals, existed in every port, together with officially recognized bodies whose purpose was to ransom fellow countrymen or coreligionists. Escaping was always risky and fugitives could expect savage treatment if apprehended. In Algiers recaptured runaway slaves could expect mutilation, severe beatings and even death. Cosimo I de' Medici ordered the ears and noses of two recaptured Turks to be cut off 'as an example for the others'.[50] These instances of extreme brutality coexisted with examples of great chivalry. Courage, generosity and sticking to one's principles were qualities everyone admired, and allowed for courteous behaviour between otherwise bitter enemies. Illustrative of this is the letter sent in 1576 by the Ottoman corsair Cara Assam Reis to the grand duke of Tuscany Francesco I de' Medici.*

> A few days ago arrived here a Turq asked [i.e. called] Sinan of Mythilene, once a slaiv on the Grand Duke of Tuskany's galleys. The said Turq has made himself yours reccomendation for which we thanck you verry particullarle the Captain Caraasam. Iff you shuld need anythung from here I am willings to serve you. Iff you shuld disere to do me a favour helping theis *rais* for which we would consider donne it to ush beeng an old man. Nothung else; if you should neid something in Barbary or Turquey I am entirrely at your servise. God keep you in health.[51]

Such civility was customary between gallant and worthy foes, particularly people of rank, and transcended the fact that important captives were a source of ransom money. The well-known exchange between Dragut and La Valette when the former was a prisoner of Giannettino Doria (La Valette: 'Mister Dragut, custom of war.' Dragut: 'Yes, and reverse of fortune.')[52] is only one of many examples. La Valette himself had just been released from the captivity of a Muslim galley, and so could appreciate Dragut's plight. The fact was that both Christians and Muslims were confident in their beliefs allowed them to treat their religious enemies with assurance.

~

Even before its official ratification all of the Holy League's signatories had started enlisting soldiers on a grand scale. Recruitment officials were busy everywhere in search of suitable candidates for

* The original Italian is full of misspellings and lacks punctuation. My translation tries to capture the flavour of the document.

the colours: feudal lords ordered their retainers out; states levied military contingents from subject communities; aristocrats from all over Europe – including some French, thus defying their government's veto – eagerly joined the anti-Ottoman expedition, some leading parties of soldiers, others simply as volunteers. If it had not been for the looming war, the gathering of the league's fleet would have been the most fashionable event of the season. Reasons for enlisting were many, ranging from lofty crusading ideals to rather more prosaic motives: Knight of St Stephen Luigi della Stufa joined the allied fleet to redeem himself from some sort of misdemeanour that had cost him two years of exile from Florence.[53] But everyone, whatever their motives and whether from the top echelons of society, the petty nobility or the lower classes, aspired to glory and money – 'in the name of God and good profit', as the Florentines would say. Their goals and aspirations were similar to those of their Muslim counterparts and typical of a world in which religion was integral to daily life.

Francesco Maria della Rovere was born 1549, the son of Guidobaldo II duke of Urbino and Vittoria Farnese, granddaughter of Pope Paul III. His father, like many Italian princes, soldiered by profession, and Francesco Maria received an education befitting someone of his station, physical activities going hand-in-hand with humanistic culture. At the age of sixteen he asked to be allowed to join the Holy Roman Emperor's forces, then busy fighting in Hungary. Guidobaldo agreed, but being then in the service of Philip II had first to seek his employer's permission. The king, wishing to keep Italy under his thumb, insisted that Francesco Maria go to Madrid. The young heir to the dukedom of Urbino arrived there at the beginning of 1570 after visiting every court in northern Italy. In Spain he befriended a number of important people, including Don Juan of Austria, but soon tired of courtly life. Having been refused permission to visit France, he decided to return to Italy and when in Genoa was the guest of Giovanni Andrea Doria. His desire was to gain experience in statecraft, 'but since his father showed no desire to employ him, he went back to his long-neglected studies'.

On hearing about the Holy League, he rushed to join Don Juan of Austria in Genoa, leaving behind his newly wed wife Lucrezia d'Este, sister of the duke of Ferrara.[54]

Not from a royal family but nonetheless someone who could boast Pope Boniface VIII among his ancestors was Onorato Caetani. Born in 1542 to Bonifazio, duke of Sermoneta, and Caterina Pio di Carpi, Onorato, like Francesco Maria, received the typical education of a Renaissance gentleman – designed to fortify the intellect as much as the body – under the direction of his uncle Cardinal Nicola, known as Cardinal Sermoneta. Sermoneta would be a crucial element in Onorato's life. Made a cardinal when only nine by his kinsman Paul III – whose mother was Giovannella Caetani, Nicola's great-aunt – he was notorious for his lechery, but nonetheless a religious reformer and a friend of the Jesuits and the Oratory of St Filippo Neri. Onorato himself was a supporter of the Oratorians and committed to his religious beliefs. Since Cardinal Sermoneta was one of those who had worked most assiduously behind the scenes for the Holy League,[55] it was not difficult for him to obtain a prestigious commission for his nephew, who happened also to be Marcantonio Colonna's brother-in-law. Onorato, one of the few Roman nobles with any naval experience, was made captain-general of the pope's maritime troops.[56]

Although Pius V had confirmed Colonna in the post of high admiral, his disappointing performance during the previous year's expedition required someone competent in maritime matters be appointed to assist him. For the sake of Colonna's dignity and the Holy See's prestige it was necessary to find someone neutral, but of recognized international standing. Pius had no doubt about the right person for the job, and on 12 June 1571 wrote to the celebrated knight of Malta Romegas, inviting him to join his fleet. Romegas did not hesitate for a minute, and ten days later climbed aboard Colonna's flagship with the rank of superintendent of the papal galleys.[57]

Fra Mathurin Lescaut, *dit* Romegas from the name of one of his family's estates, was already a legend. Born in 1528 to a French noble family connected with the great house of Armagnac, he joined the Hospitallers around the age of fourteen in 1542, being dubbed a knight four years later after completing the prescribed period of religious and military apprenticeship. Quickly making a name for himself as a redoubtable sea fighter, Romegas seemed blessed with incredible stamina. When in 1551 his galley was over-turned by a waterspout, he managed to survive underwater for twelve hours clinging to the keel with his head in an air pocket. The incident severely affected his nervous system, to the extent that his hands never stopped shaking and he could not drink from a glass without spilling some of the contents. It is unclear if the incident also affected Romegas's character, for he is reputed to have been exacting with his men and harsh with prisoners. What is certain is that he was totally committed to the defence of the Catholic faith, fighting with unbounded zeal Protestants and Muslims alike. Con-sidered by all one of the greatest mariners of his age, he knew intimately every nook and cranny of the Mediterranean.[58]

Equal to Romegas in maritime skill but on the Ottoman side was the *beylerbey* of Algiers Uluç Ali Pasha. Originally Luca (or possibly Giovanni Dionigi) Galeni, he was born in Le Castella in Calabria, the tip of Italy's boot, around 1511 into a family of fishermen, reputedly becoming a Dominican friar. Captured by Barbary corsairs and chained to a rowing bench, he converted to Islam – according to one unconfirmed story, his decision motivated by the wish to hide under a turban the ringworm on his head – managed to obtain his freedom and married the daughter of his former master. After fighting at the battle of Preveza he became one of Dragut's associates and soon one of the most feared men in the Mediterranean. It was thanks to his advice that Piyale Pasha decided to attack the Christian fleet at Djerba in 1560, and in June of the same year during a raid against Villafranca Uluç Ali nearly managed to capture the duke of Savoy Emmanuel Philibert. As a reward for his services the sultan made him commander of the Egyptian fleet based at Alexandria, and after Dragut's death at the siege of Malta Uluç Ali succeeded him as governor of Tripoli. Two years later he became *beylerbey* of Algiers and in 1570 captured Tunis for the Ottomans. Of average height, well built with a thick beard, reputed to be at the same time 'most cruel and inhuman' and 'indefatigable and very generous', he was universally recognized as one the ablest naval tacticians of his day.[59]

Equally experienced if not as famous was the commander of the Egyptian fleet Şuluç Mehmed Pasha, better known in Christian Europe as Maometto Scirocco. Another of Dragut's associates, he had been at sea since his teens, operating mainly against the Genoese in Liguria and Corsica. Present at the siege of Malta, after the fall of Fort St Elmo he was given the task of relaying the good news to the sultan in Constantinople. Promoted to governor of Alexandria, during the Cyprus campaign he commanded the Chios and Rhodes squadrons after their commanders' disgrace following Querini's exploit at Famagusta. The Venetians had a particular grudge against Scirocco for his 'insolent' attitude towards them even before the outbreak of the war. Skilled in naval affairs and a devout Muslim, Şuluç was a foe to be reckoned with.[60]

Religion also motivated others. Pompeo Floriani, born in Macerata in 1545, at seventeen had gone to France with the expeditionary force sent by Pius IV to fight the Huguenots. Having risen to company commander, Floriani, a skilled architect and engineer, was once more facing battle against the infidel under his old colonel Paolo Sforza, count of Santa Fiora. Knight of St Stephen Bernardino Antinori came from an old Florentine family with a military background; his cousin Amerigo had fought under Henry VIII of England and the Emperor Charles V. Bernardino, a cultivated man and a poet in his own right, was the son of one of Cosimo I's most trusted servants and had entered the Tuscan order in 1567, following in the footsteps of his older brother Alfonso. After the statutory period of religious and military training, which included the study of history, astronomy, navigation, geometry, arithmetic, drawing and the art of war, fencing with a variety of weapons, shooting with the harquebus, crossbow and the 'Turkish' bow, and wrestling, he went to sea hoping to gain sufficient reputation and seniority to allow him to enjoy the revenues of one of the order's commanderies.[61]

Seeking glory and fortune was also an obscure figure, later destined to overshadow nearly all other participants in the expedition. Miguel de Cervantes y Saavedra was born in 1547 in Alcalá de Henares, a small town near Madrid, into a family with some pretensions to nobility, even if his mother may have been descended from converted Jews. His father, Rodrigo de Cervantes, was an apothecary-surgeon of little means and often in debt, so much of Miguel's childhood was spent moving from town to town with his constantly work-seeking father. Educated by the Jesuits in Cordova and Seville, Miguel later studied under one Juan López de Hoyos in Madrid. Forced to flee from Spain to Rome at the end of 1568 for wounding another man, he entered the service of Cardinal Giulio Acquaviva in 1570. But the same year Cervantes, wishing like many young Spaniards to try his luck in war, joined a Spanish infantry regiment destined for the Levant.[62]

Men of letters could be found on both sides. The scribe Hindī (Dark) Mahmūd was born in Afyon Karahisar, in western Anatolia, to a family of local standing. Thanks to the good offices of a *kadi* (judge) uncle he managed to gain access to Prince Selim, securing employment in the latter's household. Following his master to Konya, Hindī gained experience in both clerical and diplomatic affairs. During this time he also managed to visit Mecca three times as a pilgrim, something which contributed to his rising status. Steadily advancing in the prince's service, his career took a leap forward when Selim became sultan, Mahmūd being given judicial responsibilities in the town of Diyarbakir.[63] Like all administrators, Hindī Mahmūd also had military duties, and in this capacity was on board one of the Ottoman ships.

Leaving aside slaves and convicts, not all those climbing aboard the league's galleys were there spontaneously. Venice's maritime levy required all subject communities to provide galley rowers, and the inland town of Brescia had to contribute a quota of 378 men. However, the various political and social bodies in Brescia and its territories started quarrelling among themselves over how many men each of them should provide, with the guild of notaries claiming exemption because of ancient privileges. After two months of quibbling and haggling with the Venetian authorities, in May 1571 Venice peremptorily ordered Brescia to send without further delay 338 rowers, sufficient to man two galleys, promising to resolve at a later date the matter of the forty men owed by the notaries. Given the unpopularity of naval conscription, Venice attempted to sweeten the pill by allowing galleys crewed with levied rowers to have local commanders and officers. On 3 March Brescia's city council had elected Giovanni Antonio Cavalli and Orazio Fisogni to the role of *sopracomiti*. Of the two, the fifty-year-old Cavalli was the more experienced, having participated in various naval and land campaigns, including the battle of Mühlberg. Both men started immediately to recruit sailors and other naval personnel, completing their task by the 24th of the same month.[64]

Unlike many others, the Tuscan convict oarsman Aurelio Scetti was not keen to go east. A musician by trade who had performed at various Italian courts, on 20 August 1565 'inspired by a diabolical spirit' he had killed his wife with a razor, managing to break a leg while attempting to escape by jumping out of a window. Condemned to death for murder, his friends in Florence managed to get Cosimo I to commute the sentence to life service on the galleys. Because of the lameness deriving from his broken limb, Scetti spent little time at the oars (as a matter of fact certain contradictions in his memoirs arouse the suspicion that he rowed not one day) and at some point was given some sort of minor clerical post. Endlessly complaining about his self-inflicted miserable condition, Scetti beheld the Tuscan galleys leaving port with a mixture of fear and anticipation.[65]

~

Besides artillery, the fighting capability of a galley was provided by its complement of soldiers. A normal galley had the capacity to carry up to 100–150 soldiers, up to 400 in the case of *bastarde*. With the exception of Venice, few states had troops specifically assigned to serve at sea, and crewmen other than rowers, called by the Spanish *gente de cabo* (artillerymen, sailors and galley guards), were considered combatants for all intents and purposes.[66] As we have already seen, in Venice conscript and volunteer rowers were also expected to fight in sea battles while in *ponentine* galleys convict rowers, or even *buonevoglie*, received weapons only in extreme circumstances. Spain had lost the cream of its experienced naval fighters at Djerba, and from then onward deputed regular infantry to serve on its galleys. Venice employed marines (known as *scapoli* or *uomini da spada*, swordsmen)* in large quantities, usually but not invariably recruiting them from the costal areas of eastern Italy, Dalmatia, Albania and Greece. The main difference between *scapoli* and the other soldiers to be found on Venetian galleys was that the former were intended to serve exclusively at sea.[67]

Tuscany attempted to recruit marines by introducing a levy in its coastal areas, but the resulting yield in men was never more than 650 and often less. The grand dukes could tap into the well-trained and efficient Tuscan militia for galley troops, but during the 1571 expedition the *asiento* between Cosimo I and Pius V placed the responsibility for troops squarely on the pope's shoulders. As a result, the rank and file on the Tuscan galleys came mostly from the papal states or served under papal officers. Many of the gentlemen rankers (*venturieri* in Italian, *particulares* in Spanish) and junior officers were Tuscan, approximately 100 coming from the Order of St Stephen. The Ottomans had fewer problems finding the necessary military manpower for their fleets, employing for this purpose *timar* and *kapıkulu* troops and normally only sixty per galley. In addition, the

---

* Sir John Hale aptly describes *scapolo* as 'a chameleon-like term', appropriately translating it as marine. HALE (1983): 312. Yet *scapolo* in the rest of Italy usually meant what it still means today, bachelor. Thus in Tuscany an order to select *scapoli* for galley service from the ranks of the militia meant choosing unmarried men. See for example: ASF, MM, 370, ins. 40, segn. 46, nn.ff. 'Ragguaglio della spesa della Banca al tempo del Gran Duca Francesco, Gran Duca Ferdinando, e del Gran Duca Cosimo' (1620).

sailing crews and free rowers were expected to fight alongside the professional combatants.[68]

With war raging in the eastern Mediterranean, Spain and Flanders, raising enough soldiers to serve on the league's galleys was not easy. For those recruiting for the papal fleet difficulties were increased by Pius V's order 'not to enroll any beardless boy', and scores of soldiers already enlisted had to be dismissed. Many of the Spanish troops were green, Don Garcia de Toledo commenting that they hardly knew how to fire their harquebuses, and that if he had to fight the seasoned Ottoman soldiers he would much prefer to have some veterans from Flanders. Yet the Ottomans, although daunting enemies, were not as formidable as Don Garcia painted them. Their galleys had been at sea since the spring and badly needed maintenance. Ill feeling was rampant among the *sipahi*s and janissaries allotted to serve with the fleet, many of whom had been on campaign for more than a year and seen scores of their comrades die in Cyprus.

Venice had similarly serious problems, many of its subjects recruited the year before having fallen victim to the epidimic which had ravaged the republic's fleet. The solution, of course, was to enlist foreigners. But the recruitment campaign produced disappointing results, the Venetians paying through the nose for often inferior and untrustworthy soldiers. To make matters worse, 4,000 men destined for the galleys would not reach them due to an Ottoman foray into the Adriatic that July. As a result, the Venetian vessels were undermanned – Caetani calculating just sixty to eighty fighting men each – forcing their commander Sebastiano Venier to accept Don Juan of Austria and Colonna's offer of extra manpower.[69]

Soldiers were supposed to come with their own weapons, but every galley kept stocks of arms to equip soldiers, sailors and other members of the crew. The 1562 statutes of the Order of St Stephen stated that on each galley there should be seventy-five sets of body armour plus fifty helmets and fifty bucklers, one hundred pikes or 'short weapons' and as many harquebuses. The previously mentioned 1588 inventory of two Spanish galleys lists fifty harque-buses, sixty-six edged weapons including sixteen pikes, a two-handed sword and forty-six helmets. Similar weapons in type and number, with the addition of some fifty breastplates for each ship, were also stored on the Lomellini galleys in 1575. The evidence points to a reduction in the number of pikes versus firearms in the latter part of the sixteenth century, following the universal trend in this direction. Indeed, a memorandum directed to Don Garcia de Toledo in the early 1560s stated clearly the need that all the soldiers on a galley 'should be harquebusiers'.[70]

The harquebus used a matchlock mechanism and fired a lead ball of approximately half an ounce capable of killing an unprotected man at 200 yards, even if it would take an exceptional marksman to hit a target at more than sixty. Another of the harquebus's drawbacks was its slow rate of fire, although a skilled individual in ideal circumstances could shoot three times in a minute. Maintaining a steady rate of fire was considered more important than accuracy, the tactical employment of firearms calling for formations a number of lines deep delivering massed volleys. Around the 1590s the Dutch would realize that rotating the ranks of their soldiers, moving them to the rear to reload after shooting, could increase the volume of fire.[71] But this was nearly impossible to do on a narrow galley bridge, and even the galley's forecastle was too cramped to allow for such manoeuvres. Seeking ways to keep the bullets flying, navies came up with some ingenious solutions. One is described in a 1570 report by Giovan Francesco Morosini, Venetian ambassador at the court of Savoy:

In addition to the sixty sailors on each of His Excellency's [Emmanuel Philibert] galleys, there are also eighty to one hundred soldiers. Each of these carries two harquebuses with fifty charges, powder and shot being tied together in a piece of paper. Thus once the harquebus has been fired, nothing remains to do but load it up again by placing the paper wrap in the barrel with unbelievable speed. And if need be, this operation is done by one of the oarsmen on each bench specifically assigned to this task. In this manner, while the soldier fires his piece, the rower has already loaded and primed another one, so that shots rain without interruption and much damage for the enemy.[72]

Ottoman janissaries, as we have already seen, also made extensive use of firearms, but for the *sipahis* matters were different. Due to a misguided sense of honour and military conservatism, for a long time the *timar*-holding cavalrymen spurned firearms, relying on their traditional weapons even when serving dismounted on galleys. This was less of a disadvantage than may at first appear, since the Turks made extensive use of the composite recurved bow. Often seen as an anachronism by those who believe in technological progress at all costs, in the sixteenth century the bow was still a formidable weapon. An Ottoman bowman could deliver something like six aimed arrows a minute, even more when employing barrage shooting against a dense mass of men or ships. The effectiveness of composite bows is proved by the fact that the Venetians were still storing them on their galleys after the Cyprus war. The bow's main defect was that it needed brawn and lengthy training to function effectively, its draw force of approximately 150 pounds draining a man's energy with each arrow fired. Besides, it took several years for a bowman to learn to handle his weapon properly, while a good instructor could train a reasonably able harquebusier in a few days.[73] With the benefit of hindsight, it is easy to assert the clear superiority of firearms over other types of projectile weapons, yet at the time of the Cyprus war this was far from a foregone conclusion. The effectiveness of the harquebus against Ottoman troops was more a consequence of the latter's use of light or no body armour than the firearm's intrinsic qualities; a harquebus ball could easily pierce the coats of plate or mail worn by those *sipahis* who could afford them. On the other hand, the cuirasses, breastplates and helmets worn by Western infantrymen gave considerable protection against arrows, unless they happened to strike an exposed part of the body such as the face. It is also true that many harquebusiers or even pikemen wore open helmets and no body armour except for leather or quilted cotton jackets.[74] Arrows could easily pierce these sorts of garments, and soldiers would try to exploit the protection of the thick planking typical of the high gunwales found on Western galleys.

Arming a galley fleet was a hugely expensive and lengthy operation. As Grand Vizier Koja Sinan Pasha would write in 1589, 'One can launch a campaign on land by a mere command: everybody mounts his horse and sets off. A naval expedition is not like that . . . however great the material investment and human efforts made, it can only be realized in seven to eight months.' Rulers across the Mediterranean would have agreed. Efficient states like the Ottoman empire had developed elaborate logistics systems to feed their armies on campaign, and alternatively soldiers could always live off the land.[75] Naval warfare, on the other hand, required considerable forethought, since once at sea a fleet could not replenish its supplies, with the exception of water, until it reached a friendly port. In addition, even a small fleet could be a considerable burden on a country's budget. The few galleys that the Medici put to sea every spring cost around 15 per cent of Tuscany's annual revenues. During the Cyprus war arming and manning ninety-six galleys consumed 13–14 per cent of Spain's income including that of Naples, Milan and Sicily, plus the monetary yield of the Three Graces.[76]

Since galleys relied at least as much on human as on natural power, the oarsman's diet had to provide him with the necessary strength to do his work properly. The basic component of every rower's meal was biscuit, of the hard tack variety, often broken up and mixed with water to create a kind of bread soup. But biscuit only provided carbohydrates, and an oarsman's dietary needs also included sufficient protein. Tuscany, like other Mediterranean states, recognized this by regulating the daily amount of food each crew member was to receive.

> Three pounds [a Florentine pound was 339 grams] of black bread a day, or alternatively two and a half pounds of biscuit. On Sundays, Wednesdays and Fridays, three pennies of rice for their

soup, or six of beans with five ounces of oil. At Easter, Christmas and Carnival they receive an extra allowance of one pound of fresh meat, half a measure of pure wine, and a soup. When required to perform extra efforts, half a ration of biscuit and half a measure of pure wine; as an alternative, half a measure of acid wine and two pennies of oil for each bench.[77]

The relatively small allocation of meat was not unusual, flesh not being a normal component of the diet of the poorer classes at the time. Oarsmen on Savoyard galleys received thirty-six ounces of bread a day, often selling the excess to buy wine, while those in Giovanni Andrea Doria's fleet received only thirty ounces. The dietary situation was not as grim as might appear, since crewmen could easily supplement their daily ration with the fish readily obtainable all over the Mediterranean. The *gente de cabo* on Spanish galleys, in addition to their bread ration, also got bacon, cheese, fish and beef. Soldiers received similar allowances. Fresh meat was provided by the livestock carried on board, chickens, rams and calves, slaughtered according to need [78]

All this resulted in galleys being veritable money and food sponges. In 1571 the twelve belonging to Giovanni Andrea Doria received from the Spanish Crown 40,000 pounds of biscuit, 9,000 litres of wine, 3,100 pounds of salted meat, 1,535 pounds of dried herrings, 2,940 pounds of cheese, 4,600 pounds of oil, 810 litres of vinegar, 2,400 pounds of fava beans and 240 pounds of salt, costing in total nearly 1,000 pieces of eight. But all these supplies were sufficient only for a fortnight, just the biscuit consumption of the rowing crew of an ordinary galley being in the range of 7,500 pounds a month. In other words, the victuals consumed by twelve galleys during a three-month cruise would cost more than 6,000 pieces of eight, keeping in mind that food prices fluctuated according to the availability of certain agricultural products in a given place. However, such sums did not represent a straight loss for galley owners, since oarsmen, crewmen and soldiers were supposed to pay for their living. This could be cripplingly expensive for those concerned. In 1615 a Venetian *galeotto di libertà* spent more than three quarters of his wages on the necessary drink 'to sustain himself during efforts'. In 1572 a soldier on a Tuscan galley received a monthly salary of twenty-one Florentine lire (three and a half pieces of eight), but spent nearly nineteen just on food. No wonder so many of those serving on galleys descended into chronic debt, especially when employed by governments, like the Spanish crown, notorious for being bad paymasters. On 18 March 1571 Giovanni Andrea Doria was informed that two companies of Spanish infantry he had left in Palermo the year before were owed eight months' pay, and that the little money they had received in the meantime had barely covered the debts incurred to buy food during the previous three months.[79]

The galley's main logistical problem, and one of the reasons it generally hugged the coastline, was its constant need to replenish its water supply. A normal galley needed between 230 and 280 men to function properly, two thirds of them rowers.[80] Given that rowing is extremely dehydrating work, the men at the oars needed a constant intake of liquid. Water was also used to prepare the soup that constituted the main meal of oarsmen, sailors and soldiers alike. But a galley had limited storage space and also had to accommodate all sorts of stores, ropes, gunpowder, weapons and ammunition. This meant that every few days a galley had to interrupt its progress to land parties of men to search for water, a time-consuming operation which was also fraught with danger if undertaken in enemy territory. For such reasons a galley captain's reputation rested not so much on his success as a tactician – albeit an important factor – as on his ability to keep his vessel in operational order. A galley in good shape, with adequate provisions, well-maintained ordnance and a trained fighting complement was a formidable war machine, one destined to dominate Mediterranean warfare even after the appearance of the great men-of-war from the Atlantic.

8. BRAGADIN'S HIDE

~

As the long line of seventeen galleys approached the mouth of the port of Naples on 24 June 1571, shots rang out in salute from the nearby fortresses. People of all social classes gathered on the shore to behold this living theatre of gilded wood, muscle and metal. Two galleys were from the Neapolitan squadron, but from the mainmasts of twelve others fluttered the papal banner, and the remaining three proudly sported the white cross of the Order of Malta.

The papal high admiral Marcantonio Colonna had departed from the port of Civitavecchia three days before at the head of His Holiness's fleet (courtesy of Cosimo I de' Medici), picking up the other galleys on the way, having spent the previous two weeks raising men and gathering victuals. In fact the infantry companies on board were under strength, but Colonna, remembering what had happened the previous year and fearing that the long voyage between Civitavecchia and Cyprus could result in the death of many men, had correctly calculated that he could fill his ranks by recruiting in Sicily.

The viceroy of Naples Cardinal Granvelle had come to the port in person to greet the papal commander, but the animosity between the two men, thinly disguised under a veil of courtesy, prompted the papal admiral to refuse the viceroy's invitation to stay in his palace. Colonna's intention was to wait in Naples for Don Juan of Austria, but on receiving fresh instructions from Rome he departed for the Sicilian port of Messina, reaching it on 20 July. In Naples he had managed to replace a dilapidated Maltese galley with a new one, but otherwise his stay could hardly be described a success. No sooner had he arrived that a brawl erupted between some papal soldiers and the Spanish of the local garrison; this quickly escalated into a battle with dead and wounded on both sides. The pontifical troops even broke into Granvelle's palace, and only Colonna's timely arrival avoided more violence and bloodshed. Tempers were still running high, however, and following another scuffle in Messina between Spaniards and Italians, Colonna was forced to send the culprits to the gallows or the oars.[1] It was not the ideal start for what was supposed to be a long-term collaboration between Christian princes against the infidels.

The Venetians reached Messina three days later. Captain-General Sebastiano Venier had arrived in Corfu in April, and after receiving the banner of command from the hands of Agostino Barbarigo had immediately set to work to get his fleet in fighting condition. By all accounts the seventy-five-year-old Venier was the quintessential man of action, often to the point of rashness. Born in 1496 into one of the most distinguished patrician families of Venice, Venier, a lawyer by training, had an impressive record of public service. Governor of Crete from 1548 to 1551, he later administered the cities of Brescia and Verona, plus holding a number of other posts. Created *procuratore di San Marco*★ for his services to the republic, the outbreak of the 1570 war found him in charge of Venice's fortresses, and in March of the same year he was elected governor of Corfu. Designated governor of Cyprus in place of Niccolò Dandolo, he was unable to reach the island due to illness and Doria's delaying tactics, and after Girolamo Zane's disgrace stepped into his shoes as captain-general of the Venetian fleet.

★ *Procuratore di San Marco* was the highest dignity of the Venetian republic after that of doge, and was likewise for life. It was bestowed on prominent individuals with a distinguished record of public service.

Although inexperienced as a warrior, he was a first-class administrator and an aggressive commander, both much-needed qualities in the spring of 1571. Venier was also a staunch patriot, old enough to remember Venice's golden days before her humiliation during the war of the League of Cambrai. The anti-Ottoman conflict of 1537–39 had fostered his mistrust of the Habsburgs and the Genoese, the latter Venice's traditional enemies, his animosity towards the former growing stronger while serving as one of the delegates to the inconclusive mid-1560s Venetian–Habsburg talks over a disputed border in Friuli. It would emerge time and again during the 1571 campaign.[2]

To counter Venier's lack of military expertise, not to mention lack of diplomacy, the Venetian government had installed as his deputy Agostino Barbarigo. Twenty years younger than Venier, Barbarigo also came from an illustrious family, one of his relatives and namesake having been doge at the beginning of the sixteenth century. More important, he had considerable experience both in diplomatic and seafaring matters, having among other things served on an ambassadorial mission to France in 1557 and navigated on galleys since his youth. As *provveditore generale da mar* he was subordinate to the captain-general, but due to Venier's abrasive character destined to become the main representative of Venice's interests within the allied fleet.[3]

Venier had been dissatisfied with what he had found in Corfu. There were twenty-eight galleys in the harbour, all of them in bad condition and lacking provisions. The fortress's defences and artillery also left much to be desired, but Venier could do little to improve the situation until the arrival of reinforcements from Venice. The captain-general was not a man to remain idle, and in the meantime busied himself by reinforcing the garrison of Sopot and trying in vain to take the Ottoman port of Durazzo (Durrës). The Ottomans were successful in repulsing the sallies of Sopot's garrison, on one occasion killing or capturing twenty Venetians.

At length more ships arrived from Venice, together with orders to reinforce with thirty galleys the squadron stationed in Cretan waters. On 6 May Venier received an urgent request for help from Famagusta, the message stressing that the Ottomans had only 100 galleys available to support the besiegers. The captain-general wanted to depart immediately, confident that his ninety-four galleys – including those in Crete – would be sufficient to force the Turkish blockade, but his war council opposed the decision. Paolo Orsini in particular objected that such an enterprise required a fully equipped fleet of at least 130 galleys, ten galleasses and ten transport ships. Venier bowed to the majority will, although later he would complain that had his idea been accepted, Famagusta would have been saved and Venetian territories spared from Ottoman depredations. However, Orsini and the others were probably right to be cautious, since Venier himself admitted that he did not even have forty *scapoli* on each galley, even after the disarming of three of the worst galleys had put at his disposal 386 sailors, marines and rowers. In fact, to reach the barely acceptable number of sixty *scapoli* per galley he would have needed some 800 extra men. Given the shortage of manpower, tackling the Ottoman fleet without the aid of the heavily armed galleasses would have been extremely risky, not to say suicidal.

In any case, the captain-general already had his hands full trying to defend Corfu and the other Venetian possessions in the area, especially after an expeditionary force of 3,000 men was repulsed by the Ottomans near Kotor with heavy losses. To make matters worse, at the end of June Venier received news that Ottoman galleys had ravaged Crete and were moving towards the Ionian Sea. Realizing that he risked being bottled up in Corfu, he sent orders to the Cretan squadron to meet him in Messina, overruling his war council's proposal that the fleet should move to Brindisi instead. As he awaited Barbarigo's return from a scouting mission, six galleasses under Francesco Duodo arrived in Corfu and on 11 July Venier departed for Messina with fifty-eight galleys and the six galleasses. The latter's slowness – being rowed *alla sensile* with only three men to each bench – meant not only that they had to be towed by galleys, but also that the whole fleet's cruising speed was much reduced.[4] Once Venier arrived in Messina twelve days later he immediately set to work with Colonna's aid to recruit soldiers, although managing to find half of the number he needed. To save on provisions he paid his soldiers extra, which in the long run proved a wise decision since the arrival of the allied fleet in Messina sparked a dramatic rise in food prices. Having joined hands, the only thing Colonna and Venier could do was wait for the arrival of the Spanish and their allies.[5]

Don Juan of Austria departed from Madrid on 6 June, but despite the pope's urgings that he reach Italy with the utmost haste Philip II's half brother took nearly three months to reach Messina. This was partly due to the many ceremonies and receptions he attended en route – a necessary component of any royal progress of the time. But many suspected that once more the king of Spain was employing delaying tactics to block any expedition to the Levant, the pope and the Venetians in particular taking Don Juan's endless delays as a sign of the king's lack of commitment.[6] Their distrust was not unfounded, since Philip's aim was to put off the fleet's departure without increasing the Venetians' already strong suspicions.

In Barcelona Don Juan received a letter from Philip ordering him to listen to Giovanni Andrea Doria's advice and on no account to risk battle without the unanimous consent of Doria, the *comendador mayor de Castilla* Luis de Requesens y Zuñiga and the marquis of Santa Cruz.[7] Given Doria's well-known prudence, ordering Don Juan to pay heed to his advice was tantamount to telling him to avoid battle at all costs. Besides, both Doria and Requesens were tied to the duke of Alva, and thus not in favour of a sustained Spanish commitment in the Mediterranean.[8] By stressing the need for unanimity, the king was also curbing the aggressive Santa Cruz. Don Juan took these instructions as a personal affront, and in two letters – of 8 and 12 July, the first to Philip's secretary Ruy Gómez de Silva, the other to the king himself – complained about his brother's lack of trust in him, even suggesting to Gómez that he was ready to resign from his position but telling Philip, 'I will obey, as far as possible, whatever they may be, the orders which Your Majesty may give.'⁹ This was rather less petulant than it may at first appear. Once the league's fleet was at sea, it would be up to Don Juan to interpret the king's instructions according to the changing situation. In any case, the king must have been aware that should the league's other military commanders decide to fight, it would be difficult for the Spanish to refuse to do so without losing face. From Philip's point of view, the best way to avoid risking his ships was to delay as much as possible his brother's arrival in Messina.

Despite Don Juan's best intentions, it would be almost another month before he left Barcelona. No move was possible until the arrival of the Cartagena squadron under Santa Cruz, and that of Mallorca commanded by Don Sancho de Leyva. Besides, the galleys needed provisions and troops, and finding both kept Don Juan busy until the middle of July. Gathering victuals for a fleet was never an easy task in Early Modern Spain, as Miguel de Cervantes would later discover at his own expense when acting as royal purveyor at the time of the 1588 Armada. Communities were supposed to provide food, drink and other goods, and suppliers were expected to pay for what they solicited or seized. In reality, general mistrust, administrative delays, legal obstructions and the frequent lack of ready cash hindered the work of the purveyors, who resorted to bullying, cajoling, pleading and negotiation to obtain the necessary supplies.

In any case, transporting victuals to ports was never an easy task, particularly in the Spanish crown's domains. On 30 July the viceroy of Sicily's wife wrote on behalf of her ailing husband to Giovanni Andrea Doria that it would take eight to ten days to load foodstuff on the galleys once they arrived in Palermo, all victuals being still 'in the mountains' lest they rot in the summer heat. A few days later the count of Landriano informed Doria that since he had no way of collecting these provisions, Colonna and the Venetians should send some galleys to Palermo. Eventually, Colonna allotted four of his galleys for the task, gathering extra supplies in the port of Milazzo.¹⁰

Don Juan sailed from Barcelona on 20 July, arriving in Genoa on the 26th. He spent the next five days attending parties given in his honour and receiving delegations from various Italian states. For some governments Don Juan's arrival was a source of apprehension; they feared that 'the stateless prince' had no intention of sailing on to Messina, but instead would use his forces in Italy. Tuscany had mobilized its militia and reinforced its fortresses, anticipating a possible Spanish invasion. Instead, Don Juan's reception of Crown Prince Francesco de' Medici, sent by his father to pay homage to the league's commander, turned out to be of the outmost cordiality, doing much to allay Cosimo's worries. Don Juan dispelled many fears by announcing that he intended to move on to Naples as quickly as possible, stopping in Tuscany only to pick up soldiers from the Spanish-held fortress of Porto Ercole.[11] True to his word, Don Juan left Genoa on 31 July accompanied by, among others, Doria, Alessandro Farnese and Francesco Maria della Rovere. Santa Cruz had already departed for Naples with his own squadron to deal with a number of logistical matters. Don Juan arrived in Naples on 9 August, and on the 14th, after the now usual festivities in his honour, solemnly received the banner of the Holy League from the hands of Cardinal Granvelle. The need for extra soldiers and supplies caused further delays, and eventually Santa Cruz had to be left behind to complete the task. Don Juan reached Messina on the 23rd, a month after the arrival of the Venetian fleet, greeted by the guns of the fortress and of the other galley squadrons.

The next day a meeting to assess the situation was held on the Spanish flagship. Don Juan stated that he had eighty-four galleys including those, still to arrive, of Doria and Santa Cruz, plus 20,000 good Spanish, German and Italian infantry. Colonna had only twelve galleys, but all in excellent order. Venier was not so enthusiastic. He was still waiting for the rest of his ships, had few men, and had been hindered by the viceroy of Naples in his recruitment and victualling efforts. However, he was expecting the 5,000 troops promised him by Pompeo Colonna and other captains, and in any case his need for soldiers was not as pressing since

Venetian rowers were trained to fight. Don Juan offered to make good with his own troops any gaps in the Venetian ranks, and volunteered to help solve the supply problem. It would have been better for Venier had he been more economical with the truth, since those hostile to the Venetians immediately circulated his frank statements in a distorted fashion. The young inexperienced Francesco Maria della Rovere would write to his father the duke of Urbino:

> We found the papal and Venetian fleets in this port, but both in bad shape and in particular the Venetians. They have forty-eight galleys, six galleasses, and three round-ships, but without soldiers and few, sad, crewmen. Sixty galleys from Crete are expected, but up to now their whereabouts are unknown. Our fleet is very well equipped with men and everything else, being of eighty-one galleys and twenty round-ships, with 20,000 infantrymen on board.[12]

Colonna's galleys were certainly not as run-down as della Rovere, a friend of Doria and his clique, would like us to believe. Moreover, the poor condition of Venier's ships was not due to the commander's sluggishness. Ever since his arrival in Messina he had done everything in his power to bring his squadron up to scratch, only to be systematically stonewalled in his victualling efforts by the local authorities. In frustration he had sent Barbarigo with six galleys to the nearby port of Patti, while he in person with thirty other warships sailed to Tropea in Calabria, being told he could find soldiers and supplies there. Tropea had no harbour, but given the summer season the captain-general considered it safe to anchor his ships near the shore. No sooner had he arrived than a sudden storm threw his galleys against the coast, wrecking six of them. The same ill wind also hit Barbarigo's squadron, sending one of his vessels to the bottom. As ill luck would have it, another two galleys and as many round-ships loaded with supplies were captured by the Ottomans near Corfu. Venier managed to recover all the artillery, masts and other equipment from his foundered ships, but many crewmen, having already endured enough, deserted, thus contributing to Venier's despondency.[13] Francesco Maria della Rovere's patronizing attitude towards the Venetians was ignorant and unjust, to say the least.

The allied commanders having made their points, it was decided that future discussions about the campaign should be postponed until the arrival of Santa Cruz, Doria and the galleys from Crete. At the same time two galleys under Knight Commander Gil de Andrada, captain of Don Juan's flagship, were sent to discover the Ottomans' whereabouts. Don Juan's advisers, ever mindful of Philip's instructions about not risking his ships, welcomed the decision to wait. Requesens was firmly reminded in writing by Don Garcia de Toledo of the king's orders, the former viceroy stressing the importance of not accepting battle unless under totally favourable circumstances, and not to trust the Venetians, 'more used to saying, than doing' – an unfair and dishonest comment. Don Garcia's advice to Don Juan was not very different concerning the Venetians: since they were unreliable it would be better to give them the vanguard of the fleet should they request it; at the same time it would be wise not to inform the Venetians that the vanguard was up for grabs, lest they become suspicious and decline to take it. But Don Garcia also offered the young prince some very sound tactical suggestions. Remembering Barbarossa's formation at Preveza, he recommended the Christian armada be divided into three squadrons, all sailing in one line but with sufficient distance between them to allow room for manoeuvring.[14] Don Juan, as we shall see, would profit considerably from this advice.

The Spanish also tried to isolate the Venetians by bringing Marcantonio Colonna over to their side. The papal admiral was in a particularly difficult position, being grand constable of the kingdom of Naples and, more important still, a candidate for a number of prestigious posts within the Spanish domains in Europe. A wrong move on his part could jeopardize any chance of future preferment. In distress, he would write to his friend Francisco Borgia – general of the Jesuits, future saint and great-grandson of the lecherous

Alexander VI, for this reason subsequently known as the revenge of the Holy Spirit – about the letters he had received from Philip II, 'always putting before me the obligations which bind me to his service'. He added that he had given the king no offence, yet 'having last year saved the honour of his fleet, and this year helped to conclude the league, I find myself called upon to write a justification of my conduct'. He also expressed the intention of giving up his command, but would wait and see how the situation in Messina evolved. The reference to the 'honour' of the Spanish fleet was a thinly veiled criticism of Doria's dithering behaviour the year before, disingenuously omitting the fact that the Genoese admiral had preserved his master's ships. Luckily for Colonna, Don Juan was itching for action, despite the contrary opinions of his increasingly irritating advisers. In fact the prince found in the papal admiral a precious ally, both men being anxious to accomplish some memorable enterprise which would increase their prestige. At the same time, Colonna's excellent rapport with the Venetians would prove an immense asset for Don Juan in the weeks to come.[15]

~

The Ottomans, meanwhile, had not been idle. Like Venice, the Porte possessed an extensive and elaborate espionage network, and by February of 1571, despite the fact that the league was not yet officially concluded, the Ottomans were taking active steps to stymie a possible allied offensive in the Levant to relieve Famagusta. In mid-February twenty galleys were sent to reinforce the Rhodes squadron, in charge of watching the Venetians in Crete, and all the naval forces in the area put under the command of the governor of Alexandria Şuluç Mehmed Pasha. On 21 March Müezzinzâde Ali Pasha left Constantinople with thirty galleys, reaching Cyprus at the end of the month. He remained in those waters until mid-May, disembarking troops and supplies for the army besieging Famagusta, before sailing towards the port of Karystos (Castelrosso), located at the southern tip of Evvoia, with a force of fifty-five vessels. There he met the second vizier Pertev Pasha, who had left Constantinople at the beginning of the month with 124 galleys and the title of *serdar*. At the same time an army under the third vizier Ahmed Pasha was assembling in Skopje, in Macedonia, ready to operate in conjunction with the fleet against Venetian possessions in Greece. Müezzinzâde Ali spent a few weeks in Karystos, repairing his vessels and waiting for reinforcements. Eventually, with the arrival of Uluç Ali together with a number of Anatolian corsairs, he would have approximately 250 oared vessels of various types, with another twenty left to cover the siege operations in Cyprus. The *kapudan paşa* also carried with him orders 'to find and immediately attack the Infidel's fleet in order to save the honour of our religion and state'. With Famagusta still holding out, the last thing the Ottomans wanted was another Querini-style relief expedition.[16]

Müezzinzâde Ali's next objective was Crete. A raid on the settlements at Souda Bay netted a number of prisoners, and from them he managed to find out the exact strength of the Venetian naval forces based on the island. Boldly, the *kapudan paşa* split his forces into two divisions: one to attack the ports of Chania and Irakleio, while the second, under Uluç Ali, was given the task of capturing the fortress of Rethymno. On 20 June Müezzinzâde Ali tried to take Irakleio by surprise, but the alertness of *provveditore* Querini foiled his plan, forcing him to call off the assault after sustaining losses. Another attempt against the fortress of Turlurù was equally unsuccessful, and to make matters worse a sudden squall drove twelve of his galleys against the shore reducing three of them to splinters. Uluç Ali was more fortunate, sacking and burning Rethymno and capturing twenty-two artillery pieces. Gathering his fleet, the *kapudan paşa* proceeded to pillage the islands of Kythira, Zakynthos and Kefallonia, before making for Corfu.[17]

Deciding that Corfu was too tough a target, Müezzinzâde Ali opted for an amphibious operation to recapture Sopot. The Venetian garrison put up a stiff fight but was eventually forced to surrender to overwhelming numbers. The Ottomans, angered by their losses, put most of the garrison to the sword. Uluç Ali in the meantime was busy operating in nearby waters, capturing the

Venetian *Moceniga* with 800 soldiers destined for Corfu, after a battle lasting eleven hours which resulted in the death of more than half of those on board. After this success the *beylerbey* of Algiers sailed towards Dubrovnik, chasing into the harbour a Venetian galley that had happened to cross his path. The Ragusei, appealing to their neutrality, refused to hand over the ship but nonetheless provided the Ottoman commander with information concerning the league's fleet. Sometime later Uluç Ali was joined by the *kapudan paşa*, who in conjunction with Ahmed Pasha had been busy capturing Venetian fortresses on the Adriatic coast. The capture of Ulcinj (Dulcigno) was considered particularly important, and the occasion for much rejoicing in Constantinople. Still, the taking of Dulcigno had been costly in terms of manpower, the fortress resisting for a fortnight. In addition many Ottoman naval personnel had deserted, leaving the galleys undermanned.[18]

Once the Ottoman forces were reunited the commanders agreed to pursue a dual course of action: Müezzinzâde Ali with the bulk of the fleet would retreat to Herceg Novi for some much-needed caulking, while the *beylerbey* of Algiers and the famous corsair Kara Hodja were given the task of penetrating deeper into the Adriatic to harass Venetian lines of communication. Kara Hodja and Uluç Ali had much in common, including the fact that both were allegedly former Dominican friars, veterans of the battle of Preveza and the siege of Malta. The two redoubtable Ottoman naval commanders were also famous for their daring and guile. Five years before, Kara Hodja had come with a galley and a *fusta* to Pesaro, on the Adriatic coast of Italy, telling the local inhabitants that he simply wanted to trade. His plan was to attract as many people possible on board and then sail off with an easy catch of slaves. The scheme was thwarted by the arrival of a Venetian galley, forcing the corsair to leave empty-handed. As a token of thanks to their protector St Terence, the citizens of Pesaro commissioned an ex–voto painting, still to be seen in the cathedral.

Cunning was not confined to one side. During his foray into the Adriatic Uluç Ali first attacked Korcula (Curzola), but retreated after being tricked by local commander Antonio Balbi into believing that the garrison was more numerous than in reality it was; Balbi used the old ruse of dressing women in military dress and parading them on the walls. Next, the *beylerbey* and Kara Hodja attacked Hvar (Lesina), capturing the island but losing 300 men in the process. At the same time the Ottoman army tried to take the important coastal town of Zara (Zadar), but the Venetian garrison managed to repulse the attackers. The Ottomans were now within striking distance of Venice, as the city frantically prepared itself to beat off the imminent invasion. Citizens were called up and troops raised; a force of fifteen galleys was made ready and other vessels pressed into service; the forts at the mouth of the lagoon were filled with men, artillery and munitions.[19] The Ottoman fleet was not strong enough to capture Venice, but its actions effectively disrupted Venice's war efforts. In particular, the attack against Crete forced the Venetians back on the defensive and stymied any future attempt Querini might have made to relieve Famagusta. From the strategic point of view, there was no doubt that the Ottomans had the upper hand.

It was now too late to save Famagusta.[20] With no relief in sight Marcantonio Bragadin agreed to exchange hostages and discuss terms for the city's capitulation. The Venetians asked for safe conduct and enough ships to transport to Crete all those who so desired; the Italians should not be harassed but allowed to embark to the beat of the drums, with colours unfurled, taking with them their arms, artillery, families and possessions; those Greeks and Albanians who wished to depart should be free to do so, and likewise those Italians who wished to remain; no Greek should suffer loss of freedom, honour or property, and if after two years he decided to leave, the Ottoman authorities should not hinder his departure, but instead provide safe passage to his final destination. Mustafa agreed to everything except the removal of the artillery, although he apparently allowed the defenders to take away five guns, together with three of their finest horses. The treaty signed, the Ottomans sent ships into the harbour and started embarking the defenders. Everything seemed to be going smoothly in the harbour, but for the Famagustans things were getting ugly. No sooner had the Ottomans entered the city than they started misbehaving, looting homes and churches, robbing people and billeting themselves on households. This would be taken as another example of Ottoman treachery, but more likely it was simply a case of soldiers running amok after months of hardship and slaughter.

Worse was in store. On 5 August, following Mustafa's request for a formal surrender ceremony, Bragadin left the city followed by numerous gentlemen, including Baglioni, and accompanied by an escort of harquebusiers and halberdiers. Bragadin was clad in crimson, as befitted his senatorial rank, and over his head stood a parasol, a symbol of authority. The defenders of Famagusta marched between two lines of angry Turks hurling insults at them, but once they arrived at Mustafa's pavilion the Pasha showed nothing but courtesy, the unsuspecting Venetians oblivious of the tragedy about to befall them. The various accounts of what followed conflict on a number of details, but all agree on the final outcome of the exchange between Mustafa and Bragadin.

According to the Ottoman historian Peçevî Ibrahim Effendi the Pasha asked that the young Antonio Querini remain as a hostage until the ships with the Venetians had returned, to which Bragadin is supposed to have answered, 'You can't order a *bey* or a dog for that.' The reply enraged Mustafa, who demanded the restitution of fifty Muslim pilgrims captured by the Venetians at the beginning of the war. When Bragadin answered that they had all been killed, the Pasha ordered his arrest and that of all those with him. Venetian historians instead maintain that Mustafa had never intended to keep to the terms of surrender and that the pilgrims' alleged execution was not the real reason for his ire; rather, the Pasha was enraged by the number of his casualties and the scantiness of the booty left by the Venetians in Famagusta.[21] Interestingly, Mustafa's report to Pertev Pasha (intercepted and translated by the Venetians), while emphasizing Bragadin's killing of prisoners and his refusal to deliver hostages, stresses that his order to arrest the Venetian commander was triggered by the latter's statement, 'that if I [Mustafa] wished to abide by the articles of surrender, it would be fine with him; but if otherwise, he did not care if they were revoked'.[22] Thus, from a strictly legal point of view Mustafa believed that he was within his rights to act as he did, given that Bragadin himself had broken the truce with these words.

It is quite possible that Mustafa – by all accounts a nasty piece of work – had been waiting for such a chance. Although some historians have justified the Pasha's request for hostages as an accepted practice,[23] by asking for something not mentioned in the surrender terms he was behaving like a loser overturning the poker table in the middle of a game. In any case, Mustafa's subsequent behaviour was nothing short of unwarranted savagery. All those with Bragadin, including Astorre Baglioni, were bound, taken out of the pavilion and beheaded on the spot. The Venetian soldiers shared their officers' fate, and caught up in the slaughter were also a number of innocent Cypriots carrying victuals to the Ottoman camp. Only a few prominent Greeks of Bragadin's party were spared, in an attempt by the Pasha to win over the sultan's new subjects. Bragadin expected to share his companions' fate, but for the time being Mustafa was satisfied with cutting off his ears.

The Ottoman commander had issued strict orders that there should be no more looting in Famagusta, but as soon as news of what had happened spread through the army the soldiers took matters into their own hands. The unfortunate Italians waiting to embark were slaughtered; the Greeks were spared, but many saw their wives and daughters raped in front of them. All those already on board the ships were enslaved, the strongest men being sent straight to the oars. The next day Mustafa entered Famagusta, displaying in the main square the heads of the executed Venetians and hanging a few more found in the city. Some managed to save their skins by pretending to be Greek or through the complicity of Ottoman officials more interested in profit than blood. Count

Ercole Martinengo was hidden by one of Mustafa's dragomans until his master's fury abated, while the French consul, on friendly terms with the Pasha, managed to ransom Alessandro Podocattaro.

Bragadin's fate was the most tragic of all. With other Christians he was forced to clear debris from the ruined walls and carry on his shoulders sacks of earth from the cavalier at the Limassol gate all the way to the arsenal at the opposite end of the city's southern wall. During the ordeal he suffered taunts, insults and physical abuse, his captors attempting to force him into accepting Islam. According to one source, eight days after the fall of the city Bragadin made it known that he wanted to become a Muslim. When an imam arrived, Bragadin asked him which were the first words of the Gospel of St John. The puzzled cleric, possibly a renegade Christian answered, 'In the beginning was the word . . .'

Bragadin, turning towards the Pasha cried, 'So, you treacherous dog, if in the beginning was the word, and the word is God, why, treacherous dog, did you renege on it? But you are a treacherous dog, an enemy of God and of your currish law. Cunning scoundrel, why did you kill those poor Christians? If I offended you, then you should have killed me alone, not all the others. But these are thievish actions worthy of you. Dog, dog, disgusting fucking cuckold.'

Apparently impassive, Mustafa asked Bragadin if it was true he had said that had their roles been reversed he would have had the Pasha carry on his shoulders all the earth he had piled up in front of Famagusta's walls. The proud Venetian answered that not only had he said that, but also that he would have used Mustafa's beard 'to clean out the shit from latrines'.[24] Whether this story is true or not, there is no doubt that Bragadin's defiant behaviour enraged Mustafa; and there was the added insult, one could argue, of having made the imam an apostate by tricking him into saying the first words of the Gospel of St John, according to many Muslim legal scholars of the time the speaker's intention being irrelevant.[25]

On 15 August the captive Venetian, already seriously ill from the infection deriving from his amputated ears, was taken to the harbour and hoisted to the main yard of a galley so that all could see. Ottoman soldiers below shouted up mockingly, asking if from there he could see Christ. After an hour he was taken down, dragged to the main square and tied to a column. Mustafa, watching the scene from the balcony of a nearby palace, shouted once more the request that Bragadin convert to Islam, but the Venetian's answer was to raise his voice in prayer. Then two executioners started to flay him alive. First they stripped the skin from his skull, then did the same with his back and arms. They had reached his navel when Bragadin shouted, 'In your hands, Lord, I commend my spirit,' and expired. The executioners laid the lifeless body on the ground and proceeded methodically to finish their grisly work. The body was then quartered, and the pieces displayed in various parts of Famagusta. Bragadin's skin was pickled, stuffed with straw, clad in its owner's crimson robes and carried through the town on top of an ox, preceded by a Turk carrying a parasol. Then it was hoisted once more to a galley's main yard and paraded around the coast of Cyprus before being taken to Constantinople with the booty from Famagusta.

Many at the time compared Bragadin's death to Christ's cruci-fixion. Sokollu Mehmed Pasha – possibly with a keener eye for political expediency than Christian theology – would express his contempt of Mustafa's behaviour to Marcantonio Barbaro, talking about 'the cruel martyrdom inflicted on the most illustrious Braga-din'.[26] Mustafa's brutality towards Famagusta's defenders was widely discussed at the time. The well-informed Venetian historian Paolo Paruta suggested that Mustafa's display of savagery was but a show of force to regain standing with his soldiers, having denied them the opportunity to sack the city. Another possibility is that the Pasha was simply exacting revenge for all his soldiers killed during the ten-month siege – a staggering 80,000 according to one source,[27] although even half that number would have been a terrible toll. Paruta also believed that Mustafa, an extremely choleric man, had been enraged by Bragadin's display of pomp when arriving at his tent, 'as befitted a victor, not a vanquished'.[28] The Venetian historian could have perhaps added another reason. Mustafa was a sworn enemy of Sokollu, and within the *dîvân* a member of the war faction opposed to any deal with Venice. His behaviour at Famagusta can be seen as his way of sabotaging in the immediate future any possible agreement between the Republic of St Mark and the Porte. Whatever his motives, Mustafa's actions would for a long time be cited as an example of Ottoman – indeed Muslim – duplicity, and even today Bragadin's straw-stuffed hide casts a shadow over East–West relations.*

~

Oblivious of the fall of Famagusta the Christian fleet was still in Messina at the end of August, waiting for the arrival of its remaining squadrons. In the meantime Don Juan had been busy inspecting the various forces under his command. He was satisfied with the papal contingent, but could not hide his misgivings about the Venetian ships. In particular he wrote to Don Garcia de Toledo complaining about their lack of men and their indiscipline, with each galley 'doing very much as it pleases', ignoring the fact that when it came to battle the *levantine* method employed by the Venetians, allowing greater independence to individual captains, was as good as any other. Don Juan hoped that the galleys from Crete – which he erroneously believed were from Cyprus – would be in better shape, although he admitted that Ottoman activities in the Adriatic had compelled the republic to concentrate many of its forces in Venice. The young man was also concerned about the best tactical use of firearms, prompting Don Garcia to answer that harquebus fire should be withheld 'until you are near [enough] to the enemy to be splashed with his blood' and that 'the crash of the galleys' rams and the sound of their guns should be heard at the same time'. He added, however, that the artillerymen should not fire until Don Juan ordered them to.[29] Since this last letter was written on 13

* Bragadin's skin was eventually recovered by his family, and now rests in the church of SS Giovanni e Paolo in Venice.

September, it is unlikely that Don Juan received it before his departure from Messina. In any case, the number of expert seamen with the fleet more than compensated for Don Juan's ignorance in naval matters.

Giovanni Andrea Doria entered Messina harbour on 1 September with eleven galleys, and the sixty Venetian galleys from Crete turned up the next day, in good shape and well equipped with rowers. Some had a few Cretan archers, and most the normal complement of fifty *scapoli* 'but no other soldiers'. Prospero Colonna had also arrived from Naples with the infantrymen he had managed to recruit in that kingdom. But even with these troops and the 1,200 'bellicose Calabrian soldiers' recruited for Venier by Baron Gaspare Toraldo, the Venetian ships were still short of fighting men. The difficulties experienced by the Venetians in filling their ranks were partly due to the bouts of disease that still afflicted their fleet, but also to the fact that few people were willing to face the apparently invincible Ottoman navy. As a result, the soldiers enlisted were green and, according to the Savoyard admiral Provana de Leynì 'of the worst type seen at sea for a long time'. Wishing all galleys to have at least 100 soldiers on board, Don Juan reiterated to Venier his former offer to provide the necessary troops: 2,000 Germans, 1,500 Italians and 1,500 Spanish. The Venetian captain-general was loath to accept, mistrustful of the Spaniards' real intentions; but thanks to the mediation of Marcantonio Colonna agreed to embark the Italian and Iberian soldiers, on average forty men to each galley. Santa Cruz's thirty galleys made their way into Messina on the 6th, bringing the league's fleet to its full fighting strength.[30]

More or less at the same time Knight Commander Gil de Andrada returned from his scouting mission with news of the Ottoman fleet. He had stopped in Corfu, where the governor Benedetto Orsini informed him that the Ottomans had nearly 300 vessels, but only 150 galleys, the rest being round-ships or galliots with few soldiers on board. From other Venetian outposts the knight commander had also received word that the Ottoman ships were ill-equipped with artillery and riddled with disease. Having delivered his findings, Gil de Andrada set out for some more scouting, leaving Don Juan to ponder what to do next. On the 8th a general review took place, but those who expected an immediate departure were disappointed, for Don Juan told Venier and Colonna that he wished to convene a general conference of all the league's senior officers to decide on a course of action. Don Juan was not just bowing to his advisers' appeals for prudence; he was also aware that any major decision taken by a small council would inevitably arouse the resentment and jealousy of those left out. Indeed, a few days later the Venetian *provveditori* Antonio da Canal and Marco Querini would write to the senate complaining that Venier and Barbarigo were excluding them from the restricted meetings they held with the other commanders.[31]

The general conference took place on 10 September, with some sixty senior officers gathered on the Habsburg flagship. Don Juan postulated two alternative courses of action: seek battle with the enemy or remain on the defensive. The prince's advisers immediately raised a number of objections to any sort of venture in the Levant, arguing that the strength of the Ottoman fleet, the insufficient victuals and soldiers, and the approaching autumn pointed instead to a more profitable attack against Tunis. The other participants, especially the Venetians, rejected this idea out of hand and the discussion shifted to whether battle should be sought or not. Again Don Juan's counsellors expressed objections, despite the fact that later Don Luis de Requesens would maintain that he always advocated fighting.[32] It is easy, as many have done, to accuse the Spanish of sabotaging the league's efforts for their own parochial interests, but it should be remembered that North Africa was among the league's objectives and that the conquest of Tunis had some very sound strategic merits. Besides, the idea of engaging the intact Ottoman fleet in battle was enough in itself to encourage caution.

Shrewdly, Giovanni Andrea Doria approached the problem from a different angle. He did not reject the possibility of a sea battle, but pointed out that 'even if we should be victorious, we would in any case have to retreat and this will allow the Turks to recover their strength'. He suggested instead sailing to Cyprus and trying to relieve Famagusta, thus disrupting the Ottoman war effort.[33] Doria had apparently gone over to the Venetians, but his words belied his real intentions: he understood perfectly the Ottomans' potential for recovery, but also knew that the fleet would never make it to Cyprus before the bad weather set in. By backing the Cyprus option Doria was attempting to erase the accusations of cowardice levelled against him the year before, without exposing his ships, and Philip's, to excessive risks. Other commanders, including Santa Cruz, advocated battle against the Ottoman fleet, and Don Juan concluded the meeting by stating that he was resolved, with the aid of the Venetian and papal squadrons, to seek out the enemy.[34]

The prince could not have done otherwise without a colossal loss of face; the Venetians had made it known that if the league fleet should delay its departure any longer, they would go hunting the Ottomans alone. Colonna was also under pressure from the papal authorities to get moving, and it was more than likely that he would join Venier's venture. Thus, as the Savoyard commander Andrea Provana di Leynì had a few days before informed Duke Emmanuel Philibert, 'not everyone willingly agrees to fight, but nonetheless [is] forced and pressured by shame to do so'.[35] Meanwhile, to be sure that nothing was decided contrary to Spain's interests, Philip II had written to Don Juan ordering him to dismiss the league's non-Spanish contingents and move his own forces into winter quarters in Sicily.[36] But the prince did not receive this letter until the end of October, by which time the situation had changed completely.

On 14 September Don Juan issued the official order of movement and combat. The fleet was to be divided into four squadrons – three front line and one reserve. During the voyage Doria would occupy the vanguard, Don Juan the centre and Barbarigo the rear. Santa Cruz with the reserve was to follow, accompanied by twenty-six ships with 3,000 German infantry. Each front-line squadron was allocated a pair of galleasses, navigating a mile ahead. In the event of battle, Doria would have the right wing, Barbarigo the left and Don Juan the centre, or 'battle', with Santa Cruz placing himself behind the main line with the reserve. The sailing ships' position was on the wings, to avoid the Christian line being outflanked, exploiting the wind to manoeuvre with the galleys. Alternatively, they were to use their boats to feed troops into the fight. The galleasses had the task of disrupting the enemy line with their artillery fire before the two fleets came to blows. It was a well-designed plan, which Doria would later claim as his, although it owed much to Don Garcia de Toledo's suggestions.[37]

Two days later the fleet finally set sail from Messina, with an impressive show of strength, music and colour. Slowly the vessels exited the harbour, blessed one by one by the papal nuncio Giulio Maria Odescalchi, whom Pius V had sent to join the Christian armada with the aim of hastening its departure. In front of the nuncio's eyes passed 207 galleys, six galleasses, twenty-eight round-ships and thirty-two smaller vessels (frigates and brigantines), with on board some 30,000 fighting men and about 50,000 sailors and rowers.[38] Doria's squadron led the way, his flagship displaying at the stern the rich celestial sphere – a gift from his wife – he used as a recognition sign. The galleys under his command were Genoese (his own, plus those of other *asientistas* such as the Lomellini, Negroni, Grimaldi and De Mari), papal, Savoyard and Venetian, the latter making up half his squadron. This is hardly surprising, since Venice provided 50 per cent of all the galleys present. By dividing the various national units among the four squadrons Don Juan was insuring himself against the possibility of one contingent deserting en masse. By all accounts Doria's division was a very mixed and ill-balanced formation. The light, plain Genoese galleys contrasted with the heavily armed, refined Venetian vessels.* The papal (Tuscan) galleys, loaded down with ordnance, proudly flaunted at

* The stern of Genoese galleys usually lacked the decorations and gilding typical of these vessels. Cfr. ASF, MP, 2426, n.n.f. (Vincenzo Graffigna to Domenico Pandolfini, 13 November 1650, from Pisa).

their sterns the Medici coat of arms. Two of the Savoyard ships, the *Piemontesa* and *Margarita*, were small – with their eighteen rowing benches more galliots than galleys – and the *Margarita* decrepit. Admiral Provana di Leynì had tried to replace her in Naples with a new galley, but had been thwarted by lack of funds.[39]

In the middle of the fleet in the central division stood Don Juan's majestic *Real*, its stern decorated in true humanistic fashion with a mixture of motifs borrowed from both pagan and Christian traditions.[40] It was preceded and followed respectively by Colonna's and Venier's flagships. These were large galleys, with full sets of heavy and light ordnance and fighting contingents of over 200 men each, the *Real* having 400 harquebusiers from the *tercio* of Sardinia. Some of the most important galleys were in the central squadron, although these were not necessarily the strongest. Bunching together well-equipped powerful vessels was a way to archive tactical superiority at a specific point of the line of battle, but often matters of precedence prevailed over military expediency. The *capitana* of Savoy with its twenty-five rowing benches was little more than a glorified *galea sottile*, but Admiral Provana, following Duke Emmanuel Philibert's instructions, had insisted that it should take position immediately to the right of the papal flagship. On a previous occasion the Maltese commander Fra' Pietro Giustiniani had tried to usurp Provana's place, causing a diplomatic scuffle. The impenitent Giustiniani tried the same trick again after the fleet left Messina, forcing Don Juan to put his foot down in the Savoyards' favour. Perhaps for this reason the Maltese flagship was placed on the extreme right of the central division, another honourable position.[41]

The three galleys deployed by the Order of Malta belied its real strength within the coalition. All the Knights of St John came from the ranks of the European aristocracy – although the majority were from the petty nobility – and trained as soldiers from birth. Adding this to the traditional religious monastic vows of chastity, poverty and obedience made them formidable fighters, reckoned as among the toughest in Europe. Everyone was keen to exploit the knights' expertise in naval matters, and as a result scores of them could be found throughout the allied fleet, sometimes as galley captains but in many cases simply as volunteers. Gil de Andrada, Pagano Doria (Giovanni Andrea Doria's brother) and Luigi Mazzinghi were just three of the Maltese scattered throughout the galleys, and on more than one occasion during the forthcoming battle their presence would make a significant difference.

Once the whole fleet reached the high seas it spread out in accordance with Don Juan's orders. The vanguard, with fifty-seven galleys, sailed six miles from the coast; the centre, with sixty-four, was four miles from the shoreline; the third division, with fifty-six, two miles. The reserve squadron brought up the rear, keeping the same distance from the coast as the central division. Four to six miles separated each squadron from the others. Eight of the best galleys from Doria's and Barbarigo's squadrons scouted ten miles ahead of the vanguard, while the galleasses sailed a mile in front of their respective squadrons. Battle formation could be adopted by halting Doria's division and allowing the others to catch up.[42] Should the van stumble upon the Ottoman armada, there was enough time for the Christian fleet to meet the enemy in an orderly fashion. Don Juan was confident about his chances of success, writing to Don Garcia de Toledo on the day the fleet left Messina that although the Ottoman fleet was superior in numbers, the quality of its ships and of the men on board was not good.[43]

What the league's commanders ignored was that the enemy knew of their whereabouts and probably their planned tactics. By mid-September the Ottoman fleet was at Preveza, where Müezzin-zâde Ali Pasha received the latest intelligence about the allied forces. Executing a daring cloak-and-dagger operation, the corsair Kara Hodja had managed to penetrate the port of Messina at night in an all-black galliot in order to assess the strength of the Christian fleet. Not detecting Barbarigo's squadron, at anchor in the inner part of the harbour, Kara Hodja estimated the league galleys at not more than 140. Puzzled by the report, Müezzinzâde Ali decided to retreat to the logistics base of Lepanto to replenish his ships with victuals and men.[44] He may also have managed to obtain one of the broadsheets printed at some point before the fleet's departure from Messina showing the allied battle plan★ – with so many people attending the general conference of the 10th it was inevitable that news should leak out, to the advantage of the efficient Ottoman spy ring present in every port of the Mediterranean.[45] In fact, both sides were under the impression that they were dealing with a numerically inferior enemy, a factor that would crucially influence their subsequent decisions.

Don Juan learnt with displeasure about Kara Hodja's exploit while passing Santa Maria di Leuca, at the tip of Italy's heel. But there was nothing he could do at this point, except stop to embark 500 Calabrian infantrymen and send twelve galleys to Brindisi to take on 1,500 more. When the league's fleet reached Corfu on the 26th it lacked a third of its force, inclement weather and victualling delays accounting for many of the missing galleys. The galleasses had also lagged behind, and a total of thirty-six galleys had to be sent to take them in tow. Once the whole fleet gathered in Corfu there was some talk about attacking Sopot or Margariti, the excuse being that it was late in the season and that little bread remained. Venier would have nothing of it, insisting that the advance be resumed. Corfu's bread supplies would be sufficient for another two months, and Venier was eager to catch the Ottomans before it was too late. Besides, thanks to the liberation of two important Venetian prisoners, exchanged for a high-ranking Ottoman officer, fresh intelligence had become available.

The freed gentlemen had managed to observe closely the Ottoman fleet and reported that it counted more than 300 sail, including 160 galleys, but lacked fighting men. The Venetian commander grudgingly agreed to take on six siege pieces from the

★ I have come across two versions of this broadsheet. One, giving the strength and disposition of the allied fleet in great detail, was published in SALIMEI between pages 96 and 97. The other, with the names of the Ottoman squadron commanders, can be found in QUARTI, between pages 568 and 569. I thank Admiral Tiberio Moro for pointing out to me the existence of the latter. Both versions show the Ottoman fleet in a crescent formation.

fortress of Corfu, since Don Juan wanted at the very least to reduce a fortress or two before the end of the campaign. Venier immediately pointed out that landing infantry and artillery with an unbeaten fleet of over 200 sail in the rear was courting disaster. Receiving another demand for pikes and powder, in order to avoid further delay he decided to leave five galleys in Corfu with orders to rejoin the rest of the fleet once they had finished loading the armaments.[46]

The allied armada sailed to Igoumenitsa, where it stopped for water and fuel, Christian troops skirmishing with local Ottoman forces sent to harass the foraging parties. What happened next nearly wrecked the league for good. Ever since the Venetians had agreed to embark Spanish soldiers on their galleys, the tensions already existing between the two nationalities had increased by the day. Tempers were already running high when on 2 October Giovanni Andrea Doria visited Venier's galleys demanding to see if they were in fighting order. The captain-general could hardly contain his ire in the face of such a blatant breach of protocol, his anger worsened by Venier's personal animosity towards the Genoese admiral. Venier, according to his own report, nevertheless allowed the inspection to take place, although other sources state that he flatly refused to receive Doria, agreeing however that the inspection be conducted by Luis de Requesens. Worse was to come.

Around four o'clock in the afternoon a scuffle started on one of the Cretan galleys between crew members and some Italian soldiers in Spanish pay led by one Captain Muzio Alticozzi from Cortona, which quickly degenerated into a fight with dead and wounded. When Venier sent some officers to see what was happening, Alticozzi attacked them, shouting, 'I am not obeying these fucking cuckolded Venetians.' For Venier it was the last straw. Surrounding the Cretan galley with other vessels and threatening to sink anyone who tried to stop him, he managed to capture Alticozzi and four of his accomplices after a stiff fight. Some days before, a similar incident had resulted in the killing of some Venetian crewmen by Spanish soldiers, but the intervention of Don Juan's advisers had got the culprits off scot-free. Venier was determined not to allow such a thing to happen again. Paying lip service to legal niceties, he organized a drumhead court martial which promptly sentenced Alticozzi and three others to death. The punishment was executed immediately, and the four men found themselves dangling from a yardarm.

Don Juan's representative arrived soon after to see what had happened and immediately reported his findings to his master. The prince was understandably enraged. Not only had Venier flouted the commander-in-chief's authority, but Alticozzi held a Spanish commission and thus did not fall under Venetian jurisdiction. Such was Don Juan's fury that, according to some, he swore to hang Venier in reprisal for his dead men. For a few hours everyone thought that a full-blown battle was about to erupt between the Spanish and the Venetians, both contingents standing at the ready with guns loaded and matches lit. It is unlikely that Don Juan would have carried out his threat, if he ever made it in the first place – executing an allied commander would have had incalculable consequences. Eventually cooler heads prevailed, Marcantonio Colonna and Barbarigo doing much to soothe the prince's ruffled feathers. In any case, as Colonna pointed out, the Spanish would be fighting more than 100 Venetian galleys and six galleasses. Still, Don Juan was not to be appeased so easily, informing Venier that from then on he would only deal with Barbarigo. The captain-general shrugged his shoulders, commenting that if such were His Highness's desires he would not object.[47]

Once the tension between Spaniards and Venetians abated the fleet resumed its voyage south. On reaching Capo Bianco, Don Juan ordered a general rehearsal of the battle formation, with the squadrons taking up their positions along a five-mile front. The squadrons were distinguished by flags of different colours: Doria's ships sported green pennants at the peak of each mainyard; Don Juan's had blue ones at each masthead; Barbarigo's flew yellow banderols from their foreyards; and Santa Cruz's ships hoisted white pennants from a flagstaff over the stern lamp. Gil de Andrada rejoined the fleet, having shadowed the Ottoman armada until forced to retreat by the arrival of a strong enemy squadron. Some Greek locals he had encountered on his way told him that the Ottoman fleet was at Lepanto and assured him that if the Christians attacked they had a good chance of winning. Little did Andrada know that those same Greeks were also keeping the Ottomans informed of the league's movements, assuring them also that victory was at hand. On the afternoon of the 4th the allies reached Kefallonia and received a rude shock. A frigate sent by the *provveditore generale* of Crete Marino Cavalli was in the Bay of Guiscardo, carrying letters of 24 August with news of the fall of Famagusta and the fate of its defenders. When the tidings were made public a wave of indignation swept through the fleet. Old rivalries vanished in a flash, the Spanish shared the rage of the now vengeful Venetians.[48] If Lala Mustafa had indeed intended by his actions to provoke the allies to battle he had certainly accomplished his goal, but now the Ottomans faced a swarm of angry hornets.

The anger of the rank and file was not shared by all senior officers. Indeed, the fall of Famagusta had to a great extent pulled the strategic rug from under the allies' feet. That evening a restricted conference was held aboard Don Juan's flagship to discuss what to do next. With Cyprus lost any foray into the Levant was now pointless, leaving two possible options open: attack some Ottoman fortresses in the area or continue searching for the enemy. Predictably, most of Don Juan's advisers favoured the first choice, but in the face of the Venetian commanders' opposition it was decided to continue towards Lepanto.

Next day the allies managed to advance twelve miles before being forced to drop anchor due to bad weather. The Spanish were clearly frustrated by the Venetians' stubborn determination to seek battle, especially given the presence of many other juicy, easier targets in the area. That evening Barbarigo went to Venier and told him that Don Juan's advisers had been spreading the rumour that the Venetians had no stomach for a fight, and that all their assertions to the contrary were but a sham. Writing to the doge the captain-general vented his spleen against the Spaniards' attitude: 'for thanks to all these delays the enemy will look after his own business, and Christendom will lose the best chance it has ever had'. He added that he was ready to be relieved, 'believing that those who desire this post will be more suited than myself to be overawed, and see Your Lordship's state destroyed by vain hopes'. In truth Venier was being rather unfair to Don Juan, since a few hours before the prince had discussed with Barbarigo and Colonna the best way to engage the Ottomans. The three had agreed to sail up to the mouth of the Gulf of Lepanto to taunt the enemy fleet into fighting; should this not work, they would capture the two fortresses guarding the entrance to the gulf. When Barbarigo informed Venier of the plan the old man grudgingly agreed, given also that according to recent intelligence Uluç Ali had departed east with eighty galleys. However, the *beylerbey* of Algiers had in the meantime returned to Lepanto unnoticed by the Christians, who believed it unlikely that a heavily outnumbered Ottoman fleet would risk battle.[49]

The bad weather conditions lasted until the evening of the 6th, when 'God showed us a sky and a sea as not to be seen even in the finest day of spring.' Under oars the allied ships started moving south, but slowly in order not to overtire the crews of those galleys towing the galleasses, and hampered in their progress by a headwind. As they directed their prows towards the Curzolaris islands at the entrance to the Gulf of Patras, the galleys of the advanced guard under Juan de Cardona managed to bottle themselves up in a small cove,[50] rejoining the fleet just moments before battle was joined.* Four of these galleys were part of Doria's squadron, and their absence would have a telling effect on future developments. In fact, the Christian armada had lost rather more than its vanguard. The round-ships, with nearly 5,000 German troops on board, had failed

---

* In Doria's report (ADP, 79/53, int. 5A, 'Particolare relazione', f. 3) the original phrase 'due to a mistake of their pilots found themselves inadvertently inside a small cove, with no exit except from the entrance', has been deleted and substituted by 'the galleys of the vanguard remained somewhat behind'.

to keep up with the rest of the fleet even before it reached Corfu, and the Venetians' determination to push forward meant that these ships and soldiers would not be available in the event of a fight. Also the temporary loss of Cardona's galleys meant that the original battle plan devised in Messina was now irremediably damaged, with what consequences still remained to be seen.

The Ottomans had been lurking in the shadow of the fortress of Lepanto since 27 September, retreating there after the allied fleet's presence in the Adriatic had forced them to abandon operations against the Venetian port of Kotor. Speculation about the Christians' moves and objectives had been rife throughout the summer, the Ottomans being at one stage convinced that the league's objective was the Dalmatian coast. As a result, reinforcements, victuals and munitions had been sent to various garrisons in the area. The *kapudan paşa* himself was short of supplies and men. Believing the campaign season over, many *sipahi*s had been allowed to return home, and the Ottoman ships badly needed repairs after being constantly at sea since March. On receiving the news that the enemy fleet was approaching, the Ottomans had hastily conscripted men from the local fortresses and population.

Müezzinzâde Ali could look back with pride at the accomplishments of his fleet in the last four months, but now he was grappling with the various directives he had been receiving from Constantinople. A message of 19 August had ordered him to 'display all his courage and intelligence' when facing the enemy, and also winter his fleet in the still-unconquered Kotor. The next instruction he received confirmed Kotor as a winter base, but at this point the league's fleet was already approaching Corfu, making it impossible for the *kapudan paşa* to execute the order. In fact, a later directive that Müezzinzâde Ali never received gave him the choice of Kotor or in 'another port after consulting with Pertev Pasha'. The same letter ordered him to attack the Christian armada 'after getting reliable news about the enemy' and consulting the other commanders of the fleet 'all in perfect agreement and unity, in accordance with what is found most suitable'.[51]

Much has been made of Müezzinzâde Ali's alleged slavish adherence to the letter of these orders to explain his subsequent decision to fight – a consequence, it has been suggested, of the Ottoman central authorities trying to micromanage a campaign being fought hundreds of miles from the capital. In fact, the instructions to the *kapudan paşa* allowed him considerable latitude, not least because they specified that all decisions should be taken in accord with the other commanders. The military situation had changed since May, when the sultan had ordered him to seek out and destroy the enemy fleet; besides, Ottoman pragmatism permitted the man on the spot to act according to circumstances. This emerges forcefully from the records of the war council held on 6 October in the castle of Lepanto with the participation of all the most important Ottoman officers, a number of whom would later report the details of the meeting to their Christian captors. Present were the *beylerbey* of Algiers Uluç Ali Pasha; two of Hayreddin Barbarossa's sons, Mehmed Pasha and the corpulent Hasan Pasha; Salihpaşazâde Mehmed, *bey* of Negropont; Pertev Pasha, Kara Hodja and many others.

Kara Hodja, just back from another reconnaissance mission, reported that the Christian armada numbered 150 galleys at most. By interrogating prisoners previously captured near Igoumenitsa he had also discovered that the fleet was short of water, most supplies having remained with the round-ships, and in need of repairs. Pertev Pasha argued against attacking the enemy, pointing out that the Christians were not there for fun. Other reports estimated a force of some 200 galleys, and he worried about the presence of the Venetian galleasses. The Ottoman fleet was admittedly larger, but not in pristine condition. He added that many of the *sipahis* had gone home, the remaining soldiers were inexperienced, and even the veterans had not much practice in sea fights. Moreover, the Christians were heavily armoured and equipped with harquebuses, while the Ottomans had mostly bows and lacked bodily protection. Pertev also suggested that the many enslaved oarsmen in the Ottoman galleys could be a potential source of trouble, should they manage to free themselves during the battle. His conclusion was that although the sultan had ordered the fleet to fight the Christians, he did not wish to see it in ruins.

Salihpaşazâde Mehmed Bey agreed with Pertev Pasha about the perils of an attack, stating that it would be better to find out the enemy's intentions under the shelter of the guns of Lepanto. Şuluç Mehmed Pasha and others also advised prudence, and the North African Abd el-Malik – who would feature as Mulay Maluco in Cervantes' play *Los Baños de Argel*[52] – stressed the foolishness of attacking fresh forces with battle-weary troops. At this point Hasan Pasha intervened, stating that he not only believed Kara Hodja's report, but that it was a known fact that the enemy fleet was riddled with dissension. Besides, as his father had proven, the Christians were no match for the Ottomans. Uluç Ali also wanted battle, but was against the Ottomans attacking first.

Once everyone had given his opinion Müezzinzâde Ali rose to speak. He pointed out that although the enemy fleet was of considerable size, it was nonetheless rent by jealousy and discord. Besides, according to his spies, Giovanni Andrea Doria was still far away escorting the sailing vessels. Dismissing the galleasses as worthless, the *kapudan paşa* stated that it would be better to attack the Christians before the arrival of their round-ships. He admitted that many of his soldiers were green, but they would be fighting alongside veterans; in any case, they had always been victorious, even without armour. Bows were better weapons than harquebuses, having a rate of fire thirty times greater. The Christian slaves were not a problem, since they would be forced on pain of death to lie under their benches once the fleets clashed. Given these favourable circumstances and the sultan's wishes, the Ottomans should not hesitate to fight the Christian armada: 'For what shall the world say if we, used to provoking the others to battle, now challenged by such despicable enemies should refuse to fight?' Besides, should the Ottomans be victorious the whole of Italy would be theirs to invade. With this the meeting broke up, everyone falling in with the *kapudan paşa*'s bellicose proposal 'either because convinced, or in order not to be accused of cowardice'.[53]

Müezzinzâde Ali has been criticized for his decision, which many have attributed to rashness and/or inexperience. Some Turkish historians have even seen Sokollu Mehmed Pasha's Machiavellian hand in this: by appointing Müezzinzâde Ali and Pertev Pasha, both new to naval warfare, the wily grand vizier had created conditions likely to lead to the Ottomans' subsequent defeat. Michel Lesure has dismissed this idea as a mere conspiracy theory, pointing out that if such a plan ever existed it would have been a risky one to implement.[54] Still, Sokollu had already tried before the stratagem of giving someone a difficult task with the hope of discrediting him – Lala Mustafa's appointment as *serdar* in the Yemen expedition of 1567 being a case in point – and according to Marcantonio Barbaro, Müezzinzâde Ali, originally one of Sokollu's protégés, had sided with the grand vizier's enemies over going to war with Venice.[55] If this was indeed the case, then Sokollu had every interest in making the *kapudan paşa*'s life difficult.

It is also possible that Müezzinzâde Ali was acting out of personal ambition. The son of a *muezzin* in Edirne, he had entered the Porte's corps of gatekeepers (*bevvab*), apparently thanks to the patronage of Süleyman I's powerful wife Hürrem. From there he had advanced by merit to become a taster (*çasnigir*), steward of the gatekeepers (*kapıcılar kethudası*), commander of the janissaries (*yeniçeri ağası*), governor (*beylerbeyi*) of Algiers and grand admiral. However, he was looked down upon as an outsider by those state officials who had been trained in the inner palace service (the *birun* as opposed to the *enderun*, to which the gatekeepers belonged), for not having been recruited through the *devşirme*.[56] From contemporary accounts it is clear that the *kapudan paşa* used the sultan's order to attack in order to silence his opponents, not because he feared Selim's wrath. Indeed, according to Katib Çelebi his attitude was cavalier to say the least: 'Is there no zeal for Islam and for the sultan's wishes?' he is supposed to have cried. 'What does it matter if there are five or ten men missing from every ship?'[57] The same author describes the admiral as being an inexperienced, rash and stubborn man. These are unfair accusations, for while Pertev Pasha had little knowledge of maritime matters, Müezzinzâde Ali had participated in the Djerba and Malta campaigns, acted as Piyale Pasha's deputy and been *kapudan-ı deryâ* since 1567. Clearly he had some understanding of naval affairs, and his decision to attack was also based on the opinion of some of the most distinguished mariners of the time. Given the intelligence at his disposal, taking the offensive was as good a choice as any other.

That evening the Ottoman fleet sailed out of the Bay of Lepanto, galleys, galliots and other smaller vessels making it 300 strong. Many on board were happy that battle was about to be joined 'for they believed that victory was theirs'.[58]

9. THE 7TH OF OCTOBER

~

As the allied fleet moved into the Gulf of Patras, Marcantonio Colonna was sure something big was about to happen. The renowned mariner Cecco Pisano had just returned from a scouting mission, bringing news of the enemy's strength. Not wishing this intelligence to become public – lest Don Juan be swayed by his cautious advisers – he cryptically whispered to Colonna, 'Sir, you will need to bare your claws and fight'. Don Juan, however, had also received fresh information. Requesens' secretary together with Romegas had been spying on the Ottomans, and reported having seen the enemy vanguard sailing out of the port of Lepanto.[1] Still, Don Juan ignored the size of the force he was about to encounter, like his adversaries convinced he was dealing with a weaker foe.

As the first rays of the sun lit up the sky the Christian lead division under Doria was approaching the northernmost of the Curzolaris islands, sailing through a seascape now much altered by nature. Since Harold Edgerton and Peter Throckmorton conducted their pioneering archaeological research at the site of the battle scholars have accepted the fact that the shoreline has changed significantly from what it was in 1571. At the time of the battle the coast was roughly one to three nautical miles north of the present shoreline. The silting of the river Acheloos has since turned the island of Koutsilaris into hills a short distance inland from the coast,

Oxia being the only isle left of the original archipelago.[2] Ignoring this fact, in 1888 the admiral and scholar Jean-Pierre Edmond Jurien de La Gravière reconstructed the Christian approach to the Curzolaris[3] according to the shoreline of his own time, a theory slavishly followed by other authors over the years. According to Jurien de la Gravière's reconstruction, the league's ships sailed north from Kefallonia, then south through some offshore islands which he thought to be the Curzolaris, to pass between today's Point Scropha and the isle of Oxia before deploying in the Gulf of Patras. In reality the allied armada navigated straight from Kefallonia to south of Petala, at least part of it passing through the channel separating the then island of Koutsilaris from the mainland. Given the slowness of its progress, if the fleet had taken the route described by Jurien de la Gravière it would not have managed to arrive in the Gulf of Patras by the morning of 7 October.

Approaching the Curzolaris, Don Juan ordered lookouts to land on the islands and climb the peaks. No sooner had Giovanni Andrea's lead galleys debouched from the narrow channel separating Oxia from Koutsilaris than from the crow's nests sails were sighted to the east. With the increasing light it became clear that the whole Ottoman fleet had exited the Gulf of Corinth, advancing under sail 'like a forest' in no apparent order. Waiting for the news to be confirmed, Don Juan halted his flagship in order to allow the rest of the fleet to catch up. As more reports confirmed the sighting and the increasing strength of the enemy fleet, Don Juan ordered a green banner to be unfurled on the mainmast of his flagship and a gun fired, in this manner signalling the fleet to ready itself for battle.

The prince then called a conference on his flagship to decide the best course of action. Asking Romegas what he thought should be done, the fire-eating Gascon answered, 'What I think? That if the emperor your father had seen such an armada like ours, he would not have stopped until he had become emperor of Constantinople, and done so with ease.' 'You mean we must fight, Monsieur Romegas?' enquired the prince again. 'Yes, sir.' 'Let's fight then.' When asked the same question Marcantonio Colonna answered laconically in Latin, paraphrasing the Gospel, 'Even if I should die, I will not deny you.' Some of Don Juan's advisers, still remembering Philip II's instructions, tried to dissuade the prince from joining battle, pointing out that in the event of defeat the Ottomans could still retire to the haven of Lepanto while the Christians had nowhere to go if beaten. (Sarcastically a contemporary French author described Requesens as 'considering all the possible options, in true Spanish fashion'.) Don Juan, however, was determined to implement the course of action decided upon in Corfu, cutting short the conference with: 'Gentlemen, this is not the time to discuss, but to fight.'[4]

In the meantime the galleys' decks and bridges were being cleared for battle, and some of the rowers' benches covered over with planking to allow the soldiers greater freedom of action. Offensive and defensive weapons were stacked in the prescribed areas of each vessel, as men checked their arms and donned armour. Gunners loaded their pieces with round, chain and canister shot, and prepared anti-personnel fire pots and fire trumpets. Wine, water, cheese, bread 'and other necessities' were stored on the bridges, fighting being a terribly tiring and thirst-inducing activity. Convicts on the *ponentine* galleys were unchained and provided with weapons, Don Juan having promised a general amnesty if victorious; Muslim slaves, on the other hand, found themselves manacled to their oars. The prince's promise was to a degree fraudulent, for although the league's commander-in-chief he only had the power to liberate those convict rowers under his immediate jurisdiction, certainly not those belonging to others.[5]

Don Juan, reputedly following a suggestion of Giovanni Andrea Doria, also ordered the removal of the rams from the bows of the Christian galleys, so that their guns could be depressed to hit the Ottoman vessels at the shortest possible range. William Prescott commented in 1855, 'It may seem strange that this discovery should have been reserved for the crisis of a battle.' Actually, according to one source, the Venetians had already removed their rams sometime before, since they 'do not allow the use of the centreline gun, a much esteemed and feared weapon, and time is needed to remove them'. Captain Pantero Pantera would comment a few years later that in most cases they were but ornamental objects, and in any case it would appear all the Christian galleys managed to cut off their rams before the battle began.[6]

As soon as the conference ended, Doria informed the prince that he would be moving towards the open sea to allow the Christian fleet room to draw up for battle. Still nourishing some doubts about his decision to fight, Don Juan then boarded a frigate and was rowed over to Venier's flagship. A few words exchanged with the Venetian admiral were sufficient to dispel the prince's misgivings and reconcile him to Venier, mutual need dispelling the animosity that had existed between the two men since the troubles at Igoumenitsa. Don Juan remained on the frigate for some time, offering encouragement to each galley as it passed. The ships moved slowly towards their assigned stations, so as not to create confusion, following a more or less south-easterly course. Barbarigo, instead, probably took a more northern route, skirting the shallows at the mouth of the Acheloos. The narrow channels separating the Cuzolaris only allowed for the passage of a few galleys at a time, making rapid deployment impossible. In any case, the slow-moving galleasses needed time to reach their battle stations ahead of the fleet, and the galleys had to trim and close their ranks 'to stop the enemy from entering the line and striking them in the flank'.[7] The advance party of eight galleys under Cardona was expected to split in two, half being allotted to Barbarigo and the rest to Doria. In fact, those assigned to Doria never made it to their stations, taking position instead on the right of the Christian centre. Thus Doria was deprived of four galleys, at least two of them heavily armed *bastarde* with strong fighting complements.[8]

Delays and problems also hampered the galleasses' deployment; in fact it is by no means certain that those allotted to Doria's wing actually managed to reach their prescribed battle station in time. Most modern authors, following Jurien de La Gravière's reconstruction, based on Benedetto Veroggio's very biased and imprecise work written to justify Giovanni Andrea Doria's actions, maintain that these galleasses remained behind Doria's line.[9] Contemporary accounts contradict this, and even those most favourable to Doria admit that at least one galleass made it to the front of the Christian right. Due to the contrary wind the galleasses took time to reach their assigned posts a mile ahead of the Christian line, and two of them were so far behind that Don Juan, 'uttering holy curses', ordered the nearer ones to move ahead. Doria himself was concerned about the delay, and sent repeated requests that the galleasses make haste. Eventually it proved necessary to tow them into place, but since it took around three hours for the Christian fleet to complete its deployment the four galleasses allotted to the centre and left wing managed to move into position in time, a mile ahead of their respective divisions. As for the other two they certainly reached the front of the right wing, but probably only a few hundred yards from it.[10] Subsequent events would appear to confirm this.

The Christians' southward movement did not go undetected by the Ottomans, who initially had not spotted the enemy forces in the fast fading darkness. 'Allah, Allah,' they cried, 'these dogs are running. Let's go and catch them.' Under the false impression that the allied fleet was trying to escape towards the open sea, the Ottoman armada adopted a south–west course in an attempt to cut off the imagined Christian escape. As the other Christian ships slowly came into view, Müezzinzâde Ali realized his mistake and quickly realigned his fleet onto a course parallel to the enemy's. He also started to have misgivings about joining battle, but Uluç Ali reassured him that the Christians were craven scoundrels, ready to run at the first chance. The *kapudan paşa*'s doubts derived also from the many crows seen hovering over the fleet when departing from Lepanto, considered an ill omen by the Ottoman mariners. Müezzinzâde Ali had tried to reassure his men that there was nothing to fear, similar signs having been seen on other occasions when the Ottomans had been victorious, but had only partially managed to allay their fears. The *kapudan paşa* was worried that many of his men were unhappy about the prospect of a naval battle, and a number had been tricked on board the galleys while carrying on ammunition and flags. Animosity was also present between the Ottoman commanders. Abd el-Malik was accused behind his back of being a coward and in cahoots with Don Juan of Austria. Discovering this, Abd el-Malik publicly berated his critics: he was no coward or traitor, but a good Muslim descended directly from the Prophet Muhammad, while most of the Ottoman commanders were Christian renegades 'with pork flesh still stuck between their teeth'.[11] Abd el-Malik's words reveal a certain amount of ethnic and social tension, the North African aristocrat looking down on those he considered mere upstarts, often by-products of the *devşirme*.

The Ottomans took roughly the same time as the allies to deploy their fleet, Uluç Ali's Algerian contingent moving out first to face Doria's division. The Christians in turn interpreted their opponents' deployment as an escape attempt 'and because of these erroneous thoughts, each side took heart to fight the other'. To both contenders battle now seemed inevitable. Müezzinzâde Ali called his sons to him and reminded them of who they were and their duty. Having listened with humility, they took their leave with the promise to bring back the papal flagship and the simple words, 'Blessed be the bread and the salt you have given us.' Like their Christian counterparts the Ottomans were getting ready for battle. A large number of the fighting men on each galley took position on the bow platforms, while on the decks, from bow to stern, stood paired archers and harquebusiers in groups of four. Ottoman galleys lacked pavisades (large wooden planks along the sides of the rowing benches) and usually did not reinforce their forecastles with movable ramparts of reinforced timber – both features typical of western Mediterranean galleys – leaving the men on board exposed to firearms.[12]

The Ottoman fleet was now deployed in a crescent shape, apparently a much favoured formation, the right wing under Şuluç Mehmed Pasha with fifty-five galleys and one galliot; the centre, commanded by the *kapudan paşa*, with ninety-one galleys and five galliots; and the left under Uluç Ali with sixty-seven galleys and twenty-seven galliots. A small reserve under Murad Dragut with eight galleys, five galliots and eighteen *fuste* was placed behind the central division. Smaller vessels with extra fighting men stood ready to assist wherever needed, making a total of about 300 ships. There is no doubt that the Ottoman fleet was numerically stronger, many galliots being no different from normal galleys – some of them having up to twenty-five rowing benches – except possibly in the amount of ordnance carried.* The league definitely held the upper hand in ordnance; while archival evidence has laid to rest Alberto Guglielmotti's tidy estimate of the guns present (1,815 for the league and 750 for the Ottomans), it is probable that the Christians held a two to one advantage in artillery pieces.[13]

Having disposed his forces for battle, Müezzinzâde Ali issued his orders. The two wings were to advance and envelop the Christian flanks, while his division would tackle the enemy centre. The simple Muslim tactical plan was to break through the enemy line by skilful use of numbers, isolating and destroying the allied ships piecemeal. Şuluç's and Uluç Ali's divisions were to move first, immediately followed by the *kapudan paşa*'s. By exercising enough pressure on Don Juan's centre and left the Ottomans calculated that he would be forced to commit his reserve prematurely to aid these divisions. Should this happen, then Uluç Ali could deal unhindered with an outnumbered Doria. The Algerian *beylerbey*'s galleys were to pin down the Genoese admiral, allowing his galliots to swing round the allies' right flank and fall upon their rear. Should the manoeuvre succeed, then the hapless allies would be pinned against the shore, and cavalry units had been stationed on the coast with the task of rounding up the stranded Christians.[14] Alternatively, if Don Juan sent Santa Cruz to help Doria, then the *kapudan paşa* would attempt to smash through the enemy centre by sheer weight of numbers causing the disintegration of the Christian line.

---

* This is probably the reason why estimates of the Ottoman fleet vary significantly in the various contemporary sources.

The crescent formation initially adopted by the Ottomans was, in theory, ideal for enveloping manoeuvres, allowing, in the words of a near contemporary, 'in different directions but at the same time to invest the front of the enemy, while the horns on the side surround him, or retreat should there be the need'.[15] Yet the size of the Ottoman fleet meant that the tips of the crescent would come too early into contact with a much stronger enemy and possibly be severely mauled before the rest of the armada could come to their aid. To be successful the *kapudan paşa*'s plan called for good timing and the whole fleet to work in unison for the Ottoman punch to be delivered with full force. Müezzinzâde Ali therefore altered his fleet's formation, dividing it into three divisions mirroring the Christian deployment. He also ordered that no one should overtake his galley on pain of death, reserving the same fate for any enslaved Christian oarsman who should turn his head towards the enemy fleet – something that inevitably would cause a drop in speed. A good psychologist as well as a humane and generous person, Müezzinzâde Ali promised freedom to all his slaves if victorious. Since the Ottomans were convinced that the Christians were lambs to the slaughter, the *kapudan paşa* was banking on having enough prisoners to take the place of the liberated slaves.[16]

Yet the *kapudan paşa* was worried. He could not understand the galleasses' tactical role in front of the enemy line, and was bemused that what he believed to be vessels had been placed in such an exposed position. It was common knowledge that the Venetians had armed some *galie grosse*, a number of his officers expressing concern about their presence. But prisoners recently captured near Igoumenitsa had told him that these big galleys had only three artillery pieces at the stern and three at the bow, hardly something to be worried about. Müezzinzâde Ali was more anxious about the number and position of the *ponentine* galleys, having little regard for the Venetian ones 'even if there had been a thousand of them'. The *kapudan paşa*'s dismissive attitude may appear strange, but the poor performance of the Venetian fleet during the 1570 campaign should be borne in mind. Müezzinzâde Ali was certainly aware of the many problems still afflicting the republic's ships, including the scarcity of fighting personnel, and was thus puzzled to discover that the allies had intermixed *ponentine* and *levantine* galleys. His decision to strike Barbarigo's wing first and with the same number of galleys as his adversary could also have resulted from the belief that the Venetians represented, in every sense, the league's soft underbelly.[17]

Not everyone approved of Müezzinzâde Ali's plan. As he watched the Ottoman fleet deploy, Uluç Ali was unable to hide his concerns from the *kapudan paşa*. In particular he had serious misgivings about Şuluç's wing being placed so near to the coast, urging his commander-in-chief to move the fleet towards the open sea. Otherwise, not only would the Ottoman right have little manoeuvring space, but the crews would also be tempted to make for the shore should the tide of battle turn against the Turks. Müezzinzâde Ali stubbornly stuck to his plan, causing Uluç Ali to tear at his beard crying in despair, 'Why don't those who learnt their trade with Hayreddin and Dragut speak out?'. This story may have been concocted at a later date and with the benefits of hindsight, but the contemporary Genoese author Foglietta would also stress that by deploying near the coast the Ottomans had provided their crews with an irresistible escape route.[18]

The Christian fleet was now fully arrayed. On the left stood the fifty-seven galleys of Barbarigo's division, four placed behind the front line as an immediate reserve, the Venetian commander having moved as close to the shore as he dared to avoid envelopment. But Barbarigo, not knowing the coast well and wary of sandbanks, made the mistake of leaving a gap between the left of his squadron and the shore wide enough to allow a few galleys at a time to slip through. The central division under Don Juan of Austria numbered sixty-two galleys, two at the stern of the prince's *capitana*, many being the flagships of the various contingents. Doria with fifty-three galleys was to the right, still lacking four of Cardona's vessels. Seeing that the opposing Ottoman division under Uluç Ali far outnumbered his own, Doria extended himself to the south, thinning his ranks and creating a gap between the Christian right and centre. But the Genoese admiral sent word to Don Juan not to commit his reserve unless the Ottomans managed to break through in force, it being more advantageous to meet any threat with fresh forces than having to do so with battle-weary galleys and men. Doria's suggestion was sound given that the absence of the round-ships and of Cardona's group had weakened the whole Christian front, but he still believed that the vanguard would eventually reach its assigned position, and was probably counting on the galleasses to plug the hole developing to the right of the allied main division. Behind the main line stood Santa Cruz's reserve with thirty galleys, plus some forty brigantines and frigates, each loaded with ten harquebusiers and a couple of small guns, whose job was to tackle the enemy's light craft 'doing as much damage possible'.[19]

The centre of both fleets was heavily larded with *capitane* and *padrone*, eighteen on the allied and twenty-two on the Ottoman side, all lantern galleys. John F. Guilmartin in his seminal study of galley warfare describes the latter as not necessarily larger than ordinary galleys – nor were *bastarde* necessarily lantern galleys – but as 'invariably exceptionally heavily armed and . . . [playing] an important role as tactical focal points in battle'.[20] While the second part of this statement is to an extent true, the first assertion is debatable. As we have seen, the *capitana* and *padrona* of the Lomellini family, both lanterns, were small and carried limited amounts of ordinance. The same was true of the twenty-five-bench *capitana* of Savoy, but in the Christian battle array it occupied the place immediately to the right of the papal flagship. The Lomellini *capitana* also occupied a particularly exposed position on the extreme left of the central division, where one would have expected to find a more powerful vessel. The answer to this riddle lies in the complicated system of precedence, typical of the age. Significantly, Doria's and Barbarigo's galleys stood on the extreme flanks of their respective divisions, Cardona's flagship should have been placed at the extreme left of Doria's wing, and the Genoese republic flagship stood beside Venier's galley – all these dispositions proving how tactical needs had to take into consideration social conventions. This was not limited to the West, the Ottomans also having to deal with problems of hierarchy when deploying their fleet, although they tended to group together the galleys of the various contingents making up their armada. Nor were the Ottoman lantern galleys necessarily all *bastarde*; for many independent captains the stern lamp represented a status symbol, even if their command be just one vessel.[21]

The exact number of soldiers on each side remains a matter of debate. Alfonso Salimei, writing in 1931, estimated 34,000 Christian soldiers present, a figure accepted by some Turkish historians as proof that the Ottomans were quantitatively inferior in troops. However, Salimei, while undoubtedly a thorough researcher, based his estimates on theoretical calculations and overtly attempted to claim the so-called battle of Lepanto as an Italian victory 'with Spanish help'. Salimei, after all, wrote during the Fascist period, glossing over the fact that in the Early Modern age – and to an extent today – Italy was but a cultural and geographical expression, and also that many of the Italians participating in the 1571 campaign were Neapolitans, Sicilians and Milanese, all subjects of the king of Spain.[22] Contemporary documents show the league having between 28,000 and 31,000 soldiers, and the Ottomans fielding 25,000 *sipahis* and janissaries. To the latter should be added a few thousand Algerian, Tunisian and Tripoli corsairs, plus an unknown number of garrison soldiers taken from nearby fortresses. A few years after the battle Mario Savorgnan estimated the fighting complement of the standard Ottoman galley present as on average 120 'swordsmen', lantern galleys boasting up to 300, yet we know that the crews of a number of Ottoman galleys were under strength. In reality, calculating the exact number of fighting men is virtually impossible: not only were Venetian and Ottoman sailors and free rowers trained combatants, it was also customary for commanders facing a difficult situation to augment their forces by unchaining and arming *buonevoglie* (on *ponentine* galleys) and convict oarsmen.

Thus, it is safe to say that the two forces were more or less equal as to fighting men, although the Ottomans probably had more seasoned veterans.[23]

Both sides aimed to reduce the enemy's combat strength by the use of artillery before the fleets came into contact. Since the Ottomans relied more on hand-to-hand fighting, they preferred to load their naval ordnance with stone balls, 'considering that by shattering into pieces, smashing the timber and sending splinters flying through the air they do more damage than iron balls, that pass clean through the wood'. For this reason the Ottomans preferred firing their guns at close range in one single volley, leaving their boarding parties to finish off a stunned and decimated foe. Western tactics emphasized damaging vessels as much as crews, galley ordnance being loaded with different types of shot and discharged at various moments during a battle. In his fighting orders Don Juan allowed every captain 'to fire when they believe it will most damage the enemy' but ordered them to reserve at least one piece for the final clash.[24] Events would prove which of the two philosophies was best.

On his flagship Don Juan donned a suit of mirror-polished armour and then, crucifix in hand, climbed on a swift frigate. Marcantonio Colonna and Requesens also boarded frigates, each of the three men travelling to one of the divisions division to ascertain that the galleys were in fighting order and to encourage those on board. Back on his galley, Don Juan heard mass, and on both sides men bowed their heads in prayer, asking God to aid them in their cause. On Christian vessels priests, many from the new Jesuit and Capuchin orders, heard confessions, while the Muslims performed ritual ablutions. Pius V's bull of general indulgence and absolution for all those who should happen to die in battle against the infidels was read aloud on each of the league's ships. The Muslims did not need such reassurance, believing that dying in battle for their faith would automatically allow them into heaven.[25]

It was now about eleven in the morning, and the two fleets had slowly been moving towards each other for at least three hours, the allies still hampered in their movements by a headwind. The league's fleet had taken up position, its extreme left wing close to the northern shore of the Gulf of Patras, and it now awaited the enemy onslaught. As soon as Müezzinzâde Ali was sure his fleet was ready he ordered a blank shot to be fired in the direction of the enemy, formally challenging his opponent to battle. Immediately the *Real* answered with a shot loaded 'with ball'. To confirm his intentions, the *kapudan paşa* had another blank shot fired, and again Don Juan answered with a fully loaded artillery piece. In this way not only did the prince signal to his opponents the position of the allied flagship – since the Ottomans' vision would soon be impeded by the sun shining in their faces – but the water columns produced by the impacting balls allowed him to adjust his guns' elevation for maximum effect. Trumpets sounded, and the great banner of the league, displaying Christ crucified accompanied by the coats of arms of Habsburg Spain, the pope and the republic of Venice, was hoisted on the *Real*'s mainmast.[26]

At a signal the whole Ottoman fleet advanced towards the Christian array. It was an impressive and daunting sight, enough to make even the bravest man quake, made of multicoloured banners, robes and turbans, accompanied by the sound of drums, horns and other instruments. From the mainmast of Müezzinzâde Ali's flagship (called in the west the *Sultana*) flew the Ottoman battle standard, on which the name of Allah was embroidered 29,800 times. The Ottomans moved at a leisurely pace, exploiting the favourable wind to advance without having to tire their crews, galleys using oars only to keep in line. Suddenly the wind changed, a breeze starting to blow in the Ottomans' faces. Hastily the *kapudan paşa* ordered all sails furled and the fleet to continue under oars. The Christians were quick to see the change in weather as a sign of divine favour and took fresh heart. Apparently calm and relaxed, Don Juan watched from the poop deck of the *Real* the Ottoman fleet pause. Calling for his musicians, he went to the *arrembata* and there, in a supreme example of what the Italians call *sprezzatura*, he danced a galliard together with two other Spanish gentlemen.[27] But very soon everyone would be dancing to the tune of the *Totentanz*.

~

It was nearly midday, and the Ottomans were about a mile and a half from the Christian line, galleys oars dipping into the sea in constant, long strokes, the beating of drums giving the rhythm to thousands of free and forced rowers.[28] The Christian galleasses lay in the middle of the sea like sleeping castles, but the men on board were awake and alert, impatiently waiting near their guns or at the pavisades for the enemy to approach. Tension was evident on the face of Master Gunner Zaccaria Schiavina, the inventor of a new aiming system 'to shoot at the enemy creating the outmost damage'.[29] Now the moment of truth had arrived, the Ottomans being little more than half a mile away and steadily moving in for the kill. Francesco Duodo, commanding the galleasses, uttered a brisk order and the Venetian gunners' lit matches struck the touchholes.

The effect of the galleasses' fire on the advancing Ottomans was devastating, the last thing many of them saw being the flash and the smoke of the Christian bow pieces. Most did not even hear the thunder of the guns before being hit. The flying iron balls easily found targets in the formation of densely packed Muslim ships, smashing through timber and flesh. Shouts of '*mavna, mavna!*' rose from the Ottoman vessels, mingling with the screams of the wounded and the sound of splintering wood. 'God allow us to get out of here in one piece,' cried Müezzinzâde Ali, seeing a shot carry away the central lantern of his flagship.[30] Beholding the destruction around him, Pertev Pasha tugged at his beard in consternation. In one case, the impact of Venetian shot lifted a galley out of the water, its oars waving helplessly like the legs of a wounded centipede, before sending it to the bottom with all hands. In another, a galley was blown sky-high after a ball penetrated its ammunition magazine. At least two other ships were lost to the galleasses' fire, and many more damaged. Other galleys, their coxswains dead, caused havoc by colliding with those adjacent to them.

Scores of Ottomans were crushed or torn apart; masts toppled into the sea; water poured into smashed hulls. The drums on the Muslim ships stopped beating, and a number of galleys started to backwater; others instinctively converged towards the galleasses, discharging their guns as they did. Slowly Duodo's six ships made a half-turn, oars moving the vessels in unison as if in a pirouette, before delivering another volley from the port side. Again the gentle manoeuvre, and the process was repeated with the aft and starboard artillery, the relentless Venetian fire making the galleasses look like 'all one flame'.[31] Duodo had dealt the Ottomans a dizzying upper-cut; not yet a knockout, it was a blow that brought the enemy to his knees. Acting quickly, Müezzinzâde Ali barked out orders, and the rowers on the Ottoman vessels increased their stroke rate in an attempt to get away as quickly as possible from the hellish galleasses. But as the Ottoman fleet pushed on, full speed ahead, formation was irremediably lost; many galleys, at sea for too long now, lagged behind. The *kapudan paşa*'s plan lay in ruins, together with its formation the Ottoman fleet having lost much of its punch. However, with grim determination it pressed ahead towards the waiting Christian galleys to see what the remainder of the battle would bring.

Attempting to avoid the devastating Venetian heavy ordnance the Ottoman right and centre had to run the gauntlet of swivel guns and harquebuses fired by the men posted on top of the galleasses. The galleys passing nearest to the big vessels were the worst hit, single leaden balls and grapeshot opening gaping holes on the densely packed decks and forecastles. No sooner were they free of the galleasses' steely claws than the Ottomans started being pounded by the allied galleys' centreline guns. By this point nearly a third of the Muslim ships had been sunk or damaged to a greater or lesser degree; worse still the smoke from the league's ordnance was blowing in the Ottomans' faces, hiding the Christian fleet from sight and impeding the aim of archers and gunners. But despite its losses the Ottoman armada still had plenty of fighting spirit in it, as the allies were soon to find out.

No sooner had the galleasses opened fire than the allied fleet began slowly to advance towards the now broken enemy line. The unhurried pace had the purpose of keeping a tight formation, although according to one source the Christian fleet would have done better fighting closer to the galleasses 'which could have been of greater aid in the battle'.[32] Because of the fleet's size, perfect alignment proved impossible, much to Venier's chagrin. The *capitana* of Malta moved 'the length of two galleys' ahead of the line, as did Marco Querini's group on the extreme right of Barbarigo's wing. From a nearby galley Count Ferrante Caracciolo noticed Querini's escapade, potentially very dangerous for the whole allied fleet, and immediately sent a message to Barbarigo allowing him to redress the situation in time by ordering Querini to fall back into line.

In an attempt to avoid the galleasses' murderous fire, Şuluç Mehmed Pasha swung his division towards the coast. To an extent he managed to get out of the range of the Venetian heavy guns, but the *beylerbey* of Alexandria's move also had another purpose. Exploiting the nautical knowledge of the Genoese renegade Caur Ali, Şuluç passed under the promontory of Malcantone, braving the shallows at the mouth of the river Acheloos with the intention of turning Barbarigo's flank. The Venetian commander saw the peril and reacted quickly. The four Venetian galleys of Cardona's vanguard had just reached the Christian left and had positioned themselves to the rear of Barbarigo's flagship. Being the nearest at hand, Barbarigo ordered them to stop the Muslim outflanking manoeuvre. It was a timely decision. As the Ottomans rounded Malcantone, they found their way blocked by the first of these vessels, the *Santa Maria Maddalena* under Marino Contarini. Counting on superior numbers they attacked it immediately, and very soon Contarini's men were fighting for their lives. Barbarigo understood that if he did not stop the advancing Muslims in their tracks all would be lost. Turning his flagship – easily recognizable because of its sides painted Venetian red, the colour of ordinary Venetian galleys being brown – towards the coast, he signalled to the nearest galleys to follow

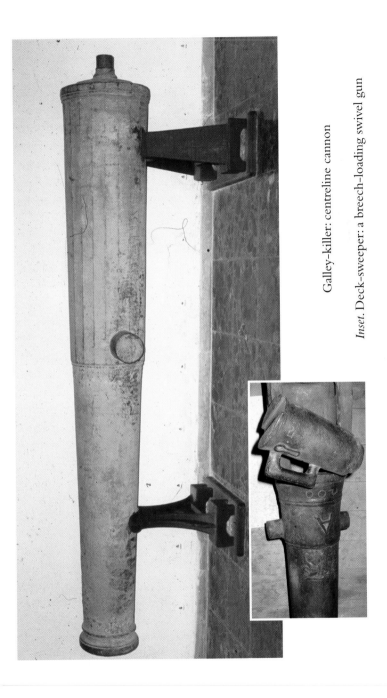

Galley-killer: centreline cannon

Inset. Deck-sweeper: a breech-loading swivel gun

The League's soldiers
Left to right: Venetian
Galeotto di Libertà;
Italian galley captain;
Spanish junior officer
(drawings by Bruno
Mugnai)

Ottoman soldiers
Left to right:
North African corsair;
janissary on naval duty;
topçu (artilleryman)
(drawings by Bruno
Mugnai)

The galley's 'muscle': rowers on a Tuscan vessel

RITRATTO
D'VNA LETTERA SCRITTA ALL'ILL^{mo}
ET ECC.^{mo} S.^{re} AMBASCIATOR CESAREO
DALLA ARMATA.

Donde si hanno molti nuoui, belli, & particolari ragualgi
circa la Vittoria hauuta contra Turchi.

In Roma Appresso gli heredi di M. Antonio Blado Stampatori Cameral
Con Priuilegio.

The core of the matter:
the Holy League's Banner
as reproduced in a
contemporary pamphlet

Saint Mark's marines:
Venetian *scapolo*

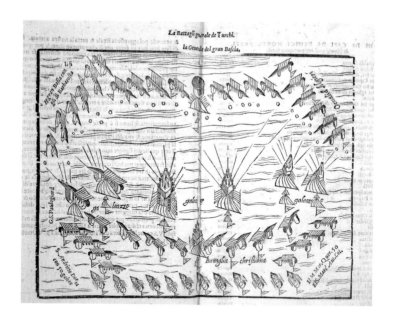

Crude but clear:
a contemporary sketch
of the Battle of the
Curzolaris

A better view:
Genoese print of the
battle showing the fleets'
initial disposition and
Uluç Ali's manoeuvre

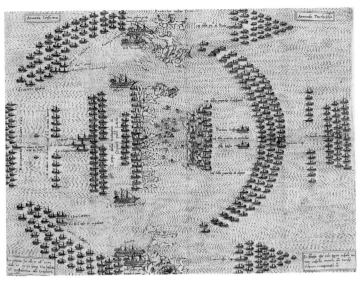

Winning tactics: the galleasses' opening barrage

Gruelling match: galley melee at the Curzolaris

High noon: the climax of the battle

Sadness in victory: Agostino Barbarigo's death

Privilege of holiness:
Pius V's vision

Half-hearted
celebration: Philip II of
Spain offering the infant
Don Fernando
to victory

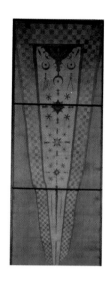

Full-blown celebration:
Francesco Maria della
Rovere with his gilded
victory armour

Surviving trophy:
standard taken from
Müezzinzâde Ali's *Sultana*

Breaking the news:
one of the many
contemporary pamphlets
describing the league's
victory

him. With guns blazing he headed for the flank of the advancing enemy galleys and then placed himself squarely in their path 'so that not even a small boat could pass'.[33] It was an act of desperate courage, for now he was pitted against a far superior foe.

It did not take long for the *Santa Maria Maddalena* to resemble a charnel house. Marino Contarini himself was killed almost immediately by a harquebus shot, the same fate befalling many of the galley's officers. Colonel Paolo Orsini, in command of the Venetian infantry on board, received a ball in the right shoulder and burns all over his body from a fire pot. Then *Il Sole* captained by Vincenzo Querini emerged from the smoke, crashing into the Ottoman ships and relieving the pressure on Contarini. Thanks to their plentiful small-calibre artillery firing at point-blank range the Venetians managed to keep the Muslims at bay, but *Il Sole* in its turn suffered grievous losses from Ottoman harquebusiers, archers and swordsmen. Querini was killed, and for more than a hour the Venetians desperately tried to push back their Ottoman assailants. Nevertheless, with their determined stand Contarini and Querini's men had bought precious time for the rest of the Christian left wing.

Seeing Barbarigo's galley approaching, Şuluç had swung his galleys round to confront the Venetian. Hit by the withering fire of eight Ottoman galleys, Barbarigo's ship was soon in the centre of a maelstrom. Muslim soldiers poured over the gunwales and the forward platform, pushing back the Venetian defenders. Barbarigo himself was in the thick of the fight, constantly encouraging his men and leading them in one counter-attack after another. More Venetian galleys joined the fray, fresh troops allowing Barbarigo to push back his attackers. Şuluç realized that he had to finish the job quickly, lest he lose his chance of turning the Christian left flank. Exploiting local tactical superiority he redoubled his efforts to capture Barbarigo's flagship, hoping that this would lead to the collapse of organized resistance in that sector. But for the *beylerbey* of Alexandria time was running out fast, more and more Christian galleys engaging the Muslim vessels or helping the ships thus occupied by feeding troops into the fight.

Meanwhile, below Malcantone, the two Venetian galleys pro-
tecting Barbarigo's left flank had prevailed over their enemies.
Locked together side by side they had provided mutual support to
each other, repulsing attack after attack with the aid of the galleys
Santa Caterina and *Nostra Donna*, all originally part of the vanguard.
As the Alexandrian galleys attempted to prise apart *Santa Maria
Maddalena* and *Il Sole*, Paolo Orsini exploited a momentary lull in
the fighting to organize a counter-attack with his surviving men.
Taken by surprise, the Ottomans attempted to resist, but suddenly,
having somehow managed to break open their shackles and grabbing
the weapons of the fallen, Christian slaves attacked their former
masters from all sides. Caught unawares the Muslims quickly succumbed, the Ottoman galleys near Malcantone falling one by one
to the Christians. The *Santa Caterina* and *Nostra Donna* now turned
to Barbarigo's aid.

More help was on its way. Santa Cruz, already engaged with
the Ottomans in the centre, had sent ten galleys of the reserve to
plug the potential gap developing on the left wing. Meanwhile,
Provveditore Marco Querini was also arriving, having on his own
initiative swung his detachment towards the coast. The *Santa
Caterina* and *Nostra Donna* joined the hard-pressed Barbarigo, but
nearly immediately their *sopracomiti* Marco Cicogna and Pier Francesco Malipiero were struck down. To make matters worse, an
Ottoman galley under the cover of thick smoke managed to round
Malcantone and ram Barbarigo's galley at the stern. Once again the
Christian left was at risk, the Ottomans still having enough advantage in numbers to execute a breakthrough, with potentially incalculable consequences for the battle's outcome. Marco Querini's
manoeuvre had also opened a large gap to the left of the Christian
central division. Should Müezzinzâde Ali be able to exploit this
chance and unite with Şuluç's forces at the rear of the allied battle
line, all would be lost for the league.

A hail of arrows fell on Barbarigo's ship as the Ottomans once
again tried to take it by storm. Rallying his men Barbarigo raised
the visor of his helmet to make himself heard. His aides warned him

of the peril. 'Better to be hit than not heard,'[34] answered the feisty Venetian. No sooner had he uttered these words than an arrow pierced his left eye. Collapsing into the arms of his secretary Andrea Suriano, he was hastily carried below with the help of Colonel Silvio da Porcia. Dismay struck the defenders, and the Ottomans exploited the confusion to board the galley, fighting their way up to the mainmast. It was now up to Barbarigo's deputy Federico Nani to repel the Ottoman assault – Nani himself having been wounded several times – but luckily for the Venetians relief was at hand. With all guns firing, the galley *Dio Padre e la Trinità* under Giovanni Contarini del Zaffo struck Şuluç's galley at the stern, carrying away its rudder. Behind this vessel was the galley of Provveditore Antonio da Canal, who having just dispatched an enemy vessel went straight for the *capitana* of Alexandria, ramming it amidships. But immediately da Canal was in turn attacked from the rear, and it was left to Nicolò Avonal's Cretan vessel and to the galleys of the vanguard to fight off the ships attacking Barbarigo's galley.

Slowly the tide was swinging in the allies' favour. Marco Querini had reached his beleaguered companions, and the ten galleys from the reserve led by Martin de Padilla were bearing down on the wavering enemy line. The Neapolitan and papal galleys of both Querini's and Barbarigo's squadrons – *ponentine* with strong fighting contingents – engaged Şuluç's front and right, the Spanish harquebusiers pouring pounds of lead into the Ottoman ranks. The galleasses of Antonio and Ambrogio Bragadin also joined the fray, their heavy guns disabling one galley after another. But the Ottomans were not prepared to give up, and scores of impatient Venetians fell trying to board the enemy vessels.

Exploiting a gap in the Muslim line created by galleass fire, the Tuscan *Elbigina* charged through followed by a number of other galleys. Swinging to the right they went for a contingent of Anatolian vessels commanded by Salihpaşazâde Mehmed Bey. On one of the allied galleys, the *Marchesa* owned by Giovanni Andrea Doria, lay the ailing Miguel de Cervantes. Rising from his sick bed to join the fight for the Anatolian galleys, his left hand was permanently crippled by a harquebus shot. 'For the glory of the right one,' he would later comment, proudly showing his wound.[35] The *Elbigina* and her companions intercepted a group of about thirty Ottoman galleys escaping from the centre,★ and after a stiff fight captured the *capitana* of Rhodes, commanded by Hasan Bey, with a fighting contingent of 250 men. On board, the victorious soldiers found rich booty, including four falcons and as many greyhounds. Salihpaşazâde Mehmed was also captured, and now the Neapolitans of Padilla's squadron were busy wrapping things up on the left.

By now the Ottomans in this sector of the battle were thoroughly demoralized. As a small group of slow and undermanned Turkish galleys approached the battle, the crews realized that the game was up. Believing discretion the better part of valour, they headed straight for the shore, abandoning their galleys without a fight. The rest of the Ottoman right was likewise being pushed towards the coast by the allied galleys, some of the latter running aground in their haste to come to grips with the enemy. A shot from Giovanni Contarini's ship sent Şuluç's galley to the bottom, but it didn't sink far, the sea at that point being less than two metres deep. Badly wounded, Şuluç was dragged from the water onto Contarini's galley. Antonio da Canal, dressed in a quilted cotton jacket and hat, had meanwhile donned a pair of rope shoes so as not to slip on the blood-soaked planks and was busy clearing the enemy decks with a two-handed sword. Hundreds of Ottomans jumped into the sea in an attempt to reach the safety of the nearby coast. Many got trampled by their comrades and drowned in the shallow waters; others were chased and killed by the pitiless Venetians; others still, wounded or not knowing how to swim, surrendered, trusting in their enemies' mercy. The Venetians had little, but the soldiers of the other contingents were happy to take as many prisoners as possible. The slaughter on the Christian left had been

---

★ This could explain why Ferrante Caracciolo states that Şuluç had seventy galleys with him. (CARACCIOLO: 37. Cfr. ADRIANI: 885).

great, but was nothing compared to what was still happening elsewhere.

~

Rowing furiously and in some disorder, the Ottoman main division hit the allied centre just after midday. Accompanied by a group of powerful *lanterne*, the *Sultana* went straight for the *Real*. As they approached the enemy line, the Ottomans had been subjected to a continuous bombardment from the Christian vessels, some of which managed to shoot up to five times at the advancing Muslims. The latter, having retained their galleys' rams, could not depress their guns sufficiently to reply, in most cases the Turkish shots sailing clean over the decks of the Christian ships. Besides, the allied artillery fire had been mainly directed at the front of the advancing Ottoman galleys, killing many gunners before they could fire their pieces, a number being found still loaded at the end of the battle. But still the Ottomans came on, until the fleets clashed with an ear-splitting cacophony of sound. Giovanni Battista Contarini has left us a vivid image of the scene:

> There happened a mortal storm of harquebus shots and arrows, and it seemed that the sea was aflame from the flashes and continuous fires lit by fire trumpets, fire pots and other weapons. Three galleys would be pitted against four, four against six, and six against one, enemy or Christian alike, everyone fighting in the cruellest manner to take each other's lives. And already many Turks and Christians had boarded their opponents' galleys fighting at close quarters with short weapons, few being left alive. And death came endlessly from the two-handed swords, scimitars, iron maces, daggers, axes, swords, arrows, harquebuses and fire weapons. And besides those killed in various ways, others escaping from the weapons would drown by throwing themselves into the sea, thick and red with blood.[36]

The air was dense with gunpowder smoke, engulfing all combatants without distinction. Often men knew that they were under attack only when they felt their galley struck by an enemy vessel, seconds before being hit by a storm of arrows, harquebus or artillery fire. In the confusion it was difficult to distinguish friend from foe, although the league's ships displayed sheep's fleeces as field signs.[37] It would be wrong to think that the combatants were only intent on boarding each other's vessels. Storming an enemy galley was not easy, unless its fighting crew had been substantially reduced in numbers. The Ottomans were more inclined to employ boarding tactics, after thinning the enemy ranks with guns, bows, flaming pots and fire tubes. Muslim archers were particularly active, one source describing the Christian galleys as being so studded with arrows as to resemble hedgehogs.[38] The allies preferred to keep the Muslims at a distance with a continuous barrage of grapeshot and small-arms fire: at close range one well-directed harquebus volley was enough to clear an opponent's bridge, even if in the confusion many fell victim to friendly fire.[39]

With banners fluttering in the wind, Müezzinzade Ali's galley now descended on the *Real*, striking it diagonally at the bow. The *Sultana*'s guns thundered, one ball smashing through the *Real*'s *arrembata*, wounding and killing a number of rowers; another went wide and the third sailed clean over the gunwales. The *Real*'s artillery also did considerable damage to the enemy flagship, the advantage gained from having no ram being evident. Shouting like madmen, the *Sultana*'s janissaries leapt onto the *Real*'s foredeck, trying to storm the *arrembata* and engaging Don Juan's soldiers in a furious hand-to-hand fight. Marcantonio Colonna moved his galley in to assist Don Juan, but was hit by Pertev Pasha's vessel. The blow caused the papal flagship to turn sharply to its left and in turn strike the *Sultana* at the second bench from the bow, just as another Ottoman galley crashed into Colonna's stern. On Don Juan's left, Sebastiano Venier also attempted to engage the *Sultana*, counting on the support of Genoa's *capitana* commanded by Ettore Spinola. But seeing Spinola already engaged with four other enemy galleys and himself about to be intercepted by a group of Ottoman vessels, he sent for two Venetian galleys of Santa Cruz's squadron. As

Venier pushed forward a small mastless boat managed to reach undetected the starboard side of the Venetian flagship, slipping under its oars to prevent the galley from moving. Never lacking initiative, Venier ordered all his men to the starboard side, tilting his galley onto the boat until it sank.

Meanwhile on the *Real* the harquebusiers had repulsed the Ottomans, and now counter-attacked under the command of Maestre de Campo (Colonel) Don Lope de Figueroa. His 400 Sardinian harquebusiers were augmented by a number of gentlemen volunteers and their retainers, bringing the *Real*'s fighting complement to 800 men. Battling furiously they boarded the *Sultana*, pushing back the Ottomans to the mainmast. With the arrival of Muslim reinforcements from the galleys coming up behind Müezzinzâde Ali's flagship, the allies were in turn forced to retreat as the Turks once more gained a foothold on the *Real*. From the Christian galleys at Don Juan's stern came more troops in support of their hard-pressed companions, and again the allies boarded the *Sultana* only to be pushed back once more. This deadly see-saw continued for some time, neither side managing to gain the upper hand as more and more men were pushed into the battle, often to their deaths. The bridges of both flagships had makeshift pavisades at three different places, and were covered with fat and oil to cause assailants' to slip and fall.

Having managed to free his vessel, Venier headed once more for the *Sultana*. En route, he noticed four enemy galleys moving to intercept him but 'thank God they all went by my stern'.[40] Pushing ahead, Venier struck the *Sultana* amidships but was in turn hit in the prow by a Turkish lantern galley, and by another towards the stern. Now Venier had to fend off attacks from two sides, and to make matters worse the four galleys which had previously failed to intercept him reversed course, heading for his stern. Luckily the two galleys Venier had sent for arrived just in time to stop the Ottoman vessels in their tracks, engaging them in furious combat. Both their *sopracomiti*, Cattarin Malipiero and Giovanni Loredan, were killed, with their sacrifice saving Venier from almost certain destruction. But in the meantime other Ottoman galleys were attacking the allied command squadron, one of them striking the *Real* at its stern. The Christian centre had been pierced, and should the gap in the line become wider the Ottomans could still exploit their superiority in numbers to stage a major breakthrough.

Malipiero and Loredan's galleys were followed by Santa Cruz's whole squadron. Whether the leader of the Christian reserve simply followed the two vessels or made a deliberate decision to engage his division is unclear. He had been ordered 'with the greatest attention and care to see which section be the weakest, where his intervention be necessary, and with what number of galleys ... leaving every decision to the aforesaid marquis's prudence, only if it coincides with what we expect and confide he shall do'.[41] Santa Cruz had been given complete freedom of action, but he knew that he had to use it shrewdly. Committing the reserve too soon or unnecessarily could mean having nothing left to stop the Ottomans should they manage to turn one of the allied flanks. On the other hand, Santa Cruz could not stand by idly while the Christian centre was penetrated and possibly annihilated. In the event, seeing the Ottomans pierce the allied line, the marquis moved his galleys forward and pushed back the enemy – something for which his political adversary Requesens would later criticize him.[42] Santa Cruz soon had his hands full, and was saved from a bullet only thanks to his buckler. For others even the strongest armour was no protection. Virginio Orsini died when a ball sailed clean through his buckler and breastplate – which speaks volumes about the poor quality of both. Don Bernardino de Cardenas was hit in the chest by a shot fired from a swivel gun, and although his armour withstood the blow the unfortunate gentleman died from shock.

Marcantonio Colonna had meanwhile forced Pertev Pasha to pull back, but was still faced by other Ottoman galleys. On his right the *capitana* of Savoy had been fending off the attacks of one commanded by Mustafa Esdey, paymaster general of the Ottoman fleet, and another vessel. The Savoyard galley was nearly overwhelmed, and its commander, Provana di Leynì, received a harquebus ball in his helmet that left him stunned for half an hour – he was still suffering from headaches a few days later when he wrote his report to Duke Emmanuel Philibert. The timely arrival of one of Santa Cruz's galleys restored the situation, allowing Provana to repulse his assailants.[43] On the left of the *Real* Sebastiano Venier was busy encouraging his men, shooting with a crossbow at enemy soldiers. Standing on his bridge he received an arrow in the leg but refused to leave his post.

To the right of the *capitana* of Savoy was the *Grifona*, one of the galleys leased by Cosimo I de' Medici to Pope Pius V. It was a powerful vessel and a gift to the grand duke from his rich and powerful supporter Ugolino Grifoni. Captained by Alessandro Negroni, it had on board also Onorato Caetani and Bartolomeo Sereno, who later would leave detailed accounts of the fight. Kara Hodja and the galley of the corsair Kara Deli attacked the *Grifona* head on, meeting the stiffest of resistance. The papal soldiers poured harquebus and artillery fire into the Muslim ranks, already depleted since the Ottoman galleys had already fought two Venetian vessels. True to his reputation, Kara Hodja led his men from the front until shot by an Italian harquebusier. The arrival of a Venetian galley from the reserve commanded by the confusingly named Giovanni Loredan (a relation of his recently killed namesake) put an end to the matter, allowing the capture of the Turkish vessels. Onorato Caetani paid tribute to the Ottomans' fighting spirit, writing that between the two galleys 'no more than six Turks remained alive'.[44]

Leaving other galleys to deal with Colonna's, Pertev Pasha sailed round to the stern of the *Sultana* with the intention of bringing aid to the *kapudan paşa*. It was a mistake, for Pertev had already suffered considerable losses at Colonna's hands and now found himself subjected to devastating fire from Venier's *capitana*. Already in bad shape, Pertev's galley was also set upon by the *capitana* of the Lomellini under Paolo Giordano Orsini (son-in-law of Cosimo I) and a Venetian vessel from Sebinik commanded by Cristoforo (or Michele) Lucich. Still, it took some time for the Christians to subdue their adversaries, Orsini suffering a leg wound from a spent arrow. In the end Pertev, having lost his rudder and nearly all his men, badly burnt in the shoulder by a fire trumpet and 'berating the folly of the rash, and cursing [Müezzinzâde] Ali's obstinacy', abandoned ship together with his son. Climbing into a boat rowed by a Bolognese turned Muslim the two men passed unscathed among the allied ships, the Italian renegade shouting 'Don't shoot. We also are Christians.'[45]

Harquebus and cannon fire was slowly turning the battle in the Christians' favour. The gunpowder smoke prevented the Ottoman archers from aiming properly, and fatigue made their shooting weaker by the minute. To the left of the *Real* Ettore Spinola had managed to drive away his assailants after a fierce fight during which he had been struck three times in the leg by arrows, one of which 'was my saving grace, for while stooping to pull out the arrow, a harquebus shot passed over my head grazing my morion; and if I had been standing I would have been in great peril'.[46] Under oars he moved nearer to the *Real* so as to provide Don Juan with assistance. By now Christian galleys were converging on the *Sultana* in numbers, while the stream of reinforcements sent by the other Ottoman vessels to its aid was rapidly declining to a trickle. Allied gunfire had effectively stopped men from reaching the *Sultana* by boat, and those who tried to do so by swimming were shot as soon as they attempted to climb the ship's sides. The galleasses allotted to the centre were now fighting the rearmost Ottoman vessels, effectively preventing them from assisting their flagship. On the papal *capitana* Romegas turned to Colonna, who had just finished dealing successfully with an enemy ship. 'That galley is ours,' he said. 'Shall we seek another one, or help our still embattled *Real*?' 'Let's help our *Real*,' answered Colonna. Personally taking the tiller, Romegas directed the galley against the *Sultana*'s stern.[47]

For the Ottoman flagship the end was approaching fast, even if a number of Turkish galleys tried to interpose themselves between the *Sultana* and the advancing Christian vessels. Allied soldiers poured onto the *kapudan paşa*'s galley, pushing the defenders back towards the poop deck. There the remaining janissaries managed to throw up a makeshift barrier made of satin mattresses, from behind which they shot arrows at the Christian soldiers to slow down their advance. Seeing this, Filippo Venier loaded one of the Venetian flagship's *petriere* with canister shot and fired it at the resisting Ottomans. The barrier went down in a flurry of fabric, blood and bone, as the allies once more surged forward. Müezzinzâde Ali fought to the last, discharging arrow after arrow until killed, the circumstances of his death constituting one of the minor mysteries of the battle. Did he die outright from a harquebus ball in the head? Was he wounded and then beheaded by a Spanish soldier – who is supposed to have brought the bloody trophy to Don Juan, only to receive a frosty rebuke? Did he commit suicide by slitting his throat after throwing his valuables into the sea? Whatever the truth, his head was stuck on a pike and raised high for everyone to see, while from the *Sultana*'s mainmast the Ottoman standard was taken down and replaced with a Christian banner. At these sights Ottoman resistance started to crumble, as the shout of 'Victory! Victory!' rang from the Christian galleys.

But Nike's price was to be hefty, and had not yet been paid in full.

~

Advancing towards the Christian right wing Uluç Ali started receiving shots from the two galleasses placed in front of Doria's division. As the balls from the heavy Venetian guns found targets among his ships, the *beylerbey* of Algiers quickly changed course, pushing his force south towards the open sea. Giovanni Andrea Doria noticed the move and immediately took a course parallel to his adversary's. Their galleys slowly rowing towards the south, each commander, 'attempting to catch out (*uccellarsi*) the other',[48] kept a constant eye on his opponent's movements, the gap between the Christian right and centre increasing to roughly a mile. Uluç Ali was careful to stay out of the range of the *galie grosse*,[49] but every now and then stopped to exchange gunfire with the Christian galleys. The heavily outnumbered Doria was successfully managing to keep Uluç Ali at a distance, relying on his galleasses' firepower to thwart any outflanking movement and buying precious time by keeping his opponent from joining the battle. Uluç Ali's movements appear incomprehensible if one excludes, as many have done, the galleasses' presence in front of the Christian right. Without their presence, it would have been easy for Uluç Ali to surround and destroy Doria, as subsequent events would prove.

Doria's actions would afterwards be the subject of much discussion and recrimination, the Order of Malta and his old enemy Marcantonio Colonna – rather than the Venetians, despite what is usually believed – accusing him of having behaved with suspiciously excessive prudence.[50] The accusation that he was reluctant to risk his galleys is disproved by the fact that more than half were serving in the other two divisions. As for the suggestion of a secret agreement between him and Uluç Ali – Doria being part of Philip II's secret plan to bribe the *beylerbey* of Algiers into switching his allegiance from the Ottomans to the Spanish – first suggested by Cesareo Fernandez Duro at the end of the nineteenth century,[51] it ignores the fact that the two commanders could not possibly have known in advance they would be facing each other; indeed, according to Ottoman intelligence Doria was not even supposed to be present. Given the circumstances, the Genoese admiral could not have acted differently faced with Uluç Ali's outflanking attempt. Still, his southward move worsened his numerical disadvantage vis-à-vis the Algerian, since a number of galleys, largely Venetian, became separated from the division's main body. It is uncertain whether this happened because they were unable to keep up with the rest of Doria's ships, Venetian oarsmen having to row wearing armour, or because their recalcitrant captains had decided to join the fight in the centre. Whatever the truth, these vessels were now scattered along a mile-long front. It was a chance that no commander worthy of the name would let slip through his fingers, and 'the most cunning' (furbaccio)[52] Uluç Ali seized it with both hands.

Suddenly reversing course, the Algerian headed straight for the stragglers. It would appear that Doria did not notice the move immediately, possibly because Ali was moving behind a screen of smoke, but when at last the Genoese admiral realized what was going on, he reacted with energy. Hoisting sail, Doria with twelve of his swiftest galleys swung towards the east – in the process leaving behind the galleass of Piero Pisani – exploiting the wind to increase the speed of his ships as he attempted to catch up with Uluç Ali's rearguard. Meanwhile the Algerian was moving north-west, his vessels taking hits from the guns of Andrea da Pesaro's galleass as they passed its port side. For the Algerian it was a necessary price to pay, and his force smashed into the ships spread out between the Christian right and centre. The fight that developed was of the sort that the Ottomans had in vain sought until then. Each of the isolated Christian galleys found itself pitted against four or five enemy vessels and quickly succumbed to overwhelming numbers. Uluç Ali's galliots were all corsair ships, most of them of the large North African type, with experienced fighting crews. Against these men, the defenders of the beleaguered Christian galleys could do little except sell their lives as dearly as possible.

Losses were heavy on both sides. Benedetto Soranzo's galley went down with all on board, including the Ottomans who had captured it, when the ammunition magazine blew up. Captains fell with their crews: Girolamo Contarini, Marcantonio Lando, Marcantonio Pasqualigo, Giacomo di Mezo, Giorgio Corner and Pietro Bua. Alvise Cipico was lucky to survive with seven wounds in his body, surrendering his galley with only six of his men standing. Twelve remained alive on the *Piemontesa* of Savoy, her captain Ottaviano Moretto dying in the company of Cesare Provana di Leynì, a kinsman of the Savoyard admiral. One by one the allied galleys fell to the enemy, who started to tow away what had become floating coffins. Venier would later acidly comment that 'the galleys behind did not aid them', adding however that he had received this information from the survivors of the debacle 'for being at a distance did not see it myself'.[53] It is unclear whether Venier was pointing the finger at Santa Cruz, or at those galleys of Doria's squadron nearest to the action. His attitude was typical of many in the league and his suspicions unfair, the allied rearguard being already heavily engaged and Doria coming to the rescue as fast as he could.

Uluç Ali's plan was to keep Doria busy with the remainder of his command while he attacked the Christian centre with about thirty vessels. The first enemy galley he encountered was the *capitana* of his old enemies the Knights of Malta, sitting in the middle of the sea after having driven off two enemy ships. For Uluç Ali the standard of the Hospitallers had the effect of a red rag to a bull, and the temptation to repeat the previous year's capture of the order's galleys at Montechiaro must have been irresistible.

Four Ottoman galleys surrounded the already battle-worn Maltese flagship, boarding parties invading it from all sides. The Knights of St John fought desperately to save the sacred banner of the order, until only the captain Fra' Pietro Giustiniani and a handful of defenders remained alive. The extraordinary bravery and tenacity of the knights is exemplified by the Aragonese Don Martin de Ferrera, who defended the standard until his left arm was nearly hacked off at the shoulder and his face cut in two. The epic fight on the *capitana* became part of the order's lore, fact merging into legend. According to the latter, Giustiniani's Muslim slave saved his master by dragging him below deck and blocking a door with coats and blankets. As a token of gratitude he was presented with his freedom and money to return home, but chose instead to remain with his master for the rest of his life. In fact Giustiniani and the other knights saved their skins by bribing the Algerians with cash and silverware – something that a Barbary corsair would find much more profitable than blood – and the Ottomans' task was made easier by the revolt of the vessel's Muslim slaves. Uluç Ali also captured the order's standard, despite the knights' later claim that it was but a ceremonial banner – the real standard having been previously hidden. Myth-making was not unique to the Hospitallers. Uluç Ali made the most of his exploit, claming falsely that he had taken two Maltese galleys. Seventy years later the polymath Khatib Çeleby could even write that the *beylerbey* of Algiers had personally decapitated Giustiniani.[54]

Seeing the *capitana* of Malta under attack, Don Juan de Cardona came to its rescue accompanied by the flagship of the Imperiale family. Cardona had a reputation as a skilled commander, and his action forced Uluç Ali to stop and deal with this new foe. Once more, superior ordnance and Spanish harquebusiers proved crucial, even if the Ottomans managed to board Cardona's galley to the mainmast. On the Imperiale *capitana* losses were also heavy, the fighting contingent being nearly wiped out although the vessel was not taken. The same fate befell the isolated Tuscan galley *Fiorenza*, only the severely wounded captain Tommaso de' Medici, a kinsman of Cosimo I, and fourteen men remaining alive. With eight or so prizes in tow, Uluç Ali's force swung behind the Christian centre, mauling a number of scattered and ill-equipped Venetian galleys. Had he arrived half an hour earlier, the outcome of the battle could have been reversed.

But for the Ottomans it was now too late. All Muslim resistance in the centre had collapsed and Don Juan, Santa Cruz, Colonna and Venier turned their bows, guns firing, towards the new menace. In the meantime Doria was approaching fast, picking up on the way Andrea da Pesaro's galleass, but in his path were between fifty and sixty of Uluç Ali's still unconquered vessels, busy gobbling up isolated Christian galleys. The Ottomans tried to block Doria's advance, but with the arrival of the galleys from the allied centre the Muslim ships found themselves in turn isolated and attacked from all sides. But for the allies it was no picnic, the Muslims giving them a good run for their money. The Tuscan *San Giovanni*, riddled with bullets and cannonballs, suffered sixty killed and 150 wounded, including her captain, Knight of St Stephen Agnolo Biffoli, who received two harquebus shots in the throat.* Doria himself did not shrink from battle, fourteen oarsmen on his flagship – about 7 per cent of the total – becoming fatalities. The Genoese admiral would later remember the cacophony – the rumbling of guns, the cracking of harquebuses, the beating of drums and the shrill sound of trumpets 'that made the sea rumble and vessels shake'.[55]

Uluç Ali, behind the Christian line and under attack, realized that all was lost and decided wisely that it was time to go. But the allies' galleys were closing in on him, forcing many of his ships back towards the shores of the Curzolaris. Uluç Ali now abandoned his prizes – the Venetian galley *Aquila Nera e D'Oro* under the slain Pietro Bua had already been towed back to Lepanto – by severing the tow ropes. With a handful of vessels he passed through the channel between Koutsilaris and Oxia and aided by the rising south-south-easternly wind managed to sail to Modon. Don Juan wished to give chase, but was dissuaded by the other commanders and it was left to Onorato Caetani to go after the Algerian with a small force. By now it was after half past two in the afternoon and there was still plenty left to be done.

The Ottomans may have been defeated, but many still possessed plenty of fighting spirit. Girolamo Diedo described how those who had not taken refuge on land or were unwilling to jump into the sea obstinately refused to surrender. Lacking arrows and shot, they threw oranges and lemons at the attacking Christians, who proceeded to fling them back. 'And many of these fights happened at the end of the battle, a sight that made everyone laugh.' Amusing incidents happened everywhere. An unnamed gentleman was hit by a small wooden splinter when a shot from his harquebus hit one of his galley's flag poles, but for two months afterwards he went around with his head bandaged and later doctored the insignificant

---

* Biffoli is usually included among the fallen, although Bernardino Antinori clearly states in his letter that he was recovering. In any case, he was still alive and active in 1576 (ANTINORI: 2r. ASF, *MP*, 695, f. 341r (Piero Tiragallo to Francesco I de' Medici, 12 May 1576)).

scar to make it look like a bullet wound.[56] But death and destruction were nothing to laugh about, and both abounded in the bloody waters of the Gulf of Patras. Hundreds of bodies floated and men struggled in the sea, galleys hardly being able to move for the corpses blocking their way. The wounded Ottomans in the water were left to their fate or used for target practice by the allied harquebusiers.

The battle was still raging when the looting started, for 'as soon as the Christians knew that they were victorious and masters of the enemy, they preferred to sack and bind, than fight and kill'. Onorato Caetani bitterly commented that he 'had not come to steal, but instead to fight and serve Our Lord' after some Venetians sacked the galleys he had defeated. Sebastiano Venier wrote that 'to us has befallen to fight, die and be wounded; to others to carry away booty', adding that 'from such a victory I have gained 505 ducats, two lire and six shillings, some knives, a coral necklace, and two blackamoors hardly fit to row in the middle of a gondola'. Everywhere sailors were busy fishing Ottoman bodies out of the water in order to despoil them. It was the rank and file that benefited most from the looting, pocketing money and jewels often with their officers' complicity. In fact, sailors, soldiers and *forzati* went on looting and ransacking for another two hours after the battle had ended, and only with the greatest difficulty did galley officers manage to get their unfettered convicts to return to their benches and take the captured Ottoman galleys in tow. Prisoners were also considered valuable items, for slaves or for ransom, even if the vengeful Venetians were less keen on sparing those who surrendered.[57]

Dusk was approaching fast, and with it heavy rain clouds. Don Juan sent his fleet to find refuge for the night in a number of havens along the coast, a wise decision since a few hours later the whole area was hit by a violent thunderstorm. That evening a meeting was convened on the *Real* at which Don Juan warmly received Venier and Colonna even to the point of embracing the crusty old Venetian. The prince also thanked Francesco Duodo, stating unequivocally that the allies owed their victory to the galleasses. Don Juan was not wrong, although there were also other reasons for the success.[58] But ultimately many believed that the real winner was not of this world.

10. THE PHOENIX'S ASHES

~

On the morning of 8 October the sun shone once more on the Gulf of Patras, the previous night's storm having cleansed from the waters the blood of the fallen. Corpses littered the shores; more floated among the waves; others still had drifted out to sea, some allegedly turning up as far away as Crete. The early light accompanied a strong allied force to the site of the slaughter. The rank and file were looking forward to looting more Ottoman bodies, but their commanders sought prizes of greater importance. Presently, two stranded Ottoman galleys were sighted on the coast, one of them nearly completely burnt out, the other wedged between some rocks. Marcantonio Colonna tried to tow away the latter, but since it would not budge the allies removed its artillery and other useful items, before handing it over to looting and fire. At one point some thirteen enemy galleys came into view, probably with the intention of aiding those Ottomans who had sought refuge on the coast, but seeing the Christian array quickly turned tail towards Lepanto. Less lucky was the crew of a small Ottoman vessel which sailed unawares straight into the allies' arms.

Having scoured the whole coast, the reconnaissance force returned to Petalas. There a war council was held to decide on the next objective. The Venetians were in favour of recapturing one of their former possessions; Don Juan wanted to attack Lepanto, believing it devoid of troops as Müezzinzâde Ali had embarked its garrison on his galleys. Others thought that due to the advanced season and the condition of the fleet it was time to go home. In the end it was agreed to capture the island of Levkás (Santa Maura), on the way to Corfu. The Christian armada sailed there on the 12th, towing the captured Ottoman galleys, together with those friendly ones too damaged to move under their own power. However, it soon became apparent that at least a fortnight would be necessary to take Levkás and eventually the decision was taken to postpone all further operations to the following spring.[1]

For the victorious allies it was time to count their gains and losses. A total of 117 galleys and thirteen galliots had been captured, being divided as follows: nineteen galleys and two galliots went to the pope; the Spanish got fifty-eight and a half and six and a half of each; thirty-nine and a half and four and a half went to the Venetians. Between eighty and ninety enemy vessels had sunk or been wrecked on the shore, around forty or fifty managing to escape. Of the captured ordnance, Venice, Spain and the pope received as many centreline pieces as galleys, and proportional shares of the remaining 256 small guns and seventeen *petrieri*. The pope got 881 prisoners, Spain 1,742 and Venice 1,162. All these numbers are open to question, various sources giving sometimes significantly different totals and portions. Besides, not all the guns were accounted for, and not just the small pieces – in John Guilmartin's words, 'light enough to manhandle out of their mounts and carry off as loot'. In fact, the Venetians (and probably not just they) managed to surreptitiously remove at least eleven large and medium-sized guns, something about which Requesens would complain to Philip II; Venier for his part would protest about the Spaniards wanting more than the lion's share of the booty. The pope had placed a ban of excommunication on anyone who illegally held on to spoils of war, but this had little effect on these hard-bitten warriors. Similarly, not all the prisoners were accounted for, 'many having been left to die, and others hidden by their captors'. Şuluç Mehmed Pasha, concealed by the Venetians on board Marco

Querini's galley, died of his wounds a couple of days after the battle.* It is unclear how many men the Ottomans lost dead, captured or missing, but including oarsmen their casualties can't have been less than 35,000, including most of their senior officers.[2]

Disagreements arose over the division of forty important prisoners, and in the end it was decided to entrust them to the pope's care. Among these were Müezzinzâde Ali Pasha's sons, Salihpaşazâde Mehmed Bey, Caur Ali and Hindī Mahmūd, who would later write, 'While fighting for the faith, I was taken prisoner on the sea – I fought hard but I was overcome.' The Ottoman prisoners appear to have accepted their fate with remarkable fortitude. One day the seventeen-year-old Ahmed Bey, Müezzinzâde Ali's eldest son, saw Don Bernardino de Cardena's son in tears, and enquiring what had happened was told that the boy's father had been killed in battle. 'So,' answered the Turk, 'I know someone who lost his father, property and freedom, yet does not cry.' Don Juan treated the two youths with the respect due to royalty, their father being related to the sultan by marriage, allowing their old tutor to return to Constantinople to inform their mother that they were still alive. Don Juan was genuinely sad about Müezzinzâde Ali's death, not only for his value as a prisoner but also because he believed the *kapudan paşa* to have been a worthy and chivalrous person 'more loved than feared' by his own slaves.[3]

Allied losses were also heavy, an approximate count giving 7,650 killed and 7,800 wounded on the Venetian, papal and Spanish ships. The Venetians had paid the highest price with 4,836 dead and 4,604 wounded, including oarsmen, a witness to the savagery of the hand-to-hand fighting, 'where swords proved particularly effective, and harquebuses little used'. On the papal galleys 800 died and some 1,000 were wounded; on the Spanish, 2,000 and 2,200 – the *Tercio de Sicilia*'s total casualties alone amounting to 600 hundred men. To these numbers should be added the losses suffered by the Maltese,

* This may be the reason why there are so many different versions of his death: fallen in battle, drowned, captured and immediately executed, or dispatched to spare him from more suffering.

Genoese (private and public), Savoyard and Tuscan crews. Given the majority of forced oarsmen on *ponentine* galleys, it is only possible to make an educated guess at how many of them died on the benches or fighting weapon in hand. Giovanni Andrea Doria's eleven galleys lost a total of seventy-four rowers killed, roughly seven each. Thus probably at least 700 rowers were killed in the approximately 100 *ponentine* galleys present at the battle, probably more if one takes into account the larger crews of the *bastarde*. It should be remembered that the complements of some galleys, for example the Maltese *capitana*, the Tuscan *Fiorenza* and the Savoyard *Piemontesa*, were all but wiped out. In contrast, the commander of Genoa's state contingent Ettore Spinola, after stating in his report that on his galleys 'blood flowed from stern to bow', admitted nonetheless that while a number of sailors had been wounded he had lost only one oarsman.[4]

Of the officers, sergeants and gentlemen present only a few hundred died or suffered wounds, thanks to the fact that many wore bulletproof armour. A record of the losses incurred by two Spanish *tercios*★ lists a total of fifty-seven, including Don Lope de Figueroa and Pagano Doria. Don Juan himself received a dagger wound in the ankle, something he would later report to his brother in an off-hand manner. Of the roughly 100 knights of St Stephen involved, fifteen died. At least forty knights of St John lost their lives, the majority on Giustiniani's *capitana*. Some fifty Venetian officers and gentlemen were killed, including Barbarigo, or seriously injured. The galleasses also had their share of casualties, some of them the result of an explosion of a powder magazine which killed nearly fifty men. Thus, between dead, wounded and captured (the few taken by Uluç Ali), allied casualties must have been around 20,000 men. In addition, the Christians lost between twelve and sixteen galleys – according to Bartolomeo Sereno, 'thanks to those who refused to fight', – an incorrect and unfair comment – including those sunk, captured or so badly damaged that they had to be destroyed. Among the latter was the *Fiorenza*, which after being stripped of everything

---

★ *Tercios* were Spanish infantry units roughly equivalent to regiments.

useful served as a bonfire during the celebrations held at Levkás. Thus was fulfilled the prophecy that in 1571 the Medici would lose Florence.[5]

True to his promise, Don Juan liberated all the convict oarsmen under his authority who had fought during the battle. He also ordered that all Christian slaves on the Ottoman galleys be immediately freed, possibly fearing someone would try to hold on to some extra 'booty'. The Venetians, despite the pope's objections, treated as slaves all captured Ottoman subjects, including non-Muslims. Between 12,000 and 15,000 Christians were liberated, the Ottomans having compensated for their end-of-campaign shortage of free rowers by chaining to galley benches the prisoners taken during their raids the previous summer. Venier also tried to free eighty of the bravest convicts on his galleys, but had his request turned down by the Venetian authorities. Although not bound by Don Juan's promise, Cosimo I de' Medici later liberated a number of his own *forzati*. One who did not regain his freedom was the musician Aurelio Scetti, despite the fact that 'he had captured two Moors and brought them to his galley saying, "If not in the other way, at least for this I shall be free."' Scetti was probably lying, since it is difficult to see how he could have accomplished such a deed with his crippled leg, although it could also be that in his memoirs he exaggerated his lameness. Given that he clearly enjoyed the protection of someone at the Tuscan court, had Scetti's claim been true he would certainly have reaped the benefit of his actions. Quite a few unfettered convicts deserted in the heat of the battle or immediately afterwards. Giovanni Andrea Doria lost to desertion the same number of oarsmen as killed in battle – the equivalent of the rowing crew of one of his galleys. Scetti would attribute these desertions to the *forzati*'s mistrust of their commanders' promises, but one should also keep in mind that many convicts had acquired booty and were unwilling to share their new-found wealth with anyone else.[6] Scetti's account is also disingenuous in other ways, since it is impossible to know how many 'deserters' lay instead on the seabed of the Gulf of Patras.

The harmony between the Christian commanders did not last long, factional interests soon raising their ugly heads once more. Venier had immediately insisted that news of the victory be sent to the various governments. Three days later, seeing that nothing had been done, he took matters into his own hands and dispatched to Venice the galley of Onfrè Giustinian. When he found out Venier's escapade Don John was positively livid, considering this behaviour a breach of protocol and an attack on his own prerogatives as commander-in chief. In the meantime the supply problem was becoming acute. Provisions found on the captured Ottoman galleys had come in handy but were hardly enough for a prolonged campaign. The allied fleet sailed from Levkás on the 21st, reaching Corfu three days later. On the way it ran into three other Venetian galleasses and thirteen galleys, stranded in the port of Paxoi by contrary winds. Their crews stated that on the day of the battle they had heard the rumbling of the guns from the Gulf of Patras. Once in Corfu the division of prizes was finally settled, although not without problems. Venier protested bitterly about the Spaniards' claims, even accusing Don Juan of intercepting and reading letters sent to him by his government. In the end, thanks once more to Colonna's mediation, Venier agreed to sign the document concerning the division of spoils. Don Juan gave the Order of Malta thirty slaves to replace their losses during the battle, encouraging the other confederates to do the same. Prisoners were allotted also to various officers and officials, and it was decided at the same time that any future claims would be resolved in Messina It was high time for Don Juan to go, having finally received Philip II's orders about wintering in Sicily. On the 27th he took his leave of Venier, who had been instructed by the Venetian government to remain in Corfu, and set off for Italy.[7]

By now news of the Christian victory was common knowledge. Onfrè Giustinian had arrived in Venice on the 19th, finding the city in a state of shock over the loss of Famagusta. However, people immediately realized that something important had happened when they saw Giustinian's galley trailing in the water

Ottoman banners, and in their hundreds rushed to the port to hear the news. As soon as Giustinian delivered his report to the Senate, the whole of Venice exploded in spontaneous rejoicing. Bells were rung, bonfires lit and masses celebrated. Mourning was forbidden, even for close relatives. The festivities continued for three days and nights, the city a fantasy of colours, banners and music. Turkish carpets, standards and turbans were displayed on the Rialto bridge for all to see. The only people who did not take part in the celebrations were those Ottoman subjects still at liberty in Venice. Fearful of being stoned by the crowds, they locked themselves in their quarter, displaying their grief by beating their breasts, shaving their moustaches and scratching their faces and bodies.[8]

In Rome there was also much rejoicing. Pius V had miraculously known about the outcome of the battle since the evening of 7 October (evidence of this being later used during his beatification trial), but he nonetheless prudently waited for the arrival of official reports before starting any celebration. The dispatch from the nuncio in Venice was brought by fast courier on the night of the 21st, and Pius reportedly exclaimed, cited once more the Gospel, 'Nunc dimittis servum tuum, Domine . . . quia viderunt oculi mei salutare tuum' (Now, Lord, you can take your servant, for my eyes have seen your salvation). As soon as the news became public the populace lit bonfires, accompanying the flames with artillery salvos, although the pope considered this cannonading a waste. Pius was also concerned that the victory would count for nothing should the allies not press home their advantage, but realized that nothing could be done before the spring. The pontiff was soon busy with thanksgiving celebrations, and as more details of the battle arrived his joy only increased. Referring to Don Juan's role in the victory, he is supposed to have quoted from the Gospel, 'Fuit homo missus a Deo, cui nomen erat Johannes' (God sent a man by the name of John). More significant was his decision to dedicate 7 October, the feast of St Justine, to Our Lady of Victory. Later, his successor Gregory XIII would change the dedication to Our Lady of the Rosary, thus recognizing the role played by this devotion in the Christians' success.[9]

Philip II received news of the battle on 2 November, at the same time as the Venetian ambassador Leonardo Donà. No sooner had the latter read his dispatches from Venice than he rushed to the royal chapel where the king was attending vespers, appropriately arriving as the Magnificat was being intoned. Philip waited for the end of the service to hear Dona's report in full, and then asked him to participate in the recital of the Te Deum. Don Lope de Figueroa arrived with more news on the 22nd, the king questioning him closely about Don Juan, the prince's health and the battle. In the meantime festivities were held all over Spain, particularly in Seville, in honour of the Christian victory, while Philip graciously bestowed honours, benefices and monetary rewards on those officers and men who had most distinguished themselves in the battle. The king also ordered the dean and chapter of Toledos cathedral to institute a service to be performed in perpetuity every 7 October.

Despite his apparent elation over the Christian victory, the king was not totally happy about the league's success. Don Juan had put the Habsburg galleys and soldiers at considerable risk by deciding to join battle – a rash decision to say the least, especially for *el rey prudente*, and according to a number of Philip's councillors the prince could only thank God if he had come out of it alive. Significantly, the king commissioned only one work of art to commemorate the victory – Titian's *Philip II, after the victory of Lepanto, offers the prince Don Fernando to victory*, now in the Prado – and to celebrate more the continuity of the Habsburg line than the Ottoman defeat. The six large canvases of the battle by Luca Cambiaso, now in the Escorial, were probably gifts of Giovanni Andrea Doria to the royal secretary Antonio Pérez, acquired by the king at a later date.[10] One has the distinct impression that for Philip the league victory represented a potential source of political trouble, possibly because by weakening the Porte's navy it had altered the balance of power in the Mediterranean and loosened Spain's grip on Italy.

Things were seen differently by the veterans of the 1571 campaign. Many celebrated their participation in the battle of the Curzolaris (although the name Lepanto was used almost immediately – and misleadingly, since Lepanto was forty miles away from where the battle was fought) by commissioning paintings, sculptures and literary works – the latter, according to Sereno, much favoured by those whose fighting achievements were somewhat doubtful. The Barbarigo family had a hall of its country villa near Vicenza frescoed with scenes exalting their kinsman's role in the battle. So did the relatives of Ascanio Della Corgna, in their palace on Lake Trasimene. The marquis of Santa Cruz had the battle painted on one of the walls of his palace at El Viso – sadly these frescoes were destroyed by an earthquake in the eighteenth century. The popes after Pius V were also active proponents of the battle's artistic merits, the Vatican palaces and the church of Santa Maria Maggiore, for example, receiving their share of images commemorating the league and the victorious fight. Works of art on the same topics are scattered in churches all over Italy, some of them ex-voto offerings by those who had managed to bring their skins back home. Similarly, the various Italian rulers commissioned works exalting their involvement in the battle. Ferdinando I de' Medici, Cosimo I's son and successor, added a scene from it to the paintings exalting the deeds of the knights of St Stephen in the order's church in Pisa. Francesco Maria della Rovere had himself portrayed proudly wearing a splendid suit of gilded 'victory' armour.

Marcantonio Colonna outdid everyone, commissioning celebratory frescoes for his castle of Paliano and entering Rome in a triumphal procession worthy of ancient Rome. In reality Colonna would have preferred to enter the city privately, fearing that the envy of his adversaries at the Spanish court could endanger his future preferment, but the pope was adamant about giving Marcantonio his due. Accordingly, on 4 December 1571 a long cavalcade entered Rome from the San Sebastiano gate, passing under the arches of Constantine, Titus and Septimius Severus. Skirting the Capitol, it proceeded to Monte Giordano and then St Peter's, where the pope was waiting to celebrate a solemn Te Deum. Along the route were inscriptions comparing Marcantonio to the great Roman generals of the past; the sound of musical instruments and the booming guns of Castel Sant'Angelo accompanying 'an exhibition of barbaric and exotic opulence'. The whole Colonna clan participated in the event, including those related by marriage like Onorato Caetani. Marcantonio brought up the rear, mounted on a white horse and wearing a simple black robe. The triumph differed from classical Roman parades in that it lacked carts filled with the spoils of victory, this 'for respect of the most serene Don Juan of Austria', although a few Ottomans in chains were included in the procession. Conspicuous was the absence of most of the Roman nobility, unwilling to pay even token homage to their successful peer – something that Don Luis de Requesens, always Colonna's enemy, would not fail to report to Don Juan in Messina. Philip II, evidently irritated by Colonna's elevation, found it expedient to wait a while before sending him a brief note of thanks for his role in the allied victory.[11]

~

While much of Christian Europe rejoiced for the league's success – even Charles IX of France, despite his worries about Spain's power in the Mediterranean and the alliance treaty between France and the Porte, having a Te Deum sung in thanksgiving for the victory – in Constantinope the mood was very different. Selim II is supposed to have received official news of his fleet's destruction on 23 October while in Edirne, thanks to a special courier sent to him by Uluç Ali. There is evidence that the sultan had already found out about the disaster a few days before, at least according to some chronicles.[12] Information sent by Jews in Constantinople to their brethren in Venice would appear to confirm this.

> The Great Turk [Selim II] one night having heard much wailing
> and screaming coming from the city, the next day asked about
> the noise. It was answered that some important citizens had died,

and that their relatives had done what was appropriate in these cases. The next night having heard greater commotion and louder crying, he enquired again about the reason for such a din. It was answered that rumours had it that his fleet had joined battle with ours [the allied], and in the fight both had been badly mauled with great loss of life on each side, although the details were unknown. The third night, with the whole city wailing and screaming because no one could hide any more the grief for such a loss, the Great Turk, concerned and irked by all the moans and tears, demanded to hear the truth. It was answered that it was impossible now to hide the news that his fleet had been all burnt, sunk and taken by the Christians, with the death of all his great soldiers, captains and his General [Müezzinzâde Ali Pasha]. Hearing this he gave a deep sigh and said, 'So, these treacherous Jews have deceived me!' And having the Lord's utterance spread through the palace and the streets, everyone started shouting, 'Death to the Jews; death to the Jews!' and there was much fear that this would degenerate in a general massacre.[13]

In mentioning Jews, was Selim referring to Joseph Nassi? Certainly the fortunes of the duke of Naxos declined after 1571, and maybe the sultan made him a convenient scapegoat for the losses sustained in the war. In any case, while we may doubt the details of this particular report, there is no doubt that the debacle shook the Porte. Dimitri Cantemir, writing 150 years after the event, would describe how the downcast Selim refused to eat for three days, until he found consolation and encouragement in a passage of the Koran: 'it may be that you dislike a thing while it is good for you'. But the sultan could not afford to grieve for too long; in fact he decided to return to Constantinople in some haste, according to one source covering in less than a week the roughly 250 kilometres separating Edirne from the capital, entering it on the 28 November.[14] In the meantime, the imperial *dîvân* was taking energetic measures to address the crisis.

There were a number of matters that needed to be settled

urgently. The reconstruction of the fleet was top priority, and a new *kapudan paşa* was needed. The fact that Uluç Ali had managed to salvage part of the Ottoman fleet helped solve the second problem. Many were convinced that having survived the battle, the *beylerbey* of Algiers would be executed for his share in the rout. But Uluç Ali not only had fifty vessels with him, but also – equally important from a psychological point of view – the Maltese standard. As a result, the Algerian not only retained his master's favour, but was also made *kapudan paşa* with the new name of Kılıç Ali – Ali the Sword – although shrewd and malicious observers would comment that Uluç Ali's elevation to grand admiral had less to do with his abilities than to the fact that nobody else was available for the job. The sultan would later order the captured banner of the Knights of Malta hung in the old cathedral (now mosque) of Hagia Sophia, in an attempt to minimize the extent of the defeat. The arrival on 3 November of sixteen ships loaded with the booty of Famagusta further aided Selim's propaganda efforts: after all, by conquering Cyprus the Ottomans had attained what, ostensibly, had caused them to go to war in the first place. As for the disaster at the Curzolaris, the sultan could write to Pertev Pasha, 'the results of a war are uncertain. God's will manifests itself in these occasions, as appears in destiny's mirror.' For the Ottomans the Curzolaris would simply be *sıngın donanma* – 'the dispersed fleet'.[15]

But if misinformation could to an extent appease the populace, the military emergency could not be ignored. Sokollu Mehmed Pasha's well-known exchange with Marcantonio Barbaro was an admission of uneasiness despite the grand vizier's apparent confidence. Sokollu acknowledged that the Christians had given the Ottomans 'a close shave', adding however that by losing Cyprus the Venetians had been deprived of an arm. The fleet, like a beard, could grow again thicker and stronger 'if the forests don't fail us', but a lopped-off arm would never do so.[16] The simile was only partially apt. Cyprus was an extremely important commercial centre in the Levant, and by the loss of its ports, produce and salt mines Venice's economy suffered a serious blow. However, by holding on to Crete and Corfu the Venetians could still imperil Ottoman maritime routes towards the west. Rather than an arm, for Venice the Porte's conquest of Cyprus was more akin to the loss of a couple of fingers. Besides, certain beards could take time to grow again; and, if thicker, were not necessarily stronger for that.

Words could not rebuild fleets: material resources and resolve were needed, both of which the Porte possessed in abundance.[17] Kılıç Ali had been ordered to gather together all the surviving ships and stay on guard in the Aegean, but once the allied fleet moved to its winter quarters in Messina he returned to Constantinople. The historian Selânikî Mustafa Efendi was there when he arrived on 19 December, at the head of forty-two vessels including *bastarde*, galleys and galliots all firing their guns in salute 'as if they had been two hundred'. The salvos also served to drown the wailing of the many who had come to the port looking in vain for a husband, a father or a brother.[18] The rebuilding of the fleet had been in progress since the end of October, orders having been sent out to various governorships to cut the necessary timber with the utmost haste. Wood abounded in the Ottoman empire – Sokollu had not been wrong to mention the forests – and so did oakum, pitch, hemp, sailcloth, awnings, nails and other iron parts. The losses in artillery incurred at the Curzolaris were quickly made good, orders for the production of enough thirty-pounder cannon to arm 100 galleys being issued as early as 24 October. The bronze necessary for the casting appears to have been obtained by melting down a number of church bells previously stored in Trebizond.[19]

Despite their abundance, the huge demands for all these materials imposed a severe strain on the Porte's resources. Kılıç Ali expressed his concerns about this to the grand vizier: 'Building the hulls is feasible, but to find 500 or 600 anchors, the materials of war and the sails for 200 ships is impossible'; to which Sokollu Mehmed is supposed to have glibly retorted, 'My dear Pasha. You do not yet know this state. Trust in God. This is such a state that if desired there would be no difficulty in making all the anchors in the fleet of silver, the ropes of silk and the sails of satin. For whatever materials of war or sails are lacking from any ship, ask me.' Then Kılıç Ali answered, 'I now know that if anyone can complete this fleet, you can.'[20] Although Sokollu was clearly boasting for rhetorical purposes, he was not exaggerating the Porte's resources. On 5 January 1572 Marcantonio Barbaro would inform the Venetian government that the Ottomans had eighty-one galleys ready, old and new, and another thirty-eight in various stages of construction.[21] The many arsenals along the Anatolian coast allowed for the simultaneous building of large numbers of vessels, the imperial arsenal in Istanbul only adding the artillery and final fittings. Still, the high demand for timber forced the builders to use green wood, causing the new vessels to be susceptible to rot and infestation, making them slow, difficult to steer and short-lived. Cordage was another problem, the only material in short supply. Orders to the hemp officials in Sinop produced only partial results, demand being greater than supply, and even at the end of March 1572 the ships at Amasra and Kefken lacked their rigging.

The Ottomans had been deeply impressed by the volume of fire produced by the Venetian galleasses at the Curzolaris, and were soon busy on their own version of the new weapon.[22] Apparently this would not be too difficult since the Ottomans already knew how to build the large merchant galley from which the galleass had originated. Yet in building these vessels the Ottomans made the erroneous assumption that they were simply modified *galie grosse* with all-round shooting capabilities. Instead, as we have seen, Venetian galleasses were the product of a long tradition of naval engineering debates and experiments, and not of a single stroke of genius. By April 1572 the Porte could field half a dozen modified *maone*, but their construction left much to be desired and the Ottomans soon found that they lacked the necessary naval skills to operate them. The Curzolaris veteran and engineer Pompeo Floriani could write around 1580 that the Ottomans 'don't know how to fabricate galleasses'. In this they were not alone. The battle inspired the Tuscans to build their own galleasses, even creating a special arsenal for them on the isle of Elba, only to discover that they did not know how to handle them. When they tried the experiment again in the 1630s, the sailors and pilots had to be brought in from Venice. The Spanish appear to have been more successful in copying the new Venetian vessel, the English being much impressed by the performance of four Spanish galleasses during the Armada campaign of 1588.[23]

Manning the new Ottoman fleet proved to be the biggest problem of all. The heavy losses in manpower suffered by the Porte during the previous year meant that naval personnel was in short supply. Those *sipahis* who had survived the Curzolaris were tired, dispirited and naturally unwilling to face another maritime campaign. Eventually the government managed to find 4,396 *sipahis* and some 3,000 janissaries to serve at sea, a far cry from the roughly 20,000 troops required by the fleet. The only alternative was to enlist volunteers, something that had already been done in the years before the Cyprus war. Learning from the abundant crop of lives reaped by the repeated allied harquebus volleys, the government's intention was to raise as many men possible armed with bows or firearms. The plan was to have 150 soldiers for each galley, placing between each thwart two harquebusiers and one bowman. Firearms were distributed to the *sipahis*, but despite the Porte's efforts it would appear that the traditionally minded *timariots* were more than reluctant to accept the new weapons. This would explain the increase in the number of volunteers in the years ahead. Certainly the number of soldiers now equipped with firearms struck European observers. On 10 June 1572, François de Noailles, bishop of Dax and the French envoy in Istanbul, wrote that the Ottomans were putting 20,000 harquebusiers aboard their fleet – an exaggerated number, perhaps, but evidence of the Ottomans' shift in naval tactics.[24]

Oarsmen were also in short supply. The navy needed some 20,000 every year, normally raising them through conscription from the ranks of the non-military population. It was a much-resented blood tax, made worse by the terrible losses suffered by rowing crews at the Curzolaris. Each new galley required a force of about 150 oarsmen, but raising them through traditional means proved an impossible task. Some local notables managed to exchange the levy for a cash payment, the resulting money being used to raise volunteer rowers at ninety *akçe* a month. But even with this method results proved disappointing, while in some cases oarsmen already recruited never made it to the capital due to the negligence of their overseers. Resistance to the levy was such that the Porte was forced to look elsewhere for the necessary manpower. War prisoners were one source, but with not enough available the government took the unprecedented step of sending large numbers of criminals to the galleys. *Kadis* (judges) from all over the empire were ordered to send to Constantinople all convicts whose crimes did not carry the death penalty. It was not a measure the government took willingly, since rowing gangs made up of convicts or war prisoners were more likely to mutiny than crews of conscripts or volunteers. Still, extreme situations call for extreme means, and there is no doubt that in the winter of 1571–2 maritime affairs looked grim for the Porte.

However, thanks to the energy and administrative skills of Sokollu Mehmed Pasha and Kılıç Ali's maritime experience, by the beginning of spring 1572 the Ottomans could field a fleet of 134 galleys plus a number of large galliots owned by Muslim corsairs from Anatolia and Rumelia, with more vessels being added each day. The effort to accomplish this had been enormous in every sense, and all those in positions of power had been asked to share in the endeavour: 'The leading viziers . . . committed themselves as their wealth permitted', in the historian Selânikî's succinct words.[25] One captain volunteered to build two *bastarde*, and the grand vizier's chief clerk paid out of his own pocket for the construction of a galliot. In less than six months the Porte had managed the impossible – although Giovanni Andrea Doria had predicted that such a thing could happen – and like a phoenix the Ottoman navy was rising from its ashes. Admittedly, its ships were poorly built, undermanned and no match for the Western vessels. Nonetheless, it was a fleet in being, and that's what ultimately mattered.

~

While the Porte was busy rebuilding its naval forces, the Venetians were taking measures to nip in the bud a resurgence of Ottoman maritime power. On 22 October 1571 the Council of Ten ordered the captain-general of the Venetian fleet that 'with the utmost caution, deft and secret manner he immediately kill first Captain Şuluç'. On the same day the council wrote to Venier to make sure that no 'prisoner of importance, galley captain or corsair' be freed or ransomed without the Ten's authorization, and ordering him to execute immediately those already in Venetian hands 'so that they will no more be able to inflict damage on Christendom'.[26] Şuluç was already beyond the council's reach, having died of his wounds four days after the battle. Still not happy the Ten harassed the pope and Don Juan of Austria to kill the Ottoman captives in their custody. Ostensibly the Venetians ordered the executions because they mistrusted their own galley captains not to accept ransom money 'since everyone desires profit', although they admitted that they were taking revenge for what had happened at Famagusta. But if the papal nuncio in Venice was perturbed by the Ten's decision, Pius V was positively shocked: it was one thing killing an armed enemy in battle, quite another murdering powerless prisoners. The pope adamantly refused to have anything to do with the matter, while Don Juan answered that one should take pity on a defeated enemy; besides, given the fickleness of the fortunes of war, there was always the possibility of being captured oneself and so it was better not to invite reprisals. Don Juan could have also pointed out the foolishness of eliminating potential bargaining chips, and in any case the Ottoman captives were worth quite a bit of ransom money. In the end it would appear that the only important prisoner the Venetians managed to execute was the renegade Dimo Baffo, although it is possible that some other unnamed captives also lost their lives. As for the other Ottoman prisoners of rank, the papacy treated them with all due honour and respect, housing them in a palace in Rome.[27]

For the whole of the winter of 1571–2 the Venetians were active on the Dalmatian coast, Venier managing to recapture Sopot and Margariti and giving support to the rebellions which had flared up in various parts of Albania and Greece. These revolts were partly religious in nature but had also a material side, the rebels for instance refusing to pay taxes or provide oarsmen for the new Ottoman fleet. Ultimately, the disturbances were settled by the Porte by the use of carrot-and-stick policies, aided by the league's incapacity to support the rebels in any significant way. The Venetians lacked enough men and resources to exploit their temporary advantage after the Curzolaris, and had to settle for limited goals. The Spanish, on the other hand, did not have a clear idea of what to do next. Their primary objective was the Barbary Coast, but they were afraid that any such proposal would rekindle the pope's suspicions about Spain not having the 'general interest' of Christendom at heart. Don Juan was of the opinion that it would be best first to capture and fortify some strategic positions in the Levant to keep the Ottomans distracted, and then take Algiers. In Western capitals there was much discussion of the league's future plans – the Venetians, rather too optimistically, going as far as contemplating the capture of Constantinople – but everyone agreed that it was vital not to allow the Ottomans any respite. As it happened, when the league's capitulations were renewed in Rome on 10 February, the Spanish agreed that in 1572 all military operations should take place in the Levant with a force of 250 galleys, nine galleasses and 32,000 men.[28]

The superficially friendly dealings barely hid the deep suspicions and resentments existing between the allies, not just on a national but also on a personal level. Giovanni Andrea Doria was the first victim of a smear campaign. Already on 13 November 1571 Giovanni Andrea had complained to Marcantonio Doria, prince of Melfi, that in Rome and elsewhere 'for the evil of this world' somebody was trying to diminish his role in the victory; he hoped Philip II had been informed of the truth. Likewise, writing to Donna Costanza d'Avalos, Doria begged her not to believe all the malicious gossip circulating in Rome that 'he had been the last to fight, and the first to run'.

The whole anti-Doria campaign owed much to Marcantonio Colonna, who in his various reports to Pius V had done everything to boost his own role, at the same time lambasting the Genoese admiral for his – according to Colonna – overcautious behaviour during the battle, prompting the misinformed pontiff to comment that Doria had behaved 'more like a corsair than a captain'. Pius's secretary of state, Cardinal Girolamo Rusticucci, on 16 December wrote to the papal nuncio in Madrid that Doria had 'tried more to save himself than fight the enemy', implying also that he had chosen the right wing in order to escape more easily. The Spanish faction in Rome rushed to Giovanni Andrea's aid, Luis de Requesens writing to Don Juan on 15 December that he had defended Doria as much as possible, and now nobody dared to speak ill of him in his presence. However, Requesens added, the pope had already made up his mind, and since 'His Holiness sometimes speaks freely', Giovanni Andrea had been advised not to show his face in Rome. In order to avoid friction within the league the Genoese commander left the allied fleet, his place being taken by his cousin Antonio Doria.[29]

Venier's head was the next to roll. Don Juan had never forgiven him for the Igoumenitsa hangings, nor for his breach of protocol after the battle. The Spanish wanted Venier to go – Cardinal Granvelle describing him as an old fool with no more brains than an ape – and, *pro bono pacis*, so did the pope. But understandably the Venetians were loath to recall their captain-general – after all, he had defended Venice's interests within the league, and he enjoyed wide popularity within the city. Instead, the Venetians chose a dual-command solution, nominating a second captain-general in the person of the *provveditore generale* of Dalmatia, Giacomo Foscarini.

Furthermore, in an attempt to sweeten the bitter pill for Venier, the Venetian senate offered to entrust him with an independent force of ten galleys.[30]

Dramatic changes were also about to take place on the international scene. On 1 May 1572 Pius V died after a brief illness, and with him disappeared the driving force that had kept the league in existence. While committed to the anti-Ottoman alliance, the new pope Gregory XIII did not possess his predecessor's charisma and austerity. The cracks that had always existed in the alliance became more apparent. Philip II was worried about the prospect of war with France over Flanders, the French Protestants' active support for the Flemish rebels being an open secret. Rumours were circulating that Charles IX – or at least his Huguenot subjects – were about to launch a military campaign in the Netherlands, something the Ottomans were hoping would occur. Should war erupt on the Franco-Spanish border, Philip could not afford to have nearly 20,000 men somewhere in the Levant. For this reason, Philip II wrote to Don Juan in Messina on 17 May, ordering him to delay his departure for the east using as much secrecy and deceit as possible. In the meantime he could busy himself by collecting victuals and munitions for the fleet. Don Juan, who had spent the whole winter 'looking over old papers and passed life feeling more and more lonely each day', was none too happy. In other letters to Granvelle and Juan de Zuñiga, the king wrote that in the event of the pope's death it would be better to strike at Algiers, so as to get something back for the huge sums spent on the league. A few days later he informed Don Juan that with Pius dead he intended to attack Bizerte and Algiers. The king was not inspired exclusively by selfish reasons, since in Western diplomatic circles there was a widespread belief that Uluç Ali was ready to go over to the Christians. Despite Philip's orders that lips remain sealed about the planned Barbary expedition, it did not take long for his intentions to become common knowledge. The Venetians were deeply alarmed by this apparent Spanish volte-face, while the new pope sent the king a stiff reminder of his duties. Cosimo I de' Medici was of the opinion that the French threat should not stop Philip from joining forces with the Venetians, believing that giving the Ottomans another licking was the best way to keep the Valois at bay. But at this point, with reports coming in about the Ottoman fleet's activities, the king had already written to Don Juan giving him the green light to sail for Corfu, taking with him part of the force assembled in Messina.[31]

What happened next can only be described as a series of misunderstandings and blunders. Marcantonio Colonna had received express orders from the pope to go to Messina and convince – or order if necessary, using the league's clauses – Don Juan to give him the necessary galleys for a Levant expedition. Cardinal Granvelle had the new pope in his pocket, and was actively manoeuvring to discredit the Roman admiral in every possible way. Colonna, with an eye to future employment with the Spanish, reluctantly obeyed, and managed to convince Don Juan to let him go to Corfu with fifty-seven galleys, the prince caving in to allay Venetian suspicions about the Spaniards' endless delaying tactics. Colonna departed east on 6 July, while Don Juan, having not yet received his brother's most recent instructions, sailed west towards Palermo with twenty-six galleys, twenty-two other ships and most of his infantry, still convinced that Philip II wanted him to attack a Muslim base in North Africa. Indeed, Cosimo I de' Medici, always good at guessing which way the wind was blowing, on the 17th had written to the pope attempting to convince him of the need to take Algiers.

No sooner did Don Juan arrive in Palermo than he received the king's message with orders to depart for the Levant. Meanwhile, Colonna had sailed for Otranto with the intention of embarking the infantry waiting there, but since the necessary orders from Cardinal Granvelle had not yet arrived the papal admiral continued on towards Corfu empty-handed. En route he met Santa Cruz, who added four more galleys to his fleet. Colonna arrived at his destination on the 13th, joining forces with Foscarini's seventy-four galleys, six galleasses and twenty-five galliots. From there the allied armada moved in the direction of Igoumenitsa, where the commanders received a letter from Don Juan ordering them to wait for him in Corfu. The Venetians were unwilling to agree to this since it would delay even further an encounter with the Ottoman fleet, while Colonna wished to enhance his reputation with another victory that would silence his enemies at home. For these reasons the decision was taken to disobey the prince's orders and seek the enemy instead.[32]

Receiving some reinforcements on the way, on 7 August the allied fleet of 145 galleys, twenty-two round-ships, six galleasses and twenty-five galliots and *fuste* finally met the Ottoman armada, 200 sail strong, off the Venetian-held island of Kythira. The Christian order of battle followed the one used at the Curzolaris. Colonna, with fifty-eight galleys and two galleasses, took the centre; on each wing, flanked by eleven round-ships, were forty galleys and two galleasses; a mere seven galleys made up the reserve. Kılıç Ali, although possessing a numerically superior fleet, refused to close with the enemy, employing instead hit-and-run tactics in an attempt to break the allied formation. Hampered by the slow galleasses, Colonna was unable to catch his crafty opponent, and at nightfall the Ottomans withdrew towards the Gulf of Lakonia. Two days later the allies left for Corfu, and on the morning of the 10th again encountered the Muslim armada off Cape Matapan (Akra Tainara). This time the eagerness of Giacomo Soranzo, commanding the Christian right, to come to grips with the enemy nearly cost him his life when the apparently retreating Ottomans pounced on his exposed force of eleven galleys and one galleass. Superior Venetian firepower managed to keep the Ottomans at bay long enough for Colonna to bring up the remaining galleasses. Again Kılıç Ali refused to engage in a full-scale battle, retreating under cover of a smoke screen with the loss of seven galleys. The Ottomans had suffered a tactical defeat, but strategically for them it was at worst a draw. With news that Kılıç Ali's fleet was growing daily, after further debate the allies decided to sail to Corfu, reaching it on 31 August.[33]

In Corfu Colonna and Foscarini found Don Juan, furious that

his orders had been disobeyed. Colonna tried to blame the Venetians, but by now his stock with the Spanish had plummeted. Don Juan waited only long enough to repair and resupply his fleet before setting out in search of the enemy. Arriving off Navarinou on 16 September, the allies found that the Ottomans were now in the securer haven of Methoni. Attempts to force the latter harbour resulted in nothing, and the rest of the campaign was spent in desultory skirmishing, with the Christians finding the enemy forces becoming increasingly strong. The only bright spot was the capture on the anniversary of the Curzolaris of an Ottoman lantern galley outside Methoni. But by now the campaign season was over, and on 26 October the allied fleet dropped anchor in Messina.[34]

The Venetians were exhausted and eager to reach a deal with the sultan. The victory at the Curzolaris had in no way offset their huge military expenses, since it was apparent that it would be impossible to dislodge the Ottomans from Cyprus. Also in Constantinople the political situation was ripe for peace talks. The sultan had gained territory but his losses in military personnel and war materiel over the past two years had buried any Ottoman chances of conquering more Venetian possessions in the short run, and a plan to attack Crete was shelved in consequence. Besides, the possibility of war between Spain and France was appearing more and more remote. On 17 July a Huguenot force had crossed the border between France and the Netherlands, only to be routed by the Spanish, who also discovered evidence of Charles IX's involvement. The French king quickly distanced himself from the enterprise, and the mass killings of the Huguenots in Paris on the night of 24 August (the St Bartholomew's Day massacre) radicalized religious divisions in France. The Valois now had too many domestic problems to contemplate fighting Spain. The Venetians knew that with France out of the way the Ottomans were diplomatically isolated in the Mediterranean; and despite the fact that both the Holy Roman Emperor and the king of Poland had refused to join the league, should war break out in Hungary the Porte would be in a very sticky position, given also the enormous sums spent on its new fleet. In addition, Sokollu Mehmed had prevailed over his adversaries within the Imperial *dîvân*, and was now in a position to negotiate unhindered a treaty with Venice.[35]

Diplomatic feelers had been put out practically on the morrow of the Curzolaris. In September 1571 the bishop of Dax had appeared in Venice on his way to Constantinople, ostensibly to secure the release of the Ottoman ambassador but really to try and sabotage the league by brokering peace between the Venetians and the Porte. Dax was unsuccessful in his efforts, but on his arrival in Constantinople the following March he had immediately started exploring the possibility of a settlement by meeting both Barbaro and Sokollu. In Venice the Council of Ten was also working behind the scenes, on 6 June instructing the imprisoned *bailo* to investigate the possibility of a deal with the Porte. On 22 August the Ten wrote again to Barbaro, ordering him to work secretly with Dax towards this goal, and on 19 September, at the height of military operations in the Levant, the *bailo* was given a free hand to negotiate a peace treaty with the Ottomans.

The republic was working behind its allies' back, but the Spaniards' procrastinations over the previous months had made the Venetians suspicious of their intentions, while Gregory XIII's openly pro-Spanish stance was far from reassuring. By starting peace talks the Council of Ten was bowing to the mercantile lobby in Venice, and by employing secrecy it was acting in the republic's best interests. Keeping things completely confidential was not easy, however. Already at the end of June the papal nuncio in Venice had an inkling of an imminent Venetian–Ottoman rapprochement, a suspicion that became more and more pronounced during the following months. By the beginning of 1573 an agreement between the Porte and Venice was considered imminent in European diplomatic circles.[36]

The ensuing treaty had been negotiated by the *bailo* with Sokollu through his Jewish doctor Solomon Ashkenazi, always very well disposed towards the Venetians. Dax was not present at the beginning of the talks, having left the Ottoman capital on 20 September 1572. He returned the following February, after learning in Dubrovnik of the St Bartholomew's Day massacre, but arrived too late to influence the negotiations. However, he had managed to talk the sultan out of an offensive against Corfu and attacking Venice's home territory, since this would have meant passing through the Holy Roman Emperor's possessions. The last thing the French wanted was a military alliance between the two branches of the Habsburg dynasty.[37]

It took some time to hammer out an agreement satisfactory to both Venice and Istanbul, due in part to the slowness of communications between the two capitals, but also because the Ottomans' initial requests included the surrender of the fortresses of Kotor and Corfu. Barbaro refused outright, knowing that accepting would have turned the Adriatic into an Ottoman lake. Sokollu backed off a bit, requesting Sopot plus an indemnity of 300,000 ducats, but even this the *bailo* found unacceptable. Both parties were trying not to appear weak, since the warmongers in Venice and Istanbul were still active. When Kılıç Ali was informed of the negotiations he asked Sokollu why he had not yet hanged Ashkenazi, flying into a rage when the latter suggested that the Ottomans were no match for the allied fleet. Sokollu then suggested reconfirming the territorial boundaries of the treaty of 1567, with the exception of Cyprus and the other recently captured territories, the surrender of Sopot and the 300,000-ducat indemnity. At this point Dax intervened in the negotiations, although by now the treaty was virtually a done deal. The *bailo* had initially welcomed the bishop's efforts, believing that with the French as guarantors any settlement would carry greater weight, but later he would write off Dax as a meddlesome pest. The treaty between Venice and the Porte was finally settled on 7 March 1573. The Venetians regained most of their lost territories in Albania and Dalmatia. Ulcinj and Bar remained in Ottoman hands, and the Venetians agreed to pay 1,500 ducats a year for the possession of the island of Zakynthos. Arrangements were made for the exchange of prisoners; merchants were to be released, and their goods restored or compensation paid.[38]

These terms may seem harsh on Venice, but should be considered in context. The Ottomans had gained Cyprus and other territory, but the republic had saved Crete, Corfu and Kotor, regained its commercial rights, and become once more the Porte's privileged trading partner. The loss of possessions may have been hard to swallow, but at least now Venice did not have to pay for their defence and the 300,000-ducat indemnity was a fraction of the republic's war costs. It is significant that the peace treaty was ratified in Venice with little opposition.[39]

Having signed a separate treaty with the Porte in blatant violation of the league's terms, it was now up to the Venetians to get their allies to swallow it. When informed of the deal by the republic's ambassadors Leonardo Donà and Lorenzo Priuli, Philip II took it with good grace, listening to them without showing any emotion except for a slight twist of his lips. He had been expecting the news for some time and was probably sympathetic to the Venetians' excuse that the peace had been done 'out of need and to avoid greater damage'. After listening carefully to the diplomats, the king dismissed them saying that he needed to meditate on the matter before giving an answer. Philip had no reason to be unhappy. For the Spanish crown the league had been a financial liability – although its costs had been partly covered by the Church – producing little in return, since the Venetians had reaped most of the benefits. In any case, with Ottoman naval power humbled and trouble brewing in Flanders, Philip was happy to close this chapter of his Mediterranean policy. Gregory XIII's reaction to the news was far more heated. When the Venetian ambassador Paolo Tiepolo told him about the deal, the pope rose screaming from his chair and ordered the diplomat out, cursing the Venetians and threatening excommunications left, right and centre. But apart from this there was little Gregory could do, except take away the subsidies granted to the republic by his predecessor. Excommunication is a serious matter, but sixteenth-century Catholic politicians saw it as a risk intrinsic to their job.[40]

The Venetian defection killed the league, but the Spanish still had a substantial military force in the Mediterranean. In October a fleet under Don Juan took Tunis and Bizerte practically unopposed, effectively blocking Ottoman access to the western Mediterranean. But the new acquisitions could not be defended without huge monetary investment, something the Spanish could ill afford. Besides, their capture was a challenge the Ottomans could not ignore, as the Curzolaris veteran Pompeo Floriani noted. Sure enough, nine months later a huge armada under Kılıç Ali arrived off Tunis, capturing it in two months together with the island of La Goleta, a Spanish possession since 1535. By now Philip II was embroiled in Flanders, and by 1580 Spain and the Porte had agreed on a truce that, despite its ups and downs, was destined to become permanent.[41]

~

For many of those present, the battle of the Curzolaris was an experience never to be repeated. Many would have agreed with Cervantes's comment on the event,* some to the point of paying ghost writers to describe their real, or imaginary, participation in the fighting, or would claim that some wound on their body dated back to that bloody October day. Others did not need to feign, their reputation assured by three gory hours of fighting over crimson waters.[42]

After Tunis, Don Juan of Austria served as viceroy of Naples, and there was even talk of him marrying Mary, queen of Scots; Philip II was not interested in the match, however. In 1576, following the death of Luis de Requesens, he was sent to Flanders as governor-general. He tried to pacify the region through a combination of force and clemency. Some of the insurgents were appeased, but many others, led by William of Orange, refused to

* See page vii.

lay down their arms. On 31 January 1578 Don Juan routed a rebel army at Gembloux, regaining the southern portion of the Netherlands for the Spanish crown. But by now his health was failing, and intrigues in Madrid had deprived him of Philip II's trust. After another, useless attempt to settle the Flanders rebellion peacefully, he died, a broken man, on 31 October 1578. He was first buried at Namur, but a year later his body was taken to Spain and interred in the Escorial, where he lies to this day.[43]

Marcantonio Colonna's political fortunes nose-dived after 1572. The league's collapse made his military position redundant, and the intrigues of his many political enemies in Rome, Naples and Madrid prevented him for some time from finding employment with the Spanish crown. Don Juan never forgave Colonna for challenging his leadership, and the Roman nobleman's offers to join the Tunis expedition were met with cold refusals. However, he was still grand constable of Naples, and for some time Philip II employed him to raise troops and inspect fortresses in that kingdom. At last, Colonna's endless nagging got him in 1577 the job of viceroy of Sicily, but he soon managed to get embroiled in a running fight with part of the Sicilian ruling elite. Accused of mismanagement and of usurping the king's authority, Colonna was on his way to Madrid to justify his actions when he died of a fever in Medinaceli on 1 August 1584.[44]

Sebastiano Venier was finally recalled to Venice at the end of 1572. He remained fiercely anti-Ottoman, adamantly opposing all peace deals with the Porte to the point of offering his personal fortune to help the war effort. Although considered something of a crank, he was also a national hero and one of those selected to receive King Henry III of France during his visit to Venice in 1574. Three years later, following the death of Alvise Mocenigo, he was unanimously elected doge. During his short term of office he displayed all the virtues and defects he had been known for during his spell as captain-general – a proud patriot who ignored protocol and showed little regard for political niceties. He died nine months after his election, some say from grief after a fire nearly burnt the ducal palace to the ground. True to his simple lifestyle, he was originally buried in a modest tomb on the island of Murano. With him was interred a rosary, made from the coral necklace he had won at the Curzolaris. In 1907 his body was solemnly moved to its present resting place in the church of SS Giovanni e Paolo in Venice.[45]

Giovanni Andrea Doria never lost the king of Spain's favour. He participated in the Tunis expedition and was one of those who advocated a negotiated solution of the Genoese civil war of 1577. In 1582 he ceded most of his galleys to Philip II – managing at the same time to retain control over them – and a year later the king chose him for the prestigious post of captain-general at sea. Also a member of the *Consejo de Estado*, Doria asked to retire in 1594, claiming ill health, but his request was turned down. In 1601 he planned and organized an expedition against Algiers, but the enterprise was sabotaged by bad weather. Finally allowed to retire, he spent the last years of his life augmenting the already considerable family fortune. He died in 1606, possibly the last of the great Italian sea captains of the sixteenth century. Nonetheless, doubts about his behaviour at the Curzolaris followed him to the grave and beyond, despite all the efforts to clear his name.[46]

Don Álvaro de Bazan, marquis of Santa Cruz, also remained persona grata with Philip II, having to his credit a continuous record of victories. He commanded the Spanish fleet during the invasion of Portugal in 1580, and two years later won a brilliant naval battle against a combined French and (unofficial) English fleet off Punta Delgada, in the Azores islands. A superb administrator, as well as a brilliant tactician, in 1587 Santa Cruz was chosen to lead the Armada being put together to invade England the following year. His death, on 9 February 1588, possibly changed the course of European history, for who can say what the Armada might have accomplished had Santa Cruz, and not the uninspiring duke of Medina Sidonia, been in command?[47]

Kılıç Ali, Doria's old adversary, remained *kapudan paşa* until his death. Under his energetic leadership by 1576 the Ottoman fleet was completely back to its pre-Curzolaris strength, the sultan now having 300 galleys plus a number of smaller boats at his disposal, while the pool of expert naval officers had been replenished thanks to the arrival of many corsairs from North Africa. Ottoman galleys now had also more artillery and men. In 1582 Kılıç Ali sailed to the Crimea to install the Ottoman-appointed khan of this vassal state, before going into semi-retirement. Like many Ottoman officials he spent the last years of his life erecting and endowing religious buildings. He died in July 1587, the last of the great Ottoman admirals from the school of Barbarossa and Dragut, and was buried in Constantinople near the Tophane – the cannon foundry – at the side of a mosque allegedly erected by the great architect Sinan. In 1989 a monument to him was erected in his native town of Le Castella in Calabria.[48]

Pertev Pasha, the other major Ottoman commander to survive the Curzolaris, was not so lucky. Returning to Constantinople, he was employed for a while during the emergency period following the battle, but having disgraced himself his life was now in jeopardy, and he owed his survival to his many connections at the Ottoman court. Dismissed from his position of second vizier, he died in obscurity in 1574. Barbaroszâde Hasan Pasha, reported to have died in the fight, actually managed to escape, being appointed *beylerbey* of Algiers in place of Kılıç Ali. Already sick, possibly as a result of wounds received at the Curzolan's, he never managed to occupy the post, expiring at the beginning of 1572. Abd-el Malik also survived the battle, participating in Kılıç Ali's 1574 Tunis campaign. Later with the aid of Ottoman troops he managed to become sultan of Morocco by capturing the city of Fez.[49]

Fortune distributed her favours unevenly to other veterans. Francesco Maria della Rovere was recalled by his father to Urbino in 1572, succeeding him two years later. His marriage on the rocks, the duke spent the rest of his life administering his state and collecting works of art, becoming more and more devout as the years went by. His only son (from his second wife) turned out a debauched individual, expiring because of his own excesses at the age of eighteen. Francesco Maria survived him by eight years, and on his death the duchy of Urbino was incorporated into the papal territories.[50]

Onorato Caetani's later history was grim. Received by Philip II into the Order of the Golden Fleece, he had nonetheless incurred Marcantonio Colonna's displeasure for the shoddy way he had handled the recruitment of soldiers in 1571. Colonna had him replaced as general of the papal infantry with Pius V's nephew Michele Bonelli, a veteran of the Curzolaris. With the election of Gregory XIII Caetani's fortunes went further downhill, the new pope distrusting Onorato partially because he was at loggerheads with the latter's uncle Cardinal Sermoneta. Without employment and faced with increasing family expenses, by the time of his death in 1592 Caetani had been forced to sell much of his property to pay his debts.[51]

Romegas got embroiled in the internal politics of the Order of Malta, in 1581 heading a revolt against the then grand master Jean de La Cassière. Called to Rome to answer to the Pope for his actions, he died there in November of the same year. After recovering from his wounds Miguel de Cervantes remained a soldier for some time. In 1575 he was captured by Muslim corsairs while on his way to Spain, spending five years as a slave in Algiers until ransomed. Cervantes passed the rest of his life eking out a living by working for the Spanish government, suffering bankruptcy and imprisonment. He died poor in 1616, but not before having acquired international fame with his immortal *Don Quixote*. Bernardino Antinori, another soldier-writer, was not so lucky. Some time after his return to Florence he got embroiled in a passionate love affair with Eleonora de Toledo 'the younger', wife of Cosimo I de' Medici's son Pietro. Eleonora was allegedly murdered by her enraged husband, and Grand Duke Francesco I had Antinori strangled in prison soon after. The same week as Eleonora's death, the Medici suffered another family tragedy when Isabella, Cosimo I's daughter, was murdered by her husband, the Curzolaris veteran Paolo Giordano Orsini, who suspected her of adultery. Orsini then embarked on a long affair with Vittoria Accoramboni, then married to Francesco Mingucci, a nephew of the future Sixtus V. Paolo Giordano duly arranged the murder of Vittoria's husband – or at least so it was believed at the time – and eventually married his lover. Orsini died in Venetian territory in 1585 and Vittoria joined him soon after, murdered in Padua by one of her first husband's kinsmen.[52]

Others fared better, and indeed connections made during the campaigns of 1570–2 helped many a career. Pompeo Floriani became sergeant major general of infantry in the Holy Roman Empire, and in 1573 was entrusted by Antonio Doria, on the suggestion of Paolo Sforza, with devising ways to defend the newly captured Tunis. Returning home, Floriani held a number of military/administrative posts all over Italy, gaining a reputation as an expert in fortifications. He died in 1600, his fame as an engineer subsequently eclipsed by that of his son Pietro Paolo. Francesco Duodo also enjoyed fame and public employment, crowning his career in 1587 when elevated to the dignity of *procuratore di San Marco*. He died in November 1592 while inspecting fortifications on the Venetian mainland. Juan de Cardona continued in command of the Sicilian galley squadron for some years before returning to Spain. In 1587 he was viceroy and captain-general of the kingdom of Navarre, dying some time at the beginning of the seventeenth century. For a number of Ottoman survivors of the Curzolaris, career advancement was due as much to ability as to the battle leaving many places vacant. Ahmed ben Sinan rose to the rank of galley captain after serving as helmsman on the *Sultana* and distinguishing himself with an harquebus during the fight.[53]

The important Ottoman prisoners were not liberated until some years after the battle. Müezzinzâde Ali's elder son died in captivity, while the younger regained his freedom after his sister sent a written plea to Don Juan of Austria. Eventually most were exchanged for high-ranking Christians captured at Famagusta or Tunis. Not many of the lesser captives had such luck, most facing a life of toil, often on a galley bench, away from their families and homes. Count Silvio da Porcia brought back two slaves whom he employed as masons and bricklayers for his home. In time they became Christians, and the count threw a party (costing him a substantial amount of money) to celebrate their baptism. In 1610 the Venetian authorities liberated three Ottomans enslaved after the battle, housing them in hospices on the mainland.[54]

By then all the main protagonists in the Cyprus war had died: Philip II in 1598, Selim II in 1574 and Cosimo I' de Medici the same year. Mehmed Sokollu was stabbed by an assassin in 1579, his power by now on the wane. His old enemy Lala Mustafa managed to become grand vizier after his demise, but died after only a few months in office. Joseph Nassi, often thought the villain of the piece, did not retain his influence under the new sultan, and when he passed away in 1579 Murad III seized all his possessions. As for the thousands of common soldiers on both sides, after their brief moment in the spotlight they quickly slid back into obscurity.

EPILOGUE

~

The league was finished, Tunis recaptured, the Ottoman fleet rebuilt, the Porte still firmly entrenched in Europe; the Christian effort, the innumerable deaths, the economic drain, had been for nothing. Indeed Voltaire would comment that it seemed as if the Turks had been the real victors at the Curzolaris. But how much of this is true? Fernand Braudel would appositely remark that instead of scoffing at the battle's apparent lack of consequences, one should look instead at the situation before: Cyprus captured, Crete, Corfu, southern Italy, Spain, Venice, Vienna and ultimately a way of life threatened by the Muslim advance.[1] Now the Ottoman onslaught had been stopped in its tracks; its rebuilt fleet was unable to dominate the Mediterranean as before, the recapture of Tunis, brilliant as it may appear, being due more to Spain's mistakes than Kılıç Ali's ability. The Ottoman beard had indeed grown again at lightning speed, yet was no stronger; and not due to the scarcity of skilled personnel – North African corsairs and ransomed prisoners could plug that gap – but because of the Porte's lack of a long-term naval policy. Even more important, the battle of the Curzolaris had not just been a psychological success; it had also confirmed the viability of Western military strategy and tactics.

The reasons for the Christian victory at the Curzolaris include: galleass fire, better tactical use of artillery, harquebusiers, body pro-

320

tection and Ottoman overconfidence. Most important was that the allies largely succeeded in stopping the Ottomans from exploiting their skill in hand-to-hand fighting, something at which they were the undisputed masters. The Europeans had realized that they could not win in a sword fight with the Ottomans and that in the long run it was not worth trying. In the Hungarian war at the beginning of the seventeenth century, Western field tactics forced the Ottomans to adapt their war machine, not always successfully, to the changed situation. Military initiative was now in European hands, although ultimate success was not assured. Western military superiority would not be a confirmed fact until the end of the eighteenth century, and until then the Ottomans remained a formidable foe.

Christian Europe would find other allies in its struggle against the Porte. In the 1580s the Ottoman empire was hit by a serious economic crisis, in the long term producing much political and social unrest. By the beginning of the seventeenth century the financial burden of maintaining simultaneously a numerous army and a large fleet had become intolerable. Something had to give, and that was the navy. In 1600 *kapudan Paşa* Cigalazâde Sinan (originally captured at Djerba with his father, Visconte Cigala) was going to sea with a mere sixteen galleys 'and then more as a corsair than as the sultan's admiral'. The Ottomans would not be the only ones forced to make such a choice. By 1650 Tuscany had sold or scrapped two thirds of its fleet to meet the costs of a substantial army.[2] Long wars between Constantinople and Persia did not help a situation made worse by the crisis in leadership that plagued the Porte in the first half of the seventeenth century, with sultans, grand viziers and government continually toppled and killed by palace conspiracies and army revolts. To many Western observers, by 1640 the Ottoman empire appeared on the verge of collapse.

But the Porte proved more resilient than people thought, the Ottoman state still capable of functioning with the right people at its helm. These were the grand viziers of the Köprülü 'dynasty', who ran the empire for nearly half a century. Thanks to them, the Porte was able to resume its role in Europe, indeed make the continent shudder once more. In 1645 the Ottomans attacked Crete, and although the city of Irakleio resisted until 1669 it was clear from the beginning that the Venetians would eventually lose the island. True, whenever the Ottomans encountered the Venetians at sea they invariably came off worse, but they proved unbeatable when it came to amphibious operations. On land the Porte suffered a few defeats at the hands of the Habsburgs, but in 1683 a huge Ottoman army penetrated Austria and besieged Vienna. The timely arrival of a makeshift army of Saxons, Poles and Austrians restored the situation, the Ottomans suffering a major defeat and in the years to come losing most of Hungary to Austria and large chunks of Greece to the Venetians.[3] But Venice was no longer the military power it had been, and in 1718 a whirlwind Ottoman offensive recaptured nearly all the lost territories in Greece. The Porte also made headway in the Balkans, in 1738 retaking Belgrade from the Austrians.

By now in the West the Ottoman Empire had become an intellectual curiosity, seen within the frame of the Enlightenment as an exotic culture. Mozart would compose a 'Turkish March' and write the score for the opera *The Abduction from the Seraglio*. Coffee houses, an idea imported from the east, sprang up everywhere in Europe, and Turkish objects were eagerly sought after by collectors. From a military standpoint the Ottomans now faced not only Austria but also a resurgent Russia, as attempts to reform the state apparatus failed in the face of internal resistance. Sultan Selim III tried to modernize the army, navy and public administration, with partial success.[4]

In 1797, Venice, by now only a shadow of its former greatness, fell to Napoleon's revolutionary army practically without a fight. The following year it would be Malta's turn, the knights cowering from the French fleet behind their hitherto impregnable fortifications. Having overrun Italy and Malta, Napoleon now attacked Ottoman Egypt, defeating the army sent against him but then unable to advance further after a British fleet under Horatio Nelson destroyed a French one at the battle of the Nile. Now at war with

France, the Ottoman empire joined forces with the Austrians and Russians. In 1799 Ottoman soldiers fought side by side with papal troops near Ancona, collaborating also with a Russian contingent to rid Rome of its French-sponsored republican government. Turkish units fought alongside anti-French Tuscan insurgents, who advanced to the battle cry of 'Viva Maria'; others operated in the south of Italy with the army of the Catholic/Bourbon 'Army of the Holy Faith'. The wheel had come full circle. The Ottomans were now allies of those very forces they had always opposed as enemies of their religion, but by recognizing the heathen French Revolution, that monstrous offspring of Western civilization, as the enemy of both Christianity and Islam they had acknowledged Europe's true soul.

~

The battle of the Curzolaris is still very much a presence in the Mediterranean. Many palaces, houses, churches and museums, especially in Italy and Spain, display relics, real or alleged, of the fight – weapons, banners, pieces of Turkish cloth. The Turks, understandably, prefer to remember the epic exploits of people like Hayreddin Barbarossa, the Turkish navy celebrating as its own day the anniversary of the battle of Preveza. In the naval museum in Istanbul one can admire some well-preserved seventeenth-century rowing vessels, the only ones in such a state left in the world. The same institution holds the banners captured by the papal contingent at the Curzolaris, and returned in 1965 by Pope Paul VI. One of the standards from Müezzinzâde Ali's flagship is still to be seen, together with many other Muslim banners, in the church of Santo Stefano in Pisa. The great Ottoman banner sent to Spain by Don Juan of Austria was destroyed by fire at the end of the seventeenth century. Marco Antonio Colonna's much frayed standard is still visible in the Pinacoteca Comunale of Gaeta.

By taking the ferry from Brindisi to Patras it is possible to follow more or less the route of the league's fleet in 1571, passing Corfu, Igoumenitsa and Kefallonia. Entering the Gulf of Patras, the boat skirts the southern tip of the isle of Oxia, the only one of the original Curzolaris not to have been consumed by the silt of the Acheloos, and crosses over what once was the battlefield. The ferry's wake appears profane, stirring as it does the waters where so many fell. But the depths of the gulf placidly guard the eternal resting place of all the brave men who lost their lives fighting for their beliefs on a distant October day.

APPENDIX 1. BATTLE ARRAYS

~

A — HOLY LEAGUE

LEFT WING

State/Owner	Number	Guns	Lanterns
Genoa (private)	3	9	0
Naples	10	30	0
Tuscany (Papal)	1	5	0
Venice	43	215	3
Total	57	259	3

NOTE: Included the four Venetian galleys of the vanguard.

GALLEASSES OF THE LEFT WING

Name/Captain	Guns
Bragadina (Antonio Bragadin)	32
Bragadina (Ambrogio Bragadin)	27
Total	59

NOTE: Originally positioned one mile ahead of the division.

CENTRE

State/Owner	Number	Guns	Lanterns
Genoa (private)	9	27	5
Genoa (public)	2	10	2
Malta	3	15	1
Naples	3	11	1
Savoy	1	3	1
Sicily	4	16	2
Spain	9	35	4
Tuscany (Papal)	7	35	1
Venice	26	130	1
Total	64	268	18

NOTE: Included the three Sicilian and one Genoese (private) galleys of the vanguard, originally allotted to Doria's division.

GALLEASSES OF THE CENTRE

Name/Captain	Guns
Guora (Jacopo Guoro)	23
Duoda (Francesco Duodo)	28
Total	51

NOTE: Originally positioned one mile ahead of the division.

RIGHT WING

State/Owner	Number	Guns	Lanterns
Genoa (private)	13	39	7
Genoa (public)	1	3	0
Naples	7	21	0
Savoy	2	2	0
Sicily	1	3	0
Tuscany (Papal)	2	10	0
Venice	27	135	0
Total	53	213	7

NOTE: Many of the Venetian galleys appear to have been undermanned, and possibly with less ordnance than usual.

GALLEASSES OF THE RIGHT WING

Name/Captain	Guns
Pesara (Andrea da Pesaro)	26
Pisana (Piero Pisani)	23
Total	49

NOTE: Supposed to be one mile in front of the division, but probably positioned just ahead of the line.

RESERVE

State/Owner	Number	Guns	Lanterns
Naples	11	33	1
Sicily	2	6	0
Spain	3	9	0
Tuscany (Papal)	2	10	1
Venice	12	60	0
Total	30	118	2

NOTE: Ten galleys were sent to aid Barbarigo, soon after the initial clash.

BREAKDOWN OF HOLY LEAGUE'S FORCES

Division	Galleys	Galleasses	Lanterns	Guns
Left	57	2	3	318
Centre	64	2	18	319
Right	53	2	7	262
Reserve	30	0	2	118
Total	204	6	30	1,017

B — OTTOMAN

RIGHT WING

Provenance	Number	Guns	Lanterns
Alexandria	21	63	2
Istanbul	11	33	2
Tripoli (Syria)	8	24	1
Anatolia	13	39	0
Negropont (Evvoia)	1	3	1
Galliots, Alexandria	2	4	1
Total	56	166	7

NOTE: Probable estimate. Some galleys from the Ottoman battle may have joined the right trying to escape the galleasses' cannonade.

CENTRE

Provenance	Number	Guns	Lanterns
Istanbul	41	120	15
Rhodes	11	33	2
Napulia	12	36	1
Gallipoli	10	30	1
Mytilene	10	30	1
Tripoli (Libya)	6	18	1
Avlona	1	3	1
Galliots, Istanbul	5	5	0
Total	96	275	22

NOTE: The Ottoman battle was on two lines. The first, with 62 galleys; the second, with 29 galleys and 8 galliots. At least six lanterns were bunched together in the middle of the division.

LEFT WING

State/Owner	Number	Guns	Lanterns
Avlona	2	6	1
Anatolia	12	3	0
Istanbul	26	72	2
Algiers	7	15	4
Negropont	13	6	0
Tripoli (Syria)	6	18	1
Izmir	1	3	1
Galliots, Avlona	8	16	0
Galliots, Algiers	9	9	0
Galliots, Anatolia	10	25	0
Total	94	173	9

NOTE: The Ottoman left was on two lines. The first, with 67 galleys; the second, with 27 galliots.

RESERVE

State/Owner	Number	Guns	Lanterns
Chios	1	3	1
Istanbul	6	18	3
Tripoli (Libya)	1	3	1
Galliots, Istanbul	3	3	0
Galliots, Tripoli (Libya)	2	2	0
Total	13	29	5

NOTE: The Ottoman reserve included also 18 *fuste*.

BREAKDOWN OF OTTOMAN FORCES

Division	Galleys	Galliots	Lanterns	Guns
Left	67	27	9	173
Battle	91	5	22	275
Right	54	2	7	166
Reserve	8	5	5	29
Total	220	39	43	643

The number of artillery pieces is a rough estimate, give or take 5–6 per cent, and includes only the main gun batteries. As explained in the text, lantern galleys were not necessarily more heavily armed than other vessels of the same type, their function being more command centres of a particular unit. The large number of Ottoman lantern galleys is due to the fact that they were also a symbol of rank, befitting the many dignitaries of the Porte present at the Curzolaris. It should be stressed, however, that, despite some recent, admirable attempts to produce the exact order of battle of the two forces,★ the precise strength of the two opponents is likely to remain a mystery. For instance, the League departed from Messina with 207–208 galleys, but apparently a couple of those sent to Apulia to embark troops did not manage to rejoin the allied fleet in time for the battle. Other two were disarmed in Corfu to allow, at Don Juan's request, the loading of the siege artillery taken from the fortress. As for the Ottomans, we have estimates ranging from 180 to nearly 300 fighting vessels. Guido Antonio Quarti would sum up the matter by commenting: 'The confusion is such, that we don't know whom to believe.'†

★ BICHENO: 306–318. GARGIULO: 189–197.
† QUARTI: 590–591. 616–617. Citation: 591.

APPENDIX 2

~

A — GALLEY ARMAMENT

Country	Main Battery[*]	Secondary Armament[†]	Weight of Shot, Centreline Gun(s)[‡]	Equivalent, UK/USA pounds
Algiers, *sottile*	1–3	2+	–	15.0–30.0
Algiers, *bastarda*	1–3	2+	–	30.0–35.0
Algiers, *galliot*	1	2+	–	15.0–30.0
Florence, *sottile*	5	4+	40–50 pounds	30.0–37.5
Florence, *bastarda*	5	10+	40–50 pounds	30.0–37.5
Genoa, *sottile*	3	2+	20–40 pounds	13.5–27.5
Genoa, *bastarda*	3–5	4+	30–50 pounds	20.5–34.5
Malta, *sottile*	5	4+	50–60 pounds	29.0–35.0
Malta, *bastarda*	5	10+	50–60 pounds	29.0–35.0
Naples, *sottile*	3	2+	20–50 pounds	14.0–35.0
Naples, *bastarda*	3–5	10+	40–50 pounds	28.0–35.0
Ottoman, *sottile*	1–3	2+	9–11 *okka*	25.5–31.0
Ottoman, *bastarda*	3	2+	11–21 *okka*	31.0–60.0
Ottoman, *galliot*	1–3	2+	9–11 *okka*	25.5–31.0
Savoy, *sottile*	1–3	2+	20–40 pounds	14.0–20.5
Sicily, *sottile*	3	2+	25–60 pounds	15.5–35.0
Sicily, *bastarda*	3–5	10+	50–60 pounds	29.0–35.0
Spain, *sottile*	3	2+	15–30 pounds	15.5–30.5
Spain, *bastarda*	3–5	10+	30–40 pounds	30.5–40.5
Venice, *sottile*	5	10+	40–50 pounds	27.5–34.5
Venice, *bastarda*	5	15+	50–60 pounds	34.5–40.0
Venice, *galleass*	12–18	5–22+	20–60 pounds	13.0–40.0

[*] The fixed artillery of the galleys or galleasses.
[†] Swivel guns and anti-personnel light artillery.
[‡] For Algiers the estimate is based on captured artillery pieces.

It would appear that at this date *ponentine* galleys had a main battery of three guns with the exception of the Maltese and Florentine/Tuscan galleys, specifically designed for hunter/killer operations against Muslim shipping.* The normal Spanish, Neapolitan, Sicilian and Genoese galley had the same number of guns as its Ottoman counterpart, and mounted lighter pieces than those found on Venetian vessels. For this reason they often beefed up their hitting power by mounting a pair of heavy *falconete* swivel guns.† In general Venetian galleys sported more and heavier artillery, between main and secondary armament, than *ponentine*, to compensate for their lack of fighting men. Only in the 1590s did the five-gun main battery become the standard armament of western galleys,‡ although to generalize would be risky: galleys were armed with whatever was available, standardization not being a feature of early-modern warfare.

From the above chart it is clear that every country in the Mediterranean employed guns of more or less equivalent calibre, as shown by the table below. The only exception would seem to be that of the Ottomans with their gargantuan 60-pounder. But this particular piece weighed only 4,782 Venetian "heavy" pounds (other two Turkish 35-pounders weighing 4,799 pounds each), which suggests it was intended to fire stone balls, and may have been one of the 20-*okka* (1 *okka* =2.83 UK/USA pounds) guns cast for naval use in 1538.§ What made the difference at the Curzolaris was not the size or the number of guns, but instead the tactical use of firearms in general. The concentrated bombardment of the Venetian galleasses, the long-range shooting of the other western galleys, swivel guns and massed harquebus volleys proved superior to the Ottoman short-range artillery fire, arrow barrage and hand-to-hand fighting.

---

* ASF, *MP*, 220, f. 33rv (Cosimo de' Medici to Francesco di Ser Jacopo, 19 April 1564).
† *CN*, VIII, 14, ff. 114r-118r. (1580).
‡ Cfr. PANTERA. CRESCENZO. *CN*, VIII, 23, ff. 156r-157r. (1590).
§ ASV, *CX, Parti Comuni*, filza 122, n.n. f. (25 February 1575). ÁGOSTON: 77.

B — THE SOUTHERN EUROPEAN POUND

Country	'Heavy' Pound (kg)	Ounces	'Light' Pound (kg)	Ounces
Genoa	0.317664	12	0.31675	12
Florence	–	-	0.339542	12
Malta	–	-	0.26447	12
Naples	–	-	0.32076	12
Rome	–	-	0.339072	12
Savoy (Nice)	–	-	0.311628	12
Sicily	–	-	0.26447	12
Spain	0.4601	16	–	-
Venice	0.476999	12	0.30123	12

Where the division between 'heavy' (*libbra grossa*) and 'light' (*libbra sottile*) pounds existed, the former was usually employed for metals, and sometimes spices. In Venice, however, 'heavy' pounds were used to establish the weight of artillery pieces, but 'light' ones for shot, possibly because in origin ordnance was supposed to fire stone balls. The Spanish pound is equivalent to the standard UK/US one: 0.4536 kg. (16 ounces). The Spanish also had the *libra carnicera* ('butcher's pound') of 32 ounces, used for meat.

GLOSSARY

~

a scaloccio Italian (probably from *scala* = ladder) referring to the rowing arrangement on a galley (q.v.) with one oar per bench handled by several rowers.

ağa Head servant of a household. Also commander of certain military units.

akçe Silver coin, the main unit of currency in the Ottoman empire.

akinci Light cavalryman from Rumelia (q.v.) engaged in permanent warfare along the Habsburg–Ottoman frontier in the Balkans.

alla sensile Italian (from the Spanish *sencillo* = simple) referring to the rowing arrangement on a galley (q.v.) with more than one oar per bench each handled by an individual rower.

arrembata Italian (Spanish *arrumbada*) for the elevated forecastle at the bow of a *ponentina* (q.v.) galley (q.v.).

askerî Military, in the Ottoman empire all those, with their retainers and families, not part of the *reaya* (q.v.) class.

azab Galley (q.v.) officer under a *reis* (q.v.); provincial soldier on garrison duty.

bagno Corral-type building for housing galley convicts and slaves.

bailo Venetian, a resident diplomat.

bastarda A galley (q.v.) with more than twenty-six rowing benches on each side (from the Italian for mongrel).

Bektaşi Dervish sect, its beliefs incorporating elements of Islam, Christianity, Buddhism and pre-Muslim Turkish paganism.

bey *See sancak bey.*

beylerbeik Ottoman province.

beylerbey Governor of a *beylerbeik* (q.v.).

buonavoglia Volunteer oarsman, especially on a *ponentina* (q.v.) galley (q.v.).

capitana Galley (q.v.) designed as a flagship, usually but not invariably a *bastarda* (q.v.) and a *lanterna* (q.v.).

çavuş Official of the Ottoman *dîvân* (q.v.).

cebelü Armed retainer in the service of a *timar*-holding *sipahi* (q.v.).

chief mufti (Turkish *şeyhü'l-islam*) The mufti (q.v.) of Constantinople, in the sixteenth century the highest religious and legal authority in the Ottoman empire.

condottiere (plural *condottieri*) Italian military entrepreneur.

culverin Artillery piece, approximately one third longer than a cannon.

darülharb The world not under Muslim rule.

darülislam The world under direct Muslim rule.

devşirme The forced recruitment of Christian youths for service, after conversion to Islam, in the *kapıkulu* (q.v.) corps or the Ottoman administration.

dîvân Council.

dîvân-ı hümâyûn The sultan's council, meeting under the presidency of the grand vizier (q.v.).

fanale *See lanterna.*

fatwa In Islamic law an opinion, given by a competent religious authority.

forzato (plural *forzati*) Convict oarsman on a galley (q.v.).

fusta Small galley (q.v.) with between twelve and fifteen rowing benches.

galeotto Galley (q.v.) oarsman.

galia grossa *See* galleass.

galley The standard vessel of the Mediterranean for many centuries, powered by oars and sail and with approximately twenty-five rowing benches.

galleass Large and heavily armed galley (q.v.) also known as a *galia grossa*, created by the Venetians by modifying transport galleys.

galliot Smaller galley (q.v.) with between sixteen and twenty-three rowing benches

gaza Raid, an alternative term for jihad.

gente de cabo Spanish for the artillerymen, sailors and guards on board a galley (q.v.).

grand vizier (Turkish *sadr-ı azam*) The chief vizier and the sultan's deputy.

harquebus Portable gun fired from the shoulder shooting a ball of approximately half an ounce.

has The largest fief within the Ottoman system, with a revenue of more than 100,000 *akçe* (q.v.).

imam Muslim prayer leader in a mosque; Muslim doctor of divinity.

janissary (Turkish *yeniçeri*) Ottoman infantry soldier recruited through the *devşirme* (q.v.) and part of the *kapıkulu* (q.v.) corps.

jihad Islamic term (Arabic *jahd* = effort) for holy war against the infidels.

kadi Ottoman judge.

kapıkulu ('slave of the Porte') In the Ottoman empire an individual recruited through the *devşirme* (q.v.) and employed in the sultan's army, administration or palace.

kapudan-ı deryâ Ottoman title for the grand admiral of the Mediterranean fleet.

kapudan paşa The *kapudan-i deryâ* (q.v.) when entrusted with a *beylerbeik* (q.r.)

küreçi azab Ottoman levied oarsman.

lanterna (also *fanale*; Venetian *fanò*) The lantern at the stern of certain galleys (q.v.); galley acting as a command vessel, usually a *capitana* (q.v.) or a *padrona* (q.v.).

levantina Type of galley (q.v.) used mainly in the eastern Mediterranean.

maona Vessel akin to a transport galley (q.v.) (Turkish *mavna*); Ottoman name for a galleass (q.v.); in Chios under Genoese rule, the body ruling the island.

mariol Ottoman volunteer oarsman.

mavna See *maona*.

moschetto da zuogo Small artillery piece used on Venetian ships.

moschetto da braga Venetian type of swivel gun.

mufti Religious authority with the power to issue a fatwa (q.v.).

padişa Official Ottoman title for the sultan.

padrona Galley (q.v.) designed as a deputy flagship, usually but not invariably a *bastarda* (q.v.) and a *lanterna* (q.v.).

Pasha/*paşa* Ottoman title given to viziers and major provincial governors.

piece of eight (Spanish *peso de ocho*) Spanish silver coin worth eight *reales*, and the standard medium of exchange in the Mediterranean of the sixteenth century.

ponentina Type of galley used mainly in the western Mediterranean.

Porte The Ottoman government and state.

provveditore Term used mainly in Venice to indicate the chief administrator of a certain body or place.

reaya In the Ottoman Empire all those, with their retainers and families, not part of the *askerî* (q.v.) class.

reis Ottoman naval captain.

Rumelia The part of Europe under Ottoman rule

sancak Subdivision of a *beylerbeik* (q.v.), comprising a number of *timar* (q.v.).

sancak bey Governor of a *sancak* (q.v.)

Safavid The dynasty ruling Persia in the sixteenth and seventeenth centuries.

scapolo Venetian term for a marine.

Schmalkaldic Bund Defensive league of German Lutheran princes.

serdar Ottoman commander with extensive powers in charge of a military expedition.

şeyhü'l-islam *See* chief mufti.

sharia The body of Islamic law.

sipahi Cavalryman; cavalryman holding a *timar* (q.v.) in exchange for military service.

Sipahi of the Porte Member of one of the Six Cavalry Divisions (q.v.).

Six Cavalry Divisions Mounted units of the *kapıkulu* (q.v.) military corps.

sopracomito Captain of a Venetian galley (q.v.).

tercio Spanish infantry unit akin to a regiment, with between twelve and fifteen companies and a theoretical strength of 3,000 men.

timar Ottoman military fief worth less than 20,000 *akçe* (q.v.) a year.

uomini da spada In Venice an alternative name for *scapoli* (q.v.); all fighting individuals (i.e. other than rowers) on board a galley.

vizier One of the sultan's ministers, with both military and political authority, and a member of the *dîvân-ı hümâyûn* (q.v.).

wagenburg Field fortress of fortified carts joined together.

yeniçeri *See* janissary.

yeniçeri ağasi The officer in command of the janissaries.

zeamet Military fief valued at more than 20,000 *akçe* (q.v.) a year.

NOTES

~

ABBREVIATIONS

ADP: Archivio Doria-Pamphilij, Rome

AFMC: Archivio Floriani, Macerata

AGF: Archivio Guicciardini, Florence

AGS: Archivo General de Simancas, Simancas (Valladolid)
    SE: Secretaría de Estado

ASF: Archivio di Stato di Firenze, Florence
    CS: Carte Strozziane
    DGA: Depositeria Generale, parte antica.
    GCS: Guicciardini-Corsi-Salviati
    MM: Miscellanea Medicea
    MP: Mediceo del Principato
    SFF: Scrittoio delle Fortezze e Fabbriche

ASG: Archivio di Stato di Genova, Genoa
    NA: Notai Antichi

ASTr: Archivio di Stato de Trieste, Trieste
    TT: Torre e Tasso

ASV: Archivio di Stato di Venezia, Venice
    CCX: Capi del Consiglio dei Dieci
    CM: Cariche da Mar
    CLS: Collegio Lettere, Secreta
    CR: Collegio Relazioni

CX: Consiglio dei Dieci

MC: Miscellanea Codici

MdM: Milizia da Mar

SAPC: Secreta, Archivi Propri Contarini

ScMN: Scritture Miste Motabili

SD: Senato Dispacci

SDM: Senato Deliberazioni Mar

SM: Senato Mar

SMMN: Secreta, Materie Miste Notabili

SS: Senato Secreta

ST: Senato Terra

BAV: Biblioteca Apostolica Vaticana, Rome

BMCCV: Biblioteca del Museo Civico Correr, Venice

BMrF: Biblioteca Moreniana, Florence

BNCF: Biblioteca Nazionale Centrale, Florence

BNMV: Biblioteca Nazionale Marciana, Venice

BOA: Basbakanlık Osmanlı Arşivi, Istanbul

    MD: Mühimme Defterleri

CLDSP: *Calendar of Letters, Despatches, and State Papers, relating to the negotiations between England and Spain*

CN: *Colección de documentos y manuscriptos compilados por Fernandez de Navarrete*

CODOIN: *Colección de documentos inéditos para la historia de España*

CSPV: *Calendar of state papers and manuscripts, relating to English affairs, existing in the archives and collections of Venice*

DBI: *Dizionario Biografico degli Italiani*

EI²: *Encyclopaedia of Islam*, 2nd edition

f.: folio

MS.: manuscript

n.: number

n.n.f(f.): non numbered folio(s)

r: recto

RBM: Real Biblioteca, Madrid

    EBG: Ex Bibliotheca Gondomariensi

reg.: registro

SOCSS: Statuti, capitoli, et constitutioni, dell'Ordine de' Caualieri di Santo Stefano.

v: verso

PROLOGUE

1 SELÂNIKÎ: I, 84. BNMV, Ms It. VII, 11, c. 204r. 'Lettera di Sultan Selim imperator de' Turchi, presentata alla Signoria di Venetia, 1570 a' 28 marzo'.

2 Venier's report, in: MOLMENTI, (1899): 311.

3 ARROYO: 61r.

4 MONGA: 59.

5 *Intiero, e minuto ragguaglio*: f. IV.

6 CATENA: 215–16.

1. THE WAXING CRESCENT

1 ASF, *MP*, 1171, ins. 5, f. 235 (Lorenzo Pagni to Pierfrancesco Riccio, undated, but early February 1545).

2 MACHIAVELLI (1524): Act III, Scene 3.

3 EMMERT. ATIYA.

4 BABINGER (1978). INALCIK (1960).

5 BARBARO. PERTUSI.

6 SIRE.

7 LAGGETTO. FONSECA.

8 E. TYAN (1965). KHADDURI.

9 INALCIK (1980).

10 BARTUSIS.

11 IMBER (2002): 194–8. INALCIK (2003): 113.

12 MACHIAVELLI (1994): 14.

13 KÁLDY-NAGY (1977). MATUZ: 177.

14 MÉNAGE (1965). MÉNAGE (1966). MÉNAGE (1956). repp. wittek.

15 GOFFMAN: 68.

16 ALBERI (1844a): 48–58. UZUNÇARŞILI (1984). AKGÜNDÜZ. For the

strength of the janissaries, as well as for other troops, I have relied on: MURPHEY (1999): 43–9, Table 3.5. IMBER (2002): 257–67. For an example of rewarding troops in the field, see: GIOVIO (1564): II, 580–1.

17 *Ibid.*: 8.

18 *Ibid.*: 134.

19 *Ibid.*: 39.

20 FISHER: 45.

21 *Ibid.*: 52.

22 ALLOUCHE.

23 BIRGE: 66–7.

24 FISHER: 88.

25 TEKINDAĞ. FISHER: 90–1.

26 HESS (1973).

27 FODOR (2000b): 119.

28 LABIB.

29 Quoted in: KÁLDY-NAGY (1974): 55.

30 FODOR (2000b): 119–20.

31 KNOLLES: I, 404.

32 PERJÉS: part II. NEGYES. Süleyman's retreat baffled his contemporaries, as well as future historians. For a discussion of the problem, see: FODOR, (2000b): 119–20.

33 SEYYD MURAD.

34 GIOVIO (1564): II, 423–6.

35 GULLINO. TURAN.

36 KHALILIEH: 133–48. SANTILLANA: I, 421. BRAUDEL (1976): I, 103. ROSSI.

37 BELLINGERI. GOKBILGIN: 57–9. KÜTÜKOLU: 148–9.

38 PRYOR: 165–74.

39 ÖZBARAN (1978).

40 KATIB ÇELEBI (1911): 159. ALBERI, (1844a): 291–5.

41 IMBER (2002): 298–302.

42 IMBER (1996a): 23–33.

43 PRYOR: 176–7.

44 See on this problem: FODOR (2002).

45 BRUMMETT. HESS (1970).

46 LUFTI PAŞA: 31–2.

47 ÖZBARAN (1994).

48 ALBERI (1844b): 100.

49 FODOR (2000b): 131–43.

50 BEBINGER.

51 IMBER (2002): 53–4.

52 INALCIK (2003): 37.

53 ALBERI (1844b): 98.

54 For a summary of the Djerba operation, see: GUILMARTIN (2003): 137–48.

55 IMBER (1996a): 48–9.

56 AGS, SE, 1325, n. 122 (Garcia Hérnandez to Philip II, from Venice, 23 November 1565). KATIB ÇELEBI (1697): 149.

2. A HOUSE DIVIDED

1 PARISOT DE LA VALLETTE: 71–3.

2 AGS, SE, 1325, n. 117 (García Hernández to Philip II, 29 September 1565, from Venice).

3 GUICCIARDINI (1949): 41.

4 MACHIAVELLI (1994): 45.

5 EVERT-KAPPESOVA: 245.

6 BROQUIERE: 149.

7 PIUS II: 11–12.

8 BISAHA.

9 See, for example: RUNCIMAN: 467–8.

10 For the Italian Wars, see: PIERI.

11 BOCCACCIO: 33.

12 For Savonarola, see: RIDOLFI.

13 ERASMUS: 319.

14 LUTHER (1957): 91–2. LUTHER (1967): 205.

15 LUTHER (1961): 47. See also: SETTON: III, 189–90.

16 For Hadrian VI, see: PASOLINI.

17 CLDSP, III, 2: 201–2.

18 For the Pontificate of Clement VII, see: GOUWENS AND REISS.

19 For the Schmalkaldic Bund, see: SCHLÜTTER-SCHINDLER.

20 MSETTON: III, 484, 502—4.

3. MEDITERRANEAN MEDLEY

1 *CSPV*, VI-2, n. 791, pp. 907—8.

2 PEPPER: 43—4.

3 *Ibid.*: 52—3.

4 PRETO (1975): 36—45.

5 PRETO (2002): 3.

6 CAPASSO.

7 PAOLETTI: 49.

8 BORNATE. ORESTE (1953).

9 MANFRONI (1898): 757—82, 809—56.

10 BASSO: 1—2.

11 *Ibid.*: 4.

12 PICCINO: 5—6.

13 HALICZER.

14 HESS (1968): 1—7.

15 OLESA MUÑIDO: I, 364.

16 MICCIO.

17 CANTAGALLI: 14—15.

18 TOGNARINI: 32—3.

19 SETTON: IV, 635.

20 NORES: 35—43.

21 ALBERI (1846): 389.

22 For the papal—Spanish war, see: PAOLETTI: 63—8.

23 SETTON: IV, 672.

24 The bishop of Lodève, French ambassador in Venice, to Henry II, in: RIBIER: II, 673—5.

25 NORES: 481—500.

26 DUMONT: 10—13.

27 BAZZANO: 74—6.

28 For the text of the treaty, see: DUMONT: 34—57.

29 MALLETT.

30 ASF, *MP*, 5, f. 194rv (Cosimo I de' Medici to Francisco Alvarez de Toledo, 4 July 1543).

31 AGLIETTI: 60.

32 CAMERANI: 86.

33 ASF, *MP*, 186, f. 46rv (Cosimo I de' Medici, to Alfonso Berardi, 16 September 1547).

34 ANGIOLINI (1996): ch. 1.

35 ASF, *MM*, 264, ins. 29, 'Ristretto delle Entrate Ordinarie e Straordinarie di S.A. Ser.ma, si come di tutte le Uscite Calculate dall'anno 1625 a tutto l'anno 1650', n.n. ff.

36 For the Spanish espionage ring in Istanbul, see: FLORISTAN IMIZCOZ: 579–737.

37 AGS, *SE*, 485 (Francesco Franchis to Philip II, 21 January 1559); (Memorandum of Gonzalo Pérez to Philip II, 5 March 1559); (Philip II to the duke of Sessa, from Brussels, 6 March 1559).

38 GUILMARTIN (2003): 145–6.

39 AGS, *SE*, 1068, doc. 5, 'La respuesta del Duque de Terranova sobre el estrado que quedan las cossas del Reyno de Siçilia' (1576).

40 ASP *Segretari del Regno – Ramo Protonotaio*, 47, n.n.f. (30 June 1565).

41 GUILMARTIN (2003): 203–5.

4. BUILD-UP TO DRAMA

1 I have taken most of the information concerning the Ottoman take-over of Chios from: ARGENTI (1949); ARGENTI (1958).

2 DOUAIS: I, 61–2. For the Corsican rebellion, see: BRAUDEL: II, 1001–4.

3 BORNATE (1939).

4 BOSIO: III, 757.

5 See on this matter: MILLER.

6 BRAUDEL: 625. Many thanks to Gabor Ágoston for pointing this out to me.

7 The struggle for Süleyman's succession is described in detail in: TURAN.

8 cfr. IMBER (2002): 108.

9 IMBER (1997).

10 DOUAIS: I, 49.

11 ZRINYI.

12 This section is based mainly on: HAMMER: VI, 149–58.

13 ALBERI (1844a): 360–1.

14 CHARRIERE: III, 259.

15 ALBERI (1844a): 401.

16 WOODHEAD (1995): 131–2.

17 KRAMER: 720.

18 OSLARAM: 571–2.

19 ALBERI (1844a): 299. HAMMER: 156. BABINGER (1993b): 316.

20 See, for instance: PEDANI (2003): 287.

21 CHARRIERE: II, 735–7; III, 80–4. ROMER.

22 CHARRIERE: III, 14–15, and notes.

23 KRAMER: 720–1.

24 SERRANO (1914): I, 87.

25 GRENTE.

26 For the Council of Trent, see: JEDIN.

27 SERRANO (1914): I, 28–30.

28 GOODMAN: 56.

29 SERRANO (1914): I, 152–4, 187.

30 AGS, SE, 530 (Margaret of Parma to Philip II, 18 August 1566).

31 For the Flanders revolt, see: PARKER (1977).

32 SERRANO (1918): 57–9.

33 SERRANO (1914): II, 132–3, 180.

34 Ibid.: II, 524–5.

35 MARRANA-ROSSI.

36 ASF, MP, 5040, f. 199 (Bernardetto Minerbetti to Cosimo I, from Madrid, 28 December 1561).

37 ANGIOLINI (1999).

38 AGLIETTI: 62–3.

39 ASF, MP, 211, f. 59r (Cosimo I de' Medici to Albertaccio degli Alberti in Constantinople, 11 July 1560). Ibid., f. 60r (Cosimo I de' Medici to Angelo Biffoli, 11 July 1560).

40 ASF, Manoscritti 127 'Settimanni vol. III:' ff. 272r–273v.

41 ASF, *MP*, 2077, ff. 347r–352r. FONTANA: 31–2. GUARNIERI (1960): 99–100.

42 AGLIETTI: 71–3. GOODMAN: 55–6.

43 Quoted in: SETTON: IV, 823.

44 FRIEDA: 47–9.

45 DIAZ: 187–8.

46 AGLIETTI: 85.

47 ASF, *MP*, 615, ins. 3, f. 528rv (Cosimo I de' Medici to Queen Catherine de' Medici, 15 September 1570).

48 The whole Don Carlos affair can be found in: GACHARD.

49 ELLIOT: 231–6. KAMEN: 128–9. HESS (1968): 13.

50 For the Morisco revolt see: CARO BAROJA. DOMINGUEZ ORTIZ, VINCENT.

51 AGS, SE, K 513 (Francés de Alava to Philip II, from Paris, 9 December 1569). HESS (1968): 13–16. CARO BAROJA: 188.

52 KAMEN: 130–2. VINCENT.

53 HAËDO: 78v–79v. BRAUDEL: II, 1068.

5. CYPRUS

1 ASV, *CCX*, *Lettere da Costantinopoli*, 3, n.n.f. (Vettore Bragadin to the Council of Ten, 13 January 1566).

2 ASV, *SS*, reg. 75, ff. 28v–29r (26 July 1567). STELLA (1963): 255.

3 PRETO (1986): 80–4.

4 I am grateful to Professor Maria Pia Pedani for this information.

5 SETTON: IV, 934–5.

6 ASV, *CX*, *Parti Secrete*, reg. 8, ff. 118v–119r (4 June 1568). BNMV, Ms. It., VII (390), *Copialettere di Marc'Antonio Barbaro*, (19 December 1569).

7 PEDANI (2003): 288–9.

8 FAROQHI: 7–10.

9 PEDANI (2003): 289.

10 PARUTA: 11–17. HAMMER: 196. FODOR (2000d): 201.

11 STELLA (1972): 124–5. PARUTA: 21–3. TOSI.

12 CHARRIÈRE: III, 84, 87.

13 ASV, *SD*, *Costantinopoli*, 4 (Marcantonio Barbaro to the Venetian Senate, 31 January 1570). STELLA (1972): 187–8.

14 Quoted in: FODOR (2000C): 218.

15 HAMMER: 197.

16 PEDANI (1994): 199–203. CANOSA: 59–62.

17 QUARTI: 110–11; quote: 111. MACCHI: III, 9.

18 CONTI: II, 74r–75v. On Salomon Ashkenazi's influence, see: ASF, *MP*, 4274, ins. 1, f. 23rv (Bongianni Gianfigliazzi to Francesco I de' Medici, 14 September 1578, from Constantinople).

19 STELLA (1972): 215–16.

20 PIOT, POULLETT: IV, 51–2.

21 SERRANO (1914): III, 248–50, 275–7.

22 DRAGONETTI DE TORRES. SERRANO (1918): 82–115. SERRANO (1914): III, 295–9.

23 VARGAS-HIDALGO (2002): 656.

24 SERRANO (1914): III, 335–51.

25 SERENO: 393ff. SERRANO (1918): 85–94. SETTON: IV, 962–3. GATTONI: 626–8.

26 PIOT, POULLETT: IV, 81. BAZZANO: 129–31.

27 ASV, *CLS*, 25 n.n.f. (The collegio to Michele Surian in Rome, 6 June 1570). ASV, SS, reg. 76, f. 121r (Alvise Mocenigo to Gerolamo Zane, 22 July 1570). SERRANO (1914): III, 446–7.

28 HALE (1990): 353.

29 CARRIERE: III, 113. SERENO: 51.

30 GUGLIELMOTTI (1887): VI, 30–1. DUMONT: V (1), 192b. DRAGONETTI DE TORRES: 104–5. SERRANO (1914): III, 479.

31 STELLA (1965): 383, and note 27.

32 ADP, 69/32, 3, ff. 12v–14r (Giovanni Andrea Doria to the Prince of Melfi (Marcantonio Doria del Carretto), 8 August 1570).
ADP, 69/32, 3, f. 22rv (Giovanni Andrea Doria to Philip II, 11 August 1570, from Messina). AGS, *SE*, 1399, n. 74 (Diego Guzmán de Silva to Philip II, 28 July 1570, from Genoa). ADP, 69/32, 3, f. 19rv (Giovanni

33 Andrea Doria to Stefano De' Mari, 11 August 1570, from Messina).

34 BOSIO: III, 855–65.

35 BMCCV, 3596, G. SOZOMENO, *Della Presa di Nicosia*.

36 GUILMARTIN (2003): 204.

37 QUARTI: 263. Quote in: PARUTA: 101.

38 PROMIS: 410. Quote in: FARA: 45.

39 HAMMER: VI, 205.

40 KALDY-NAGY.

41 CONTI: 87v.

42 QUARTI: 319–20. KATIB ÇELEBI (1911): 88.

43 HALE (1990): 298.

44 ASV, SM, reg. 39, f. 149v (4 April 1570). PARUTA: 128.

45 ASV, *Annali*, 1566–70, f. 501r. SERRANO (1914): III, 447. Quote in: PARUTA: 73–4.

46 DOGLIONI (1598): 826.

47 GUGLIELMOTTI: 29.

48 ADP, 69/32, 3, f. 25r (Giovanni Andrea Doria to Count Giuseppe Francesco di Landriano, 22 August 1570, from Otranto).

49 CAMPANA: I, 56.

50 LO BASSO: 279–80.

51 ASV, *CM*, *Processi*, 4, f. 18r.

52 ASV, *Annali*, 1566–70, f. 523r (8 September 1570). PARUTA: 128. CONTARINI: 14r.

53 IBÁÑEZ DE IBERO.

54 GUGLIELMOTTI: 58–64. SERENO: 67.

55 ADP, 69/32, 3, f. 26rv (Giovanni Andrea Doria to the viceroy of Sicily, 17 September 1570, from Crete).

56 AGS, SE, 1133, n. 107 (Marcantonio Colonna to Philip II, 29 September 1570, from Crete). ASV, *CM*, *Processi*, 4, ff. 39v–40v.

57 DORIA: 359. ASV, *CM*, *Processi*, 4, ff. 37v–38r. SETTON: IV, 984–5. ADP, 70/25, int. 8 (Giovanni Andrea Doria to the viceroy of Sicily, 17 October 1570, from Cape Spartivento).

58 CONTARINI: 12r.

59 GUGLIELMOTTI: 91.

60 TUCCI.

61 PARUTA: 133.

62 GUGLIELMOTTI: 107. CONCINA: 127. SERENO: 72.

6. A LEAGUE OF MISTRUST

1 BAZZANO: 133–5. PIOT, POULLETT: IV, 81. CAETANI, DIEDO: 151.

2 ADP, 69/32, 3, f. 42v (Giovanni Andrea Doria to the viceroy of Sicily, 14 November 1570, from Genoa). STELLA (1966): 391. MOLINI: 481–4.

3 SETTON: IV, 990–1.

4 SERRANO (1914): IV, 21–5.

5 AGLIETTI: 85–7. FRIEDA: 104.

6 SETTON: IV, 994. WANDRUSZKA.

7 ASF, MP, 4901, 'Instruttione al Cavaliere de Nobili sopra 'l negozio delle galere' (17 March 1569). Ibid, (Crown Prince Francesco de' Medici to Leonardo de' Nobili in Madrid, 14 August 1570).

8 AGLIETTI: 88, 90–1.

9 SERRANO (1914): IV, 175–85.

10 GATTO: 45. ASV, Annali, 1571, f. 460r (25 January 1571).

11 SERENO: 124. CONTARINI: 22r.

12 ASV, SM, I reg. 39, f. 256r.

13 TENENTI (1972).

14 BNMV, cl. VII, 391, f. 116r (Report by Marcantonio Barbaro to Venice, 8 January 1571).

15 ASV, CX, Secreta, reg. 9, f. 144v (7 March 1571). ASV, SD, Costantinopoli, reg. 4, c. 271v (4 March 1571). STELLA (1972): 456–7.

16 BNMV, cl. VII, 391, c. 136v (Giacomo Ragazzoni to the Venetian Senate, 7 May 1571).

17 QUARTI: 406–11.

18 ASV, SS, Deliberazioni, Costantinopoli, 1569–75, I. f. 29.

19 KAMEN: 134–5.

20 PIOT, POULLETT: IV, 50–1. CAETANI, DIEDO: 155–9.

21 BRUNETTI, VITALE: i, 176–7. AGS, SE, 917, n. 36 (Cardinal Granvelle to Philip II, 9 March 1571, from Rome).

22 BAZZANO: 143.

23 Quote in: GÓMEZ-CÉNTURION: 57.

24 Cfr. PARKER (1998): 123.

25 BAZZANO: 143.

26 STELLA (1972): 490–1. AGS, SE, 1329, n. 34 (Diego Guzmán de Silva to Philip II, 24 April 1571, from Venice).

27 AGS, SE, 914, n. 318 (Philip II to Juan de Zuñiga, 24 September 1570, from Madrid). ASF, MP, 4901 (Cosimo I de' Medici to Leonardo de Nobili, 13 February 1571, from Pisa).

28 AGLIETTI: 106–12. The text of the *asiento* is in: ASF, MP, 2131, ins. 5.

29 SERRANO (1914): IV, 183–4.

30 GATTONI: 631. ASF, MP, 3596, n.n.f. (Piero Usimbardi to Cosimo I de' Medici, 18 May 1571).

31 SERRANO (1914): IV, 272–3. QUARTI: 423–5.

32 The text of the treaty was widely publicized, both in manuscript and print, and translated into many languages. The original Latin text may be found in: SERRANO: IV, 299–309.

33 *La batalla naval*: 194.

34 For this section I have relied on the accounts by: MARTINENGO; AGOSTINO DA FAMAGOSTA; GATTO; VISINONI; FOGLIETTA; plus large sections of the account by Pietro Valderio transcribed and translated by SETTON: IV, 1027–36.

35 ASV, MC, 100, f. 130r (Marcantonio Bragadin to the doge, 8 October 1570, from Famagusta).

36 AGOSTINO DA FAMAGOSTA: 20.

7. THE CUTTING EDGE

1 PANTERA: *proemio*, n.n.p.

2 See on this matter: BOTTI.

3 'R.C.' GUILMARTIN (2003): 210–14, 219. RODGERS: 232.

4 PRYOR: 210.

5 See for instance: ASF, MP, 5153, ins. 1, f. 126rv (Grand Duke Ferdinando I de' Medici to Don Giovanni de' Medici, 16 August 1597).

6 ASF, Guidi, 97, n.n.f. (Cammillo Guidi to Grand Duke Cosimo III de' Medici, beginning of March 1703).

7 ASV, CR, 57 'Arsenale', n.n.f. (Report by Andrea Morosini, 12 March 1628).

8 ASF, *MP*, 2131, part 1, n.n.f. (Inventory of the Florentine galleys, 20 May 1558). FODOR (2000a): 186. *ASF*, MP, 2426, n.n.f. (Vincenzo Graffigna to Domenico Pandolfini, 13 November 1650, from Pisa). ÇIZAKÇA: 777. Cfr LANE: 264.

9 GUILMARTIN (2003): 231.

10 ALBERI (1844b): 335–8. ALBERI (1855): 152–3, 191–4. ASV, *CR*, 57, *Arsenale* (Report by Andrea Querini, 1580). GOODMAN: 112.

11 ASV, *CX*, *Parti Comuni*, reg. 27, f. 165v (11 January 1566); reg. 31, f. 95v (30 December 1573). ADP, 76/21, int. 2 'Inventarii delle due galere di S. Altezza Santa Caterina e Santa Margherita, fatto alla fine di febraro 1588'. cfr VIOLA: 4. Cfr. also ASV, SCMN, 13, 'Scritture diverse di Giulio Savorgnan', ff. 16v–17v (13 January 1588).

12 ADP, 70/25, int. 9 bis 'Inventari delle galere' (1582).

13 ASG, *NA*, 3150 (Notary Domenico Tinello, deed of 23 April 1575).

14 COLOMBINA: 470–3. SARDI.

15 MORIN (2004): 74. HALL: 85–7. RUSCELLI: 215.

16 MORIN (2004): 71–2. OLESA MUÑIDO: 318–21.

17 PANTERA: 87.

18 ÁGOSTON (2005): 53, Table 2.3. ALBERI (1844b): 100. BELHAMISSI: 59. AGS, *SE*, *Napoles*, 1049, n. 175, in: CONIGLIO: II, 363–70.

19 ASV, *CX*, *Parti Comuni*, reg. 30, f. 156v (28 November 1572). ASV, *SDM*, 689, n.n.f. (20 January 1690). ASV, *CX*, *Parti Comuni*, 122, n.n.f. (25 February 1574).

20 ÁGOSTON: 187.

21 ASV, *SM*, 95, n.n.f. (26 May 1587).

22 BNCF, *Magliabechiano*, cl. XIX, 12, *Armar d'una galea sottile, di Giovanni Brandimarte Franconi Fiorentino*, f. 14v.

23 HUGHES: 36. MORIN (2004): 73.

24 GIOVIO: II, 55.

25 PEDROSA: 331. PANTERA: 90.

26 See for example: ASF, *SSF*, *Fortezze Loronesi* 1928, ins. 38, n. 58, n.n.f. (Michele Grifoni to Alessandro Nomi, 1 April 1643).

27 ASV, *SM*, 226, n.n.f. (Petition of Antonio Surian's son to the Senate, 20 August 1616).

28 ASF, MP, 238, f. 67v (Cosimo I de' Medici to Bartolomeo Concini, 27 February 1572). Many thanks to Dr Maurizio Arfaioli for this document.

29 ASV, SDM, reg. 39, f. 180r (April 1570).

30 ASV, ScMN, 18 bis, n.n.f. (1570).

31 Unless otherwise indicated, for this section I have relied on Luca Lo Basso's excellent study on galley oarsmen. See: LO BASSO.

32 ALBERI (1844b): 100.

33 IMBER (1996a): 53–4.

34 ASF, MP, 2084, part 1, n.n.f. (Admiral Lodovico da Verrazzano to First Secretary Andrea Cioli, 29 June 1630, from Livorno).

35 ADP, 70/25, int. 24 'Notta de le chiusme che vi sono datte per la rassegna delle undice galere dell'Ill.mo Sig. Giovanni Andrea . . .' (no date, but early 1560s).

36 DORIA: 19, 185.

37 ASF, MP, 2077 f. 396r.

38 MAFRICI: 196–8.

39 ASF, MP, 627, ff. 25, 36, 56 (Inventory of the Florentine galleys, April–May 1555).

40 ALBERI (1855): 192.

41 FONTENAY. DAVIS.

42 IMBER (1996a): 54. SOCSS: 242. Cfr. Table 5.

43 ASV, MdM, 707 'Carattade diverse de galeotti fatte in diversi tempi . . .' Census of 1545. Again many thanks to Luca Lo Basso for this document.

44 IMBER (1996a): 52–3. ALBERI (1855): 152.

45 DA CANAL.

46 ASF, MP, 627, ff. 25v–62r (April–May 1555).

47 ASF, MP, 638, f. 199rv (Cosimo I de' Medici to Pier Francesco del Riccio, 3 March 1548).

48 FRATTARELLY FISCHER. FRIEDMAN.

49 HAEDO (1612): 42.

50 ASF, MP, 2426, n.n.f. (Giuseppe Orsati to Secretary Domenico Pandolfini, 2 August 1645, from Livorno). CANAVAGGIO: 77–97. DAVIS: 129. ASF, MP, 211, f. 110rv (Cosimo I de' Medici to Piero Machiavelli, 29 May 1561).

51 ASF, MP, 695, f. 264r (Cara Assam Reis of Istanbul to Francesco I de' Medici, 9 September 1576, from Algiers).

52 BOSIO: III, 213.

53 ASF, GCS, 128, ins. 1 (Luigi della Stufa to Agnolo della Stufa, 5 February 1569, from Rome); Ibid (Luigi della Stufa to Lena Strozzi-della Stufa, 10 July 1571, from Rome).

54 ASF, Urbino, I^a, X, n. 6/22, 'Vita di Francesco Maria 2° da Montefeltro della Rovere, Duca Sesto et ultimo di Urbino, signore di Pesaro', ff. 625r–627v.

55 ASF, MP, 3596, n.n.f. (Piero Usimbardi to Cosimo I de' Medici, 1 April 1570, from Rome).

56 CASTANI, DIEDO: 11. BRUNELLI: 39. DE CARO.

57 TESTA: 126. DAL POZZO: I, 11.

58 TESTA: 46–8, 63. VIANELLO.

59 SOUCECK.

60 SAGREDO: 396.

61 ADAMI: 333. BNCF, Passerini, 47: 'Antinori', 97–101. SOCSS: 269–73.

62 CANAVAGGIO: 14–53.

63 MEREDITH-OWENS: 456–61.

64 PASERO: 35–44.

65 LO BASSO: 357–8. MONGA: 107.

66 GUILMARTIN (2003): 264 note 6.

67 HALE (1983): 312–13.

68 ASF, MP, 2355, Capitoli della Nuova Militia Marittima. Nuovamente Stabilita da Sua Altezza Serenissima, Firenze 1586, ff. 305r and 306v. FERRETTI: II, 69. GUILMARTIN (2003): 145. IMBER (1996a): 46–50. IMBER (2002): 303–4. ÁGOSTON: 53.

69 CAETANI, DIEDO: 83–8. CODOIN: III, 8–10. ERCAN: 3. HALE (1990): 44, 154.

70 SOCSS: 242. ADP, 76/21, int. 2, 'Inventarii delle due galere di S. Altezza Santa Caterina e Santa Margherita' (1588). ASG, NA, 3150 (Notary Domenico Tinello, deed of 23 April 1575). CN, XII, 83, f. 311v. cfr. PARKER (1990): 274–6.

71 GUILMARTIN (2003): 160–1. PARKER (1996): 19–20.

72 ALBERI (1841): 131–2.

73 ÁGOSTON (2005): 57–8. GUILMARTIN (2003): 161–4. BNCF, *Magliabechi-ano*, cl. XIX, 12, *Armar d'una galea sottile*, f. 11r.

74 STANLEY: 350–2. OLESA MUÑIDO: 793.

75 FODOR (2002a): 174. MURPHEY: 93–100.

76 ASF, *MM*, 264, ins. 29, 'Ristretto delle Entrate Ordinarie e Straordinarie di S.A. Ser.ma, si come di tutte le Uscite Calculate dall'anno 1625 a tutto l'anno 1650', nn.ff. PARKER, THOMPSON: 15–16.

77 ASF, *MP*, 1802, part. 2, 'Instrutione delle parti si danno al Generale, Commissario, Capitani, e tutti li altri offitiali di Galera, e in che consistono' [1601], n.n.f.

78 ALBERI (1841): 134. BNCF, *Rossi-Cassigoli*, 199: ff. 132–45. ASF, *mp*, 49, f. 102r (note dated 16 June 1558). GUILMARTIN (1993): 121–2.

79 ADP, 79/37, int. 1, 'Copia della relazione delle vettovaglie che furono date alle galere del sig. Giovanni Andrea Doria il 1571, 1572' (16 June 1573), n.n.f. BNCF, *Magliabechiano*, cl. XIX, 12, *Armar d'una galea sottile:* f. 9v. LO BASSO: 126. ASF, MP, 2131 (Register dated 1572 on galley provisions), c. 44r. ADP, 22/40, int. 7 (Paolo de Guirardi to Giovanni Andrea Doria, 18 March 1571, from Palermo).

80 BNCF, *Magliabechiano*, cl. XIX, 12, *Armar d'una galea sottile:* f. 17v.

8. BRAGADIN'S HIDE

1 CAETANI, DIEDO: 86–95. SERENO: 115–18. MOLMENTI (1899): 80–1, 353–5.

2 MOLMENTI (1899): 1–30.

3 STELLA (1964): 49–50.

4 ASV, *Secreta, Archivi Propri Contarini*, reg. 25. ff. 3v–4r.

5 Venier's report to the Senate (29 December 1572), in: MOLMENTI (1899): 295–9.

6 Cfr. SETTON: 1019–22.

7 SERRANO (1914): IV, 429–30. VANDERHAMMEN: 42–4.

8 BAZZANO: 148.

9 Don Juan of Austria to Ruy Gómez de Silva (8 July 1571), and Philip II (12 July 1571), in STIRLING-MAXWELL: II, 376–83.

10 FERNÁNDEZ-ARMESTO: 1–4. ADP, 22/40, int. 7 (The Marchioness of Pescara to Giovanni Andrea Doria, 30 July 1571 from Palermo). ADP, 22/40, int. 7, (The Count of Landriano to Giovanni Andrea Doria, 3 August 1571, from Palermo). *Batalla Naval*: 120. CAETANI, DIEDO: 116.

11 AGLIETTI: 114–23. See also: PANICUCCI.

12 ASF, *Urbino*, Iª, 112, f. 199rv (Francesco Maria della Rovere to the duke of Urbino, 27 August 1571, from Messina).

13 Venier's report in: MOLMENTI (1899): 207. *Batalla naval*: 121. CAETANI, DIEDO: 120.

14 CODOIN: III: 8–10, 11–15.

15 BAZZANO: 144–6, 152, 381 note 120. Marcantonio Colonna to Francisco Borja, 4 September 1571, from Messina, in: GUGLIELMOTTI: 180.

16 INALCIK (1974): 187–9. QUARTI: 446.

17 SERENO: 126. CONTARINI: 29r. PARUTA: 103.

18 SERENO: 128. LESURE: 81–2. INALCIK (1974): 187–8. SELÂNIKÎ: 81.

19 STELLA (1977): 72–3.

20 For this section I have relied mainly on: GATTO: BNMV, MS. It. VIII, 399 ff 236r – 240r. 94–101. AGOSTINO DA FAMAGOSTA: 24–8. MARTINENGO. VISINONI: 35–42. *Il crudelissimo assedio*. TOMITANO. CONTARINI: 30r–31r. SETTON: IV, 1030–43.

21 PEÇEVÎ: I: 490–1. CONTI: 131.

22 ASV, *Annali*, 1571, f. 204r.

23 PEDANI (2003): 295.

24 AGOSTINO DA FAMAGOSTA: 25–6.

25 cfr. IMBER (1996c): 220.

26 BNMV, MS. It, VII, 391 f. 426r. (Marcantonio Barbaro to the doge of Venice, 27 March 1573).

27 GATTO: 54–7.

28 PARUTA: 260–1.

29 CODOIN: III, 15–18, 21–6.

30 CAETANI, DIEDO: 125. COSTO: 24. SEGRE: 134.

31 ASV, *Annali*, 1571, ff. 196v–197v (Dispatch from Messina, 13 September 1571).

32 Don Luis de Requesens to Pedro Fajardo, 28 December 1571, in: MARCH: 19–21.

33 VENTURINI: II, 130–2.

34 SERENO: 190. STIRLING-MAXWELL: 383.

35 QUARTI: 490.

36 VARGAS-HIDALGO (2002): 768.

37 CONFORTI: 40. CARACCIOLO: 18. SALIMEI: 51. *L'Ordine che ha tenuto l'armata*: ff. 1r–3v. ADP, 79/53, int. 5A, 'Particolare relazione del viaggio e della vittoria dell'armate della Lega contro gl'Infedeli', ff. 1–2.

38 Numbers deduced from various sources, including: CODOIN: 26–7, III, 203–15. ADP, 79/53, int. 5A, 'Particolare relazione', f. 1. CARACCIOLO: 24. SALIMEI: passim.

39 CAETANI, DIEDO: 210. GUILMARTIN: 255. MANUELE: 46.

40 CALANDRIA.

41 GUILMARTIN: 256. SALIMEI: 89. ALBERI (1841): 131. MANUELE: 52.

42 *L'Ordine che ha tenuto l'armata*: ff. 1r–3v. *Ordine che si debbe tenere*: f. 5r. ADP, 79/53, int. 5A, 'Particolare relazione', f. 2. SETTON: IV, 1047–8, note 16. CONTARINI: 37r–39r. SEGRE: 136.

43 Don Juan of Austria to Don Garcia de Toledo, 16 September 1571, in: CODOIN: III, 27.

44 MONGA: 110. QUARTI: 497–8.

45 IPSIRLI: 471.

46 ASV, *Annali*, 1571, f. 216r, (Sebastiano Venier to the senate, 29 September 1571). Venier's report in: MOLMENTI (1899): 307.

47 ASV, *Annali*, 1571, f. 219r, (Sebastiano Venier to the Senate, 3 October 1571). TORRES Y AGUILERA: 64r. CARACCIOLO: 25. Venier's report in: MOLMENTI (1899): 308–10. CAETANI, DIEDO: 130–1, 184. VANDERHAMMEN: 173. ROSELL: 92.

48 ADP, 79/53, int. 5A, 'Particolare relazione', f. 3. CONTARINI: 40r. ROSELL: 93. TORRES Y AGUILERA: 63rv.

49 Venier's report in: MOLMENTI: ASV, *Annali*, 1571, f. 221v (Sebastiano Venier to the doge, 5 October 1571). *Il Successo della nauale vittoria christiana*: f. 1. CAETANI, DIEDO: 192–3.

50 ADP, 79/53, int. 5A, 'Particolare relazione', f. 3. ASF, *Urbino*, C, ff. 1525r–1526r, 'Per lettere d'Anibal Protetico da Corfù, li 3 di ottobre 1571'.

51 INALCIK (1974): 188. LESURE: 80−1.

52 CERVANTES (1984).

53 There are many versions of what happened during the meeting, but, with the exception of Uluç Ali's position, they differ only in detail. My reconstruction is based on: *Intiero e minuto ragguaglio*: ff. 1−2. CAETANI, DIEDO: 184−92. SERENO: 170−82. TORRES Y AGUILERA: 55r−62r. ADP, 79/53, int. 5A, 'Particolare relazione', ff. 3−4. HERRERA: 30−1. SAGREDO: 396. CARACCIOLO: 31. CONTI: 138v−141v. KATIB ÇELEBI (1911): 93. PEÇEVÎ: 496. SELÂNIKÎ: 82.

54 DANIŞMEND (1948): 402−20. LESURE: 64−5.

55 ALBERI (1844a): 299.

56 PEÇEVI: I, 443. UZUNÇARSILI (1995): 182.

57 CONTARINI: 44r. KATIB ÇELEBI (1911): 93. Cfr. SELÂNIKÎ: I, 82.

58 *Del successo dell'armata*: f. 4.

9. THE 7TH OF OCTOBER

1 SERENO: 188. *Il successo della navale vittoria*, n.n.f.

2 EDGERTON, THROCKMORTON, YALOURIS. MORIN (1985): 210. PIERSON: 13−14. CONTARINI: 50r.

3 See for example: CARRERO BLANCO.

4 BRÂNTOME: II, 112−13.

5 CONTARINI: 48v−49r.

6 PRESCOTT: I, 622. HERRERA: 30. COLLADO, f. 50. APARICI: 98, note 38. PANTERA: 71.

7 ADP, 79/53, int. 5A, 'Particolare relazione', f. 4.

8 CAETANI, DIEDO: 133. SERENO: 192. *Ordine che si debbe tenere*: f. 5r. CARACCIOLO: 37.

9 JURIEN DE LA GRAVIÈRE: II, 150−210 VEROGGIO. GUILMARTIN (2003): 258.

10 ADP, 79/53, int. 5A, 'Particolare relazione', f. 4. *Copia d'una lettera*: f. 2. FOGLIETTA: 349, 361. *Del successo dell'armata*: f. 2. ADRIANI: 884. CAETANI, DIEDO: 133. ASV, MC, 670, 'Relazione Particolare delli successi dell'armata cristiana dell'anno 1571', f. 97. ORESTE (1962): 228.

CONTARINI: 51r. LESCAUT DE ROMEGAS: f. 2r. SERENO: 193. RBM, EBG, II/2211, n. 56 (Nicolás Augusto de Benavides to Lope de Acuña, from Portofigo, 10 October 1571). BNMV, *Ms. It.*, cl. VII 2582, f. 25r. *Discorso sopra due grandi battaglie navali*: 30. APARICI: 31. CODOIN: III, 242. *Batalla naval*: 190.

11 *Avvisi Particulari*: f. 1. CARACCIOLO: 33. SAVORGNANO: 221. HERRERA: 31.

12 CARACCIOLO: 36–7. GUILMARTIN (2003): 163.

13 CONTARINI: 40r–44r, 49r. *Ordine che si debbe tenere*: f. 6r. SORANZO: 12. GUGLIELMOTTI: 211–12.

14 CONTARINI: 52r.

15 PANTERA: 355.

16 SORANZO: 14. *Ragguaglio particolare*, n.n.f. ROSELL: 101. MONGA: 115.

17 *Intiero, e minuto ragguaglio*: f. IV. CARACCIOLO: 33. FIGUEROA: f. 2v.

18 PEÇEVÎ: 497. FOGLIETTA: 357.

19 CONTARINI: 37r–40r. FOGLIETTA: 347–8. CONTI: 144. *Ordine che si debbe tenere*: f. 6v.

20 GUILMARTIN (2003): 87.

21 *L'Ordine che ha tenuto l'armata*: ff. 1r–4r. *Ordine che si debbe tenere*: ff. 1r–4v. CONTARINI: 37r–40r. ASTr, TT, 264, n. 1 (Anonymous report about the Ottoman navy; no date, but beginning of the seventeenth century. Again; many thanks to Luca Lo Basso for this document.) n.n.f.

22 SALIMEI: 57–63. ERCAN: 7.

23 CODOIN: III, 203–15, 250. *Del successo dell'armata*: 4. CAETANI, DIEDO: 126. SAVORGNANO: 220. FOGLIETTA: 357. Cfr. PARKER (1996): 50–1.

24 FIRPO: 622. *Ordine che si debbe tenere*: f. 6r.

25 CONTARINI: 49v. CARACCIOLO: 33. *Il successo della navale vittoria*, n.n.f.

26 CAETANI, DIEDO: 202–3.

27 CARACCIOLO: 36. CODOIN: III, 270–2.

28 Since any description of the battle requires an endnote for practically every other phrase, I have limited notations to quotes, or when discussing specific points. Among the many sources used to reconstruct the event, see in particular: ADP, 69/32, ff. 146r–147r (Giovanni Andrea Doria to Stefano di Mare, 13 November 1571, from Naples). ADP, 79/53, int. 5A, 'Particolare relazione', ff. 4–6. ASF, *Manoscritti*,

127 'Settimanni, vol. III', ff. 541r–550v. ASF, CS Iᵃ, 137, ff. 138r–140r (Fra Luigi Mazzinghi to Fra Emilio Pucci, from Messina, 15 November 1571). ASF, CS Iᵃ, 145, 'Imprese delle galere', f. 11r. ASF, CS Iᵃ, 254, ff. 129r–130r (letter of 29 November 1571). ASF, *Urbino*, Iᵃ, 112, f. 110r (Francesco Maria della Rovere to the duke of Urbino, 8 October 1571, from the Curzolaris). ASV, *ANNALI*, 1571: ff. 224r–228v. ASV, *MC*, 670. BAV, *Barb. Lat.* 5367, f. 108r. *Relazione dell'Ucciali.al Gran Turco della rotta della sua armata l'anno 1571*. RBM, *EBG*, II/2211, n. 56 (Nicolás Augusto de Benavides to Lope de Acuña, 10 October 1571). AMMIRATO: XI, 329–36. ANTINORI: IV–2v. *Ritratto d'una lettera*: ff. 1r–2v. CARACCIOLO: 38–43. CONTARINI: 49r–54v. FOGLIETTA: 352. F. HERRERA: 350–82. ILLESCAS: 353r–355r. KATIB ÇELEBI: 94. LÓPEZ DE TORO: 18–20. ORESTE (1962): 227–33. PEÇEVÎ: 495–9. SAGREDO: 396–401. SELÂNIKÎ: 84. SERENO: 194–216.

29 ASV, *CX*, *Parti comuni*, 138, n.n.f. (Testimony of Paolo Orsini, 20 November 1579).

30 *Discorso su due grandi battaglie*: 40. *La batalla naval*: 180.

31 SAGREDO: 397.

32 FOGLIETTA: 353.

33 CONTARINI: 51v.

34 CAETANI, DIEDO: 205.

35 CERVANTES (1980): f. 5v.

36 CONTARINI: 52r.

37 TESTA: 140, note 21.

38 FOGLIETTA: 361.

39 CARACCIOLO: 39. ASF, CS Iᵃ, 145, 'Imprese delle galere', f. 11r.

40 Venier's report in: MOLMENTI (1899): 311–12.

41 *Ordine che si debbe tenere*: f. 6r.

42 MARCH: 52–3.

43 Provana's report in: SALVO: 78.

44 CAETANI, DIEDO: 135.

45 VANDERHAMMER: 181. SERENO: 199. CARACCIOLO: 38.

46 Spinola's report in: SPINOLA 7.

47 CARACCIOLO: 38.

48 FOGLIETTA: 355.

49 CONTI: 150v. CAETANI, DIEDO: 210.

50 Cfr. ASF, CS Iª, 137, f. 139r (Fra Luigi Mazzinghi to Fra Emilio Pucci). DAL POZZO: I, 25–7. SAVORGNANO: 222. CAETANI, DIEDO: 210–11. CONTARINI: 51v. Cfr. LESURE: 139.

51 FERNANDEZ DURO: 184.

52 *Ritratto d'una lettera*: f. 2r.

53 Venier's report in: MOLMENTI (1899): 313–14.

54 DAL POZZO: I, 26. ASF, CS Iª, 137, f. 139r (Fra Luigi Mazzinghi to Fra Emilio Pucci). SAFVET: 561, doc. III. KATIB ÇELEBI (1911): 43r.

55 ADP, 79/53, int. 51, 'Morti et fuggiti nelle galere di Gio. Andrea d'Oria al di 7 Ottobre 1571', n.n.f. ADP, 69/32, f. 146v.

56 CAETANI, DIEDO: 212. SERENO: 214.

57 CONTARINI: 52v. CAETANI, DIEDO: 136. Venier's report, in MOLMENTI (1899): 314. SERENO: 216. CARACCIOLO: 44. TORRES Y AGUILERA: 76v. BMrF, 269, *Priorista della città di Firenze a Tratte*, 'Rotta del Turco nel Golfo di Lepanto', f. 367v.

58 CARACCIOLO,: 45.

10. THE PHOENIX'S ASHES

1 SERENO: 216–20. CARACCIOLO: 47–51. ADP, 69/32, ff. 138r–139r (Giovanni Andrea Doria to unidentified recipient ['Molto Maggior Signore'], 28 October 1571, from Levkás).

2 CONTARINI: 55rv. CODOIN: III, 227–30. GUILMARTIN (2003): 245. ASV, CX, *Parti Comuni*, 122, n.n.f. (25 February 1575). SERRANO (1914): 684–5. AGS, SE, 1501, n. 201 (Decree by Don Juan of Austria, 15 October 1571). Venier's report in: MOLMENTI (1899): 316–17. ADRIANI: 887.

3 CARACCIOLO: 39, 52, 56. MEREDITH–OWENS: 462. *L'ordine che ha tenuto l'armata*: f. 4v.

4 CONTARINI: 55r. QUARTI: 725. *Copia d'una lettera*: f. 2r. AGS, SE, 1135, n. 70, n.n.f (Juan de Cardona to Philip II, 8 October 1571, from Petalas). ADP, 79/53, int. 51 'Morti et fuggiti nelle galere di Gio. Andrea d'Oria', n.n.f. Spinola's report in: SPINOLA: 8.

5 ADP, 70/25, int. 13 n.n.f. (List of Spanish officers, sergeants and

gentlemen killed and wounded). APARICI: 27. GUARNIERI (1965): 193–6. DAL POZZO: I, 26. CONTARINI: 55r. ASV, *ST*, 237, n.n.f. (Petition by Girolamo d'Adorno to the senate, 12 November 1577). QUARTI: 726. SERENO: 217. *La batalla naval*: 194.

6 AGS, *SE*, 1501, n. 201 (Decree by Don Juan of Austria, 15 October 1571). ASV, *SS*, reg. 78, f. 51v (The senate to Sebastiano Venier, 29 December 1571). Da Canal's report in: PRASCA: 128. Venier's report in: MOLMENTI (1899): 316–17. MONGA: 118. ADP, 79/53, int. 51 'Morti et fuggiti nelle galere di Gio. Andrea d'Oria', n.n.f.

7 SERENO: 220–4. Venier's report in: MOLMENTI: 315–18. CODOIN: III, 230–5. BRUNETTI, VITALI: I, 360. TORRES Y AGUILERA: 78rv.

8 BENEDETTI.

9 STELLA (1977): 121. SETTON: IV, 1062–4. SERRANO (1914): IV, 493. ASCF, *MANOSCRITTI*, 127 'SETTIMANNI, VOL. III' F. 550V. CAETANI, DIEDO: 223. CARACCIOLO: 54.

10 BRUNETTI, VITALI: I, 372–5. ROSELL: 208–10. MULCAHY.

11 BAZZANO: 158–61. ALBERTONI. TASSOLO. ROSELL: 208–10.

12 SELÂNIKÎ: 84.

13 ASF, *Urbino*, Iᵃ, 217, f. 935rv (Don Cesare Carafa to the duke of Urbino, 19 November 1571, from Venice).

14 CANTEMIR: 224. KORAN: II, 216. SELÂNIKÎ: 88–90. FOGLIETTA: 384–5.

15 *L'ordine che ha tenuto l'armata*: f. 4v. BRÂNTOME: 59. BOA, *MD*, 16: 316, n. 559 (Order to the *kapudan paşa*, 29 October 1571). FOGLIETTA: 384–5. INALCIK (1974): 192. TESTA: 132. BOA, *MD*, 16: 323, n. 568 (Order to Pertev Pasha, 28 October 1571).

16 CANTEMIR: 224, note 20.

17 Unless otherwise indicated, for this section I have relied mainly on Colin Imber's study of the reconstruction of the Ottoman fleet. See: IMBER (1996b).

18 SELÂNIKÎ: 84. PEDANI-FABRIS (1996): 167.

19 BOA, *MD*, 16: 75, n. 151 (Order of 24 October 1571). ALBERI (1844a): 421.

20 PEÇEVÎ: I, 498–9.

21 BNMV, MS. It. 391, f. 244r (Marcantonio Barbaro to the doge, 5 January 1572).

22 BAV, *Barb. Lat.* 5367, f. 108r, *Relazione dell'Ucciali*.

23 ALBERI (1855): 222. AFMC, 0002/004/534, segn. 17 'In due modi le forze delli Principi Cristiani sono superiori a quelle del Turco' (n.d. but early 1580s). FARA: 20. ASF, *MP*, 238, ff. 67r–68r (Cosimo I de' Medici to Bartolomeo Concini, 27 February 1572). ASF, *MP*, 1803, segn. 64, n.n.f. 'Condizioni accordate con il Comito Giorgio Condocali, Veneziano, che partì alli 22 novembre 1631 per andare a servire S.A. Ser.ma'. ASF, *DGA*, 658, n. 1097, n.n.f. (Muzio degli Agli to Ferdinando II de' Medici, 7 January 1633, from Pisa). AGS, SE, 1134, n. 150, n.n.f. (Don Juan of Austria to Philip II, 21 November 1571, from Messina).

24 CHARRIÈRE: III, 271–3.

25 SELÂNIKÎ: 85.

26 ASV, *CX*, *Parti Secrete*, reg. 9, f. 182v (22 October 1571). ASV, *CX*, *Parti Secrete*, 15, n.n.f. (The Council of Ten to Sebastiano Venier, 22 October 1571).

27 STELLA (1977): 123–5. CANOSA: 189, note 266. LESURE: 152. PRETO (2004): 26.

28 Venier's report in: MOLMENTI (1899): 315–27. LESURE: 191–211. ROSELL: 217–29. CANOSA: 188. ASV, *SS*, reg. 78, ff. 24r–25r (The senate to Sebastiano Venier, 22 October 1571). SERRANO (1914): 656–9.

29 ADP, 69/32, f. 148r (Giovanni Andrea Doria to the prince of Melfi, 13 November 1571, from Naples). ADP, 69/32, f. 149r (Giovanni Andrea Doria to Donna Costanza d'Avalos, 15 November 1571, from Naples). PARUTA: 292. ROSELL: 223. VARGAS-HIDALGO (2002): xxx–xxxi.

30 AGS, *SE*, 1328, n. 62, n.n.f. (Cardinal Granvelle to Diego Guzmán de Silva, 31 October 1571, from Naples). SETTON: IV, 1073–4.

31 FRIEDA: 246–7. MANFRONI (1893): 395–7, 402. SERRANO (1918): I, 294–300, 363–70. DORIA PAMPHILI: 27. LESURE: 226–7. CHARRIÈRE: III, 287–9, 363. GUARNIERI (1960): 296–7. DONÀ: II, 473–6, 500–13.

32 BAZZANO: 163–8. AGS, *SE*, 1505, n. 102, n.n.f. (Don Juan of Austria to Philip II, 6 July 1571, from Messina). GUARNIERI: 297–8. AGS, *SE*, 1331, n. 77, n.n.f. (Diego Guzmán de Silva to Philip II, 14 July 1572, from Venice).

33 CODOIN: XI, 372–7. SERRANO (1918): II, 35–46. SERENO: 285–91. LONGO: 35–40. MANFRONI (1893): 427–32.

34 SERRANO (1918): II, 47–60. SERENO: 291–327. AGS, *SE*, 1138, n. 183 (Marcantonio Colonna to Philip II, 18 August 1572).

35 IMBER (1996**b**): 85. FRIEDA: 246–75. INALCIK, QUATAERT: 94.

36 CHARRIÈRE: III, 175–9. AGS, *SE*, 1329, n. 94, n.n.f. (Diego Guzmán de Silva to Philip II, 15 September 1572, from Venice). AGS, *SE*, 1332, n. 6, n.n.f. (Diego Guzmán de Silva to Philip II, 2 January 1573, from Venice). ASV, *CX*, *Parti Secrete*, 16, n.n.ff. (The Council of Ten to Marcantonio Barbaro, 6 June 1572; 22 August 1572). TENENTI: 405–7. STELLA (1977): 225–7, 318–19, 329–30, 369–75.

37 BNMV, MS. It. VII, 391, f. 261r. CHARRIÈRE: III, 261 and note, 286–7.

38 BNMV, MS. It. VII, 391, ff. 372r–417r. SETTON: 1091. ROSI (1901): 29–32.

39 SETTON: 1092–3.

40 DONÀ: II, 677–80. GARCÍA HERNÁN, GARCÍA HERNÁN: 81–155. SERRANO (1918): II, 413–14.

41 FLORIANI. BRAUDEL: 1143–85.

42 SERENO: 213–14.

43 PETRIE: 260–329.

44 BAZZANO: 182–333.

45 MOLMENTI (1899): 221–59. MOLMENTI (1915).

46 SAVELLI: 371–5. VARGAS-HIDALGO (2002): XXXI–XXXIV.

47 Cfr. IBÁÑEZ DE IBERO.

48 PEDANI-FABRIS (1996): 197–8. SOUCEK: 811.

49 BABINGER (1993**a**): 296. LESURE: 182. BNMV, MS. It. VII, 391, ff. 233v–234r. LE TOURNEAU, ORHANLU: 252. HESS (1972): 65.

50 AGS, *SE*, 1483, n. 167, n.n.f (Duke of Urbino to Philip II, 28 May 1572). ASF, *Urbino*, Iª, X, n. 6/22 'Vita di Francesco Maria 2° da Montefeltro della Rovere, Duca Sesto et ultimo di Urbino, signore di Pesaro'. PIERACCINI: 453–4, 459–70.

51 BRUNELLI: 42–3. CAETANI, DIEDO: 70.

52 BNCF, *Passerini*, 47: 'Antinori', 101. PIERACCINI: 163–87. LITTA: tav. XXIX.

53 AFMC, 0001/001/053 (Letter patent to Pompeo Floriani as sergeant major general, 25 August 1574). ADAMI: 335–6. GULLINO (1993): 31–2. SCICHILONE: 794–5. IMBER (1996**a**): 39–40.

54 ROSELL: 237–9. ROSI (1897). ROSI (1901). DE PELLEGRINI. ASV, SDM, reg.
    69, f. 88rv (7 June 1610).

EPILOGUE

1 BRAUDEL: 1088.
2 ALBERI (1840a): 429. N[iccolò] CAPPONI (2004).
3 EICKHOFF.
4 SHAW. ARTAN, BERTKAY.

BIBLIOGRAPHICAL NOTE

~

Much has been written on the battle of the Curzolaris, and tackling the various sources can be risky without adequate historiographical skills. Indeed, in this particular case the well-known quote attributed to the Duke of Wellington about the impossibility of accurately describing battles and balls, rings as something of an understatement. The encounter of 7 October 1571 was fought on a front of nearly ten kilometres, the main clash lasting roughly ninety minutes with the two opposing fleets engulfed in smoke. Thus, witnesses had a limited vision of what was happening, and for this reason the letters and reports written immediately after the battle provide few details. Yet all those present immediately understood the importance of the event and within a few weeks detailed descriptions of the battle were circulating in print or as manuscripts. Unfortunately, the political or personal bias of some of these accounts means that they have to be taken with more than a grain of salt. Even the battle's name was not immune from distortion, the original 'Curzolaris' being quickly replaced by 'Lepanto' (forty miles to the east), possibly giving the impression that the allied fleet had penetrated deeper into Ottoman waters than in reality.

Amongst the earliest printed reports the most complete is by Girolamo Diedo, written a couple of months after the battle and based on the recollections of survivors on both sides. The *Discorso sopra due grandi e memorabili battaglie navali*, published a little later, is less comprehensive but also relies on eyewitnesses' testimony. The account by Giovanni Andrea Doria's secretary provides some interesting details, one suspects to justify his master's behaviour. Doria, trying to counter Marco Antonio Colonna's accusations, prepared his own version of the 1571 campaign, apparently it never went to print. It is preserved in the Doria-Pamphilij archive in Rome, catalogued under *scaffale* 79/53, int. 5A. Giacomo Contarini published in 1572 a detailed description of the previous year's military operations against the Ottomans, a fountain of information from which many would drink. In the years following the Curzolaris a number of the participants divulged their own accounts of the event, including Ferrante Caracciolo, Fernando de Herrera and, in an original manner, Miguel de Cervantes. The war of 1570–3 found its place in general histories of the time, the various authors usually emphasizing aspects relevant to their country. For instance, Uberto Foglietta's work has a strong Genoese slant, whilst Giovan Battista Adriani exalts Florence's role. Pro-Venetian, but nonetheless an excellent piece of historiography, is Paolo Paruta's *Storia della guerra di Cipro*, the author having access to the official documentation of the Venetian Republic. Natale Conti's *Istorie* is valuable not just for the details it includes, but also for the author's understanding of the military/political situation of the time. Several other histories of the Cyprus War still remain in manuscript form, a number being preserved in the Biblioteca Nazionale Marciana in Venice.

From the Ottoman side information is scant and sketchy, the Porte being unwilling to remember a defeat. Still, the works of Kâtib Çelebi, Peçevî Ibrahim Efendi, Selânikî Mustafa Efendi and Dimitri Cantemir provide some useful information. Unfortunately, most of these sources are not available in a western language. There is an early Italian edition of Kâtib Çelebi's historical chronology, whilst James Mitchell translated the first four chapters of his *Thufat al-Kibar fi Asfar ad-Bhihar* into English under the title *The History of the Maritime Wars of the Turks* (London, 1831). Mitchell's version stops in 1560, but is useful for an overall picture of Ottoman naval organization before the Cyprus War. Some time after the Curzolaris Western chanceries managed to obtain Uluç Ali's alleged report on the battle, and more Ottoman documents ended up in Venetian hands. It is quite possible that writings like Seyyd Murad's biography of Hayreddin Barbarossa may still be gathering dust in some unknown repository. One may hope that in the future more translations of Ottoman sources will be available.

The advent of Romanticism in the nineteenth century, often coupled with a growing national sentiment across Europe, produced a renewed historical attention to the struggle between East and West. From the 1840s onwards the Cyprus War became a hot topic amongst historians, greatly aided by the steady publication of archival documents. Unfortunately, the prevailing nationalistic feeling pervading the Western world caused historians to focus on their fellow countrymen's role, conversely undermining everyone else's. Instead of treating original sources as elements of a complex jigsaw puzzle, most writers used them as one employs letters in a game of scrabble.

This was not apparent initially. In 1853 Cayetano Rossell published *Historia del combate naval de Lepanto*, the first comprehensive monograph on the Curzolaris and perhaps the most balanced account of the battle itself. The author relied heavily on primary sources, not just Spanish ones, and although understandably partial to Philip II's subjects tried to give everyone his due. Sadly, mainly thanks to Italian historians, this example was not followed. In 1862 father Alberto Guglielmotti published his *Marcantonio Colonna alla battaglia di Lepanto*, which over the years went through a number of reprints. Guglielmotti's work on Colonna was an integral part of his history of the papal navy. A Dominican friar living in a time when the papacy was politically and culturally under constant attack from the most nationalistic elements of Italian society, Guglielmotti, by an extensive – if somewhat arbitrary – use of archival sources, argued instead that without Rome's commitment and Colonna's ability Italy would have been lost to the Ottomans. In order to do this he purposely diminished everyone else's contribution to the League's victory, with the notable exclusion of the Venetians, given their general good relationship with Colonna. The villain of the piece was, of course, Giovanni Andrea Doria (the Spanish, Doria's employers, getting a respectable second place), whom Guglielmotti squarely accused of cowardice and treachery for his behaviour at the Curzolaris.

The popularity of Guglielmotti's work ignited a heated row between Doria's detractors and supporters. Prominent amongst the latter was Benedetto Veroggio, a retired Genoese army officer, whose *Giannandrea Doria alla battaglia di Lepanto* was little less than Guglielmotti's argument turned on its head. For Veroggio the Christian victory could only be attributed to Doria and, to an extent, the Spanish. Belittling Colonna and the Venetians' contribution, he also created the myth that the two galleasses allotted to Doria never reached their battle stations. Veroggio was a polemicist not a historian, and as a result his book is of little worth. Unfortunately, its influence would have long-standing consequences, thanks to another serviceman turned historian. In 1889 Jean Pierre Edmond Jurien de la Gravière published his *La guerre de Chypre et la bataille de Lépante*, destined to become the main reference source on the Curzolaris outside Italy. Jurien de la Gravière's authority derived from being an admiral, as well as a hydrographs expert. His reconstruction of the Curzolaris was the result of this, but La Graviere wrongly assumed the coastline around the Acheloos was the same as in 1571, ignoring the extent of the silting at the river's mouth. As a result he moved the battlefield a couple of miles to the south, thus altering the structure of the fight. This, and his use of Veroggio as a *bona fide* source (evidently trusting a fellow military man), effectively marred Jurien de la Gravière's conclusions. In particular, he perpetuated the myth that the two galleasses of Doria's division did not arrive in time, ignoring all other evidence to the contrary. Despite these mistakes La Gravière's book was a solid piece of scholarship, and since it was written in French (a language which the majority of the educated classes in the West understood), his account of the Curzolaris became internationally accepted and, with a few variations, repeated to this day. Even more telling, his reconstruction of the 1571 campaign became the official version in Spain after the civil war of 1936–9. In 1948 Luis Carrero Blanco published *La victoria del Christo de Lepanto* (reissued in 1971 with the more sober title *Lepanto, 1571–1971*), to all intents and purposes La Gravière all over again, maps included, and with an even more pronounced Spanish slant. For Carrero Blanco Europe's civilization had been saved at the Curzolaris thanks to the Spanish and Don Juan de Austria, a resounding victory like the Nationalists one in the Spanish Civil War (dubbed the *cruzada*) under the leadership of Francisco Franco.

As befitted their parochial nature, few Italians bothered to publish anything equivalent to La Gravière's account, concentrating instead on publishing the exploits of particular individuals during the Cyprus War: Neapolitans, Sardinians, Sicilians, Romans, Lombards, Tuscans, and others, received their share of attention, and so did some key characters like Sebastiano Venier. Most of these studies contained useful information, and many included original documents in full. But nobody attempted to weave all this material together, until the publication in 1935 of Guido Antonio Quarti's *La guerra contro il turco in Cipro e a Lepanto*. Whilst mirroring the nationalistic psychology of its times, there is no doubt that Quarti's work was an impressive piece of research. Ploughing through libraries and archives, the author added greatly to the historical knowledge of the Cyprus War. In particular he challenged, although without mentioning him directly, La Gravière and his interpretation of the battle, but at the same time criticized Guglielmotti and gave a balanced assessment of Doria's behaviour. Quarti's main limitation was that he relied nearly exclusively on Italian primary sources, and often was careless in his footnoting. Besides, his study never circulated in sufficient numbers to make a real historiographical impact.

Following the end of the Ottoman Empire after World War I,

a few scholarly works appeared in Turkish on the 1570–3 conflict. Most of these consisted of published documents with a commentary, but only in 1973 did Halil Inalcik produce an article in English on the battle of the Curzolaris based on Ottoman documents. At the same time Michael Lesure came out with his *Lepante et la crise de l'empire ottoman*, in which Ottoman archival sources figured prominently. With the voice of the vanquished now available to Western scholars, the Ottomans' strategic and political goals became clearer. Lesure structured his book as a collection of original accounts interspaced by a commentary, which sometimes makes it difficult to follow the sequence of events. Besides, one is puzzled by the author's theory that the defeat at the Curzolaris shook the Ottoman Empire at its roots, and that the Holy League failed to exploit the situation. Colin Imber's essay *The Reconstruction of the Ottoman Fleet after the Battle of Lepanto*, also based on Ottoman documents, makes it clear instead that the Porte had little difficulty making good its material losses, something impossible to do in a situation of chaos.

Lesure added new fuel to the historical debate (as old as Voltaire) about the long-term effects of the Curzolaris' outcome. The most often repeated story dismisses the League's victory as nothing more than a psychological success – for Carrero Blanco, quoting Cervantes, it showed that the Ottomans were no longer invincible – given that the Venetians lost Cyprus while the Ottoman fleet was rebuilt within six months, and after the Western powers had incurred huge expenses. Echoes of this attitude can still be found in Andrew C. Hess's article *The Battle of Lepanto and its Place in Mediterranean History* (1972), and Geoffrey Parker's essay *Lepanto (1571): The Cost of Victory*, (1978). Turkish historians, understandably, tend to agree. However, already Fernand Braudel in his *The Mediterranean and the Mediterranean World in the Age of Philip II* had pointed out the obvious: instead of looking at the situation after the battle, one should look at the one before: to all extents and purposes the League's victory at the Curzolaris helped to stop the Ottoman advance in the Mediterranean. As a historian of economics, Braudel understood that war is made of men and materiel, and both cost money. Despite their conquest of Cyprus, the destruction of their fleet imposed a heavy strain on the Ottomans' war effort that could not be sustained indefinitely (Braudel also pointed out that Spain's many military commitments had been the cause of the League's inability to exploit its victory).

In his 1974 study *Gunpowder and Galleys*, John Guilmartin took Braudel's argument one step further, underscoring how the huge losses incurred by the Ottomans in skilled naval personnel had lasting effects on the efficiency of the Porte's fleet for many years afterwards. While Guilmartin's book contained a chapter on the Curzolaris its focus was not so much on the fighting itself, but instead discussed the logistics, technology and tactics peculiar to galley warfare (these matters had already been tackled a few year before by Francisco Fernando Olesa Muñido in his encyclopaedic *La organización naval de los estados mediterráneos*). Although Guilmartin's description still followed La Gravière's outline, his book laid the ground for a reinterpretation of the battle. The survey of the site done in 1971–2 by Throckmorton, Edgerton and Yalouris successfully challenged the acquired knowledge about the battlefield's outline, thus clarifying the movements of the contending fleets. Marco Morin added to this in his 1985 article *La battaglia di Lepanto*, which included some pointed criticism of previous scholarship. In particular, Morin made clear that without a profound knowledge of the weaponry involved it was impossible to understand what had happened at the Curzolaris. He also took to task those who had written about the battle without making proper use of primary and archival sources. Despite Morin's warning, some recent monographs on the Curzolaris still repeat the dated story popularized more than a century ago by Jurien de La Gravière. But such a historical attitude is not limited to the battle of 'Lepanto'.

BIBLIOGRAPHY

~

For abbreviations used in the Bibliography see the list at the start of the Notes on page 340–42.

ARCHIVAL SOURCES

Archivio Doria-Pamphilij, Rome
> *Scaffale*: 22/40, 38/32, 69/32, 70/25, 76/21, 79/17, 79/37, 79/53, 93/37
> *Bancone*: 72/5, 72/6

Archivio Floriani, Macerata
> 001/001/053
> 002/004/534

Archivio Guicciardini, Florence
> *Miscellanea*, II, n. 24

Archivo General de Simancas, Simancas (Valladolid)
> *Secretaría de Estado*: 485, K 512, 530, 914, 917, 1049, 1058, 1068, 1133, 1134, 1135, 1325, 1328, 1329, 1332, 1399, 1483, 1501, 1505

Archivio di Stato di Firenze, Florence
> *Carte Strozziane*: Iᵃ serie, 137, 145, 254
> *Depositeria Generale, parte antica*: 658
> *Guicciardini-Corsi-Salviati*: 128

Guidi: 97

Manoscritti: 127

Miscellanea Medicea: 264, 370

Mediceo del Principato: 211, 238, 615, 627, 638, 695, 2077, 2084, 2131, 2355, 2426, 3596, 4274, 4901, 5040, 5153

Scrittoio delle Fortezze e Fabbriche: Fortezze Lorenesi 1528

Urbino: Iᵃ serie X, 112, 132, 201, 217; C

Archivio di Stato di Genova, Genoa

Notai Antichi: 3150

Archivio di Stato di Trieste, Trieste

Torre e Tasso: 264

Archivio di Stato di Venezia, Venice

Annali: 1566–70, 1571

Capi del Consiglio dei Dieci: Lettere da Costantinopoli, 3

Cariche da Mar: Processi, 4

Collegio Lettere, Secreta: 25

Collegio Relazioni: 57

Consiglio dei Dieci:

Parti Comuni: reg. 27, 30, 31; filza 122, 138

Parti Secrete: reg. 8, 9; filza 15, 16

Miscellanea Codici: 100, 670

Milizia da Mar: 707

Scritture Miste Motabili: 13, 18 bis

Senato Dispacci: Costantinopoli, 4

Secreta, Archivi Propri Contarini: reg. 25

Senato Deliberazioni Mar: reg. 39, 40, 69; filza 689

Senato Mar: I, reg. 39, filza 95, 226

Senato Secreta: reg. 39, 75, 76, 78; Deliberazioni Costantinopoli I

Senato Terra: filza 237

Başbakanlık Osmanlı Arşivi, Istanbul

Mühimme Defterleri: 12, 16

Biblioteca Apostolica Vaticana, Rome

Barberiniani Latini 5367

Biblioteca del Museo Civico Correr, Venice

Ms. 3596

Biblioteca Nazionale Centrale, Florence

    Magliabechiano, classe XIX, 12

    Passerini, 47

    Rossi-Cassigoli, 199

Biblioteca Nazionale Marciana, Venice

    Ms. Italiani, classe VII: 11, 390, 391, 2582

Real Biblioteca, Madrid

    EGB: Ex Bibliotheca Gondomariensi: II/2211

PRINTED PRIMARY SOURCES

ADRIANI, G. *Istoria de' suoi tempi di Giouambatista Adriani gentilhuomo fiorentino* (Florence, 1583).

AGOSTINO DA FAMAGOSTA (Fra) *La perdita di Famagosta e la gloriosa morte di M. A. Bragadino. Nozze Lucheschi-Arrigoni*, ed. A. MOROSINI (Venice: Ferrari, 1891).

A. AKGÜNDÜZ, (ed.) *Kavanin-i Yeniçeriyan-i Dergah-I Ali*, in A. AKGÜNDÜZ, *Osmanli kanunnâmeleri ve hukukî tahlilleri*, vol. 9, (Istanbul, 1996): 127–367.

ALBERI, E. (ed.) *Relazioni degli Ambasciatori veneti al Senato raccolte, annotate ed edite da Eugenio Alberi*, 15 vols. (Florence, 1839–66): vol. 2, 1st series (Florence, 1840), vol. 3, 2nd series (Florence, 1846), vol. 6, 3rd series (Florence, 1844**a**); vol. 7, 3rd series (Florence, 1844**b**); vol. 9, 3rd series (Florence, 1855).

ALBERTONI, F. *Lentrata che fece l'ecellentissimo signor Marc'Antonio Colonna in Roma alli 4 di decembre 1571* (Viterbo, 1572).

AMMIRATO, S. *Istorie fiorentine*, 11 vols. (Florence, 1824–27).

ANTINORI, B. *Copia d'una lettera scritta dal sig. cavaliere Antinori ai suoi fratelli. Qual narra la felice, et gloriosa vittoria, che ha hauuto l'armata christiana contra alli nemici perfidi della fede di Giesù Cristo* (Florence, 1571).

APARICI, J. *Colección de Documentos Inéditos relativos a la célebre Batalla de Lepanto sacados del Archivo de Simancas* (Madrid, 1847).

ARGENTI, P. P. *Chius vincta* (Cambridge, 1941).

BIBLIOGRAPHY

– *The occupation of Chios by the Genoese and their administration of the Island 1346–1566* (Cambridge, 1958).

ARROYO, M. A. *Relacion del progresso de la Armada de la Santa Liga . . . con un breve discorso sopra el accrescentamiento de los turcos* (Milan, 1576).

AVENA, A. *Memorie Veronesi della guerra di Cipro e della battaglia di Lepanto* (Venice, 1912).

BARBARO, N. *Diary of the Siege of Constantinople, 1453*, J. R. JONES (trans.) (New York, 1969).

La batalla naval del señor don Juan de Austria: Según un manuscrito anónimo contemporáneo. Homenaje del Instituto Histórico de Marina. IV Centenario de Lepanto (Madrid, 1971).

BENEDETTI, R. *Ragguaglio delle allegrezze, solennità e feste fatte in Venetia per la felice vittoria* (Venice, 1571).

BERGENROTH, G. A., GAYANGOS, P. DE, HUME, M. A. S., TYLER, R., (eds.) *Calendar of Letters, Despatches, and State Papers, relating to the negotiations between England and Spain, preserved in the Archives at Simancas and elsewhere*, 12 vols. (London, 1862–1916).

BOCCACCIO, G. *The Decameron*, G. WALDMAN (trans.), J. USHER (ed.) (Oxford, 1999).

BOSIO, G. *Dell'istoria della sacra religione et ill.ma militia di San Giouanni gerosolimitano*, 3 vols. (Rome, 1594–1602).

BRÂNTOME, P. DE BOURDEILLE, SEIGNEUR DE *Oeuvres complètes: publiées d'après les manuscrits avec variantes et fragments inédits pour la Société de l'histoire de France*, L. LALANNE (ed.), 11 vols. (Paris, 1864–68).

BROQUIERE, B. DELLA *Le voyage d'outremer de Bertrandon de La Broquiere*, ed. C. SCHEFER (Paris, 1892).

BROWN, R., BROWN, H. F., HINDS, A. B. (eds.) *Calendar of state papers and manuscripts, relating to English affairs, existing in the archives and collections of Venice and in other libraries of Northern Italy*, 38 vols. (London 1864–1947).

BRUNETTI, M., VITALE, E. (eds.) *La corrispondenza da Madrid dell'-ambasciatore Leonardo Donà: (1570–1573)*, preface by F. BRAUDEL, 2 vols. (Venice & Rome, 1963).

CAETANI, O., DIEDO, G. *La battaglia di Lepanto, 1571* (Palermo, 1995).

CAMPANA, C. *Volume primo, che contiene libri dieci: ne' quali diffusamente si narrano le cose avvenute dall'anno 1570 fino al 1580. Nuovamente stampate, con gli argomenti a ciascun libro. Con una tavola de' nomi proprii, e delle materie* (Venice, 1599).

CANTEMIR, D. *The history of the growth and decay of the Othman empire*, 2 vols. N. TINDAL, (trans.) (London, 1734–35).

CARACCIOLO, F. *I commentarii delle guerre fatte co' turchi da D. Giouanni d'Austria, dopo che venne in Italia, scritti da Ferrante Caracciolo conte di Biccari* (Florence, 1581).

CATENA, G. *Vita del gloriosissimo papa Pio quinto . . . Con una raccolta di lettere di Pio 5. a diversi principi, e le risposte, con altri particolari. Et i nomi delle galee, et de capitani, cosi christiani, come turchi, che si trovarono alla battaglia navale* (Mantua, 1587).

CERVANTES SAAVEDRA, M. DE *Los Baños de Argel*, J. CANAVAGGIO (ed.) (Madrid, 1984).

– *Viaje del Parnaso: facsimil de la primera edicion Madrid, Viuda de Alonso Martin, 1614* (Madrid, 1980).

CHARRIÈRE, E. *Négociations de la France dans le Levant*, 4 vols. (Paris, 1848–60; repr. New York, 1965).

Colección de documentos inéditos para la historia de España, 113 vols. (Madrid, 1842–95).

Colección de documentos y manuscriptos compilados por Fernandez de Navarrete, 33 vols. (Madrid, 1946).

COLLADO, L. *Pratica manuale di arteglieria; nella quale si tratta della inventione di essa, dell'ordine di condurla, e piantarla sotto a qualunque fortezza, fabricar mine da far volar in alto le fortezze* (Venice, 1586).

COLOMBINA, G. B. 'Origine, eccellenza, e necessità dell'arte militare', in B. GIUNTA (ed.) *Fucina di Marte, nella quale con mirabile industria, e con finissima tempra d'instruzioni militari, s'apprestano tutti gli ordini appartenenti a qual si voglia carico, essercitabile in guerra. Fabbricata da' migliori autori e capitani valorosi, ch'abbiano scritto sin'ora in questa materia, i nomi de quali appaiono doppo la Lettera a' lettori* (Venice, 1641): 440–92.

CONFORTI, L. *I napoletani a Lepanto: ricerche storiche. Lettera di Bartolommeo Papasso* (Naples, 1886).

CONIGLIO, G. (ed.) *Il viceregno di Napoli e la lotta tra Spagnoli e Turchi nel Mediterraneo*, 2 vols. (Naples, 1987).

CONTARINI, G. P. *Historia delle cose successe dal principio della guerra mossa da Selim Ottomano a' Venetiani, fino al di della gran giornata vittoriosa contra Turchi* (Venice, 1572).

CONTI, N. *Delle historie de' suoi tempi di Natale Conti. Di latino in volgare nuouamente tradotta da m. Giouan Carlo Saraceni. Aggiunteui di piu e postille*, 2 vols. (Venice, 1589).

Copia d'una lettera del Signore Secretario dell'Illustrissimo Signore Giovanni Andrea Doria. Con il vero disegno del luogo dove è seguita la giornata, che fu il dì de S. Marco Papa, e confessore il dì 7 Ottobre 1571, 40 miglia sopra Lepanto (Rome, 1571).

COSTO, T. *Del compendio dell'istoria del regno di Napoli, di Tomaso Costo napolitano. Parte terza* (Venice, 1613).

CRESCENZIO, B. *Nautica Mediterranea* (Rome, 1607).

Il crudelissimo assedio, et nova presa della famosissima fortezza di Famagosta (Milan, 1571).

DAL POZZO, B. *Historia della sacra religione militare di S. Giovanni Gerosolimitano detta di Malta, del signor commendator Fr. Bartolomeo Co. Dal Pozzo veronese, cavalier della medesima*, 2 vols. (Verona, 1703–15).

Del successo dell'armata della Santa Lega dell'anno 1571 (Rome, 1571).

Discorso sopra due grandi e memorabili battaglie navali fatte nel mondo, l'una di Cesare Augusto con M. Antonio, l'altra delli sig. venetiani, e della santissima Lega con sultan Selim signor di Turchi (Bologna, 1572).

DOGLIONI, G. N. *Historia venetiana scritta breuemente da Gio. Nicolo Doglioni, delle cose successe dalla prima fondation di Venetia sino all'anno di Christo 1597* (Venice, 1598).

DORIA, G. A. *Vita del Principe Giovanni Andrea Doria scritta da lui medesimo*, V. BORGHESI (ed.) (Genoa, 1997).

DORIA PAMPHILJ, A. *Lettere di D. Giovanni d'Austria a D. Giovanni Andrea Doria* (Rome, 1896).

DOUAIS C. (ed.) *Lettres de Charles IX. à M. de Fourquevaux ambassadeur en Espagne, 1565–1572; publiées pour la première fois*, 2 vols. (Paris, 1897).

DRAGONETTI DE TORRES, A. *La Lega di Lepanto nel carteggio diplomatico inedito di Don Luys De Torres nunzio straordinario di S. Pio 5. a Filippo 2* (Turin, 1931).

DUMONT, J. *Corps universel diplomatique du droit des gens contenant un recueil des traitez d'alliance, de paix, de treve, de neutralite* . . . vol. 5 (Amsterdam & The Hague, 1728).

ERASMUS OF ROTTERDAM 'On the War against the Turks', in E. RUM-MEL (ed.) *The Erasmus Reader* (Toronto, 1990): 316–32.

FERRETTI, F. *Della osservanza militare del capitan Francesco Ferretti d'Ancona, cavallier dell'Ordine di San Stefano* . . . (Venice, 1577).

FIGUEROA, L. DE *Relatione fatta in Roma a sua santità dal s. maestro di campo del terzo di Granata Don Lopes di Figheroa imbasciatore del signor don Giovanni d'Austria mandato alla catolica maestà del re Filippo* (Florence, 1571).

FIRPO, L. (ed.) *Relazioni di ambasciatori veneti al Senato: tratte dalle migliori edizioni disponibili e ordinate cronologicamente. Vol. 13: Costantinopoli, 1590–1793* (Turin, 1984).

FLORIANI, P. *Discorso della goletta, et del forte di Tunisi* . . . (Macerata, 1574).

FLORISTAN IMIZCOZ, J. M. *Fuentes para la política oriental de los Austrias. La documentación griega del Archivo de Simancas (1571–1621)*, vol. II (León: Universidad de León, 1988).

FOGLIETTA, U. *Istoria di Mons. Uberto Foglietta nobile genovese della sacra lega contra Selim, e d'alcune altre imprese di suoi tempi, cioe dell'impresa del Gerbi, soccorso d'Oram, impresa del Pignon, di Tunigi, & assedio di Malta, fatta volgare per Giulio Guastauini nobile genovese* (Genoa, 1598).

FONTANA, F. *I pregi della Toscana nelle imprese più segnalate de' cavalieri di Santo Stefano* (Florence, 1701).

GATTO, A. *Narrazione del terribile assedio e della resa di Famagosta nell'anno 1571 da un manoscritto del capitano Angelo Gatto da Orvieto*, P. CATIZ-ZANI (ed.) (Orvieto, 1895).

GIOVIO, P. *Delle Istorie di Mons. Giovio*, 2 vols. (Venice, 1564).

GÖKBILGIN, M. T. (ed.) *Osmanlı İmparatorluğu medeniyet tarihi çerçevesinde Osmanlı paleografya ve diplomatik ilmi* (Istanbul, 1979).

GUEVARA, A. DE *Arte de marear*, R. O. Jones (ed.), (Exeter, 1972).

GUICCIARDINI, F. *Ricordi*, N. H. THOMSON (trans.) (New York, 1949).

HAËDO, D. DE Topographia, e historia general de Argel, repartida en cinco tratados, do se veran casos estranos, muertes espantosas, y tormentos exquisitos . . . (Valladolid, 1612).

HERRERA, F. Relación de la guerra de Cipre y sucesso de la batalla Naval de Lepanto, in Colección de documentos inéditos para la historia de España, vol. XXI: 243–382.

HERRERA Y TORDESILLAS, A. Segunda parte de la historia general del mundo, de 15. anos del tiempo del senor rey don Felipe 2. el prudente, desde el ano de 1571. hasta el 1585 (Valladolid, 1606).

ILLESCAS, G. DE Segunda parte de la historia pontifical, y catholica: en la qual se prosiguen las vidas, y hechos, de Clemente Quinto, y de los demas pontifices sus sucessores hasta Pio Quinto. Contienese ansi mismo la recapitulacion de las cosas, y reyes de Espana . . . (Madrid, 1613).

Intiero e minuto ragguaglio della vittoria contra Turchi, con alcuni versi sopra il signor Don Giovanni d'Austria (Rome, 1571).

KATIB ÇELEBI Cronologia historica scritta in lingua turca, persiana, e araba, da Hazi Halife Mustafa, e tradotta nell'idioma italiano da Gio. Rinaldo Carli nobile justinopolitano . . . (Venice, 1697).

—— Thufat al-Kibar fi Asfar ad-Bhihar (Istanbul, 1911).

KNOLLES, R. The Turkish history, from the original of that nation, to the growth of the Ottoman Empire: with the lives and conquests of their princes and emperors, by Richard Knolles . . . 3 vols. (London, 1687).

KÜTÜKOGLU, M. S. Osmanlı belgelerinin dili (diplomatik) (Istanbul, 1994).

LA BROCQUIERE, B. DE Le voyage d'outremer de Bertrandon de La Broquiere, C. SCHEFER (ed.) in Recueil de voyages et de documents pour servir a l'histoire de la Geographie depuis le XIIIe jusqu'a la fin du XVIe siecle, vol. 12 (Paris, 1892).

LAGGETTO, G. M. Historia della Guerra di Otranto nel 1480, Come fu presa dai Turchi e martirizzati li suoi fedeli Cittadini (Maglie, 1924).

LECHUGA, C. Discurso del capitan Cristoual Lechuga, en que trata de la artilleria, y de todo lo necessario a ella. Con un tratado de fortification, y otros advertimento . . . (Milan, 1611).

LESCAUT DE ROMEGAS, M. Relatione della giornata delle Scorciolare, fra l'armata Christiana e Turchesca alli 7 d'Ottobre 1571, ritratta dal Commendator Romagasso (Siena, 1571).

LESURE, M. *Lepante et la crise de l'empire ottoman* (Paris,1972).

LONGO, F. *Successo della guerra fatta con Selim Sultano Imperator de' Turchi e giustificazione della pace con lui conclusa di M. Francesco Longo, fu di M. Antonio a M. Manco Antonio Suo fratello*, in *Archivio Storico Italiano*, 17, appendice al tomo IV (1847): 3–58.

LÓPEZ DE TORO, J. *Lepanto y su héroe en la historia y en la poésia: José Lopez de Toro. Hallazgo de la crónica inédita de un soldado en la batalla de Lepanto*, J. GUILLÉN TATO (ed.) (Madrid, 1971).

LUFTI PASHA, *Das Asafname des Lufti Pasha*, R. TSCHUDI (ed. and trans.) (Berlin, 1910).

LUTHER, M. *Luther's Works*, vol. 31: *Career of the Reformer I*, H. J. GRIMM (ed.) (Philadelphia: Muhlenberg Press, 1957); vol. 46: *The Christian in Society III*, R. C. SCHULZ (ed.) (Philadelphia, 1967).

—— *Martin Luther: Selections From His Writing*, J. DILLENBERGER (ed.) (Chicago: Quadrangle Books, 1961).

MACHIAVELLI, N. *Comedia facetissima intitolata Mandragola et recitata in Firenze* (Rome, 1524).

—— *The Prince*, G. BULL, (trans.) introduction by A. GRAFTON (London, 1999).

MARCH, J. M. *La batalla de Lepanto y Don Luis de Requesens, lugarteniente general de la mar: con nuevos documentos historicos* (Madrid, 1944).

MARTINENGO, N. *L'Assedio et presa di Famagosta doue s'intende minutissimamente tutte le scaramuccie, batterie, mine & assalti dati ad essa fortezza: et quanto valore habbiano dimostrato quelli signori, capitani, soldati: popolo: e infino le donne . . .* (Brescia, 1571).

MICCIO, S. *Vita di Don Pietro di Toledo*, in *Archivio Storico Italiano*, 9 (1846): 1–143.

MOLINI, G. *Documenti di storia italiana copiata su gli originali autentici e per lo più autografi esistenti in Parigi*, 2 vols. (Florence, 1836–37).

MONGA, L. (ed.) *Galee toscane e corsari barbareschi. Il diario di Aurelio Scetti, galeotto fiorentino 1565–1577* (Fornacette, 1999).

NORES, P. *Storia della guerra di Paolo IV, sommo pontefice, contro. gli Spagnuoli*, in *Archivio Storico Italiano*, 12 (1847): 1–303.

L'ordine che ha tenuto l'armata della Santa Lega, cominciando dal di che si partì da Messina, con li nomi di tutte le galere, e di tutti li capitani di esse.

Aggiuntavi ancora la relatione, che ha fatta a sua Beatitudine il signor don Lope Fighuerola nel passar per Roma, portando lo Stendardo della Reale del Turco, a sua Maestà Cattolica in Spagna (Rome, 1571).

L'ordine che si debbe tenere per il serenissimo don Giovanni d'Austria generale dell'armata della s.lega nel navigare in dar la battaglia all'armata del Turco. Col numero delle galere, e nomi, e capitani d'esse, e del modo tenuto nell'accompagnarle nelle squadre a tutte le nationi di detta lega (Florence, 1571).

ORESTE, G. 'Una narrazione inedita della battaglia di Lepanto', *Atti della Società Ligure di Storia Patria*, 76, 2 (1962): 209–33.

PANTERA, P. *L'armata nauale, del capitan Pantero Pantera gentil'huomo comasco, e caualliero dell'habito di Cristo. Diuisa in doi libri . . .* (Rome, 1614).

PARRISOT DE LA VALLETTE, J. 'An Unpublished Letter of Jean de La Valette', B. C. WEBER (ed.), *Melita Historica*, 3, 1 (1960): 71–3.

PARUTA, P. *Storia della guerra di Cipro libri tre di Paolo Paruta* (Siena, 1827).

PEÇEVÎ İBRAHIM EFENDI *Tarih*, 2 vols. (Istanbul, 1864).

PEDANI-FABRIS, M. P. (ed.), *Relazioni di ambasciatori veneti al Senato*, vol. XIV, *Costantinopoli. Relazioni inedite (1512–1789)*, (Padua, 1996).

PEDANI-FABRIS, M. P., BOMBACCI, A. (eds.) *I 'documenti turchi' dell'archivio di Stato di Venezia* (Rome, 1994).

PIOT, C., POULLET, E., (eds.) *Correspondance du cardinal de Granvelle, 1565–1586*, 12 vols. (Bruxelles, 1877–96).

PIUS II (AENEAS SILVIUS PICCOLOMINI) *Epistola ad Mahomatem II (Epistle to Mohammed II)*, A. R. BACA (ed. and trans.) (New York, 1990).

PRASCA, E. *Nuovi documenti sulla battaglia di Lepanto* (Padova, 1909).

RIBIER, G. *Lettres et mémoires d'estat, des roys, princes, ambassadeurs, et autres ministres, sous les regnes de François premier, Henri 2. & François 2*, vol. II (Paris: Clousier, 1666).

Ritratto d'una lettera scritta dall'Ill.mo et Ecc.mo Ambasciatore Cesareo dalla Armata. Donde si hanno molti nuovi, belli e particolari ragguagli circa la Vittoria avuta contra Turchi (Rome, 1571).

SAGREDO, G. *Memorie istoriche de monarchi ottomani* (Venice, 1673).

SANSOVINO, F. *Gl'Annali ouero le Vite de' principi et signori della casa Othomana di m. Francesco Sansouino. Ne quali si leggono di tempo in tempo tutte le guerre particolarmente fatte dalla nation de' Turchi, in diuerse prouincie del mondo contra i christiani* (Venice, 1571).

SARDI, P. *L'artiglieria di Pietro Sardi romano divisa in tre libri* . . . (Venice, 1621).

SAVORGANO, M. *Arte militare terrestre e marittima* (Venice: Francesco de' Franceschi, 1599).

SELÂNIKÎ MUSTAFA EFENDI, *Tarih-i Selânikî*, M. İPŞIRLI (ed.), 2 vols. (Istanbul, 1989).

SERENO, B. *Commentari della guerra di Cipro e della lega dei principi cristiani contro il turco, di Bartolomeo Sereno; ora per la prima volta pubblicati da ms. autografo con note e documenti per cura de' monaci della Badia Cassinese* (Monte Cassino, 1845).

SERRANO, L. *Correspondencia diplomatica entre España y la Santa Sede durante el pontificado de S. Pio V*, 4 vols. (Rome, 1914).

—— *La liga de Lepanto entre Espana, Venecia y la santa sede: (1570–1573): ensayo historico a base de documentos diplomaticos* (Madrid, 1918).

SEYYD MURAD *La vita e la storia di Ariadeno Barbarossa*, G. BONAFFINI (ed.) (Palermo, 1993).

SPINOLA, E. *Lettera sulla battaglia di Lepanto*, A. NERI (ed.) (Genoa, 1901).

Statuti, capitoli, et constitutioni, dell'Ordine de' Cavalieri di Santo Stefano, fondato e dotato dall'illustr. e eccell. S. Cosimo Medici, duca 2. di Fiorenza, e di Siena, riformati dal sereniss. Don Ferdinando Medici, terzo Gran duca di Toscana, & Gran maestro di detto ordine. Et approvati, & pubblicati nel capitolo generale di detto ordine, l'anno 1590 (Florence, 1595).

STELLA, A. (ed) *Nunziature di Venezia*, F. GAETA (general editor), vol. VIII (Rome, 1963); vol. IX (Rome, 1972); vol. X (Rome, 1977).

Il Successo della navale vittoria christiana, contra l'armata turca; occorsa (mercé divina) al golfo di Lepanto; di nuovo ristampato, e aggiontovi più particolarità secondo varij riporti (Venice & Brescia, 1571).

TASSOLO, D. *I Trionfi feste, et livree fatte dalli Signori Conservatori, e Popolo Romano, e da tutte le arti di Roma, nella felicissima, & honorata entrata dell'illustrissimo signor Marcantonio Colonna* (Venice, 1571).

TOMITANO, B. *Resa di Famagosta e fine lagrimevole di Bragadino e di Astorre Baglioni, Per le faustissime nozze Marcello Zon* (Venice, 1858).

TORRES Y AGUILERA, G. DE *Chronica, y recopilacion de varios successos de guerra a que ha acontescido en Italia y partes de leuante y Berberia, desde que el turco Selin rompio con venecianos . . .* (Caragoca, 1579).

TOSI C. O. (ed.) *Dell'incendio dell'Arsenale di Venezia nel 1569: due nuovi documenti inediti pubblicati da Carlo Odoardo Tosi* (Florence, 1905).

VANDERHAMMEN Y LEON, L. *Don Juan de Austria, historia* (Madrid, 1627).

VARGAS-HIDALGO, R. *Guerra y diplomacia en el Mediterráneo: Correspondencia inédita de Felipe II con Andrea Doria y Juan Andrea Doria* (Madrid, 2002).

—— *La battalla de Lepanto: segun cartas ineditas de Felipe 2, Don Juan de Austria y Juan Andrea Doria e informes de embajadores y espias* (Santiago, 1998).

VENTURINI, T. N. *Storia, grandezze, e miracoli di Maria Vergine del Santissimo Rosario secondo il corso delle domeniche, e feste di tutto l'anno* (Venice, 1732).

VISINONI, L. A. (ed.) *Del successo in Famagosta, 1570–71: diario d'un contemporaneo, Nobili nozze Gozzi-Guaita* (Venice, 1879).

ZRINYI, M. *Szigeti veszedelem. Az torok afium ellen valo orvossag* (Budapest, 1997).

PRINTED SECONDARY SOURCES

ABOU-EL-HAJ, R. A. *Formation of the modern state: the Ottoman Empire, sixteenth to eighteenth centuries* (Albany, 1991).

ADAMI, G. 'Floriani, Pompeo', in *DBI*, XLVIII (Rome, 1997) 49–52.

AGLIETTI, M. *La partecipazione delle galere toscane alla battaglia di Lepanto*, in D. MARRARA (ed.) *Toscana e Spagna nell'età moderna e contemporanea* (Pisa, 1998) 55–145.

ÁGOSTON, G. *Guns for the Sultan. Military Power and the Weapon Industry in the Ottoman Empire* (Cambridge, 2005).

ALLOUCHE, A. *The Origins and Development of the Ottoman–Safavid Conflict: 906–962/1500–1555*, in *Islamkundliche Untersuchungen*, vol. 91 (Berlin, 1983).

R. C. ANDERSON, 'The "Mahona"', *The Mariner's Mirror*, 5, 3 (1919): 59.

—— *Naval Wars in the Levant* (Liverpool, 1952).

ANGIOLINI, F. *I cavalieri e il principe. L'Ordine di Santo Stefano e la società toscana in età moderna* (Florence, 1996).

—— *Il Granducato di Toscana, l'Ordine di S. Stefano e il Mediterraneo (secc. XVI–XVIII)*, in *Ordens Militares: guerra, religião, poder e cultura – Actas do III Encontro sobre Ordens Militares*, vol. I (Lisbon, 1999) 39–61.

ARENAPRIMO DI MONTECHIARO, G. *La Sicilia nella battaglia di Lepanto* (Pisa, 1886).

ARTAN, T., BERTKAY, H. 'Selimian times: a reforming grand admiral, anxieties of re-possession, changing rites of power' in *The Kapudan Pasha: His Office and His Domain* (Rethymnon, 2002) 7–45.

ATIYA, A. S. *The Crusade of Nicopolis* (London, 1934).

BABINGER, F. *Mehmed the Conqueror and His Time* (trans.) R. MANN-HEIM (trans.)(Princeton, 1978).

—— 'Pertew pasha', in *EI²*, vol. VIII (Leiden, 1993a) 295–6.

—— 'Piyâle pasha', in *EI²*, vol. VIII (Leiden, 1993b) 316–17.

BARTUSIS, M. C. *The Late Byzantine Army: Arms and Society, 1204–1453* (Philadelphia, 1992).

BASSO, E. 'L'ochio drito de la città nostra de Zenoa: il problema della difesa di Chio negli ultimi anni del dominio genovese' in *Le armi del sovrano: armate e flotte nel mondo tra Lepanto e la Rivoluzione francese, 1571–1789* (Rome: Assostoria, 2001): 1–9. http://www.assostoria.it/Armisovrano/Basso.pdf

BAZZANO, N. *Marco Antonio Colonna* (Rome, 2003).

BELHAMISSI, M. *Histoire de la marine algérienne, 1516–1830* (Algiers, 1986).

BELLINGERI, G. 'Il Golfo come appendice: una visione ottomana', in *Mito e antimito di Venezia nel bacino adriatico (secoli XV–XIX)*, S. GRA-CIOTTI (ed.) (Rome, 2001) 1–21.

BENZONI, G. (ed.) *Il Mediterraneo nella seconda metà del '500 alla luce di Lepanto* (Florence, 1974).

BERENGER, J. 'La Collaboration Militaire Franco-Ottoman a l'Epoque de la Renaissance', *Revue Internationale d'Histoire Militaire*, 68 (1987) 51–70.

BICHENO, H. *Crescent and Cross: The Battle of Lepanto, 1571* (London, 2003).

BIRGE, J. K. *The Bektashi Order of Dervishes* (London, 1996).

BISAHA, N. 'Pius II's Letter to Sultan Mehmed II: A Reexamination', *Crusades*, 1 (2003) 183–200.

BONO, S. *Corsari nel Mediterraneo. Cristiani e musulmani fra guerra, schiavitù e commercio* (Milan, 1993).

BORGHESI, V. 'Le galere del Principe Giovanni Andrea Doria (1540–1606)' in *Le navi di legno. Evoluzione tecnica e sviluppo della cantieristica nel Mediterraneo dal XVI secolo a oggi* (Grado, 1998) 91–100.

BORNATE, C. 'La missione di Sampiero Corso a Costantinopoli', *Archivio Storico di Corsica*, 15, 3 (1939) 472–502.

—— 'I negoziati per attirare Andrea D'Oria al servizio di Carlo V', *Giornale Storico e Letterario della Liguria*, XVIII, II, (1942) 63–84.

BOTTI, F. 'Come non ci si prepara a una guerra', *Storia Militare*, 2 (4) 1994: 42–50.

BRAUDEL, F. *The Mediterranean and the Mediterranean World in the Age of Philip II* (New York, 1976).

BRUMMETT, P. *Ottoman Seapower and Levantine Diplomacy in the Age of Discovery* (Albany, 1994).

BRUNELLI, G. *Soldati del Papa. Politica militare e nobiltà nello Stato della Chiesa (1560–1644)* (Rome, 2003).

CALANDRIA, E. C. 'Nuevos Datos Sobre Pintores Españoles y Pinturas Mitológicas en el Siglo XVI. La Galera Real de Don Juan de Austria', *Goya*, 286 (2002) 15–26.

CAMERANI, S. 'Contributo alla storia dei trattati commerciali fra la Toscana e i Turchi', *Archivio Storico Italiano*, XCVII, 4, (1939) 83–101.

CANAVAGGIO, J. *Cervantes*, J. R. Jones (trans.) (New York, 1990).

CANOSA, R. *Lepanto: storia della Lega santa contro i turchi* (Rome, 2000).

CANTAGALLI, R.3 'LA GUERRA DI SIENA', IN L. ROMBAI (ED.) *I MEDICI E LO STATO SENESE, 1555–1609. STORIA E TERRITORIO* (ROME, 1980).

CAPASSO, C. 'Barbarossa e Carlo V', *Rivista storica italiana*, 49 (1932) 169–209.

CAPPONI, N[eri] 'Il Sacro Militare Ordine di Sa. Stefano Papa e Martire e il Sacro Militare Ordine Costantiniano di S. Giorgio quali enti canonici' in *Gli Ordini dinastici della I.E.R. casa granducale di Toscana e della reale casa Borbone Parma* (Pisa, 2002) 39–60.

CAPPONI, N[iccolò] 'Strategia marittima, logistica e guerra navale sotto

Ferdinando II de' Medici, 1621–1670' in *L'Ordine di Santo Stefano e il Mare* (Pisa, 2001) 114–29.

CARO BAROJA, J. *Los moriscos del Reino de Granada: ensayo de historia social* (Madrid, 1985).

CARRERO BLANCO, L. *Lepanto, 1571–1971* (Madrid, 1971).

CHIAVARELLO, G. *La Battaglia di Lepanto (7 ottobre 1571): apporto decisivo della tecnica del fuoco napoletana; localizzazione dello specchio d'acqua ove avvenne lo scontro* (Naples, 1976).

CIRAKMAN, A *From the 'Terror of the World' to the 'Sick Man of Europe': European Images of Ottoman Empire and Society from the Sixteenth Century to the Nineteenth* (New York, 2002).

ÇIZAKÇA, M. 'Ottomans and the Mediterranean: An Analysis of the Ottoman Shipbuilding Industry as Reflected by the Arsenal Registers in Istanbul' in R. Ragosta (ed.), *Le genti del mare Mediterraneo*, vol. II (Naples, 1981) 773–88.

CONCINA, E. *Navis: l'umanesimo sul mare, 1470–1740* (Turin, 1990).

DANIŞMEND, I. H. *Izahlı Osmanlı tarihi kronolojisi*, vol. II (Istanbul, 1948).

DAVIS, R. C. *Christian Slaves, Muslim Masters: White Slavery in the Mediterranean, the Barbary Coast and Italy, 1500–1800* (London, 2003).

DE CARO, G. 'Caetani, Onorato' in *DBI*, XVI (Rome, 1973) 205–9.

DIAZ, F. *Il Granducato di Toscana: i Medici* (Turin, 1987).

DOMINGUEZ ORTIZ, A., VINCENT, B. *Historia de los moriscos: vida y tragedia de una minoria* (Madrid, 1985).

EDGERTON, H. E., THROCKMORTON, P., YALOURIS, E. 'The Battle of Lepanto. Search and survey mission 1971–2', *International Journal of Nautical Archeology*, 2, 1 (1973) 121–30.

EICKHOFF, E. *Venezia, Vienna e i turchi: bufera nel sud-est europeo, 1645–1700* (Milan, 1991).

ELLIOTT, J. H. *Imperial Spain, 1469–1716* (New York, 1966).

EMMERT, T. A. *Serbian Golgotha: Kosovo, 1389* (New York, 1990).

ERCAN, Y. *Power balance between east and west: the Lepanto naval battle*, paper presented at the international conference: *Le armi del sovrano: armate e flotte nel mondo tra Lepanto e la Rivoluzione francese, 1571–1789*, Rome, 5–8 March 2001.

EVERT-KAPPESOVA, H. 'Le tiare ou le turban', *Byzantinoslavica*, 14 (1953) 245–57.

FARA, A. *Portoferraio. Architettura e urbanistica, 1548–1877* (Turin, 1997).

—— *Il sistema e la città. Architettura fortificata dell'Europa moderna dai trattati alle realizzazioni, 1464–1794* (Genoa, 1989).

FAROQHI, S. *Pilgrims and sultans: the Hajj under the Ottomans, 1517–1683* (London & New York, 1996).

FERNÁNDEZ ARMESTO, F. *The Armada Campaign. The Experience of War in 1588* (Oxford, 1988).

FERNÁNDEZ DURO, C. *Armada española desde la unión de los reinos de Castilla y de Aragón*, 9 vols. (Madrid, 1896).

FISHER, S. N. *The Foreign Relations of Turkey, 1481–1512*, in *Electronic Journal of Middle East Studies*, III, 3 (originally published in *Illinois Studies in the Social Sciences*, XXX, 1, 1948).

FODOR, P. 'An Anti-Semite Grand Vizier? The Crisis in Ottoman–Jewish Relations in 1589–1591 and its Consequences' in *In Quest of the Golden Apple: Imperial Ideology, Politics and Military Administration in the Ottoman Empire* (Istanbul, 2000d) 191–206.

—— 'Between Two Continental Wars: The Ottoman Naval Preparations in 1590–1592' in *In Quest of the Golden Apple: Imperial Ideology, Politics and Military Administration in the Ottoman Empire* (Istanbul, 2000a) 171–90.

—— 'The Organization of Defence in the Eastern Mediterranean (end of the 16th Century)' in *The Kapudan Pasha: His Office and His Domain* (Rethymnon, 2002) 87–94.

—— 'Ottoman Policy Towards Hungary, 1520–1541' in *In Quest of the Golden Apple: Imperial Ideology, Politics and Military Administration in the Ottoman Empire* (Istanbul, 2000b) 105–69.

—— 'Sultan, imperial Council, Grand Vizier: Changes in the Ottoman Ruling Elite and the Formation of the Grand Vizieral Telhis' in *In Quest of the Golden Apple: Imperial Ideology, Politics and Military Administration in the Ottoman Empire* (Istanbul, 2000c) 207–27.

FONSECA, C. D. (ed.) *Otranto 1480: atti del Convegno internazionale di studio promosso in occasione del 5°centenario della caduta di Otranto ad opera dei turchi. Otranto, 19–23 maggio 1980* (Galatina, 1986).

FONTENAY, M. 'Chiourmes turques au XVIIe siècle' in R. Ragosta (ed.) *Le genti del mare Mediterraneo*, 2 vols. (Naples, 1981) 877–903.

FRATTARELLI-FISCHER, L. 'Il bagno delle galere in 'terra cristiana'. Schiavi a Livorno fra Cinque e Seicento', *Nuovi Studi Livornesi*, 8 (2000) 69–94.

FRIEDA, L. *Catherine de Medici* (London, 2003).

FRIEDMAN, E. 'Christian Captives and "Hard Labor" in Algiers, 16th–18th Centuries', *The International Journal of African Historical Studies*, 13 (1980) 616–32.

GACHARD, L. P. *Don Carlos et Philippe II*, 2 vols. (Brussels, 1863).

GARCÍA HERNÁN, D., GARCÍA HERNÁN, E. *Lepanto: el día después* (Madrid, 1999).

GARDINER, R. (ed.), *The Age of the Galley: Mediterranean Oared Vessels Since Pre-classical Times* (London, 1995).

GARGIULO, R. *La battaglia di Lepanto* (Pordenone, 2004)

GATTI, L. *Navi e cantieri della Repubblica di Genova (secoli XVI–XVIII)* (Genoa, 1999).

GATTONI, M. 'La spada della croce: la difficile alleanza ispano-veneto-pontificia nella Guerra di Cipro. Politica estera e teoremi filosofica nei documenti pontifici', *Ricerche Storiche*, 29 (3) 1999 611–50.

GOFFMAN, D. *The Ottoman Empire and Early Modern Europe* (Cambridge, 2002).

GÓMEZ-CÉNTURION, C. *Felipe II, la empresa de Inglaterra y el comercio septentrional 1566–1609* (Madrid, 1988).

GOODMAN, D. C. *Spanish naval power, 1589–1665: reconstruction and defeat* (Cambridge & New York, 1997).

GOUWENS, K., REISS, S. (eds.) *The Pontificate of Clement VII: History, Politics and Culture*, 2 vols. (London, 2005).

GRENTE, G. *San Pio 5, 1504–1572* (Alba, 1932).

GUARNIERI, G. *I Cavalieri di Santo Stefano* (Pisa, 1960).

—— *L'Ordine di Santo Stefano nei suoi aspetti organizzativi tecnici-navali sotto il gran magistero mediceo*, vol. I (Pisa, 1965).

GUGLIELMOTTI, A. *Marcantonio Colonna alla battaglia di Lepanto, 1570–1573* (Florence, 1887).

GUILMARTIN, J. F. *Gunpowder and Galleys: Changing Technology and Mediterranean Warfare at Sea in the 16th Century* (London, 2003).

—— 'The Logistics of Warfare at Sea in the Sixteenth century: The Spanish Perspective' in J. A. LYNN (ed.) *Feeding Mars: Logistics in Western Warfare from the Middle Ages to the Present* (Boulder, 1993) 109–37.

GULLINO, G. 'Duodo, Francesco' in *DBI*, XLII (Rome, 1993): 30–2.

—— *Le frontiere navali* in *Storia di Venezia. Dalle origini alla caduta della Serenissima*, vol. IV, *Il Rinascimento. Politica e cultura* (Rome 1996) 13–111.

HALE, J. R. 'Men and Weapons: The Fighting Potential of Sixteenth Century Venetian Galleys', in J. R. Hale (ed.) *Renaissance War Studies* (London, 1983) 309–32.

—— *L'organizzazione militare di Venezia nel '500* (Rome, 1990).

HALICZER, S. *The Comuneros of Castile: The Forging of a Revolution 1475–1525* (Madison, 1981).

HALL, B. S. *Weapons and Warfare in Renaissance Europe: Gunpowder, Technology and Tactics* (Baltimore, 2002).

HAMMER, J. V. *Histoire de l'empire ottoman, depuis son origine jusqu'à nos jours*, vol. 6 (Istanbul, 1999).

HESS, A. C. 'The battle of Lepanto and its Place in Mediterranean History', *Past and Present*, 57 (1972): 53–73.

—— 'The Evolution of the Ottoman Seaborne Empire in the Age of Discovery', *American Historical Review*, 75, 7 (1970) 1892–1919.

—— *The Forgotten Frontier: A History of the Sixteenth Century Ibero-African Frontier* (Chicago, 1978).

—— 'The Moriscos: an Ottoman Fifth Column in Sixteenth-Century Spain', *American Historical Review*, 74 (1968) 1–25.

—— 'The Ottoman Conquest of Egypt (1517) and the Beginning of the Sixteenth Century World War', *International Journal of Middle East Studies*, 4, 1 (1973) 55–76.

HILL, G. *A History of Cyprus. Volume III: The Frankish Period, 1432–1571* (Cambridge, 1972).

IBÁÑEZ DE IBERO, C. *Santa Cruz, primer marino de España* (Madrid, 1946).

IMBER, C. 'Four letters of Ebu's-su'ud', *Arab Historical Review for Ottoman Studies*, 15–16 (1997) 177–83.

—— 'The Navy of Süleyman the Magnificent' in *Studies in Ottoman History and Law* (Istanbul, 1996a) 1–69.

—— *The Ottoman Empire, 1300–1650. The Structure of Power* (Basingstoke & New York, 2002).

—— 'The Reconstruction of the Ottoman Fleet after the Battle of Lepanto' in *Studies in Ottoman History and Law* (Istanbul, 1996b) 85–101.

—— '"Involuntary" Annulment of Marriage and its Solutions in Ottoman Law' *Studies in Ottoman History and Law* (Istanbul, 1996c) 217–51.

INALCIK, H. 'Lepanto in the Ottoman Documents' in G. BENZONI (ed.) *Il Mediterraneo nella seconda metà del '500 alla luce di Lepanto* (Florence: L. S. Olschki, 1974) 185–92.

—— 'Mehmed the Conqueror and His Time', *Speculum*, 35, 3 (1960) 408–27.

—— *The Ottoman Empire. The Classical Age, 1300–1600* (London, 2003).

—— 'The Question of the Emergence of the Ottoman State', *International Journal of Turkish Studies* 2 (1980) 71–9.

INALCIK, H., QUATAERT, D. (eds.) *An Economic and Social History of the Ottoman Empire*, 2 vols. (Cambridge, 1997).

İPŞİRLİ, M. 'Observations on the Ottoman Secret Service during World War I (organization and activities)' in *Military Conflicts and 20th Century Geopolitics* (Athens, 2002) 471–4.

JEDIN, H. *A History of the Council of Trent*, 2 vols. (London, 1957–61).

JURIEN DE LA GRAVIÈRE, J. P. E. *La guerre de Chypre et la bataille de Lépante*, 2 vols. (Paris, 1888).

KÁLDY-NAGY, G. 'The First Centuries of the Ottoman Military Organization', *Acta Orientalia Academiae Scientiarum Hungaricae*, 31 (1977) 147–83.

—— *Szulejmán* (Budapest, 1974).

KAMEN, H. A. F. *Philip of Spain* (New Haven, 1997).

KHADDURI, M. 'Harb. I – legal aspects', *EI²*, vol. III (Leiden, 1971) 180–1.

KHALILIEH, H. S. *Islamic Maritime Law: An Introduction* (Leiden-Boston-Cologne 1998).

KRAMERS, J. H. 'Mustafa Pasha, Lala', *EI²*, vol. VII (Leiden, 1991) 720–1.

LABIB, S. 'The Era of Suleyman the Magnificent: Crisis of Orientation', *International Journal of Middle East Studies*, 10, 4 (1979) 435–51.

LANE, F. C. *Venetian ships and shipbuilders of the Renaissance* (Baltimore, 1992).

LE TOURNEAU, R., ORHANLU, C. 'Hasan Pasha', *EI²*, vol. III (Leiden, 1971) 251–2.

LITTA, P. *Orsini di Roma* (Turin, 1847–8).

LO BASSO, L. *Uomini da remo: galee e galeotti del Mediterraneo in età moderna* (Milan, 2004).

MACCHI, M. *Storia del Consiglio dei Dieci*, 9 vols. (Milan, 1864).

MAFRICI, M. *Mezzogiorno e pirateria nell'età moderna, secoli XVI–XVIII* (Naples, 1995).

MALLETT, M. E. *The Florentine Galleys in the Fifteenth Century: With the diary of Luca di Maso degli Albizzi, Captain of the Galleys, 1429–1430* (Oxford, 1967).

MANFRONI, C. 'La Lega cristiana del 1572', *Archivio della Reale Società romana di storia patria*, 16 (1893) 412–32; 17 (1894) 38–54.

—— 'Le relazioni fra Genova, l'Impero Bizantino e i Turchi', *Atti della Società Ligure di Storia Patria*, XXVIII, 3 (1898) 577–858

—— *Storia della Marina italiana, dalla caduta di Costantinopoli alla Battaglia di Lepanto* (Turin, 1897).

MANTRAN, R. 'L'écho de la bataille de Lépante à Constantinople', in G. BENZONI (ed.) *Il Mediterraneo nella seconda metà del '500 alla luce di Lepanto* (Florence: L. S. Olschki, 1974): 243–56.

—— *L'Empire ottoman du XVIe au XVIIIe siècle: administration, économie, société* (London, 1984).

MANUEL, J., BLECUA, A. (eds.) *Cervantes y Lepanto* (Barcelona, 1971).

MANUELE, P. *Il Piemonte sul mare. La Marina sabauda dal Medioevo all'unità d'Italia* (Cuneo, 1997).

MARRARA, D., ROSSI, C. 'Lo stato di Siena tra Impero, Spagnae Principato Mediceo (1554–1560): questioni giuridiche e istituzionali' in D. MARRARA (ed.) *Toscana e Spagna nell'età moderna e contemporanea* (Pisa, 1998) 5–53.

MASALA, A. *La banda militare ottomana (Mehter), con l'aggiunta di testi musicali e di uno studio di Cinucen Tanrikorur sulla musica classica ottomana* (Rome, 1978).

MATUZ, J. *Das Osmanische Reich: Grundlinien seiner Geschichte* (Darmstadt, 1985).

MÉNAGE, V. L. 'Devshirme', *EI²*, vol. II (Leiden, 1965) 210–13.

—— 'Sidelights on the *Devshirme* from Idris and Sa'duddin', *Bulletin of the School of Oriental and African Studies* (1956) 181–3.

—— 'Some Notes on the *Devshirme*', *Bulletin of the School of Oriental and African Studies*, 29 (1966) 64–78.

MEREDITH-OWENS, G. M. 'Traces of a Lost Autobiographical Work by a Courtier of Selim II', *Bulletin of the School of Oriental and African Studies*, 23 (3) 1960 456–63.

MILLER, W. *The Latins in the Levant: a history of Frankish Greece, 1204–1566* (New York, 1979).

MOLMENTI, P. *Sebastiano Veniero dopo la battaglia di Lepanto* (Venice, 1915).

—— *Sebastiano Veniero e la battaglia di Lepanto* (Florence, 1899).

MORI UBALDINI, U. *La marina del Sovrano militare ordine di San Giovanni di Gerusalemme, di Rodi e di Malta* (Rome, 1971).

MORIN, M. 'La battaglia di Lepanto: alcuni aspetti della tecnologia navale veneziana' in M. SBALCHIERO (ed.) *Meditando sull'evento di Lepanto. Odierne interpretazioni e memorie* (Venice, 2002) 69–77.

—— 'La battaglia di Lepanto' in *Venezia e i Turchi: scontri e confronti di due cività* (Milan, 1985) 210–31.

MULCAHY, R. 'To celebrate, or not to celebrate: Philip II and representations of the Battle of Lepanto', paper presented at the Renaissance Society of America annual conference, Cambridge, 7–9 April 2005.

MURPHEY, R. *Ottoman warfare, 1500–1700* (New Brunswick, 1999).

MUSCAT, P. B. J. *Food and Drink on Maltese Galleys* (Valletta, 2002).

NANI MOCENIGO, M. *Storia della Marina veneziana, da Lepanto alla caduta della Repubblica* (Rome, 1935).

NEGYESI, L. 'A Mohacsi Csata', *Hadtortenelmi Kozlemenyek*, 107, 4 (1994) 62–79.

OLESA MUÑIDO, F. F. *La organización naval de los estados mediterráneos y en especial de España durante los siglos XVI y XVII*, 2 vols. (Madrid, 1968).

ORESTE, G. 'Genova e Andrea Doria nella fase critica del conflitto francoasburgico', *Atti della Società Ligure di Storia Patria*, LXXII, 3 (1950) 2–71.

ÖZBARAN, S. 'Kapudan Pasha', *EI²*, IV (Leiden, 1978) 571–2.

— *The Ottoman Response to European Expansion: Studies on Ottoman – Portuguese Relations in the Indian Ocean and Ottoman Administration of the Arab Lands during the Sixteenth Century* (Istanbul, 1994).

PAOLETTI, C. *Gli italiani in armi: cinque secoli di storia militare, 1494–2000* (Rome, 2001).

PARKER, G. *The Army of Flanders and the Spanish Road, 1567–1659* (Cambridge, 1990).

— *The Dutch Revolt* (London, 1977).

— *The Grand Strategy of Philip II* (New Haven & London, 1998).

— *The Military Revolution: Military Innovation and the Rise of the West, 1500–1800* (Cambridge, 1996).

PARKER, G., THOMPSON, I. A. 'Lepanto (1571): The Cost of Victory', *The Mariner's Mirror*, 64 (1978) 13–21.

PASERO, C. *La partecipazione bresciana alla guerra di Cipro e alla battaglia di Lepanto: 1570–1573* (Brescia, 1954).

PASOLINI, G. *Adriano VI* (Rome, 1913).

PEDANI, M. P. 'Tra economia e geo-politica: la visione ottomana della Guerra di Cipro', *Annuario dell'Istituto Rumeno di Cultura e Ricerca Umanistica di Venezia*, 5 (2003) 287–97.

PEDROSA, F. G. 'A artilharia naval portuguesa no século XVI', in *A Guerra e o Encontro de Civilizações a partir do Século XVI* (Lisbon, 1999).

PELLEGRINI, A. DE, *Di due turchi schiavi del conte Silvio di Porcia e Brugnera dopo la battaglia di Lepanto* (Venice, 1921).

PERJÉS, G. *The Fall of the Medieval Kingdom of Hungary: Mohács 1526–Buda 1541*, M. D. Fenyö (trans.) in *War and Society in East Central Europe*, vol. 26 (1989).

PEPPER, S. 'Fortress and Fleet: The Defence of Venice's Mainland Greek Colonies in the Late Fifteenth Century' in D. S. CHAMBERS, C. H. CLOUGH, M. E. MALLETT (eds.) *War, Culture and Society in Renaissance Venice. Essays in Honour of John Hale* (London, Rio Grande, Ohio, 1993) 30–55.

PERTUSI, A. *La caduta di Costantinopoli*, 2 vols. (Milan, 1976).

PETRIE, C. *Don Juan of Austria* (New York, 1963).

PICCINNO, L. 'I rapporti commerciali tra Genova e il Nord Africa in età moderna: il caso di Tabarca', *Quaderni di ricerca della Facoltà di Economia dell'Università degli Studi dell'Insubria*, 15 (2003) 1–21.

PIERACCINI, G. *La stirpe de' Medici di Cafaggiolo. Saggio di ricerche sulla trasmissione ereditaria dei caratteri biologici*, vol. II (Florence, 1986).

PIERI, P. *Il Rinascimento e la crisi militare italiana* (Turin, 1952).

PIERSON, P. 'Lepanto', *MHQ: The Quarterly Journal of Military History*, 9 (1997) 6–19.

PILONI, G. *I bellunesi a Lepanto. Episodi tratti dalle storie inedite* (Belluno, 1892).

PRESCOTT, W. H. *History of the Reign of Philip the Second, King of Spain*, 3 vols. (Boston, 1855–58).

PRETO, P. 'La guerra segreta: spionaggio, sabotaggi, attentati', in M. REDOLFI (ed). *Venezia e la difesa del Levante. Da Lepanto a Candia: 1570–1670* (Venice, 1986) 79–85.

—— *Venezia e i Turchi* (Florence, 1975).

—— 'Venezia, i Turchi e la guerra di Cipro', in M. SBALCHIERO (ed.) *Meditando sull'evento di Lepanto. Odierne interpretazioni e memorie* (Venice, 2002).

PRYOR, J. H. *Geography, Technology and War. Studies in the Maritime History of the Mediterranean* (Cambridge, 1992).

QUARTI, G. A. *La guerra contro il turco in Cipro e a Lepanto 1570–1571: storia documentata* (Venice, 1935).

RANKE, L. V. *The Ottoman and the Spanish empires in the sixteenth and seventeenth centuries*, W. K. KELLY (trans.) (New York, 1975).

'R. C.' 'Sull'impiego economico delle nostre navi da guerra', *Rivista marittima*, 8 (9) (1875) 238–9.

REDOLFI, M. (ed.) *Venezia e la difesa del Levante: da Lepanto a Candia 1570–1670* (Venice,1986).

REFIK, A. 'Kıbrıs seferine aid resmi vesikalar', *Istanbul Universitesi Darül-fünun Edebiyat Fakültesi Mecmuası*, 5 (1927): 29–75.

REPP, R. C. 'A Further Note on the *Devshirme*', *Bulletin of the School of Oriental and African Studies*, 31 (1968): 137–9.

RIDOLFI, R. *Vita di Girolamo Savonarola* (Florence, 1997).

RODGERS, W. L. *Naval warfare under oars: 4th to 16th centuries: a study of strategy, tactics and ship design* (Annapolis, 1967).

ROMBAI, L. (ed.) *I Medici e lo Stato Senese, 1555–1609. Storia e territorio* (Rome, 1980).

ROMER, C. 'A Firman of Suleyman the Magnificent to the King of France preserved in an exercise book of the "K. K. Academie Orientalischer Sprachen" in Vienna, 1831', *Turcica*, 31 (1999) 461–70.

ROSELL, C. *Historia del combate naval de Lepanto y Juicio de la Importancia y Consecuencias de aquel suceso* (Madrid, 1853).

ROSI, M. 'Alcuni documenti relativi alla liberazione dei principali prigionieri turchi presi a Lepanto', *Archivio della Reale Società Romana di storia patria*, 21 (1898) 141–220.

— 'Nuovi documenti relativi alla liberazione dei principali prigionieri turchi presi a Lepanto', *Archivio della Reale Società Romana di storia patria*, 24 (1901) 5–47.

ROSSI, E. 'La leggenda turco-bizantina del pomo rosso', *Studi bizantini e neo-ellenici*, 5 (1939) 542–53.

ROSSI, E., ALBERANI, M., FELLER, A. M. *Le galee: storia, tecnica, documenti* (Trento, 1990).

RUNCIMAN, S. *A History of the Crusades: Volume 3, The Kingdom of Acre and the Later Crusades* (Cambridge, 1987).

SAFVET, A. 'Sıngın donanma harbi üzerine bazi vesikalar', *Tarih-i Osmani Encümeni Mecmuası*, 2 (1926–27) 558–62.

SALIMEI, A. *Gli italiani a Lepanto: 7 ottobre 1571* (Rome, 1931).

SALVO, U. *Alpignano e Andrea Provana: le straordinarie imprese del conte di Alpignano il grande ammiraglio Andrea Provana nel quarto centenario della sua morte 1592–1992* (Susa, 1992).

SANTILLANA, D. *Istituzioni di diritto musulmano malichita con riguardo anche al sistema sciafiita*, 2 vols (Rome, 1926–38).

SAVELLI, R. 'Doria, Giovanni Andrea' in *DBI*, XLI (Rome, 1992) 361–75.

SCARSELLA, A. (ed.) *Quixote/Chisciotte, MDVC-2005* (Venice, 2005).

SCHLÜTTER-SCHINDLER, G. *Der Schmalkaldische Bund und das Problem der causa religionis* (Frankfurt-am-Main & New York, 1986).

SCICHILONE, G. 'Cardona, Giovanni', in *DBI*, XIX (Rome, 1976) 792–6.

SEGRE, A. 'La Marina Militare Sabauda ai tempi di Emanuele Filiberto e l'opera politico-navale di Andrea Provana di Leyni' in *Memorie della Reale Accademia delle Scienze di Torino*, second series XLVIII (Turin, 1899).

SETTON, K. The Papacy and the Levant, 1204–1571, vols. III, IV (Philadelphia, 1984).

SHAW, S. *Between Old and New: The Ottoman Empire under Sultan Selim III, 1789–1807* (Cambridge, Massachusetts, 1971).

SIRE, H. J. A. *The Knights of Malta* (New Haven, 1994).

SOUCECK, S. 'Ulûdj 'Alî', in *EI²*, vol. X (Leiden, 1998) 810–11.

STANLEY, T. 'Men-at-arms, hauberks and bards: military obligations in The Book of Ottoman Custom' in Ç. BALIM-HARDING, C. IMBER *The Balance of Truth: Essays in Honour of Professor Geoffrey Lewis* (Istanbul, 2000) 331–63.

STELLA, A. 'Barbarigo, Agostino', in *DBI*, VI (Rome, 1964) 49–52.

—— 'Gian Andrea Doria e la Sacra Lega prima della battaglia di Lepanto', *Rivista di Storia della Chiesa in Italia*, 19 (1965) 5–29.

STIRLING-MAXWELL, W. *Don John of Austria, or Passages from the History of the Sixteenth Century, 1547–1578*, 2 vols. (London, 1883).

TAMBORRA, A. *Gli stati italiani, l'Europa e il problema turco dopo Lepanto* (Florence, 1961).

TEKINDAĞ, Ş. 'Şah Kulu Baba teseli ispani', *Belgelerle Türk Tarih Derisi*, 3 (1967) 34–9; 4 (1967) 54–9.

TEMIMI, A. 'Le gouvernement Ottoman face au problème morisque' in *Les Morisques et leur temps, U.E.R. des Langues, Littératures et des Civilisations de la Méditerranée (4–7 juillet 1981)* (Paris, 1983) 297–311.

TENENTI, A. 'La Francia, Venezia e la Sacra Lega' in G. BENZONI (ed.) *Il Mediterraneo nella seconda metà del '500 alla luce di Lepanto* (Florence, 1974) 393–408.

TESTA, C. *Romegas* (Sta Venera, 2002).

TOGNARINI, I. 'La guerra di Maremma' in L. ROMBAI (ed.) *I Medici e lo Stato Senese, 1555–1609. Storia e territorio* (Rome, 1980) 23–34.

TUCCI, U. 'Il processo a Girolamo Zane, mancato difensore di Cipro' in G. BENZONI (ed.) *Il Mediterraneo nella seconda metà del '500 alla luce di Lepanto* (Florence, 1974) 409–33.

TURAN, Ş. *Türkiye-Italya ilişkileri, I Selçuklular'dan Bizans'ın sona erişine* (Istanbul, 1990).

TYAN, E. 'Djihad', *EI²*, vol. II (Leiden, 1965) 538–40.

UZUNÇARSILI, I. H. *Acemi ocagi ve Yeniçeri ocagi* (Ankara, 1984).

—— *Izahlı Osmanlı tarihi kronolojisi*, vol. 5 (Istanbul, 1975).

—— 'Kıbrıs Fethi ile Lepant (İnebahtı) muharebesi sırasında Türk Devletiile Venedik ve Müttefiklerinin Faaliyetine dair bazı Hezine-i Evrak Kayıtları', *Türkiyat Mecmuası*, 3 (1935) 257–92.

UZUNÇARŞILI, I. H., KARAL, E. Z. *Osmanli Tarihi*, 9 vols. (Ankara, 1947–73).

VEROGGIO, B. *Giannandrea Doria alla battaglia di Lepanto* (Genoa, 1886).

VINCENT, B. 'L'expulsion des morisques du royaume de Grenade et leur répartition en Castille (1570–1571)', *Mélanges de la Casa de Velázquez*, 6 (1970) 211–46.

VIOLA, O. *Il governo delle galere e la guerra di corsa sulle coste di Barberia nel secolo XVI illustrati da un ms. della Biblioteca civica di Catania* (Catania, 1949).

WANDRUSZKA, A. 'L'Impero, la casa d'Austria e la Sacra Lega' in G. BENZONI (ed.) *Il Mediterraneo nella seconda metà del '500 alla luce di Lepanto* (Florence, 1974): 435–43.

WITTEK, P. '*Devshirme* and *Shari'a*', *Bulletin of the School of Oriental and African Studies*, 17 (1954) 271–8.

WOODHEAD, C. 'Selim II', *EI²*, vol. IX (Leiden, 1995) 131–2.

INDEX

~

For reasons of space the index has been limited to people, places or events of importance. For clarity, Ottoman names have been indexed with their given name first, instead of last. For instance: Sokollu Mehmed Pasha, instead of the more correct Mehmed Pasha, Sokollu.

PICTURE CREDITS

~

Section 1. *Devirme*: Topkapi Library, Istanbul; *Lala Mustafa*: Topkapi Library, Istanbul; *Sultan Süleyman*: from J. SCHRENCK, *Augustissimorum imperatorum* . . . (Innsbruck, 1601); *Sultan Selim II*: Topkapi Library, Istanbul; *Pius V*: copy after El Greco, private collection; *Grand Vizier Sokollu Mehmet Pasha*: from J. SCHRENCK, *Augustissimorum imperatorum* . . . (Innsbruck, 1601); *Cardinal Granvelle*: print by Martin Rota, 1543; *Marcantonio Colonna*: anonymous print, 1569; *Giovanni Andrea Doria*: from D. CUSTOS, *Atrium heroicum Caesarum* . . . (Augsburg, 1600–02); *Cosimo I de' Medici*: from A. MANNUCCI, *Vita di Cosimo I de' Medici* . . . (Bologna, 1586); *Don Juan of Austria*: from J. SCHRENCK, *Augustissimorum imperatorum* . . . (Innsbruck, 1601); *Sebastiano Venier*: print by Cesare Vecellio, 1572; *Francesco Duodo*: from J. SCHRENCK, *Augustissimorum imperatorum* . . . (Innsbruck, 1601); *Uluç Ali Pasha*: print by G. Guzzi, 19th century; *Marcantonio Bragadin*: from G. HILL, *A History of Cyprus*, vol. III (Cambridge, 1948); *Müezzinzâde Ali Pasha*: print by Martin Weigel, c. 1572; *Álvaro de Bazan*: painting by Rafael Tejeo (1528), from an anonymous portrait; Museo Naval, Madrid; *Sultana*: after a print by Melchior Lorch (1572); *galleass*: drawing by Ignazio Fabbroni, Biblioteca Nazionale Centrale, Florence.
Section 2. *centreline cannon*: Museo Storico Navale, Venice; photo by M. Morin. *swivel gun*: Museo Storico Navale, Venice; photo by M. Morin; *League's soldiers*: illustration by Bruno Mugnai (2006); *Ottoman soldiers*: illustration by Bruno Mugnai; *Rowers*: drawing by Ignazio Fabbroni, Biblioteca Nazionale Centrale, Florence; *Venetian scapolo*: from C. VECELLIO, *Degli habiti antichi et moderni* (Venice, 1598); *Banner*: from a contemporary pamphlet, 1571; *sketch*: from a contemporary pamphlet, 1571. *Better view*: anonymous print, 1571; *Barrage*: anonymous print, 1571; *melee*: print by Jacques Callott, c. 1615; *High noon*: arras, Palazzo de Principe, Genoa; copyright Arti Doria Pamphilj s.r.l; *Sadness in victory*: Fresco, Villa Barbarigo, Comune di Noventa Vicentina; photo by M. Morin. *Privilege of holiness*: painting by Lazzaro Baldi (1673), Collegio Ghislieri, Pavia; photo by M. Morin; *Half-hearted celebration*: painting by Titian (1572–75), Museo del Prado, Madrid; *Francesco Maria della Rovere*: painting by Federico Barocci (1572); Galleria degli Uffizi, Florence; *Ottoman standard*: Church of Santo Stefano, Pisa; *Breaking the news*: from a contemporary pamphlet, 1571.

Virgin

by

Pam Keevil

Virgin At Fifty

First published in October 2017 by Black Pear Press
www.blackpear.net

ISBN 978-1-913418-51-9

Cover design by Black Pear Press

Black Pear Press

Dedication

This book is dedicated to anyone who has ever wanted to forge a new life.

Chapter One

Angie Jarvis, age forty-nine and three-quarters, teetered on the edge of the kerb, her heels planted firmly on the pavement, her toes in free fall. She looked right, left and right again. The road was clear. Her feet refused to move. How could starting a new life be so hard?

'It's just a street,' she whispered under her breath. It was more than that. On this side, safe in the shadows, was Sister Ruth, former nun, former dutiful daughter. On the other side, appropriately the sunny side, was a doorway to a new life.

'Don't be melodramatic,' her inner voice said. 'It's a coffee bar and you are meeting someone you knew at school. People do that all the time.'

'People do, virgin nuns don't.'

'Shut up the pair of you' said a third voice; 'I'm Angie, the new me and I don't plan on remaining a virgin for much longer. Enough with the voices, I'm not crazy. I've sold my dad's old house and bought a bungalow, I've torn up my habit, I can cross a bloody road when I want to.' And swear too. She smiled. That might come in very useful one day.

Angie took a deep breath and stepped across the empty road, into the sunlight heading for the newest café in town. Ironically, it stood on the site of the shop where she used to gaze longingly at the toys with her Christmas or birthday money clutched in her hand. Of course, her parents always made her buy a book or something educationally useful. In the window she could see piles of brightly coloured cakes that had replaced the toys and even in the street the

1

aroma of chocolate and homemade soup made her mouth water.

It was inviting, but she was about to meet the first old friend that had replied to her post on the school Facebook page, Maggie Henderson. She'd been the queen bitch of her year group. Her sole interest, apart from fags and boys, was making kids' lives a misery, unless they were in her gang. Why did it have to be her?

It was a long time ago. Surely they'd both changed and besides, it was only for a coffee. She had earned some time off. She checked herself. Did it have to be earned? She'd taken enormous piles of rubbish to the dump, cleared and sold the old house. She deserved a break and a new life had to start somewhere. Was Maggie the same girl who used to emerge from behind the bike shelter each lunchtime in the arms of a different boy, hurriedly pulling down her skirt or tucking in her school blouse?

I'm a twice-married and now a very single mum of three kids. Ellie, the eldest followed in my footsteps and is a nurse in the States. The younger two, Tasha and Gareth, live at home. Tasha is at college and Gareth is copying my dreadful record at school and doing as little work as he can get away with.

It was impossible to read between the lines of that message, maybe she'd changed, maybe not. Wasn't she allowed a little curiosity? Ugh, there it was again, "allowed". Angela Jarvis might need permission, Angie can think for herself. She straightened up, opened the door and smelt the full bouquet of coffee and cake. She paused to savour the mix of chocolate,

2

almonds, sugar and warm milk and to get her bearings. There are worse ways into a new life.

Sitting in the corner was a plump woman with rich red hair. This had to be her. It was definitely not the teenage couple in the corner or the old gentleman reading the paper. The Maggie she'd known had mouse-brown hair and was slim. People change. Or she hoped they did as all her old teenage anxieties of being picked on—or, worse, being left out—came back. Angie walked over to the table. 'Maggie?'

The woman looked up. The hairstyle can change, the face adapts to ever increasing years whereas the eyes remain the same. Even though they were no longer caked in mascara and black eyeliner, they were unmistakeable. They had always reminded Angie of cat's eyes, hazel flecked with gold. Except instead of being cold, they were just wary. A flicker of a frown crossed her face before it was replaced by a broad smile of recognition. She stood up. 'Angela Jarvis? Is it really you?'

For a split second, there was silence as each took in the appearance of the other. Maggie was smaller than Angie had remembered and her red hair showed brownish grey roots that said the colour was the product of a bottle rather than nature. Although she was plump, she was dressed in a plain black jacket and trousers with a red sweater and a grey scarf knotted in a manner that Angie envied.

'Yes. It's me, *Angie* Jarvis.'

Maggie pulled out a chair for Angie to sit down. 'Let me get these. What do you want?'

'Just white coffee, please.'

'One regular Americano with milk and one medium cappuccino, double shot,' Maggie called out.

3

Angie must have looked confused because Maggie added. 'I suppose as a nun you didn't get out much?'

'How did you know?' Angie fought to control the waver in her voice. Maggie was nothing if not direct and it was unnerving.

'I've got a long memory. It was the talk of the town at the time.'

There was a pause and Maggie shifted in her chair as they waited for the coffee. Angie folded and unfolded her arms, crossed and uncrossed her legs and tried to look interested in the coffee machine as it hissed in the corner. This had all been a mistake. She should have stayed at home, polished the front door, done anything except allow herself to come under the scrutiny of Maggie's gaze. 'Ta, love, over here,' Maggie called out to a slender girl in black trousers and a large white apron who deposited a huge bowl in front of Angie and an even larger bowl of white froth in front of Maggie.

'Do you want to order lunch?' The girl offered them card menus. At least this would give them something to do before they had to think of a new topic of conversation. Angie seized one and studied it.

'I can recommend the ciabatta with goat's cheese, rocket and red onion marmalade.' Maggie was turning the menu over and studying every offering.

Angie tried not to pull a face again, she was totally out of her depth. Maggie must have realised as she leaned forward and whispered, 'Think of it as a posh cheese sarnie with a bit of greenery and pickle and heaps better than what we had at school.' She smiled. 'Do you remember the caramel pie that stuck to the spoon?'

'Or the coconut custard?' Angie said.

'We used to call it toenail soup.'

'What about chocolate concrete, that cake stuff that nearly broke your teeth?'

'And the stew where you had to send out a search party to find any meat?'

They both giggled. The spell was broken. 'I used to reckon if you could put up with school dinners, you could put up with anything in life. If that's what you recommend, I'll be guided by you.' Angie sat back. Perhaps this wasn't going to be so bad after all.

'Two ciabattas, please.' Maggie called out and turned her attention back to Angie. 'Before you tell me anything there is one question I have to ask. Why did you leave? No, forget that question. Why the hell did you ever join the Holy Joes in the first place? A clever kid like you could have done anything? Not like me, thick as...you know.'

For a moment Angie was tempted to lie, she had a feeling that underneath all the bravura, Maggie could turn out to be a good friend so she wanted to be honest from the start. 'I had to get away. First from home and then from the convent. I thought it would be a serene place, full of love and God's protection. He let me down.' She stirred her coffee. It gave her hands something to do to stop them from trembling as memories surfaced of her last conversation with Sister Catherine who again denied she'd ever suspected their priest of any wrongdoing.

'I never had much interest in the God stuff—in my book it's people who let you down.' Maggie took a sip of the froth before she dabbed at the brown and white moustache that was deposited on her top lip. 'Why did you go there in the first place?'

5

Angie sighed. 'I'd always been more religious than the other girls in my year and when I was at college, there was a man.'

Maggie leaned forward, her eyes wide open, the cup poised half way to her lips. 'Yeah? Man trouble eh? Did he break your heart?'

'No. It was nothing like that.' Maggie's face fell. 'The chaplain at the college encouraged me.'

'Is that all he did?'

'With me, yes. Though not with some of the more nubile members of the student body. I seem to remember that he liked them with big breasts. I always thought that I could be a better role model than him and so joined.'

Maggie let out a long whistle. 'So what next?'

'I want to get my life back, or rather get a life,' Angie corrected herself. 'I've got a lot of living to do.' She took a deep breath. There was no going back. 'That includes meeting men.' Her cheeks felt like she'd accidentally rubbed chilli on them and she waited for the reaction. It came and it was not the one she had expected.

Maggie clapped her hands. 'Well, you've got some fun times ahead of you. Where do we start?'

Over the ciabattas, which Angie had to admit were like posh cheese sandwiches, Maggie revealed how she'd got pregnant in the last year of school, kept it quiet until she'd left and married the father. They divorced within two years. She'd married again and produced two more children. She was living on the same estate where she'd been brought up and now worked as a care assistant in the Crystal Hill Care Home. 'Today is my much-needed day off,' she said.

'A care assistant?' Angie remembered the

placement she'd been offered for her father in the last days of his illness and screwed up her face.

Maggie noticed. 'It's not like that.' She spoke briskly. 'We're a small family-run business and take a pride in what we do. We get to know our clients and what they like and never, ever stick them in front of the television unless we're all there and we watch as a family, like the Jubilee and the Olympics.' She stopped. 'Sorry. It's one of my bugbears. I don't think I could work anywhere else.'

'I wish my father had been offered a place with you.'

'We've got a waiting list as long as your arm,' Maggie said. 'Even so, money is very tight and I don't know how long we can keep going.' She stopped. 'I'm sorry, I'm hogging the conversation, as always. What about you?'

'After school I got a degree and qualified as a teacher. Most of my life's been spent as a nun. I quit for a while to nurse my dad, who soon died.' Maggie nodded sympathetically. Angie continued. 'Since then I've sold his house, bought a bungalow with a dishy neighbour and I've left the convent for good.' As Angie said the words, she realised they could never convey the enormity of what she had done and crossed her fingers Maggie would not press her for more details. She wouldn't know what to say.

Maggie's interest lay elsewhere. She leaned forward like a cat about to pounce. 'What's he like? Oh and by the way, *fit* is what the kids say today. Or *hot*, not dishy.'

'Oh my age, slim, greyish hair. He drives a very smart new car.' Angie hoped to put Maggie off. For some reason she didn't want to say anymore. She'd

7

been standing outside the bungalow with the estate agent when she'd spotted him. He had turned and looked at her. In that second, something had stirred deep inside, although she had no idea what it was.

'Is he single?'

'His wife died a few years ago.' Angie would forever be grateful that the estate agent had leaked information. It was good to know that Paul Buchannan, as she'd found out he was called, was proof that there was at least one attractive and unattached male in town.

'Way to go, kid.' Maggie paused. 'What happens next?'

'That's the problem. I'm so out of touch with modern life that I have no idea where to begin. Selling and buying houses sounds big, yet other people really do most of the work. The thought of shopping, especially for things like clothes or make-up, frightens me silly.'

'Shopping?' Maggie sat up, her eyes alight. 'You've come to the right person here. If you've got your car, we can go to the retail mall and I'll direct you to the places with the best bargains.'

'The retail what?'

'The cut-price designer outlet. No one pays full price nowadays. Check this.' And she showed Angie the label on her jacket. 'Fifty quid reduced from two hundred. These trousers, fifteen from ninety and...' she stretched out a foot encased in red leather pumps, '...twenty quid. Job lot, bought special. Eat up and we can get going. You'll get twice as much there as you will in any ordinary shop and it's good stuff.'

Angie looked at the way Maggie knotted her scarf and how she pushed up the sleeves of her jacket to reveal the slimmest part of the body. She had to admit, Maggie had a sense of style. She always did, even when she had to wear the regulation school uniform. She looked down at her baggy black trousers and the sweater that covered all the lumps and bumps of the female anatomy and hid her away from the eyes of the world. 'I can't...' She felt the air squeezing out of her body. Everything was happening too fast. 'I can't possibly take you away from your day off.' Angie relaxed. It was a good excuse.

'What about a time next week? I'm free on Thursday again? It'll give you chance to find out what you really want. Check out the latest trends, you know?'

'It's very kind of you but—'

'—but nothing.' Maggie leaned over and patted Angie's hand. 'It'll make a change to go shopping with someone and not have to foot the bill.'

The hand remained where it was, a touch of reassurance as if Maggie knew instinctively what Angie was feeling. With that, Angie got out her diary and circled the date. She could always back out later. After exchanging phone numbers, they parted and Angie watched as Maggie disappeared down the hill. With a sinking feeling she realised she didn't want to go back to an empty house. She'd spend a bit more time in the town and perhaps find a hairdresser. As she poked her nose into Cuts R Us, the sight of the skinny assistants in black and grey with their multicoloured or artfully piled up hair made her feel even more dowdy. She closed the door and scurried away.

By the time she got back to the car park, a light drizzle was falling. She climbed into the car and turned the ignition. It growled, wheezed and stopped. She did it again. There was a clunking sound as if something important had fallen off. She turned the engine again and again, as a mounting feeling of desperation and irritation rose in her. 'Stupid bloody car!' she yelled and yanked on the ignition key. The engine screamed its indignation.

A hand tapped on the window. 'Don't do that. It just sounds a bit damp to me.' She looked up into the face of a young man, a beanie hat pulled down over his head. Despite numerous piercings in his ear, and *Bryony* tattooed on his neck, he looked clean.

'Sorry. What did you say?' Angie wound down her window but stayed in the car. At least she could lock the doors and would be safe in case he started to behave strangely.

'Open the bonnet and I'll take a look at it,' the young man said. He stood up, noticed her reluctance and added, 'My grandad had an old Ford like this and they're always tricky in the damp.' Angie did not move. 'I'm training to be a mechanic,' he added as if to reassure her.

Angie stayed where she was and unlocked the bonnet. The young man fixed it in place before ducking his head inside the engine. He fiddled, twiddled and wiped something on a dirty rag he pulled out of his pocket. 'Try again,' he called. She turned the ignition. The engine sprang into life.

'How did you do that?' She got out and came to the front of the car and looked inside.

'It just needed a dry and a tweak.' He closed the bonnet with a bang. 'Good as new.' He turned to go.

'How can I repay you?' Angie asked. There was no reply. Her Good Samaritan was already heading off.

'Thanks anyway,' she called out to the departing figure. She raised her eyes to heaven and nodded her thanks before stopping. 'What the hell are you doing that for? Stupid, stupid, stupid,' she scolded herself. As she drove home though, she felt a twinge of gratitude that she'd found Maggie or Maggie had found her.

Chapter Two

As soon as Angie parked the car at the retail outlet, Maggie was ready for action, like a runner in the starting blocks. She'd dressed for the occasion too in jogging bottoms, a fleece and trainers. 'Lesson number one, never,' she grabbed Angie's arm and propelled her towards the revolving doors that were swallowing up the latest coach load of visitors, 'and I mean never, ever just wander about. You'll end up buying stuff you don't need.'

'You make it sound like a military campaign.' Angie puffed along at Maggie's side, relieved she'd worn flat shoes.

Maggie stopped abruptly and swerved to avoid a mother and grandmother with a buggy and two toddlers and turned to face Angie. 'That is exactly what it is. If you want a bargain, you have to plan. Come on, this way.'

She dived into a shop that announced discounts of seventy per cent. It wasn't long before Angie understood Maggie's method. Select your shop, go inside, check prices and leave. Repeat until you have done a complete circuit before you decide which garments you want to try.

Maggie marched them into a dress shop, ignoring Angie's pleas that all she needed were a few simple trousers and tops. 'Nonsense. Every woman above forty needs at least two good dresses that show off what she's got while she's got it.'

Rails of skirts, dresses and trousers hung on chains from the ceiling like a fabric rainbow. In the centre of the shop floor stands of neatly arranged sweaters in

12

sweet shop colours called out to be touched. Shoes and bags, carefully selected to tone with the outfits on display, further tempted the unwary shopper. Maggie, however was a match for any marketing expert who thought he or she knew how to prise even more hard-earned cash from already overstretched budgets. She strode past the assistants in their uniform of black dresses and selected two items from the rails. 'Try these for size,' she said and directed Angie to a cubicle of pale wood, bright white lights and purple velvet curtains. At least there were none of the communal changing rooms that had filled Angie with dread as a youngster. The lucky ones with stunning figures strutted whilst those with bulges or washboard thin chests cowered in corners and hid their eyes from the kaleidoscope of bums and boobs that the 360-degree mirrored walls provided.

'Put this on.' A hand thrust a red dress into the cubicle where Angie was struggling with a back zip on a pale blue creation. She held the dress up in the light. It had long sleeves and was made of stretch material that would hug every curve.

'I can't…isn't it going to be a bit…revealing?' she said, hoping Maggie was in earshot.

Maggie pulled back the curtain. 'Give us that blue thing. This is much better and yes, it will show off what you've got. Now get into it.' She watched as Angie slid the red dress on and smoothed it down over her bust and thighs. 'That is one helluva *fuck-me* dress,' she whistled. 'Although not if your tits droop. What bra are you wearing?'

'First what is a *fuck-me* dress and secondly what is wrong with my bra?' Angie folded her arms to hide the alleged drooping breasts.

'It's one that you'll only ever wear on a date that ends in the bedroom.' Maggie spoke slowly as if Angie was a small child. 'Tits need to stand up, not rest on your midriff. Shape wear, that's what you need. I reckon you're a medium.' And the curtains closed.

As she waited, Angie looked at the mirror and sucked in her stomach. Never mind the many bulges of flesh that might have been camouflaged by something more voluminous, it was the face staring back at her that demanded attention. The chin was pointed. The eyes were larger and had lost their dark shadows. There was a rosiness about the cheeks and the lips were parted in a slight smile. After years of ignoring her appearance, apart from checking if she was clean and presentable, the unfamiliar person staring at her was *attractive* if only in a homely sort of way. She tried to quell the excitement welling up inside her. She fiddled with her hair, smoothed down the dress and went on tiptoe to see what effect that would have. She turned this way and that to get a better view of the creature she'd become. Her reverie was cut short.

'Take your bra off and put this on.' Maggie handed over a tiny packet that contained a flesh-coloured top. It would have fitted Barbie.

'I can't get into this.' Angie dangled the offending object between her fingers.

'Yes you can. Strip off, pull it over your hips and bum and yank it up. Smooth the wobbly bits flat and make sure your tits are in the little pockets, not squashed. It works for me.'

Angie did as she was told. It was a strange sensation, like being encased in an elastic second skin

14

that held everything in place even though some flesh did have a life of its own and tried to fight back. With a bit of pushing and poking, she inched the garment into position. Angie stood back to check her image. Somehow she looked smoother and the unwanted lumps and bumps had been tamed. She pulled the dress over the top. 'Wow.'

Angie gazed at the figure in the mirror. The red dress shimmered in the light and reflected on her cheeks, which glowed. The breasts were firm and stood out. The hips were voluptuous rather than podgy and even her stomach was flatter. She looked down. She'd got legs. The dress hovered just above the knee, revealing calves that were slim and firm after years of taking PE lessons in all weathers. She would have to do something about the covering of hair. That was a minor problem. Only a few weeks ago her body had been shrouded. Now, released from its prison it was rewarding her in ways she'd not thought possible. She was at least halfway to looking a quarter decent.

Maggie drew back the curtains. 'Bloody hell, Ange. If that doesn't get the men queuing up with their tongues lolling out, nothing will.'

'Really?' Angie looked again at the image in the mirror as the taunts of her youth floated back. 'Nobody will ever snog frumpy Jarvis.' Perhaps if she'd looked like this it might have been different. Did she want men to think she was attractive and dare she say it, sexy? She paused. 'Yes I bloody well do,' she said under her breath and stopped. She glanced at Maggie who was gazing at her legs and so lost in her own train of thought she couldn't have heard. Angie pretended to clear her throat.

15

'You'll need to get your legs waxed and find some decent heels.' The hairy calves had not gone unnoticed by Maggie's sharp eyes. 'Get changed and we'll pay up. I spotted a great place in the South Mall for shoes.' The curtains closed. Angie peered down at her legs again. Waxing hurt and it would cost a fortune. She made a mental note to see if she'd got any of her father's razors. That would do for a start.

Shoes, jackets and bags followed in the shopping frenzy and it was gone four o'clock when they drew up outside the house where Maggie lived. It was a 1950s council house on an estate where there was a noticeable demarcation between those with a neat lawn, tidy hedges and fresh paintwork and others that were in need of some care and attention. Maggie's was one of the latter. As she pulled up in the driveway behind a battered estate car, Angie turned to Maggie. 'Today has been great. Thank you so much.'

'My pleasure. Like I said, I always enjoy spending someone else's money. The next thing we need to sort out is your hair.'

Angie ran a hand through her curls which after years of the shortest cuts possible were growing at a remarkable rate. She shook her head. 'I popped into a salon but I didn't know what to ask for and I—'

'My daughter's doing a hair and beauty course at the local college. She'll help you decide on a cut and a colour and it'll be cheaper than any shop.' Maggie paused. 'She does a lot at home. Better money…no tax. I'll ask her, if you like?'

Angie smiled. All memories of Maggie and her teenage behaviour were a distant memory. 'I'd appreciate that,' she said and for the first time in years allowed herself the luxury of believing that she might have found a friend.

'Let me ask her when she's in next and I'll email or text you some times and we can make an evening of it.' With that she climbed out and Angie drove home with the piles of brightly coloured bags wobbling on the back seat. At least it made a change from bin bags of rubbish. So what if she'd spent more than she'd planned? She'd soon have plenty of money from the sale of the house. Tonight she would try on some of the new clothes and treat herself to a glass of sherry.

***

Wednesday arrived and Angie turned up at Maggie's with a bottle of wine and a Chinese takeaway, both bought on advice from Maggie. The door opened and a sullen-looking youth stood there. 'Yeah?' His school shirt was untucked and the front bore the marks of a hastily eaten burger with ketchup. He must have had a growth spurt in recent days as his neck stuck above the collar like a giraffe. He was undoubtedly Maggie's son as he had her eyes under a shock of black hair which was gelled in a style that defied gravity.

'I'm Angie. I'm here to see your mum.'

'Mum,' he called before he turned back to Angie. 'Come in.' He showed Angie into the lounge where a television was playing to no one. 'Mum,' he yelled again. 'Your friend's here.'

'I'm coming, just putting the washing out,' a voice called from the back of the house.

'She's coming.' And he headed towards the stairs, fiddling on a machine that looked like a miniature set of handlebars with buttons.

'Is that a PlayStation?' Angie asked.

The youth turned. 'Naaa.' He grunted something that Angie failed to understand. 'Wanna look?' He handed it to her.

'Do you play computer games on this?' she said.

'What?' A hand reached up and scratched the gelled spikes. 'That's what it's for.' His lip twisted and his mouth hung open.

'I've never played a computer game before,' Angie explained.

'What never?'

Angie shook her head. 'Never, ever.'

'Wanna go?'

'Please.'

By the time Maggie arrived, they were both ensconced in Wargame 45 and sounds and images blasted through the small room.

'Gareth, switch that thing off and get upstairs and do your homework.' Maggie flopped down on the sofa.

'Just let's finish this will you?'

'I told you to switch it off.' Maggie's voice had an edge that Angie remembered from those times when she'd been reprimanded for wearing the wrong uniform.

'Gotcha.' Gareth punched the air as the images on the screen exploded into fragments and died away.

'Does that mean I lost?' Angie said.

'You were splattered.' Gareth took the consoles and packed them in a box stored under the television. 'What you should have done is take your army and go to the west. You'd have a better chance against my attack. You walked straight into it.'

'I think I've got a lot to learn,' Angie said and smiled.

'Not bad for a first time, though.' He slunk out of the door.

18

'Was it really your first time playing that game?'
Maggie shook her head from side to side.

'First time for that game and any game.' Angie
looked away. 'In fact there are lots of other things I've
never done,' she said.

'Such as?' Maggie's eyes were out on stalks.

'Had a manicure, waxed my legs, worn a thong,
been to a rock concert...the list is endless.' Angie
ticked them off on her fingers. 'Until we met, I'd
never had a cappuccino and...' she held up the glass
of red wine that Maggie had poured, 'I don't usually
drink wine.'

'What do you drink then?'

'In the convent we used to have a small glass of
port on Christmas Day and my parents always had
sherry in the house.'

Maggie pointed to the glass, 'You'd better go easy
on that stuff.' She paused, 'Boy have you got some
fun times ahead...Does that mean you...?' Her voice
dried up and for once she seemed uncomfortable as if
there was something she wanted to ask but couldn't
bring herself to.

Angie hurriedly filled the gap. 'I suppose my life
stopped in the 80s. The sort of everyday stuff that
people do, is just not on my radar.' Angie paused and
studied her finger nails, anything to avoid Maggie's
gaze. 'I've got a lot to er...experience.' She crossed
her fingers that Maggie would be satisfied by her
answer. The last thing she wanted was to be quizzed
on the lack of her sex life and her desire to remedy
the situation.

'You sure have.' Maggie stood up and Angie
relaxed. 'That requires another *very* small, glass of
wine with the meal. Let's get it heated up and I'll call

the gang down.'

Five minutes later, Angie, Maggie, Gareth and Tasha were squashed at a table that was clearly designed for two people. Tasha looked just as Angie had expected from someone doing a beauty course. Not a hair was out of place, her eyebrows were teased into neat arcs that framed huge, brown eyes, fringed with spiderlike fake lashes and her fingernails, although devoid of varnish, sported a shine that would have graced a car showroom. Beside her Angie felt like the ugly duckling.

'Bloody good food,' Gareth spluttered, shovelling rice and chicken into his mouth from the huge mound on his plate.

'Gareth, manners and no swearing,' Maggie corrected him. She turned to Tasha who was picking at the handful of vegetables on her plate. 'Well, love, what would you do with Angie's hair?'

'I've been thinking about that. I'd get a new colour, not too bright, just enough to tint the grey a pearly silver and blend into the blonde, with a neat bob that falls below the chin.' She stared at Angie, her head on one side. 'You should use soft natural eye make-up and a neutral lipstick; modern and classic, that's what you want. It'll be a great new picture for your Facebook page.'

'I haven't got a personal Facebook page.' There was silence. Gareth looked up from his plate, a forkful of food half way to his mouth.

'Everyone's got a Facebook page. I mean how do you keep up to date with what people are doing, like your friends?' Tasha said.

'I suppose I don't have any friends and only a few relatives I write to at Christmas...' Angie's voice tailed away.

'You've got us,' Maggie insisted. 'We're your friends aren't we?'

'Yeah.' Tasha said and smiled. 'When you get a Facebook page you'll be amazed at how easy it is to collect friends.'

'That's settled. Gareth, when you've stopped feeding your face and you've done your homework, set up a Facebook page for Angie. We can take a photo of her tonight to upload.' Maggie stood up to clear away the plates.

'Can I take this upstairs?' Gareth added two pancake rolls and more rice to his plate which he was guarding from Maggie's attempts to create a space on the table.

'All right but no mess or you're grounded.' She turned to Angie. 'Are you ready? Tash will get your hair washed in the kitchen sink as there's more space down here than in our bathroom.'

'I didn't expect anything tonight. Isn't it too late?' Angie glanced from Tasha to Maggie and back again. Now she knew what it felt like to be a small deer, eyed up by two very hungry lions. For a moment she was tempted to escape.

'It'll take a couple of hours but not if you're unsure.' Maggie looked at Tasha.

'If you don't like it, I'll change it, no charge.' Tasha said and smiled again. Angie knew she could trust her.

'I'm in your hands, then, literally.'

'Atta, girl.' Maggie punched the air.

As Angie drove home that night, she kept glancing in the rear mirror at her new appearance. She had instructions as to what make-up to buy and how to put it on. Her new image sat on the front page of her

Facebook profile with three friends (Maggie, Gareth and Tasha) and a warning from Gareth about the need to keep safe on line. Why that was important she'd no idea.

Before going to bed, Angie was about to pour herself a sherry when she stopped. She sniffed the bottle and pulled a face. She went to her shopping list for the week and next to MAKE-UP wrote RED WINE before tipping the rest down the sink. 'Another bit of my past life going down the plughole,' she said and giggled.

Chapter Three

Angie swerved and slowed down as she approached the roundabout outside the local college. A banner strung along the wall announced an open evening tonight for anyone to find out about the courses on offer. All the websites for single people had stressed the importance of taking up hobbies or learning new skills as a way of meeting people. This was the chance she needed. She made a note of the time. It would be worth going along.

It took the whole afternoon to apply her make-up the way Tasha had instructed her although she was certain she resembled a clown. What to wear was another problem. She finally decided on a pair of jeans, flat boots, in case she had to walk or stand for a long time and a black polo neck sweater. As she did up the jeans, she noticed the waistband no longer fitted snugly. She turned this way and that to see her figure and, unless she was imagining it, she did look thinner. Must be all the shifting and carrying she'd been doing. Although the fact that she was no longer tempted by Sister Agnes's puddings, smothered in custard might also be a factor. She frowned. The only downside of losing weight was the need to replace her meagre collection of clothes, yet again. With the sale of the house going through, her bank balance might eventually be a bit fatter. She shrugged. 'We'll cross that bridge when we come to it, Sister Ruth,' was something Sister Elizabeth always used to say at such times. She would do the same.

Angie grabbed her leather jacket, added a cerise scarf and stepped out into the night air. She breathed in, wrinkling her nose at the smell of wood smoke and damp earth and climbed into her car, keeping her fingers crossed it would start. A quick turn of the key, a splutter and it sparked into life. She eased it into gear and set off through the town.

The college was a blaze of light as Angie negotiated her way to the last space and parked her tatty hatchback between a series of shiny vehicles that made her wonder if she'd come to a car sale by mistake. What if everyone was a frightful old bore that needed a social life? She smiled. She'd fit in perfectly. She walked across the car park and past the shelter where the smokers congregated, their cupped hands shielding glowing butts from the icy drizzle. She ran up the steps and pulled open the swing doors to be met with a babble of voices.

Signs directed her to a series of rooms where tutors congregated and smiled in welcome as she walked past. She wandered from room to room for over an hour collecting leaflets, not daring to sit down at any of the desks that were manned in case she was pounced on. There was everything from printmaking, painting and decorating to an assortment of GCSE classes, vying with languages for the holidaymaker. She'd go home and take her time before coming to any decision. Besides, white flakes were fluttering down and had already covered the paths.

She reached the front door and pushed it open. Wind whipped a few snowflakes against her face. She pulled the leather jacket tighter and wished she'd worn her old coat. After all, there had been no one to impress. She hurried down the steps and stopped. Someone was shouting down a phone, 'You bastard. Where the fuck can I go? You'd better not let my stuff get messed up.' The speaker thrust the phone in his pocket. He looked familiar.

'Excuse me?' Angie stepped forward. 'You're the young man that helped start my car, aren't you? You really have the knack with vehicles,' she added.

He turned. 'Are you the old lady with the red hatchback?'

'Not so much of the old! Yes, that was me. I'm Angie by the way.'

'Yeah? And?'

Conversation was obviously not one of his strong points. She persevered, 'I just want to say thank you.' She paused. 'I heard what you were saying. Is something wrong?' The old instinct was coming back. Here was someone in need of help.

'None of your business.'

'Fine. Can I give you a lift anywhere? This stuff's coming down pretty fast.' She indicated the large white flakes that fluttered through the air.

'Where to?' His answer came in a snarl.

'Home?'

'Got no home. Stepdad just chucked me out.'

Angie went and stood on the step next to him. He was not much taller than she was and slightly built. 'I'm sorry to hear that. Won't your mum be worried though?'

'Stepdad and me don't get on and she won't say anything.'

'So where will you go?'

'I'll sleep somewhere and sort it out tomorrow.' The boy turned up his collar, thrust his hands in his pockets and walked off in the direction of the town. The snowflakes were getting larger. Angie shivered. No one should have to sleep out on a night like this.

'Wait a minute,' Angie yelled after him. 'I've got a spare room. You can stay there tonight. At least you'll get a good sleep ready to find a place tomorrow.' Even as Angie heard herself saying the words, a small voice inside was keeping up the infernal chatter that this was madness, crazy, she'd get murdered, robbed, beaten up or worse. Deep inside she knew this was not going to happen. She and Sister Elizabeth had never been afraid of the waifs and strays that turned up unannounced at the convent. It was as if they shared a sixth sense and could pick out those who needed help. That intuition was working again now. He turned and looked at her.

'You don't know me. I might be a murderer.' A hint of a smile curled over his lips.

'One good turn deserves another and anyway, I don't think you're the murdering type.'

The boy walked back towards Angie. 'I don't need a bed. Just a sofa, so don't go to any trouble.'

'It's no trouble and if you can give me some advice about driving in this stuff, I'd be grateful.' Angie kicked at the snow that dusted the road surface.

'Done.' He went to the passenger door and got in. 'First steady on any braking, right? Keep to second until we get out onto the main road. We'll check what it's like from there.'

'What's your name?' Angie did up her seat belt and turned to look at her passenger.

'Jason.'

'Well, Jason, at least if the old girl doesn't start, I'm sure you can give me a push.' She put the car into gear and edged forward.

By the time they got back to Angie's house, the snow was falling heavily. 'You got me here,' she said and heaved a sigh of relief as the car turned into the driveway.

She unlocked the front door and went in, followed by Jason. He gazed at the hallway with its tiles and stained glass. 'Nice place you got. You lived here long?'

'Most of my life,' Angie said as she pulled off her boots. 'How about a cup of tea before I show you to your room? The toilet is through there.' She pointed to the downstairs cloakroom. Jason followed her into the kitchen and leaned against the table. She'd just filled the kettle and switched it on when she heard a movement behind her. She turned to see Jason move closer. He fixed his lips on hers and placed his hands on her shoulders.

'Get off!' She pushed him away. 'If you do that again, it'll be me that is up for murder.' He stepped back.

'I thought that's what you expected? You know as payment?' He pushed the beanie hat back off his head to reveal short, dark hair.

'Whatever gave you that idea?' Angie leaned against the sink and folded her arms. This was something new.

'An older woman and a young man, you know?'

'No I do not know and at nearly fifty, I do not call myself an old woman although I am old, er, I mean *mature* enough to be your mother,' Angie said.

'My mum's only thirty-seven,' Jason added as if by way of an explanation.

Angie blanched. 'All right, grandma but do that again and you're out. Understand?' She didn't wait for a reply. 'Think of this as one good turn deserving another, like the proverb.'

27

'What?'

'Proverb, like *A stitch in time saves nine,* things like that.' By the perplexed look on Jason's face she realised he hadn't a clue what she was talking about. What on earth had he been doing in school all those years? She was about to ask him, then thought better of it. He was a guest and probably wouldn't appreciate an inquisition. 'Make yourself useful. Cups and saucers are in the dresser and milk is in the fridge.' Jason didn't move. 'Look lively or this water will have gone cold.'

'You don't want me to go?'

'You need a place to stay and I've got plenty of spare rooms here. As far as I'm concerned, there's no more to be said.' She turned back to the sink to make the tea, aware of some shuffling and the clatter of crockery that told her Jason was doing as he was told. Angie poured the tea and opened the biscuit tin. Jason sat down and wolfed three biscuits. 'When did you last have a meal?' He shrugged. 'Fried egg sandwich do you?'

'Yeah. Lovely.'

'That's what you'll get as long as you tell me a bit about yourself.'

Angie busied herself with the frying pan while she listened to Jason explain how he was desperate to get an apprenticeship, there was nothing available at the moment and all he ever wanted to do was be a mechanic. 'I've got to keep looking for a job or go on a training course.' She placed the plate in front of him; all bluster had gone. He sat slumped, his head bowed.

She pushed the plate towards him. 'Cor great.' And a smile crossed his face as he reached for the ketchup.

The recuperative effect of food never failed to amaze Angie. Nothing more was said while he demolished two fried egg sandwiches with tomatoes and mushrooms. When the plate was cleared, he sat back. 'That was excellent.'

'Good. Let me show you to your room.' Angie led the way upstairs and got out a towel, soap and a toothbrush from the store her father always kept *just in case* and which she hadn't the heart to throw away.

'Good night. See you tomorrow.' She went into her own room to get ready for bed and wedged a chair under the door handle *just in case*. As she snuggled down into bed, there was a strange reassuring feel about having someone else in the house. She realised that she'd never slept in an empty house until the last few weeks. First there were her parents, followed by fellow students and flatmates and finally the other nuns. Even the house seemed to acknowledge the presence of another person and the usual bumps and creaks that regularly disturbed her sleep were not there.

Angie woke with a start. She checked the clock. It was already gone eight. She hadn't slept so long since she'd been in the convent with the other nuns. She leapt out of bed. The boy. Was he here? She threw on a sweatshirt and trousers and crept along the hallway. His door was closed. Had he done a runner? Had she been robbed? So what? There was precious little to take apart from a few bits of jewellery and a credit card or two. She listened outside the door. There was no sound yet she sensed someone was there. She knocked. 'Jason? I'm getting breakfast.'

'What?...Ta…Be down in a sec.' The voice was muffled and sleepy. He'd obviously had a good night too. An idea struck her. It was one that might help them both. She'd have to talk to him once he'd had a good breakfast.

Ten minutes later Jason came down the stairs, dishevelled and smiling. 'Good morning,' Angie said, avoiding his gaze and concentrating on the porridge as it bubbled and spat.

'Morning. Is there anything I can do to help?' Jason looked around at the kitchen.

'Orange juice in the fridge, glasses and plates in the cupboard and placemats and cutlery in the dresser. Lay the table and the porridge and toast will be ready in a moment. There's tea in the pot.' There was a clatter as drawers and cupboards opened and closed, then silence. 'Is anything the matter?' She glanced over her shoulder to see Jason peering into the drawer that contained her mother's lace tablecloths.

'What's a placement?' he mumbled.

'Placemat,' Angie corrected him. 'Those things you put on a table instead of a cloth when you eat.'

'Never ate at the table.' Jason continued to search. Angie went over and pulled open the middle drawer of the dresser which contained a dozen ethnic designed placemats in rattan, souvenirs from her parents' many trips abroad. She took two out and handed them to him.

'If you didn't eat at the table, where did you eat your meals?'

'On our laps in front of the telly. Here?' He indicated the kitchen table where Angie had already laid out butter, jam and honey. She nodded and he spread them out, taking care to put them dead square on the table and arranging the cutlery on one side.

'In this house, I eat at a table and you can join me.'

30

She collected two willow pattern bowls and poured porridge into them and placed one on each place mat. 'There's sugar or honey to sweeten it and jam for the toast. Can you pour me a tea?'

Jason sat down and poured the tea and added milk from the jug, watching as Angie added honey to her porridge. He did the same and tasted it. 'Nice. Better than cornflakes and it's hot.'

'Don't you have a hot breakfast in the winter?'

'Don't have breakfast.'

'So what do you have in the morning?'

'Used to be a fag and a cup of tea or a bag of crisps on the way to school. When I was with Gran she'd make toast and I'd have cornflakes. Mum doesn't have breakfast and if I bought something she and Les would eat it all and in a day or two it'd be gone.'

'Who's Les?'

'My stepdad,' his voice hardened and Angie let him eat in silence before she passed a huge pile of toast in his direction which he buttered, added jam and devoured.

'So what is your plan today?' she asked, pouring him a second cup of tea. Now seemed the right time to talk.

'Job centre and housing association to see if there's anything for me. There won't be so I'd better see if a mate can take me in.'

'And if they can't?'

'On the streets. I've done it before; I can do it again.'

'Over my dead body.' Angie fought to control the anger that was bubbling up inside her. 'Aren't there any hostels?'

'They're full at this time of the year. I might get a B and B paid for by the social. There's no guarantee. It's my fault you see. I can't get on with my stepdad and so I've walked out and made myself homeless. I'm over twenty-one so I don't count as a kid.'

'Could your girlfriend help? I take it Bryony is the name of your girlfriend?'

Jason ran a finger over the tattoo on his neck and a smile spread across his face. 'Yeah. Me and Bry have been going out since school. Her place is chock full. Her mum and dad split and her mum moved in with this new bloke. He's got two kids and they had a baby together so there's six kids and the two adults in a three-bed place.'

'And here am I in a six-bedroom pile, rattling like a pea in a pod.' It wasn't fair.

'What?'

'Oh nothing.' Angie hadn't realised she'd spoken out loud. She coughed and cleared her throat. 'What about money?'

'If I get job seekers I can't go to college and that's what I want to do, see, to go to college. The places are there and they'd be free.'

'You can't live on the street,' Angie said.

'Don't worry, I can look after myself. You've been kind, thanks, I'd better be off.' Jason stood up and held out his hand. 'Thanks for everything.'

'You're not going anywhere. Sit down, I've got an idea; it needs a fresh pot of tea. Stack the dishes in the dishwasher and I'll pour us both a cup and this time we'll sit in the conservatory because there's something I want to discuss with you.'

Angie waited until they were both sitting down in the conservatory. Outside last night's snow was already beginning to thaw in the warmth of the morning sunshine. Small birds squabbled over the remains of some fat balls that swung from the old plum tree. Telltale drips of water spattered the wooden floor and as Angie looked up she spotted more leaks between the glass and the metal panels as the winter weather continued to take its toll on the old house. Thank God it wouldn't be her responsibility for much longer. She touched her chest before she realised the crucifix was no longer there. It felt strange. She pointed to a white wicker chair with a faded mirror work cushion and sat down on the sofa, curling her feet underneath her. She waited till Jason was seated, took a sip of tea and began, 'You need a place to stay, right?'

'Yeah.'

'And if you don't have a job, you can go to college, right?' Angie leaned forward.

'I can get an allowance to cover college expenses. The training I really want to do takes six months with an apprenticeship at the end.'

'If you claim benefits, you can't go to college?'

'Right.' A wary note crept into Jason's voice. 'What's this got to do with you?'

Angie sat back and held up one hand. 'This is my proposal. I need help clearing this house and moving into my next one. That place needs some work inside and out.' She shuddered at the memory of the purple bedrooms and the hall painted in a murky green, like a stagnant pond. Anyone can splash a bit of paint on a wall, can't they?

'Like what?'

'It's easy stuff; there's just too much for me to do and I need to…let's say I need to do other things.'

She didn't think it would be wise to reveal the more sensual elements of her life plan; if she did, Jason would probably know a man who could oblige.

'What sort of stuff?' Jason spoke slowly as if he was weighing up Angie's words.

'The bungalow I've bought needs completely re-decorating. It's only painting and I've never done that before. The garden needs a bit of work too.' She crossed her fingers Jason wouldn't ask any more questions. She hated lying. Clearing the bramble infested garden and cutting back the ten-foot high Leylandii hedge was probably better described as a hell of a lot of work. Removing the branch from the huge beech tree in the next-door garden so that it didn't scrape against her roof might be more of a challenge though she was sure a strong lad like Jason could sort it out.

Jason nodded. 'I used to help my grandad with his garden.'

'What if I take you on as a handy man? You get your board and lodging and your college allowance covers your day-to-day stuff.' Angie knew she was gabbling, she couldn't stop herself.

'Are you for real?' His eyes were wide open and his voice was little more than a whisper.

'I am very *for real* as you say.' If she was breaking some laws of employment and not following red tape she'd cross that bridge when and if they got to it. 'Besides, it's only for six months while you're on this course, isn't it?'

Jason nodded. 'I've got an offer of an apprenticeship with a flat if I can get the first training done. It's my best mate's dad.' His voice bubbled with enthusiasm and his eyes shone as he talked. 'His place keeps getting burgled. If I was living above the workshops, his insurance would go down.'

'That's settled.' Angie clapped her hands together. 'I reckon it'll take about six months for my new place to be sorted, so until that time you get a home. What do you say?' She crossed her fingers.

Jason stared at her, at the floor and back at her. 'I could be a maniac. How do you know I won't murder you in your bed or nick your stuff?'

'First I reckon after all the years I've spent with people, I'm a pretty good judge of character,' said Angie as she remembered the countless times strangers had turned up at the convent. It was always when she was with Sister Elizabeth and they'd have to decide if it was a genuine case of need or just a chancer, out to rob and make a quick getaway. 'We never make a mistake do we, Sister Ruth?' She could hear Sister Elizabeth's breathless voice, her head perched on one side like an inquisitive bird. Angie snapped back to the present. 'Second, you could have done both of those things last night. You didn't. I reckon you're worth a chance. Any funny business though and you're out, understand?'

'Yeah. Agreed.' He drew in a breath. 'Fucking Jesus, I can't wait to tell Bry.'

Old memories stirred again as Angie immediately made the sign of the cross at the profanity. She caught sight of Jason staring at her, a puzzled look on his face. She pretended to rearrange her scarf and stood up. 'Come on. Let's go and collect your stuff.'

Chapter Four

Angie drove Jason to the college for him to sign up on the day course and to check the starting date and times. Once all the paperwork was completed, she followed his instructions to an old estate on the outskirts. They were former council houses, built in a circle with a playing field in the centre. Later designers had installed a skate park and an adventure playground that was now broken down and covered in graffiti. She stopped in front of number seventeen. 'Do you want me to come in?' Angie asked.

Jason shook his head. 'Better not. Les can get a bit angry sometimes.' He got out of the car, went up to the front door and knocked on it. The poor kid hadn't even got a key to his own home. From inside the house a dog barked. Jason shifted from one foot to the other and knocked again.

'Heard you the bloody first time,' a voice yelled and the door opened. 'What the fuck are you doing here?' A bald man folded his tattooed arms over a vest-covered paunch, leaned against the doorframe and waited for an answer.

'Can I see Mum?'

'She's asleep.'

'I just want to tell her I've got a place to stay and I'm starting at the college tomorrow.' Angie stared ahead. Out of the corner of her eye she could see Les peering in her direction.

'You'd better come in.' He added something in a quieter voice which she couldn't hear. He opened the door wider and Jason disappeared inside. Les looked up and down the road before he slammed the door shut.

Twenty minutes later the door opened and Jason came out, carrying some boxes and a case. He staggered over to the car and stowed everything in the boot. Angie wound down the window. 'Mum says she'd like to say thanks.'

'What about Les?'

'If Mum says you're welcome, it's her house, he can't do anything.' Angie got out, double-checking she'd locked the car as she followed Jason up the path.

A smell of stale smoke, fried food and sweaty bodies greeted her in the sauna-like heat of the hallway. Furious barking and the sound of a dog hurling itself against a closed door suggested that animal behaviour management was not a priority in this house. The floors were bare and the walls once had wallpaper. Now only faded strips remained. The door to the small front room was open and a television was blaring away. The curtains had not been opened and as she stepped inside, she saw a stick thin woman, dressed in leggings and an oversize shirt with the words *Sexy Babe* emblazoned over her chest. She was sitting on a huge sofa which apart from the television was the only other piece of furniture in the room. A cigarette was clamped in her mouth and an overflowing ashtray was perched on the arm of the sofa. Her face was criss-crossed with lines and her front teeth were missing. She looked up as Angie entered. 'Thanks for helping my boy out. It means a lot to me.'

'Bloody do-gooder,' the man snarled.

'Les, shh.' She looked across from Angie to Les who was standing, his arms tightly folded, his lips contorted around the smouldering butt of a cigarette. 'He doesn't mean what he says.'

'Yes I do. She'll get the Social on us, or the plod.'

'Why would I do that?' Angie turned to face him.

Les drew himself up and wagged a nicotine stained finger. 'Cause that's what you social workers do. You always blame us and you don't know what a little sod he's been.'

Angie refused to flinch from the accusing finger. 'For your information, I am not a social worker and I do not care how you live your life. If you want to know the truth Jason will be doing me a favour.' She looked Les straight in the eye. All the bruising encounters she'd had with kids not to mention their parents fighting and swearing on the playground and numerous school inspectors had been good practice. She'd eaten little boys like him for dinner and would do so again.

She turned to Jason's mother and fished in her bag, for a pen and paper. She scribbled down her address and phone number and handed it over. 'This is where he'll be staying. I'll let you know the address of the new place when I've moved in. If you're worried at any time, that's my number. You're quite welcome to visit as long as you let me know in advance in case I'm out.'

'You're an angel.' Jason's mum struggled to her feet, pulled Angie to her and hugged her for a few seconds before sinking back onto the sofa. 'He's a good boy really.' A snort from Les told Angie all she needed to know about his feelings on the matter.

'We'd better be going. I'll wait for you in the car.' She nodded to Jason, turned and left.

Once outside Angie sucked in huge gulps of fresh

air and sniffed at her clothes. Even after such a short time, the smell of the house permeated her sweater and as she breathed in the aroma she remembered where she'd smelt it before. It had been in the houses she visited to ask about the children and their links with Father Benedict. It was the smell of fear, distrust and poverty. She got into the car and waited till Jason reappeared and she could escape.

Nothing was said until they had been driving for ten minutes. It was Angie who broke the silence. 'Your mum does care, you know.'

'She did until Dad died. Gran brought me and my brother up.'

'Where is he?'

'Army. He did two tours in Afghan and is in Cyprus now.' There was no mistaking the pride in his voice.

'Your gran did a good job. What happened to your mum?'

'When Dad died, she started drinking and that was it.'

Angie sighed, 'Wasn't there anyone she could talk to? A neighbour, a doctor or someone from the local community? There's a support group for the bereaved, you know and…' her voice faltered, 'the church will always help out.'

'Never believed in all that God mumbo jumbo. Do you?' he asked.

'I used to.' One hand instinctively went up to the space where her crucifix would once have rested. It only found the material of her scarf.

'Why did you stop?'

'I discovered some terrible things had been done by people in the church.' Angie drove on, focussing her eyes on the road as the memory of her last meeting with Sister Catherine came into her mind. She gripped the wheel. Father Benedict had been there. His pale blue eyes, shot through with red lines had scrutinised her as she took the clammy hand he offered and shook it. He had made his excuses to go soon after and had sidled out without a backward glance, secure that whatever he had done would never come to light. She was jolted back to the present by Jason's insistent voice.

'That's people…not God. My gran used to tell me it was people what messed up this world and I reckon it's probably the same with all the God stuff, if he does exist.'

'Perhaps you're right.' The empty space where her crucifix had been felt strange. It wouldn't do any harm if she wore her little gold cross from time to time, would it? She'd find it tonight.

They continued in silence until they got back to Angie's house and Jason unloaded the boxes and cases from the car. 'Welcome home,' she said as she opened the front door. 'Remind me to get you a key cut.'

'Home?' he said. 'I suppose it is, for now.'

'For as long as you need it. Let's put the kettle on and I'll show you just how I like my tea.'

Later that night Angie opened the top drawer of her bedside table and pulled out the small jewellery box that held her childish gems. She lifted the lid. Inside was a small crucifix and chain that had been a present for her confirmation, a ring with an amethyst birthstone that she'd begged her mother to buy for her tenth birthday and a seed pearl brooch in the shape of a leaf from an aged aunt who had lived in

Spain. She lifted
chain run throu
back and closed
was there. If sh
would ever find

It was Wednes
Angie was sitti
emails. A lamb
bubbling away
dumplings was
when she wou
stir fry the shr

some time if you like. Nex
Brian

The picture o
length image o
He gave ver
pictures.
in her
ove

Jason got in. Thank God she'd spent Saturdays and Sundays helping in the kitchen rather than in the chapel. It had worked out far more useful to be able to cook rather than know the Bible readings by heart. 'Sorry, God,' she said and just managed to stop her hand from crossing herself again.

She scanned the emails one by one, deleting the endless junk until she came across a Facebook message from someone called Brian with a *Friend Request*. She hit *Accept* and read the message.

Dear Angela,
I don't know if you remember me but I remember you.
We both sang in the choir when St Winifred's and St Joseph's joined together to raise money for Live Aid. We sang a medley of Beatles songs. I started at college as a trainee engineer but it wasn't for me so I joined the family business. Now all these years later I'm divorced with two lovely kids who wind their old dad around their fingers when they come to stay. I only live twenty minutes away from the town so we could have a drink

his Facebook page showed a full
a man with a dog in front of a lake.
little else away and there were no other
Angie's stomach lurched. Her heart pounded
chest and her hands shook as they hovered
the keyboard. If this is just what the thought of
meeting a man was doing to her, what on earth would
the real thing be like? The last time she'd felt like this
was when she fell in at the deep end of the pool
before she'd learnt to swim. She closed up the laptop,
opened the window and gulped down the fresh air.

After a few deep breaths, she re-opened the laptop
and typed *dating tips for the mature woman* in the search
engine. Within half a second over four million sites
had shown up. She read a few and pushed the laptop
away. She was being silly. It wasn't really a date. It was
just a drink with an old friend. She would have to
show Maggie the message when she went to see her
again and find out what she could remember about
Brian. Maggie would be her lifeboat; she would know
what to do.

Meeting Maggie every Friday evening for a chat
about the week had become a bit of a habit, along
with a glass or two of wine which Angie had to admit
was miles better than sweet sherry. She was waiting
for the right time to tell Maggie about her houseguest
as she suspected she would not approve.

Gareth opened the door. 'Hi, Angie. Come on in.'

'You sound cheerful, Gareth, good week at
school?'

He shrugged. 'So-so. I'm in my room, Mum, OK?'

And he galloped up the stairs as if someone was after him.

'In here, Angie,' Maggie called from the kitchen and Angie walked in and sat down at the table. 'Open the wine. I need it after the week I've had.'

Maggie was bundling washing from the machine into a red laundry basket. Angie squeezed past her, fetched glasses from the cupboard and poured the wine. 'Cheers. Gareth's in a good mood. What's up?'

Maggie plonked the basket on the work surface and grasped at the glass. She took a big drink and swallowed. 'That's better. Oh her name's Hermione and, yes, she has a brother called Harry, before you ask.'

'Are they boyfriend and girlfriend?'

Maggie sat down at the kitchen table and cleared a space amongst the circulars, pizza adverts and assorted junk mail that littered the top. 'I think she's a friend. He'd like her to be more than that.'

'Poor lad, unrequited love is tough at any age,' Angie said. She twiddled the stem of the glass and pushed a stray wisp of hair out of her eyes. 'Talking of friends, can you remember anyone called Brian from school? He went to St Joseph's; left before the sixth form. He reckons we were in the upper school joint choir together.'

'Brian? Not stinky breath Brian?'

Angie shrugged. 'Your guess is as good as mine.'

Maggie suppressed a chuckle. 'The only Brian I know is that one. He moved away and came back a few years ago after his marriage broke up. Why?'

'He wants to meet up.'

'Go girl, give it a try.' Maggie raised her glass.

'What will happen?'

43

'You'll go for a drink, perhaps have something to eat, chat and decide if you want to see each other again. Where's the harm in that?'

'What if he tries to kiss me?' Angie cradled the glass in her fingers and watched the red liquid leave a trail as she swirled it to and fro.

'If he's drop dead gorgeous, you can give it a try but if it's who I think it is, unless he's got rid of the breath problem, you'll need a gag for him and a sick bag for yourself.' Maggie drained her glass. 'Who's for a top-up?'

Maggie refilled their glasses as a thousand questions fought for space in Angie's head. She'd start with something easy. 'What should I wear?'

'Good question. From what I remember your wardrobe consists of a few decent pieces, which I helped you buy and the rest is a uniform shade of *greige*.'

'*Greige?*' Angie scowled. Sometimes Maggie seemed to be on a different planet to her or perhaps she was the one who was not on the same planet as everyone else.

'Yes, where all you ever wear is either grey, beige, sage or a curious pale blue that looks better on a two-month-old baby than on anyone with their own teeth. At least you have a decent hair style and,' Maggie peered at Angie, 'you are slowly getting the hang of wearing make-up without looking like a pantomime dame.'

'What do *you* suggest I wear?' Angie bristled.

'You know I'm right. Remember that black dress, the one with the short sleeves to cover the bingo wings…?'

'What bingo wings? My arms are quite taut…'

44

Angie flexed her muscles to check, 'apart from a few areas that could do with tightening.'

'Everyone over the age of fifty has bingo wings. Get over it. Team that dress with a necklace and the smart patent heels. Add the red jacket, pulled in at the waist, and you'll look great.' Maggie sat back, a self-satisfied grin spreading over her face.

'Now you have sorted out my clothes, what else should I learn from your vast experience of dating?' Angie folded her arms and waited.

'Hang on, don't get uppity. I happen to be an expert on first dates. I just never get asked out on a second,' Maggie said and for a moment she was silent, her eyes downcast until her usual exuberance bubbled up again. 'Follow my instructions and you'll be fine.'

'Go ahead. I'm all ears.' Angie recalled the numerous websites with advice on what to do on a first date. Somehow it all seemed complicated. Just how do you show you're interested by being flirty? What's being flirty? Angie had tried twirling her hair in front of the mirror; it looked as if she was sifting through it for nits and just how long was eye contact supposed to last? She waited for Maggie's advice.

'First choose a small glass of white wine—shows you are both careful in what you drink and not a complete turn-off and party pooper, insisting on something non-alcoholic. Sip it, don't neck it down. Try to make it last.'

'I don't neck it down,' Angie protested, holding up her empty glass. 'Oops, point taken.'

'Ask questions about what he does, show an interest in his work and tell him about yourself...' she paused. 'It's probably best that you don't mention being a nun.'

'Why?'

'Let's say, it might be interpreted as a red rag to a bull, you know, female hasn't had sex for ages, guy thinks it should be him to show her a good time. You might not find he's interested in you as a person, just a repository for his cock.'

Angie felt her skin flush. Is this how you spoke about the male anatomy? She imagined herself using the word. The warm flush on her cheeks had turned into a raging fire. What else could you say? *Penis?* Too medical. *Willy?* More like a friendly uncle. Maggie's words interrupted her thoughts. 'Are you listening to me?'

'Yes. Sorry what were you saying?' Angie looked up to see Maggie glaring at her.

'I said all you are going to do is have a nice evening getting reacquainted with an old friend. Keep it simple and casual and you can't go wrong. However,' Maggie eyed Angie over the top of her glass, 'if it starts to get serious, for God's sake be careful.'

'What do you mean?'

'Just be careful.'

When Angie got home she reread Brian's message. 'Oh what the hell,' she said and typed her reply.

Hi Brian, Lovely to hear from you and yes it would be great to meet up for a drink. Next Saturday would be fine. I'll leave it to you to suggest a place. I'm sure you know the local area much better than me!
Angie

Chapter Five

Angie spent Saturday practising with her make-up and resisting the impulse to go out and buy something new to wear. At seven o'clock she tottered down the stairs and checked her hair in the mirror. There was an appreciative whistle from Jason who was sprawled out on the sofa, catching up with the football results. 'Nice one, Ange. You look good. Who is he?'

'Thanks. He's an old school pal and we're off for a drink. I'll be back about ten.'

'He'll be daft if he lets you back before tomorrow morning. Bugger, City lost again.'

'We've only just met!'

Jason shrugged. 'It happens.'

'Wish me luck' Angie called out as she opened the front door.

'Good luck and be careful.'

There was the same message again to be careful. Angie got into her car. There was nothing to worry about. She was simply meeting up with an old acquaintance over a casual drink. At least that was what her head was saying although judging by the adrenalin coursing through her system, if she'd been entered for the Gold Cup she'd have romped home. 'Get a grip,' she said out loud and started the engine.

By the time she got to the wine bar, her stomach was flip flopping and her legs were so wobbly she'd have felt more at home in an aquarium with the jellyfish. She peered in through the window. It was very quiet. What if Brian didn't turn up? Could you be stood up for a date before you'd ever been on one? She rubbed her hot hands down her dress. She could go home. Or stay for a few seconds, say it was all a mistake and make up a story about a sick relative. No. That was being cowardly and she'd hate herself tomorrow if she wimped out. She had to go through with it. If it was really dreadful, she'd stay for one drink and leave. 'Here goes,' she said and pushed open the door. A portly man was ordering a drink at the bar. He turned. Angie recognised him instantly. 'Brian?'

'Angie?' He walked over and planted a wet kiss on her lips before depositing an equally sloppy one on both cheeks.' A pungent aroma drifted her way. She forced herself not to recoil. 'You haven't changed a bit. Drink?'

'Please. Small glass of house white.' She waited while he collected the drinks, paid and they found seats at one of the tables at the back of the room and sat down. She was now able to get a good look at him. Brian's face was florid; his eyes were a soft hazel colour and his brown hair had more grey than his photo had suggested. He was dressed in a pale blue sweater, a candy-striped shirt and navy trousers. She racked her brains to think of something to say.

Brian held up his glass. 'To old friends.'

'Old friends,' Angie replied and sat back, twiddling the stem of the glass and smiling what she hoped was the relaxed smile of a confident, mature woman.

She opened her mouth to ask him if he'd come far but Brian got in first and launched into a blow-by-blow account of his life past school, including what a success he had made in the butchery business. Any attempts to add a comment or to interrupt him in full flow were brushed aside. Most people stop to take a breath from time to time. Brian appeared not to need

48

oxygen, he was so pumped up with his own worth. An involuntary sigh brought him to his senses.

'Sorry this has all been about me, hasn't it? You shouldn't let me carry on like this. My kids tell me I can talk for England. If there was an Olympic medal in talking, I'd win hands down.' He brayed at his own weak joke and a waft of sewage floated her way. The breath problem had not improved over time and she made a mental note to tell Maggie. 'So what have you been up to?' he said.

'I was a teacher for many years. Being with young children is so funny...there was this one time...' Angie crossed her fingers that she was coming across as witty and entertaining. Everything she'd read said men expected their prospective dates or friends to have a good personality or some such description. 'It was Christmas and...' She stopped. Brian's eyes were no longer focussed on her. He was scanning the bar. 'Are you expecting someone?' Angie said.

'There is a slim chance my ex-wife might pop in. She and her new partner often come here. She was at Chatsworth Park High School on the opposite side of the town and knows everyone. I can introduce you.' He stopped for a breath. 'What were you saying?'

Angie opened her mouth to speak when Brian leapt up. 'There she is. Pat, over here,' he called out to a lanky woman in paint-spattered dungarees. Her grey curls were escaping from a knitted hat and slung over her shoulders was a poncho that had seen better days in 1970. She looked over at them and gave a half-hearted wave. She turned to say something to the man behind her and they came over. 'What a coincidence. I was just telling Angie that you two ought to meet and here you are.' Angie fixed a smile on her face. If Brian had a tail it would have wagged. 'Pat, Tom, this is Angie. Can I get you a drink?'

'No we're not stopping, just popped in to see if our friends are here. They've got the tickets for the Arts Space poetry event. Tom is going to read.' Pat had a machine gun style of speaking. She glanced at Angie and a flicker of a frown crossed over her face before she turned back to Brian.

'Pity,' said Brian. 'Perhaps another time?'

'Can I have private word with you?' Pat ignored his question. 'There seems to be a problem with the allowances you're paying, or rather *not* paying.' They went off to the opposite part of the bar where Pat could be seen gesticulating, her face getting redder by the minute.

Tom held out his hand to Angie. 'Pleased to meet you.' Behind the dark-rimmed glasses, green eyes, like a cat's, shone and with the long tail of greyish black hair that snaked down his back he would not have been out of place in the zoo.

'What sort of poem are you reading?' Angie said.

'It's very experimental. With lots of sounds. It's performance art really.'

'How fascinating.' Angie hoped she sounded knowledgeable. 'What's the subject?'

'The myth of the female orgasm, seen from the perspective of the penis,' Tom spoke in such a deadpan voice that Angie had to lean forward to hide her face and disguise the peals of laughter threatening to engulf her. She coughed several times and took a long drink of wine. 'Are you all right? Do you want some water?'

Angie shook her head. 'Went down the wrong way, that's all.' She just had time to compose herself before Brain and Pat returned. By the looks on both of their faces, the discussions had not gone well.

Pat looked at the other people in the bar again. 'Our friends aren't here. We'd better go.' She put a hand on Tom's arm. 'Come on, you've got to set up the stage for your performance.' Angie must have looked confused as she added in a tone of voice you'd use to soothe a child struggling over their spellings. 'He does it in a bed. Nice to meet you.' She nodded to Angie and left with Tom trailing in her wake.

'They seemed a very pleasant couple,' Angie said as Brian sat down. His previous good humour had evaporated and he looked like a baggy balloon on the day after the party.

'She says she wants more money.'

'Oh.' Angie tried to think of something to say. 'Perhaps you can provide all the meat she needs? Kids love burgers, don't they? Surely that would save her a lot of expense?' She prattled on in a vain attempt to lift Brian's spirits.

'She's a vegetarian and so are the kids.'

'That would make it more difficult.' There was silence. The evening was not going to improve from here on so Angie stood up. 'It's been very nice meeting you, Brian. I must go. Thanks for the drink.' She was hoping to make a discreet retreat when Brian jumped up.

'Thank you so much.' He grasped both her hands in his and squeezed. 'It was good for Pat to see me with a new and...' he leaned forward, 'a very attractive lady. It might make her realise I've moved on. Can we meet up again sometime?'

'Perhaps,' Angie replied, kicking herself that she didn't have the courage to tell him what a boring, self-centred slob he was. Brian pulled her closer and hugged her tightly, running his hands over her back and letting one linger on her bra strap before it slid down to her bottom. Angie pulled back and held his hands in hers to stop them from wandering back to her body before she moved out of reach. 'It's been very interesting catching up with you, now I really need to get back home. Take care and goodbye,' she said, turned and clattered across the wooden floor in her high heels.

Once outside, she looked back to check he had not decided to follow her. He was nowhere to be seen. She pulled her jacket tighter; it was no protection from the wind which dragged the wrappings from the overflowing bins outside the takeaways that were strung along the road. She picked her way over the chicken bones and styrofoam containers, past the pubs and bars from where raucous laughter fought with pounding beats as makeshift discos pretended they were upmarket clubs. Burly, bald men in black overcoats with flashing blue lights in their earpieces hovered outside the open doors. She hurried past, looking neither to left or right, anxious to get away from the tide of pheromones flowing down the street as noisy groups of drunken men and women trawled up and down in search of entertainment.

Once back in the car though she began to giggle. She gripped the wheel as waves of laughter swamped her. She, Angie, the ex-nun had been asked out on a date to make another woman jealous. She shook her head and wiped her eyes, smearing mascara over her fingers. She blew her nose as the giggles subsided. The idea that someone, even if it was only Brian, had thought she was attractive was the best thing that had happened to her in years. With any luck, the next time she was asked out on a date, it might be because the person was interested in her. 'Well done, me,' she said out loud and headed for home.

As the car pulled into the driveway, Angie noticed that the lights in the house were on. 'Silly boy,' she said. Jason must have forgotten to switch them off. She unlocked the door, stepped into the hallway and kicked off her shoes. Sounds were coming from the lounge. He must have left the television on too. She stood quite still and listened again. It could be the television. The tingling along her spine, however, told her that she was not alone. She picked up one of her father's walking sticks from the hall stand and gripped it with two hands.

Padding along the hallway, the walking stick raised and ready, she slowed down. The noises were not those of a burglar ransacking the place nor did they come from the television. She stopped at the lounge door, took a deep breath and flung it open. 'I've phoned the police, so no funny business,' she called out, brandishing the walking stick aloft.

On the carpet in front of the fire, was a naked Jason and a young lady in the throes of making noisy and very passionate love. They stopped and looked up. 'Shit. Sorry, Ange.' Jason made to move.

'Whatever you do, don't get up.' Angie turned and slammed the door behind her.

Muffled voices could be heard and scrabbling sounds before the door opened. Jason, his face now pale despite the exertions of a few minutes ago, had his trousers on. The young lady was wearing his shirt and was sitting, knees tucked up on the floor that had till recently been the scene of their lovemaking. All Angie could think of was what her father would have said about his beloved Persian rug being used in such a way. She felt her face begin to break into a smile and forced herself to appear stern and angry.

'Sorry, Ange.' Jason looked down.

'At least you can introduce me.'

'Ange, this is Bryony. Bryony, Ange my landlady,' Jason grunted and looked away.

'Hi,' Bryony smiled and pulled the shirt tighter over her naked body. For the first time, Angie could get a good look at her. She was small and slightly built with short dark hair that framed a heart-shaped face. Soft brown eyes flecked with yellow were set under arched eyebrows which gave her a startled look. Everything about her said sweetness and softness except for her lips which were set in a firm line and suggested a very determined nature.

'Bryony...that's the name tattooed on your neck, isn't it?'

Jason ran his hand over the place where the tattoo was visible. 'Yeah. We've been together since school.' He paused and his skin flushed pink. 'It won't happen again.'

Angie nodded to acknowledge the apology. 'I hope you're using something,' she said knowing she sounded like a disapproving mother, 'and that you are over sixteen?' The last remark she addressed to Bryony.

'I'm on the pill and yeah I'm the same age as Jase.'

'In that case, you are both adults and I have no objection to you bringing a friend or your girlfriend home from time to time,' Angie said in what she hoped was a sympathetic yet fierce voice. 'Only at weekends, mind.' The last thing she wanted was to have a free house for all the waifs and strays of the town. 'Jason and I have a lot to do during the week and I'm sure you have work to go to, don't you?'

'Bryony's a receptionist at the Feathers Hotel in the High Street,' Jason announced as his chest visibly swelled with pride. 'She's at college too and doing her NVQ.'

'I want to go into management really,' Bryony explained.

'Does that mean she can stay?' Jason asked.

'Yes. Next time just tell me in advance and please confine your...' Angie paused, 'er, exploits to the bedroom.'

'Awesome, Ange.'

'I'll leave you to clear up down here.' She indicated the clothes that had been hurriedly discarded. 'I'm going to bed.' She closed the door behind her, fetched a glass of wine and went to her room.

Twenty minutes later there was the sound of muffled giggling coming up the stairs and Jason's door slammed. If Angie thought that they had slaked their passion she was wrong. Rhythmic grunting and groaning soon told her that they were up for a repeat performance. She tried not to listen. It was impossible. Perhaps she shouldn't let them sleep together, although there wouldn't be much sleeping going on tonight. She turned over, punched the pillows and covered her head with them to block out any more sounds. Except now her interest had been awakened. Her body was asking for something although she'd no idea what that something was...

If Angie had been expecting Jason and Bryony to show any embarrassment the following morning, she was mistaken. She was sitting in the conservatory, reading the Sunday papers online when the pair came downstairs. 'Can I make Bryony some breakfast?' Jason called, poking his head round the door.

'As long as you clear up afterwards and call me when you make some fresh coffee, I could do with a top up.' She went back to the business news. Her father's investments hadn't taken into account a worldwide recession. If the interest rates didn't go up again soon, she'd be in need of some cash. She could always take out a couple more credit cards and there were a number of store cards that might fill the gap until she was more flush. Yes, that would have to do. She pushed the idea out of her head. She'd be fine. She checked out Facebook, wincing at the occasional crash coming from the kitchen and salivating as the smell of bacon drifted her way until Jason called her to say the coffee was ready.

As Angie entered the kitchen, Bryony was stacking the dishwasher with the air or someone who knew what she was doing. Her make-up was smudged but she had a glow about her, a bloom that Angie did not recognise. 'Thanks for letting me stay, Miss...er,' her voice petered out.

'Call me Angie,'

'Thanks...Angie.'

Angie poured herself a coffee and sat down. Bryony joined her as Jason tidied away the marmalade and placemats which he had used on the table. Bryony cradled her cup of coffee, her brown eyes darting from side to side as they flitted from Angie to Jason.

'I'll give you a lift home, Bry, just got to sort the car out. Wouldn't start yesterday that's why we stayed in.' Jason nodded to Angie before he disappeared outside to attend to the ancient vehicle that had arrived the previous day.

Angie wracked her mind about what to say. She was tempted to ask how Bryony had slept and then smiled to herself as sleep had been the last thing on their minds. She was surprised they were up so early. 'I hope we didn't disturb you,' Bryony said, her face turning pink.

'I did hear some things.'

Bryony blushed. 'Sorry.'

'Don't be.' Angie said. 'In fact it was good to hear you having such a great time. Can I ask you something?'

Bryony jumped like a startled deer, then checked herself as if she must have realised she was not in a bargaining position. 'Go ahead.'

'Was it as good for you as it sounded?'

'What do you mean?' A car engine revving outside broke the silence.

Angie felt herself blushing to the tips of her newly tinted hair. 'Please don't think I'm some sort of pervert, asking you all these questions...there's so much in the media about sex and what to do and what not to do.'

'Oh. You mean did I have an orgasm?' Bryony relaxed. 'Don't believe everything you read or see.'

'That's just it. Where is the truth?' Angie was warming to her theme. 'My generation led such a sheltered life.'

Bryony sipped her coffee. 'Anyone would think a man just had to touch you and you have an orgasm. It isn't like that. Well, not all the time.'

Angie paused and nodded in what she hoped was an understanding manner, before continuing, 'So how

57

did you know what to do?' She tucked the cross she was wearing inside her sweater. This wasn't what she'd imagined she would be talking about on a Sunday morning.

'Sex toys. You buy them, practice and when you have sex you can tell him what to do and if he can't do it, he can use it on you.'

'Really? Interesting…' Angie was trying to think of something else to say when Jason reappeared.

'All done. Come on, Bry. Your mum's cooking us lunch. Thanks for last night, Ange.'

'It's quite all right.' Angie smiled at Bryony. 'Thanks for the chat.'

'I bet you two have been having a girly gossip about make-up and shoes, eh?' Jason ruffled Bryony's hair and Angie felt a pang of envy. Here were two people who openly cared for and were attracted to each other. She'd be lucky to find any man who was not totally repugnant and who had a pulse.

'Yes. Something like that.' Bryony winked at Angie and put her empty mug in the dishwasher.

Angie went back into the conservatory and sat down. There was far more to this sex lark than she'd realised. It was as if she was a novice again; all eagerness and no knowledge. She shuddered as the memory of her first few months at the convent came back. She'd sat down when she should have been standing, spoken on silent days and eaten on fasting days. The other nuns were sweet and helpful but she didn't want to feel embarrassed and foolish like that again, ever. She was certainly a novice as far as sex was concerned. She picked up her laptop. Not for long. She'd search online and sex toys might be a good place to start.

Chapter Six

The trouble with the internet was that it had great pictures of sex toys and nothing that Angie could really imagine. Her research needed a more practical approach. The following Monday after Jason had left for college, Angie set off for the nearest town where there was a sex shop. She'd put on a dark brown coat with a hood in the hope of blending with other middle-aged shoppers although she doubted they'd be heading to the same place. Her plan was to go into the shop, look at what was on offer, go home and buy online as she couldn't imagine handing over cash in such an obvious way. As she passed the hall table she slipped off the cross and chain and left it on the polished surface. This was not a place for religion, although Mary Magdalene might have approved.

The shopping centre was quiet with only a few people wandering about dressed in winter clothes despite the windows proclaiming that spring had arrived. She followed the main drag past familiar stores and turned sharp left by the Post Office to where she knew the shop was located. From the street, it looked as if it only sold sexy lingerie and Angie walked slowly past several times trying to peer inside. It was no good. The window dressers did a very good job of hiding the more intimate purchases from the prying eyes of casual passers-by. She would have to go in.

Angie walked up the street and down the other side, stopping to look at the display in the card store opposite as a thousand fears tumbled through her brain. Would she meet anyone she knew? Would the assistants laugh at the woman who obviously hadn't a clue about sex? And what was worse, could people tell she was a virgin? She paced up and down the street again and hovered in front of the Post Office. It would be so easy to go home, guess and order online. She checked her watch. She could be back by midday. She turned and was about to leave when she stopped. It would be such a waste of the money she'd already spent on petrol and a car parking space. 'You can do it,' she said under her breath and, taking a deep breath, she crossed the walkway and plunged in.

The interior was dark with small spotlights trained on the display units. Bras, thongs and crotchless panties in pink, red and black dangled from the ceiling. There was nothing seedy or sinister here. The music playing made it more like the boutiques of her youth. Angie stopped and gazed at the nightdresses in satin, net and lace with spaghetti straps hanging next to suspender and stocking sets in a rainbow of colours. She reached out her hand and touched one. The material was silky smooth.

'Nice ain't they?' The shop assistant looked up from the till where she was checking stock.

Angie withdrew her hand as if it had been stung. 'Very nice,' she murmured.

'We sell a lot for wedding nights,' the assistant said and went back to her work.

Angie walked on past the rows of fancy dress outfits where you could go from a nurse to a naughty schoolgirl via rubberised cat suits and wet look Santa outfits. She moved further to be confronted by packets of jelly willies, fur handcuffs and bras made out of sweets. She clamped her mouth shut or her jaw would have been on the floor. She slowed down even more as she approached a screen with a notice. *Beyond this point are things of a highly sexual nature.* 'Forgive me, Father,' Angie whispered and stopped. There was nothing to forgive, except if it was about being human.

Female voices floated from the other side of the screen. Angie walked over to a display of books and picked one up. She thumbed through the pages as she listened to their conversation.

'Don't bother with that little thing. This is better.'

'Yeah…is it noisy?'

'They all buzz but you'll be making so much noise that you won't care.' The last exchange was followed by peals of laughter.

'Right, I'll get this one and plenty of batteries.'

From behind the screen came two women, both in their mid-forties. Neither would have looked out of place at a PTA fete or a church rummage sale as they were dressed in waterproof jackets and jeans with pastel pashminas slung over their shoulders. One was carrying a box. 'That's a good book,' she said as she passed Angie. 'Plenty of ideas in there.'

Angie looked at the book in her hand. *How to have a Good Orgasm* was emblazoned on the cover. She dropped it back on the pile. Thank God no one had spotted her.

The two women went across to the cashier. 'Extra batteries for this one, please,' the one carrying the box said. If they could do it, so could she. Angie walked past the screen.

Models of the male anatomy in all shapes and colours greeted her. Some had small arms that looked like ears and which she discovered were called rabbits and others were simple wands. She picked one up and

61

ran her hands over the surface. Pink and purple were the colours of choice and at eye-watering prices which was not surprising since they all promised pleasure, thrills and satisfaction. She picked up a pink wand and turned it over in her hands. Everything was so much easier than when she was young. She remembered the hours she'd spent poring over the problems pages of her mother's magazines and exchanging teen magazines with her friends, anything to find out what this mysterious thing called sex was all about.

She put back the wand and looked at the other models on display. Some were too realistic and some needed a degree in anatomy to figure out. She picked up one and read the blurb on the box.

> *For a sensual massage that leaves you tingling, enjoy the wiggling, rotating or whirling motions and with its new extra slippery smooth finish you can be assured of a pleasurable fit.*
> *Suitable for beginners.*

That would do and she'd get it now. If she slunk out without buying something, it would hardly give the impression of the liberated woman she wanted to appear. Even so, she turned the box over so that the picture was obscured as she handed it to the cashier. Within seconds it was all done. She left the shop, her head held high and her purchase tucked away in a discreet bag

At home she unpacked her new toy and looked at it. She inserted the batteries and pressed a switch. There was a whirring and a buzzing sound. Some parts twisted and turned while others rotated to a slower rhythm. She locked the front door, switched on the central heating and went upstairs to her bedroom. She peeled off her trousers and pants and climbed into her bed, pulling the covers over her. She switched on the trembling ears and moved it slowly towards her crotch. Once it was close to her pubic zone, she pressed it down. She pulled her hand away as if she'd been stung. Bloody hell, was it supposed to feel that weird? She tried again. It was about as comfortable as a nest of wasps attacking her and the buzzing was louder than she expected. She stretched out. She'd get used to the sound in time. Besides, practice made perfect, didn't it?

'Have you done your hair different, Ange?' Jason said that evening as she ladled meat and vegetables onto a plate, already groaning with cabbage and mashed potatoes.

'No.'

'Oh. You just look different.' He peered at her. 'No it's make-up. You've got blusher on that's why you look a bit pink.' Satisfied with his summary, he attacked the food and all went quiet. Angie said nothing. Her trip to town today had been worth it if it had that effect so early on in her experimentation.

***

It was early Wednesday evening and Angie was in the kitchen. A lone blackbird warbled outside in the garden. The rhythmic clatter of knife on chopping board as she diced onions and carrots harmonized with the lazy tick-tock of the kitchen clock. A pan of meat sauce bubbled on the hob; its savoury smell mingling with the candied aroma of a treacle tart that was baking in the oven. A jug of custard stood ready to be poured over it. Jason was partial to a pudding and it would help fill up his ever-hungry stomach.

Angie chopped onions with a spoon in her mouth because she'd read somewhere it stopped you crying. It didn't so she leant back to stop the tears falling into the onions. There was a hammering at the door. Angie checked the time. It was gone six and no one was expected. 'Jason,' she yelled and the spoon fell out and clanged on the floor. 'Get that will you?'

She tipped the vegetables into the sauce and stirred, straining to hear the hushed conversation that was happening at the front door. 'It's someone for you, Ange,' he called out before the door slammed and footsteps thumped down the hall.

Angie turned to see Maggie standing in the doorway. She had on her green work overalls and her hair had been pulled back in a tight ponytail. For once there was not a scrap of make-up on her face and if Angie didn't know her better she'd have sworn Maggie had been crying. 'Maggie, what's up? Are the kids OK?'

Maggie slumped down at the kitchen table. Angie noticed she'd given the room a quick appraisal. 'Nice place you've got here and yes the kids are OK, up to a point. Although if you think bunking off school and failing his mocks is doing OK then yes Gareth is absolutely hunky dory.'

Angie put a lid on the sauce and switched on the kettle. 'Tea first.' She got out cups and saucers. Maggie sat and stared out of the window. She'd never been like this before. Something must be very wrong indeed. It was only when she'd poured them both a cup and was sitting down that she spoke again. 'Come on, Maggie, tell me what's up.' She clapped a hand over her mouth, 'Oh God, you're not pregnant are you?' She was about to make the sign of the cross when she stopped herself and turned it into a rearrangement of the sweater over her chest.

'Bloody hell, Ange. I've had less sex than you…no, that can't be true. I am certainly not pregnant.' There was silence again as Angie waited for Maggie to take another sip of her tea. 'Remember I told you the place where I work had a few money worries?'

'I thought you said the family who owned it weren't in it for the cash?'

'Wrong. It turns out that they are selling to the highest bidder and that bidder is about to do a hatchet job on the place.'

'What do you mean?' Angie filled up their cups again.

'They're closing it down, chucking everyone out or *rehoming* them as they're calling it.' She shook her head. 'What on earth will happen to Mr James? The place has been his home for nearly ten years.' She looked up. 'He feeds the ducks every morning and they come right up to his hand.' The clock wheezed and struck six, each chime ringing through the silence that hung between them.

Maggie spoke first. 'After a brief refurbishment, they're reopening under new management.'

'That will be good won't it? You're always telling me that you could run it more efficiently.'

'Yes and we could. There's plenty of ways to save money.' She pulled a face. 'No one ever listens to us. Instead, they've got this new guy coming in and he's been told to slash costs. I reckon it'll end up like all the other places where the clients get fed, watered, toileted and left in their chairs or beds for hours at an end. Mind if I have a fag outside?'

'Smoke in here if you like. I think I've got an

ashtray.' Angie scrabbled in the dresser cabinet and found one that had been her father's before he decided the habit was filthy and forbade her to date anyone who indulged. Maggie lit up and smoke spiralled above her head.

Angie checked the oven and removed the treacle tart. She didn't know what to say. She had been used to dealing with any number of upset people when she'd been at the convent. This was different. Maggie was a friend and somehow that made it harder to find the right words. 'This might sound crazy but can't you get another job? There must be better places.' Angie leaned against the sink and watched as Maggie blew a smoke ring. The look on Maggie's face was enough. She knew the answer before it came.

'It's not as easy as that. If I don't accept the new regime, I'll be making myself redundant. That means no benefits until I can find an alternative and there's no shortage of cheaper agency staff.'

'With your experience, surely you'll be snapped up?' Angie made her voice sound as upbeat as she could.

'My CV is hopelessly out of date.'

'That's easy to change.' Angie noticed Maggie's raised eyebrows. 'I used to help some of our parents with stuff like that to get them back into work,' she explained. 'I can do the same for you.' Angie tasted the sauce and added more pepper. She turned to face Maggie. 'It could just be rumours, couldn't it?'

'No.' Maggie crushed the cigarette into the ashtray. 'The Hatchet Man's second in command came to talk to us today.'

Angie filled another pan with water, set it to boil and fetched a packet of spaghetti from the cupboard.

She wasn't used to seeing Maggie so downhearted. 'There must be something we can do?'

Maggie shrugged. 'Such as?'

'What about a bit of publicity? Something like… Excellent care home forced to close with shocking reduction of facilities for the clients?'

'I'm not sure. I've never been a campaign sort of person.' Maggie shook her head.

Angie paused, spaghetti in her hand and watched as the water bubbled in the saucepan. 'Isn't it worth a try? The very least it'll do is embarrass Hatchet Man. What's his name by the way?'

'He's called Paul Buchannan.'

Angie curled the spaghetti into the bubbling water and pressed it down. The name sounded familiar. 'Is he local?'

'Dunno.' Maggie looked at her watch. 'Hell, I'd better be going. The kids will be starving.' She hugged Angie. 'Thanks for letting me explode like that. I needed it.' She picked up her bag and was about to leave when Angie called after her.

'I'm serious about the publicity. There's been far too much in the news about poor quality care homes.' Angie folded her arms and leaned against the cooker. 'The local press loves a bit of juicy gossip.'

Maggie looked at Angie. 'How come you know so much about this sort of thing?'

Angie stroked the cross that was hidden under her sweater. 'We had plenty of dealings with the press when there was an alleged scandal with a priest and some young parishioners.' The memories were as raw as ever and she tried not to flinch. 'At one time they were even camping outside the convent. It was my job to deal with them.'

Maggie picked up her bag and headed off down the hallway. She stopped and turned back. 'I often wonder where I'd have ended up if I'd taken a bit more notice of school. At least you've got a career to fall back on, not like me.'

Angie followed. She had come to expect Maggie to be the strong one, forever coming up with a sharp retort, ready to take on the world. Not this time. She had to do something to help. 'Think about what I said. A campaign might just work.'

'I will. See you on Friday as usual?' Maggie fumbled in her bag for her car keys.

'Not this Friday. I'm moving, remember?'

Maggie clapped a hand to her head. 'Yeah, sorry. I'm too caught up in my own troubles.'

'I know you offered to help so if you've got other things to do, it'll be all right. Jason and I can manage.'

Maggie leaned on the car door. 'Never. I said I'd help and I will. I've got a day owing me from all the overtime I did so it won't cost. I'll be there.' She got into her car and Angie watched as it spluttered down the road.

Angie closed the door. What on earth could she do to help? Any further thoughts were swept aside as a fierce hissing sound from the kitchen told her the spaghetti was boiling over.

'I've got it, Ange,' called Jason. He was standing at the range and mopping at the sticky liquid that oozed over the top of the pan. 'Trouble?' he asked.

'Jason, you've lived here all your life, haven't you?' Angie leaned against the dresser.

'Yep. Will this be ready?' He poked at the pan with a wooden spoon.

'Test it. What I want to know is if you can

remember any scandal, stuff about hospitals in the area closing…things like that?'

Jason twirled a strand of spaghetti around a fork and dropped it into his mouth. 'Done.' He drained the spaghetti and tipped it back into the pan, adding the sauce which he stirred. 'My gran would have known. She read the local rag every week. You could try there.' He stopped, the spoon in mid-air. 'Any use?' He went back to his stirring.

'It's certainly worth a try.' An idea was forming in her head. It would take some research though. Once the house move was out of the way, she'd check out the local papers. She would not sit back and do nothing. Maggie needed her and a warm fuzzy feeling spread through her, like the feeling she used to get when a pupil read a difficult word, mastered the seven times table or did a forward roll for the first time. 'Right let's eat,' she said and got out the plates.

It was only as she lay in bed later that night that she realised where she'd heard the name Paul Buchannan before. He was going to be her new neighbour.

Chapter Seven

On Friday that same week the removal van arrived. Maggie had offered to help by waiting at the bungalow while Angie stayed behind to hand the estate agent the key to the old place. The two young men made light work of packing up the van and Angie waved them off. There was just one black bag that sat waiting on the front step. Whether it was destined for the bin or the back of her car, she hadn't decided. She opened it up. It was full of the reporter's notebooks that contained the record of her life. She selected one at random.

Tuesday 22nd March 1989

Bright day. School staff full of plans for new curriculum.
Father Benedict not at confession. Monsignor officiated.
Compline chant 45. Sister Dominica has flu.

What a bloody pointless existence. She had been so desperate to make a difference and it had all gone sour. Angie threw the notebook back in the bag, tied up the top and dumped it by the bin. She wanted to take a final walk through the garden.

The grass sank under her feet as she headed towards the plum tree that stood in the centre. She leaned against its damp, cold bark and breathed in the earthy smell. She ran a finger along the groove in the thick branch where her rope swing had been. She closed her eyes as unwelcome voices floated from the past.

'Don't go too high, Angela...'

'Don't twizzle like that, you'll be sick...'

'Don't ride your bike on the lawn, it'll make such a mess...'

'Don't…don't…don't.' The familiar refrains echoed in her ears and she shook her head to chase away the sounds, except more joined in a steady chorus of disapproval.

'Why waste your time on the arts, a business degree is the way forward…'

'What a pity you didn't make Oxbridge, such a disappointment to us all.'

Angie swallowed hard and blinked back the tears. How could she be the perfect daughter? Such a person didn't exist although perhaps if she'd been funnier, cleverer, more hardworking, less dreamy it might have been different. Now she'd never be able to win her parent's approval. She'd always feel a failure and that thought hurt like hell.

'Mum there's a tree. A proper tree. Can we have a swing?' Angie was jolted back to the real world by voices as a tumble of bodies hurtled round the corner of the drive into the back garden. She wiped her eyes on her sleeve. The voices stopped. A bundle of fur and energy did not and bounced at her, leaping up with dirty paws leaving muddy prints on her sweater.

'Down, Bobby, get down. I'm so sorry.' A tall woman sprang forward and dragged Bobby away. She was dressed in leggings, a huge stripy sweater that hung down to her knees and furry boots. A small child, no more than five, looked up at Angie.

'Why 'ith that lady in our garden?' His squeaky voice had a slight lisp and as he opened his mouth Angie could see he was in the gappy phase of childhood.

'Shh. That's rude.' She held out her hand. 'I'm Jane and this is Sam and you've already met Bobby. We've just arrived.'

71

'Oh heavens. I am sorry. I was just saying goodbye to the garden and the house.' Angie forced a smile. 'I meant to wait at the front to give the keys to someone.' She fumbled in her pocket and handed them over.

'Please don't rush away. As long as we can get into the house and let the removals men in, we can get started,' Jane said. 'The older two will be home from school soon and it'll be chaos.' She ran a hand through her brown hair and grinned. 'It's a lovely house. We're so excited. The children can have a bedroom each at last. That should stop a load of arguments.' She ruffled Sam's hair and he squirmed away from her.

'I'd better go and catch up with my removals men or everything will be in the wrong place tonight.' Angie bent down to speak to Sam who was glaring as much at his mum as Angie. 'If you want to make a good swing, ask your dad to put the rope over this branch, it will fit in the groove here. If you swing high enough, you can see the whole world.' She winked at the woman and turned to go. 'I hope you will be very happy here.'

'I'm sure we will,' the woman said and hugged Sam to her.

Angie walked away, her head held high. Without another backward glance, she picked up the black bag, slung it into the boot and got into her car. 'And if ever you start feeling sorry for yourself, read that lot,' she said and drove off with the radio turned up loud to drown out the cries of any remaining demons that wanted to follow.

The removal van was already parked in front of the driveway when she arrived at the bungalow, and

Maggie was standing by the open back, directing operations. 'Thank goodness you're here. We have a slight problem.' She jerked her head in the direction of the neighbour. '*Mr. Helpful Next Door* has complained that the van is blocking the road and what would we do if there was an emergency?'

'We'd move it, wouldn't we?'

'That's what I said to him. He whinged about the length of time it was taking before he slunk away.' Maggie glared in the direction of the neighbour's bungalow.

Angie's heart beat faster. This was not the time for there to be aggravation between her and Paul Buchannan. For the moment it was essential that she kept his identity from Maggie as that might scupper the plan that had been forming in her head over the past few days. 'I'd better go and say sorry.'

Angie left Maggie to continue organising the removal men and walked across what would now be her front lawn. As she approached the driveway of Paul Buchannan's house, she slowed down. The path to the front door was newly paved in a pattern of hexagons, interspersed with squares and all in muted shades of reddish browns. The lawns were edged with meticulous precision and even the plants in the black ceramic bowls on the doorstep were devoid of any brown leaves or dead heads. She paused for a few minutes to pluck up courage and spotted the curtains moving. A face peeked out from behind them and withdrew. Angie walked up to the porch and took a deep breath. She rapped on the front door using a brass knocker that gleamed against the white paint. The door opened. 'Yes?'

'Hi. I'm your new neighbour, Angie.' She held out

her hand. 'I just want to apologise for the van parked in the road. It won't be there for long, I haven't got a lot to unpack.'

Blue eyes, etched at the corners with fine lines glared at her. He ignored her outstretched hand and nodded. 'Thanks for the information.' The door closed.

Angie shrugged and walked off. 'Welcome to the neighbourhood. Nice to meet you,' she murmured under her breath. Didn't it say in the Bible that even in Paradise there was a snake? There was no way she was going to let a miserable old git like him spoil her new life, even though she did not fail to spot that for someone in his early fifties, he was a very slim, elegant gentleman with longer than usual greying hair that gave him a distinguished look. 'Let's hope you've got a single brother,' she said under her breath as she rejoined Maggie to continue to oversee the removals.

Maggie was busy unpacking glasses and putting them into the kitchen cabinet when Angie remembered the notebooks. She heaved the bag into the largest bedroom which would be hers. The ancient brass bedstead with its lumpy mattress was placed against the long wall and her father's school trunk, rescued from the attic in the old house, was in the middle of the floor. She opened it, tipped the notebooks inside and slammed the lid down. They could stay there until she was ready to get rid of them. She shoved the trunk under the bed and went to help Maggie sort out plates and cutlery or they'd have nothing to eat with for the rest of the day.

The kitchen was full of empty boxes and Maggie was humming as she sorted and stacked the contents. 'I can't thank you enough,' Angie began. She was cut short.

'I'm glad to be here.' Maggie wiped a shelf with a cloth and arranged some etched wine glasses in order of size. 'Work will be a bloody nightmare today.'

Angie picked up a box and flattened it. 'Why?'

Maggie stopped. 'We all got an email yesterday from the takeover company. We've got three months before the sale goes through and that will be it.'

Angie punched another box flat. 'Are you sure?'

Maggie sniffed and picked up another glass. 'Yes, so any help with my CV would be appreciated.' Her voice was quiet.

Angie went over and placed her arms round her shoulders. 'I'm sure it will work out all right,' she said.

'Have you got a special arrangement with him upstairs?' Angie flinched. 'Sorry that was uncalled for.' Maggie looked down.

'Something will turn up.'

Maggie broke away. 'We'd better get a move on or you'll be eating your breakfast off paper plates tomorrow. Shove that box over here.'

It was gone six when the removals van drew away and Maggie and Angie sank down on a rug that they had unrolled in the lounge. The table, chairs and old wardrobes in heavy dark wood had gone to a recycling charity and the sofa and armchairs had been collected by the council and taken to the tip. Everything else was in boxes piled up in each room; at least she and Jason would have a bed to sleep on and they could eat in the kitchen at the breakfast bar.

Maggie produced a bottle of wine and a corkscrew and poured them both a glass. 'Here's to new beginnings.' She clinked her glass against Angie's. Before Angie could raise the glass to her lips, a

75

clanking and clattering like someone shaking a load of rusty nails in a bucket could be heard from outside.

Angie got up and went to investigate. Parked on her driveway and surrounded by stinking black smoke was Jason's car. An armchair was lashed to the top of the roof. The stuffing bulged out from a series of holes and the pink roses of the upholstery were almost obscured by brown stains. From time to time a strange rumbling coming from the engine broke the quiet of The Close. Jason looked up as Angie opened the front door. 'Hi Angie. Trouble with the old car. Shouldn't take too long to mend.' He looked up and down The Close. 'It's nice here. Me and Bryony would like a place like this eventually.'

'What is that?' Angie pointed to the chair.

'It's all right, Ange, I've got one for you too.' Another chair was poking out of the back of the car.

'How the hell did you—?'

'I went real slow and we both need somewhere to sit and watch telly don't we?' he said. He disappeared under the bonnet again and tweaked something. The engine revved and more black smoke pumped from the exhaust.

It was at that point Angie spotted a figure crossing the front lawn. It was her neighbour. 'Could you explain what is the meaning of this noise and this smell?' he demanded.

'Sorry, mate. Won't take long.' Jason looked up.

A red flush began to spread over Paul Buchannan's face. 'First I am not a mate and secondly this was a pleasant, quiet area until you and your son arrived.' He turned to Angie and stood as if waiting for an apology.

This was too much for Angie. She stepped

forward, pulled herself up to her full height and stared straight at him, before answering, 'Let's get something clear, can we? First he is not my son and second if Jason says it won't take long, believe me it won't. We've just moved in and we are carrying out our business on our land and if you cannot put up with a few minutes of noise, I am sorry. However, there is nothing I intend to do about it.' He was just a typical bully. Call their bluff and it's like pulling the plug on a bouncy castle—all the hot air leaves and the thing collapses. She folded her arms and waited.

'In that case, tell your boyfriend this has always been a respectable neighbourhood and it had better stay that way.' He turned to go then spun round. 'And if you don't get those damned trees cut back, I'll come and cut them down myself.' He pointed to the Leylandii dominating the fence that divided their back gardens.

'I find what you have said offensive. I agree there's a bit of noise, knowing Jason and his brilliance with engines, if he says it will only take a few minutes he means it. As for the matter of the trees, I will deal with them if you address the issue of those branches overhanging my roof.' Angie glared at him, defying him to answer back. 'Finally, you are on my property without an invitation and so are technically trespassing. If you do not leave and indeed if you come onto my land again without an invitation, I will have to call the police.'

As if on cue, Jason slammed the bonnet down. The chair jolted and slid from the top of the car. It landed on the grass at Paul Buchannan's feet. He jumped out of the way just in time. Angie heard Maggie snigger before she turned it into a cough and felt the corners of her own mouth twitch. 'All done. Sorry about that, mate.' Jason wiped his greasy hands down his jeans as Paul Buchannan's mouth opened to say something and snapped shut again.

'Let's go inside, Jason.' Angie put a hand in the centre of his back and propelled him towards the door. 'You're wasting your breath.'

Chapter Eight

On Monday morning, Angie set off for the library. It was a modern building with a plate glass frontage that looked out over the High Street. Beanbags were lying on the floor of the children's area, a coffee machine bubbled in the corner and computers were dotted along the sides of the room. She waited until a young woman, dressed in a red pencil skirt and yellow blouse came over from where she had been sorting a pile of picture books. 'Good morning. What can I do for you?' The name on the lanyard hanging from her neck said she was called Lisa and was the chief librarian.

'I used to visit the library here before I moved away and there was a reference section. Does it still exist?' Angie said.

'What were you looking for exactly?' Lisa pushed her dark hair back behind her ears and smiled.

'I wanted to find out about recent campaigns against the cuts, closures, things like that.'

'You want the local paper.' She handed over a card with a login and password.

'Thanks.' Angie went and sat down at a terminal and logged on.

'It might be useful to check out the campaign to save the local maternity hospital. There was a real battle over that and the campaigners won,' Lisa called out.

'That's where I'll start.' Angie typed in *maternity hospital* and began to read.

One name that kept cropping up was Polly Cadwallader. With her hair swept up into a bun and the gold-rimmed spectacles perched on the end of her nose, she looked like a retired teacher. Numerous quotes were splashed across any page where she was featured and they all focussed on her argument that small was good and local was best. She was just the person Angie needed. Finding her proved remarkably easy too. A quick search on the name and the area provided three results: only one was over sixty. A registration to 192192 and she had a phone number.

Once home, Angie checked the clock. It was 1.30 pm and lunchtime for a lot of people. She'd leave it until mid-afternoon which would give her the chance to tackle the unappealing task of trying to clean one of the chairs that Jason had brought home. Armed with a bowl of soapy liquid, a sponge and industrial strength rubber gloves she set to. While she was scrubbing away at decades of encrusted dirt, the sound of a car engine starting and stopping accompanied by a clinking sound intrigued her. Sponge in hand, she sneaked a peek through the curtains. Paul Buchannan was outside rattling the door of his car. He switched the engine on and she watched as the passenger window jolted and jammed open. He got out and looked over at her place. She stepped back and hoped he hadn't spotted her. She shrank against the wall as footsteps crossed the gravel drive and someone thumped on her door.

'Coming,' she said as breezily as she could, took a deep breath, wiped her hands down her trousers and opened the door. Paul Buchannan was standing there dressed in a grey suit, white shirt and a grey and red silk tie. She waited for him to accuse her of spying and wondered what excuse she could give.

'I'm sorry to bother you in the middle of your

cleaning.' Angie put down the sponge and peeled off the rubber gloves. The look on his face was enough to tell her what he thought of her appearance. 'I realise we haven't got off on a very good note and I apologise.' He paused. 'I am in a bit of a fix though and I was wondering if your young guest was here?'

For a second Angie was tempted to tell him to get lost. His speech sounded too rehearsed. 'He left for college ages ago. Why?'

'The window on my car has jammed open and I just thought he'd be able to work some magic. It doesn't matter, I'll get a taxi to the station.' He turned to go.

'Wait a minute,' Angie called after him. 'I can take you. It could be tricky to get a taxi at this time of the day.' She put down her gloves and grabbed her keys off the hall table.

'You're very kind. I can't possible take you away from your...' he gazed at Angie's faded sweatshirt and stained trousers.

'I'll be glad to get away from the dirt.' She slammed the door shut. It could prove very useful to be in a car with Paul Buchannan. Somehow the closed interior encouraged intimacy. People talked more and she might learn something about his plans for the care home.

'That's very kind of you. I might not make the two-thirty train if I have to wait for a taxi. I'll just grab my bag.'

Angie stuffed the cardboard boxes that were destined for the tip onto the back seat and waited while Paul locked up. He clambered in beside her. 'You must let me pay for the petrol.'

Angie put the car into gear and reversed down the

drive. 'There's no need. Give it to a favourite charity instead, if you have one.'

They lapsed into silence until they reached the main road and headed towards the centre of town. 'You're off to London then?' Angie said in what she hoped was a disinterested yet neighbourly voice. 'Business?'

'Yes and no. My brother is in poor health and I need to see him. While I'm up there I can visit head office.'

'Head office, eh?' Angie swerved to avoid a kamikaze cat that had shot across in front of her. 'What's your line of business? No, let me guess.' She pretended to think hard. 'Something in investment banking?'

'I wish. Nothing as lucrative as that. I specialise in takeovers, cost cutting, getting a dead-end business and pulling it back into shape. I work for a company of investors, as a freelance. They buy. I make it a viable business on paper and they get on with the rest.'

'What sort of businesses?' Angie said.

'Anything. In the past I've dealt with a printing company, a small pottery, a chain of hairdressers and a nationwide furniture store. Now there's a growing market in care homes. That's what this is about.'

'Care homes are different aren't they. The very word is *care* isn't it?' Angie hoped he'd take the bait and let slip something.

'Same thing, profit or loss makes the world turn. I just do a job, that's all there is to it.' Paul spoke without any emotion.

'Oh I see.' They drove on in silence for a short time. He'd given her an idea for a possible campaign.

The gist would be how unscrupulous it was to treat humans with the same ideas of profit and loss that you would use for sofas or beds. She pulled into the car park opposite the small station. 'You'll make the afternoon train.'

'I really can't thank you enough.' Paul came over to the driver's side and Angie wound down the window. 'I'll make a very big donation to my favourite charity.'

'And what is that?' Angie half expected it to be for a self-interest group of bastard businessmen.

'It's for children who've been abused.' Angie froze. She was back at the convent, standing in front of Sister Catherine, begging her to make sure Father Benedict was not left alone with young children. *Shut up, shut up* her mind screamed. Paul did not shut up, and she gripped the wheel as he looked away for a few seconds before continuing. 'My brother was abused at school by the parish priest and he's never got over it.' She held her breath as his words ripped open wounds she thought had been healed. 'Thanks again.' He slung the bag over his shoulder and headed into the station.

Nausea swept over Angie. Her head slumped on the wheel and she closed her eyes. She'd been a fool to think the past was behind her. Seconds ticked past and turned into minutes and she stayed where she was, motionless, lost in the pain of her memories. Sounds of a train arriving and departing filtered through. She took a deep breath and looked up. The anguish was no longer just for her. Nor was her sympathy for Paul Buchannan. She put the car into gear and pulled away. She couldn't do anything to help Paul's brother. She could damn well help

Maggie. As soon as she got back home she'd call Polly Cadwallader.

Inside the hall she dialled the number she'd found. The phone was picked up on the third ring and a breathless voice shouted out, 'Yes? Down you two, sorry, caller, not you, the dogs. I've just got back after lunchtime walkies. Can you hang on while I get them a drink?' Without waiting for a reply the phone was put down and Angie could hear frantic barking and a clatter, like a metal bowl being dropped on a stone floor.

'There, all done,' the voice came back and was less breathless this time. 'Polly Cadwallader here. What can I do for you?'

'I hope you don't think I'm being presumptuous,' Angie said, 'I remember reading a lot about you when there was the campaign to save the local hospital and I wondered if you had any tips?'

'Got something in mind?' Angie could hear the mounting excitement in Polly's voice.

'Yes. It's about a care home.'

'That's a new one on me. I've saved fields, hospitals and some crumbling buildings of dubious historical interest…never a care home. What's the problem?'

Angie crossed her fingers and explained the situation. There was a pause before Polly answered. 'Come and see me. Can you make this afternoon about four? I know it's short notice but there's a couple of Council meetings coming up and I'd love to see old Jenkins get his comeuppance. I bet he's got his snout in the trough.'

'Jenkins?'

'Councillor William Jenkins, Chair of the Planning

Committee. We've crossed swords a number of times. Can you get over here?'

'Yes. I can—'Angie was cut short.

'Littlecote Mill, just off the main road before you get to The Common.'

'Right, I'll be there.' Polly rang off. Angie replaced the phone. She only hoped she had not started something she couldn't finish.

Littlecote Mill was up a bumpy drive that was more like a dirt track, made worse by the previous three bad winters. Even the potholes had potholes. She negotiated the car past the worst, bumped and splashed her way through others as any different manoeuvre would take her perilously close to the edge and a precipitous slide into the mill race that bubbled along the bottom of the valley. She pulled into a wide space in front of a three-storey, redbrick building that huddled under the trees growing on the hillsides. Their branches stretched up to the sky where a dim sun struggled to pierce the dank clouds. Even at this time of the year, when the hedgerows were bursting with the sounds of songbirds, only a crow's squawk disturbed the silence. Angie shivered and hoped it wasn't a bad omen.

A studded wooden door was set into the wall and a bell with a rope clapper hung by the side. Angie rang it. There was the sound of ferocious barking, the pattering of paws and a thump, followed by another as a dog or two launched themselves at the intruder who dared to disturb their peace. Thank God the door was sturdy. She crossed herself to apologise for the profanities which she noted were becoming more numerous. 'Satan, Beelzebub, down, do get down,' a male voice shouted as the door opened a crack. 'Ah you must be here to see Polly.' A white-haired gentleman in a long grey cardigan, a pipe clamped between his teeth, was holding onto the collars of two very lively brown and white boxer dogs. He opened the door fully and dragged the dogs back as they strained to get closer to Angie; whether it was to tear her apart or lick her to death she didn't want to find out. 'Polly, your girl is here,' he called as Angie stepped inside. 'This way.'

Angie picked her way between piles of newspapers, books, seats overflowing with jackets and coats, muddy boots and shoes, a large stand with walking sticks and umbrellas and boxes of empty tins and bottles, destined for recycling. Her optimism was fading. If Polly's organisation was as good as her housework, Maggie might as well turn up at the job centre next week.

For some reason Angie's legs were now shaking as she continued down the hallway under beams adorned with cobwebs and it wasn't from a fear of spiders. Hanging on tobacco-smoke-stained walls were a series of portraits in ornate gilt frames. Faces of what must have been ancestors frowned down as she passed. With each step she was getting more and more anxious. Her pathetic attempts to help Maggie couldn't possibly be of any use. She'd make a fool of herself. Polly would tell her it was impossible. The hall opened into a lounge with a roaring fire and it was too late for any further thoughts.

'Ahh there you are.' A woman stood up from the seat in front of the fire and stepped forward. Polly Cadwallader's hair was swept up into a messy bun and framed a face that was once beautiful and even now could be described as handsome. A purple velvet skirt and black velvet jacket accentuated a slim figure. Heavy silver and wooden beads hung from her neck. Purple Doc Marten shoes and black fishnet tights showed off shapely legs. Her eyes fixed on Angie with a burning intensity that would have scared the life out of any wrongdoer or anyone that wanted to pull a fast one on Polly Cadwallader. 'Let's go into the garden room. John, get us some tea can you?' She swept out as the dogs fought over the seat she had recently vacated.

The garden room was an octagonal conservatory that looked out over the back lawn and down to the stream. It was furnished with white metal seats and an inlaid table was set in the middle on which was perched a laptop. 'The WiFi is fine here,' Polly said as she sat down and indicated a chair for Angie. 'I've been doing a bit of googling.' She reached for her laptop. John came in with a tray, two mugs and a plate of homemade flapjacks. Angie accepted the tea but declined the flapjacks as the plate had some strange dried scraps attached to it. Polly took one and snapped her fingers. The two dogs bounded in and gobbled up all the remaining flapjacks then chased the plate over the floor before John picked it up and shooed them back to their place on the couch.

Polly tapped at the keyboard. Mesmerised by the flying fingers, Angie counted her rings. An emerald the size of a small egg and a sapphire encircled by glittering diamonds fought for space with three silver bands. How could she type so fast? Polly pushed the screen over to Angie. 'Look at this. The planning is done and dusted. There's nothing we can do about that. Cost cutting, however, is never a popular item. What else can you tell me?' She leaned back and waited.

Angie told her the facts as far as she knew them and at the news that all the residents were to be rehoused Polly's eyes lit up. 'That's what we need...the human touch. No one likes to think of poor old Aunt Mavis or Uncle Bert being shifted from pillar to post.' She pulled the keyboard towards her, tapped away and paused to read. 'Just as I thought, there's a Friends Association. I wonder how much they know about all this?' She studied the webpage again. 'Here's what we need. There's an email and a phone number of the chair. Damn me. Now I know why the planning got through so easily. The chair is none other than Billy Jenkins who just happens to chair the Planning Committee. I wonder how many feathers we could ruffle at the next meeting by staging a small demonstration and letting the Friends know too. Got your diary?'

Two hours later Angie had been initiated into a world of which previously she had been totally unaware. Polly had been able to rustle up a dozen or so committed protesters who would bear placards against the sky being blue if they had the chance. Their motive was to embarrass the current administration over anything and everything before the next election. It was left to Angie to get Maggie and the staff on-side as their support was crucial for the success of the plan. If they could prove there was a better way and save money, they were on to a winner. She needed to get them ready for action before the next Council meeting.

Angie stood up. 'I really can't thank you enough.'

'Nonsense. I'd love another crack at old Billy Boy and it's a damn sight more interesting than doing the bloody crosswords.' She led Angie out through the lounge where two dogs and John Cadwallader were snoring on the sofa. 'See what I mean?' She didn't wait for an answer. 'You married?' Angie shook her head.

'When you get asked, make sure he's younger than you. Get a toy boy.' She stood aside to let Angie out.

'Er, there's one thing I'd like to know.' Angie paused on the doorstep. 'Why do you call your dogs Satan and Beelzebub?'

Polly frowned. 'Because they're bloody devils.' And she shrugged as if explaining the obvious to a simple child. 'Give me a call next week when you've spoken to your friend.'

Angie got into her car. Dusk was falling and the sound of a lone blackbird pierced the gloom. She listened to the flute-like notes. It was a call to action. Polly knew just what to do and Angie's fears faded away. It was going to be fine. All she had to do was talk to Maggie.

She manoeuvred the car onto the main road and headed back towards the town. As she drove, traces of her conversation with Paul Buchannan came back. With her knowledge of the inner workings of the church, she might just be able to point him in the direction of some help or at the very least a sympathetic ear for his brother. She checked the time. It was too late to cook. She'd stop at the chippie and Jason would have to make do today. She had bigger fish to fry. She smiled at the unintended joke as she let the clutch out and headed home.

Chapter Nine

'Why do you look like the cat that's got the cream?' Maggie asked on Friday evening as she and Angie relaxed with a glass of wine. 'Is it a man?' She looked at Angie over the rim of the glass, her eyes wide open and her eyebrows nearly touching the lines on her forehead.

Angie shook her head, pleased that Maggie was in a lighter mood although the shadows under her eyes suggested a different story. 'I've been to see someone who might be able to help with the plans for the care home.'

'Really?' Maggie sat up. 'Tell me more.'

Maggie listened, perched on the edge of her seat as Angie described her meeting with Polly Cadwallader. 'So everything is set up and ready to go. I really need you to get *your* team on our side, if you can?' Angie didn't have to wait long for a reply.

'They'll be champing at the bit,' Maggie said, rubbing her hands together. 'We've banged on for years that we could save money and maintain the quality of care needed.' She sat back in her seat. 'You just wait 'til I tell the others. You can bet we'll get a damn good turnout.'

They sat in silence for a while. Angie was sure that Maggie's eyes were damp and she was using the time to compose herself. Even so, when she spoke there was a slight tremor in her voice. 'You know I can't thank you enough for all of this. You didn't have to do it. God knows you've enough to get on with in your own life.'

Knowing she was of use produced a familiar inner

glow. 'Somehow this feels more real than anything I've done in a long time and who knows I might get swept off my feet by one of these protesters? They can't all be students, can they?'

'From my knowledge they'll be either very rich with trust funds and Daddy is a banker sort of thing or they're old hippies who've got lost in some time warp and think the revolution is just about to happen.' Maggie held out her glass and Angie refilled it. 'No matter, as long as they've got a pulse…' There was a pause. 'You know what you need, don't you?

'I'm sure you're going to tell me,' Angie said and smiled. Maggie was back to her usual brash and bossy self.

'Internet dating.' Maggie helped herself to a handful of nuts.

'Really? I suppose you've had extensive experience of this?'

The sarcasm was not lost on Maggie. 'Don't get all 1950s. Just hear me out will you?'

'Go on then,' Angie sniffed. 'I suppose I've got lots to learn about…dating and all that.'

Maggie leaned forward, her eyes sparkled and her voice was as excited as a child's on Christmas morning. 'It's all the rage. Everyone's doing it.' She stopped as Angie raised one eyebrow.

'Is this something that you have personally done?' Angie asked, picking an imaginary fleck from the immaculate white sweater she wore with her very first pair of skinny jeans.

'Not exactly me, but I know plenty of people who have.' Maggie poured nuts into her mouth and chewed.

'I'm not sure…I suppose I think Mr Right will

somehow just turn up.'

'For heaven's sake, Angie, it's the modern way. Did you know almost twenty per cent of relationships begin online?'

'You sound like one of those adverts on the telly.' Angie swirled the wine in her glass, avoiding Maggie's insistent gaze. There were times when Angie felt that she was a gauche teenager back at school and Maggie was about to make a withering comment over something she was wearing. She remained silent.

Maggie was the first to crack. 'At least have a look at one of the sites and if it isn't for you, I promise not to say anything else, ever,' she said and ran a hand through the red hair that was desperately in need of a retouch at the roots.

'I suppose it won't do any harm just to take a look. Though I'm not promising anything.'

'That's my girl. We'll soon get you fixed up with some dates. A hot looking lady like you will be snapped up in no time.' Maggie leaned over and refilled Angie's glass. She opened her laptop and tapped away.

Angie had to admit that Maggie's advice on clothes and Tasha's make-up and hair together with the weight she'd lost made her look less than her forty-nine years. Whether that was enough to attract a discerning male and not just any old fruitcake that fancied sex was in doubt in her mind. As for being described as a hot looking lady, she shuddered. She felt as hot as a wet Sunday in November.

'Take a look at these sites.' Maggie passed over her laptop.

Angie scrolled down, reading out loud. '*Flirty dating? Fun dating? For serious relationships only?*' She stopped and looked at Maggie. 'Are these all genuine?'

'They certainly are. That one would suit you, wouldn't it?' Maggie pointed to a site that was for Christians only.

Angie pulled a face and carried on reading, '*For urban singles who want action,* that's not me. This one says it is for *Educated Singles.*' That sounded more promising. She clicked on the icon.

'Move over.' Maggie came and sat down by her side and together they read in silence, each taking in what they needed to know. 'It's very reasonable for twelve months.'

'Will I need that long?' Angie's face fell.

'You don't want to go straight into something serious do you? After all this time you want to play the field a bit, surely?'

'I've never really thought about it.'

Maggie took a deep breath. 'Remember what we used to say at school about kissing a whole pond full of frogs before you meet a prince. You haven't even found the pond yet, have you? I mean you're inexperienced…not that it matters.'

Angie frowned. Maggie had no idea just how inexperienced she was, thank goodness. 'So basically you're saying that I need to get plenty of experience before any commitment? Right?'

'Yes,' Maggie said and smiled, 'I knew you'd come to see it from my point of view. Get out your credit card and we can get started.'

'Isn't that a bit quick? It says here that I can register and have a look.' Angie needed time to think and to stop the panic that was taking hold.

'Come on, let's just dive in and see which frogs are in the pond, ready and waiting.'

After several hours it was obvious that there were more people out there looking for dates than Angie had imagined in her wildest dreams. 'What about him, Angie, he looks good?' Maggie pointed out a handsome man in his late fifties. 'His profile is just right for you.'

'I'm not sure. Somehow I just think I'll end up meeting someone by bumping into them in the supermarket queue.' Angie knew she sounded pathetic.

'Oh look a blue moon,' Maggie said, 'or are there pigs flying about?' She giggled. 'This isn't the 1960s or even the 70s or 80s. Those days are long past. You've probably got more chance of winning the lottery.'

'It worked all right when we were younger, didn't it?' Angie could not believe that all this was necessary.

'That's because there were so many single people available,' Maggie said. 'At our age, you've got to understand that the pond of single and available frogs has shrunk to the size of a puddle, and a rather muddy, shallow puddle at that. The internet expands it to the size of an ocean.'

'Frogs don't like salt water,' Angie pointed out.

'A big lake then. Satisfied?'

'Point taken.' Angie laughed and fell silent. A knot had formed in her stomach. There was something that she had to ask. 'You've dated men recently, I mean as an older woman, what's it like?'

'You've been on dates before, haven't you?' Maggie frowned.

'It was a long time ago. I was a kid and they were just boys, well young men,' Angie said.

'What did they all want?'

'To get past first base, I suppose.' Angie looked

down as her cheeks flushed.

'Exactly. So what do you think Mr *I haven't had my hands on a woman in ages* will want?' Maggie took a large gulp of wine and waited for Angie to answer.

'Surely not the same?'

Maggie nodded and a smile played over her lips as Angie choked back her surprise. 'I thought that they'd be more interested in getting to know me first...so we can forge a relationship...'

'They'll have your pants off as soon as look at you. The ones I date always do,' Maggie said.

Angie took a deep breath. It was now or never. 'That's what I'm afraid of.'

'It's like riding a bike. You don't forget what to do,' Maggie said.

'That's exactly the trouble. I don't know how to...' Angie paused, 'ride a bike, if you see what I mean. I've never been on one.'

There was a moment's silence as Maggie digested Angie's last comment. 'Are you saying what I think you're saying?'

For an answer Angie looked away not wanting to meet Maggie's piercing gaze. The hiss of the gas fire filled the silence between them until Angie became aware of a bubbling sound. She looked up to see Maggie laughing and the sight started her off too until they were both convulsed. It was several minutes before Maggie managed to speak. 'Bloody hell, this puts a whole new meaning on first date nerves. It's first shag nerves we've got to sort out.'

***

Saturday morning dawned bright and breezy with a fierce red sky that promised unsettled weather. 'What are your plans this weekend, Jason?' Angie asked as she poured coffee and served their Saturday breakfast of eggs and bacon with buttered toast. Jason looked up from his phone which he'd been studying all the time she was cooking.

'Me and Bry are off to a party tonight and staying over. Tomorrow I'm having Sunday tea at her mum's so...' he looked up, 'I thought I could get started on the garden. A couple of hours and I'll have the place cleared of all them brambles.'

By the time Angie went out with some coffee at eleven, there was a huge mound of cuttings. 'I told you it would be easy. I reckon this lot will go up like a rocket with the few dry days we've had lately. Have you got any newspaper?' Jason added another branch to the pile.

'That is precisely what you will not do, young man,' a voice floated from the other side of the hedge. The branches parted and a head appeared in the gap. Paul Buchannan eyed Angie and Jason. 'There is a clause in the deeds of the bungalows in this small and what-was-once-exclusive estate that stipulates no bonfires will be lit during the hours of daylight.'

Jason shrugged. 'Fine. Just as long as I know, I can do it one evening this week. I'll go and clear the front instead.' And he went off whistling.

Angie gripped the tray with the coffee mugs. 'Thank you for the information, however, I'd just like to point out that you interrupted a private conversation.'

'That everyone could hear,' Paul Buchannan added.

'Only if they were listening with their ear pressed up against the fence.' Angie kept her voice as calm

96

and firm as she could.

'I assure you that I have far more important things to do than to take note of your every trivial move. I was just being a good neighbour and I was about to thank you again for your help the other day.' Angie watched as he stumped back to the house. No chance of any romance there. Perhaps Maggie was right. The pond had got very small. She went inside and logged on. It was time to bring her love life into the 21st century.

The morning flew past. Jason was as good as his word and cleared the front garden while Angie was hunched over the screen, setting up her profile. The photos were easy once she had spotted the rules; make sure there is at least one full length shot as well as one with head and shoulders. There was the question of what to put in her profile. What did she like? What sort of man? Were there any things that were a big *no no*? Hairy nostrils were a turn off, yet she hesitated. Would that come across as freaky?

The back door flew open and Jason crashed in, pulling off his boots and showering the kitchen floor with twigs and dead leaves. 'Is lunch ready?' he asked.

Angie shook her head. 'I'm sorry, Jason, I've been er...'

'Setting up online dating?' He peered over her shoulder at the screen on the laptop. 'Good on you, Ange. What sort of bloke do you want?'

'That's the trouble.' Angie got up and went over to the fridge, pulling out salad, bread and ham. 'I don't want some guy who's creepy...how do you say that without appearing a sad old obsessive?' She cut some thick slices of bread and spread them with butter before adding salad and ham. She passed the plate to

Jason. 'Tea coming up.'

'So, what would be a turn off?' Jason bit into the sandwich. 'Any ketchup?'

Angie passed the bottle to him. 'I don't want someone who is scruffy, fat or dresses like an old man in brown slacks and...' she shuddered '...wears open toe sandals and has hairy toes and lumpy feet.'

Jason tapped at the keyboard. 'Smart appearance, slim build and has good personal grooming.' He wiped at the keys with his sweater. 'Sorry, Ange.' Angie reached for a paper towel and cleared away the smear of ketchup that had transferred itself from Jason's hand to her precious keyboard. She poured two mugs of tea and sat down beside him.

'Go on, I think you've got something there.'

'What else?'

'I want someone who is open to going out and trying new things, not just heading off to the pub or slumped on the sofa watching football.'

He tapped again. 'Must be open to new experiences and be happy to spend time with family and friends, just hanging out.'

'What is *hanging out*?'

'You know, like chilling?' Jason said, in a weary voice. Angie pulled a face. 'Chilling is spending time at home watching a film, having a beer, eating popcorn, stuff like that.'

Angie didn't but decided it was better to let Jason have his head so she just nodded and hoped she appeared more worldly than she felt. Three more sandwiches, two more cups of tea and Angie's post was complete apart from what Jason said was the stuff that would get her really noticed.

'Can't help you there, Ange,' he said, 'cos that's

about you. What you want…Look up some on the internet and check out what they say.' He stood up to go. 'Lovely lunch. I'm off to have a shower before meeting up with Bry.'

'Jason, one thing before you go, how come you are so good at this?'

He grinned, his smile almost splitting his face. 'Me and my mate Jack did it for his mum when she divorced. We got good at it too. She had twenty dates in a month and met her new partner.' He turned. 'See you tomorrow evening.'

Angie stacked the dishwater and cleared away. She got out a piece of paper and pencil and wrote at the top of the paper *What I want in a relationship with a man.*

The sun was setting when she finally finished. She had given herself the screen name of Angel 30 after her birthdate and the tag line of *Willing to Lie About How We Met!* She read through her profile.

I'm slim, blonde (ish) and neither old nor young—sort of in-between. I'm a trained teacher and have spent many years with young children and young adults so I like to think some of their enthusiasm for life has rubbed off on me. I still get a real wow from going out in the snow, splashing in the sea on a hot summer's day and looking up at the stars on a winter's night. I like music from the 60s, 70s and 80s and spicy food, though not all at the same time.

I'm looking for a date who is strong enough to be the man and willing to show his sensitive side. I want to find a person that I can connect with on an emotional, intellectual and physical level. Someone who is intelligent, active and passionate as well as genuine and sincere. Someone who can make me feel like a woman as much as I can make him feel like a man.

I'm a 'one at a time' kind of woman so if you want to date, bed and leave for someone else, I'm not for you. However, if you want to take the time for us to get to know each other, try out some fun activities and see if we share that special magic, I might just be the right one.

She sat back. It was perfect. A smug sense of satisfaction spread through her. It was easy really, when you got the hang of it. Just wait 'til she told Maggie. She uploaded the words, selected the most expensive option which would allow access to the greatest number of profiles, entered her credit card number and hit *submit.*

The words *card refused* appeared on the screen. She checked the expiry date and the card number and did it again. It wouldn't go through. She pulled out another and crossed her fingers. *Card accepted* flashed on the screen. She stuck the offending one at the back of her wallet. She'd have to transfer more cash from the house sale. So what? This was too good a chance to worry about penny pinching.

She went into the kitchen and filled the kettle. As she waited for it to boil she gazed out at the darkening evening sky. A light was shining from Paul's bungalow. He was at home. Snatches of the conversation she'd had with him about his brother floated back. There had to be something she could do to help him. She got out her mother's old recipe book and switched on the oven. It was time she and Paul Buchannan came to a better understanding.

Chapter Ten

An hour and a half later Angie carried a plate of warm, chocolate chip cookies to Paul's bungalow. She had already changed into her new jeans with a loose sweater that slouched over her shoulders in what she hoped was a chic manner. She'd put on some make-up and swept her hair back in a small bun at the nape of her neck. She slowed as she approached his front door. This was going to be tricky. She shifted from one foot to the other. There had to be some way to approach the whole business of his brother without giving the game away about her past life yet she wasn't sure what it was. 'Come on, Angie, give it a go,' she said under her breath and rang the bell. The door opened and Paul Buchannan looked out. 'Yes?' he said. 'Is there a problem?

'Why should there be?' Angie felt her irritation with this man returning. Why did she let him do this to her when all she wanted was for them to get on well? She swallowed and smiled. She had to make this work. People's lives depended on it. 'For some reason, we haven't got off on the right footing and this is just to say I'm sorry if I don't know what the rules are...I'm new to this home ownership lark. So this is from me.' She held out the plate.

For a moment Paul stood there, his mouth gaping open slightly before he spoke. 'No, it's for me to say sorry too. And I can think of no better way than to invite you in for a tea or a coffee and we can taste one of your biscuits.' He stood aside and let Angie step into the hallway.

'Can you take these?' She thrust the plate at him as

she bent down and took off her shoes, hoping her socks didn't have holes in them.

'There's really no need. You're a guest.'

'With carpet this colour,' Angie indicated the deep cream pile, 'it would be sacrilege to walk on it in shoes. Besides,' she added, 'I can let my toes sink in.' She wriggled them.

To her surprise Paul burst out laughing. 'Now I know what they mean when they refer to *happy feet.*' Angie couldn't remember the last time a man had laughed at something she'd said, not because they thought she was stupid but because she was funny. It felt good. She looked up at him. He was certainly hot as Maggie might say and Angie knew her cheeks were going pink as something that was more than neighbourly friendliness flickered inside her.

'Come this way.' Paul led her down the hall into a large kitchen that overlooked the garden. 'Take a seat and I'll make the tea or would you prefer coffee?'

'Tea will be fine.' Angie sat down on a metal chair with a black seat that was the perfect height for the black marble-topped island that served as a table. She looked at the white cupboards and shiny silver appliances. Everything shouted *no expense spared.* She sat not daring to move, terrified in case any feather light touch would make the drawers and cupboards glide open. The usual assortment of kitchen equipment that cluttered her work surfaces was hidden away. There was no sign even of a tea towel. Paul busied himself with filling a bright red enamel kettle and laying out black and white cups and saucers decorated with dots of colour. He set one down in front of Angie and she picked it up. 'These are lovely.'

'Made at the little pottery on the farm next to

junction seventeen on the motorway. My late wife knew the potter. They were friends at school.' He fell silent.

'I'm sorry about your wife.'

'Thanks. It was nearly three years ago now. It seems like yesterday sometimes.' A pang of disappointment hit Angie in the solar plexus as a thought flashed through her mind that he was still in mourning. She looked at the clutter-free, spotless surfaces. Anyone who liked their house as neat and tidy as this wasn't going to be comfortable with her more casual approach.

She changed the subject, reminding herself that she had a duty to Maggie and perhaps to Paul's brother too. 'Did you get to London on time?'

'Yes, and it was thanks to you.' Paul filled the teapot and arranged milk and sugar on a tray. He carried it to the counter and sat down.

'This is very nice. I usually just dunk a tea bag in a mug.' Angie twisted on the seat, swinging her feet like a kid on a chair that is too big for them and feeling she needed to lighten the atmosphere a bit.

'When I have a guest I do things properly.' He poured the tea. 'Let's try those biscuits.'

Two cups of tea and two biscuits later and Angie felt she had made enough small talk for her to broach the subject of Paul's brother. 'You can say I'm nosy or it's none of my business but I remember you telling me about your brother. How did it all start?'

There was silence and Paul seemed to shrink. He looked at her, his head on one side. She would never have believed that this was the same man who had been so belligerent with Jason earlier on. She let the silence hang between them, knowing he'd talk when and if he was ready.

'It's a long story.' Paul's voice was flat. His contorted face did nothing to mask his true feelings.

'I'm listening.' Angie folded her hands and waited.

'Ben was a pupil at a cathedral school in the Midlands. He was a gifted musician and went from a bright, lively kid to someone who…well he gave up, withdrew and got hooked on drugs.'

'Did you suspect anything at the time?'

Paul shook his head. 'We all thought it was just a very bad attack of adolescent anger. He was thirty-three before he told me what had happened. All that stuff about kids being abused by celebrities and politicians made him determined to speak out and get some justice, I suppose.'

Angie nodded. 'I think it helped a lot of people do the same.'

'He went to the police and named the priest. It was just his word against the priest's and no one will take notice of an ex-junkie. Besides, the priest always had an excuse for when Ben claimed the abuse took place. He said he was at confession at some convent and no one can trace that back.'

As he spoke Angie felt a creeping sickness crawl and lodge in her throat. It was not just the similarity with what she had suspected of Father Benedict, there were too many other coincidences. She squeezed her hands together to stop them from trembling and asked the question that was burning in her brain. 'What was the name of the priest?'

'Father Benedict. I think he was the parish priest of—'

'St Ced's?' Angie willed him to deny it.

'That's right. How do you know?'

Angie looked up into eyes that were as full of pain as the sensations coursing through her body. 'I knew him,' her voice wavered, '…and I think I might be able to help.'

'How?' Paul's eyes were fixed on Angie's face.

This was not the question Angie'd been expecting. 'Er, I taught at a school nearby. There was a priest with the same name who was responsible for hearing confession in my church.' She sent up a prayer hoping he wouldn't press her any further.

'What makes you think you can help when God knows how many experts have trawled over the case?' The old Paul was back, defensive and angry.

'I may be able to find some evidence. Father Benedict was often booked for events with us and he would cancel at the last minute. We did the best we could without him. It wasn't the same.'

'Whatever you find, it would be appreciated.' Paul's face softened.

Angie stood up to go. 'I'll be in touch if I think of anything.'

Paul accompanied her to the front door. 'I need to thank you once again, not just for the biscuits but for listening.'

'Thank you for your hospitality and for being so understanding about Jason and me,' Angie said as she slipped on her shoes and stepped outside.

'It was good to have someone to talk to and if you can do anything that would help Ben, I would be extremely grateful,' Paul said as he closed the door.

Angie walked slowly back to her home. There was only one thing she knew she would have to do: trawl through her meticulous diaries. Somewhere she must have made a reference to Father Benedict not turning up for an event and if it coincided with Ben's account, it would be a chance, a slim chance that someone might take his accusations more seriously.

Later that evening she hauled out the trunk where she had stowed the notebooks, one for every year of her life in the convent. All the frustration she had felt came flooding back. This time it was accompanied with a growing sickness. If she found dates when Father Benedict didn't turn up, was that because he was with Ben? She pushed the obscenity from her mind. 'Focus, focus, focus,' she said out loud.

She flicked through the contents, skimming over the dates and religious festivals, the weather and the day-to-day goings on. She didn't have to read many entries. The evidence was there in black or rather blue biro and white. Between 1990 when Father Benedict first arrived at the parish and 2005, there were plenty of occasions when he had arranged to come and take either confession or to join in with a service and had cancelled at the last moment. Angie surveyed one of the entries:

Friday 15th February 1992
Cold, bleak day. Some snow. Half-term began. Sister Mary has flu. Vespers led by Sister Catherine as Father Benedict not able to attend. Very difficult chant. Evening discussion on creating care facilities in the building as way of generating income. Very lively.

There were others in the same fashion. It may not be much but it might help. If Paul could get some dates from his brother, she could check against her records. Angie swallowed hard. It would mean she would have to trawl through page after page of the

106

notebooks and suffer the painful memories that would be dredged up. She had to do it. She would go and see Paul again tomorrow.

Angie pressed her hands to her temples and shook her head to blot out the image of Father Benedict's pale skin, the touch of his clammy hands and the syrupy voice as he absolved them of their paltry sins. She was back in the convent. Voices singing the familiar chants floated through the air from the chapel. She was alone in her cell, kneeling by the bed as the rosary beads slipped through her fingers and words formed automatically on her lips:

Hail Mary, full of grace.
The Lord is with thee.
Blessed art thou amongst women,
and blessed is the fruit of thy womb, Jesus,
Holy Mary, Mother of God,
pray for us sinners,
now and at the hour of our death.
Amen.

She screwed up her eyes to push the memory back where it belonged, in the dark, undisturbed corners of her mind. A sound brought her back to the present. She had been saying the words out loud. She threw the books in the trunk, slammed the lid and shoved it under the bed. Even if it took all her strength, even if it brought back memories that still had the power to torment her in the middle of sleepless nights, she would find the information she needed. It might just provide enough evidence to put Father Benedict in prison once and for all. She looked up. 'You'd better not let me down this time,' she said.

Chapter Eleven

Angie checked the clock. 8.30 was far too early on a Sunday morning to go and see Paul. She pushed the duvet away and yawned. The sheet was crumpled under her body and the pillows which she had repeatedly punched to find some scrap of comfort in a restless night were twisted in their cases. She'd have to wait until at least ten, that meant keeping occupied. What the hell could she do?

She wandered downstairs, made a coffee and logged on in case there were any messages from the dating site. Emails tumbled into her inbox and the bubbling feeling of anticipation coursing through her body chased away any tiredness. She scanned the contents. As soon as she saw the photo of Leo she stopped. It showed a man leaning on a walking pole, overlooking a lake with snow-topped hills in the background. A close-up revealed good teeth, a lovely smile, deep brown eyes and dark hair threaded with grey. She read his profile.

I'm Leo from the West Country. I've been single for five years since my wife died and in that time I've focussed on getting the kids (aged nineteen and twenty-two) to university, and now I feel I can spend the time to meet some interesting ladies with a view to friendship and possibly romance. Friendship comes first. Please do get in touch, as I'm sure we would have a lot in common.

Her hand hovered over the *reply* icon. He sounded interesting. At fifty-two he was the right age and he looked *fit*, to use Maggie's word. What if it all went wrong? She shook herself. 'Angie Jarvis, you haven't even met the man and here you are worrying about the future,' she said out loud. Sister Elizabeth's words floated back. 'There's no time like the present, Sister Ruth.' She was right. Angie clicked on *reply*.

Hi Leo, I'm Angie. Is the photo of you from a holiday in Scotland? I used to go there regularly as a child when my father wanted to bag another Monroe. I like walking too although it has lapsed lately.

Angie let out a sigh. It was done. She leaned back and checked the other responses again. No, she had made the right decision. She was about to get up when her laptop signalled an incoming email. Leo had replied already.

Hi Angie, Yes indeed it is a Monroe that you can see in the distance. I must confess my walking is much more down to earth and always ends with a hearty pub lunch. I wonder if we should meet up? I would like to get to know you as we seem to share the same outlook on relationships, and possibly life in general. Perhaps a drink sometime next week would suit you? I am free on Wednesday and Thursday evening. Leo

Angie pulled her hands back as if the keyboard were alive. This was all happening too quickly. She picked up her phone. Maggie would know what to do. It rang five times before a sleepy voice answered, 'Angie what do you want at this ungodly, oh sorry, bloody awful time of the day?'

Angie ignored the god word. 'What do I do? I've got someone asking to see me.'

'What are you talking about?' There was the sound of a stifled yawn.

'Internet dating, remember, I said I'd probably set up a profile? I had a go yesterday and I've already got some replies.'

'Bloody hell, that was quick,' Maggie now sounded wide awake. 'So what's the problem?'

'I said what should I do?' Sometimes she wondered if Maggie wasn't a bit slow on the uptake.

'Hold your horses. Don't reply again for a while. Wait 'til later, play hard to get and when you do email, ask him a few more questions about himself. If you arrange to meet up, go to a place that is likely to be busy, like a pub or a bar. Tell me the name and address and I can call you during the evening in case you need rescuing.'

'You make it sound dangerous.' First Gareth, then Jason and now Maggie sounded like prophets of doom. Angie's previous excitement was eroding fast.

'It can be. Do as I say and you'll be fine.' She hung up.

Angie went back to the computer screen and logged off. She'd do as Maggie advised and would wait. She checked the clock again. It was just gone nine. Already her fingers were twitching to email Leo and find out more. She'd go and see Paul instead. She looked out through the front window. His car wasn't in the driveway. 'Damn!' she spoke out loud. Now what could she do?

She paced up and down the hallway. The sounds of rumbling snores told her Jason was fast asleep so he was no distraction. In the end Angie washed the kitchen floor, dusted the living room, stacked the recycling tins and bottles outside and was about to clean the hall window when she stopped and looked at the slime green paint on the walls. She pulled a face. What would Leo think if he came to collect her for a date? He sounded a very cultured and elegant man and probably had a house to match. She ran a finger over the surface. It was only paint. Anyone can paint a wall, can't they? She looked down at the baggy sweatshirt and faded jogging bottoms. Leo was out there somewhere and it would just be her luck to bump into him or someone like him, dressed in items a charity shop would consign to the bin. A bit of grooming was required.

She changed into clean jeans and a new lacy top, grabbed her car keys off the hall table and opened the front door. She stopped and breathed in the warm spring air. It would be good to get out, even if it was only a trip to the DIY store. The Close was quiet as either the other residents were having a late breakfast or had gone out for the day. Paul's car was nowhere to be seen. She'd wait until afternoon and check on him again.

Ten minutes later she pulled into the car park of the store that doubled up as both garden centre and DIY outlet. Others had had the same idea and a procession of visitors with trolleys laden with everything from plants and compost to fence panels and paving slabs trundled past. Angie went inside, pushing the smallest trolley she could find, as all she needed was a tin of paint.

She gazed at the rows of tins stretching along the aisles. How on earth did anyone know what to buy? She picked up one that announced it was vinyl paint called *Champagne Truffle*. She'd only ever heard of vinyl flooring. She turned the tin over and read the instructions. Nothing made any sense. A couple were standing nearby, arguing about the choice. They were middle-aged and had adopted the elastic waists and shapeless tops beloved of many of that generation. Their language too owed more to the roles that they had lived for the past thirty years as parents rather than partners. 'You said you're fed up with Magnolia.' The man ran a hand through his hair before he folded his arms and waited.

'It's such a sensible colour and we could add a feature wall in this shade of blue.' The woman held up a tin with a blue flash that was just the colour of the Police boxes Angie remembered from her childhood.

Angie put her own tin back and picked up another, before letting out an exasperated sigh. The man must have heard. 'Are you stuck, love? Need a hand?' He moved closer and Angie noticed how he had glanced at her figure. It felt uncomfortable. She pulled her top down over her hips. Men never looked at Angela Jarvis.

She pointed to a row of tins. 'I want this colour but I've no idea how much to buy.'

He picked up a five litre tin marked *Matt.* 'If it's a small room, this is plenty. Have you got brushes?'

'No. I've never decorated before.'

'Oh a virgin, then?' He winked.

'What?' She was about to turn and run in the other direction when she noticed he was smiling.

'Sorry, just my little joke. At interior decorating, I meant.' He sounded flustered.

'Yes and there are plenty of other things I've never done before so I suppose you're right.' Angie smiled back. This was fun.

'Get yourself a pack of brushes, some white for the ceiling, a gloss for the woodwork, a paint can, roller and tray and you can't go wrong.' He ticked off the items on his fingers. 'Just make sure the surface is clean and smooth and keep the roller for the large areas and the brush for the skirting.'

'Don...what are you doing?' His wife's voice was sharp and as Angie smiled in her direction, the glare that she received was far from friendly. In fact it was downright hostile.

'Thanks,' Angie said. She collected the paints, piled them onto her trolley and headed towards the display of brushes. As she turned she heard the man say to his wife, 'Why don't you ever wear jeans?' She didn't stay long enough to hear the reply. So men did look at Angela Jarvis. No, she corrected herself. They looked at *Angie* Jarvis. A warm feeling spread through her and she walked away from the store with a jauntiness that she would not have thought possible a few months earlier.

By the time she got back to the bungalow Jason was standing outside the kitchen, his phone clasped in his hand, as usual. He looked up, pointed to the phone and mouthed something about a weak signal in the house. She nodded.

Angie heaved the paint and brushes on the kitchen table. Jason came in. His usually cheerful face was pinched. 'What have you got there?'

'It's time I got this place the way I like it and I'm going to start on the entrance hall. It'll make the right impression, won't it?' Angie laid out her purchases like a hunter returning with her kill.

'Who for?' Jason scratched his head.

'Anyone who comes to visit.' Angie unwrapped a

bush and held up the paint can. 'Just what am I supposed to do with this?'

'I'll get changed and give you a hand.'

'Aren't you going out with Bryony today?'

'She says she's got something she needs to do first and won't tell me what it is,' he shrugged. 'That's not like my Bryony.' He drained his mug of tea and taking a slice of toast and marmalade, went into his room.

It was just as well that Jason did help. Washing down the walls and the skirting board was easy enough. Paint, however, had a life of its own. Jason pulled up the old carpet and deposited it in his car to take to the tip. He covered the floorboards with newspaper to collect the spatters. That didn't stop paint running down her hand and over her arm which meant she had to find a cloth to clean up and inevitably, left to its own devices the brush fell into the pot. Jason was making good progress on the ceiling and the walls and soon the hallway looked clean, fresh and larger than Angie had realised.

She watched as Jason dipped a brush in the paint can and squeezed off the excess before he tackled the wall, stroking the bristles over the surface so that it left a creamy stripe. He repeated the action, covering a small area at a time with neat, even movements. Angie moved the paint tray closer and copied him. This time there was no sticky mess running down the brush and onto her hand. The paint soon covered a small section which grew until she realised she had painted a door-sized portion of the wall. 'Piece of cake,' she said under her breath and stepped back to admire her work. Her left foot landed on the edge of the tray of paint that was on the floor. It flipped upwards and the contents sprayed over her leg and onto the newspaper. A few blobs even managed to find the only bits of the wooden floor that had not been covered. 'Bugger.'

'What's up, Angie?' Jason turned, took one look at her and exploded into laughter.

'Just what is so funny?'

'You are—' he managed to get out between splutters. 'Go and get cleaned up and I'll carry on here. There's more paint on you than on the walls.'

Angie fled to the bathroom and stripped off. The paint had soaked through parts of her clothes and stuck to her body. She stood in the bath and scrubbed away at the creamy marks. Next time she'd paint in the nude. Jason was as good as his word though and by the time Angie had cleaned herself up, he'd finished the ceiling. Soon the hallway had been transformed under one coat of paint. It was mid-afternoon when Jason called her in and they both stood to admire his handiwork. 'Where did you learn all of this?'

'When Granddad was alive, I'd go and help him. After he died, I used to do all the decorating for my gran. She liked cream too,' he added. 'I'll try and be home early this week and give it another coat and then you'll be ready to get some carpet on the floor.'

'I can't thank you—' before she could say anymore, Jason's phone rang.

He listened. His face went pale and his voice dropped to a whisper. 'I'm coming over.' He turned to Angie. 'Gotta go.' And he rushed out of the front door.

'Is everything all right?' she called out. He took no notice. She followed and watched as he sped off. Something was very wrong. Angie was about to close the door behind him when she spotted Paul's car in the driveway. She hitched up her trousers and straightened her sweatshirt. What a pity she wasn't wearing the same clothes that had impressed the man who'd helped her buy the paint. It was too late now. She crossed the lawn and rang the doorbell.

'Hi, Angie. What can I do for you?' Paul leaned against the doorframe.

'I think I've found the evidence we might need. I've got a question for you or rather for Ben.'

'You'd better come in.' He ushered her into the lounge. 'Sit down.' Paul indicated the cream leather sofa. 'Drink?' Angie shook her head. 'Well I think I need one.'

While he poured himself a whisky, Angie perched on the edge of the seat and allowed herself a quick glance at the pale walls, the Persian rug on the thick carpet and a few carvings that suggested someone had visited Africa. A small brass-topped table in front of the matching cream sofa was smothered with the sort of books that would have graced a stately home. They were filled with glossy prints of exotic gardens and idyllic homes, with a sprinkling of upmarket travel destinations. Dominating the room was a curved screen television and a sound system that obviously played records and CDs. Someone who liked and could afford a bit of luxury would never be interested in her. She pushed the self-pity aside. She was here for Ben and Maggie.

Paul sat down opposite her. 'So what have you found out?'

'I really need to know the dates and times that your brother claims the priest was...' she wasn't sure what to say '...was with him. If you know what I

116

mean?'

Paul nodded. 'I know *exactly* what you mean.'

'I've found plenty of evidence between 1990 and 2005 when Father Benedict missed events that he had planned to take.' Paul stood up and switched off the music that was playing softly. 'Is that possible?' Angie said.

There was silence as Paul sat back down and processed the information. 'I'm sure Ben can do that.' He took a sip of his drink and his eyes narrowed as he looked at Angie. 'How do you know all of this?'

It was the question Angie had dreaded. 'I was a teacher, not at Ben's school,' she added hastily, 'at the Catholic junior over the other side of the town. I used to spend some time at the convent and Father Benedict would visit and take services.'

'You must have one hell of a good memory.'

Angie studied her feet on the soft carpet. 'I kept a diary of odds and ends, little scraps of information about the day and the weather, school events, things like that…' She'd probably given Paul the impression that she was a pathetic old spinster with nothing better to do than to write a *Dear Diary* every day. For some reason, the thought saddened her.

Paul seemed satisfied by her answer. 'I can ask Ben and let you know. It might be some time. He's back in hospital after another bout of depression so I won't disturb him for a while.'

'I'm sorry,' she said and felt her fists clench. Father Benedict's legacy had to be stopped.

'It's been going on for such a long while, another few weeks won't matter.' Paul corrected himself, 'That doesn't mean I'm not grateful. I'm very, very appreciative of anything that might help but we've been let down before.'

'I won't let you down.' Angie pursed her lips. Why did he have this effect on her?

'I know you won't…the system might…thank you, anyway and from Ben too, when I tell him. I'm sure he'll be pleased.' He paused. 'Were you attached to the convent in any way?'

Angie jumped up. 'Is that the time? Jason will be home soon. I haven't even started cooking and he was so good helping me to decorate today.'

'That explains the paint. Nice colour by the way.' Paul's eyes twinkled.

Angie frowned. 'What paint?'

'Your hair…or is it a new fashion?'

Angie put her hand to her hair and felt a sticky blob and some strands that were stuck together. She looked at her fingers, now streaked with paint. 'I'd better go,' she mumbled.

'White spirit will do the trick,' said Paul as he showed her out.

It was only when she got back to the bathroom and took a good look she realised that her hair was matted with cream streaks that only a badger might have found attractive. Her heart sank. Yet again, Paul had seen her in a mess.

Angie was washing the residue of white spirit from her hair when the front door banged. Jason was back. She wrapped her head in a towel and went to find him. He was in the lounge, sitting in silence.

'Jason, what's up?'

'It's Bryony.'

'Is she all right? Has there been an accident?' Angie sat down on the arm of the chair and waited.

'There's been a bloody accident all right.' Angie

118

grabbed his hand. 'No, not that sort. She's pregnant.'

Angie squeezed his hand. 'Are you sure?'

'Yeah, we just did a test. Twelve weeks.'

'That's ages. Didn't you suspect before?'

'No. She was on the pill but she had food poisoning a while back and we reckon it must have stopped working. She didn't think anything was wrong until yesterday. She did a test just in case and it came back positive.'

'What are you going to do?'

'What can I do? I've got no home, no money, no job, nothing. Her mum will kill me.'

'Do you want to keep it?' Angie fought off the feelings of disgust rising in her throat at the thought he might say they both wanted an abortion. She had not been brought up a good Catholic girl for nothing.

He looked up, his eyes shining. 'Course we do. It's part of me and Bry and I've always wanted to be a dad,' he corrected himself, 'I mean to be a better dad than I ever had.' He placed his head in his hands and Angie was sure she heard a sniff.

She grasped him by the shoulders. 'Listen to me, Jason. You've got a home here and you'll be finished your training in a few months, won't you?' The words rattled out. 'Until you can afford a place of your own, you can stay here, all of you. There's plenty of room.' Angie sat back and let her words sink in.

He looked up. 'Do you mean that?'

'Yes I do.' As soon as she had said the words she knew it was the right thing. 'Go and call Bryony and together you can think of how you'll tell her mum.'

Jason flung his arms around her neck and kissed her cheek. 'Thank you.' He got out his phone. She could hear him as he went out of the door. 'Ange says we can move in here if we have to so it's going to be all right. I'm coming over. We'd better tell your mum.'

It was only when Angie collapsed into bed that night that she realised she hadn't replied to Leo. What had Maggie said? Play hard to get? She turned over in bed. Tomorrow would do.

Chapter Twelve

Monday morning dawned and Angie was desperate to hear how Bryony's mum had taken the news that she was to be a grandmother. She set about getting breakfast ready before Jason appeared for college. 'Well?' Angie asked when he dragged himself out of his bedroom. 'How was Bryony's mum?'

He scratched his head, poured himself a cup of tea from the pot and added two sugars before answering, 'First she threatened to cut my dick off and told me I was stupid. When she realised Bry was on the pill and it was an accident, she calmed down a bit. She reckons Bry should stay there until the baby is born. After that it's up to me and her.'

Angie placed a bowl of porridge in front of him and passed the honey. 'I'm serious about you both coming here.'

Jason stopped, the spoon in mid-air, half way to his mouth. ' But a baby in the house? What about the noise and—' he shuddered, 'the smell of all those nappies?'

'As I don't expect to be doing nappy changes and they can be disposed of very easily, I don't think that will be a problem. Besides,' Angie gazed into space, 'a baby in the house might be fun.'

'You might have one of your own one day,' Jason said. The corners of his mouth twitched as he suppressed a smile.

'At my age? By the time I've found a partner I'd be its grandma. It's easier for men.' Angie's eyes glazed over as she continued, 'You can have kids until you're ancient. I won't ever have children so the odd cuddle with one that lives here will have to be enough.'

'If you're sure?'

Her attention snapped back to Jason. 'As you said it's only for a few months so even if you do my head in, it won't be for very long.' She patted his hand. 'Discuss the matter with Bryony *and* her mum and find out what they think.'

'I reckon I know what they'll say. There's no room at her place for me and the baby.'

There was a ping and the comforting smell of toast filled the air. 'I suggest you talk it over and if you all agree, you'd better get cracking on your room and the smallest bedroom will do for the baby.'

'Like a nursery?'

Angie put down a plate of toast in front of Jason. 'Why not? The baby will need its own room after the first few months, won't it?'

'We can all muck in and make the place baby proof.' He took a piece of toast and heaped jam on it. 'How do you know so much about kids, you not having any I mean?'

Angie poured herself a coffee and sat down. 'I did a lot of work helping young mums,' she said remembering the times she and Sister Elizabeth had visited the flats where the authorities stuck vulnerable girls with their babies, next to drug addicts and God knows who else. She crossed herself and noticed Jason watching her.

'Why do you do that sort of...?' He made a movement across his chest.

'It's an old habit.'

'Yeah like what?'

'It's what Catholics sometimes do.' She changed the subject. 'Make sure you talk to Bryony today and

122

tell me what the result is.'

'Funny I don't remember anything like that with my mate Dean. He was a Catholic too.' Jason finished his tea, spread another piece of toast with jam and stood up. 'Thanks, Angie. I really do mean that.' He went out whistling. If only her dating problems could be solved so easily. It was time to email some questions to Leo before she made any decisions about what to do next.

It was gone midday when she received a reply.

Dear Angie,

Thank you for getting back to me so soon. I'm happy to answer any questions you might have so here goes.

My children are both now settled at university and enjoying the lifestyle of typical students although they do assure me, when they decide to turn up for clean clothes and a good meal, that they are studying in between partying.

My wife died when they were only teenagers but she would have been so proud of them.

As for the farm, it's mixed—that's animals and crops. I'm a beef cattle man—easy to look after. It's close to the motorway off junction 18 which is only a few miles away from where you live, according to your profile, so it will be very easy to meet up.

Can I suggest this Wednesday, 7.30pm at The King's Head in the High Street?

Leo Wilson

Angie read the email again. This was a proper date. She couldn't fudge the issue any longer.

Dear Leo,

Thank you for getting back to me so promptly.
Wednesday evening will be fine. I look forward to
meeting you in person.
Angie

She hit *send*. She jumped up and punched the air. At last she'd got a date with a man who was interested in her. She ran to her wardrobe and pulled out some clothes. She held up one garment after another and slung them back. Nothing looked right. She sat down on the bed. The euphoria evaporated. Something else had taken its place and that was fear. A call to Maggie was needed.

Angie was chopping red cabbage and apples to go with the shepherd's pie she'd made for Jason's supper. That was the good thing about cooking. She had to concentrate or risk losing a finger. The clatter of the knife on the board was the only sound in the room until the back door burst open. Jason came in, followed by Bryony. 'Do you want to stay for some food, Bryony, there's plenty?'

'That would be lovely and I just want to say that our answer is yes. I'd love to come here when the baby is born.' Bryony came up to Angie and hugged her. 'You've been so good to Jason. You're one of the few people who really believe in him. You don't know what that means to me and to him,' she added in a whisper.

'That's settled then. Jason, put the kettle on and let's talk arrangements.'

As soon as Jason left to take Bryony home Angie called Maggie. She opened a bottle of wine and poured herself a glass, ready for the onslaught of information that she was bound to receive. What she hadn't expected was that Maggie had already arranged a meeting with her co-workers to discuss the arrangements for the care home. Angie would need to get in contact with Polly Cadwallader again. That would have to wait. She had enough to worry about with her upcoming date with Leo.

By the time Wednesday evening came, Angie had been through every emotion known to womankind and probably a few more besides. At 7.30 pm she walked into the wine bar, making sure that she had parked her car in a very well-lit part of the street (Maggie's advice again). She was dressed in a slim-fitting, blue dress, thick black tights and flat ballerina pumps in case she needed to get away. From what she was not sure. Her leather jacket was slung over her shoulder in what she hoped was a stylish and youthful manner without looking like a middle-aged teen.

She wiped her clammy hands down her thighs and pushed open the door. Angie vaguely remembered the King's Head from earlier days when it was easy to pretend you were eighteen and sneak a half of lager with your mates in the hope of appearing grown-up. So many places had undergone a transformation Angie sometimes felt she was in a parallel universe.

She crossed her fingers for a second and stepped inside. There were a number of couples sitting at the polished wooden tables while the booths along the side of the wall contained a group of young women celebrating with pitchers of a lurid blue cocktail. A lone man was seated at the bar, cradling a whisky in one hand while the other was alternately smoothing his hair and checking his watch. If that was Leo, he looked as nervous as Angie felt.

She ignored her wobbly legs and walked over. 'Excuse me, are you Leo?' she said.

He turned and she looked into brown eyes, set within laughter lines that had taken years to create. 'You must be Angie.' He took hold of her hand and squeezed it. 'How lovely to see you.' He smiled and pulled up a seat next to him. 'What would you like to drink?'

'A glass of red wine, please' Angie stammered out. She was taken aback. She had half expected that his photo had either been touched up as Gareth had shown her how to do or it was from decades earlier. He was a few inches taller than she had expected and his hair had more grey than black, otherwise his photo was a good likeness. For the first time in more decades than she cared to remember, Angie felt a tremor in the pit of her stomach. It reminded her of the times when a smile from a certain boy on the local bus had the power to turn her day upside down. She was seventeen again.

Angie slid onto the stool and pretended to take an interest in the bottles on display while she waited as Leo went to the other end of the bar and ordered. At least it meant she could take a better look at him. His immaculate blazer was worn with an open neck white shirt tucked into a pair of chinos. Leo placed the small glass of red wine in front of Angie and sat opposite her. She glanced down at her fingers and hoped he hadn't noticed her gawping at him before she raised the glass. 'Cheers.'

'Cheers.' He smiled again.

There was no going back. 'So, Leo, tell me more about your job?'

'I suppose you could call me a gentleman farmer.' His voice was soft with a slight West Country accent. The small gold signet ring on the third finger of his right hand matched his cufflinks. His watch had the word *Rolex* on the face. Farming was more lucrative than Angie had realised unless they were both fakes. 'What about you?'

They were the words that Angie had been dreading. She forced a smile and went into her well-rehearsed reply. 'I was a teacher. I left to look after my father when he fell ill.'

'I'm sorry. Is he better?' Leo's voice was a whisper.

'He died last year. No,' Angie corrected herself, 'it was only a few months ago. Somehow it seems like a different world.'

Leo placed his hand on hers and squeezed it gently. 'I am very sorry. My parents died when I was young. I lost my wife a while back and whatever people say, the sadness changes although the feelings of loss never go away.'

'Thank you. You are the first person I've spoken to who hasn't either told me it will get better or that I'll get over it soon.' In that instant, Angie knew that whatever the future would hold between her and Leo, she had found someone who understood exactly what she had been going through. It was both comforting and a relief.

Leo nodded. 'I understand. Now tell me more about yourself.' He stood up and ushered her to a seat away from the bar where they could talk and not be interrupted.

Whether it was the wine or his company, the time flew past. A buzzing sound came from Angie's phone. She scrabbled in her bag. 'Excuse me, my friend said she would call.'

'In case I turned out to be a double-headed monster or about to whisk you away to my secret lair? Please answer it.' Leo leaned back.

Angie stood up, turned away and hissed into the phone, 'Everything is all right. I'll call you tomorrow.' She rang off. 'Let me get you a drink, whisky?' She scuttled off to other end of the bar where the bartender was chatting up a voluptuous blonde. She felt her cheeks flush, embarrassed that Leo knew exactly why she was being called. She came back with their drinks. 'You must think I'm terrible, getting someone to check up like that.'

Leo waved his hand. 'I told my daughter the same thing when she was younger. Believe me, there are some strange characters out there in cyber world.' He patted her hand. 'You can't be too careful.' Angie relaxed. He understood. 'You're very lucky to have such concerned friends. I shall have to be on my guard, won't I?'

It was a strange thing to say so Angie changed the subject. 'You said both children were at university, what are they studying?'

'My son is in his final year at Sheffield reading engineering and my daughter is a fresher at Aberdeen reading law.' Angie noticed how he used the old fashioned terminology and didn't just say they were at *uni*. They continued to chat, discovering that they had many things in common. Both liked spicy food, preferred live music and theatre to cinema and enjoyed reading crime novels. Leo played tennis, not golf, and was a fan of rugby and cricket. Talking to him was easy and she allowed herself a small smile of self-satisfaction. Why on earth had she allowed herself to get all worked up? Internet dating was simple.

By the time the landlord called last orders, Angie had not enjoyed herself so much in a long time and she was happy to allow Leo to escort her to her car. He waited for her to unlock it before he opened the door for her. 'Thank you for a very pleasant evening, Leo.'

'It's been delightful and I hope that we can meet up again soon.' Leo pulled her close and brushed her cheek with his lips which left Angie wanting more. She wasn't sure if you kissed on dates like this so let it go. Standing back, he waved as Angie's car pulled out of the car park.

Angie drove home, feeling light-headed and it was not from the two small glasses of wine. Could she be attracted to someone she'd met only today? It wasn't *the knock you off your feet, love at first sight* experience that she'd read about when she was younger. Instead there was something stirring in her. It was exciting, scary and intriguing all at the same time. She'd definitely see Leo again, if he asked her.

Once back in her own home she got out her laptop and logged on. She'd email a quick thank you for the date. Leo had already sent her a message asking if she would like to go for a meal on Friday the following week. She replied, thanking him for the date and agreeing, providing that they split the costs. He must have been online because his answer pinged back immediately:

Dear Angie,
Much as I prefer to be the gentleman and pay, I appreciate that I have met a very independent and

129

charming lady whom I would hate to annoy in any way.
How about Italian? Just say the word and I will make
the arrangements.
Leo

Dear Leo,
Italian will be fine.
Good night.

She hit *send.*
A new message came back.

Goodnight and sleep well. I will email you the time later
in the week.
Love Leo xxx

Angie looked at the email again. He'd signed it
with three kisses. She sat bolt upright. Kisses on
paper were fine. They were not the real thing. Was it
tongues straight away and where would he put his
hands? She curled down in bed and pulled the pillow
over her head. Apart from a few slobbers under the
mistletoe and chaste fumblings as a teenager, she was
a virgin kisser too.

Chapter Thirteen

After seeing Jason off to college at the start of the new term, Angie was about to begin painting the bathroom when the letterbox clanged. A brown envelope was lying on the floor. She picked it up to see her name handwritten on the front. She peered out through the hall window. The Close was deserted. Inside the envelope was a note and scrawled at the top was a message from Paul.

Ben insisted on sending you this although he is far from well. I hope it's what you need. Paul.

Dear Angie,
My brother tells me that you might have some information about Father Benedict. These are the dates as far as I can remember. Some are just days of the week in a particular month and a year as they coincided with football practice or choir. Others are more specific as they are etched on my brain. Thanks for the offer.
Ben Buchannan

There followed a list of dates spanning a decade from 1992 to 2002. The painting would have to wait.

Angie collected a pen, ruler and a pad of lined paper and placed them on the bed. She got down on her hands and knees and hauled the trunk out from underneath. She opened the lid and picked up one notebook after another, searching for the dates she needed and double-checking against the list Ben had given her. Each notebook was annotated on the front with the year and the start and end date which was underlined with a ruler. Those she needed she placed in a neat pile by the bed. She selected one dated 27th May 1991 to 17th September1993 and flicked through it.

As she scanned the neat cursive script, the years fell away and she was no longer Angie. She was just another young novitiate, eager for a life of duty and devotion to a cause she believed in. Entries showed the years rolling past in a familiar pattern with Advent, Christmas, Lent and Easter all following each other as they had done for hundreds of years, with monotonous regularity.

As she reread the entries she noticed the tetchiness she displayed at the rules and regulations and the eventual relief when she was allowed to go out into the world to teach. One simple entry 'Oh God, what have I done?' was enough for her eyes to fill with tears. If only she could have got away sooner. She sighed. That would have been impossible. The girl who wrote those entries was not the same as the woman who read them now.

She wiped her eyes on her sleeve. She couldn't change the past and that's what it was, however much it hurt. She placed the unwanted notebooks back in the trunk and closed the lid. She selected a piece of paper and drew two columns. At the top she wrote the words *date* and *event* and underlined them. She picked up the first notebook with the dates Ben had provided.

November 23 Father Benedict absent from service. Pity. Chant very difficult.

Surely it was a coincidence? Disgust mingled with

hope and fear. Yet hope was winning. It might be her only chance to get Father Benedict convicted. She read on.

December 18 No Father Benedict at Compline. Again. Weather freezing. Pipes burst in kitchen.

And there were plenty more. She flipped through the months stopping from time to time to write down the information that might just be the proof Ben needed. Occasional birdsong filtered through the bedroom window as Angie scribbled away, otherwise the house was enveloped in a comforting silence as if the world was grateful that justice was at last being done.

By the end of the day Angie had found what she hoped would be sufficient evidence for Ben to go to the police again. No one would understand her scrawls. If she typed fast, she could get it to Paul within a couple of days and it could be with Ben before the weekend. She tidied away the notebooks and fetched her laptop. Jason would have to make do with a stir-fry and noodles tonight.

It took far longer than she expected. It was nine o'clock on Thursday evening by the time Angie had double-checked and read through as many entries as she could from her diaries. The information she had uncovered stretched to twelve A4 sheets, single-spaced. She enclosed a note to Ben.

Dear Ben,
I have searched through my diaries and hope the information I've found will be of use. The one thing I'd ask is that you keep the information between ourselves and the solicitors. A lot of it is personal to me and I

don't like to think of my private thoughts being seen by everyone. I hope you understand and that all goes well.
Best wishes,
Angie Jarvis

She sealed up the envelope and slipped out of her front door.

As she approached Paul's bungalow, she noticed a strange car parked on his driveway. An easel was perched on the back seat under a portfolio of papers. On the front seat, a pile of brushes and a wooden box with paint smears jostled for a place. She tiptoed over the drive. Voices could be heard coming from the kitchen. She couldn't tell how many people it was or the gender. She stuck the envelope through the letterbox and let the flap down so as not to make any noise and crept away.

She was halfway down Paul's drive when she stopped. She turned to see shadowy figures on the curtains and a pang of something shot through her. It felt remarkably like jealousy or envy. What she had to be jealous of she didn't know. She had just been on a date with Leo and was going on another next week. She tried to shake off the distinctly uneasy feeling that engulfed her. It refused to go away. Another more curious part of her would have liked to find out who was with Paul and what they were doing. 'Christ Almighty, woman,' she swore out loud, marched to her front door, went in and slammed it behind her. This time she only half apologised for the profanity.

Maggie could not wait to hear Angie's news when they had their usual Friday evening get together. 'So what was Leo like?' They had taken advantage of the unseasonably warm evening to sit in the garden so

Maggie could indulge in a cigarette. She took a deep breath and blew a perfect smoke ring, a trick Angie remembered thinking was so glamorous when she had first seen a seventeen-year-old Maggie do it in the toilets, her head half out of the window.

'He's charming,' Angie said. 'I really think there's a connection.'

'Did he kiss you?'

'Only on the cheek.'

'Very restrained. I like the sound of him.' Maggie paused. 'Hey, you're interested, aren't you?'

'I think I am,' Angie said. 'I haven't felt like this in years.' She suspected that she might have been able to feel the same about Paul Buchannan if given half the chance. She brushed the thought aside. He was way out of her league and judging by the disparaging looks he gave her, he thought so too.

'Good for you, girl. Let me top you up and tell you about the meetings I've had with the staff.' Maggie refilled their glasses.

Angie listened. 'So what is the verdict?'

'The verdict is a unanimous *yes*. We've often felt that if we were asked more about the day-to-day running, we could do a damn sight better job than the management.'

Angie paused to take it all in. 'I suppose I need to get back to Mrs Cadwallader to find out what she plans to do next. She was talking about some meeting with the Council.'

'That meeting is about the sale of the care home. It has to be agreed by the Council. I bet I can get a few people there to demonstrate, if it's needed.' Maggie stretched and did up her cardigan. 'You can tell it's not summer yet.' She stood up. 'Let's go inside. I want to hear more about the lovely Leo.'

Angie followed. If Polly Cadwallader could organise enough of a protest, it might at least raise the possibility of alternatives for the board of the care home to consider. She took one last look at the fading light. It felt good to be of use again.

It was gone nine on Saturday when Angie awoke. The sunshine streaming in through the curtains promised another unusually fine day for the time of year. She stretched and listened. There was silence. Jason was staying with a cousin of Bryony's. She had been used to the hustle and bustle of communal living for such a long time, it came as a surprise to be able to hear nothing except the noise she was making as she stretched and rustled the covers.

Angie got up and took the longest bath she could before her skin started to get wrinkly. Once in the kitchen, she switched on the kettle and sat and waited at the table. The whole day stretched ahead of her and she could do exactly as she pleased. Through the open door she could see into the hallway that Jason had finished decorating. The rest of the house looked dingy and tatty by comparison and Angie wondered if he might be eager to earn a few more pounds if she paid him to blitz the rest of the rooms before fatherhood took over. She'd talk to him about it when he got back later. That needn't stop her from ordering some new furniture though. She opened her laptop and to hell with the expense.

Jason arrived back at mid-morning. He was not alone. 'Ange, it's me,' he called from the front porch. Angie went to meet him. 'Mikey here is Bryony's cousin and he says he can cut down those leylandii. He's got all the kit,' he added by way of explanation.

The van which proclaimed *Mike Jones, Tree Surgeon* told her all she needed to know.

'How much will this cost?' Angie said.

Mikey stepped forward. He was a tall man in his mid-thirties with a bushy beard and a red face that told of a life spent in the fresh air. He was wearing a check jacket, like a lumberjack and a woollen hat that struggled to contain his ginger curls. 'I can do it for a ton. Cash,' he added.

Angie frowned. 'He means a hundred quid,' Jason explained. 'It's a good price, Angie, and it'll get *him* off your case,' he said, nodding in the direction of Paul's bungalow. Angie was about to stick up for him when she stopped. It might not be a good idea if people thought they were on good terms in case he was involved more deeply than she realised in the proposals for the care home.

'We'll get rid of the cuttings too,' Mikey said.

'If you can do all that for a ton, I mean one hundred pounds, go ahead. I suppose you'd like a coffee or tea to start?' Angie waited for the reply although she knew what it would be.

'Tea and a couple of bacon sandwiches would fit the bill.' Jason looked over at Mikey who nodded hard enough for his hat to slip sideways. Angie went into the kitchen and was getting the frying pan out when an ear splitting scream from an engine broke the torpor of a weekend morning. She took a peek through the back door just in time to see Mikey climbing up the first Leylandii and Jason revving up a chainsaw. She shuddered and left them to it, praying to whichever god was listening that Paul was not in a complaining mood. His car was not in the driveway and neither was the strange one she had seen last night.

Three tea breaks later, accompanied by bacon sandwiches, fruitcake and a cheese ploughman's lunch and Angie was one hundred pounds worse off but the Leylandii were now no more than fence height. Jason had made two trips to the tip with the van full of cuttings and apart from a carpet of dead needles lying on the grass, the place was looking as if someone cared, at last. It was gone five by the time Jason called Angie to take a look. 'That is fantastic,' she beamed at them both. 'Can I get you two boys a meal tonight?'

'Not for us, Ange. We're going bowling and I'll stay over with Mikey so I'll see you tomorrow evening.' With that they both clambered into the van and it shot down the drive in a squeal of brakes and puffs of acrid smoke.

'What about clean clothes?' Angie shouted after them. Obviously, such things were not important to Jason and she went inside and spent the evening online, checking out what she could do to appear a mature, sexually experienced, confident woman, just in case she and Leo became more than just friends.

Spending time online meant that Angie did not hear the weather forecast and so was not prepared for the storm, brewing out in the ocean which roared inland in the early hours of the morning. Neither were many of the inhabitants of the county as the wind unexpectedly switched direction and unleashed its venom over the downs instead of along the coast.

Angie woke to darkness. The comforting light of the alarm clock was absent and when she tried the switch there was no power. A rumbling beast of a gale was careering round the house, rattling at the doors and windows. The outside gate was banging where it had slipped its latch. Angie pulled on a dressing gown and went into the kitchen. She found the torch and by its dim light she peered outside before unlocking the front door. As soon as she opened it, the strength of the wind tore her breath away and flung the door out of her hands. She dragged it back and fastened it behind her. She needed to close the gate. Heaven knows what would happen and what damage it might do if it was ripped off.

Flickering lights, like the dance of a candle flame, pierced the gloom in the windows of neighbouring bungalows and told the same story of a wakeful night for the inhabitants. Angie fastened her dressing gown tighter and battled towards the gate at the side of the house. Bins skidded over the road, scattering the contents which were pitched and tossed in the air. The debris from battered trees was spread over the grass and a small sapling in Paul's garden was bent almost horizontal. It was the noise of the wind as it pounded and raged over the hillside that frightened her most.

Split seconds of eerie silence were shattered in the relentless onslaught. Angie placed one foot carefully in front of her and bent double like the sapling, stumbled the short distance from the front door to the side gate. It was swinging wildly on one hinge. She lashed the gate to the post with her dressing gown sash and bent down to fasten the bolt. It would have to do although the way the post was swaying in its holder, it would not last the night.

She took a last look at the post, wiped her hands down her pyjama bottoms and headed back towards the front door. As she did, she heard a high-pitched whistle and the wind screamed, tugged at her and knocked her off her feet. She cowered down against a power that was stronger than any she had ever experienced. A flash of lighting and a huge crash of thunder overhead was followed by a cracking sound and as she looked up, she saw the branch from the tree that hung over the bungalow break and fall inwards, smashing through the roof and scattering tiles and debris over the garden. She waited, certain that in the next minute she would either be whisked away or flattened, and bowed her head for the punishment that she expected.

Chapter Fourteen

'My God are you all right?' Angie looked up to be confronted by neighbours in various states of undress, running towards her. Flashlights and torches shone on the devastation. She glanced back at the roof. The charred branch stuck up from the bungalow and was smoking. A shiver ran through her and her teeth started chattering. Someone put a blanket over her shoulders and guided her away. 'There's nothing we can do tonight,' a calm voice said. 'She can stay with me.' It was Paul Buchannan.

'We'd better call the Fire Brigade. I reckon the lightning's set fire to summat,' a tall man in a full length Barbour said to a murmur of approval from the others.

'What about the boy? Is he in there?' another called out. Paul's face blanched as he took in the words.

'No. He's not there,' Angie said. 'He's staying with friends tonight.' She was speaking as slowly as she could but the shivering and teeth chattering would not stop.

'If you call the emergency services and tell them what's happened, I can be here when they arrive,' Paul said to the man in the Barbour. 'It's all right everyone. I'll take care of Miss Jarvis tonight.' He waved away the other neighbours, thanking them for their promises to help when dawn revealed the truth of what had happened. They melted back into their own homes in the acknowledgement that he was now in command.

Paul put an arm round her shoulders to support

her against the ceaseless battering from the wind. He led Angie into the lounge where a wood burner glowed, sending out a welcoming heat. Small, battery-powered lights were dotted here and there. 'Sit down,' he indicated a huge cream leather recliner chair. 'I'll get you a cup of tea. That's what they recommend for shock isn't it?' He scurried into the kitchen. Angie lay back and closed her eyes, grateful for the warmth and cosiness of the room. She could hear the comforting clatter of cups. For some reason the storm didn't sound so fierce.

'Sorry it took so long.' Angie sat up and opened her eyes. 'I had to use the gas ring and a saucepan. It's a good job I was in the Boy Scouts.' Paul placed a tray with cups, saucers, sugar bowl and milk jug in pale blue onto the table. 'I can't give you a brandy as it's not good for anyone in shock. Do you mind if I have one? Tea? I know I should remember. Is it milk and no sugar?' He was gabbling on and Angie noticed him glancing at her from time to time. What did he think she was going to do? Run screaming out of the room? Faint on him?

'Milk no sugar and I don't mind if you have a drink.' Her hand shook as she took the cup and saucer and settled back into the chair to sip the scalding brew. A flashing blue light outside told her help had arrived.

Paul got to his feet. 'Let me deal with them. You sit here and I'll let you know what's happening.'

'No. It's my home. I need to be there.' Angie got up unsteadily. Paul placed his arm under hers and supported her into the hallway. He helped her into a large overcoat and together they fought their way to the front of the fire tender where a burly crew leader

142

was taking stock of the situation while the rest of the team sprang into their well drilled actions. Paul stood close by her side. Together they watched without speaking as water doused the smouldering branches and soaked the inside of the bungalow to dampen any sparks. The wind had dropped to something more recognisable as a gale. It was an hour before the emergency services finally left, reassuring Angie there was no more risk of fire.

Once back in his bungalow Paul made more tea and this time poured out an amber liquid into two cut glass crystal tumblers. He handed one to Angie and took a long drink himself. 'I needed that.' He flung another log onto the burner and the flames crackled and sparks flew up the chimney. 'I suppose it would be stupid to ask how you are?'

'I'm not hurt. I'm just worried about tomorrow and the damage.' The enormity of the task ahead was sinking in. She'd only just started to get the place decent. It wasn't fair. All Angie wanted to do was to curl up and cry like a baby.

'My guest bedroom is ready and aired so you must stay here. Tomorrow we'll alert the insurance company and get a builder to check the roof.'

'After a night like this, they'll all be busy, won't they?' For the first time Angie felt like crawling back to the convent. At least there she had Sister Elizabeth or Sister Agnes to share the burden of day-to-day living. Here she was alone and it was tougher than she'd ever expected.

'It might be hard to get someone straightaway if there is more damage like this in the town.' He took another sip of his drink and tapped the side of his nose. 'I know a few people in the building industry who owe me a good turn so don't get despondent.' Taking control sat easily on Paul's shoulders and Angie was grateful he was able to help. 'Listen to that?' He tilted his head on one side. 'I reckon the storm has passed.' The previous insistent roaring of the wind had been replaced by a slight rumble. The rain was now pouring down, finding a way into Angie's house through the damaged roof, adding to the water and foam that the fire crew had used.

'I think you're right,' Angie stifled a yawn.

Paul stood up. 'Let me show you to your room. You can sleep as long as you like as I'm working from home tomorrow.'

He fetched a torch and led her to a guest room with an en suite bathroom. Even in the dim light, it was clear that the overall cream colour was continued here accentuated by blues and navy with piles of fluffy towels waiting on the navy silk bed cover. Paul fetched a clean pair of silk pyjamas that were obviously for men and a navy bathrobe. 'You'd better get out of those.' He indicated the muddy clothes that Angie was wearing. 'There's plenty of hot water and this torch will last for hours.' He paused. A look that Angie had never seen before spread over his face. It was of concern and there was something else that she couldn't quite comprehend. 'Will you be all right?'

Angie nodded. 'You've been very kind.'

'It was the least that I could do. If I had got the damn tree trimmed earlier, none of this would have happened.' Then he added in a quieter voice, 'You could have been killed.' He closed the door.

Angie sat down on the bed. Either Paul had undergone a complete personality change or he was terrified of what could have happened. She took off

144

the dirty clothes and slipped on silk pyjamas. That was typical of her life. She had never worn silk before and here she was putting on a man's pyjamas after a night in which she had been made homeless. On a different day she would have enjoyed it and its erotic overtones more. She snuggled down into the bed. The high thread count cotton crunched under her body and the duvet and pillows moulded to her shape. It was not long before she fell into a deep, exhausted sleep.

A tap on the door woke her. Angie sat up, uncertain where she was. She looked at the strange surroundings, panic rising until she recalled the incidents that had brought her there. 'Er, yes?' She lifted herself on one elbow as the door opened a crack and Paul's face peered into the room.

'Sorry to disturb you. I managed to get my builder contact to come out and survey the site. He reckons you can go back to collect some things and he'll tell you what needs to be done. There's slippers in the cupboard,' he added and closed the door. Angie got up and pulled on the navy bathrobe. She opened the cupboard to find a pair of white slippers trimmed with fur and tiny crystals. She eased her feet into them and wriggled her toes. She could get used to this luxury.

In the kitchen Paul was leaning against the counter. A large man in a denim jacket, clutching a note pad and pencil stood by the door. 'This is Matt. He reckons we should have a look at the damage. It isn't cold and you can wear my Hunters if you like.' He held out the same overcoat that she had worn before and she snugged into its cashmere softness.

Angie changed into the boots and followed Matt

back to her house. She opened the door and stepped inside. The hall was untouched. Her own bedroom was unscathed too. It was Jason's room that had taken the brunt of the damage. There was a gaping hole in the roof and where the rain had come in, the floor was soaked. Part of a large branch had come to rest on his bed. If he had been there, he would have been killed. The branch had knocked down the large chimney pot and it had crashed with the television aerial though the roof, smashing onto the kitchen cabinets and the sink. The water and the foam had drenched the fridge and the cooker. It was likely the electrics were shot to pieces too as the water had soaked the junction box and fuse board.

All the pent-up emotions that Angie had been holding in for so long joined together in a tsunami of feeling. Her legs buckled. Tears fell in noiseless sobs as she surveyed the wreckage of her house and now her life. All the inner demons she had fought to suppress were released and ready to go on the rampage.

Paul stepped forward and placed his hands on her shoulder. 'The first thing we must do is go and rescue the important stuff from your bedroom and,' he pointed to her laptop on the table, 'anything else we can get. Matt tells me it's safe. I'll take this.' He picked up her laptop and she stumbled into the bedroom where at least she had to focus on collecting some clothes and toiletries. She opened the trunk with her notebooks. Nothing had been damaged. That was typical of her father. His old school trunk would survive the next world war. She left it where it was and collected some half-decent clothes. God knows how long she would have to wait and the insurance might take ages. This time there was no apology to God for her profanity. She had given him enough supplications over her life and a fat lot of good it had done.

The task helped to clear her mind. It might be months before she could get any semblance of normality back into her life. At the moment she didn't even know if she had the energy or the enthusiasm. It would be easier to give up and go back. Paul's voice filtered through. He chatted on, keeping his comments light and practical as if recognising her distraught state of mind. 'Matt will make the house secure and watertight so that no more damage is done. The insurance will take care of it all and it'll soon be better than ever.'

'What about Jason's stuff?' Angie turned to face Paul. 'He's only got an overnight bag with him. Can't we get some things from his room?'

Paul shook his head. 'Matt says it's too risky. Let's get back to my place. You get dressed while I make breakfast and you can text him.'

Thirty minutes later, Angie was sitting at the breakfast bar in Paul's kitchen, forcing herself to eat a slice of toast. She called Jason, explained what had happened and waited for his reaction. 'What about you, Ange?' His voice wobbled. 'How are you?'

'In shock. Your room and all your stuff is wet. What do you need?' She didn't have time to finish.

'What stuff? A few old clothes and some car magazines? I can get new clothes on the insurance and everything else is on my tablet and my phone. I'll borrow some jeans from Bryony's brother and her mum will put me up for a few weeks. It'll do me good to get to know her better. I'll call you later to see how you are.' He rang off.

'Everything all right?' Paul asked as he poured coffee.

Angie nodded; oh for the resilience of youth. If only a bit of it could rub off on her.

By the end of the day, it had. Angie unpacked in the spare bedroom which she would be using at Paul's insistence until the repairs were completed. She contacted the insurance office who promised to send someone out the following day and she had received an unusual text from Jason which she read and reread.

Can't believe you staying wiv old misery guts. Bet he's worried in case you sue. It's his fault innit? Best not say anything and sue him once you're back—all them accident claims bods will help. You'll clean up. See ya.
J.

It did seem strange how Paul had changed. Angie would need to discuss arrangements with him and perhaps she might get some idea why he was being so helpful. She spent the rest of the day arranging for quotes, phoning the insurance company, speaking to a loss adjuster and explaining to Maggie what had happened. It was gone five before she finished.

Paul had ordered them a takeaway as he rarely cooked during the week. He was pouring a glass of wine when Angie came into the kitchen. 'Beer or wine?' he said.

'A glass of wine would be lovely.' Angie perched on the stool at the counter. 'Can I ask you something?'

'Go ahead.' Paul handed her a glass of red wine.

148

'We haven't exactly hit it off since I moved in here so ...' she faltered. 'Why are you doing this for me?'

'You mean why the sudden change to Mr Nice Guy?'

'Well...yes.' His honesty had caught her off guard.

Paul sat opposite her at the counter, took a sip of wine and ran a hand through his hair before answering, avoiding her gaze as he spoke. 'There are two things. First, if I hadn't been so pig-headed, this would never have happened. The last people promised to trim their hedges and I'd do the same with the tree. Nothing happened. I suppose I expected you to be the same.'

'You said there were two things. What's the second?'

'Ben got your letter. He reckons it's just what he needs.' He looked back at her. There was no mistaking the pain in his eyes. 'For the first time he has a ray of hope that someone might take him seriously. You'll never know how much that means to me. So you can stay here as long as you like and I promise I won't get in your way.' He got to his feet. 'Let's eat or this will be getting cold.'

'I really can't impose on you like this.' Angie took another sip of her wine and crossed her fingers for some good old-fashioned courage.

'Nonsense. It won't be as long as you think. Matt says he'll get started straight away with the clean-up and making everything safe so that you can move back.' He opened the tops of the plastic containers and a smell of Chinese food wafted out. 'The repairs can be done when the insurance is settled which will be in a week or two. I know it looks a mess but apart from the hole in the roof and the fuse box, everything else is cosmetic.'

'At least let me cook for you in the evening and pay proper rent. I'm sure a diet of takeaways isn't healthy.'

'It's my fault, remember.' He handed her a plate.

'I can't accept.' Angie folded her arms. Perhaps Jason was right and he did have a guilty conscience or was worried in case she sued him.

Paul stopped ladling the food onto his plate. A smile crossed his face. 'You really are a very formidable lady. I bet the kids in your class took notice of you. Am I right?'

'Something like that,' Angie replied. 'Stop changing the subject.'

Paul held up his hands. 'Yes, boss.'

Angie ignored him and continued. 'We'd need to split the grocery bills. Agreed?' She held up her glass.

Paul clinked his against hers. 'You're a hard taskmaster. I know when I'm beaten.' He did a mock bow. 'It's agreed.' As he smiled Angie noticed what beautiful eyes he had, fringed with long lashes and how his hair had threads of gold. Maggie's words came back to her. 'Fit, is what they say, Angie, not dishy or hunky.' Well Paul was definitely *fit* and she was enjoying experiencing the kinder side to his nature. She raised her glass to heaven. God was certainly working in a mysterious way. Perhaps she had been wrong about both of them after all.

Chapter Fifteen

For nearly two weeks Angie and Paul fell into an amicable arrangement. At weekends he disappeared for hours to play golf or visit friends. During the week he rose early and she would hear him getting ready and going off to work. She would wait until he left before getting up herself. After breakfast, she tidied the bungalow before she turned her attention to shopping for their evening meal. It was strange to be in someone else's home yet pleasant to be in a place where everything worked and was up to date. The washer drier had more cycles than she had clothes and the vacuum cleaner was so strong it practically sucked the carpet off the floor. There was a complex coffee machine that used small pods; Angie left that alone.

She was busy dusting the lounge one day when she stopped. There were only two family photos on display. One was of Paul and his wife on their wedding day. The other one was a group photo with two teenagers who bore a striking resemblance to Paul. It must have been taken on a holiday as the foursome were standing against a backdrop of whitewashed houses and cobalt sky. Every time she flicked the duster over them she felt sad and she didn't know why.

Only when she had finished preparing their evening meal did she feel that she could do what she wanted to do. That meant checking her inbox and keeping up to date with any messages. Her first thought was Leo.

Hi Leo,

Sorry about not getting in touch sooner. The recent storm has caused havoc in my place and I have to stay with friends for a few days. I will be in touch towards the end of the week when I should know what is happening. I'm really sorry but the meal will have to be postponed for a while. I'll be in touch.

Angie

His quick reply intrigued her. Either he must have lots of staff or he was one of those people who were constantly checking their phone. She only hoped he wasn't mucking out or castrating a bull at the time.

My dear Angie,

How dreadful for you! We'll simply delay our next meeting until you are settled. If there is anything I can do to help, please let me know. I love a bit of DIY as it's an excuse to buy another power tool, really. Seriously, I am at your disposal.

Fondest wishes,

Leo xxx

She thanked him again and declined the offer of help. Although it had nothing to do with Paul, she felt there was something tacky about arranging a possible romantic meeting when she was staying in another man's house.

Paul was nothing if not punctual and would arrive back at 6.30pm. Angie made sure he had a drink. They would eat and discuss the day's events (on his part) and the news, since Angie felt she had nothing much to tell him about her day. They would finish their wine watching the television, just as Angie imagined thousands of other couples did every evening.

It was Thursday and Paul was checking his emails. 'Damn,' he swore. 'Sorry.'

Angie looked up from the book she was reading. 'Bad news?'

'I suppose you could say that. There's a comedy event at the Retro Club on Saturday night and I must have missed the email alerts. The tickets are all gone. Pity. There's a good line-up. How on earth did the emails end up in junk mail?' he grumbled.

It gave Angie an idea. The following day after he had left for work, she searched online and there was a site offering tickets. She clicked on the link and gulped. Did people really pay that much? She shrugged. It was worth it. Paul had been the perfect gentleman and the bungalow would probably be safe for her to return to sometime next week if all went to plan. This would be a fitting thank you for helping her out. She entered her credit card details and held her breath in case it didn't go through. It did and she printed out the eticket for two people so that he wouldn't be on his own. She couldn't wait to tell him tonight. First she had to see Maggie.

It was to be a short visit so Angie had bought cakes to go with their tea. She had explained what had happened to her house and knew Maggie would now want all the gory details. 'So how are you and how is your new landlord?' Maggie plonked herself down at the kitchen table and helped herself to a cake.

'He's very sweet.' Angie paused, 'At least he has been so far.'

Maggie pulled a face. 'Yeah right.' She took a bite

153

of the cake.

'He's not half as bad as I'd expected.'

'Hmmm, must be hiding something. Is he married?'

'He was at one time…she died.'

'Is he marriageable material?' Maggie picked up the crumbs on her plate with one finger and licked them off, 'or more to the point is he bed worthy?'

Angie chewed on her slice of cake. 'I've never thought about him in that way.'

'Liar. Even if you don't admit it, you've got that dreamy look on your face that says if he asked you out, you'd agree straightaway.' Maggie paused to gather breath. 'What would you do if he made a move on you?'

'I don't know.' It was a lie. She might be ready to go on a date with Leo but as the days went past, Paul was becoming more and more attractive in her eyes. She was beginning to feel a connection with him. The trouble is she didn't have a clue if he felt the same.

'Dare I ask what is happening with the lovely Leo?' Maggie's words broke into Angie's thoughts.

'I said I'd email him again once I'm back home. I didn't feel I could go out on the…' Angie stumbled over the words, not certain what to say.

'Pull, shag, date even if you insist on being very Jane Austen about it,' Maggie suggested.

'I didn't think it was right to go out dating when I'm in another man's house.'

'Very Jane Austen. I bet he wouldn't think twice if the shoe was on the other foot. Make sure you don't lose him by being coy. If he's as good as you say, he'll soon be snapped up.'

Angie checked the time. 'Heavens I must dash.

I've got masses to do. We'll be back to normal soon and I'll bring a very large bottle of wine to celebrate.' She kissed Maggie on each cheek.

'Make sure you can bring me some good news on the Leo front,' Maggie called as Angie closed the back door and went to her car. As she started the engine, she checked herself. Her stomach was doing a flip and she knew why. She was looking forward to going home, cooking and presenting Paul with the tickets.

They ate at the kitchen counter. Conversation ebbed and flowed which helped deflect Angie's attention away from the shifting sand of emotions she was feeling. Afterwards they moved into the lounge. Paul had lit small candles and a jazz quartet was tinkling over the sound system, its syncopated rhythm filling the space. Angie loaded the dishwasher, switched it on and went and fetched a piece of paper from her room. She came back in and sat down. 'Did you say you wanted tickets for the Retro Club on Saturday?' she asked.

Paul rolled his eyes in exasperation. 'Yes and more fool me for not checking my junk mail. There might be a chance next year, if the line-up tour again.'

Angie held out the paper. 'This is for you,' she said.

Paul did a double take. 'What is for me?'

She wiggled the paper. 'This-'

He looked more closely and took hold of the paper to read it properly. A smile creased his face. 'How on earth did you get these?'

'I found a website where they sell spare tickets.'

'It must have cost a fortune.'

'A bit more than usual,' Angie lied. 'It was worth it though, as now, Cinderella, you can go to the ball.'

155

She did a mock bow.

'I'll go on condition you come with me.' Paul fixed her with a steely gaze, his eyes never leaving her face,

'I can't...I mean what about taking a friend?' Angie felt her face burning up and she knew she was blushing.

'I can't think of anyone who would be better company.' Paul continued to look at her. 'Agreed?'

'Only if I can treat us to a meal, too. Is there a restaurant nearby?'

Paul got out his phone and tapped away. 'It says here that there is a chippie, a Chinese takeaway, an Indian and a new Italian called Luigi's. Would Italian suit you?'

'Yes, and if you let me drive, you can have a glass of wine.'

Paul pulled a face. 'In your car? Isn't it a bit unreliable?'

'I'd prefer to call her temperamental.'

'I tell you what, we'll have a bottle ready for when we get home and we can both enjoy it.'

Saturday evening arrived and Angie wore her skinny jeans with a lacy top and her leather jacket with pumps. She added a scarf which she hoped she had draped elegantly over her shoulders although Maggie did say that she wore scarves like someone out on a day's grouse shoot; more for comfort and warmth than style. She squirted on some perfume and gave her hair a final pat before grabbing her bag. Paul was already by the front door. 'You look nice,' he said and looked her up and down.

'Thank you. My friend Maggie helped me choose the jacket.' She looked away in case he caught her blushing. She wasn't used to men paying her compliments.

Paul was dressed in black trousers, a blue check shirt with a blue sweater and a tan leather jacket. His feet were encased in black loafers with a tassel and with his greying hair he could have passed for an Italian any day. 'Ready?' He opened the door and Angie stepped outside. She cast a glance at her home and watched as the tarpaulin over the roof flapped in the chill breeze. 'Not long now,' Paul said, as if reading her thoughts. 'I reckon you can move back within a few days, if you want to that is—' he added.

He opened the car door and Angie slid into the seat, luxuriating in the feel of the rich, black leather. 'It will be nice to get my life back on track,' she admitted.

Paul let the clutch out and the car purred into life. He was a good driver and the car ate up the miles to the city centre. Paul parked near the Club. Over dinner he entertained her with stories of backpacking in India when he and his wife were young. Angie listened with a twinge of envy. It was too late for her to make memories like that.

The Retro Club was down a small side street. It had once been a cinema and stone steps led to double doors set between two stone columns. The foyer was painted in red and gold and cherubs decorated the wrought iron staircase that led to the upper tiers of seats. They went through another set of double doors that said *stalls* which opened onto a space in front of the stage. The seats had been replaced by tables and chairs set in cabaret style with a bar along one wall. The place was packed and Paul steered Angie to a space where they perched on two metal chairs. Paul nudged her. 'There's someone I know. I'd better go

157

over and say *hello* just to be polite.' She watched as he headed towards a table where a florid man was sitting with a woman his age and three young people. Two must have been his children as the family resemblance was evident in the shape of the faces. She saw Paul nod in her direction and she waved as the man acknowledged her presence. Paul chatted for a few minutes before he patted the man on the shoulder and came back.

'Is he a friend?' Angie asked.

'No. He's chair of the committee I'm working with on my latest project.'

Angie was about to ask if it was anything to do with the Crystal Hill Care Home but changed her mind. She'd keep business and pleasure separate.

Nervous laughter from the audience filled the air and gestures were getting bigger and more expansive as the voices grew louder. Paul leaned forward, his mouth opening and shutting. Angie had no idea what he'd said. 'Sorry. I can't hear you,' she mouthed.

Paul got closer so that his face was next to hers and she could feel his breath on her cheek. 'Can you see from where you are sitting?'

His closeness was unnerving and Angie swallowed hard to compose herself before she replied. There was no time to speak. The compere burst onto the small stage and everyone in the audience stood up to get a better view of the first act. Angie simply nodded and with relief turned her attention back to the stage. As they watched the different acts, Angie was aware of Paul close beside her and something awoke inside. It had been years since she had experienced this sensation, like an invisible current passing from one person to another, a hyperawareness of their every

158

move. It was both unnerving and exhilarating.

The last ripple of applause died away and the lights came up, a signal for everyone to leave. Paul and Angie made their way back to the car park and he opened the door for her to get in. 'All I can say is a very big thank you,' he said. 'It's a dream come true to see those acts, all in one line-up without having to travel to London or Manchester.'

'It was my pleasure,' Angie said, 'and now I can let you into a secret. That's the first live comedy act I've ever seen.' Before Paul could interrupt, she carried on, 'You see I've lived a very...' she paused, 'I suppose you'd call it a very sheltered life.'

'Let me take it upon myself personally to change that. The next good act that comes here we'll go and see together, it will be my treat.' He let the car into gear and joined the stream all jostling to get out of the car park.

It was gone midnight when they got back. 'How about a glass of wine, since we've been so abstemious tonight?' Paul asked.

'That would be lovely,' Angie said.

'You go and put some music on and I'll fetch the drinks.' Angie wandered into the lounge and kneeled down in front of Paul's huge collection of music. She was flicking through the vinyl records when he returned and handed her a large goblet of wine, so thick and red that it left traces as it swirled round the glass. 'Are you looking for anything in particular?' Paul asked as he perched on the seat of the armchair next to her.

'Yes I am. The name begins with A and there is a picture of someone holding a hawk on the cover against lots of water.'

'*Avalon* by *Roxy Music*,' Paul said and selected the disc which he slipped from its sleeve and placed on the turntable in the record unit. The sound filled the space and Angie was transported back to her first term at university. She had been crammed into a bedsit along with a dozen other students and was squashed up against a young man called Dan. For the first time she had felt the delicious sensation of the close proximity of someone of the opposite sex she found very attractive. That was what she had felt again tonight with Paul.

As she leaned back and listened to the music, she closed her eyes and wondered what it would be like if Paul kissed her. She snapped her eyes open. That was just a silly dream and life never resembles dreams. They sat in silence, each listening to the music until the last strains died away. Angie stood up. 'Time for me to go to bed,' and she went into the kitchen to put her glass in the dishwasher.

As she opened the front, Paul leaned over to put his glass inside and his arm brushed hers. He looked at her and for a moment Angie was convinced he was leaning closer. Time slowed down, hovered as if deciding whether to stop. She held her breath and willed him to kiss her. 'Good night.' He moved away. Time continued on its journey. The spell was broken. 'Thanks again for the tickets.' It was the way you might talk to a distant neighbour and Angie felt the disappointment well up inside her. 'Everything's locked up,' he said and hurried off to his room at the end of the hall.

Angie switched off the lights and went into her room. She sat down on the bed. 'Damn, damn, damn.' Her instincts told her Paul was attracted to her

160

although the way he had just spoken to her contradicted that. She cringed. She could so easily have made a fool of them both. She undressed slowly and got into bed. She was now sure of one thing; whatever Paul felt about her, she was very attracted to him. The familiar pain of unrequited love that had haunted her youth came flooding back and she covered her head with the pillow.

Chapter Sixteen

After that night nothing was quite the same again. Paul worked later and later each day. Angie left him some food which he heated up in the microwave. Gone were the evenings spent chatting and either she had embarrassed him by making her feelings obvious or he was fed up with her being there. She longed to be back in her own home and away from the shame that sent her scurrying to her room as soon as she heard his key in the door.

It was Thursday morning when Matt the builder knocked on the door. He was smiling. 'It's ready for you to go back. Want a look?'

Angie walked over to her bungalow where tarpaulin flapped over the hole in the roof. 'Are you sure it's safe?' Her stomach churned as she waited for his reply.

'The electrics are fine and the roof will be done within a couple of weeks.'

She followed Matt as he walked through the hall and into the kitchen pointing out what he'd done. With each step her excitement rose. The place only needed a good clean. After that it would be more than ready for new carpets and curtains and some decent modern furniture. She beamed at Matt. 'You've done a great job.'

'I bet you can't wait to get home,' Matt said as he handed her the keys.

'Yes. It will be lovely to be in my own place again.' Even as she said the words, she knew she'd been secretly hoping that with a few more days, she and Paul could have…She stopped. This was no time to get all gooey eyed with some teenage fantasy. It was time to get back to normal. She closed the door and texted Jason to tell him. His reply came back by return:

Bloody good thing Bry's mum is doing my head in I've slept on all me mates floors and I've got no clean clothes C U 2 nite.

Angie went back to Paul's house and collected up her belongings. She scribbled a note in case she didn't manage to see him as she didn't have his number to call.

Matt told me that I can go back today so I won't outstay my welcome. Jason has had it tougher than me. I've been very lucky and it's all down to your excellent hospitality. I will catch up with you later. Thanks for everything and will probably see you at the weekend. Angie
PS I've not cooked so I'll bring something over later.

She left the note with his keys on the hall table and went back to her home, parroting Sister Agnes' advice whenever anyone looked miserable. 'Hard work will soon put paid to that, my girl.' She just hoped she was right.

By six o'clock she had shopped and was in the middle of preparing a meal for Jason when she heard a car draw up outside. She ran to the front door. Her heart pounded and she just knew a grin like the Cheshire Cat from *Alice in Wonderland* was spreading across her face and could not be stopped She opened the door and called out. 'Paul?'

163

He turned. 'What the hell are you doing over there?' He checked himself. 'I mean is it safe?'

Angie wiped her hands on her jeans and looked up at him. 'Yes it's quite safe so I can move back. It means Jason can come home too. I left you a note because I didn't have your number and …' her voice trailed off as Paul's face hardened.

'I see. Thanks for letting me know,' he added. His blue eyes were as cold and unfeeling as they had been when they first met.

'I didn't leave you anything to eat. I can bring you some chilli later, if you like?'

For a second Paul's face softened. It soon changed. 'I've already eaten, thanks for the offer.'

Angie wanted to keep him talking. 'Or perhaps I can invite you over for a meal as a way of saying thank you.'

'That's very kind of you except I'll be working in the north for a few weeks so it will have to wait.' Paul's voice registered no enthusiasm whatsoever.

'I understand. I wouldn't want to put you out.' Angie's previous excitement had morphed into irritation.

'Very well. That's settled.' He turned and went inside.

'Thank you once again for your hospitality,' Angie's voice faded away as the door closed. A plume of black smoke greeted her in the kitchen. She had left the onions sautéing and they were now a burnt mess. She stuck the pan under the tap where it hissed accusingly. She got out another onion and began to chop. Her eyes watered and her cheeks were soon wet; whether it was from the onions or another reason, she preferred not to know. She forced herself to concentrate and block out the jumble of feelings careering through her body. Relief at being back home was battling with regret over Paul and at the moment regret was winning hands down.

An hour later a key clicked in the latch and the sound of a large bag being dropped in the hall announced that Jason was back. He burst into the kitchen and enveloped Angie in a bear hug. 'Great to be home, Ange. What's for dinner?' He let go and lifted the lid on the pot of chilli Angie was cooking. 'I've had enough takeaways to last a lifetime.'

'Get the table laid and pour us both a beer and this will be ready in about five minutes. I've made up a bed in the spare room as yours really isn't habitable until the roof is mended.'

Jason disappeared and reappeared a few seconds later shaking his head. 'What a bloody mess.' He took a swig of the beer from the bottle. Angie pushed a glass towards him. 'Have you decided what to do about suing him next door?' He jerked his head in the direction of Paul's bungalow.

'Can you lay the table please?' Angie switched the conversation and pretended to be very busy tasting and stirring. The last thing she wanted was to discuss Paul with Jason and yet at the same time she desperately wanted to talk about him. The clattering behind her said the table was laid and so she doled out a huge plate of rice and chilli and put it down before Jason. She ladled herself a small portion and sat opposite him.

'Not hungry, Ange?' Jason asked as Angie pushed the food around her plate.

She sat up. 'Not really. Tell me all about Bryony's mum and how you two have been getting on.'

165

As Jason talked she listened yet found her thoughts drifting back to what Paul was doing. What was he eating? What music was he playing?

'Ange, is something wrong?' Jason's voice broke into her dreams.

Angie shook her head. 'I'm just tired that's all. I need an early night before I get cracking on this place. Everything needs cleaning.'

'Tell you what, why don't we have a clean-up and house warming party? You can invite Maggie, me and Bry and we'll all pitch in and clean and you can feed us?' He helped himself to more chilli.

Angie clapped her hands together. 'Jason that is the best idea you've ever had. I can include the rest of the neighbours who were so kind on the night of the storm.' She was careful not to say it also meant she could invite Paul informally. This could be the chance she needed to get talking to him again. By then she might have worked out exactly what she wanted to do about those feelings that he so easily aroused.

Later that evening she called Maggie to tell her she was back home. 'What happened with that miserable old so and so next door?'

For once, Angie wasn't quite sure just how much she wanted to tell Maggie. 'He was a gentleman, a real gentleman.'

'So all that *Mr Grouchy Old Man* was a front?'

'I don't think so. I reckon he just likes his privacy and…' she paused, 'I don't think he's over the death of his first wife, yet.'

'Ahha, you are in with a chance, if you want it…' Maggie said.

'What do you mean?' Sometimes Angie reckoned she and Maggie were living on a different planet.

166

'You can be the understanding friend... like a patient often falls in love with the nurse or doctor that helped them, he might feel the same way about you.'

Angie felt her cheeks get warm. 'I don't think he will, ever.' She knew her voice was wavering and hoped Maggie wouldn't spot it.

There was no such luck. 'Did something happen or did you want something to happen?'

'Yes, no, oh I don't know...' Angie stammered out.

'For heaven's sake, which is it?'

'I don't know what to think. I'm supposed to be interested in Leo but I feel something for Paul.' She sighed. 'I thought this was going to be so easy, meeting someone, falling in love, like they do in films.'

Maggie snorted. 'Lies, all lies.'

'So what is the truth?'

Maggie sniffed. 'It's far more complex than you think. Why don't you go out with Leo, see what happens and carry on being friendly with Paul?'

'You're probably right,' Angie said and hoped to hide her disappointment from Maggie. Her head might be able to tolerate just being friends with Paul, the rest of her did not agree.

'I know I am.'

'Jason has this idea for a house warming and cleaning party and I was going to invite Paul too. I suppose that would be a start, wouldn't it?'

'Brilliant idea,' Maggie said. 'Don't invite him to clean, just for the meal afterwards. It would be a way of saying thanks. As you've invited the rest of the neighbours, it won't seem like you've singled him out.'

Angie thought for a few moments and a smile spread across her face. 'I'm just extending the hand of friendship, really, aren't I?'

'Exactly.'

'What could we eat?' Visions of her poisoning the inhabitants of The Close crowded in.

'Easy. Have you got a pen ready?' Within half an hour, Angie had a shopping list and a menu that Maggie assured her would suit Gareth, Tasha and the more discerning palate of Paul. 'Get those invites out tonight. There's no guarantee he hasn't got other plans. Didn't you say he used to play golf at the weekends?'

'I hadn't thought about that.' For once Angie felt the need for a quick prayer, except God didn't interfere in affairs of the heart. He had bigger things to do. Besides she didn't believe in all that stuff. Her fingers went instinctively to the cross under her sweater; she pulled her hand away.

'There's plenty of invitation templates you can use. You can print and deliver them tonight, can't you?'

All was quiet when Angie crept out and pushed the invitations through the door of every bungalow in The Close. She lifted each letterbox flap as carefully as she could and let the envelope slip to the floor, hoping no one had a zealous dog ready to snatch it from her hand. She worked fast. Paul's car was nowhere to be seen. The last thing she wanted was for him to spot her strange behaviour. It would only add to his poor opinion of her.

By the time she got to Paul's bungalow her heart was pounding and any minute she expected his car to sweep into the drive and she would be caught. She stopped. This was ridiculous. She was only inviting him to a simple meal with all the neighbours. There was no harm in that. She shoved the envelope through his door, straightened up and walked back to her home as calmly as she could and just hoped he hadn't got a prior invitation.

It was nearly eleven when the lights of a car flashed through the curtains of the lounge. She went into the hall and through the small glass panel she could see Paul get out and go into his house. She waited until he had closed his door and she knew he would have spotted her note. She skipped into her bedroom and imagined him opening it and reading it. Was he smiling? Was he checking his diary? Would he pop over with a note to accept? If he was free, she'd have to decide what to wear. She wanted to look smart and the word that popped into her brain was one she never thought Angela or even Angie Jarvis would use about her appearance. She wanted to look *sexy*. She stopped and sank down on the bed. Now she knew what those feelings were careering through her body. She had fallen in love with Paul Buchannan.

Chapter Seventeen

By the time Jason arrived with Bryony on Sunday morning, Angie had checked the timings for the meal twice, re-arranged the table four times and polished the cutlery and the glasses so that they shone like the crown jewels. She had sent a quick prayer of thanks back to Sister Constanta whose ability to organise and create a party out of nothing had helped her through the last twenty-four hours. Jason and Bryony set to with a duster and polish while Angie got in their way as she re-folded her mother's damask serviettes and counted the knives and forks in case she needed to call Maggie and ask to borrow more.

She was fretting over whether she should have made some non-alcoholic punch when the neighbours who had come to her rescue on the night of the storm arrived, swiftly followed by Maggie and her crew. Angie was plunged into a frenzy of introductions and panic over whether she could remember if Bob was married to Glenda or Susie with Mike, not to mention Gail and Steve or was it Stuart? In the end it didn't matter as they kept referring to Maggie, who had set herself up in charge of directing operations. It was left to Angie to supply the endless demands for hot water, sponges and polish.

For two hours they all worked together. The men traded jokes and the latest football news with Gareth and Jason as floors were washed and walls were cleaned down. The women fussed over Bryony, telling her their own experiences of feeding on demand as cupboards were emptied, shelves lined and the contents washed, dried and repacked. They even insisted that Angie should find Bryony a job sitting down at the kitchen table so that she could take the weight off her feet. Eventually the last vestiges of the storm damage were laid to rest, apart from the tarpaulin over Jason's bedroom which would remain in place for a few more weeks.

Everyone crowded into the sparkling kitchen as the food was laid out and Angie bustled about making sure that they had cutlery and drinks. An insistent ringing at the front door made Angie jump. 'You go,' Maggie said, winking, 'and take that apron off. You look like a tea lady. Gail and I can handle everything here.'

Angie opened the door to see Paul standing there with a large bunch of freesias. Her heart thumped and she knew a stupid grin was spreading across her face. 'You got my note?' she managed to stammer out.

'Yes and the flowers are for you, to make up for me being a little bold and asking if I could bring a friend over.'

'By all means. The more the merrier as they say.' Angie took hold of the flowers and buried her face in their fragrant blooms, avoiding his gaze and wondering what on earth he was talking about.

'Thanks, this is Fleur.' Paul stood aside and from the shadow of the front door stepped a tall woman with a long horse-like face. Her greying auburn hair was swept up in a smart roll and she was dressed in shades of green and cream.

'My dear, this is too kind of you,' she patted Angie's arm, 'especially after you've had such a difficult time.' She held out her hand. 'You're Angela?'

'I prefer to be called Angie.' She took the

proffered hand and held it for a millisecond.

'Paul has been very concerned about everything.' Fleur placed a proprietorial hand on his arm. 'It seems like things can get back to normal now, can't they, darling?' She flashed a smile at Paul and Angie caught a whiff of a very strong perfume that smelt expensive.

For a moment Paul hesitated before he spoke again. 'I really should have let you know there would be an extra person. I hope it won't put you out.'

'Really, Paul, you are such a fusspot. Everyone always cooks far too much for a party, don't they?' She bared her teeth and Angie was tempted to fetch her an apple or a carrot. She pushed aside the thought and instead smiled in what she hoped was a friendly way.

'It really is no trouble at all.' Angie wafted a hand towards the kitchen. 'This way,' and she ushered them inside. At the entrance she stopped and took a deep breath. 'This is Paul everyone,' she announced to the assembled crowd, 'and this is Fleur his er, his...' she faltered.

'I suppose we could say fiancée, couldn't we?' Fleur looked up at Paul who said nothing.

'You're both very welcome,' Angie said as brightly as she could when she really wanted to curl up in a ball and cry. 'You probably recognise most people here so get some plates and help yourselves.' She turned to the spread on the table and ignored the look of surprise on Maggie's face. She kept her head down and pretended to fuss about the food, moving serving dishes and glasses in an attempt to appear busy and in control while her hands shook and her knees threatened to give way. She'd been a fool to imagine Paul might have any feelings towards someone like her. Thank God nothing had happened.

Maggie sidled over. 'Did you know about her?' she hissed under her breath.

'No, it doesn't matter, Paul and I are just friends,' Angie spoke in what she hoped was as cheerful a manner as possible but she couldn't fool Maggie.

'Liar. Do you want me to spill something on her so she has to go home?'

'Don't you dare.'

'If you do want me to do anything, tell me,' Maggie continued, adding under her breath, 'all that stuff about being good friends is crap. Paul hasn't taken his eyes off you while you've been doing your Nigella impersonation. Unless he has a fascination for table arrangements, he's more interested in you than just as friends.'

Angie looked up. Paul's eyes were focussed on her while Fleur was deep in conversation with Tasha. For a spilt second she thought he looked sad or wistful. She dismissed it and simply smiled back before resuming her manic table clearing. She glanced at the clock. If only everyone would just go away and leave her alone. Unfortunately that wasn't going to happen. Somehow she had to get through the next hour or two.

Two hours passed. Everyone stayed and ate more. Maggie made coffee and they all sat in Angie's front room. Jason got out his games console and challenged Gareth to endless battles of Wargame 45. Tasha and Bryony holed up in another corner, engrossed in their phones; Fleur shared stories of her holidays in France with the Glendas, Susies and partners. Maggie was deep in conversation with Steve about the issues facing the care of the elderly. Angie couldn't join in with any of those conversations and so sat back and listened, aware that Paul was not involved either. He was also listening and glancing at her from time to time. 'More coffee anyone?' She jumped up, eager to escape from his prying eyes.

'Lovely,' Maggie said to a chorus of approval from the rest. It was obvious they were not planning on going just yet. Angie stepped over various pairs of outstretched legs and sought refuge in the relative peace and quiet of the kitchen.

'I'll give you a hand,' Paul said and followed her. Angie filled the kettle and rinsed out the cafetières. She stretched up to the top kitchen shelf where Glenda had stacked the packets of ground coffee. 'Let me.' Paul reached out and went to grab the same packet as Angie. His hand closed over hers. She pulled her hand away and the packet fell onto the counter top. It split open, bounced and the contents sprayed over the floor.

'Damn,' Angie swore and went to rescue the packet before any more escaped. Paul bent down at the same time.

Angie and Paul both scraped at the pile of coffee grounds. 'Have you got a dust pan and brush?' he said.

'Under the sink.'

'You make the coffee and I'll do this.'

Angie stood up and turned her back on Paul, eager to avoid any more contact although she was acutely aware of every sound as he cleaned up the mess. She stayed where she was until the reassuring clang of the bin lid told her he had finished. 'Paul, do come and tell Susie about that wonderful vineyard we visited last year. What was it called?' Fleur was leaning against the doorway in a way that Angie reckoned was deliberately designed to show off her slender figure in the fitted trousers.

Angie pulled her stomach in. 'Go on,' she called over her shoulder as she spooned ground coffee into the cafetières. 'This isn't a job for two people.' His footsteps echoed over the floorboards as Fleur announced to the assembled company that Paul was an expert on all things Gallic. Angie focussed on the coffee. Keeping busy had always been a trick of hers when things were fraught and she fussed over the coffee like a mother hen with some wayward chicks before selecting Bryony and Tasha for a quick update on their lives as a way of keeping her mind off Paul.

It was gone five o'clock when Maggie finally stood up and called to Gareth, 'Right you, it's home time. You've got coursework to do and Tasha, you promised to give me a hand with my hair tonight. I'll just help Angie load the dishwasher and we'll make a move.'

Paul stood up. 'No, leave it to me.'

'I'm fine,' Angie said as she collected up mugs and cups.

Paul ignored her and took the cups from her. His hand brushed hers and her stomach twisted and turned. She looked away and scurried into the kitchen where she began to load the dishwasher, her head bent over the machine, avoiding his gaze. He stood by her and handed her more plates and mugs. 'I want to thank you for what you did for Ben.'

Angie froze. 'What did he say?'

'Just that the information you gave him is with the solicitors. Whatever you found out, I can't tell you how grateful I am.'

'Will it help?' She stood up and leaned against the kitchen sink.

'Yes I think it will. The solicitors reckon it could lead to an arrest or at the least some very difficult questions.'

'I'm glad.'

'You've done so much for someone you don't know. That means a lot to me.' He took both her hands in his. 'Thank you.'

Angie pulled her hands away and folded her arms across her chest. 'It was nothing. Please don't mention it again.' In her head the words *Go away and leave me alone* had formed and she only wished she had the courage to say them out loud.

There was an uneasy silence. 'I hope I haven't upset you in any way, by inviting Fleur I mean,' Paul added.

'No. Why would I be upset?' Angie hoped he wouldn't notice the slight tremor in her voice. She bent down and pretended to rearrange the crockery in the dishwasher. The last thing she wanted to do was to look up at him.

'I just thought that you and I were getting along so well that…'

'That what?' She heard the brittleness in her voice and could do nothing about it. 'We're neighbours, aren't we?' Angie slammed the door closed and pressed the start button. 'I really think you went beyond the call of duty to look after me, but the damage was caused by your negligence, wasn't it?'

She leaned against the dishwasher, her head tilted on one side as she scrutinised his face for any signs of emotion. There was none. The old implacable Paul had returned. 'It'll be good for me to be back here, even though it's not exactly the way I want the place, it soon will be ...' she paused, 'I'm sure Leo will be able to give me some help.'

A flicker of a frown crossed Paul's face. 'Leo?'

'Yes. Didn't I tell you about him? It must have slipped my mind. He's just someone I've been seeing for a while,' she said, hoping she could keep up the pretence that she was a confident woman of the world with a multitude of eager suitors all baying for her company. There was a pause. The sound of water pouring into the dishwasher finally broke the silence between them.

'That's great...I'd better go. I suppose I'll see you sometime?'

'Of course. After all we live next door to each other, don't we?' Angie fixed a smile on her face.

'I'll be off. Thanks for the meal,' and Paul left. Angie followed him and went through the ritual of farewells and thanks with everyone which must have taken over ten minutes as people hung back, reluctant to make the final move. Eventually there was only Maggie left. She kissed Angie on both cheeks. 'Chin up, kid. Call me before Friday if you need me.'

As Angie closed the door and the house descended into silence, a wave of exhaustion flooded over her. She wandered back into the kitchen, poured herself a large glass of wine and sat at the kitchen table to the sound of the gurgles and splashes of the dishwasher as it cleaned away all traces of her guests. One thought filled her mind; she was a fool. She'd been building up this event with the secret dream that something would happen between her and Paul. It hadn't.

She raised a glass to herself. 'Welcome to the

world of relationships,' she said out loud and, draining the glass, she went and ran herself a long hot bath. Holy Water could wash away sins. She held out little hope that bubble bath would cleanse her of the lingering sadness that nothing would ever happen between her and Paul.

As she soaked in the water and tried to banish thoughts of Paul and the fragrant and elegant Fleur in a cosy tête-à-tête over an expensive meal, the front door slammed and all went quiet. This was not like Jason. He usually called out when he got back home. A sixth sense that she had discovered when she was little and used to keep out of her parent's way when they were arguing or just silently resenting each other's presence kicked in. Something was wrong. She got out of the bath and dressed. So much for a long leisurely soak.

She opened the lounge door. 'You can tell me to mind my business or that it's got nothing to do with me but what's up?' She went and sat down on the arm of the other chair.

Jason was channel hopping. 'It's Bry and her mum.'

'What is?' Angie removed the remote from his hands and switched the sound to mute.

He took a deep breath. 'Her mum's new boyfriend, Gary, has a daughter, Courtney by his first wife. She's just been kicked out by her partner who is a real bad 'un.'

'What do you mean?'

'He's a right druggie.'

Angie nodded. 'So?'

'Courtney's got nowhere to stay with the two kids unless she goes in a B and B and Bry's mother doesn't want that.'

Angie didn't see where all this was leading. 'What has this got to do with Bryony?'

'Courtney is moving in with the kids and will have to share with Bry. They can put an extra small single bed under the window and the kids can sleep on the floor.'

'What? Do you mean a pregnant girl will have to share with a mother and two young children? Over my dead body. Tell Bryony to come here, tomorrow.'

'But Ange—'

'No buts. You were planning on moving in when the baby arrived so why not now? You'll have to use the small box room until the roof is fixed.' The disappointment over Paul had changed into full-blown anger at the fecklessness of some adults. If a table had been close by she would have slammed her fist on it. She made do with saying as firmly as she could, 'Bryony comes here.'

'If you're sure?' Jason looked confused. 'We'll pay our way. I don't sponge off anyone.'

Angie softened her voice; it was not his fault. 'I know you don't. We can talk about money later. Just tell Bryony she's very welcome.' Anger now subsided, swept away by an overwhelming feeling of tiredness. Today had just been too much for someone used to a more sedate life. 'I'm off to bed. Don't be late up. You've got work tomorrow.'

'You sound just like my gran.' Jason smiled as he got out his phone. 'Ange?'

'Yes?'

'I won't mess up my kid's lives like that, I promise.'

'I know. Goodnight.'

Angie crawled into bed and curled up. With a

shock she realised that for a few minutes she hadn't thought about Paul. She'd have to forget him and get on with her life. It was the only way forward but it wasn't going to be easy.

Chapter Eighteen

It was gone nine when Angie woke up. She wandered downstairs without bothering to get dressed. An old envelope lay on the kitchen table amongst the debris of Jason's breakfast. Scrawled on it was a message.

Ange,
Bryony is happy to move in here earlier than planned. It will make it better for everyone and she never really hit it off with her mum's new fella. Tell you more about it tonight.
J

Angie made coffee and as the caffeine coursed through her system, bringing her sluggish brain and body back to something resembling life, she flipped open her laptop and downloaded her emails. Most were junk though there was one from Leo and one from Polly Cadwallader. She opened Leo's first.

Sorry about your bad luck. Anything I can do? Even if it's only to invite you to a meal one evening. I'm a bit tied up for a while. Usually any day except Monday will suit. Get back to me ASAP.
Leo.
xxx
PS I'm very handy with a hammer and nails if that's any use?

Angie hit reply.

Hi Leo, It's good to hear from you. The place is getting

181

back to normal—if there is such a thing! Thanks for the invitation. I'd like that. Thursday would be great.

Another email bounced back by return. Either he was at home today or he was doing emails while he worked. She frowned. How can anyone do emails while feeding a cow? She shrugged. She had a lot to learn.

Thanks for getting back to me so quickly. I will book a table at 7.30 pm at Botticelli's in the High Street for Thursday week and I'll arrange the taxi to get you home so we can share a bottle of wine. If there's a change of plan, I'll email you later. I look forward to making a fuss of you after all this trouble—you deserve a bit of spoiling.
Leo xxx

This felt like a proper date at last. Angie cradled the cup and sipped the strong liquid as all her fears came tumbling back. Would he kiss her? Would they argue? What could she wear? A new outfit would solve the clothes problem. What might happen on the date was harder to predict. She opened Polly's email and hoped it would distract her.

My dear Angie,
Great news. The Council have set the date for the hearing about the sale of the care home for the 17th June at 4.00 pm. We need a battle plan so have gathered the troops for a meeting on Tuesday this week to discuss tactics. Hope you can make it. 8.00 pm at mine.
Polly

Angie scrawled the date and time in her diary. It was all starting to take shape, just as she'd hoped.

'There's nothing like a bit of graft to banish the blues, Sister Ruth,' she remembered Sister Ursula saying when she first entered the convent. That's what she'd do now.

She took a colour chart into her bedroom and stared at the assortment of paints and shades. With a large black felt tip pen she crossed out anything that reminded her of a classroom or a hospital. Pink was too sickly and any bright colours would probably bring on a migraine. That left shades of brown and beige. She ran a finger over a creamy brown called *Samarkand Sand*. Samarkand sounded so romantic. Like Fiji, Bali, Zanzibar, Marrakech…names she remembered from the hours she'd spent poring over an old atlas while her parents argued or endured sullen, resentful silences. She paused. There was nothing stopping her from finding out if these places were as glamorous as their names. With Bryony and Jason living with her she'd have built-in house sitters. She'd dreamed of travelling when she was younger. She'd never had the chance or the cash until now. India would be interesting. Switzerland and all those mountains with white snow on them would be fun. Australia? Iceland? She stopped. 'Come on, Angie, get a move on,' she said and opened a tin of white emulsion to tackle the ceiling.

She dipped her brush in the paint and watched as the mauve turned to dazzling white under her touch. The sun streamed in through the window and warmed the room. It had been years since she had luxuriated in the heat of a sun that could turn her pasty skin to gold in a matter of days. A beach holiday would be a good place to start. A blob of paint hit her nose. She rubbed it away with her hand. Travelling could be scary. Perhaps she ought to start with a holiday company. That would be best. She slapped paint on the ceiling and imagined herself sipping a cocktail and relaxing on a white sandy beach, under a blue sky with a group of like-minded men and women. She stood back. The ceiling was a bit patchy in places. Not bad for a beginner though. She put the lid back on the paint. That was enough for today. It was time to order some new furniture and she was going to have none of that flat-pack rubbish.

At five to eight on the following day Angie drove up to Littlecote Mill. Although the parking area was packed she managed to squeeze into the final space. If Polly Cadwallader could gather this amount of support, the Council had better make sure they had an alternative plan in mind. She sat for a few moments to calm her nerves and pluck up courage to go inside. What if no one spoke to her? Or they asked questions she couldn't answer? 'Stop it,' she said out loud. 'This is for Maggie, not you.'

She walked up to the front door. It was open and a cacophony of sound disturbed the evening air. Angie stepped inside as two dogs bounded towards her and pinned her against the porch wall. 'John, I told you to tie the dogs up, Beelzebub, Satan get back in here,' Polly Cadwallader's voice rang out. Angie remained where she was, oblivious to everything except two lolling tongues and four eyes.

A round, pale face appeared from behind the door. 'Here let me.' Two huge hands grabbed at the collars of the dogs and pulled them away. 'Sorry about that. Do come in. I'm Henry Porter-Asquith.

I'd shake hands but yours appear to be full,' he said and laughed.

'I'm Angie Jarvis.' Henry had bent down and was putting leads onto the dogs. Angie stayed where she was, relieved that Henry was now between her and the two animals. With his pale skin, red sweater and yellow cord trousers he reminded her of Rupert Bear. All he needed was a checked scarf to complete the image.

'Oh so you're the angel that alerted us to this injustice.' He stood up and lashed the leads round his hands so that the dogs were kept close to his side. 'This way.'

'I'm hardly an *angel*.' Angie took a deep breath and followed him along the hallway and into the lounge.

'Angie's here,' he said to the crowd that had squashed into the low-ceilinged room.

'So glad you could come,' Polly called out from the wing chair that was next to the fireplace. Her silver hair was scraped back in its usual messy bun and she was dressed from head to toe in black velvet with a waistcoat that shimmered with a thousand tiny mirrors. 'Sit here and let me introduce you to everyone,' she indicated a second wing armchair next to her. Angie avoided looking at anyone as she picked her way across the splayed legs of those who preferred the floor to a seat. For some reason her own legs felt wobbly. She'd try to act confident and knowledgeable but if anyone asked her details about the care home, they'd soon find out she was a fraud. She perched on the seat next to Polly and folded her hands to stop them from shaking.

For the next five minutes although it seemed longer, Polly called out names and heads bobbed in

185

recognition or murmured *Hello, Hi* or she thought she even heard a *What Ho* from someone in the assembled company. Angie gave up concentrating after person number two and wondered what had happened to all the old names like Mary, Barbara, Peter and Dave. There appeared to be four categories of people grouped by name and appearance. Poppies, Daisies and Lilies wore flowing skirts, hand-knitted sweaters and crocs. Imogens and Victorias preferred tight jeans, riding style boots and furry waistcoats. Joes, Sams not to mention a Baz and a Desi were dressed like urban guerrillas in combat trousers and black hoodies. Cord trousers, brogues and check shirts were reserved for the Henry and Harvey fraternity. 'Now we all know each other, let's get down to business. We've got one chance to get our viewpoint across so let's make sure it is heard, loud and clear,' Polly said as she looked at the assembled company.

Angie was not prepared for what took place next. She had imagined that at this meeting there would be some general discussion about what might happen. There would be a sharing of ideas and someone would allocate tasks before the following meeting. Polly was a force to be reckoned with and events had moved fast. 'Imogen, you're the expert on social media. What's the state of play?'

Imogen unwound her long legs, encased in the skinniest jeans Angie had ever seen and stood up, a small tablet in her hand. She tossed back her long auburn hair and slid her fingers over the surface. 'Sorry, the kids have been playing games on the thing. Won't be a sec.' From the way everyone was waiting without a sound, Imogen was held in high esteem.

186

'Here it is.' She read off the tablet, 'We have a Facebook page entitled "Save the Crystal Hill Care Home", and this is linked to our Twitter feed, Instagram and Pinterest. Sam will be filming the protest and this will go up on YouTube, linked into these sites as things happen. I want everyone to go onto Facebook and like the page and mention us on any of their sites.'

Angie bit her lip and hoped they wouldn't ask her opinion. She hadn't got a clue about half of the stuff that had been mentioned. Imogen smiled at the assembled company and sat down.

'Good work, Imogen. Harry, what about the placards?' Polly beamed from her throne-like chair. So it went on. Cars would be leafleted at each of the supermarkets in the town over the next few weeks and someone called Jimbo had written a piece for the local rag which included first-hand accounts from people whose family members had been at the home. 'So we will be meeting at 3.30pm on Wednesday 17th June in the car park at the back of the fire station. It's free after three o'clock so won't cost us a penny and we can walk to the front of the Town Hall ready for the start of the Council meeting at five.' She paused, with theatrical effect. 'I believe Baz has a very special announcement to make.'

A voice floated up from somewhere on the floor. Angie looked down as a face half covered in a hat spoke. Baz raised himself on his elbows and looked up. 'Unless there is a murder, a local politician defects or a crash on the motorway, Midlands Today are planning to send a film crew for the 6.30pm broadcast. After all the bad press lately about care homes and cuts, this is just what they want to film

187

and the footage may be part of a documentary on the state of care in our nation.'

Applause rang out and Baz did the peace sign as he sank back on the floor. 'If there are no more questions, I suggest we get a drink and circulate. Food is in the conservatory unless the dogs have eaten it,' Polly said. She waited for two seconds. 'Good. Let's socialise.'

As if on cue, John entered with a tray of glasses of wine. 'There's beer and cider in the kitchen if anyone prefers it,' he said, 'and you're welcome to smoke in the garden.'

Angie stayed where she was. It was all over and she hadn't made a fool of herself after all. Feelings of relief mingled with gratitude. All these people had come together to help and her eyes prickled. She blinked hard and turned to Polly. 'How did you get all this done so quickly?'

Polly folded her hands and sat back, like a schoolteacher about to give her verdict on a student's essay. 'It's touched a nerve, my dear. There but for the grace of God goes some mother, father, husband or wife.' She pushed a stray hair back from her face. 'Come to think of it, it could even be me. People don't like to imagine their loved ones being pushed from pillar to post as they say. They might not be in a position to look after them personally and so want them to live with dignity and compassion. You'll see...'

'I do know what you mean,' Angie said. 'I gave up my er ...job to care for my father.'

Polly spread out her hands, as if in supplication. 'Would it have helped if you'd felt he could be taken care of properly?'

'I'm not sure. I think I was looking for an excuse to get out.' Although Angie had never voiced this before, she now knew it was true. Even if her father hadn't needed her, she had been searching for a reason to leave the convent.

Any further conversation was stopped by the figure of Henry bearing down on them. 'Sorry to interrupt but Satan has got rather over excited and is making a nuisance of himself under ladies' skirts.'

'Bloody dogs. Look after Angie will you?' Polly stood up stiffly and headed to the conservatory.

'Let me get you a drink. Red suit you? The white is ghastly. Polly may be a brilliant organiser but her housekeeping skills are non-existent.' He waited for Angie to agree and went to the kitchen. Angie looked at the people standing or sitting in small groups. Some were deep in conversation and others were laughing at shared jokes. She knew she should mingle. She stood up and sank back down again. She couldn't do it. The old insecurities from her past came flooding back. It was like making a late entry to a party when everyone else has settled for the evening and you are the interloper. She was pleased to see Henry returning with her drink.

He handed her the glass. 'There you go.'

She took it and sipped. Her mouth puckered into a small circle. 'This is better than the white?'

'Infinitely,' Henry said as he settled in Polly's chair. 'Now tell me all about yourself.'

A bit of her longed to tell the truth, to say *Actually I've been in a convent for most of my life*. She daren't. 'I was a teacher,' she replied. 'Not here,' she added as she saw a glint of interest in his eyes.

'Oh. Pity. I hoped you might be able to give me

189

and my ex-wife some advice on educating twins.' He paused for a second, 'What would *you* advise about sending twins to different schools?' For the next ten minutes Angie talked education with Henry before she was rescued by Polly who insisted on introducing her to everyone again. With Polly in tow, it wasn't so bad. Either that or it was the effect of the wine. By the time Angie left she had an invitation to lunch, two coffee mornings and a poetry evening, all of which she planned to attend.

The bungalow was silent and dark when she got back. As she switched on the light she noticed an envelope addressed to her on the hall table. A note had been scrawled on it.

Sorry. New postmen sent it to number 6 not number 16.

It was from the bank. She knew she was slightly overdrawn. What was the fuss about? She went into her bedroom and stuffed the letter into a drawer under a pile of knickers. She'd sort it out later.

Chapter Nineteen

On the day of her date with Leo, Angie had spent all morning dithering over what to wear until her bed was piled high with rejected outfits. She had finally chosen a cream dress with black side panels and black patent high-heeled shoes. Panic had set in during the afternoon and she'd dashed to the shops to splash out on a new cream leather jacket. It would be more use than the black one now that summer was here and wouldn't add much to the overdraft. Avarice was a sin, anyway, so the money was better off being spent.

At five o'clock Jason's car, packed with bags and boxes drew up outside. Her dinner date with Leo would at least give Jason and Bryony some space as they began to move her stuff over and if Leo asked to come back for coffee, she'd have a ready-made excuse. She opened the front door and a smile crossed her lips. Instead of dashing in, Jason walked to the passenger door, opened it and helped Bryony out. He grabbed hold of her arm which she shook off. 'For God's sake, Jay, I'm not dying.' Then she noticed Angie standing in the doorway. She waved and her face broke into a broad grin. 'Honestly he thinks I'm ill or something.' She walked forward, stopped in front of Angie and without warning hugged her. 'Thank you so much for your help.'

'You're welcome.' Angie disengaged herself and looked at Bryony. Her slim figure was softer and more curvy than usual and her face was glowing. Motherhood or impending motherhood suited her.

'You might not say that when the baby is yelling blue murder,' Jason said.

'Come on in, you two. Let's get you something to eat and you can start unpacking.' Angie led the way into the kitchen.

She brought a bubbling lasagne out of the oven and placed it on the kitchen table. Jason helped himself, added salad and took four slices of garlic bread. Bryony raised her eyebrow at Angie. 'What?' he said aware of the unspoken communication, not the message going between Angie and Bryony.

'Are you sure you've eaten this year?' Bryony said.

'I suggest we let him tuck in while you tell me about your plans for the future,' Angie said and winced. She sounded like her own mother.

'What plans?' Bryony looked up from her plate.

'Are you two going to get married?' As soon as she had finished asking the question she realised by the looks on their faces that she was talking a different language.

'No. Why?' Jason asked.

'It might be nice for the baby,' Angie suggested.

'It won't know.' Jason looked from Angie to Bryony, shrugged and turned his attention back to his plate.

'I don't mean that; I mean what about the name?'

'Oh that's easy,' Bryony explained. 'If it's a girl we'll call her Noelle because I reckon it was over Christmas when I got pregnant and if it's a boy, we'll call him Robin 'cause it's wintry. We've decided not to find out the sex 'til it's born.'

'I meant whose surname will it take?'

The young couple exchanged glances before Bryony continued, 'We'll call it after Jason as he's the daddy,' and she squeezed his arm. They ate in silence until Bryony put down her knife and fork and spoke,

'Angie, it's really good of you to let us stay here, we need to work out how much to pay you.'

Angie leaned back in her chair. 'If you two can help me with the food bill and the gas, the rest can be taken up with you two looking after the place when I'm away.'

Jason's fork clattered to the floor. He burrowed under the table to retrieve it and came up with his mouth wide open. 'Where are you going, Ange?'

Angie shrugged. 'Nothing's planned, yet. When I was a little girl I used to dream of exotic places like India and Fiji.' She stopped. 'I might just treat myself to a holiday from time to time.' She collected up the plates and put the kettle on for tea. 'I reckon the roof will be mended within a few weeks and you can get properly settled.'

'Nice one, Ange. I'll make the tea. You go and get ready. The taxi will be here soon,' Jason said.

Angie went into her bedroom. She ran a comb through her hair and added a touch of lip gloss. If only dating could be as easy as her domestic arrangements, she'd be fine. She added a squirt of perfume, picked up her bag and went outside.

Despite Jason's offer of a lift, Angie had insisted on booking a taxi to take her to the restaurant. As she waited she looked up and down The Close. Even at this time a few keen gardeners were busy snipping and weeding and the air was full of evening birdsong. Borders were ablaze with the jewel colours of marigolds and geraniums. Laughter echoed from a back garden where a barbecue was taking place and its pungent aroma drifted over the evening air. The sound of an engine made her turn her attention back to the road. It was not her taxi. Paul's car came to a halt on his driveway.

Angie pretended to study her watch as she worked out what to do. She wanted to run back inside. It was ages since she'd seen Paul. Judging by the way her stomach was flipping about, the feelings he had aroused were alive and well. She'd never been a coward. She'd brazen it out somehow. She lifted her hand and gave a slight wave. If her luck was in, the taxi would miraculously appear and she would be whisked away before she could speak to him. Or perhaps he wouldn't see her or didn't want to see her. She fixed a smile on her face and pretended to search in her bag. 'Angie?' A voice called out. She looked up.

'Hi, Paul, how are you?' She didn't care that the smile was making her jaw ache.

'Busy, and you?' he said and smiled back.

'Very good. I'm going out for a meal with Leo. We're trying the new Italian in the High Street. Have you been there?' Her voice was shrill and squeaky.

His smile disappeared. 'No, I haven't. I've read some very flattering reviews.'

He was dressed immaculately as always and with the sun glinting on his hair, he really did look attractive. She banished those thoughts. 'How is Fleur?' Paul shifted from one foot to the other.

'She's fine and she wanted me to thank you for the lovely afternoon she spent at your place.' He ran a hand through his hair. 'I would have said something earlier except I haven't seen you lately.'

'I've had so much to do on the bungalow, it's all been a bit frantic.' With any luck she was giving the impression of a confident, mature woman, though she wasn't sure. 'We've both got very busy schedules, haven't we?' she added and checked her watch.

He nodded. 'How is the redecorating coming along?'

'Fabulous. I've nearly got it all done and the carpets are on order. Once they're down, the new furniture can arrive.'

Paul nodded. 'About Fleur,' he began and ran his tongue over his lips before taking a deep breath.

'Yes?' Angie's heart pounded as the thought flashed through her head that he was about to tell her that Fleur wasn't his fiancée after all.

At that moment the taxi drove into The Close. 'Nothing. I'll let you get off. Have a good evening.'

Angie bit back the disappointment. She had got her silly hopes up again for nothing. She climbed into the taxi and closed the door. She turned back to wave. Paul had already disappeared. As the taxi drew out of the cul-de-sac and into the main road, Angie was left with the niggling suspicion that perhaps all was not well with the fragrant Fleur. She pushed the idea from her head. After all, she was about to meet Leo again.

The taxi drew up at the restaurant and Leo was standing outside. He was dressed in a navy blazer, cream trousers and a sharp pink polo shirt. He was even better looking than Angie had remembered and as she walked towards him, she felt a slight flutter in her stomach. He handed her a bouquet of flowers and planted a kiss on each cheek before offering his arm as they walked into the restaurant. It was only after the flurry of the waiter showing them to the table, sitting down, being offered menus and selecting drinks that she was able to relax and look at him again as he studied the menu through the rimless glasses that he had taken out of his pocket.

Distinguished was the word she'd use to describe him to Maggie next time they met. And perhaps sexy. She liked the way a few dark hairs could be seen underneath the opening of his polo shirt and when he slipped off his jacket, his arms were muscular without being lumpy. His hands were smooth and his nails were very neatly cut for a farmer. Angie didn't know much about what they did nowadays. Leo might not be the sort that had his hands up a cow's backside on a regular basis. An indentation where he had worn a wedding ring showed on the third finger of his left hand. His voice jolted her back to reality.

'Can I suggest we share a starter as the platter of antipasto is supposed to be superb. It will go well with this dish here,' Leo pointed out chicken in a rich tomato sauce.

'Whatever you suggest, I don't know a lot about Italian food apart from pizza and I suppose that doesn't really count.' Angie closed her menu.

'I must say you're in for a real treat. This place is highly recommended and if the chicken is anything like the one I had in Florence last year, it will be divine. Now for wine, let me suggest, ah…this one, a Montepulciano.' He gave their orders to the waiter and sat back. 'I must say you look wonderful in that colour and have you got a new hairstyle?'

'Thank you.' Angie felt her cheeks flush. She was still not used to being paid a compliment on her appearance. She'd better change the subject. 'Do you know Italy well?'

'The usual summer holidays with the family…last year I was on a cruise and we stopped in at Livorno so I could pay a hasty visit to Florence.'

Angie was about to ask how he could have a

summer holiday in August which was supposed to be a farmer's busiest time when the wine waiter arrived. She let Leo focus on the wine. He lifted his glass to toast her and she felt mean. She knew nothing about farmers and rich farmers at that. She'd say nothing and let him tell her about his work in his own time.

There was no shortage of things to talk about and the hours flew past again. As they waited for the taxi to arrive outside the restaurant, the fresh night air that often follows a warm day made Angie shiver. 'Are you cold?' Leo asked and without waiting for an answer, slipped off his jacket, placed it over Angie's shoulders and held it in place with one arm across the back of her neck. He was so close Angie could feel his breath on her cheek and his chest moving in and out. It was both comforting and disturbing and she took a deep breath to calm the fluttering sensations in her stomach.

She was not certain who moved first. They both turned and his arms went around her as her hands reached up to the front of his shirt. Their heads moved closer so that their lips brushed lightly before they drew apart. 'I think we can do better than that,' Leo's voice was a low growl, 'if you want to?'

'I'd like that,' Angie replied and closed her eyes as their lips met again. This time she realised he was trying to push his tongue into her mouth. She opened hers slightly and his tongue wriggled into it. The sensation of a demented eel thrashing about, bumping up against her tongue and teeth, made her open her eyes. She broke away as she saw the taxi coming up the street. 'The taxi is here,' she added as brightly as she could as Leo's hand brushed over one breast.

'I could always come back in the taxi with you for a night cap,' Leo said.

'My lodger and his girlfriend will be up and besides, I've an early start tomorrow,' Angie lied. 'It's been a lovely evening.'

'Perhaps we can do it again?'

'Yes, perhaps,' Angie said as she dived into the taxi. She looked back for a second in case Leo waved and saw that he was checking the bus times. Surely he couldn't be catching a bus all the way back to his farm at this time of night? She really didn't know where he lived and made a note to ask him.

As the taxi sped away, she sank back in the seat, relieved to get away after a slobbery kiss that had left her embarrassed and slightly ashamed. She'd found a man who was good-looking but when it came to the physical, there was little or no attraction. If this was how she felt after a kiss, she'd never be able to have sex.

***

'Have you given up smoking?' Angie said as she and Maggie were sitting in the kitchen for their regular Friday evening catch-up session.

'I can't moan at Gareth when he snitches a crafty fag if I'm hooked on the stuff, can I?' Maggie said. 'And this is needed to stop me from losing it. Today has been a bitch.' She drew in a deep gulp of nicotine-laced air from an e-cigarette.

'Sister Constanta used to say there were good days, bad days and days you shouldn't even get out of bed,' Angie said. So far Maggie had not asked about the date with Leo and she was trying to keep her off the subject for as long as possible.

'She's right.' Maggie puffed on the e-cigarette again

before she tilted her head on one side and looked at Angie. 'I often wished I'd been more like you at school.'

'Me? At least you had some fun.'

'Yeah and ended up in a dead-end job. I wonder if I could have gone to university.'

'It's not too late. You could always do something part time?' Angie said as the sounds of music blasted from the upstairs. She pointed. 'What happened to Wargame?'

'Our Gareth's into music now but he's not doing enough work. The school want to set up a weekly meeting to discuss his progress. In other words, get me to check he's doing what he should be. Why don't they just shove him in detention? A few Saturday mornings cooling his heels in a deserted school hall and he'd soon buckle down.'

'I don't think they can keep kids in if they don't want to, human rights and all that,' Angie explained.

'Human rights?' Maggie snorted. 'More like you can't make me do anything I don't want to do.' She paused. 'That's enough of me, tell me more about your Leo?'

Angie took a deep breath. She was going to be honest, however embarrassing it felt. 'First he's not my Leo and secondly he tried to kiss me and it was revolting.' There was silence followed by a snigger and Maggie burst out laughing. 'What's so funny?' Angie frowned.

Maggie wiped her eyes with the back of her hand. 'Tell me more,' she begged.

Angie hesitated and took a deep breath. 'It was like a soft sausage waggling about in my mouth.'

Laughter exploded again though more controlled.

199

'Didn't you kiss him back?'

'What do you mean?'

'For God's sake, Angie, get your tongue and his touching and doing all the stuff we used to talk about at school.'

'It was disgusting.'

Maggie was serious now. 'You don't fancy him enough. Thank God you didn't go to bed with him. I'd hate to hear what you thought about him coming towards you with…' she paused and laughter escaped again, 'evidence of his excitement.' She chuckled. 'That is providing he could get it up.'

Angie looked at her. 'What on earth do I do now?'

'Either you go on another date and see if you do end up getting the hots for him or you use him, lose your virginity and you can start again with someone different. I mean you're not really expecting to find the love of your life, go out for a respectable time and lose your virginity like some romantic novel, all swooning and heaving bosoms as the hero bears down on the heroine?'

Angie was about to say that was exactly what she was hoping to do. The look on Maggie's face made her change her mind. 'I suppose I did want the first time to be special.'

'You sound as if you're living in the 1950s. Sex is part of life and not something to be kept for the one and only. It hasn't been like that for decades and there's no guarantee that Mr Right will come along anyway.'

'What would you do?'

'Me?' Maggie thought for a moment. 'Find a hot guy who is just after sex. Get laid and…'

'Get on with your life.'

'You took the words right out of my mouth.'

'I suppose these guys just materialise on street corners do they?' Angie didn't care if she sounded petulant.

'They do if you go to the right places.' Maggie inhaled and exhaled before she spoke again. 'Like holiday destinations…beaches, tropical islands where you can pick up a beach boy, have some fun and leave him. Make sure he uses a condom. You don't want to come back with a holiday souvenir in the form of an unwanted child or an unwanted disease.'

Angie sighed. This was not the romantic interlude she had imagined. She'd give Leo one more go. If nothing happened, she might have to consider Maggie's idea.

Chapter Twenty

'Summer is supposed to mean sunshine,' Angie grumbled as she watched the rain streaming down the window pain. Trees dripped and pools of water gathered on the lawn. The sky hung like an old, grey blanket devoid of any holes that might threaten to let in a chink of sunlight. The demonstration would take place today. It was their one chance to take a stand though even Polly had admitted that perhaps they had left it all too late and if the rain stopped people from turning out, they were stuck. If ever Angie needed a god or at least his blessing, it was now.

At five to four Angie parked her car and followed the Jubilee walkway towards County Hall. Sounds of chanting filtered through the pounding rain. She turned the corner and stopped in her tracks. A huge crowd had gathered in front of the glass entrance to the Council Chambers and was spilling over onto the pedestrian precinct. A police squad car was parked nearby and two policemen were standing by the front door, their arms folded A van painted with the familiar logo of the evening news team was in place with an awning that sheltered the cameraman, the sound recordist and another man whose face was vaguely familiar. Angie recognised some of the supporters from the meeting at Polly's house; it was evident their ranks had swollen tenfold. Most were holding homemade placards or signs with the message that whatever the government wanted to do, they were against it. There were a number that referred specifically to the closure of the care home and the same message was conveyed on the banner that had been tied to the handrails along the steps.

Angie spotted Polly, dressed from head to toe in olive green waterproofs and deep in conversation with the men under the awning. She made her way over and waited while Polly continued. 'If you want a really good story line, I suggest you interview—' Her eyes lit on Angie. 'Ah good you're here. This nice gentleman might want to interview you.'

'Me?' Angie froze.

The journalist held out his hand. 'I'm Owen McDonnell. We'd like to ask you a few questions later.'

'What about?' Angie spoke slowly to control the tremor in her voice.

'Angie my dear, you must do it. After all, it was your idea in the first place.' Polly patted Angie's arm.

She looked from Owen to Polly and back again. Much as she wanted to run away, she'd got herself into this so she was going to have to see it through to the end. She took a deep breath. 'All right, let me know where and when.'

'Good we'll call you to set up a shot when the members of the Council are about to go in.' He checked his tablet. 'I'll be with you later,' and he squeezed through the crowds to where a woman was waiting with an elderly man in a wheelchair holding a placard announcing, *No Cuts*.

The afternoon turned to early evening as the rain continued to fall. Protesters huddled under any makeshift shelter they could find and all except the hardiest had stopped the chanting. Angie checked her watch. It was nearly 5.30. A whisper from the crowd turned into a roar as several figures emerged from a large black car that had pulled up on the pavement.

203

'Save the care, not the costs.' Polly's voice was soon drowned out by the combined voices of over a hundred people. Banners and placards were held aloft as the Council members entered. No sooner had the car driven away than other members squeezed their way through the doors held open by the police whose numbers had increased so that they formed a chain at the entrance to the building. The crowd continued to chant as more and more delegates arrived. Angie was pushed to the front where Owen pounced.

'Right, Miss Jarvis, stand here, please.' The crew got into place. Angie shifted from one foot to the other and looked for Polly. She was nowhere to be seen. 'Now, Miss Jarvis, just why is there such concern over this project which, after all, will revolutionise care in the town?'

God help me Angie prayed and took a deep breath. 'It's er...it's been pointed out that there are alternatives to the way we deliver care...' She paused and looked again at the sea of faces. She had to get her point across. 'As you can see by the number of people here today,' she indicated the crowd with her hand, 'they want their view to be taken into account.'

'And would their ideas contribute to a viable project?' Owen held the microphone closer to Angie's face.

'What about giving those who work in the industry more say in how it is run and what is done? After all, they know the residents best.'

Owen ignored her remark. 'What would you say if I were to suggest that there are indeed tentative plans to do as you want?' He fixed his eyes on her like a card player, about to deliver a winning hand.

Angie stalled. This was the first time she'd heard

of anything like this. She looked for Polly to come to her rescue. She was nowhere in sight. She was on her own. 'If it's true it's great news.' She glanced at the crowd and an idea sprang in her mind. 'However, I'd rather wait till it's confirmed before getting anyone's hopes up.' She was beginning to enjoy the encounter. 'Besides, why does it take this sort of demonstration to get people in authority ready to talk about alternatives with those who do the jobs?'

'So you haven't heard about the new plans?'

'What bloody plans?' Polly sprang forward out of the crowd and Angie stepped out of the way, grateful to let her take control.

Owen turned to face her and the cameraman moved closer. 'The Council are considering the possibility of adopting a radical approach after the company that they had been in talks with were taken over last week.' Owen's lip curled, only the honey voice remained.

'If that happens all well and good.' Raindrops scattered off Polly's Barbour as she spoke.

Owen turned back to Angie. 'Your involvement wouldn't by any chance have anything to do with your personal interests?'

'What personal interests?' Polly pulled Angie away. 'We have no more to say and if any of this gets into the news, you will be hearing from my solicitor.' She bundled Angie to the back of the crowd. 'I think it would be better if you made a dignified exit. These guys will be sniffing for some gossip all evening.'

'I've got nothing to hide. They can say what they like.' Angie was not going to be beaten after one interview. She'd stick it out to the end.

'As long as you're prepared for a bit of dirt to be

thrown your way?' Polly placed her hand on Angie's shoulder.

'What dirt?' Angie bit her lip. What had they found out about her past?

Polly lowered her voice. 'Someone from the Council saw you and the consultant to the planning department in what they like to describe as an *intimate conversation* at a local comedy event.'

'Paul?' Angie couldn't believe what she was hearing. 'I bought him two tickets as a thank you for putting me up when my bungalow was damaged. It was late notice so he invited me.'

Polly sucked in her breath between pearly teeth. 'You stayed with him?' Angie nodded. 'Anything else?'

'What could there be? He was kind to me and even found a builder at short notice.' Paul's words about knowing a few people in the building industry who owed him a good turn came back to her. She refused to believe it was anything more than a coincidence.

'You do realise he's going to be taken on as advisor?' Polly said.

'What's wrong with that? We never discussed the matter.' Angie's voice was getting louder and shriller.

'My dear, he is implicated in any decision and so might you be.' Polly's eyes narrowed. 'Be careful. People love a good gossip and it's even better if there's a whiff of scandal.'

'Let them try.' Angie threw back her head. 'I've done nothing wrong and if they want a fight, they'll get one.'

Polly clapped her on the back. 'Good girl. Let's see what's going on.'

Angie turned her attention to the entrance where a familiar figure was walking up the steps. It was Paul

Buchannan. He was the last person she wanted to see. The gossip about them made it ten times worse. Angie was about to duck out of the way when he scanned the crowd. He looked right at her. Any flicker of recognition was extinguished. His mouth set in a line and he stared ahead.

The doors closed. The meeting was underway. There was little more to do. The protesters put down their bedraggled placards. Polly checked her watch. 'Excellent work everyone. Let's call it a day. We'll know the decision later this month. We've done all we can.' She hugged Angie. 'I'll be in touch.'

Angie trudged back alone through the rain-sodden streets to her car. She'd done the best she could. Instead of feeling happy, all she felt was disappointment and irritation. How dare anyone gossip about her and Paul? Any remaining dreams of a relationship with him were completely out of the question. 'Angie you're a fool,' she said and headed for home. A hot bath and a welcome glass of wine were waiting.

It was later that evening when there was a frantic ringing at her doorbell. It was Paul Buchannan and by the set of his jaw and the way his eyes glinted in the light from her porch, she knew it was not a courtesy visit. 'May I come in?' His voice was cold and clinical.

'This way.' Angie led him into the lounge where she indicated a new black leather couch. 'Take a seat.'

'I'd prefer to stand. This won't take long.'

She shrugged. 'What do you want?' If he was angry about the gossip, then she'd let him know she was too.

'I would like to ask you exactly what was your interest in the care home as I have spent an hour explaining my involvement with you and your gang of imbecilic friends.' He spat out the words.

Angie's jaw dropped, her fists clenched and her eyes opened wide. She paused, took a deep breath before she let rip with both barrels. 'First, let me get one thing clear, they are good people, not imbeciles. Secondly, I believe in their cause.'

'Well you've got your way. The care home will be saved.' Paul folded both arms and stood, head on one side defying her to answer.

'Good, so what's your beef?'

Paul hesitated. 'Was your concern for Ben anything to do with this interest?'

Angie could not believe what she thought he was saying. Anger had been replaced by horror that anyone half-decent could suspect another human being of behaving with such motives. 'Are you damn well suggesting that what I did for your brother was a sort of bribe?'

'It happens in business.' Paul's voice remained as flat and smooth as glass.

'Not in my bloody business it doesn't.' Angie pointed to the door. 'Get out.' Paul did not move. 'I helped your brother and Maggie because they needed help. Just that.' Paul looked up. His mouth dropped open as if to speak. Angie would have none of it. 'There's nothing more to say. Please leave.'

'I had to know. I'm sorry.' Paul's face had flushed a deep pink and there was a slight stammer in his voice. 'It's just that in my line of work—'

'Spare me the sob story. Bugger off.'

'Very well. I would suggest that we keep our interactions to a minimum from now on.' Mr Grumpy was back.

208

'Too bloody right.'

Paul left without another word.

Angie went and poured herself a drink and sat down at the kitchen table. 'To me and a Paul Buchannan-free future,' she said and raised her glass. The words sounded good. It didn't feel good. Still, there was always the prospect of another date with Leo. With any luck he might grow on her. Somehow she doubted it.

Chapter Twenty-one

The next date with Leo never took place. Angie was unpacking the groceries from the weekly shop when her phone rang. It was Maggie and she would never usually call from work unless it was something serious. 'What's up?' Angie's heart pounded as she waited for a reply, fearing the worst.

'Have you seen the news?' Maggie was practically shouting down the phone.

'I only saw the early morning bulletin. What news?'

'No, not *the* news, the *newspaper news* as in the local rag?'

'Never buy it.'

'You should, especially today. Go online, subscribe or buy a copy. Whatever you do, read the article on page four.'

'Why?'

'You might discover something about your Leo, or rather about Graham, Mike or whoever else he pretends to be. Just make sure you're sitting down when you read it. I must go. I'll pop in on my way home and check how you're getting on.'

She rang off and Angie flipped open her laptop. She scrolled down the news items. Page four revealed a story about a lost cat and one about a black widower. She clicked on that one. It was not a story of how a brave shopkeeper had found a deadly spider in a consignment of fruit. Instead, there was a picture of Leo under the headline, *Black Widower Strikes Again:*

Graham Jones, aged 53 of Rowborough Mead was arrested yesterday in connection with the deaths of his

*two former wives. Additional forensic evidence has come
to light which the CPS has described as significant. Mr
Jones' first wife, Maria, whom he married in 2009 was
found dead in their home in 2012, leaving him sole
beneficiary of her estate. Mr Jones then adopted the
name Mike Hall and remarried in 2014. His second
wife died on holiday in 2015 shortly after a large life
insurance policy had been taken out on her. Mr Jones,
posing as Leo Wilson, has recently been seen with a
number of women whom it is assumed he met on the
internet. A computer and a series of mobile phones have
been confiscated from his house. No bail has been
granted and Mr Jones remains in police custody.*

As Angie read and reread the article, an icy finger
tapped her on the shoulder and she began to tremble.
If she hadn't been sitting down her legs would have
collapsed underneath her. Had he lined her up as his
next victim? She snapped the laptop shut and
struggled to her feet. She had to do something,
anything to push the thoughts of him out of her head.

She attacked the housework. She stripped her bed
of clean linen and replaced it. She rummaged through
her wardrobe for anything that might need washing
and she scrubbed every surface in the kitchen as if it
would help erase her links with Leo. It was no good.
She would stop, a duster or a cloth posed in mid-air
as she remembered a line from a conversation with
him. More than once she found herself clutching at a
nearby table or chair as she replayed a date or scurried
to her laptop to trawl again through their messages.
There had been no clues that would have told her
what he was really planning.

By four o'clock exhaustion set in and she was

slumped flicking from channel to channel to find a programme that didn't feature a quiz in which the contestants didn't know the answer to the simplest questions or, even worse, a drama that involved a murder. A ring at the doorbell made her jump and she took a peek out of the window to find out who it was and decide if she was going to answer it. A police car was parked on the driveway. She went to the front door. The outline of a figure in blue was visible through the frosted glass. She opened the door to a young woman barely out of her teens. 'Angela Jarvis?'

'Yes. Is anything wrong?' Her stomach was in free fall as she imagined Jason or Maggie on a life support machine or even worse, in a morgue.

She flashed an ID. 'I wonder if I could ask you a few questions.'

'Of course. Let's go into the kitchen. Would you like a tea or a coffee?'

'No thank you.' Her voice was reassuringly calm and Angie relaxed a little as they sat down at the table. 'I'm PC Wanda Morris and this is my card in case you want to get in touch later.' Wanda took out a notebook and pen. 'I believe you know a man called Leo Wilson. Can you tell me how you met?'

'It was on a dating website,' Angie said and studied her fingernails.

Wanda showed no flicker of surprise. 'Did he at any time mention his past? A wife?'

Angie looked up. 'He told me he was a widower and had two children. Both were at university.

Wanda nodded. 'I see.'

'We'd only had a couple of dates and he was always the perfect gentleman, if you know what I mean?'

'What do you mean?' There was an emphasis on the word *you.*

'He made dates in advance and checked I was happy with the venue and the time. He was polite, chatty and seemed genuinely interested in me and my life…' Angie paused. 'He wasn't what my mother would have called a fast worker. He was respectful and we only kissed once or twice.'

'So it wasn't a full sexual relationship?'

'Oh no. Nothing like that.'

After a few more questions Wanda stood up. 'Thank you. You might be called to make a statement but I doubt it. We do have a number of other people to interview.'

Angie nodded. 'Can you tell me something?' A question had lodged in her mind and she had to know the answer, even though the truth might hurt.

'That depends. What is it?'

'Was I the only one he was dating?'

Wanda put the notebook in her bag. 'All I can say is that there are a number of women who are helping us with our inquiries.'

As Angie closed the door her legs buckled. She staggered to the lounge and collapsed on the sofa. She began to laugh, a high-pitched, giggling laugh that echoed through the bungalow. She'd dated a bloody murderer. The laughter subsided as small hiccups of sobs took over. They grew until Angie was bawling like a two-year-old kid. Leo hadn't even been interested in her. She had just been one of a number of single women that he'd had been stringing along for their money. And their life.

Angie dragged herself from the sofa. Jason would be home soon. She looked in the freezer and slammed the door shut. He'd have to make do with a takeaway. She sat slumped at the kitchen table going over again and again everything she knew about Leo hoping to find a clue that would have warned her off. There was nothing. She was still there when Jason breezed in the back door. 'What's for supper?' He sniffed the air and stopped. 'You all right?'

'Read this.' She opened her laptop, tapped a few keys and pushed it towards him.

There was silence for a moment. 'Bloody hell, Ange. Are you sure it's him?'

'The police were here this afternoon too, asking questions.' She leaned over and showed him Leo's profile on the dating site.

He scanned through it, swearing under his breath for once rather than out loud. 'You know what this means don't you?'

'Yes I'm a fool.' Angie sighed. 'A silly foolish, sad, old woman.'

'No. You escaped. You could have been his next victim. He was looking for number three.' Jason whistled between his teeth. 'Stick with Mr Grumpy next door.'

'Ha bloody ha.' She blew her nose on a tissue. Paul was already taken and after their last encounter, even friendship didn't seem a likely option.

'Do you want me to stay in tonight? Keep you company?' Jason asked. 'I was going to go and help Bry pack up the rest of her stuff.'

Angie shook her head. A look of relief swept over Jason's features. 'No. Get Bryony sorted out. Besides Maggie's coming over,' Angie said and on cue the back door opened and Maggie dashed in.

'If you're sure?'

'Yes. Now go and look after Bryony.' She forced a smile on her face and Jason closed the back door behind him.

'Right, one good bottle of wine, a spicy takeaway and I've downloaded a funny film. Get the plates and glasses.' Maggie bustled about and made sure Angie's glass was full before handing it to her. 'Here's to a lucky escape.' She raised her own.

'That's what Jason says.' Angie sipped the wine and stabbed at a forkful of curry and rice. 'I don't feel like it's an escape. I feel so stupid to have been taken in like that.'

'You weren't the first and you won't be the last,' Maggie said. 'There are plenty of men and women who take advantage of single people.

'Don't you mean sad, lonely people like me?'

'Everyone's been sad and lonely at some time. You're too hard on yourself. Just get out there, date a load of people and have some fun.'

Angie paused, fork in mid-air. 'Do you know what I ought to do now?

'I can't wait for you to tell me,' Maggie said.

'Why don't I just find a guy and have sex with him, like you said? No strings. Just sex.'

Maggie's mouth dropped open. 'Is that what you *really* want?'

Angie put the fork down. 'No. I suppose I had a dream that I'd find a special guy. We'd go out for a while and it would be natural to have sex with him.'

'And you'd get married and live happily ever after in a cottage with roses round the door?' Maggie's words sounded light-hearted yet her face was serious.

'Something like that.' Angie paused. The sound of a lawn mower click clacked through the open window and a single blackbird trilled a warning. 'Am I hopelessly romantic?'

'More like hopelessly out of touch with the real world,' Maggie said quietly.

'How so?'

'It just doesn't happen like that anymore.' Maggie picked at her food. They continued eating for a few minutes in silence before Maggie looked up. 'You can't just pitch up at the local pub on a Saturday night...Here I am boys, come and get it?'

'I thought you said there were holiday resorts with plenty of young men who are more than willing and very able.'

Maggie pushed her plate aside. 'Give me the laptop.'

There was a knock at the door. Angie got up. 'I hope that isn't the police back. I've had enough excitement for one day.'

She opened the door to see Paul Buchannan standing there. He must have come from work as he was dressed in a grey suit with a blue shirt and silver tie. 'Yes?' If he started whining or having a go, she'd slam the door in his smug face.

'I know we have had our differences and perhaps I was wrong to accuse you of any er...mis-doings but Steve up the road saw a police car drive away this afternoon and we wondered, I mean I wondered if anything was wrong?'

'No.' As if he cared. He'd probably been set up by Fleur to find out what the lonely, old spinster had been up to. Well she'd give him something to think about. She took a deep breath. 'Not that it's any of your business but the person I was dating has been arrested.' She waited for his reaction. 'On suspicion of murder.'

Paul's face paled and he ran a hand through his hair. 'I'm really sorry. Is there anything I can do?'

For a moment Angie was tempted to tell him where to go. *Ditch Fleur and give me a chance* would have been another option. He looked genuinely concerned. Perhaps he had a heart after all. She kept to the safe reply, 'No. It's all right.'

'If there is anything, please let me know. I mean it.'

'I will.'

If Angie thought that was the end of the conversation, she was wrong. Paul made no attempt to move away. Instead he shifted from one foot to the other before he spoke again. 'I hope you don't think I'm being presumptuous as I remember you said you had a friend called Leo and there was an article in the paper about a man called Leo? Is it the same one?'

Angie nodded. 'Yes.'

A frown crinkled Paul's forehead. 'I'm sorry.' He lifted his arm as if he was about to embrace her then let it fall to his side. 'Despite everything, I'd like to think you can count on me as a friend.'

This was too much. Angie flipped. 'What the hell are you talking about, being my friend? You've been an arsehole to Jason since we arrived. It's your fault my place was damaged and you come over all sanctimonious because you give me a place to stay. To top it all you accuse me of trying to bribe you.'

Paul flinched but remained where he was. 'I assure you I was concerned that this man—'

'—had taken advantage of a sad, old woman?'

'No, nothing like that.'

'What a pity you weren't more concerned about

217

those bloody trees and got them trimmed. Did you think I'd sue? Is that why you took me in?'

'I assure you that thought never crossed my mind.'

Angie was now in full flow. 'Or was it just a convenient way to get your meals cooked when Fleur wasn't here? Come to think of it, you were very coy about any partners.'

Paul looked away. 'It's not like that with Fleur.'

'Well as far as I'm concerned you can take your friendship and stick it.' She slammed the door and went back into the lounge.

'Wow. I heard that.' Maggie was looking impressed. 'I think I've found the place, the Gambia.'

Angie peered at the sight of palm trees and golden sand on the screen. 'How soon do you think I can get a flight booked?'

To hell with the expense.

Chapter Twenty-two

The plane bounced along the tarmac and stopped at the terminal of Banjul International Airport. Angie had endured the slow cramped flight, shoehorned into seats that were for very slim midgets, by observing her fellow passengers. There was the usual sprinkling of couples on romantic breaks, side by side with the bird watching fraternity in shades of khaki and with valuable binoculars and cameras as hand luggage. A couple of families with children risked the wrath of their schools by taking them on holiday at the start of the new academic year and there were a few single white females like Angie. She breathed a sigh of relief. She was not going to be alone.

The plane juddered to a halt. The doors opened. Angie gathered up her small flight bag and moved to the front. She passed by under the scrutiny of the cabin crew whom she suspected of exchanging glances about what she was doing, a lone middle-aged woman. She smiled brightly at them, said her goodbyes in as confident a voice as she could manage and hoped no one spotted her hands were shaking. A hazy sun filtered through the clouds as she walked out onto the steps that led down to the tarmac. A blast of hot air whipped the hair from her face. If she'd been a piece of bacon she'd have been crisped in a couple of seconds. She wiped away the beads of sweat that had already formed on her upper lip and breathed in the mix of fuel, dust and sweetness from some unseen plant.

She followed the rest of the passengers into the terminal, copying what they did and hoping they'd think she was a seasoned traveller despite dropping her sunglasses, banging her shins against a trolley and stubbing her toe on the desk in front of passport control. She had to empty her bag to scrabble for a coin to pay the kind man that helped her with her case and eventually clambered onto the coach. Twenty pairs of eyes scrutinised her. Any confidence, pretend or otherwise, instantly evaporated. She scurried towards an empty space and sank down in the seat. It was all going to go wrong, she knew it. She should never have come. A voice behind her whispered, 'You here on your own?'

Angie turned and looked into the heavily made-up eyes of a large woman with a halo of bright yellow hair. 'Yes.' It was time for the lie she'd practised. 'My last chance to get a bit of summer sun.'

The woman nodded. 'Have you been here before?'

Angie shook her head. 'What about you?'

The woman patted her straw-like hair. 'Fifth time. I've got to see my *friend*,' she winked, 'if you know what I mean. I'll fill you in over a drink if you like.' She stopped as the courier got on board and the microphone whined into life. If this woman spotted her as a sex tourist, probably everyone else did too. Angie put on her sunglasses and pretended to be fascinated by the scene in the airport car park.

The coach coughed and spluttered and turned out of the airport precinct and onto the main road. Angie pressed her nose against the dusty window and gazed at the alien sight. Groups of men squatted and chatted in any scrap of shade they could find whether it was under a tree or next to a beaten-up lorry or van. Women with children were selling huge watermelons or bunches of bananas off makeshift stalls. Slow-moving bicycles meandered through the traffic and here and there a lone goat risked death as it wandered by the side of the road. There were strange trees with huge pods hanging from the branches and palms with spiky fronds; they reminded Angie of the crosses they gave out on Palm Sunday. All were coated in a thin film of red dust. Angie glanced at her fellow passengers. No one seemed at all bothered by the unfamiliar scene outside the window. If the resort was anything like this, she'd be too scared to set foot outside the hotel. What if she got lost? Or robbed? Or everyone knew what she was there for? It was all a terrible mistake. A lump formed in her throat and she sniffed. A hand came over the top of the seat. 'Dammed dust gets everywhere. Have a wet wipe.'

'Thanks,' she managed to stammer out.

'We were all newbies once. I'm Janet by the way.'

Angie turned, grateful for the sunglasses which hid most of her face. 'Angie.'

'Nice to meet you, Angie. If we get separated, I'll be in the bar later.'

The brakes of the coach squealed and the vehicle turned into a narrow roadway lined with shops, moneychangers, banks, restaurants and bars. Boards claimed that the coldest beer, cheapest cocktails or special Gambian foods were to be found inside if only the tourist would enter. As the coach trundled on, Angie spotted some white women with local lads sitting at the tables. There was no neon light above their head saying *desperate female* nor was there anyone sniggering or pointing and saying *loser*. Perhaps Maggie was right and her attitudes towards sex and relationships were hopelessly outdated.

In the flurry of unloading cases, checking in and

getting her keys Angie lost sight of Janet. Once in her room, she walked out onto the balcony and breathed in the balmy air. Strange warbling sounds from the birds in the garden were accompanied by excited screams and splashes from the area of the pool. In the distance, the rollers of the Atlantic Ocean crashed on the beach. She flung herself down on the bed, let the warmth envelop her like a duvet and closed her eyes to gather some courage for the ordeals ahead.

The meeting with the tour rep was set for six, which coincided with Happy Hour. As Angie walked into the bar, it was obvious by the noise and clinking glasses that many of her fellow guests had already been taking advantage of the cheap booze. She tried to slip in unnoticed but Janet spotted her and rushed forward in a flurry of mottled arms and a black and orange print maxi dress. 'Come and join us over here.' She dragged Angie by the arm and propelled her to a cubicle where two other women were sitting, each with a large glass of a curious green liquid. 'Get this inside you.' She poured Angie a glass from a jug decorated with pictures of parrots. 'They call it *African Orgasm*—you'll like it—I'm not sure about the cocktail,' and she broke off in peals of laughter.

Angie sat down, took a sip and choked as a stream of sickly sweet and potent liquid fought its way down her throat. If ever she wanted to find out what paint stripper tasted like, this was as close as she would get. 'Bit strong?' Angie nodded. 'Lamu likes to sauce it up a bit. Add some more ice,' and she topped up her glass with more liquid and a torrent of ice. 'How about we all get acquainted?'

For the next half hour Angie got to know her drinking partners. There was Brenda, a slim brunette with several tattoos over her neck and chest who was fifty-two, had been divorced for ten years and was sick of internet dating and finding men who wanted sex and their washing done. She was accompanied by her friend Susie, a dental hygienist with flame-red hair that had grey roots. Susie said her last partner had tried to make off with her savings. Finally, there was Janet, her ally from the coach who was an expert in the game of *dating, mating and escaping* as she called it.

'You see I know what I want, how much I'm prepared to give them and it's strictly no strings.' She filled up her glass with more of the cocktail. 'Goodness knows what my Kevin would say if I came back with a toy boy.'

Angie must have looked confused as Janet added, 'My son's twenty-four and he wouldn't be pleased to call one of these lads *daddy*. Not that I am looking for anything long term. This is for fun, fun, fun,' and she raised her glass. 'Oh oh, sounds like the rep is ready to start. I don't want to be a party pooper.' She leaned over and dropped her voice so that Angie had to get closer to hear, 'I'm not here to be sold a trip to some overpriced market or a city tour. There's a good bar at the entrance to the hotel that sells great cocktails. Coming?'

Angie looked down at her white tailored trousers and multicoloured top and felt decidedly under dressed for an evening out. What the hell. She was damn well going to have some fun. She stood up, tipped the dregs of the cocktail down her throat and swallowed without pulling a face. 'Why not?'

Once outside the quiet confines of the hotel, a raucous sound blasted Angie's ears. Dust filled her nostrils as cars and minibuses cruised up and down, stopping to disgorge the mainly white passengers into one of the many restaurants and bars that fought for space along the road. Janet dived into one that announced it too was having a Happy Hour. 'What do you want to drink?'

Angie looked at the incomprehensible list of cocktails and ordered a gin and tonic instead. It had been her mother's favourite drink so she reckoned it was safe enough. 'Let me get this one,' she reached into her purse.

'That's sweet of you.' Janet scanned the list of drinks. '*Sex in Paradise* will do. Make it a double.' She looked at the empty tables. 'Not much of a crowd in here tonight. It'll liven up later at the Jacaranda.' Angie handed her a huge glass filled with sugar-pink liquid and topped with an umbrella, a large bendy straw and a sparkler that spluttered and scattered shards of light everywhere. 'We'll get something to eat over the road. It doesn't do to drink on an empty stomach.' She sucked on the straw and half the pink liquid disappeared. 'What's an attractive lady like you doing over here, apart from trying to find a decent guy who will at least talk to you before and after he fucks you?'

Angie took a large gulp of her drink. It sparkled on her tongue and was icy cold. She'd stick with that or beer from now on. It would be safer than the lethal alcohol content of the cocktails on offer. She swallowed and trotted out her well-rehearsed answer. 'I thought I was in a relationship. I wasn't. It turned out he had a girlfriend and that was that.' It was true, up to a point. She couldn't stop an involuntary shudder as the thought of Leo flashed into her mind.

'You all right?'

'Just a bad memory I can't seem to shake off.' Angie stared out at the road. With any luck the scene in front of her might help dispel the images of Leo and the other poor women he'd duped.

'Take it from me, the best way to get over a man is to get under another one, know what I mean?' Janet didn't wait for an answer. She stood up. 'You finished? I'll take you to a place where they sell local food. It'll give you something to tell the relatives about when you get back.'

'You're the boss.' Angie swallowed the remains of the gin. It was like being back with Maggie and she was happy to put herself in the hands of such an experienced coach.

Janet strode along the main drag, smiling and greeting the many faces that welcomed her back until they stood in front of an open space filled with plastic tables and chairs. 'It may not look much but the food is out of this world,' she said as a gangly man in a crisp white shirt and black trousers grabbed Janet's hand and pumped it up and down.

'Welcome back, Janet from Birmingham. How are you?'

'Hi, Mo. I'm fine and this is Angie and she's never tasted Gambian food before so do your best.'

They took their place at a table and Janet ordered water. She leaned over and pointed to the dishes. 'Try the vegetable domada. It's made with peanuts and tomatoes and served with rice.' Mo took their order and Janet looked at Angie her head on one side. 'Something tells me you're not here for just any old fling. Did that bastard hurt you badly?'

Mo arrived with their water and Angie waited until he'd gone before answering, which gave her brain time to think of a reply that wouldn't sound weak or unlikely. 'Let's say I'm not very confident with men. I mean I haven't had a lot of experience and now I'm free I want to make up for lost time. The trouble is I don't know how.'

'Like most of us, love. You get married, have kids, they leave home and you're stuck with someone who wants to spend all his time in the garden or bloody fishing. He wants you to cook and clean and just as you're over the worry of getting pregnant and can have some fun, he loses the drive, so to speak.'

'Did that happen to you?'

'Scratch beneath the surface of any menopausal women and you'll find a sex siren waiting to be unleashed. We're up for it and he can't get it up.'

'I didn't know that.'

'No one tells you, but believe me, us silver divorcees are on the rise and while we can, we're going to have some fun. Ahh, here's the food.'

Mo placed a huge plate in front of Angie. A mound of fluffy, white rice was encircled by a rich red brown sauce filled with courgettes, peppers, onions and carrots. She dipped her fork in the sauce and transferred a smothered courgette to her mouth. An earthy, musky flavour combined with a sweetness that came from the peanuts exploded on her taste buds. Paul would like this. She stopped. There would be no cooking for Paul ever again. She could try it on Maggie or Jason and made a mental note to ask someone in the hotel if they knew how it was cooked. She pushed all thoughts of Paul from her mind. 'Just one thing, love,' Janet said as they were splitting the bill. 'We'd better arrange to go back separately. Don't wait for me, if you know what I mean and I won't wait for you. We can meet up on the beach tomorrow and swap tales, right?'

'How long does the club stay open for?'

'Til eight.' Angie checked her watch and frowned. 'That's eight o'clock tomorrow morning,' Janet explained and patted Angie's hand. 'You *have* got a lot to learn, haven't you?'

A short taxi ride bumped them along a road and stopped in front of a two-storey building made out of concrete, shaped and decorated to look like trees. The front was open to the air and taxis, bikes and motorbikes waited to take the clientele back to their hotels or anywhere else they wanted to go. A dark alley led to the entrance where locals and tourists lounged, drinking, smoking, chatting or cooling off. 'We're here. Remember to stick to the rules.' Janet paid the taxi and clambered out.

'What rules?' said Angie.

'Make sure you agree what is on offer, don't get caught up in sob stories about medical bills, be ready to say goodbye at the end of the week and if it goes that far, always use a condom.' Janet took a breath, 'Easy eh?'

'If you say so,' said Angie to Janet's departing back as she disappeared into the club.

Although it was only nine o'clock, the place was already packed with gyrating bodies and pungent with the smell of sweat and perfume. In her early years, Angie remembered school discos with a few flashing lights and a single record deck. Here the DJ was on a huge raised dais. He was dwarfed by keyboards, consoles, decks and rows of vinyl records. Everyone in the bar was either leaping up and down in time with the music, one hand in the air or standing and nodding their heads. 'Come on,' Janet shouted above the crescendo of electronic sounds that shook the floor.

'I can't dance,' Angie wailed.

'Just follow me. You'll soon get the hang of it.' Janet pulled Angie onto the floor where she was soon caught up in the rhythmic punch of the beat. As she mimicked Janet, she looked at the scene that was unfolding. Flashing lights lit up the darker corners of the club. A few women stood at the side of the dance floor surrounded by young men. Several couples were kissing voraciously. As her eyes adjusted to the lights, she noticed how the women in the clinches would sometimes disappear out of the back door with a young man in tow. She leaned forward and tried to shout in Janet's ear.

Janet stopped and cupped her ear long enough for Angie to point and shout, 'Where are they going?'

Janet nodded. 'Back to the guy's room.'

'What?'

Janet placed her mouth next to Angie's ear and bellowed, 'Unless you fancy going onto the beach or paying the hotel a fortune for an overnight guest, they rent a room locally. There's a place at the back of the club.'

After half an hour of dancing with the young men intermingling and swapping partners as the music changed, Angie reckoned she had cracked the code. A man dances with you and because you can't hear what he's saying you have to go and sit down where you can talk. If you keep dancing, you can continue until you find someone you like. So far Angie had been accosted by two who were shorter than she was, three who were younger than Jason and one who was so tall he towered over her. By now she was dripping with sweat, her hair clung to her face like rats' tails and she just knew her make-up was a streaky mess. Her legs ached and her toes, unused to being liberated in sandals, were rubbing against the thin leather thongs that were the only means of keeping them attached to her feet.

She feigned a trip to the loo and went and sat down in the corner where she hoped she could observe what was going on. No such luck. As soon as she sat down she was accosted by several young men who insisted she dance with them. She tried saying she wanted a rest but they sat down by her side and charming as they were, it was all too much for Angie to take in. She glanced at the couples dancing, searching for Janet or anyone else she recognised. There was no one. 'No I don't want to dance,' she yelled as another young man headed her way. She ran out of the front door to where the taxis were waiting and returned to her hotel alone.

Chapter Twenty-three

The security officer at the entrance to the hotel must have been used to women arriving back looking dishevelled because he just tipped his cap and wished Angie goodnight. She went into the bar, which was quieter now, and ordered a gin and tonic. It was such a beautiful evening with the roar of the surf in the distance and the stars lighting up the sky that she wandered down to the small patio overlooking the beach. She sat on the low wall that separated the public areas from the hotel gardens.

She sipped her drink, luxuriating in the warm breeze that wafted the sounds and smells of the ocean her way. She listened. Someone was snoring on the other side of the wall. She looked down. 'What the..?' She jumped back and as she did spilt some of her drink onto the sleeping man who woke with a start and looked up at her. 'I'm sorry. I didn't mean to wake you,' she said.

The man got up and stretched. He was tall and slender with hair in neat dreadlocks. He rubbed a hand over his face and through his hair before nodding. 'Yes, ma'am, you caught me. Promise you won't tell anyone?'

'Where you sleep is your business but shouldn't you be at home?' Angie sat back on the wall.

'My home is way up country.' He waved a hand inland.

'What are you doing down here? I'm Angie by the way.'

The hand that shook hers was rough and warm. 'I was a farmer. Now all I am is a bumster.'

'What's a bumster?'

'I give the ladies a good time. They pay me,' he said without flinching

'What sort of good time?' Angie put her glass down on the wall and waited, not daring to breathe.

'What do you want? Sightseeing? Tours? Beach walks? Meals out? Trips to the market?'

Angie screwed up every last ounce of her courage, pleased it was dark and he couldn't see her blushes. 'What about …er…I mean?'

'You want fuck? I fuck you.' His eyes never left her face as he waited for an answer.

All she had to do was say *yes* and it could be over in a few minutes. It would be so easy. He was good-looking, clean and polite. He had a friendly smiling face. What more did she want? An A-list film star? She shook her head and sighed deeply. 'I don't know about that though I do need a guide.' She kicked herself for fudging the issue. Somehow she couldn't just ask him to have sex with her. She was not like Janet. She was just Angie. She'd have a holiday and go back home, her virginity intact.

'Where do you want to go?'

'I'd like to buy some jewellery for my best friend and some batik for me…if you know of anywhere?'

'Sure. You meet me tomorrow on the beach and we'll go to a market. We can get a taxi.'

'That would be great. How much would it cost?'

There was a pause as if he was eyeing her up to see how much she might be able to afford. 'Four hundred Dalasi and you pay the taxi.'

Angie did a quick calculation in her head and agreed. Even with a taxi it would be cheaper than a tour on her own. Besides, there was a chance he might be the one if she got to know him first. 'You're booked. See you tomorrow.' She turned to go, then changed her mind. 'What's your name?'

'Call me Modu.'

It was gone eight when the alarm rang and the sun was already promising another day of torpid heat. Angie roused herself and went and leaned on the balcony. The pool cleaners were busy at work and the gardeners were trimming and watering the scrub grass and the borders of flowers and shrubs. For a second, the memory of Leo flashed back, like a shadow flitting across the sky, obscuring the sun and chilling her. She shook herself. There were no Leos here. She was simply off on a trip to get some presents for her friends and she was going to enjoy the company of someone new. She pushed the thought of Leo out of her mind, went and had a long hot shower and tried to decide what to wear. By the time she had dried her hair, her bed was covered with clothes. In the end she selected cream trousers, a floral top in shades of pink and cream with flat sandals in case she had a lot of walking to do at the market.

In the dining room she spotted Janet hugging a cup of coffee. Her eyes were red and bleary, whether it was from lack of sleep or something else, Angie was not going to ask. She breezed up and plonked herself next to Janet with a cheery, 'Good morning.'

Janet raised her head and looked up. 'Is it?'

From the desolate tone of her voice, Angie knew something had happened. 'Is everything all right?'

'No and yes.' Janet replied and took another slug of her coffee. She held up the cup and called to the waiter for a refill. She took a long look at Angie. 'These boys are bastards.'

'What's happened?'

Janet grimaced. 'My boy, Edi, said he needed five thousand Dalasi for his family and when I said I hadn't got that sort of money he walked out and left me.'

'He'll come back, won't he? You've been with him for a couple of years, haven't you?' Angie said in what she hoped was her most reassuring voice.

'Yeah and as I was leaving he was curled up with some brunette.'

'What will you do now?' Angie said.

Janet shrugged. 'Find another I suppose. I'll be the same as all the other desperate women. You see, I thought he really cared about me. He was just as full of crap as the rest.' She looked at Angie over her coffee cup, her face pinched and her lips set in a narrow line.

'I'm really sorry it hasn't worked out,' said Angie and squeezed Janet's hand.

'I thought I wasn't involved...clearly I was. I'm just another sad woman who thought she'd found someone who cared for her.' Janet sniffed and wiped her eyes with the back of her hand.

'I understand.'

'Do you?'

The way Janet looked at Angie reminded her of Maggie. It was easy to be taken in by the tough exterior. Underneath was a different matter. 'Oh yes,' said Angie, remembering Leo. 'Something like that happened to me and it hurt. It still does.'

'Well perhaps you'll get lucky. Have your fun and don't get involved, remember?'

'That's what I intend to do.' Angie paused. 'What are your plans for today?'

'Top up my tan and find someone else I suppose.' Janet stopped and looked at Angie. Her head tilted on one side and a smile flickered over her lips. 'Where did you get to last night?'

'Oh I needed a good long sleep so I left at about ten.'

Janet nodded. 'Are you coming to join us on the beach today?'

Angie sipped her coffee. 'I'm going on a trip. I've got a local guide and a taxi.' She tried to sound matter of fact but Janet's eyes opened wide.

'Aren't you the dark horse?' There was no mistaking the admiration in Janet's voice and Angie allowed herself a small pat on the back. Perhaps she was becoming a woman of the world after all.

It was nearly eleven when Angie went down into the garden to find Modu. 'Angie, over here,' he called. He was dressed in a spotless white shirt and plain dark trousers. She waved back and he directed her to a waiting taxi.

On the journey Modu spent the whole time pointing out things he thought Angie might be interested in: trees; birds; food stalls with strange-looking fruits and the local houses. He stopped the driver from time to time to let her get out and take some photos on her phone. 'You'd make a damn good tour guide,' she said as they climbed back in after he'd taken a snap of Angie next to a stall with huge watermelons piled up.

'That is what I would like to be one day so I study my country and my English,' Modu said. 'Today I practice on you.'

Angie was happy to oblige until the taxi swerved to a halt on the edge of a market. Modu muttered something to the taxi driver who promptly tipped his hat over his head and went to sleep in the front seat. He led Angie through the cacophony of shouts, cries, chatter and laughter of commerce Gambian style. Her eyes were assaulted by the colours of unusual fruit and vegetables and her nose was affronted by the pungent odour of decay mixed with diesel. He cajoled the stall holders into letting her try some of their fruits, which she swallowed, crossing her fingers she wasn't going to be struck down by some lethal stomach bug. Turning a corner, he stopped at a small shack shop which had a frontage smothered in the brightest batik material that Angie had ever seen. He called out and a small woman appeared, dressed in purple and yellow, her hair swathed in a cloth of the same colour. Her wrinkled face lit up when she saw Modu and she clapped him on the back.

'This is my aunty, the sister of my father and she has the best fabric in Banjul and it is very cheap. Local price.' He winked, whether at Angie or his aunty she couldn't say. She followed the woman into the dark interior, lit only by chinks of light that squeezed between the bolts of material that were piled from floor to ceiling. The woman indicated a chair and Angie was soon swamped by material that she had to touch or stroke, accompanied by a torrent of words. After half an hour she had selected three pieces. Angie had never haggled before and reckoned she'd done well when the initial price of five hundred Dalasi each had been reduced to twelve hundred for three. She waited while the woman wrapped them up in paper and after thanking her again escaped into the bright sunlight.

It was the same with the jewellery she wanted for

Maggie. For someone who lived up country, Modu had a lot of relatives who lived locally. By the time she got back to the taxi she decided to ask Modu about his so-called relatives. He looked at her and hung his head. 'My parents live up country. I came here to be with my new family.'

'What do you mean your new family? Are you married?'

'Yes. I have two children.'

Angie felt sick. She had been prepared to consider going to bed with this young man and all the time he had a wife and children. 'What does your wife think about what you do?'

'She thinks I am a waiter. To get a job as a waiter I need contacts or references so for the moment I am a bumster.'

'I might be able to help out.'

Modu raised his eyebrows. 'How?'

'You're a great tour guide. I could write you a reference and put it on Trip Advisor,' Angie paused, 'on one condition.'

A shadow crossed Modu's face. 'What is that?'

'Invite me to your house to meet your family.' The words tumbled out. She couldn't come here and not find out about how the people lived.

'Agreed,' Modu said and clapped her on the back before he shouted something to the driver who woke up and started the engine.

The taxi wound its way through the city and out into the countryside, past whitewashed buildings with corrugated iron roofs. Open-fronted shops sold everything from batteries to soap powder. Beaten-up cars and lorries passed them by. Some were piled high with fruit or vegetables and some with scrawny animals destined for market. Despite the poverty, Angie sensed the energy of people going about their daily lives, trying to make a living for their families. She envied them. Something was missing from her own life.

After half an hour the taxi pulled off the main road and headed along a rutted track. Angie held tight as she was bounced from side to side. She clamped a hand over her mouth as the wheels kicked up copious amounts of reddish brown dust. A few minutes later it stopped in front of an enclosure with walls made from a patchwork of corrugated iron sheets. Modu got out and went up to the gate. He pushed it open and called. There were screams and shouts and two young children came rushing out followed by a beautiful woman with a baby on her hip and an old man, his toothless mouth fixed into a wide grin. Modu swung the children high in the air making them scream even louder before hugging the young woman. He went up to the old man, took hold of his hand and led him to Angie. 'This is my father-in-law, the head of the household.'

Angie held out her hand and he shook it before ushering her inside. 'Welcome, welcome,' he said. He pulled up a chair in the shade of a huge tree that stood in the centre of the compound and called out something. More chairs appeared, brought by family members who emerged from the buildings scattered at the edges of the compound. Modu sat down and pulled a child on each knee.

'My father-in-law is calling for tea and this...' he indicated the beautiful young woman with the baby, 'is my wife and these two—' he wiggled his knees so that the children giggled as they wobbled, like a boat bucking on a rough ocean, 'are my two children, Loli and Omar. The baby is my niece. My sister-in-law is working today.'

An older woman in a burka brought out a tray with tea and bananas. 'This is my mother-in-law.' She bowed. 'My mother-in-law is very traditional; she is from the older generation. Many young women, like my wife, do not wear a full covering. Enough talk. You must drink tea and eat.'

It was two hours later when Angie finally left. On the journey back, though she said little, her mind was whirring. His children needed proper books and a decent bed to sleep on if they were to succeed at school. She bit her lip. There must be something she could do to help out.

As the car drew up into the car park by the hotel she turned to Modu. 'I have an idea,' she said as she extracted money from her bag to pay him and the taxi driver. 'Let me sponsor your children to go to school, like the big charities. I'll also write you a reference so that you can get a waiter's job. At least that will be a start.'

'You will do that for me?' Modu asked, frowning. 'Why?'

Angie shrugged. 'I was a teacher. I understand just how important education is or should be.' Yet it was more than that; she wanted to be part of something again.

'Thank you.' Modu took her hand and shook it vigorously as a smile creased his face.

'There is one condition.' The smile disappeared. Angie took a deep breath. 'I want to treat you and your family to a party before I leave and invite my friends so they can see a real Gambian home.' The smile returned. It was agreed that Angie and her friends would travel to Modu's home on the last full day of their stay. She would provide chickens, rice and fruit for a meal. What they didn't know was that she was going to order a cake. It was her birthday that day and she was going to hit fifty in style.

Once back in the hotel, Angie went into the bar to get a coffee. Her hair had been tangled by the breeze in the car and her face was smudged and dusty. Her once immaculate clothes were creased and dirty and she could taste grit. As she strode up to the bar and leaned on it, aware of the curious looks that her dishevelled appearance was causing, she realised she had not felt so alive in years.

'How did it go?' Janet called from a booth where she was cradling a beer. All trace of her previous upsets had either disappeared or were hidden away. Angie collected her coffee and joined her. 'Did he give you a guided tour of his privates?' Janet winked. 'I know what you're up to over here.'

'As a matter of fact, I went to a real house, met his wife and children and we're arranging a small party and you and the gang are invited. It's on Sunday at 2pm. Will you be there?'

Janet tilted her head on one side. 'Yeah and he'll ask you for thousands for his sick mother.'

'He might but somehow I don't think so. Anyway if that happens, I promise to buy you enough cocktails to sink a ship. What do you think?'

Janet raised her bottle. 'You're on.'

It was mid-afternoon a few days later and Angie was lying on a sun lounger watching the activity on the beach. Her skin had turned golden and glistened with a mixture of sweat and sunscreen. The smell of

239

coconut mixed with the salty tang of the sea breezes and the waves were whipped into foaming crescents. However lovely it was lying here, she reminded herself, this was not real. She raised herself on one elbow and surveyed the beach scene. She was bored with her life and the whole sex thing. So what if she was a virgin? A shout made her look up from her daydreams. It was Janet staggering across the beach, laden with bags. 'I thought I'd find you here. We all reckon you're moping so you must come out with us tonight.'

Angie pulled a face. 'Not to a disco with all that thumping music, please?'

'No. It's a jazz lounge with some soulful music just right for dancing and they sell beer so cold it would freeze a snowball in hell.' She plonked herself down on the edge of Angie's lounger, her weight making the legs sink into the sand. She fished in her bag and pulled out a packet of cigarettes and lit one, blowing smoke away from Angie. 'You've been very quiet lately. What you need is cheering up.'

'What I need is something to do...' Angie pressed her feet in the sand and wriggled them as the warm grains trickled through her toes.

'Are you sure that isn't someone?' Janet sniggered then stopped. 'You're serious, aren't you?'

'Deadly serious.' Angie looked at her. 'Listen, I'm young, I've had a few months sorting my house out but there's only so many times you can get excited by soft furnishings and paint charts. I want to be of use again and I want to meet new people.' She kicked at the sand. 'The money would certainly come in handy.' For the moment she had ignored the pile of letters, the emails and phone calls from the bank, however they were not forgotten. The credit card bills for all the new clothes she'd bought for her holiday would soon be landing on the doormat. Forget the sex. She was a virgin in financial management too. She didn't just want a job: she needed one.

On Sunday Angie had arranged for a taxi to take her and the girls to Modu's home. She had taken extra care over her choice of clothes and had covered her arms in a long-sleeved cream lace top which she had teamed with a pair of flowing trousers in a jungle print, bought from the hotel shop. She had two bags with food and a large box that she had collected from the kitchen earlier in the day. It contained a pink and white iced cake with *Happy Birthday Angie* piped on it.

Modu was waiting at the front of the hotel, dressed in a white shirt and blue shorts. His dreadlocks had been cut off and he looked like a young professional about to start work. What a pity he could only get a waiter's job. It was a start. Angie waved.

He came over and took the bags from her. 'This is a very special day. My family are excited. Are these your friends?' Angie turned to see Janet and Susie in flowing printed dresses bearing down on them.

'Yes. They may look and sound a bit wild but they've had tough lives in their own way,' she said.

The three women piled in the taxi and settled down for the bumpy ride to Modu's. Even Janet was quiet as they passed through the villages where the tourists rarely visited. The wheels kicked up the dust which enveloped them all; it was too hot to close the windows. Susie held a tissue to her mouth and nose though Angie liked the pungent smell of diesel and hot earth which mingled with the faint scent of

241

roasting peanuts and frying garlic as unseen figures prepared food in the houses that lined the sides of the road.

The taxi slowed and stopped in front of Modu's compound. He got out and was assailed by his children who squealed with delight that they had another visit from their father. The taxi driver rested his feet on the dashboard and went to sleep. Modu, with a child hanging from each hand, bent down and whispered, 'Say hallo to my friends.' Their exuberance vanished as they clung to him and gazed with wide staring eyes at the strange creatures. 'You remember Angie, don't you?' The little girl nodded. 'Get her your school books.' She ran off as they walked into the compound and Modu showed them to a seat under the huge overhanging tree. He fetched glasses and squash and poured them each a drink. The little girl scampered back with her school books and approached Angie. She opened up a page of sums. As Angie bent over the familiar number lines, a thrill ran through her. If she was going back to work, it would have to be in a school.

The afternoon passed in a flurry of games as more children joined and they played a version of cricket and football until Modu's wife appeared with two dishes of spicy chicken, rice and vegetables. Angie's cake was greeted with shock by Susie and Janet who promised to treat her when they got back that evening. The sight of the family and her two newfound friends singing *Happy Birthday* as the sun set behind the trees and the whole place was bathed in the soft tropical dusk was treat enough.

Chapter Twenty-four

Angie gazed out of the window as the plane took off the following morning. If she could have willed it to fly faster, she would. Holidays were great but real life happened at home. She'd go and see Maggie, cook Jason's favourite meal, buy a decent bottle of wine and something non-alcoholic for Bryony before she set about the task of getting a job. There was no reason to hold back. She'd take up her career again and, who knows, in a couple of years she might even be a head teacher. She settled back in her seat and allowed herself to dream of having her own school until the plane began its descent through banks of clouds to reveal a rain-sodden, autumn day. Her rising excitement kept her smiling, ignoring the groans of other passengers as the plane splashed along the wet tarmac. Everything was going to be all right.

***

After the flurry of air kisses, goodbyes and exchanges of emails and soon-to-be-ignored phone numbers, Angie drove home alone. She opened the hall door and flung her case down. She sniffed. Someone had been round with the polish. She made a mental note to thank Bryony. Jason still thought a duster was something to clean his shoes or wipe the dipstick in his car. The day's post was scattered over the floor. She gathered up the assorted flyers and what looked like more letters from the credit card companies. She took a deep breath and was about to open one when she heard the tell tale beep of the answer machine in the hall. She pressed *play* as her finger hovered over the delete button. If it was another PPI reclaim offer, she'd scream. The breathless voice on the other end belonged to Sister Elizabeth.

'Hello, Sister Ruth, I mean Angela...Is this working? Can you hear me? Oh well I hope it is...My dear, be brave...I have some bad news for you.' She paused. Angie gripped the receiver wondering what was coming next. 'It's Father Benedict.' Angie held her breath. 'He's dead. He was found yesterday. He'd hung himself. It seems the police wanted to talk to him about some terrible things that happened many years ago. They've been here most of the day asking us all sorts of questions. They might want to speak to you too. Oh, I'd better go. The bell for Compline is ringing. God bless you, my dear.' The call ended. For a moment, Angie remained motionless. Dead? He couldn't be. She played the message again and let the words sink in.

She replaced the receiver and leaned against the wall. So Father Benedict had got away with his vile behaviour. She wanted to punch the wall, scream, do something, anything. It just wasn't fair. Instead, like a sleepwalker, she headed to the kitchen. She sat down at the table and rested her head in her hands. It would hit the sisters hard. Even Sister Catherine. Even worse was those poor kids whose lives he'd ruined. Like Ben. He'd never see justice done. She looked up as she had done so many times before, as if God was floating above her in some cloudy paradise. Why did you let him get away with it? At least if someone believed in divine retribution, Father Benedict would be frizzling in hell now. She stopped. She'd always been told never to think ill of the dead. Not this time. He deserved to be writhing in agony and for all eternity.

She sat for a few minutes, unable to move, unsure what to do next. Ben wasn't in the best mental health. What would happen to him? How would he cope? Paul might be able to help. She jumped up. She'd go and tell him. He might be able to soften the blow somehow. Except he was the last person she wanted to see. There was a time when all she had been thinking about was her love life. It seemed a different world and a lifetime away. She sighed. Better get it over with. She went into the hallway and looked out of the window. Damn. His car was not in the driveway. She only hoped he wasn't at work somewhere at the other end of the country. There was nothing for it but to wait.

Angie stowed her dirty washing in the machine and switched it on before going to unpack the rest of her case. She pulled open a drawer and placed her new beads inside. The old envelopes from the bank were tucked in the corner. She added the new ones to the pile. There was no need to read them. That would do later. People came first.

She pottered around, half in and half out of a dream world in which she tried to work out what to say to Paul. Everything sounded wrong. How could she tell him what she knew and not let him know about her past? Even though there was no chance of any romantic links between them, for some reason she felt uncomfortable telling anyone about her previous life. She was hanging out her clothes on the washing line in the feeble hope that they would dry in the damp evening air when she heard Paul's car pull into the driveway. A door slammed and a light went on in his kitchen. Two minutes later she was standing outside his front door. She pressed the bell. The door swung open. Before he could say anything Angie spoke, her words coming out like lava from a volcano. 'I need to talk to you. I've got some news about Father Benedict.'

'Come in, Angie,' Paul stepped aside. 'Would you care for some tea or a drink?' As always he was the perfect gentleman and the realisation he would only ever think of her as a friendly neighbour made her ache with a deep sadness she hadn't known for years.

She shook her head. 'No. I can't stop.' She swallowed hard. It didn't matter what Paul thought of her. This was for Ben. 'Father Benedict has killed himself. He was being investigated by the police for child abuse.' She took a step back. That was it. She'd done her duty.

'Yes. I know.'

'What? How?' She felt the colour drain from her face.

'Are you sure you don't want that drink?'

'No, thank you all the same.' The last thing she wanted was to spend time with Paul; her sense of dread made worse as she looked at him. Why did he have to be so damned attractive? She forced her mind back to the present. 'What's happening about Ben?'

'Ben is happy. The information you gave him was corroborated by the Mother Superior from the local convent who had worked with Father Benedict for years. He feels exonerated.'

Relief swept over Angie. Ben was going to be fine after all. Angie clapped a hand over her mouth. 'Oh my God...Did Sister Catherine provide evidence too?'

'Yes. She mentioned a sister called Ruth who had alerted her to the problem. Sister Ruth left at the start of the year.' There was a pause as Paul looked at Angie, his head on one side. 'That was you wasn't it?'

She looked down at her feet, anything to avoid his eyes. 'Yes. I am or was Sister Ruth.'

'I see.'

She changed the subject. 'The police can't prosecute, can they?'

Paul shrugged. 'The church and the police will be investigating further. The good thing is what it's done for Ben. Someone believes him at last.'

'I'm glad,' she said, so relieved she was almost lost for words. 'Not just for Ben.' She took another deep breath. 'There were others too and they'll find out what happened. Truth always triumphs. Somehow.' She was burbling on. She'd embarrass herself even more unless she shut up. 'I'd better go.' She smiled. 'Tell Ben I'm pleased for him.'

'I will,' Paul said. 'You really are welcome to stay. I feel I've got a lot to thank you for.'

'No.' Angie backed away. 'Jason and Bryony will be home soon and I've got some catching up to do. Thank you.' She turned and fled to the safety and security of her own home.

Only when she had closed the front door behind her did the significance of Paul's words sink in. Sister Catherine had finally turned against Father Benedict. She closed her eyes. 'Thank you, God,' she said and this time she meant it. She opened her eyes. Now Paul knew she had been a nun. No wonder he wasn't interested in her and never would be. She'd often read about people describing their world crashing down. They were wrong. Her life was deflating like a balloon. At least there would be no more secrets. It was like a page turning in her life story; no more

247

romantic dreams of Paul and no more nightmares about Father Benedict. Was that a fair trade?

She checked the clock. Jason and Bryony wouldn't be home until much later. She had to get out of the house. She needed company or she'd keep going over things until she was sick. She texted Maggie that she was back. The response was instant. Maggie was desperate to catch up too as she had some news of her own and insisted she came over, even though it would only be for a cup of tea.

Maggie opened the door with a smile on her face. It soon disappeared. 'My God, your face is as long as a month of wet Mondays as my old mum would say. What happened in Gambia? Bad time?' She ushered Angie into the front room.

Angie flopped down onto the sofa. 'No. It's not that...'

'Wait 'til I've got some tea,' Maggie said. 'Although I reckon a brandy is what you need.' She went into the kitchen as Angie wondered just how much she should tell her.

Maggie came back into the room and handed her a mug of tea. 'Drink this.' She sat down in the chair opposite.

'Thanks.' Angie sipped her tea. 'Aren't you going to ask how I got on?' she said and watched as Maggie nearly dropped her mug.

'I didn't like to say anything—'

'—Did I lose my virginity?' Angie butted in. 'No. As soon as I got there I realised it was never going to happen. I did meet a young man and his family and I'm sponsoring his children to go to school.'

'Oh oh, this isn't another of your rescues, is it? You do seem to have the knack of picking up waifs and strays, don't you?' Maggie shook her head.

'You mean like you?' Angie said. Maggie was impervious to the slight insult.

'No, more like Jason and Bryony. Who else are you going to help out? The whole town?'

'You're being silly, and even if it is true, does it matter if it makes me happy?'

Maggie shrugged. 'As long as you don't go handing out large amounts of cash or falling for sob stories.'

'I won't. Hang on a sec while I get your presents.' Angie scrabbled in her bag and fished out two packets; she handed them to Maggie. 'This is for you to say thank you for all your friendship and kindness to me. I don't know what I'd have done without you over the past few months.' Maggie unwrapped the packets and brought out the two necklaces, bought with Modu's help. She held up the purple one against her skin. It was perfect.

A flicker of emotion crept through a chink in the tough shell Maggie habitually wore and she wiped her eyes. 'Come here you.' She hugged Angie. They stayed together for a few moments. Neither said anything. Each gave and received from the other whatever was needed; Angie had never believed all this stuff about energy. She felt it now. It was like a current passing from Maggie to her and she knew she'd have the strength to face whatever life threw at her. 'Thanks,' she managed to whisper.

Maggie broke away first. 'You know I'm only being a misery because I care, don't you?'

Angie nodded. 'I know but you don't have to worry. I think in the future I'm going to have to take note of every single penny I spend.' It was time to change the subject. 'What about your news? It had better be good.'

Maggie sat back in the chair. 'The plan for the care home has been rejigged and,' she paused, 'the company, under the leadership of one Paul Buchannan, is to create a management committee made up of staff members with fifty per cent of the profits being reinvested. We won or rather you and Polly won.' She clapped her hands and punched the air.

Angie didn't know what to say. It was the news she'd wanted yet, somehow, she didn't feel as pleased as she had expected. 'That's great,' she managed to stammer out. And it was great. The whole day had been full of great news—great for Maggie, for Paul and for Ben. But not for her. Far from feeling as if a weight had been lifted off her, she felt it was dragging her down to unplumbed depths of sadness.

'Is there something up?' Maggie's antennae as usual were working overtime.

'I've had some news too.'

By the time she had explained about Father Benedict and Ben, it was the first occasion Angie had ever known Maggie to be lost for words. She waited for the explosion. It came. 'Bloody hell, Angie. I reckon you need another holiday to get over that.' Maggie reached out and patted Angie's hand. 'You know what this means don't you?'

'No, what?'

'It's all over.' There was silence for a moment as if Maggie was struggling to find the words to say. Eventually she spoke. 'It means there's no reason for you to have any links with the past anymore. You can finally move on.'

'I suppose I can.' Angie gazed out into the garden.

This was the fresh start she'd wanted. The whole sordid business with Father Benedict and the embarrassment with Paul were over. She was almost free, scary though it was, a clean slate beckoned her. One final task remained. The notebooks had to be burnt. When that was done, her past would finally be past.

'You look done in. Do you want to stay here tonight? I can fix up a bed. I don't like to think of you being alone.'

Angie shook her head. 'No. I'm probably just tired.' She checked her watch. 'I reckon I need a decent night's sleep in my own bed and I've got Bryony and Jason to keep me company. See you Friday as usual?'

'I'll have the wine waiting.'

Angie drove home deep in thought, forcing herself to concentrate on the road. Once back, she went straight to her father's old trunk and opened it. The smell of dust, candle wax and incense wafted up. She closed her eyes. The memory of chilled stone, dark mornings and long nights when she had forced her icy fingers to scribble each secret entry filtered back. Maggie was right. It was over. All over. She took the notebooks out and one by one she checked the dates. She'd keep three. She knew which ones. They contained most of the entries she had copied out for Ben. She wrapped them in a pillowcase and put them back in the trunk to give to him later. He might need them. The rest she took outside. Why had she written them? She couldn't even remember now except for the desire to have something that was all hers and prove she was more than Sister Ruth.

It was already dark and the first star was shining in

251

the evening sky. A faint smile formed on her lips 'Star light…star bright,' she murmured. What should she wish for? An ending? A new beginning? Both. She dropped the notebooks and knelt down on the damp grass next to the bare patch of earth where Jason reckoned he'd grow a few vegetables next year. She opened one notebook at a time and tore the pages free from the wire spirals. She scrunched some up and made a small pile on the soil. She lit a match. A flame flickered, burst into life and the paper shrivelled, turning from white to brown to black before crumbling into ash. She added more pages, oblivious to the wetness creeping through the knees of her jeans and watched as the smoke curled upwards to the sky. Sometimes she would catch sight of a word or a date. All were quickly obliterated by the fire.

'What you doing, Ange?' Jason's voice was quiet.

She kept her eyes on the flames. 'Something I should have done a long time ago. Getting rid of my past.'

'Do you want a hand? You'll be here all night at this rate'. He pointed to the pile of paper.

She looked up into his face. What would her son have looked like? It was something she would never know. She felt her lip quiver as his image blurred in the tears forming in her eyes. 'Please.' She turned back to face the flames and felt them warm the tears now trickling down her cheeks.

Jason walked back to the kitchen. She heard the door open. 'Bry order us some pizzas will you?' he called out. A smile joined Angie's tears. Thoughts of his stomach were never far away. He returned a few minutes later and made a pyramid of twigs. He took the papers, screwed them into small balls, inserted a few under the pyramid and struck a match. Soon a small blaze lit up the evening sky.

Bryony joined them and without a word, Jason continued to feed the flames until there was only one sheet left. He picked it up. Angie put her hand on his. 'No. Let me.' She dangled the sheet above the flames. The words were visible.

December 13th 2005 Press camped outside again. Sister Elizabeth and I took them cups of tea. If I told them what I knew, they'd never believe me. No one ever will.

A flame licked at the corner. The paper browned before it caught light. Angie held on until it was nearly engulfed. She dropped it onto the pile of embers. They all remained in silence until the fire had died away and the garden was in darkness. Angie stood up. As each page burnt, she had expected a feeling of release. There was none. Only a sense of loss; the pain had been with her for so long, it was part of her and at that moment she had no idea what could replace it.

She looked at Bryony and Jason, standing arm in arm watching her. It was good to have them here. 'Thank you,' she said. No one moved.

The sound of someone hammering on the door made Angie jump. 'Pizza's arrived,' Jason said. 'Hey, can we have a bonfire party this year?'

'You will have a small baby to look after.' Angie looked at Bryony for backup.

'No, Angie. I will have two kids to look after, Jason and this one,' she patted her stomach, linked her arm through Angie's and steered her back into the house. 'Come on, the pizzas are ready and we want to hear all about your holiday, don't we Jason?'

Later that evening after Bryony and Jason had gone to bed, Angie got out the envelopes she'd hidden under her knickers and spread them over the kitchen table. She opened each one in turn and checked through the contents. The banks and credit card firms pulled no punches. After a few scribbled sums on the back of an envelope, even with Jason's money, she'd need a steady cash flow for a good few years. She got out the store cards and all except one of her credit cards, cut them up and deposited the pieces in the bin. Bugger Paul, bugger bloody Leo and bugger being a sodding virgin. It was time to move on.

She knew what would replace the emptiness she felt. It was life; the ordinary, everyday events that we take for granted; getting a job, even if it was only as a supply teacher, eating pizza with Jason and Bryony, drinking wine on a Friday might with Maggie and anything else she cared to do. She paused. An image floated back into her mind. It had been January. The day of her father's funeral. She had gone upstairs to change from the unfamiliar suit and high-heeled patent shoes she'd borrowed from a cousin. The black habit and blue head covering hung on the wardrobe door. She had pressed her face into the rough material. The smell of soap, sweat and the dust of corridors where nothing ever changed represented comfort, familiarity and also imprisonment. She'd yanked the dress off its hanger, torn at the sleeves and ripped at the seams. When they would not budge, she had fetched some scissors and cut until only shreds were left. It had been the first small, faltering step to a new life.

Sister Ruth was dead and buried; the last remnants of her life had gone up in smoke. What was left was Angie and a chance to achieve her dreams even if, at the moment, she wasn't sure what they were. It didn't matter. She had the rest of her life to work things out and she'd start tomorrow.

Chapter Twenty-five

It was Sunday evening when Angie's mobile rang, shattering the peace. Jason and Bryony were seeing a film as a treat and Angie was watching a series of reruns entitled House Beautiful on a Budget in the hope of getting some ideas. It was the teaching agency. They had an emergency and could Angie cover? The young woman who had interviewed her was desperate for someone to take a class of ten- and eleven-year-olds in a small village school. With her father's SATNAV primed, Angie found herself bowling along with fellow workers at 8 o'clock on Monday morning.

She had dressed in what she hoped would be a sensible, stylish outfit. Black trousers to withstand sticky fingers and the inevitable paint sploshes were teamed with a high-necked yellow blouse thus avoiding any embarrassing fall out from a low-cut top every time she bent over to mark someone's maths. She had added flat patent shoes as teaching could involve a lot of standing up and if PE was on the timetable she wouldn't look stupid tottering on high heels as she attempted to referee a football match or demonstrate how to hit a tennis ball.

Angie drove out of the town, turned off the dual carriageway and down a narrow lane where the trees on either side of the road curved and touched in an arch of golden branches. At the end of the lane was a village with a mix of cottages and small developments of executive houses side by side with 1970s social housing. She pulled off the road into a car park. A tall hedge half obscured the sign that announced *Welcome to Rodbourne Primary School.* One other car in the car park told her that at least someone else was in the vicinity and she got out and pressed the intercom. The familiar feeling that was a combination of nerves and excitement bubbled in her stomach. As she waited, scenarios of doom and disaster came to mind. She shook them off. It was the same as the start of any new school year when you saw thirty little faces staring at you and wondered who would be the stars, who would be the class comedians and who would try your patience until the fateful day when it all snapped into place and they accepted you as their leader.

The door buzzed and swung open. She was greeted by a man a few years younger than her. He was short and fair with a wispy beard that had a reddish tinge. He held out his hand and grinned. 'I'm Nick Brown. Am I pleased to see you? This way.' He led her to the office, gave her a badge to wear which announced *Teacher* and took her into a temporary classroom off the main block. He unlocked the door and ushered Angie inside. An involuntary gasp escaped from Angie's lips as she surveyed the broken blinds, the chipped paint on the walls and the few scraps of work flapping off the display boards. The whole place said *No one cares.*

Nick must have noticed her reaction. 'I suppose it does need a bit of TLC,' he said. 'I've been here since the start of term and the class has had a succession of supply staff until I stepped in and taught them. I can't understand what the problem is. I find them amenable enough but there's so much to be done here that I can't be the head and the class teacher.' Nick flicked a lock of hair out of his eyes. 'Assembly is at 9.15 and there's a list of what they should be

257

doing today on the file marked *Class Four*. I'll log you into the system.'

As Angie surveyed the mess, she knew exactly what she was going to do. A quick search of the stock cupboards revealed maths books and text books, paper and coloured pencils. She opened the trays that held the children's work below their tables. One after another was filled with scraps of paper, unfinished stories and half-started sheets of photocopied puzzles. She rolled up her sleeves, took up a marker pen and wrote the date on the white board.

Twenty minutes later excited voices sounded outside the classroom door. 'We've got a new teacher,' was followed by sniggers and whispers. Angie checked her preparations again. Paper was ready and a list of the day's activities was on the board. She would go and meet her class on the playground as she had done on countless other mornings, regardless of the weather.

She stepped outside the door. 'You teaching us today, miss?' A dark haired boy of ten or eleven looked up at her. He was obviously the Alpha Male. His hair was gelled into small spikes that stood up from his head like a hedgehog and his deep brown eyes twinkled.

'Yes, Michael, Miss Jarvis will be here today,' Nick Brown intervened. 'Now go away and run off some of that energy. You'll be using your brain for the rest of the day, I hope.' He turned his face away from the children and whispered under his breath, 'Bright lad, needs channelling. If he's bored, he'll wreak havoc in any lesson.'

'Point taken,' Angie said, relishing the challenge of an intelligent child who could be used to set the standard. She made a note to make sure she read his poem out when they tackled English. A whistle brought the games and the chatter to an end. On the second whistle four lines formed as if by magic and Angie could see the other members of staff. One was similar in age to her and was standing by the youngest children. There were two teachers who looked as if they were straight out of university with the uniform of floppy hair, leggings and huge flat-heeled boots that dwarfed their legs.

Angie ushered her charges into the cloakroom, waited until they had divested themselves of coats and bags and led them into the classroom. 'Sit where you usually sit and I will introduce myself,' she said and ignored the hubbub of scraped chairs and squeaking trays as pencil cases and reading bags were stuffed out of sight. When all was quiet she wrote her name on the board. 'I am Miss Jarvis and as I call the register I want you to put up your hand and say *Good morning.*' It was always a winner as she discovered she had two Alexanders, two Emilys and three Alices. Each interaction enabled her to fix them with a smile and sow the seed of a relationship.

'Miss, it's time for assembly,' Michael called out.

'Thank you, Michael. Well spotted. You can be my timekeeper for the day. If I go over break and lunch time, you must remind me,' Angie said as the boy visibly preened under the unexpected praise. She'd got him on her side already.

It was towards the end of the afternoon. Angie was hearing as many children read as she could while the class were illustrating the poems they had written earlier on the subject of *The Perfect Day* when Nick Brown came in. He stood in the doorway, transfixed, a smile beaming over his face.

'Have you had a good day?'

'Yes thank you, Mr Brown,' Angie replied in the customary fashion.

'Are you free tomorrow? In fact are you free for the rest of the term?'

'Say yes, miss,' Michael called out.

'I suppose so,' Angie felt her cheeks warming.

'Right, that's settled. Come and see me in the office after school and we'll get the paperwork set up.' He left, grinning.

'Does that mean you're staying, miss?' Emily with the long brown hair asked.

'Yes I think it does and so be warned. I'm not half as nice when you get to know me,' Angie glared putting on her fierce face. 'Who's for a story?'

'Me,' they chorused and as Angie opened the dog-eared pages of one of her never-failed, tried-and-tested good reads, she felt she had come home.

Angie was so busy over the next few weeks that she had no time to think of anything other than school, doing the usual chores and helping Bryony and Jason get the nursery ready for the new baby. The occasional evening with Maggie was the sum of her social life and she didn't mind at all.

***

It was Thursday evening in late September and as Angie drove up to the bungalow she just knew something was wrong. She was greeted by a heavily pregnant Bryony. 'Thank God you're back. I think the baby's coming. I've tried to get hold of Jason but he's not picking up his calls.'

Angie put down her bag and closed the door. She took hold of Bryony's arm to steer her to the front room to sit down. 'Are you sure?'

'I spent most of the day going to the loo and I've been getting these pains. That's normal, isn't it?'

'What sort of pain?'

'Sort of—' Bryony stopped, clutched her stomach and cried out, 'The baby I think it's coming' and she took a large gulp of air.

'It can't, I mean I thought you said it was another week at least?'

'It isn't going to bloody wait,' and Bryony yelled again.

'Right, let's get you into the bedroom.'

'I can't.' Bryony sank to the floor.

'Lie down and pull off your pants and jogging bottoms and er…sit with your legs apart and…'

'I want to push.'

'Just lie still and remember to breathe. I'll call for an ambulance.' Angie picked up her phone and dialled. The signal in the house was poor as usual so she opened the back door and went outside, keeping one eye on Bryony, and waited. 'Come on, come on,' she muttered as the dialling tone sounded. A voice replied and she had to explain what was happening. 'What? Twenty minutes?' she shouted, exasperated at the wait. She flicked off her phone.

'Is anything wrong?' A voice called over the fence. It was Paul.

'Yes. I mean no. I've got a young woman in labour and it might take twenty minutes for the ambulance to get here. I don't think the baby will wait that long.'

'I'm on my way.' A door slammed, the side gate opened and Paul was standing there. 'Where is she?'

'In the hall.'

Paul knelt down by Bryony's side. 'Hey, old girl,

261

we'd better try and make you more comfortable, hadn't we?' His voice was gentle, calm and controlled. Bryony clutched his hand as another contraction took hold. Paul turned to Angie. 'Get me some cushions and a duvet or a blanket and call her partner.'

'I'm scared,' Bryony whimpered as the pain subsided for the moment.

'There's no need. Everything will be fine. Now let's time these contractions, shall we?'

Angie fetched the cushions and he arranged them round Bryony and eased the duvet under her bottom and back. 'Get me a cold towel, please.' Angie did as instructed and he dabbed Bryony's brow, talking gently to her all the time.

'It's coming, it's coming!' Bryony screamed.

'Breathe and when I say *push*, I want you to push right? Angie hold her hand.'

Angie never remembered exactly what happened next. There was the sound of a siren, a flashing light, the door of the kitchen opened and Paul was holding a screaming baby and wrapping him in a towel.

'Nice job, sir,' the paramedics said. 'We'll take over now.' Paul and Angie went into the lounge and let the professionals take charge.

'How did you know what to do?' Angie whispered.

'I had to help out on a number of occasions when I worked in Africa after college. We were miles away from hospitals and even doctors sometimes. I learnt a lot. Now you'd better call the father while I get cleaned up.'

Angie dialled Jason and relayed the news. He said he'd meet Bryony at the hospital so Angie fetched the baby bag and accompanied Bryony. Paul followed in his car to take her back. It was nearly seven when they returned to Angie's home.

'I know what you need,' Paul said. 'Tea, lots of it and it'll be very strong.' He filled the kettle and switched it on. 'Cups?'

'In the cupboard.' Angie sat at the kitchen table.

The noise of the kettle bubbling as the water heated up and the sound of cups clattering as Paul made tea focussed Angie's mind though it did nothing to quell the rising tide of nerves in her stomach. She wasn't usually this jittery. She hoped it was just fatigue but she knew it was Paul. His presence as well as his kindness to Bryony and her was unsettling.

'It's been one hell of a day.' She raised her cup. 'I suppose we should be wetting the baby's head. Tea is a bit tame.'

'It'll do for me on a Thursday night,' Paul said. 'To the new arrival. Have they thought of a name?'

They clinked cups. 'It could be Robin or Noel as Bryony thinks it was conceived at Christmas.'

Paul pulled a face. 'What's happened to all the old standard names like John and Peter or Robert?'

'The thing today seems to be to call the child after the place it was conceived. I taught a Devon once and a Paris.'

'Thank your lucky stars it wasn't conceived in…what's that place name in Wales that is the longest in Britain?'

'I know the one. Poor kid would be given their exercise books in September and probably wouldn't finish writing their name on the front covers till Christmas.' They both burst out laughing.

'See what influence you can wield,' Paul said and refilled their cups.

'I will.' There was silence as they both looked at

each other. Words were not needed. There was a connection. Angie only hoped Paul felt it as strongly as she did. She bit her lip. This was wrong. Paul was engaged. She looked away and changed the subject. 'Er, how is Fleur?'

Paul shrugged. 'I think she's all right. I haven't seen her since we had a row back in the summer.'

'I'm sorry,' said Angie. Yet she knew she was lying and her heart was pounding.

'I'm not,' said Paul. 'It started after your party.' Angie felt sick. It was her fault after all. 'She had no right to say we were an item.'

'Oh.' This wasn't what she was expecting. She dared to look back at him. She needed to know more. 'Had you been together long?'

'A couple of years but we weren't engaged and never had been. That was more in her mind than mine.'

'I don't think many women want just friendship,' Angie said and sipped at her tea, remembering Janet and some of the more desperate women, wanting a man, any man as if that would define them.

'I think she's gone to the South of France on some artist's retreat.'

A small glimmer of hope that he might now be a single man flickered…Angie pushed it aside. He wouldn't be interested in her. She wasn't as sophisticated as Fleur. 'Did you have a lot in common?'

'Not a lot. I think we were both lonely and when I met someone else…it made me realise I wanted out.'

Angie's heart sank. A man like Paul wouldn't be single for long. She stifled a yawn. 'I'm sorry.'

'No. I reckon we've had enough excitement for

one day,' Paul said and smiled.

'And we've both got work tomorrow.' Angie smiled back and looked into his eyes.

Paul glanced down and studied his fingers. 'I realise you and I have had a few disagreements but there's something I want to talk about and it involves you.'

'Yes?' Angie tried to sound upbeat yet the way Paul spoke was how you'd discuss blocked drains.

'I wonder if you'd...' He took a deep breath and the words poured out. 'How about I treat us both to a meal tomorrow night after you've visited the hospital? I can take you if you like and we can go on to a restaurant afterwards?'

'I'd love that.' Even if it was the drains he wanted to talk about, a meal with Paul might be like old times. Besides, if he was no longer involved with Fleur, there might be some chance. Angie smiled. When Sister Elizabeth was happy, she'd said she felt as if she'd lost a penny and found a pound. Angie knew exactly what she meant.

Chapter Twenty-six

On Friday, Angie was ready long before Paul was due to arrive. At precisely 6.30pm the front door bell rang. She flung it open. He was dressed in a navy jacket, dark grey cords with a pale blue sweater over a navy and white shirt. His hair was swept off his face and he sported gold-rimmed glasses. 'Ready?' he asked, holding out his arm for Angie to take. 'I've booked a table for 7.30 at *Bistro du Vin* so that'll give you about three quarters of an hour at the hospital. Is that enough?'

She closed the front door behind her and took his arm, hoping that he wouldn't notice she was shaking. 'That will be lovely. I could do with some good food and a glass of wine.' On the short drive to the hospital they slipped back into the old camaraderie they'd shared when she had stayed with him and she wondered just what on earth he wanted to talk to her about.

'Aren't you coming in too?' she asked as he bagged the last space in the hospital car park.

'I'm not family or a close friend.' He switched off the engine.

'You practically brought the poor little thing into the world. I think that makes you an adopted family member. Come on.'

Together they negotiated their way through the crowds, laden down with an assortment of presents and toys for the newcomers. As they turned the corridor to peer into the rooms where the mothers and their charges lay, Angie caught sight of Jason. He was walking up and down with the baby. A football scarf dangled from his head.

As soon as he saw Angie his face split into a wide grin and he pointed to the scarf. 'Got to get him used to the colours,' he whispered. 'Come and say hello to Bry.'

Bryony was sitting next to the bed, reading a magazine. She looked up at the approach of Angie and Paul and held out her arms to them both. Angie kissed her on the cheek and Paul took her hand and squeezed it. 'Isn't he crazy?' she nodded towards Jason. 'I reckon he's going to buy him a season ticket next year.' She turned to look up at Paul. 'I just want to say a big thank you. I don't know what I'd have done without you.'

Angie noticed a blush spreading over Paul's neck and face. She touched his arm in reassurance as he stumbled out an apology that he didn't do anything and went and sat down, leaving Angie to chat with Bryony and have a cuddle with the baby when Jason eventually relinquished him. They were still there when a thin woman whom Angie vaguely recognised burst into the room with a huge white teddy bear tucked under her arm.

'Where's my first grandchild?' she said.

'Mum.' Jason stepped forward and the woman hugged him.

'I think we had better go and leave you to your new visitors.' Paul motioned Angie to leave.

'You're my family too,' Jason said.

'That's very sweet of you, Jason. We have a table booked for 7.30. See you soon,' Angie said as she and Paul made their escape.

The restaurant was packed. Their table had been reserved in a quiet alcove from where Angie could see the open-plan kitchen. Paul ordered a glass of wine for them both and they sat and studied the menu. The wine arrived and Angie lifted her glass. 'I suppose we can officially toast the new parents and the baby? Isn't it called wetting the baby's head?'

'I think that's when the father gets treated by his mates. Somehow I don't think Jason will be spending much time away from his new arrival.' Paul lifted his glass and clinked it against Angie's. 'To Bryony, Jason and the baby.'

They were interrupted by the arrival of the waiter. For the next few minutes there was a flurry of decision making. At last the waiter shimmied away to place their orders in the shiny stainless steel and glass kitchen. Angie took a deep breath. 'So what did you want to talk to me about?'

'It's easy really.' Paul looked at her. 'I'd like to see more of you. I'm a free agent and I think you are too. I enjoyed the time we spent together and I'd like to get to know you better. What do you think?'

His directness took Angie by surprise. She had one more question to ask. 'Is that like a friend or is there something more?'

He took her hand and squeezed it gently. 'I think you are a very attractive woman and yes, I'd like to think that there is a spark or something that could develop between us. What do you think?'

Angie was pleased she was sitting down as she knew her legs were decidedly wobbly. 'I'd like that too,' she replied and allowed her hand to respond to the pressure that Paul was gently exerting.

'Good.'

If Angie had had any concerns that this new development would change their relationship, she was mistaken. Throughout the evening the conversation flowed and Angie relished the touch of a man's hand on hers, his breath gently tickling her face as he leaned forward to accept the sample of food from her plate for him to try. Despite only having drunk one glass of wine, Angie felt light-headed. As they left the restaurant later that evening, Paul slipped his arm through hers and it was natural for her to move closer so that her body touched his. By the time they got back to her bungalow, Angie's feelings had turned to panic. Her old fears flooded back. Should she kiss him? Should she invite him in? Would he want more?

Paul parked the car and went to open the passenger door. 'I can see my way home myself,' Angie stumbled over her words in her rush to get them out.

Paul pulled her into his arms. 'Don't look so frightened,' he murmured. 'I won't bite you.'

'It's not that. I'm just not used to this dating thing,' she replied,

For an answer he kissed her lightly on the lips and drew back. 'That wasn't too bad was it?'

Angie looked at him. 'No. In fact it was so nice I'd like to do it again,' she said. This time, she kissed him back. Her arms curled round him as he held her tight and pressed his tongue against her lips. Rather than be disgusted, Angie opened her mouth and let his tongue explore inside hers, allowing her own to touch his. A warm feeling was spreading through her body, reminding her of her first kiss when she was a teenager. They kissed for a few seconds more and drew apart.

'I'll say goodnight.' Paul held her hands and looked at her. 'I'll be in touch,' he said as he walked down the path, stopping at the end to turn and wave again.

The following morning Angie was struggling to coax her hair into a calmer state after the restless night she had just spent. Maggie was right. Dating was different. All you did in the 80s was wait for a phone call, a letter or just bumped into each other as you probably caught the same bus or train and possibly lived in the same street. She pushed another clip into her hair, smoothed the remaining rebellious wisps into place and went downstairs. Her stomach was churning in an interesting manner in anticipation of an email, perhaps. Her phone, which she kept by her side at all times, remained perilously quiet.

She filled up the kettle and waited for her laptop to load. As she did so, she leaned on the work surface and peered out at the early morning light. A weak autumn sun was piercing the dank grey clouds and a brisk wind swirled a flurry of brown leaves over the damp grass. Harvest festival would be over and long gone and in the convent they would be in the down time before the preparations for Advent and Christmas began. She smiled to herself, enjoying the memory and no longer with any bitterness. It was her past and it was long gone. She poured hot water over the coffee grounds, savouring the chocolatey smell and filled a cup before sitting down and logging on. A host of emails flicked onto the screen and she scrolled down to find the one she really wanted. Her palms started to sweat and her heart beat faster as she opened the one from Paul.

Dear Angie,
I just wanted to say a big thank you for your company and I look forward to getting to know you better. Any

*chance of us meeting on Friday night? I'll cook. There's
a good film to download that you might just enjoy. Let
me know by email or text as I'll be away on business
most of the week.*
Paul XXX

Angie read it through again. Did three crosses
mean anything? How long do you wait before you
answer? She decided to deal with the other emails
first and get some breakfast before answering. Didn't
Maggie say it was always a good idea to keep them
waiting? Besides she had things to think about as
Jason and Bryony were due back today and an idea
had formed in her head overnight which she wanted
to discuss with them.

It was mid-morning when the sound of a familiar
engine broke the stillness of the day. She heard the
front door open and a voice rang out, 'Ange, we're
back.' Jason lurched forward, staggering under the
weight of a baby car seat, two overnight bags and a
carrier full of toys. Bryony was behind him, cradling
her young son.

'Welcome home. You're just in time for a cuppa
before I get some food on.'

'I don't know how to thank you for letting us stay
here,' Bryony said, kissing the top of the baby's head.
'The flat won't be ready for months yet.'

'Let me get us a drink. There's something I want
to talk to you about,' Angie replied.

Five minutes later they were all in the kitchen,
seated at Angie's large table.

'I've got an idea,' she began. 'I want you to stay
here for the next six months at least. I might not be
here all the time,' she added, hoping they wouldn't ask

271

her why. If things went well with Paul, she might be spending more time at his place.

'Why?' Jason asked. 'Are you going on holiday again?'

'Jason don't be nosy,' Bryony scolded him.

'I just might be spending the odd night away.' She hoped she was vague.

'Are you hitting it off with him next door?' Jason drained his mug. Angie felt her face flush. 'It is him, isn't it? He was sniffing about most days when you were away, asking where you'd gone and when you'd be back. I told him you were on a holiday with some old friends but I don't think he believed me.'

'I think it's a lovely idea,' Bryony added. 'Why shouldn't you have a boyfriend? It's not as if you're that old. Sorry, I mean of course we can look after the place.'

'Thank you for recognising that I am not yet in my grave,' Angie said. 'In fact you'd be doing me a favour and you might save a bit of money as I won't charge.'

'Oh yes you will.' Bryony nudged Jason. 'We pay our way, don't we Jase?'

'We can talk about that later,' Angie said before he could reply. 'I'll get some lunch ready and you two need to settle this young man down.' She paused, 'Have you decided on a name yet?'

'We'd like to call him Charlie, because you're Angela Charlotte aren't you?' Bryony looked up at Angie a worried frown on her face.

'How did you find out?

'We spotted it on a letter when you were away and you've been so kind to us. Do you mind?'

'I would be delighted.' Angie bent over the sleeping baby. 'Welcome to the world, Charlie.'

It was much later when she finally answered Paul's email.

Dear Paul,
The meal was lovely and I'd enjoy sampling your cooking. Bryony and Jason have arrived back and are settling in so I'll turn up at 7.30 pm Friday starving hungry—you've been warned.
Angie

***

On Friday evening at 7.29pm Angie crossed the lawn and walked up the path to Paul's bungalow. He must have been waiting for no sooner had she reached out to ring the bell than the door opened and he was standing there dressed in a grey cashmere sweater, black chinos and a pale blue shirt that looked like silk. 'Angie, you look lovely, as always,' and he kissed her lightly on each cheek. He ushered her into the lounge where some smooth jazz was playing and the golden-syrup-like voice of a female singer was pouring out a song of longing and lust. Paul handed her a glass of white wine. Angie swirled the buttery yellow liquid in its crystal glass and took a sip.

'Lovely,' she said.

'Let's hope the food is just as good. It'll be about ten minutes so sit down here and tell me all about your day and how the new family are coping.' He patted the sofa beside her and she sank into deep cushions. He stretched out next to her, placed his hands behind his head and waited. It struck Angie how like a cat he was, languid, relaxed and, she had to admit to herself again, very sexy. With her stomach fluttering in an unusual way, she launched into her

273

account of Jason's plans to paper the nursery wall with football posters and how he had already bought a small pair of football boots as a mobile above the cot.

There was silence and she was acutely aware of Paul watching her. Before she could say anything else, the timer in the kitchen shrieked for attention and he excused himself. Angie breathed a sigh of relief. The fluttering in her stomach would not stop. The music continued in a soulful expression of unfulfilled love and longing. Angie listened and wondered when Paul would kiss her again. To her shock, there was a sensation like a hand clutching at her chest and her throat dried. She took another large gulp of wine but the feeling would not go away.

'Your meal is served.' Paul stepped into the lounge and with a flourish opened the dining room door where he had set the table with square, white plates, heavy embossed cutlery and red napkins. Red carnations in a white vase stood in the centre. A bottle of red wine was open and three red covered dishes were wafting their aroma her way. She sniffed.

'That smells good.' Angie stood up and followed Paul who pulled out her chair to let her sit down.

'Fingers crossed it will taste good too,' Paul said. 'If not, we can wash it down with more wine.' He removed the covers off the dishes to reveal a lamb casserole, rice and tiny carrots and green beans. Angie groaned with pleasure.

'If it tastes half as good as it smells and looks, it will be perfect,' she said as he passed her the serving spoons.

'I'm so pleased you're not one of those fussy women who chase a lettuce leaf round a plate.'

'After some of the concoctions Sister Agnes used to make, I can eat anything,' Angie laughed, stopped and tried to camouflage the words with a cough. Paul was listening, his head tilted slightly on one side. 'Er, as you remember I was a...' she bent her head over her meal, pretending to be fascinated by the carrots.

'I played football as a kid against a school where the nuns would referee the match. I away remember this one tearing down the sidelines with her dress or whatever...'

'Habit. It's called a habit,' Angie explained.

'Well whatever it was called, it was flying up and showed her long knickers. I tell you, that school was never beaten at footy.'

'We can be pretty fearsome,' she stopped again. Paul had not shown any surprise and he hadn't asked her awkward questions. A wave of relief swept through her. Even so, she decided a change of subject was needed. 'Tell me more about your school days, they sound fun.' She hoped he would move onto another topic. He did and so they spent the first part of the meal telling stories of their school days. By the time they had eaten the desert of tropical fruit crème brulee they had reached their university days and their first jobs.

'Coffee?' Paul asked.

'Please. Let me help you clear the table.' As Paul made the coffee, Angie stacked the dishwasher and set it going but sensed he was watching her. She turned to see him staring at her. 'Is there anything wrong? Have I made a mistake?'

Paul just shook his head, walked towards her and placed his hands on her shoulders. 'Nothing is wrong,' he said as he bent his head and kissed her on

275

the lips. Angie felt his arms go round her and she responded, enjoying the feel of his lips and his body pressed against hers. One hand slipped onto her breast and his tongue pushed against her lips. Desperately hoping she was doing the right thing, Angie opened her mouth and let his tongue enter. They kissed for a few seconds more and drew apart. 'Can we go and sit down?' Paul asked.

Angie nodded and let him lead her to the lounge where they sat down on the couch. He stretched out and she curled up next to him, kicking off her shoes before he kissed her again. This time there was no hesitation and Angie kissed him back and ran her hands along the chiselled outline of his face. A strange warm sensation pulsed through her body. Paul's hand slid to the buttons on her blouse. He undid one and his hand caressed the contours of her breasts before exploring the soft flesh beneath her bra. Drawing away, he looked deep into her eyes. 'I would love to go to bed with you. I do understand it might be too soon.'

'No. Yes. I mean I don't know.' Angie sat up and scrabbled on the floor for her shoes. 'I must get back.'

'I'm sorry. I thought you felt like me or have I misread the signs again?' Paul sat with his head in his hands. 'That's me all over, totally unable to realise what a woman wants.' He looked up. 'Please forgive me. I'm just a very unskilled male.'

Angie put her hand over his. 'It's not you, it's me. There's something...no. It doesn't matter.' She stood up to go.

'Please say you won't let this stop us from being friends. I promise, I'll never do this again.'

'I'll let myself out.' Angie scurried out, closed the

door behind her and fled back to the sanctuary of her own home. 'Stupid, stupid, stupid,' she moaned as she slammed the front door and sank back against its comforting solidity. All she had to do was tell him she was still a virgin. It would be tougher than anything she'd done since she left the convent and there was one thing she was more scared of than anything else: Paul's reaction.

Chapter Twenty-seven

For the next week Angie played cat and mouse, trying to avoid Paul at all costs. It was easier than she'd expected. His car had gone by the time she left for school and he arrived back late at night. There were no emails, texts or phone calls. He was either embarrassed or he'd written her off as a nonstarter for a relationship. Angie was uncertain what to do next.

'Why didn't you tell him the truth?' Maggie said when they met again at their usual Friday get together.

'I don't want him to think that I'm a ...'

'A bloody virgin, well you are. This is the first time you find a decent guy that you like. He likes you and wants to have sex and you run off like a scared rabbit. Honestly, what the hell do you want?' She took a long drink of wine and waited for Angie's answer.

'The truth is I feel stupid,' Angie admitted, 'and I don't want him to think I'm like that.'

'Go and see him. Tell him what the problem is and work something out together. You both fancy each other, what's the harm?'

The entry of Gareth and Tasha brought the conversation to a close but as the evening wore on and Angie had time to reflect she realised Maggie was right. It was earlier than usual when she left. Once back home she poured herself a very large glass of wine and went and sat by the front door to wait for Paul's car to draw up. Bryony, Jason and the baby were at Bryony's mum's to plan the naming ceremony as Bryony insisted they should mark the occasion with something special. Angie drained the glass and refilled it several times before she saw the telltale lights of a car turn into the driveway and stop at Paul's front door. She lifted the net curtain and peered out. For some reason her legs had decided not to work properly. She clutched at the hall table. Paul turned to glance in the direction of her house. She dropped the net curtain and turned away. Her legs collapsed beneath her and she slid to the floor giggling. She pulled herself upright and peeked out again. The light was on in his lounge. 'Come on, Angie. It's now or never.' She launched her unwieldy body out through the front door and stumbled across the lawn that separated their driveways. Her heels sank into the rain-softened grass which set her off laughing again.

She pressed her finger on the bell and kept it there as it resounded through the bungalow. 'All right, all right what's the problem?' Paul called out. There was the clanking of a chain being unfastened and the door opened.

'It's me, Angie, and I've got something to tell you,' she hiccupped and fell against the door, knocking over a plant pot in the process. 'Oops, sorry.' She bent down to scrape up the soil and stuff it back in the pot. The plant had come loose and she scrabbled about in the dark porch. 'Where are you, little plant?' she said. A sudden gleam of light from the open door showed her where it was. She grabbed it and held it aloft. 'Got you—all I need do is…' She didn't get any further.

'What the hell is going on here?' Paul did not sound pleased to see her so she tried again.

'I'm just going to put this poor little thing back in

its nice pot and then I've got something to tell you. Now where's the pot?' She crawled round on her hands and knees but was hoisted to her feet by two strong arms.

'Have you been drinking?' Paul asked as Angie steadied herself, clutching the plant, the remnants of the soil and the pot.

'Only one or two…'

'More like one or two bottles. What you need is some very strong coffee. I'll take you back once you've sobered up.' Paul closed the door behind her as Angie fell against him and promptly dropped the pot. Damp black soil fell to the floor and spread over the cream carpet.

'Oops, silly me, I seem to have made a mess of your shag pile.' Angie burst out laughing. It was the funniest thing that Angie had heard in ages. 'Shag pile. Get it? Shag pile or lack of shag is the problem,' and she burst out laughing. She was still laughing as Paul manoeuvred her into the lounge and plonked her down on the sofa.

'Stay there,' he commanded. 'I'm going to get a pot of coffee and you will drink *all* of it.'

Angie kicked off her shoes and stretched out on the sofa as the clatter of cups from the kitchen told her Paul was indeed making coffee. Angie drifted off for a few seconds and was woken by Paul bringing in a full cafetière and a cup which he filled and held out towards her. She yawned and sat up. Her head was swimming. 'Here drink this,' he said. Without letting go, he guided it to her mouth so that she could swallow the bitter liquid.

'Urgh. There's no milk,' she spluttered but took another gulp.

'Because that is what the doctor ordered,' Paul said. He poured her another cup and placed it in her hands. He went out into the hallway and came back with an old coat. He draped it over Angie's shoulders. 'You will drink two more cups and I'll take you home.'

He waited until she had finished, not talking except to encourage her to drink. On more than one occasion, Angie started to tell him why she was there but he hushed her. It was gone eleven when Paul stood up and helped an unsteady Angie to her feet and across to her house. He propped her up at the side of the porch. 'Give me your keys,' he said. Angie looked at him, a smile crossing her face.

'I don't have them. I must be homeless. Can I come home with you?' She draped herself over him. He leaned her back against the porch wall and looked at the drive.

'Jason's car is there so he must be home.' He knocked on the door and then pressed the bell.

The swimming head that Angie felt before was accompanied by a strange sensation in her mouth which felt as if it was filling with liquid. She swallowed hard as her stomach dipped and dived like a roller coaster. The door opened to reveal Jason and in the background was Bryony holding the baby. 'I think Angie needs a long sleep,' Paul said as he hitched his arms under Angie's armpits and steered her into the house.

'I think I need to be sick,' Angie blurted out.

'Get her into the cloakroom.' Jason flung open the door, grabbed her other arm and he and Paul pushed her inside. Angie collapsed to her knees grateful to see the gleaming white porcelain and blue liquid of the toilet as she threw up.

***

A weak autumnal sun filtered through the gaps in the curtains and roused Angie from her torpor. Still fully dressed, she groaned and pulled the covers over her head, anything to stop the searchlights that pierced her eyes and the thumping of hundreds of hammers that cracked her delicate skull. She ran her tongue over parched lips. She eased her legs to the floor and staggered into the en suite where she ran the tap to let the cool liquid run down her throat. It tasted foul. She looked into the mirror and pulled a face at the sight that greeted her; eyes threaded with red lines and caked with make-up, hair that would grace a scarecrow and crêpey skin that showed every day of her fifty years. She stripped off her sweaty clothes and crawled naked into the cool sheets and let the vague memory of last night percolate through her thoughts. She knew something had happened although she was not quite sure what. She turned over and closed her eyes. It would be time to remember later. All she wanted was to sleep and get rid of her king-sized hangover.

A faint tapping and the voice of someone calling her name roused her from the depths of a dreamless sleep. 'Angie?' The door opened and Jason's face peered into the half-light.

'Yes. What's up?' Angie raised herself on her elbows.

'Bry says you might need a cup of tea.' He held out a mug that steamed and filled the room with its aroma.

'God I feel awful.' Angie ran a hand through her hair. She took the cup and cradled it in both hands before sipping. 'I needed that.'

'My gran used to say there's nothing that seems so bad after a strong cup of tea.' Jason sat down on the bed.

'What do you mean, *bad*? Did I do something awful last night?'

Jason smothered a laugh by turning it into a slight cough. 'Don't you remember?'

'I knew I had a glass of wine, went next door...the rest is a bit blurry.'

'You got pissed, smashed a plant pot, dropped dirt over Paul's floor and finished off in style by puking up in the cloakroom back here. You certainly don't do things by half do you?'

Angie clasped her head in her hands. 'It's all coming back to me...I went to tell Paul...' she stopped. 'It doesn't matter. In fact nothing matters.'

'I reckon he could see the funny side like me. It wouldn't harm to apologise, though, would it?'

Angie looked at Jason. Fatherhood had had a very sobering effect on him. He was right. She had to apologise. Whether Paul would ever want to speak to her again was in the lap of the gods.

'If I were you, I'd have a long bath and take it easy today. Go and see him tomorrow. He'll understand. Bryony is getting lunch. You must be starving. Here take these for your headache.' He placed a packet of paracetamol on the bedside table and stood up. 'Soup and toast in half an hour do you?' The door slammed behind him and Angie was left with the shameful memory of exactly what she had done.

The warmth of a long bath and the power of modern chemistry soon did their magic and Angie crept into the kitchen thirty minutes later feeling brighter but just as ashamed. Bryony was serving up bowls of tomato soup and toast. The familiar aroma was both comforting and reassuring as it reminded Angie of tea with her mum after school on a winter's afternoon. The welcome she received as she slunk into her seat at the table was frosty if not glacial, at least from Bryony.

'Feeling better, Ange?' Jason asked, rocking Charlie on his lap. The baby was sleeping. Dark lashes that would have made a supermodel envious fluttered as unknown dreams played out in his mind.

'A bit,' she said and hung her head.

'Disgraceful behaviour.' Bryony crashed a plate of soup in front of Angie. Its hot contents spattered onto the polished tabletop. Angie dabbed at the drops of orange liquid with her finger.

'Come off it, Bry. You've been drunk before haven't you? I remember a time when you and the girls got paralytic on a bottle of cream liqueur. You'd pinched it from your mum's Crimbo booze store, remember?' Jason cradled Charlie in one arm as she placed another bowl in front of him.

'That was different. Give me the baby while you eat.' Jason handed him over and Bryony kissed the small head and nuzzled his neck.

'How?' Jason continued, tearing up some bread and floating it on his soup, dunking it with the spoon so that it turned from white to orange.

Angie kept her head low.

'Imagine what Charlie could have seen. It's hardly a good example to set to...' Bryony's voice faded away, 'especially since our conversation about...you know.' Silence hung in the air between the three of them until sounds that emanated from the area of the baby's bottom told everyone that a nappy needed changing.

'A good example? Charlie was asleep and is hardly likely to be damaged for life by one old lady getting ratted on the cooking sherry.' Jason exploded with laughter, letting his soup spoon clatter to the floor. The laughter that he had begun sparked a ripple from Angie.

'I'm not that old and it was a decent wine,' she stammered out between giggles. She took a deep breath and tried to look serious. 'I'm sorry. It won't happen again.'

'Apology accepted. Now I'd better go and change this smelly baby.' Bryony swept out and left Jason and Angie together.

'Sorry about that.' Jason picked up his spoon, wiped it on his jeans and carried on eating. 'She's a bit overprotective…'

'I understand.' Angie pushed her plate aside. Her appetite had disappeared. 'If that's Bryony's opinion, what on earth will Paul think?'

'Better work out a brill excuse.'

Angie knew excuses would be no use. She had to tell Paul the truth. They continued to eat in silence until Bryony came back in.

'Charlie's down for his nap,' she said as she slid into the seat beside Jason and looked hard at Angie. 'I'm sorry if you think I'm overreacting; after the conversation Jason and I had yesterday, I need to feel that you are the right person.'

'Right person for what?' Angie said.

Bryony folded her hands and looked at Angie, her head on one side as if Bryony was the older one in the relationship and Angie was the teenage tearaway.

'You know we don't believe in the church but we do want a naming ceremony. We want Charlie to have godparents except they aren't godparents.'

'They're called mentors,' Jason explained.

'We'd like you to be one for our Charlie.'

Angie felt a lump rising in her throat and her eyes prickled. 'Me?' she managed to bleat.

'Not if there is a repeat of that shameful performance in front of Charlie.'

Angie nodded. 'Point taken.'

'So will you?' Jason asked.

'I'd be delighted,' Angie said and smiled.

'Good, that's settled.' Bryony folded her arms. 'Now all you have to do is apologise to that poor man.'

It was Sunday afternoon before Angie had plucked up the courage to go across to Paul's bungalow. A cool breeze was whipping the branches of the trees and whirling twists of leaves danced at her feet as she picked her way over the grass. His car was parked in the driveway. There was no excuse: she had to apologise and explain her strange behaviour. She took a deep breath and rang the doorbell. A shadowy figure making his way across the hall could be seen through the frosted glass. Angie pulled herself up to stand tall and wiped her damp palms down the back of her jeans.

The door swung open and Angie looked up at Paul. He rested one arm against the door and raised an eyebrow. 'Yes?' A smile flickered at the edges of his mouth.

'I've come to apologise,' Angie managed to stammer out before they both exploded in peals of laughter.

'Come here, crazy lady.' Paul held out his arms and Angie stepped forward to be immersed in his embrace.

For a few seconds they stayed still. Angie relished the sensation of his arms around her, his body pressed against hers and her head resting on his shoulder before she forced herself to break away. 'I must explain,' she said.

'I can't wait. It's going to be one hell of a story.' Paul ushered her into the lounge. A wood burner was glowing. Flames licked at the glass and sent out a gentle heat. The television was tuned to a rugby match and the pile of Sunday newspapers declared that he had not yet fully succumbed to a digital habit. He switched off the screen and stretched out on the sofa. Angie perched on the edge, her hands folded in her lap. It was worse than being summoned in front of Sister Catherine to receive a severe reprimand for violating one of the countless rules of the order.

Angie cleared her throat. She was going to be blunt. This was no time for dancing on the edge of truth. 'Can you remember when you said you'd like to go to bed with me?'

Paul held up one hand. 'Yes and if that's the problem, forget I said it and let's carry on as—'

'—No. I don't want to forget and if you were going to say we should just be friends I don't want that,' Angie interrupted him.

'So what is it?'

Angie studied her hands. 'I've never been to bed with anyone before.'

There was silence for a moment as if Paul was processing the information. 'Sorry? Am I right you're telling me that you're a—'

'—Yes. I'm a virgin.' She looked up. Paul was watching her. She took a deep breath and a torrent of words spewed out. 'I went into a convent at the age of twenty-one. I never met anyone at university or at school. At least not anyone that I wanted to have sex with apart from one person and he didn't want me. This time last year I was Sister Ruth and…' This was it. She had to be honest. 'I'm scared.'

'Scared of what?' Paul asked, his voice barely above a whisper.

Angie took another deep breath. This time, she let it escape, slowly and steadily, buying herself time before she replied. 'I'm scared I'll be no good and disappoint you. Scared I'll be a failure and that's why I drank so much. I needed to pluck up courage to tell you and it went a bit wrong.' Not daring to look at him, she bent her head and waited. The leather sofa creaked and she was aware of Paul, squatting on the floor in front of her and taking her hands in his.

'Wow. Well I certainly wasn't expecting that but you've got it all wrong. Making love is just that, it's making love. And making love is about wanting to touch and hold and kiss and caress someone that you love. To feel their body and yours joined. It's not about one person or another being better and it certainly isn't one-way traffic. I want you to enjoy it too. It's about the two of us exploring what the other likes.'

Angie looked up, unable to believe what he'd said. 'You don't mind?'

'Mind? You dear, funny, crazy lady, what is there to mind? We'll take it slowly, really slowly and when you feel ready we'll go somewhere special where we can be together, just us with no one to bother us.'

'As long as you don't mind?'

'Don't be silly. It's a bit like being a teenager again with all the dating and pre-sex without the sex. If I remember rightly, teenagers spend a lot of time kissing and their hands do a lot more exploring so perhaps that is where we had better start.' He cupped his hands under Angie's chin and drew her towards him, kissing her lips and working his tongue into her mouth. Together they stretched out on the sofa and for the next hour Angie let her body respond to Paul's caresses in ways she had never dreamed were possible and it was just perfect.

Chapter Twenty-eight

Angie's car scrunched on the driveway as she pulled up in front of the hotel. Paul was right. The setting was stunning. The building was a Victorian mansion with honey-coloured walls. Beyond the hotel rolled green hills and woodlands that demanded to be explored. She looked at her watch. She could check in and go for a swim. Paul was driving down from Manchester after his meeting and would arrive later. She smiled to herself. Only Maggie knew they were together and by arriving and leaving separately, it was something they could keep to themselves, at least for a few more weeks.

She trundled her suitcase over to the entrance and up the steps. The huge double doors opened into a hallway with a sweeping staircase that led to the bedrooms. Oil paintings of various previous owners gazed down with disapproving looks on their faces as if to say, 'Who let the peasants in here?' She walked over to the reception desk, her heels clunking on the polished wooden floor. 'Good afternoon. Can I take your name?' An Eastern European twang suggested that Marika, as her badge announced, was not from the locality. Although she was dressed in the regulation uniform of the hotel chain, she wore it with a flair that went well with the red lipstick and huge lashes that fringed her green eyes.

For a moment Angie hoped she wouldn't be on the desk when Paul arrived. She checked herself. She couldn't get used to the idea he wanted to be with her, Angie Jarvis. 'There is a reservation in the name of Paul Buchannan and Angie Jarvis,' she explained.

'Yes. For two nights, we have the suite booked with the four-poster bed. Your room is ready and if you will please complete this form and sign here and here…' Angie did as she was asked and took one of the two heavy metal keys. 'Your room is on the top floor and the lift is over there. Do you need any help with your luggage?'

'No thanks. I can manage.' Angie headed towards the lift, relieved that Marika showed only a professional interest in her guests.

Angie opened the door of the suite and stopped on the threshold. She dropped her bags and her mouth fell open. It was the sort of room she'd only seen in films. A huge four-poster bed dominated the room, swathed in golden yellow drapes that were repeated in the curtains at the window and in the covers on the chairs. She checked the key. There hadn't been a mistake. Angie crept into the room as if any noise would tell the world she had never stayed in such luxury before. She placed her bags on the bed and closed the door. She prodded the duvet which crackled under her touch and ran her hands over the sheets and pillow cases which were thick and sparkling white. She poked her nose into the bathroom tiled in cream and gold with huge, fluffy, white towels hanging from the rack. She undid the tops and sniffed the array of bottles of toiletries; they'd have lasted her a whole week, let alone a weekend.

Angie undid her case and placed her wash bag in the bathroom, expecting someone to turn up and evict her at any moment. She hung up her dresses, and unpacked the silk pyjamas and dressing gown and stopped. She didn't want to put them under one of

291

the pillows because she didn't know which side of the bed Paul would want. If she left them in her bag, it might look as if she was planning to do a runner. In the end she thrust everything in a drawer and headed down to the spa to relax in the jacuzzi and the pool.

She was sitting on a lounger, flicking through a magazine when a familiar figure wandered onto the poolside. Paul waved and Angie felt a warm sensation flowing through her. He was wearing a dark blue suit with a blue and white striped shirt and a red tie. How could someone like him be interested in her, Angie Jarvis? She dismissed the thought. He *was* interested in her and she was sure as hell interested in him. He perched on the edge of the lounger and leaned forward to give her a kiss. 'You smell of chlorine,' he said.

'Sorry, I'll go and shower.'

He shook his head. 'Stay here and enjoy yourself. I'll unpack and see you back in the room in about half an hour. We can make a few plans for the weekend.' With that he drifted off, to the admiring glances of some of the ladies enjoying the jacuzzi.

Half an hour later, Angie opened the bedroom door to find Paul stretched out on the bed, deep in a Sudoku. He patted the top cover. 'Come here and let me say hello to you properly,' he said. Angie stretched out beside him. As he took her in his arms and kissed her, that same wave of warmth poured through her body. She found herself responding to his kisses and as he began to undo her top and slide his hands to touch her warm skin, she did the same, her hands desperate to touch those parts of his body she had never touched before. 'Do you want me to stop?' he murmured.

292

'No don't stop,' she said. With slow steady movements he removed one article of her clothes at a time and she followed, doing the same to him until only his white boxer shorts and her bra and pants were left. With deft fingers he undid her bra and slid her pants over her hips as he bent to kiss her breasts. Now it was her turn and she found she wanted to touch him and to touch the part of him that was pressing hard against her leg. She eased his pants down and he helped to kick them off as her hand followed the trail of hairs down his stomach. There was a warmth and firmness to her touch which she had not expected. She lay on her back and Paul moved his body on top of hers. As she guided him into her there was pain and then no pain. Only him and her, joined and moving as one as she let her body be carried away in her own pleasure, until she cried out and held him tight against her as if she would never let him go.

'I think we're going to be late for dinner,' Paul roused Angie from her doze. They were lying naked on top of the bed, their bodies warm and lightly entwined.

'Do I have time for a shower?' She sat up and clutched at the bed cover to shield her nakedness. 'Don't look. My boobs are saggy and my bum is too big.'

'You look lovely to me and besides, the hairs on my chest are going grey and my legs are too skinny. I'm hardly Mr Body Beautiful.' Paul put a kiss on the tip of his finger and planted it on her nose. 'Get a move on. Sex makes me hungry and not just for food.'

Later as they walked into the restaurant Angie

couldn't help wonder if any of the fellow diners could tell what they had been doing. As Paul held the chair for her and she sat down at the table resplendent in a crisp white cloth and crystal glasses which sparkled in the glow of a single candle, she realised she couldn't care less.

DECEMBER

Angie walked around the kitchen, putting the final touches to the buffet spread out on the counter tops. The pizzas were ready to go in the oven and jacket potatoes were keeping hot in a large earthenware dish. A pile of crackers, each named and with a small personal gift inside waited for their owner's attention. Holly sprigs hung from the tops of the units and Angie had purchased special tableware for the occasion, all with jolly pictures of Santa, for the benefit of the youngest member of the party who would probably be asleep anyway.

She walked through the hallway. The fragrance from the pots of white hyacinths she had tended since early autumn filled the air with their heady perfume. She pushed open the lounge door. Bryony was arranging glasses on the table where a bowl of punch was scenting the room with orange and cloves. In pride of place stood a blue and white iced cake with the words *Charles Jason Robin 23 September* in blue piped icing. 'Where's little Charlie?' she asked.

'Jason's on the nappy run. He's getting quite good at it even though he spends more time playing peekaboo than changing him,' Bryony said and smiled. 'It's really good of you to do all this for me and Jason. We didn't like the idea of Charlie not having a special day to celebrate his name.' She came and hugged Angie. 'You really are a good angel to all of us.'

'Nonsense, it's a good excuse for a party and especially at Christmas.' Angie turned away quickly and plumped up some cushions. Her eyes were filling with tears and she didn't want to end up snivelling like a child this early. A loud banging at the door switched her attention and she hurried to open it.

'We're here.' Maggie stepped inside, followed by Tasha and Gareth. She manoeuvred Angie into the kitchen and whispered, 'I've got a bit of news for you and a very big thank you to say.'

'Don't tell me you've got a boyfriend?'

'As if?' The contempt in Maggie's voice was unmistakeable. 'No, it's much more interesting than that.'

'Come on, don't keep me waiting,' Angie said.

Maggie hesitated for a second before she announced with a flourish, 'I'm going back to college in the spring.'

'You? What are you going to do?' Angie leaned against the kitchen counter and folded her arms.

'A qualification in caring. I reckon with the right training I could end up running one of those homes if I put my mind to it.'

'I thought you hated schools?' Angie said. 'What's changed?' Maggie never ceased to amaze her.

'This is different. I learn while I'm working. I'm ready to take a bit of control in my life.' Maggie paused and looked at her. 'I want to be more like you. If I'm honest, I've always wanted to be like you.' She looked away and Angie could see her eyes were glistening as if tears were close. 'You make things happen. I've let things happen *to* me, not anymore.'

295

'I'm pleased for you...really pleased,' Angie said. She'd never thought of herself as someone that people and especially people like Maggie could admire. It was both flattering and embarrassing and Angie felt her face flush.

'Thanks and when I get stuck on the written stuff I'll be beating a path to your doorway, OK?'

'Agreed and I'll be very happy to help.'

The bell rang. 'Go on, you've got guests to sort out,' Maggie said and turned away to blow her nose on a crumpled tissue.

The bell rang again. Angie dashed into the hallway and opened it. Janet was standing next to a bald, portly gentleman in a T-shirt that advertised an ageing rock band that even Angie recognised. 'This is Dave,' she said. There was no mistaking the pride in her voice.

'Very pleased to meet you, Angie,' he said and enveloped her in a hug.

'And you.' Angie extricated herself. 'Drinks are in the lounge, help yourself.'

'As long as we don't have too many *African Orgasms* eh?' Janet said and burst out laughing. As she went past Angie she whispered, 'I got tired of young men. Met him at the local pub on a quiz night.'

'Good for you,' Angie said and made a mental note to tell Maggie that at least some people meet up without the use of the internet.

Janet and Dave were followed by Polly and John Cadwallader, Les and Jason's mum and Bryony's very extended family. The chink of glasses, the sound of laughter and the happy buzz of conversation echoed through the house as people squeezed into the lounge or the dining room and Angie scurried back and forth making sure everyone had drinks.

She was busy cutting up pizzas in the kitchen with Maggie when there was a knock at the back door and Paul came in. 'Hi, Maggie, happy Christmas.' He pulled Angie towards him and hugged her.

'I'll take these into the front room.' Maggie picked up a plate of pizza and made her exit in as tactful a manner as she could.

'Good, now I can say hello properly,' and Paul kissed her hungrily.

Angie broke away and looked at him. 'Don't do that. There are people here.'

'No one will mind.' He kissed her again.

'I mind.' Angie pulled away. 'I have guests to feed. Take these,' and she thrust a pile of plates at Paul and pushed him towards the lounge.

'I get the message but I've got something really important to show you later,' and he winked.

For an hour the bungalow was a flurry of activity as everyone made sure everyone else had enough food. It was only after people had finished eating and had settled down with coffee or a drink that Angie allowed herself to look at the assembled group. The quest to lose her virginity seemed so silly. What she'd really wanted was a life. She looked at the crib set up under the tree. It was not God or her faith to blame for the upsets in her life. In life, stuff happens and it can be good or bad.

Paul came up and stood by her side. 'A penny for them,' he said. 'That's what my mum used to say when she caught me daydreaming.'

'I don't think they're worth a penny,' Angie said. 'What was it you wanted to show me?'

'Come with me.' Paul led her by the hand into the

kitchen and through into the back garden. 'It'll be quieter here.'

Angie shivered in the cool night air. She looked up. Pinpoints of a thousand million stars pierced the velvet blue of the sky and the moon lit a pathway over the lawn. Paul pulled a small box from his pocket and opened it. Nestled against red velvet was a large ruby ring, surrounded by diamonds. 'It's beautiful,' she whispered as he took her hand and placed it on the tip of the third finger of her left hand.

'I don't know how it will work out. I don't know how we're going to sort out living arrangements, with you and your crew. All I know is that I want to spend every minute of every day and night with you by my side. Will you marry me?'

A lump the size of a baseball was rising in Angie's throat; she managed to stammer out yes as he slipped the ring down over her finger and enveloped her in a hug.

'In the New Year my kids are back from Oz for a few weeks. They can't wait to meet you,' Paul said. 'And Ben will be here over Christmas.' Angie shuddered. 'You're cold. We'd better go back inside.'

It wasn't the cold that was making Angie tremble. The enormity of what was happening was sending out warning signals. 'Are you sure about being married…to me that is?'

'Very sure.' Paul cupped her face in his hands. 'When Sandra died, I closed off from everyone and everything. Then you came along and I realised I wanted to start living again.'

'It might not be easy.'

Paul kissed her on the nose. 'I reckon it'll be a laugh though.' He tucked her arm under his. 'Come on. We've got an announcement to make.'

They crossed the lawn arm in arm. It would be all right. They'd work something out. As Angie turned to close the door, she looked up at the sky and mouthed a silent *thank you* to whoever or whatever might be watching.

Acknowledgements

My thanks go to the excellent team at Black Pear Press, fellow students on the MA in Creative and Critical Writing at the University of Gloucestershire 2014-2016 and my colleagues at Catchwords writing group in Cirencester. Their constructive and at times challenging feedback was always accompanied by support and encouragement.